William Azuski was born in the United Kingdom, and is of British and Yugoslav descent. Travelling widely through the Mediterranean since childhood, his frequent sojourns in Greece included several months on Santorini in the 1970s, an experience that provided firsthand experience for this exceptional novel's local setting. Writing as William Miles Johnson, Azuski is also author of the critically-acclaimed *The Rose-Tinted Menagerie*, an Observer Book of the Year (nonfiction), and *Making a Killing*, an end of the world satire, both titles recently republished by Iridescent.

TRAVELS IN ELYSIUM

WILLIAM AZUSKI

iridescent publishing

Travels in Elysium

First Published in 2013 by Iridescent Publishing

www.iridescent-publishing.com

William Azuski asserts his moral rights to be identified as the original author of this work.

The characters and incidents portrayed and the names used in this work are fictitious and any resemblance to the names, character, or history of any person is coincidental and unintentional.

www.TravelsinElysium.com

Cover design: Matthias Schnellmann

ISBN 978-3-9524015-2-1 (Paperback)
ISBN 978-3-9524015-3-8 (Amazon Kindle)
ISBN 978-3-9524015-4-5 (epub)

E·ly·si·um n. 1. in Greek mythology, the home of the blessed after death. Also called Elysian Fields 2. any ideally delightful or blissful place or condition

'Beyond the Pillars of Hercules, there lay an island among islands, whose people had the means to cross one to the other...'
— Plato, Timaeus

1.

Shall I whisper its fate through the raging clouds, this mountain island with a heart of fire?

Then listen well, Stranger, for memories like us who travel dreams are but time-straying ghosts who neither know nor care that they are dead.

Summer was in the making. Catching the west wind we roamed the high bluff, lay upon the pillows of the tufted grass, infinity flooding our eyes. If ever we knew and feared this day would come, surely it could never be on a day like this, a lark's song painting the blue above our heads. People returning from the saffron fields with sunburnt faces. Drifting asleep in their gardens to the hum of the bees and the chimes of the water. A few hours in which dreams bring on the coolness of the star sown night.

I felt the tremor through the soles of my feet, so tentative at first I confused it with my own pulse. It grew stronger. I glanced across at you, wondering what kind of love could electrify the heart like that, whispering across the skin, crackling through the mind like a summer storm that will drench us in some almighty collision of fire and rain.

Then before we knew it, the ground was buckling under our feet, fissures cracking the earth, their monstrous jaws devouring anything in sight, a farmhouse, a meadow, trees torn from the soil like weeds.

Through a blizzard of petals, I caught the nose-stripping stench of sulphur, as if some malevolent daemon were now stalking the Earth. My eyes darted to the mountain heights to find liquid fire spilling between the rocks, torching the sacred trees. Then to the wide coastal plain, where among the orchards and fields of spice the waterways were bursting open; farmhouses, temples, carts, horses, boats with tattered sails, swept away on the flood wave. Villages we once knew, as puny as a child's plaything.

There was no time to think. No time to run. It was as much as we could do to stay on our feet. At the island's brink, the high cliffs were crumbling, streets, schools, workshops, temples, a thousand summers, lost to the blink of an eye.

Families still fast asleep in their beds, husbands, wives, children, lovers just like us, hushed by the sweet lullaby of the mountain's ancient sleep.

Amid a cloud of dust and rubble, they free-fall through the bloodstained dusk, eyes jarring open to find all those life-defining things that once inspired love or indifference, sublime, ridiculous, a mattress-flying child, the statue of a god, pots and pans, a tumbling donkey, a squealing pig, a flock of hens startled by their own flight.

There were numb white bodies in the water, with wide staring eyes and fronds of seaweed hair. Looming shadows through the deep cast by a sky on fire

★

I awoke with a start, still blinking back silhouettes, trying to remember who or where I was, the hypnotic clatter of the rails in my ears, the train carving its way towards Dover through the sleet, the ferry pitching across the puke-green Channel, the rippling walls of the station waiting room suddenly remembering they're made of solid stone. That's right. I remember now. February the 29th. Day two on my four-day travel plan. Brig, a bustling little town under the Simplon, its high pass lost to the snow. Waiting for my next connection heading south. My guidebook to Greece lying on the chequered floor, where it must have slipped from my sleeping fingers. Still open at the same page, that fire-breathing island in the Aegean sea: Thera, Santorini, Celeste, and whatever other names it has gone by in its tempestuous acquaintance with time.

★

Out onto the platform for a shot of frozen air, lugging my cases behind me, ticket between my teeth.

Almost time.

I glanced down at my watch as the train came thundering in on its own blizzard of snow and electric sparks. It might even have been a trick of the light, I suppose, snow falling against the sunset of a cracked sky, that lent that moment its peculiar magnification.

Time seems to quiver, then billow, a fraction of a second somehow orphaned from its own past. My father's old silver Omega, a present for my 21st; it even crosses my mind that I must have forgotten to wind it.

The second hand seems to falter, then hesitate over the XII before taking its plunge over the luminous radium dial. I blink, put it down to the eerie light, the stress, the sleepless nights that have landed me here. No, I was dead on my feet, that's all, and with another sixteen hundred miles still to go.

The train comes sweeping in on a draught of fractured light, snow and seething sparks. Carriage doors swing open, people in woollen hats, overcoats and scarves descend onto the platform, leaning forward against the cold.

Doors slam. The guard's whistle blows. The carriage jolts forward. I slip into the nearest seat, the window still all steamed up from the passengers who were sitting here before. Slide my cases between the wooden benches where they meet back-to-back, casting an eye over the open carriage, and the handful of people going on to the next stations along the line. Absently, I wind my watch, lift it to my ear, just to check it's still ticking as it should.

Moments like this, bursting with repressed chaos, that yet seem no more consequential than any other in the hours, days and weeks that have led you here.

As innocuous, perhaps, as the moment your eye caught the advertisement in *The Times* of London and you applied for the job, just on the off-chance, knowing you weren't really qualified. As routine as the call that summoned you to the interview in Cambridge, butterflies in your stomach, the dryness on your tongue sometimes making you trip over your own words, your palms all sweaty even in the cold.

As fake innocent even, as that lucky morning when the postman arrived with a registered letter all the way from Greece, the brusque scrawl less an invitation than a summons but still, it's the chance of a lifetime isn't it, a job half your college classmates would have gladly died for.

Apprentice to the archaeologist M. J. Huxley, no less, his excavations in the southern Aegean already raising a lost city, 3,500 years old, from Thera's volcanic ash.

Thera, Santorini, the southernmost of the Cyclades. An island of thousand-foot cliffs, bubbling fumaroles and black volcanic sands.

I admit, that's about as much as I knew, but it was enough for me.

From one moment to the next, everything had changed. The gravestone sky no longer had the power to entomb me. In my mind's eye, I could already see it, already feel it, summer, the curve of a blue horizon, the scattering of islands.

Moments engineered by scheming minds, by chance or serendipity, by some force greater than ourselves, who can tell?

Maybe there are even people out there who can predict them in the making, I don't know, catching the telltale movement at the corner of their eye or something, the tingle down their spine. Not me, that's for sure, making my oblivious way south, just trying to keep to the impossible timetable set by my new employers, just trying to stay awake in case I miss the next connection.

Never guessing for a moment that someone might be interested enough to record my progress, maybe that scruffy student with the goatee under the toothpowder advertisement in the Paris metro; that busker in the Gare de Lyon with the broken guitar string; that impeccably dressed valet boarding the first class carriage in Dijon with his master's cases.

No. If moments of any description entered my muddled head through the blur of the landscape or the clackety-clack of the rails, they were of the past, snatches of time just lived, that's all. Ghosts of moments, that now seemed to be struggling to keep up, flickering through me as we hurtled into the darkness of a tunnel, or emerged into bright snow-swollen light.

My final days at home, minutes, seconds, melting away with the fury of a candle left in a draught.

Eighteen hours to go and I'm racing the clock, wondering how the hell I'll ever get everything organised in time. Tossing stuff into trunks and cases, then hurling pieces out at random when the lids won't shut; cycling down to the high street for the traveller's cheques, quitting my stupid dead-end job, and I don't know, a million other things.

The great day dawns, the sun struggling through spitting clouds.

Mum's fussing over the porridge, the poached eggs, the toast, the coffee percolating on the stove. I know what she's doing; keeping busy, so she won't have to think about me leaving home; worse, leaving the country, who knows, maybe for good.

Sleepy faced, jet black hair tumbling into her eyes, Sofi gives me a playful push just at the thought of it. 'Little Brother' off to Greece; the great big brilliant adventure waiting for me at the front door. She's always been like that, ever since we were kids, visualising things abstract to the rest of us.

Have you got your passport? Have you got the tickets? Have you got the itinerary they sent you? You don't want to miss a connection, not if you can help it.

She throws me a serious look, lowers her voice so Mum won't hear: *Don't forget, Nico. It is a military junta, whatever they say in the holiday brochures. It's a police state. Just look after yourself won't you.*

There's not enough time.

There are too many things left unsaid.

Don't forget to write!

Mum's at the rain-splashed window, smiling, waving, trying not to cry till we turn the corner. Sofi at her elbow, eyes on fire, waving madly now as the taxicab sets off down the driveway.

Try to visit!

Maybe in the summer!

And the next thing I know, I'm wading through the crowds at King's Cross. *I'll never make it in time*, I'm thinking. Never. *They haven't given me enough time to change trains, change stations.*

I should have been paying more attention, that's what I'm saying, even then on the journey down, long before I ever set eyes on Marcus James Huxley.

I shouldn't have needed instruction for something as basic as this, even if I was still wet behind the ears, even if my teachers were as ignorant as I. I mean the warning was there from the start, wasn't it, long before he thrust it into my reeling senses with a vehemence that almost blew me off my feet. *Take nothing at face value. Read between the lines. Trust neither what your eyes tell you, nor the words people speak. Expect the unexpected.*

The train thunders over frost-encrusted fields in the ice-light moon, spins a vortex of snow as it crosses a viaduct built in the sky, utters a piercing shriek as it plunges into a mountain tunnel.

The carriage windows throw our reflections back in our faces and, just for an instant, just for a heartbeat, you have to wonder — *who is that, is that really me?* Nicholas Pedrosa, 22 years old, bags packed, leaving home.

Snow flakes hit us in a sudden blizzard, the line snaking the contours of the granite mountain walls, the snow valley and the river catching moonlight a breathtaking leap below.

We seem to be descending now, and on a long improbable corkscrew through the mountain itself.

11

Then just when you're thinking the tunnel will never end, out we break into the southern Alps, the air limpid, the sky a mass of crystal splintered stars.

Domodossola, all change! People hurry along the platform, all wrapped up against the cold, blowing steam. People like me, who have no idea what's awaiting them around the next corner, much less the next horizon. *All change!*

2.

When finally I set eyes on her, I assumed I was still in the wrong place, some graveyard for ships. The *Pegasus*, read the name on the prow, each letter with its trickling stain of rust. A Piraeus tramp steamer if ever there was one, her glory days beyond all recollection of the living.

Propellers frothing the putrid water, she was already getting up steam, deckhands loosening the algae-slick hawsers. There was no telling when she would be back. I ran.

A battered old Land Rover was being winched onto the aft deck in a rope sling. A few late passengers were still scurrying up the gangway, the escaping street hawkers barging past them with their trays of sesame rings and *loukoumi,* that gummy sweet the rest of us know as Turkish Delight. In a cacophony of yells, bleating, and jangling of bells, a flock of goats was being chased up the ramp and into the hold. The Captain glared down at us from the bridge. Any moment now, his patience would buckle and he would lift the gangway whoever ended up in the drink.

Dragging my stuff behind me I dashed after the goats, and had hardly stepped on deck when there was a shrill whistle from the bridge, and the funnel began panting and billowing steam.

Still winching in the hawsers, we moved across the fetid harbour, the factories on the other side belching black smoke. Past the listing and abandoned ships tied up among the graveyard quays, out past the harbour walls and then, all of a sudden, when I looked again, the whole world had turned blue.

The blue of the winter Aegean. Sea, sky, reflecting one another into infinity.

If only they could see me now, I thought, my friends, my former work mates in that dead-end job of mine. My life was just beginning.

Every so often I'd cast an eye over my fellow passengers, just to pass the time. Farmers and fishermen in Sunday-best suits two sizes too small; trouser cuffs over their ankles, spit-and-polish shoes that probably pinched the toes. A young soldier with his rifle between his knees. A gaggle of students on some class expedition to the islands. A plump man in a straw boater at the railings, round tortoiseshell glasses lending him the appearance of a pompous owl. Folded in his hands an Athens newspaper, its headline proclaiming new finds at the Theran dig. *Archaeologists Unearth Mystery Hieroglyphs.* I squinted hard. *Temple inscriptions in the extinct script Cretan Hieroglyphic, probably more than 5,000 years old. Would they ever be deciphered?*

Just how long that reptilian stare had been boring into the back of my head I had no idea, but I was aware of it now.

I shifted sideways on the bench, stealing a glance over my shoulder. So it wasn't my imagination after all. He *had* been staring at me the whole time, and continued to do so even now, sour, unflinching eyes in a speckled parchment face.

A gaunt man in a white suit and Panama hat, striking an imperious pose on the First Class deck, 80 years old if he was a day. Sitting in the wind shadow of the ship's funnel, a bronze-headed walking cane clasped tightly between bony fists and knees.

After resisting that mouldy gaze for another ten minutes or so, I gave up, retreating to the other side of the ship.

Nearing the Cyclades, we ran into a sudden gale. Demented gusts and spitting rain struck us broadside from the east and went shrieking through the wires on the upper deck. Through the doorway to the bridge, I saw the look of consternation flicker over the helmsman's face as he fought the wheel to keep us on course, the Captain at his shoulder, scanning the bruise-black horizon that seemed on the verge of swallowing us whole.

The ship pitched and rolled, the sheer force of the waves juddering through its iron hull. In the dining room, bottles, glasses and plates skated back and forth across the tables, then crashed to the floor. Passengers stumbled about as if drunk, barging into one another, collapsing into chairs. Peasant women from the islands lay supine on the floor, moaning, their olive complexions now wan and ghostly.

Others took their seasickness to the lavatories, leaving the floors and basins awash, the sight and stench so contagious there was no escaping it, stem to stern. Craving air I stumbled out onto the deck, gripping the railings with white-knuckled fists, retching over the side, knees buckling as the *Pegasus* seesawed through the waves.

A rocky island appeared off the port bow, silhouetted against the raging silver sea. Listing in the wind, the ship limped along in its cliff-bound shadow, at times so treacherously close I was certain we would be dashed against the rocks.

Smoke belching from the funnel, engines shuddering, we plunged into a maelstrom of white water, spray cascading over the decks. I saw the helmsman spin the wheel hard to port, and just as it occurred to me that he had doomed us all, we went steaming between the splintered rocks into an implausibly narrow channel.

To my untrained eye it seemed as if we had barely escaped with our lives, but at least we had reached calmer waters, a sheltered bay ringed by parched, rounded hillsides. Strung along a narrow pebble beach, a few poor fishermen's houses, bright yellow nets hanging in the sun. Above, a little village of white cubic houses nestled on the ridge of a pointed mountain.

With a clanking of chain we dropped anchor, engines hushing. Despite the enduring silence from the bridge, what with the bulk of the crew now in their bunks, it seemed safe to assume we were seeking refuge from the worst of the storm.

Through the deck railings separating First Class from steerage, I heard a man's brusque, impatient shout.

'Boy! Boy!'

The voice rose in volume.

'You, boy!' he was yelling, as though summoning some Athens shoeshine, or the servant he normally kept below stairs.

My eyes flickered towards him in irritation — only to discover that those sunken-cheeks and thin bloodless lips were actually scowling at me.

I should have known. The ancient creature in the white suit and panama hat, now striking the railings with his skull-headed cane.

I remarked it even then. His posture. Almost Napoleonic in a gaunt, moth-eaten kind of way, nose tilted several degrees above the horizon.

'On which godforsaken island are we now?' More demand than question, as though I should be any better acquainted with the Captain's charts than he. 'We are already twelve hours behind schedule, *twelve hours!*'

'One of the Cyclades, I suppose. Maybe Naxos. Maybe Paros. Maybe —'

'These Greeks!' he cried in exasperation, and now I could definitely hear the French lilt to his voice. 'It is as if their incompetence were deliberate rather than congenital.'

'You can hardly blame them for the weather.'

'The weather!' he sneered. 'There was a time, young man, when no

15

challenge was insurmountable to the warriors and visionaries of this land, philosophers who would hurl imponderable questions beyond the stars; golden heroes who would challenge even the King of Death himself. Why? Because the challenge exists and they had the soul to seek it, the resolve to demand it.' Casting a jaundiced eye over the shuffling deck hands on the lower deck, he added: 'Now, apparently, the insurmountable challenge is walking upright.'

'But we almost sank! We almost drowned!'

'If so, that would be testament to the captain's incompetence, hardly the severity of the storm. I have been through far worse in any sea you care to name.'

'At this rate,' he fumed, leaning heavily on his cane, 'we shall be days behind schedule, not hours. Are you not even vaguely curious as to the Captain's intentions?'

'Of course. I have people waiting for me on Santorini, but —'

'Then kindly spare me the trouble of negotiating those treacherous, brine-slick stairways. Go below deck and interrogate the Purser.'

Swearing, I did just that, finding the man one deck down at the reception, eating *loukoumi* and smoking cigarettes, his uniform powdered with ash and sugar dust. 'When will we get underway again, do you know? Yes, but what's our estimated time of arrival? Is it still far?'

Questions to which our Purser replied with accomplished indifference, eyebrows arching up, mouth arching down, right hand swivelling round, fingers splaying out to reveal an open palm. From what I had already learnt in evening class, this was a common expression among the Greeks, and roughly translated meant 'Who knows? Who cares? Fate alone will decide.'

Munching and smoking, his eyes drifted bleakly to the porthole at his side, and a distant patch of angry sky; conversation over.

When I reported back to the Frenchman in First Class, I expected him to rant and rave, but he merely scowled, demanding to know where I was going, who was waiting for me, and what conceivable benefit a youth could bring to something so ancient, so sacred. I made my escape.

When at last the storm blew itself out, we got underway again, pounding through the swell it had left in its wake.

I went down to my cabin, crawled onto the bunk, tried to sleep, couldn't.

Even now I could hardly believe my luck. It kept turning round and round in my head, the impression I must have made on Professor Huxley's agent at the interview, and what she had seen in me that I couldn't quite see in myself. Apart from my mediocre Greek and a four week stint at archaeological field camp on the Peloponnese when I was 19; apart from my half-completed classics course at college, what else was there?

That made me worry even more. What if there had been some kind of mistake? What if I wasn't up to the job? Maybe the obnoxious Frenchman had a point.

As interviews go, mine had been a rough ride, almost as rough as the weather out there, dashing the porthole in wind and spray.

Professor Huxley's agent turned out to be a Russian of indeterminate age, with ice blond hair, ice blue eyes and an almost translucent complexion. Aside from the flowery silk scarf bringing a splash of colour to her neck, Svetlana Bé, as she purported to be called, was dressed in black from head to foot.

Cold, yet as elegant as a fresh snow drift. You could almost imagine the ice crystals forming in the prisms of her eyes, feel the touch of the lips that would numb your skin. Fear for the cheek bones that might shatter in the event of a smile.

Nothing to do with idle vanity, this kind of elegance, but something far more purposeful. You could feel the static charge from her sheer silk stockings as she crossed her legs. See thin air make way for relentless confidence as she incised her way across the street in her stiletto heels.

As per her written instructions, we met at the old Garden House Hotel in Cambridge, overlooking the river, an incongruous setting given the barrage of questions she was about to unleash. Genteel Cambridge wives sitting down to their afternoon teas and cream cakes, all hushed voices, salmon-pink curtains, tablecloths and doilies. Beyond the French windows, a boat would sometimes glide silently through the mist, a solitary figure punting from the stern.

Svetlana Bé opened a black foolscap notebook, propping it up against the table edge so as to conceal its contents. The waitress appeared with our order. Hers, Himalayan Darjeeling with a slice of lemon. Mine, plain old tea with milk. A plate of fresh scones with strawberry jam and clotted cream was placed between us, and I could see it in her eyes, just daring me to take one.

I was aware of permed heads inclining towards us, all the better to eavesdrop on the muffled yet strangely dashing words that passed between us. I, in my mother-pressed shirt and interview tie, trying to impress or at least look the part. Grasping, fumbling for the slippery, unsettling questions being hurled at me.

Questions on my ties to England. Questions about my relationship to my family, friends and teachers. Questions on my emotional attachments, or lack thereof. At times they seemed as darkly suggestive as black chocolate. At others, as subtle as a cricket bat.

Ambition, honour, duty, love, which is more important to you? Your sexual awakening, Nicholas Pedrosa, characterise it for me. Describe your first erotic encounter; in the woods, behind the bicycle sheds, in class itself, perhaps, under the teacher's very eye, fumbling under the desk? You pleasure yourself, of course, all boys do — how many times a day?

I have to admit, it wasn't what I'd been expecting, and at first I must have looked like a stunned deer or something, caught in the headlights.

I know: that must have been the intention all along. I glanced apprehensively at the tables across the aisle, thinking how thrilled to bits the genteel ladies would be in their *'well I never!'* kind of way.

For a moment, ticking off the reaction boxes on her list and scribbling her observations, Svetlana Bé seemed satisfied, then pounced.

'How is it that a young man like you has no friends to speak of? I would consider that strange. Would you not consider that strange?'

'No, I wouldn't, not at all!' I protested, a fraction of a second off the beat. 'I only came home from college in summer —'

'Ah, yes, Aberdeen!' she said, scanning her notes. 'Such a long way from home. But why? Why a college closer to the Arctic Circle than your own home? Your dinky little village in the Cotswolds, Moreton-in-the-Marsh.'

'Because of the course,' I said, holding my breath. 'The syllabus.'

'You were not homesick?'

'No.'

'Not once? Of course, I forget. You have no attachments. No love. No friends. No passion.' If not for the midwinter frost that gripped them, the words might even have sounded sarcastic.

'Twenty-four and still living with his mother and sister.'

'Twenty-two,' I corrected her. Things were going badly. 'Where is your father? Did he desert you, you, your mother, your sister? Is that it? Is that why you ran home from college? Is that why you tore up your education, threw away your own future?' I wondered if she could hear the pounding in my chest. 'Yes.'

The second I saw the look thrown back at me across the table, I knew she knew she'd finally caught me in a lie.

'Professor Huxley demands the loyalty of his apprentices,' she went on, the ice crystals dancing sardonically in her eye. 'Boy that you are, doubtless you would expect to run home on leave every other week, back to mama, homesick, frightened, disrupting the work plan, inconveniencing everybody in sight.'

Still stumbling over the boot camp metaphor, I just managed to protest, 'No, I can go and not look back. I can.'

The pencil line eyebrows arched sceptically.

'Then what is it that attracts you most to this job that you have applied for, Nicholas Pedrosa?' A question tinged with accusation, and probably the hardest one of all to answer. In the end, thinking the job already lost, I just blurted out the first thing that came into my head.

'To know the ancient island and what it might have been.'

A hesitation. A skipped beat. The first and only one. A scrutinising look across the table, the biologist sizing up a curious bug.

'I think you cannot imagine what Greece is like,' she said in parting. 'Its identity smudged between the fog of mythology and logic as lucid as a winter sky... But look, look who I am talking to... a child.'

She took my CV and references without comment, stuffing them carelessly into her bag.

In the gathering dusk I returned home, gloomy and demoralised. Crumpling into bed that night, the encounter wouldn't leave me alone, questions, answers, bouncing around my head. What I should have said, and hadn't. The words I should have spoken, but couldn't find. There would never be a chance like this again, I knew that. Never.

The days oozed by, congealing into weeks, and I heard nothing more. I returned to my dead-end job on the high street. Junior Sales trainee at Randoor & Heaven, Estate Agents of Distinction. Mr Percival Heaven, the roly-poly Principal, his pinstripe suit so habitual he might even have slept in it for all we knew, folds of flesh sagging over his shirt collar.

If I put my mind to it, kept my nose to the grindstone, I might even make Assistant Sales Negotiator by the time I was 35. Only another 13 years to go.

'We have Rolls-Royces drawing up outside,' spluttered Mr Heaven, indignant that I had let hair, and not fat, grow over my collar. My first warning.

Second warning, late for work, an hour docked from my pay.

Third warning, unprofessionalism, blabbing to some prospective buyer that the cellar of his dream house floods in stormy weather. A bawling out from Heaven. Half a day docked from my pay.

First snows. Drifting on the hills. Christmas at home, as difficult as ever, never mind the presents under the tree, the children's carols at the door, the lights in the snow. Habit, I suppose, setting that place for him at the head of table, his favourite glass for his favourite wine. You even catch yourself looking for careless footprints in the snow. Down to the Bell Inn with the younger office staff, drinking far more than I should, who cares. It's fucking amazing to think that, of all the people you have come to know since leaving college, you have absolutely nothing in common with any of them. Nothing at all.

Monday morning. First thaw, muddy sludge along the lanes, the countryside bleak and misty.

About to bike off to work, I almost collided with the postman at the front door. A registered letter, postmark Athens. Well that's it, I thought, with a wince. This is your formal rejection. Some other lucky applicant's already heading south to the job of a lifetime.

Anxious about being late for work again, and resenting myself for it, I tore open the envelope, almost ripping its contents in the process.

When finally the swimming words began to make sense, I could hardly believe my own eyes; I had to read the letter again and again just to make it sink in. Secreted in the bulky envelope, not the booby prize brochure on the dig I had been expecting, but tickets, itineraries, everything. Boat train to Calais, then on to Paris, Dijon, Milano, Brindisi.

Within the space of that infinitesimal moment, everything had changed. Everything. Life was no longer the poison we are required to drink until it kills us. I would say goodbye to the yellowing walls that absorbed our childhood memories like blotting paper, weeping their mildewed ghosts.

Now wherever I looked, 360 degrees around my own life, I saw only one thing: horizon.

I admit, I drew some perverse pleasure in announcing my departure, effective immediately, to Heaven himself.

'Don't imagine for a second you'll be getting your last pay packet,' he blustered, the absurd originality of the moment spinning him like a top. No one had ever done anything like this before, not in all his born days. 'After all we've taught you. After all the time we've invested in you.'

'Yes. I'm leaving for Greece. I'm leaving for the islands. This time tomorrow I'll already be in Dover.'

Impressed they were not. Despite the odd envious glance from the other trainees, the smug consensus was that I had obviously taken leave of my senses. Abandoning one's career like that, without so much as a day to weigh the consequences; running off to an island you've never set foot on before, to a job you know next to nothing about, to people you've never even set eyes on before.

You'll come unstuck, my lad, you just see if you don't!

They had a point, I know, but I didn't care.

I couldn't believe my luck. I was free.

3.

Thirty-six hours behind schedule, its crescent moon outline appeared on the southern horizon. Thera. Santorini.

I hurried back to the cabin and its cubicle-like washroom, thinking, you have to make yourself look at least vaguely presentable to your new employer. Except, peering into the dimly-lit mirror, I could hardly find myself, the silver so thin it was in danger of losing its reflection altogether. I splashed water onto my face, ran fingers through my hair but still ended up looking like someone who had been sleeping rough for a week.

By the time I'd dragged my belongings to the reception area we were already reaching the northern, pincer-like tip of the island. I rushed up to the top deck to take in the sights.

At first, it was the light, not the island, that snatched my breath away. Its intensity. Its clarity. Its improbability. I squinted, shielding my eyes. It glanced off the water, off the white bridge where the helmsman stood, off the windows of the saloon in which I and my fellow deck passengers had now become silhouettes against a streaming silver sea.

And then there was the island itself, looming up at us like some eighth wonder of the world.

Long ago, it would have dominated the southern Aegean, a mountain volcano piercing the sky, its peak all snow and ice even in spring. But then, some 3,500 years ago, it went off like a Roman candle, raining fire, blowing apart, the sea flooding into its molten heart. And this was all that was left of it: a crescent shaped crater rim formed by towering, rust-red cliffs. Soon, they were dwarfing the ship.

Off the starboard bow, the Burnt Islands came into view, charred islets of solidified lava like great heaps of coal, strange obsidian sculptures and the occasional plume of drowsy, sulphurous smoke. Beyond, Thirassia, a smaller remnant of the ancient volcanic cone, a curving lava wall rising defiantly out of the sea.

With two blasts of the klaxon we hailed the inhabitants of Oia, a shabby little village of white cubic houses, domes and bell towers strung across the cliff top.

Coming from rural England, it was hard to imagine people living like this anywhere, on the brink of a thousand-foot precipice, on the lips of a volcano not dead, just sleeping.

Maybe that explained the dark superstitions that were said to infest the village streets, and why there were more churches on the island than houses. Tempting fate like that, it might have been the sensible thing to do.

Then I realised. Those grey rock caves, that appeared to honeycomb the higher reaches of the cliff face at Oia — they weren't caves at all, but the shells of ruined houses. Victims of rock slides, tremors and earthquakes that would strike inevitably sooner or later, a day, a year, a century from now.

Something was different about the sea here within the caldera. Off the Burnt Islands, it was almost as if its deeper luminosity carried an electric charge, making it hiss against the hull.

Soon we were approaching Phíra, its barrel-vaulted houses and domed churches rising over the crater wall, windows catching the winter sun.

Even here, at the main town, there was no harbour as such, just a small cement quay at the foot of the cliffs, where fishermen laid out their nets to dry. Carved out of the rust red lava, a steep pathway serpentined its way up the rock face. Squinting up, I could see, as if in miniature, a mule train being driven down to the wharf, loaded with passengers, luggage, even packing crates.

The ship edged closer until the death-defying houses were almost overhead. Then, with a clanking roar off the crater wall, we dropped anchor, probably using every link of chain to reach the seabed.

A flotilla of boats put out from the jetty. Of the smallest vessels, several looked in danger of capsizing altogether under the weight or sheer dimensions of their cargo.

I caught sight of the Frenchman whacking his way impatiently through the crowd, his luggage being towed behind him by his very own flunkey. As his head turned, I caught his profile, and the memory splashed into my head like a reluctant drip from a tap — wait, wasn't that the valet I had seen on the platform at Dijon, stowing aboard his master's suitcases, tall, self-assured, despite his apparent bondage? There was no time to dwell on it.

From the cargo hatch, crewmen were tossing suitcases, boxes and sacks onto the boats flocking below, a mess of flapping sprit rig sails, frothing propellers, colliding oars, yells and curses.

Then it was every man for himself, passengers from the flotilla leaping aboard ship with an energy and determination that defied age, weight or infirmity, passengers from the *Pegasus* shoving their way towards the boats. And somewhere in the stumbling mass, me, jumping onto the nearest caïque and almost ending up in the drink, a huge calloused hand just catching me by the wrist.

As my trunk and cases were tossed carelessly onto another boat, I wondered if I would ever see them again.

And all of a sudden, after a week on the road, there I was. Climbing out onto the dock, hands and feet meeting island for the very first time.

My eyes swept up and down the length of it, searching faces. Fishermen mending their nets, the mesh between their toes, the hemp twine between their teeth. The muleteers, fiddling with reins and saddles. The new arrivals thronging the quayside, jabbering at family, friends, lovers, whoever had braved the cliff face steps to greet them.

I suppose I had been expecting some kind of welcome as well. If not Professor Huxley himself, then at least some messenger holding up a sign with my name on it. There was no one.

Against my better judgement I joined the mule train, about to make its precipitous ascent up the serpentines. While my luggage was strapped onto the pack animal next in line, I hoisted myself up onto the crude wooden saddle. Then amid a volley of yells and lashes against hide, we were off.

For the next thousand steps up the cliff face, we clung to our lurching beasts of burden as if our lives depended on it.

At every other hairpin on the path I'd find myself teetering over the abyss, staring into thin air. When hooves lost grip, skating over the slick volcanic stones, it seemed that luck, nothing more, had saved us. Cries of dismay up and down the mule train provided little in the way of comfort.

At the summit, we entered a little square formed by an intersection of paths, and suddenly it was mob chaos again, mules snorting, bags, boxes and trunks dragged left and right, men yelling, women shrieking.

Hoping my employer might have remembered me, I scanned the faces in the crowd. In vain. As the agitated swarm abruptly dispersed, I found myself standing there alone in the middle of the pebble-dashed street, my trunk and cases in a heap beside me.

My attention was drawn to a wiry little man standing in the arched doorway of a *kafeneion* across the way, staring at me with quizzical bird-like eyes.

'Tea? Coffee?' he demanded impishly, rattling the loose change in his pocket, moustache twitching expectantly.

I stared at the heap of luggage at my feet. I could store it all inside, I thought. The little man would be sure to let me. Then scout about town for my new employer or, failing that, at least my lodgings, probably at some house without a number in some street without a name.

I wandered inside, the little man scurrying after me. It was grubby, deserted, and about as warm as a fridge. I studied the chalkboard menu on the wall, if that's the right word for a something that basically consisted of muddy Greek coffee, mountain tea, *gazoza* lemonade, and use of the *tavli* boards.

Feeling obliged to order something as I stacked my stuff in a corner, I settled on a glass of raki, some local firewater that would at least kill off any germs lurking on the grease-stained glass.

I moved towards the windows, where the afternoon light was streaming in. My heart seemed to swell over an unseen wave. Beyond the flimsy glass there was blue ethereal sky and a thousand foot drop to the caldera, that's all. I stepped back, not quite used to walking on thin air.

★

I found myself in a warren of little streets, scarcely wide enough for two mules with laden panniers to pass. They rose and fell in slopes and steps, sometimes running through archways or tunnels formed by streets and houses above.

Shrines, chapels, churches. They were everywhere you looked. Like this one, perched on a narrow ledge of rock, seemingly levitating over the precipice, the folly already apparent in the jagged crack running through its dome.

When next I looked back, it was from the heights of the town and I could see it rising across the hollow in the crater wall like an amphitheatre — barrel-vaulted roofs, domes, bell towers, cubic houses. All gaining silhouette now against the sunken crater far below, and a sea turning molten bronze in the late sun.

Just as the last of the houses gave way to barren fields, something in the distance caught my eye. A procession or something, making its way over the gashed volcanic cliffs. Twenty people, maybe more, the pathway lending them the sinuous motion of a snake.

By the time I caught up, the serpent's tail was already entering a walled field, curling under a white stucco arch.

Impulsively, I stepped through, and just as abruptly found myself wishing I hadn't.

A burial. I had blundered right into the middle of it. Silhouettes dressed in mourning, suddenly gaining flushed tearful faces. Tombs and headstones, some bearing sepia pictures of the dead. A tiny barrel-vaulted chapel, illuminated from within by a blaze of candles. The elderly *Papás*, with his flowing silver beard, chimney-pot hat and billowing skirts. And from afar, what had once resembled the serpent's angular head: six strong men, locals by the look of them, their stout shoulders bearing the crude pine coffin.

I swallowed hard. The wine coloured light, suffusing everything now, had found another angle, and with it, the profile of the face in the lidless casket.

The body, whoever it had once belonged to, wasn't Greek. Not with that straw blond hair, those finely chiselled features. A young man, hardly older than I.

Shielded by the cemetery wall, I studied the mourners one by one, thinking, *who are they?* Standing out from the rest, a young woman, far too elegant for this rough and ready place, foreign too, judging from the fair complexion and the flaxen, bun-coiled hair.

A woman in grief, yet not one whose disposition would have her keening over the grave, much less tearing her hair out by the roots. At a guess, family of the deceased, probably the young man's sister, maybe his wife. And angry, that much obvious enough from the smouldering look that swept towards me, stopping short only as it found its true mark among the mourners filing in behind her.

A shadow, eternal, passed over the dead man's face as the coffin lid was nailed shut.

A hurried ceremony got underway over the freshly dug grave, the priest delivering his singsong incantation as the coffin was lowered jerkily into the ground, a sprinkling of holy water drumming over the wood like reluctant rain.

No sooner had he recited the blessing than the bereaved woman broke away, angrily shaking off the hands that sought to comfort her. Seconds later she was marching for the gate, the sunset no match for her blazing eyes.

I heard English being spoken, and several colliding voices trying to soothe or reason.

She spun around, incensed. 'No, *no!* It is unforgivable! Who put the silver drachma in his mouth? *Who?* Who gave you the right? I should have taken his body home with me, I should never have agreed to leave him here with you godless people, *never!*'

'It is ancient custom, that's all. Benja loved the island, and everything about it, you know that.'

'The island! The island killed him! *You* killed him!'

And with that, the young woman fled along the path, choking back anger and finding tears, choking back tears and finding an anger too scalding to touch.

Call it premonition, but at that moment I knew it with utter certainty. The target of her wrath, I mean. He was the imposing, no, the almost imperious figure now blocking the gate, each calloused hand the size of a bear's paw. If youth should take a guess at age, somewhere in his early fifties. The broad shoulders telling everyone that here was a man who wouldn't flinch from swinging a pickaxe with his own hand should the mood take him. A shock of dark unkempt hair, dashed with silver at the temples. A face that has known too much dust and sun, too many sleepless nights. *Marcus James Huxley.*

A man for whom even the solemnity of an occasion like this warrants no particular deference to custom, at least to judge from the dusty boots and the donkey jacket. He stepped heavily out of the gate, casting a grim look at the receding figure who had just hurled that shocking accusation at him.

At his shoulder, other faces, unmistakeable, even if I had never set eyes on them before. My future colleagues. Archaeologists and other members of the team, handpicked by the great man himself.

I flinched as Huxley's eyes caught mine in their relentless gravitational field. For a few excruciating seconds, I don't know why, I found myself struggling to hold on to my own sense of self, as though my identity were slipping away from me.

Luckily, I was saved by the priest, who chose that moment to appear at the gates, breaking his stare. What with the grim disapproval of one and the sardonic grimace of the other, the animosity between the two almost made the air crackle.

The object of Huxley's scorn hesitated, turned.

'It is unusual to see you at any religious service, *Professor.* Even those laying the dead to rest.'

'Is that what you have achieved with your Christian ritual, *Papás?*' replied Huxley with casual contempt.

'You still have the disease of youth, Huxley, thinking you will live forever. But remember this, even you will one day meet God or the Devil through the same hole in the ground.'

A moment later I felt his penetrating eyes on me again, and had to use all my will just to meet them.

The sardonic look was still there, and for a moment I had to wonder who, exactly, it was aimed at — the Papás, me, or the whole world.

He thrust out his hand at me, no doubt recognising my face from the mug shot stapled to my job application.

'Mr Pedrosa, I presume.' The words so dry, a careless breeze might have blown them away.

A flinch of a smile, one that did nothing to dispel that air of resentful impatience about him, as if every moment here was a moment squandered on irrelevance.

His hand took mine in a powerful yet curiously sensitive grip, the mark, perhaps, of a man whose arrogance knew no bounds, yet who was accustomed to handling artefacts as delicate as eggshell.

As for idle pleasantries, there were none. The word 'welcome' passed his lips just once and with that, I was introduced to the others one by one.

Anna Trevisi, a long way from Piacenza, the charcoal scarf tied under her chin accentuating the winter paleness of her face. Henna red hair, filaments of copper where it struck grey. Emerald eyes like tropical sea anticipating the rain. Here to bury a friend, not quite ready to cry, even I could tell that; the tears held back by something, something in turmoil, something in conflict, but what?

Nestor Louganis, Huxley's right-hand man and site foreman, so tall he has to stoop as he passes under the cemetery archway. Nestled at his side, his fiancée Maria, an island beauty if ever there was one. High cheekbones, wide almond eyes, and a smile that on better days might have rivalled the dawning sun. But not today. Not with that swollen redness about them. She had been crying long and hard.

'Sam,' muttered Anna, with a vexed glance over her shoulder.

Samuel Gascon. Last known abode some attic apartment in the Paris student quarter, Saint-Michel. Half a dozen years older than me, if that. Typical Latin looks, at least if you could forget even for an instant those eyes, inherited from God knows where, a shocking blue that drew the stares, just as they drew mine now; how could they not? There was a brooding, even resentful, air about him, and he wasn't hiding it either, a bored *who cares?* curl to his lips as he slouched against the cemetery wall, rolling a cigarette.

A pudgy hand thrust its way between the milling bodies. Dr Adrian Hunt, thinning hair, waddling gait, and that pink English skin that the sun refuses to bronze even in summer. He stood there like a plump, startled bird, peering out through round tortoiseshell glasses, probably still wondering at the back of his mind why he had deserted the gothic spires of Oxford for this godforsaken place. Then it struck me, as we shook hands. This man I had seen before, on the upper deck of the *Pegasus*, his newspaper announcing those stunning hieroglyphic finds at the dig. There was a fidgety apprehension about him that somehow even this outlandish moment couldn't quite explain.

Catching a movement along the pathway I realised we were being watched by two policemen, one as round as a barrel, the other as tall and thin as a beanpole.

The moment had me in its grip. I had to say something.

'Who is it?' I asked Huxley. 'Who has died?'

His hesitation barely measured a skipped heartbeat.

'Your predecessor, Mr Pedrosa. Benjamin Randal. He has lost his life. I trust you will be more careful with yours.'

4.

Just for a second I felt myself falling, the words like brine slick rocks, my feet plunging into the foaming waters between them. Someone shot out a hand to steady me, and I heard a disembodied voice say, 'Are you all right?'

Straightening up, I mumbled my excuses, about the journey, the storm, the sleepless nights. Come to think of it, I hadn't eaten so much as a slice of bread in twelve hours.

As I looked up, I found eyes the colour of blue glass fixed on me, I don't know why, almost as if they were tapping my discomfort for their own pleasure. With a sneer, the young man stubbed out his cigarette on the cemetery wall.

'Tomorrow morning bright and early, Mr Pedrosa,' Huxley declared in parting. 'I trust you will not disappoint us on your first day.'

He turned, setting off along the path at a brisk stride.

With a stab of apprehension just at the thought at that freshly dug grave in there, I called after him: 'Do I have lodgings here? In the town, I mean?'

'A fifteen minute walk at best,' he replied sharply, pointing along the crater rim, tinged lava-red now in the dusk. 'Beyond the church with the blue dome, ask at the taverna and you'll find your accommodation.'

And with a curt nod he moved on, the others in his wake. In the gathering darkness I was left standing at the cemetery gates, the candles casting their eerie glow over the sepia faces of the dead.

Retracing my steps, the feeble lamps of the town were hardly distinguishable from the stars above.

Down below, the caldera lay in trembling moonlight, the jagged, boulder-strewn shores of the Burnt Islands engulfed in silver.

Passing the church with the blue dome, there was still no sign of Huxley's mythical taverna. The clip-clopping of hooves welled up along the narrow street, and then they appeared, barely more than shadows under the lamps. One of the muleteers, about to stable his animal for the night. Stopping him, I asked the way. About as talkative as his mule, he offered a gruff toss of the head up the street. Just as he was about to move on, I remembered my luggage at the *kafeneion* and asked if he would collect it for me. Ten drachmas, barked the stubbled face, and though it seemed a little steep, the deal was done.

I was beginning to think I'd already passed it without realising, when I came across a blue door and a glowing window filled with dusty bottles of wine. I peered inside. A few small tables, an iron stove in a corner. Then a lopsided doorway opening onto a cramped kitchen, where an elderly woman was tending her pots and pans. Hardly what anyone would have imagined as a taverna, that's for sure. To all intents and purposes, it was just a private household that had added a couple of extra tables to its living room. Just as I swung open the door, I felt a tug from the other side and a stocky man with grey-flecked hair almost barged into me. A startled expression crossed his face, momentarily chasing away the anxiousness that had set up home in his eyes.

He must have been three times my age, but still addressed me formally as 'sir'. 'We have been expecting you, *Kyrios*,' he wheezed, producing a huge iron key from his jacket pocket. A few yards up the pathway we came to a barrel-vaulted house with a small courtyard and a bare-limbed fig tree.

Oil lamp in one hand, key in the other, my landlord struggled with the lock until the door finally creaked open.

Inside, it was spartan but clean, smelling of fresh whitewash.

A half-flight of narrow stairs led to the bedroom, illuminated by the dim glow of an electric bulb. Small but functional, with a wardrobe, a chest of drawers, and a twanging, coil-spring bed.

Over the blue table in the kitchen hung a candle lamp and I wasted no time in lighting it, the sputtering wick sending our silhouettes leaping over the walls.

Like eyes preoccupied with other things, the room's twin windows stared out across the dizzying moonlit sea. From now on, I would be living here, perched on the lip of the crater, with nothing between me and the abyss but a wall made of sun brick, stucco and whitewash.

No sooner had my landlord taken his leave than I heard the echo of hooves along the pathway, signalling the arrival of my luggage.

For all his apparent surliness, the muleteer insisted on carrying in my trunk and cases on his own shoulders.

Down on the painted cement floor, I set about unpacking the essentials, but found trouble staring me in the face the moment I opened my first suitcase.

Someone had pried open the locks; their sticky fingers rifling through everything inside — shirts, pullovers, underwear, books, even my diary and correspondence with Huxley's agent, Svetlana Bé. Nothing seemed to be missing, but that left me more puzzled than relieved.

Angry, upset, I charged back into town with every intention of confronting the wiry little man in the *kafeneion*. Maybe it was just the exhaustion catching up with me but by the time I had reached the first flight of steps into town, I was already regretting my impulsiveness. *What proof do you have?* I thought. *None!*

Suddenly, I heard quarrelsome voices in the air, faint but insistent, welling up on the tail end of the gusts, then subsiding. Out of curiosity I allowed them to draw me in, along a labyrinth of narrow, dimly-lit streets.

Turning a corner, a wash of yellow light appeared and I found myself standing outside a kind of wine cellar or *kanava*, its steep flight of steps disappearing through an arched doorway. The angry voices were unmistakeable now, even as the thick stone walls continued to muffle them.

On impulse, I ventured inside; my second blunder within as many hours. On unfamiliar ground, I found myself staring up at the vaulted ceiling and the huge oak and pinewood barrels lining the walls.

The air was so thick it was almost viscous, sour from spilled wine, acrid with the smoke of cheap tobacco. But there was something else. A tension so electric it seemed to crackle between the walls.

Through the billowing smoke a dozen or so men materialised, some standing, others occupying the rickety blue tables and chairs scattered about the stone-flagged floor. My eyes were drawn at once to the ringleaders, confronting each other at close quarters at the tiled wooden bar, each trying to shout the other down.

I tried to take in what I was seeing: two sides of island opinion, cleaved down the middle, and both more than a little worse for wear after a night's drinking.

I counted myself lucky that our Greek teacher had brought such tales of island life into the classroom, telling us about the function of the village *kafeneion* or of a place like this, an exclusively male preserve where opinions not so much met in debate as in battle.

And now I was seeing it firsthand, wine and raki overflowing, tempers flaring, argument teetering precariously between dispute and brawl.

Remember, the greatest threat is not loss of life or limb, but loss of face, my teacher was saying, her amused, ironic voice far too distant for comfort.

The two protagonists were easy enough to tell apart. In the left corner, a gangling individual with a dense thatch of black hair and a Cretan-style moustache. And in the right, a thickset man in a crumpled suit, with a forehead overhang that appeared to half bury his eyes. Belly as swollen as a wineskin. Thin strands of hair slicked over his scalp to hide the bald facts from his own mind.

Around them, their enemies and supporters yelled, laughed, jeered, spat, thumped the tables. Sometimes, from one table or another, I thought I even caught appeals to reason but, if so, these were drowned as summarily as a litter of Greek kittens.

As far as I could tell, most were farmers, fishers, labourers, muleteers. The expressions etched onto their faces seemed to magnify in depth for a moment, leaping out at me, as if reflecting all the characters that the world had ever sought to create. Some smoked, others fingered their worry beads, clicking them loudly over their knuckles.

Lurid obscenities, only a quarter of which I could understand at all, were bouncing off the walls and echoing off the vaulted ceiling. Insults aimed at fate or absent enemies, curses contrived to pack a punch into their own emphatic opinions.

Confused by the bluster and noise, thrown by the unfamiliar dialect, I was struggling to understand what the argument was even about. By the time I had finally cottoned on, it was already too late. Their rage, I realised, was directed at *me* — or at least, the archaeological dig that had just hired me.

Half the eyes in the cellar were already glaring through the smoke at me, obviously sizing up the stranger in their midst.

Given half the chance you wouldn't have seen me for dust, but turning tail wasn't any option anymore. I'd never live it down.

From the greying figure behind the bar, I ordered red wine from the barrel. He was about to confuse me with varieties and vintages, for which the island is famous, but then evidently thought better of it, filling a glass from the nearest tap instead.

I caught the nonchalant gleam in his eye and I took some comfort from it. It meant he was accustomed to playing the referee, just as tradition demanded. Not that he was above taking the odd kick himself to keep the ball in play.

'Hey, Manoli,' he shouted at the beanpole Cretan, tossing his head towards me, 'look what the storm's blown in. The Professor's brand new boy.'

Reeling through a barrelful of emotions, Manolis leered through the smoke at me. Then with bared teeth, he shot out a splayed hand at the invisible Huxley, a silent yet eloquent curse of the worst possible kind. It was enough to break the tension like a downpour after a thunderclap. A jeering chorus rang off the cellar's walls.

The man in the rumpled grey suit raised his arms in mock supplication, as if appealing to reason lost among madmen.

'How can you say that?' he shouted above the din. 'Aren't your sons on the payroll there, digging down through the ash? Doesn't he pay them a decent wage? And you, Kostas, hiding back there, aren't the foreigners buying everything off your shelves, even at prices that would bring a blush to the cheeks of Lucifer himself?'

Roars of laughter, cries of protest.

'You all need him,' the stocky man went on. 'Your sons. Your daughters. He puts food on your tables, pays your bills, sends your children to school. Pah! You fools. You don't deserve such luck.'

That was too much for Manolis, and the words seemed to have sobered him, if only marginally.

'You!' he yelled, stabbing at several men at the tables with a gangling arm. 'Tell him! Tell the foreigner here what he's in for... If he lives that long!' The arm swung round to me, and I flinched.

'What's the use?' said one, with a disdainful shrug. 'Telling a boy something only a man can understand?'

More jeers, this time at my expense.

'Come on,' yelled the beanpole, 'you Nikos, and you Spyros and you too, Panos. Speak up!'

One elderly man with sad eyes and grey stubble cheeks got to his feet, the blue wooden chair scraping over the stones behind him.

'I shall tell my story,' he began.

As he spoke, a hush fell over the cellar and it occurred to me that this was somehow as ancient as mythology itself.

'It was first light. I was riding my mule to the fields, smoking a cigarette along the way, thinking about my son in Athens. You all know where my land is, just bordering the great holes they are digging to reach the towns of the ancient ones that lie beneath us. But then just as the sun was about to show its face, I saw them through the twilight, as

34

clearly as I see you now. Wraiths. Ghosts. Flocking out of the ground! Humans and animals alike, blossoming trees, rivers, escaping the shadows. As they touched the light, there was a sound like sighing, a great lament, and they were gone. After living in the earth so long, perhaps the daylight was too much for them to bear.'

A strained silence descended upon the cellar, and within it, the fear was palpable. There were whispers of curse, the dreaded word hissed between the tables on the raki damp smoke. Hailstorms destroying the first seedlings. A mad squall out of a clear blue sky, capsizing a boat, almost sending its hapless skipper to the bottom to sleep with the fishes. A child, lost in the fourth month. And now the Professor's boy, stone dead.

'They must be driven off the island before it's too late!' yelled Manolis, the words grinding between his teeth, the spent raki glass slamming onto the bar.

'You fools, just think what it will mean for our island!' parried the rumpled grey suit. 'This Professor Huxley is an educated man. When the city of the ancients is finally free of the clinging dirt, people will come from far and wide just to see it, walking the streets, scattering their dollars and deutschmarks wherever they pass. We shall be rich beyond imagining. You'll not have to grub about in the fields from dawn to dusk just to feed your families. Every home will have electricity and running water. We shall not repair our houses, but build brand new ones, two, three, four storeys tall!'

Another ear-splitting clash of words, every man shouting for all he was worth.

Just then, Huxley's foreman, Nestor Louganis, came clattering down the steps.

Greek he may have been, but to these islanders he was scarcely less foreign than I.

'Ela, drink up,' he said, gravel and treacle voice barely audible in the uproar.

He slammed a few drachmas onto the bar and began nudging me towards the steps.

Whether I was being rescued for my own sake or to prevent me hearing things I wasn't deemed ready for, who could say.

'You shouldn't have to go through that on your first night,' frustration edging his voice as we climbed up into the chill night air.

'I like to know what I'm letting myself in for,' I replied, putting a

35

brave face on things. 'The sooner the better.'

'Well, if it hadn't been for Benja's funeral today, of course we would have seen you settled in. It's hit us badly. His wife Jenna more than anyone.'

'How did he die?'

He uttered a torn sigh, running fingers through his close-cropped hair. Caught by the faint light of a street lamp, his face suddenly seemed creased by anxiety — or was it doubt?

'Just a stupid accident.'

'Island opinion seems divided,' I remarked, with unintended irony. 'It appears Professor Huxley is either going to make people fabulously rich or unleash the Devil.'

When that elicited only a disparaging click of the tongue, I added: 'So what do the local authorities have to say about it all?'

I caught his piercing glance and for a moment we stood facing each other in the street, the wind sighing forlornly between the houses, clattering the tin reflectors of the lamps.

'Those *were* the local authorities,' he replied, with just enough measure in his voice to let the bombshell hit me with its full force. 'The man in the grey suit promising them paradise — he's our mayor, Giannis Papadaikis. And Manolis the Cretan — who'd like nothing better than to throw us all off the island or into jail — well, he might be a hobby fisherman who prefers to believe that curse, not stupidity, almost sent him to a watery grave, but he's also our chief of police.'

I suppose it was that revelation that shocked me most of all. Suddenly, I remembered where I had seen that scrawny, sunken-cheeked man before; standing on the path with his barrel-round deputy, spying on the funeral of the boy I had come to replace.

What the hell was I doing here?

Back at my lodgings, I undressed, threw my clothes onto the floor and myself into bed. I was just about to fall asleep, some liquid dream already filling my eyes, when I burst awake, coughing, my eyes streaming.

'*Who put the silver drachma in his mouth? Who gave you the right?*' her distraught voice a receding echo over the grave. But it was ancient custom, wasn't it, just as one of Huxley's crew had insisted, reaching out to comfort her. The coin to pay the Ferryman. To make the crossing. A rite of passage, if you like — even if that was to the life hereafter.

36

5.

I tossed and turned, swept along in a jarring torrent of dreams. Trains heading south, my fleapit pension in Athens, the *Pegasus* pitching through the waves like a child's toy, my predecessor's dead face catching the sunset.

When the alarm clock began jangling its head off at the crack of dawn, I needed several seconds just to remember where I was.

For some time I just lay there, taking in the view from the window, the dawn light bleeding into a midnight blue sky, extinguishing stars one by one. It was a sense of tranquillity short-lived. Yesterday's events quickly began pounding through my head again, hurling questions, demanding answers. I jumped out of bed, washed, shaved, and hurried into town. It was day one in my brand new job.

By the time I arrived, the daily ritual in the town square was already in full swing, the vehicles lined up outside the post office looking like some ragtag military convoy. A couple of battered Land Rovers, and an American army jeep with the white star still painted onto the hood; then an olive green Berna truck, followed by an incongruous sky blue Morris Minor that had clearly seen better days. And, at the tail end of the column, a decrepit old bus, another War relic by the look of it, used to ferry the site labourers back and forth.

Watching them climb aboard, my encounter in the wine cellar barged its way into my head. Seconds later, I realised why. I had been catching something from them unconsciously. Rumblings of discontent. Furtive glances in Professor Huxley's direction, doubtful or suspicious. Angry mutters exchanged as they stowed their tools and lunch boxes.

'I trust you are settling in, Mr Pedrosa.'

Startled to find him standing there next to me, I blurted, 'Yes, Professor... Only...'

'Only *what?*' still glaring at the unfolding drama of the convoy.

'Only I found the locks forced on my luggage. Whoever it was, they went through everything — clothes, books, papers, even our correspondence.'

Eyes interrogating mine, he added abruptly: 'And? To your knowledge, is anything missing?'

'No, nothing.'

'Then chalk it up to experience, Mr Pedrosa. Trust no one. Believe no one. Question everything. Remember, there is nothing here you can take at face value... No — not even yourself.'

I was left gaping at his back as he strode impatiently towards the lead Land Rover — the white one of course.

The excavations lay at the farthest corner of the island, at the southern tip of its lunar crescent, Cape Akrotiri.

Grating into gear we set off, Huxley at the wheel, Nestor Louganis up front with him today, while his own vehicle was on the blocks with a cracked sump. With Sam generously sharing the next row with his own gear, that left the narrow stone-hard bench seat right at the back just for me.

Between church and school, we passed one of those garish new hoardings going up over the whole country, a rifle-toting soldier with fixed bayonet, silhouetted against a Phoenix rising from the ashes on wings of flame. Commemorating the military coup and the radiant new dawn of the Colonels, they were probably meant to be inspirational, but just ended up somewhere between kitsch and creepy.

On the outskirts of town, the tarred surface abruptly turned to dust.

'Is it always like this, every day?' I said, trying to hold on as we hit some bone-jarring rut or pothole.

'Yes, Nicky. Every day twice a day,' came the murmur from the row in front. 'What about you?' The sexual innuendo was one thing; the hostility, just baffling.

Apparently taking it upon himself to prime the new boy, Nestor called out from the front: 'Sometimes we take the caïque when the winds are favourable. But that can make for a wet and miserable crossing in winter. If the wind's gusting from the south or the east, it can get rough, too, even treacherous rounding the cape.'

But the dust track had its own pitfalls, sometimes disintegrating altogether, washed out by the rains, blocked by rock fall or landslide.

'After a storm like that,' explained Nestor, 'the one that's just hit us, you can bank on it.'

And he was right. A hundred yards on our convoy ground to a halt, the track blocked by several dislodged boulders. Not on the clock until they were through the gates, the hired hands struggled to drag them aside, using winches, levers, even the truck-mounted pulley.

Huxley sat motionless behind the wheel, staring bleakly through the windshield and becoming more irritable by the second. 'There has to be an easier way!' I caught the look reflected in the rearview mirror. That scornful defiance that crept into his eyes and tugged at his mouth, as if something out there, hidden by the sky, hidden by the rocks, were deliberately and maliciously meddling in his plans.

'I hope you are paying attention, Mr Pedrosa,' he said in that menacing voice of his, like a thunderclap sky that might blow up a great storm or just come to nothing. 'The obstacles that are thrown in our path, the obstacles that keep us from achieving what we must.'

Finally, there it was, sweeping out before us as the track took its demented hairpin turns along the mountainside.

Cape Akrotiri. Not much more than a razor cliff landmark for seafarers, a lava stone lighthouse marking its treacherous tip. Desiccated fields of charcoal soil flecked with white pumice. Crumbling dry stone walls, some almost buried by black sand drifts. A few farmer's *kalivia,* used to spend a grape harvest night, store spring hay or stable a goat or a mule.

From its northern point, what was left of the ancient crater wall went sloping back towards a rock-littered shore. There, just as the red ochre cliffs began to rise and the waters deepened, Nestor and his crew had constructed a cement dock so that freighters or fishing boats might supply the camp.

At our backs, the austere, unforgiving face of the Prophet Elias, the gashed, shrunken skeleton of a mountain that once must have towered over the Aegean in snow-capped splendour.

As we began our descent, I could even make out the excavations themselves, more striking, more brutal than anything I had imagined; like open cast mines biting into sheer cliffs, like trenches crisscrossing a battlefield.

We passed through the camp gates, thrown together with scrap metal and baling wire, and just before the track took a brief final plunge towards the excavations, parked on a small plateau of compacted ash.

I tried to take it all in. The odd holes in the ground like mine shafts. The army green tents where the visiting students and their teachers were encamped. The huts and sheds where tools were stored and artefacts sorted and catalogued. The laboratory and darkroom. The site office at the gates.

Muttering darkly, the labourers began moving into camp, several spitting surreptitiously into the dust as they hurried past the man who, they imagined, was so recklessly tempting fate. At their side, Nestor was doing his taciturn best to lift their spirits, promising mid-morning beer, bottles frosted from the dry ice machine in the mess.

The men collected their tools from the lock-ups, then headed down the slope towards a deep cleft. Burrowing into the ash as if cut with a knife, it went dipping down towards the sea, ultimately widening into the excavation zone, an area so immense it looked more like an industrial quarry than an archaeological dig.

Along the pumice-littered track the men filed in like miners, some wearing tin hats, others carrying pickaxes and shovels, the stones crunching under their feet like bones in an ancient graveyard.

At the perimeter of the site, where the volcanic ash rose like the sides of a great bowl, I gained my first awestruck impression of just how much tephra had to be shifted to reach the civilisation entombed below. Thousands, no, hundreds of thousands of tons of the stuff.

At the cliffs towards the end of the peninsula, a pair of rumbling bulldozers were driving waves of ash and pumice into the sea. On the east side, mechanical excavators were scooping up ash and lava rubble and depositing it onto a droning conveyor belt, the rollers squeaking loudly in complaint.

Despite the chill breeze off the sea, the March sun was just warm enough to remember its coming rendezvous with spring. Above our heads, the sky glowed, and I remember thinking, it is almost too blue to believe.

Here and there, Huxley's archaeologists were fussing over exposed walls and foundations with tools no more sophisticated than a garden trowel, a dustpan and brush, a garden soil sieve, a hoe.

At times, the work looked impossibly pernickety, and a stark enough contrast to the bulldozers droning away on the cliff.

Gingerly, I approached the fringes of the dig, an area marked by white demarcation lines and exposed trenches.

Sam, already up to his waist, was sifting through earth flecked with ceramic dust and coloured fragments. To my untrained eye, it seemed little more than building rubble and I was finding it impossible to visualise the ancient civilisation that was supposed to lie buried under our feet.

Huxley's other foot soldiers occupied trenches deeper into the quarry. I caught sight of Anna, hardly recognisable now in khaki fatigues, a dusty scarf tied under her chin. Head-bobbing around her, a gaggle of over-eager students, fumbling with the bulky field camera and its cumbersome wooden tripod.

Hut door slamming behind him, Huxley came marching towards us.

Just when I thought this is it, your job's about to begin, Sam uttered a piercing whistle between his teeth. Huxley veered towards his trench with a glower, not appreciating the crudity of the summons one bit.

There was a coldness, a bitterness between them like dead ash.

Against the light flushing skywards over the mountain, Sam held up a fragment of pottery, the neck and handle of a small terracotta jug, still bearing streaks of blue pigment. With an agility surprising for a man of his age and build, Huxley vaulted into the trench beside him, taking the artefact in his fingers.

One cursory glance and he pronounced judgment. 'A Roman ceramic dump.'

Sam uttered an angry sigh. 'I know that. But look at the fine work on the stem. There could be other finds here, valuable in their own right.'

'Why are you wasting your time with this? More to the point, why are you wasting mine? Dig! Dig deeper! Get the machines over here. Get the tephra shifted.'

'The trouble with you is, you can never admit you're fucking wrong!' raged Sam, proving that even dead ash can sporadically burst into flame.

Barging between us, he threw me a look of such inexplicable hatred that I almost felt the physical force of it buckling the air.

I stared into the trench that had caused such bitter dispute between them, trying to take in the idea that the artefacts of one age were about to be crushed in order to reach those of a far older civilisation lying farther below.

Anger still smouldering in his eyes, Huxley said: 'How will you ever accomplish your duties here, Mr Pedrosa, if you are too intimidated or just too downright timid to pose the questions for which you have no answer? How will you attain knowledge?' Intolerant of even the faintest hesitation, he added: 'Well? Do you have a question that is burning for an answer?'

'The Romans were here?' I was puzzled because even my limited knowledge separated these civilisations, Minoan and Roman, by two millennia or more.

'The Romans were everywhere,' he replied brusquely. 'Some might even say they are still with us today.'

While that sardonic aside went flying over my head, he added: 'Think of the strata as ages, as periods in time.'

'The picks and shovels will always hit the youngest civilisation first.'

'Yes.' The impatience still edging his voice. 'First the early Byzantine chapel or peasant's hut, their crumbling walls buried by dust storms. Then the Roman remains, an insignificant outpost that one day must have looked up into the sky to find it snowing ash. A minor eruption, but enough to bury what few buildings they had erected here — hence the broken mosaics of poor quality, the cheap ceramics...'

'Then the Minoans are deeper still.'

'Under this blanket of ash a hundred feet deep. Why else would we need all these machines to shift it? Well, you will see for yourself, soon enough. The streets, houses and temples we have already exhumed.' He cast a brooding look over the tortured landscape, over the bare rock mountain. 'At the scene of a great cataclysm, Mr Pedrosa — that is where you now find yourself. One that shook the ancient world to its core, brought about night in broad daylight, hurled flaming debris into the sky, rained fire over the Aegean. The day the island exploded with the force of a hundred thousand atomic bombs.'

'But why aren't we preserving these Roman things?'

'Because they are worthless and because we have no time,' he snapped. 'We could live another five hundred years, dig day and night and still would have exhumed only a fraction of the Minoan treasures that lie buried beneath us. So, do you think I have time to waste on this Roman gimcrack?'

I heard a plodding step behind me. It was Adrian Hunt, owl-eyed spectacles smudged with sweat, a fine film of ash catching his own careless fingerprint. 'That is an unbelievably close-minded view, Huxley. And I do not believe you should berate Sam for wanting to protect these artefacts as we dig.'

'Have you met "Hadrian"?' demanded Huxley, in a tone that escaped mockery by the skin of its teeth. I had to wonder if the tension was always like this, or whether it was just the fallout from my predecessor's death. 'Captivated by all things Roman. Wet nursed on Roman studies. And on his infrequent days off, where will you find him? Beachcombing? Walking the mountain? Sailing a boat? No. He's digging for Roman trinkets, saving them from the dump or the bulldozer, things that even the Romans saw fit to throw away before us.'

Hadrian — at least I now had an explanation for his pun-making nickname. He blinked peevishly, but then gave as good as he got, probably secure in the knowledge that, whatever their differences, he was still Huxley's second-in-command. In charge of site mapping, or stratigraphy, he was about to unfurl a huge chart, the better to harangue Huxley for his alleged vandalism, but Huxley would have none of it.

'How can you possibly know what these finds might reveal about the outpost they established here?' squealed Hadrian indignantly. 'It is reckless, unforgivably reckless!'

Huxley grunted and said: 'I cannot wait to be proven wrong, Hadrian.'

6.

I followed him into the long wooden hut, penumbral light seeping in from the narrow windows under the eaves.

Regimented columns of metal shelving disappeared into the shadows, seemingly running the length of the building, floor to ceiling.

Midpoint, enough space had been made for two trestle tables, positioned end to end and covered with green draughtsman's paper.

It was only as he flicked on the bank of lights suspended above that they emerged from the gloom. Potsherds. Fragments. Littering the tabletop from one end to the other, remnants of amphorae, vases, jugs, mixing bowls, sculptures, friezes, frescoes, and God knows what else.

Here and there they formed clusters, and elsewhere, scattered away from one another, forms of relationship and division presumably of significance to the hand that had arranged them. Huxley's.

Judging from the cardboard storage boxes stacked five high on every shelf, there must have been thousands upon thousands of them, of infinite, mind-boggling, shape and size.

'Do you know what you are looking at?'

'Potsherds?'

'Potsherds!' he retorted, as though I had said something very stupid. 'No. No. You would do better to think of them as jigsaw pieces. Parts of an immense puzzle bearing a picture we cannot yet see.'

He snatched a clay fragment from the table.

'This one, for example, offering us nothing more tangible than a glimpse of blue sky.'

He reached forward, seizing a fragment as brittle as eggshell. On it, in colours barely faded by the years, a river scene, reeds and rushes, a water bird flying low.

A moment's hesitation, and he thought better of it, plucking from the table what looked like a beach pebble, smooth, moulded, its surface bearing a line of faded script. 'Or perhaps this one here, the remains of a stone tablet that lay in water long before the great cataclysm. And freshwater, not sea, flowing, not still.'

'What does it say?'

He grunted, as though I had exposed some flaw or weakness in his abilities.

'Now you begin to appreciate the magnitude of the problem,' he replied, in a clipped voice. 'It is written in Linear A, a dead language we may never decipher.'

'But you don't really expect to find the missing pieces to all these things?' I said dumbly, casting an eye over to the door where two giant ceramic pithoi, like twin Humpty Dumpties, had obviously been put back together again after all.

'That is not the nature of the puzzle. Rather, it is the hidden picture that emerges from all the fragments. Who were these people? What did they believe? Where were they going? What was the island like before the firestorm engulfed it? Can we form a picture of its landscape and farmland, its towns and cities, gain an understanding of its economy, its philosophy, its technological achievements?'

'You can tell all that just from these fragments?'

'We begin. By a process of forensic analysis, logical deduction. The picture will emerge because we seek it, demand it. It cannot hide forever.'

★

Left to my own devices again, I began exploring the excavation site, taking care where I put my feet because of all the trenches, ditches and holes.

The more I saw, the more I began to understand the morbid superstitions of the locals. In places, weird shapes had been carved out of the lava by wind and water. Here and there, the gashed volcanic walls were encrusted with obsidian, or bore extravagant red lava or brimstone-yellow seams.

When a solitary and bloody-minded cloud chose that moment to eclipse the sun, the effect was uncanny, plunging us into a kind of ghostly twilight.

In their trenches or among the scorched walls, the crew continued to dig and sift, faces like death masks against the grey volcanic ash.

Stupid, I know, but in that air pocket of a moment I suddenly found myself entering the cemetery gates again, staring into the pitch pine coffin and the face of my predecessor, his numb skin and straw blond hair catching the sunset. *Just ancient custom*, comes the voice between the tombs.

Yet the more I twisted it now, the odder that assertion became. Benjamin Randal. The English lad with the pretty young wife. It can hardly have been *his* tradition, can it? To have been interred on this far-flung Cycladic island, in a Greek Orthodox boneyard with a pagan silver drachma on his tongue? For once, I was glad I hadn't skived off every mythology lecture at college. At least I knew the basics.

Still in the cloud's sombre shadow, it wasn't even hard to picture him trudging through the grey dust Underworld that the ancients believed lay beneath our feet. Imagination getting the better of me, I saw him reach the bog marshlands formed by the Styx and Acheron, rivers that divided the living world from the dead. Caught the dark reflection in his eyes from the black water, a cowled figure punting his flat-bottomed boat through the mist and the whispering reeds. The Ferryman. Charon, son of Darkness and Night.

Reaching the far shore, he'd enter the Kingdom of Hades, there to join the legions of the dead. Shadow beings, so the legend went, strengthless doppelgangers that death-trespassing heroes like Orpheus and Odysseus had to revive with draughts of blood, mead or wine, just to give them voice to speak.

Yes, just as that bilious old Frenchman with the wrinkled lips and parchment skin had so trenchantly pointed out in his rant against the ship's indolent crew, these golden heroes would defy even King Death in person.

On some reckless mission inspired by love, fate or a vengeful god, they would pothole through labyrinthine caves, or follow the Styx or Acheron upstream from where they empty into the world.

Battling fearsome monsters and demons along the way, some even ventured as far as the Elysian Fields, with their rounded hills, streams and asphodel meadows. Others, the Isles of the Blest, just visible from Elysium's towering sea cliffs; an archipelago in the farthest reaches of the sunset, where celestial music was said to enchant the sky, and whose ever-shifting shores would so sublimely foil the souls of the undeserving, those who were never meant to be there.

Anyway, that was the mythology, not that it offered any insights into the silver drachma on Benjamin Randal's tongue, let alone the livid accusation bereaved Jenna had hurled across the tombs. About the island killing him. About Huxley killing him. Maybe it was just emotion, the world falling in on her.

Not a moment too soon, the sun returned in a blaze of glory, chasing the cloud shadow over the peninsula like the blade of a scythe. Returning from a bad-humoured visit to the site office, Huxley was now dashing past me, telling me not to dawdle, I was with him. We crossed the excavation site, our feet raising little blizzards of dust. Past the mess tent. Past the laboratory and darkroom. Past the student encampment with the neat rows of army tents, the water cisterns, washrooms and latrines.

'The eastern sector,' Huxley announced, with a perfunctory toss of the head towards an array of elaborate trenches, half exposed walls and dunes of ash, where students from the British, French and Italian Schools were working under the supervision of their teachers; experienced archaeologists in their own right. It was a beehive, and I caught at least five languages being spoken as the various contingents worked the trenches, mapped, plotted and recorded finds within the sector zones assigned to them.

Scattered among the excavation pits were bleak, ruined shells of houses, exposed walls the colour of pallid sandstone, victims of the snowing ash, the invincible might of the lava flows or the sheer weight of the tephra. A fractured staircase, now ending in thin air. The remains of an arched doorway. A cracked amphora. He nodded a formal good morning to the archaeologist in charge of the zone we were crossing, this time a professor from Patras University, Galatea somebody, her jet-black hair so infested with ash it looked as if shock or hardship had robbed her of her youth.

The trail led us over a sand dune bluff, from whose wind-ribbed summit we could see the farthest point of the peninsula and the Aegean on three sides. What with the midnight blue sky, the Burnt Islands in the caldera, and the distant town of Phíra dusting the mighty volcanic cliffs like a fresh snowfall, the view was incredible.

He turned in an arc, his arm sweeping over the western skyline. 'Our sector. The west.'

'They're separate? Why?'

'We meet. Once a week, twice a week, when circumstances dictate. You're neither too young nor immature, Mr Pedrosa, to be ignorant of the professional rivalries that plague our oh-so principled profession. Luckily, within the zones assigned to them, they have their own petty turf wars to keep them occupied.'

In the distance stood a cluster of exhumed buildings of the same bleak colour, rising over what might once have been the peak of a hill. Houses devoured by the earth. Lying abandoned in the guts of the earth for three and a half millennia. It was as if they still possessed the death hue of the Underworld itself.

A few yards on we came across Nestor Louganis, a bunch of nails between his teeth, a tool belt slung around his hips, fixing the wooden scaffolding around a three-storey house designated '16'.

'Is it secure?' Huxley called. Leaning out from the highest platform, where he was lashing the joints together with rope for good measure, Nestor offered a taciturn if emphatic nod of assent.

As it climbed the hill, the dust track turned into an ancient street of carved geometric stone. 'The Sacred Way,' he announced, pointing out the temple at its crest. 'At least,' he added in a taut voice, 'that is the name we have bestowed upon it, as much as that can ever mean in a city without a name, on an island without a name.'

Here the preservation of the houses was of a different order of magnitude altogether, as though the falling ash might have ended up cocooning rather than crushing them. When I noted as much to my boss, he grunted and said, 'Yes, somehow or other this section of the city was spared the worst of the burning ash; so too the pyroclastic blast, an inferno of superheated gasses that swept down the walls of the volcano as the island blew apart, incinerating everything in its path.'

We entered a wide thoroughfare lined with houses, some three storeys high, the ceiling columns and flights of stairs still intact. Sometimes, the roofs gave way to sky terraces, linking this house or that. As the street narrowed, we passed under balconies left and right, and then the shop-fronts began, what had once been a bakery by the look of it, hardly different from the one in town, then some kind of ceramic workshop.

Here and there, scattered about the perimeter, he pointed to what looked like broken stone columns, some almost 10 feet in diameter.

'A ruined temple,' I said, hazarding a guess.

'Petrified tree stumps,' he replied, in that abrupt way of his, 'living things, turned to stone by hot falling ash.' Molecule by molecule, the searing ash had even captured the tree rings and the intricate pattern of the bark.

Trees? I thought, trying hard to visualise them in an ash desert like this, and wondering how tall they must have been to have a girth like that. 'What kind of trees?'

'That awaits analysis. We have sent cell structure samples to Kew.'

Without warning he veered down a narrow side street and darted through a stone-braced doorway.

Just as my eyes were becoming accustomed to the gloom, he threw aside one of the panels boarding up the house to protect it from the elements. The light came streaming in and I just stood there, blinking, disbelieving.

I was standing inside a house that hadn't been touched for the better part of three and a half thousand years. And yet everything was exactly as they had left it on that fateful day, when the world these people knew and trusted blew apart. Who knows, perhaps a day just like this, dreaming of spring.

No mistaking the purpose of this room. Amphorae of olive oil and wine, jars of grain and spice. Pots and pans, in earthenware and bronze, lined up neatly along a wall. Barley grains, in a clay crock. A well-worn marble-topped table with blue and rose veins, the criss-cross knife scores still visible. A hearth with fire-blackened cooking pots. Everything neatly in its place.

I was aware of his flecked eyes upon me again, that penetrating look that seemed to be measuring reactions, reading thoughts.

Abruptly, he turned on his heel and entered an adjoining room. The instant he wrenched the panels aside, I could feel the breath being snatched away from me, the realisation hitting me in a riot of ancient colour.

The frescoes. He may have been guilty of exaggeration in other things, but not these, bold, vibrant, the spice pigments as fresh as the day they had touched moist plaster. Swallows soaring over summer fields. On the high meadow, beautiful young women with wide soulful eyes, gathering saffron. People in the windows of the town houses, talking, gazing out to sea, here in profile, here staring right back at you with limpid eyes lined with kohl.

I was left biting my lips, struck suddenly by the uncanny sensation that we were separated from the inhabitants of this house not by millennia but by moments.

Across the street, the frescoes turned blue with sea, earning the town house a name instead of a number: *Thalassa*. Young naked fishermen on the dock, a brace of sea bream in their hands. A fishing boat with a single canvas sail and trailing oars.

In several rooms conservationists were at work, stabilising the wall

49

paintings from timber scaffolds. Among them, Sam; apparently restoration was his specialty, and he only worked the trenches at all because Huxley insisted upon it as a matter of diehard principle.

'Step forward, examine the workmanship at close quarters,' commanded Huxley.

Sun-dappled water, iridescent fish among the sea grass meadows, a solitary octopus with intelligent eyes, a school of dolphins leaping by.

'Note the subtlety with which the artist captures his subject,' he went on. 'The playful compassion in the dolphin's eye. The prisms of light over the seabed. Here and there, you can even make out the brush strokes. Do you know what that means? Once we have had time to analyse and compare, we shall even be able to differentiate between individual artists. We may never be able to give them a face or a name and yet somehow we will begin to know them. A mind will emerge from the pigment.'

Detecting our presence from ceiling height where he stood atop a scaffold bridge, Sam shot us an angry scowl, then studiously ignored us. Several students were assisting him, handing him brushes and palettes or mixing pigments; girls, boys, seventeen or eighteen years old, and I couldn't help remarking how unusually attractive they were, at least, when seen in the same place and the same time like that.

The images and colours were still tumbling through my head as we emerged into the sharp winter light. A honey bee in a blossom, children winnowing wheat. The sky-piercing mountain, and the deep green forest. Among the trees, between the waterfalls, an antelope. Peering through the dense foliage, a panther with gleaming eyes.

Back amid the ruins, in the shadow of the broken mountain, the contrast, the implications, couldn't have been starker: these ancient moments, captured in pigment. They were less an insight into changing history than changing reality, the appearance of it; even the meaning of it.

'Is that what they tell you?' demanded Huxley with a curious glance.

'Yes.'

'Then there is something else you might wish to contemplate. All of these representations are found within the same quarter of the city, many along the same street. What does that tell you about the values of our lost civilisation?'

The images ran through my head like the pigments they were made of, but I wasn't getting anywhere until finally he answered himself.

'The fisher boys and the priestess. The saffron gatherers and the philosopher. They tell us that each was held in similar regard, similar esteem. Each made this the world it was, the colour it was.'

Whoever said they depict a vision of heaven on earth was right, I reflected, as we resumed our expedition. That's exactly what they depict. That's exactly what they project.

A time-still moment of heaven before the holocaust.

7.

No sooner had we stepped out into the sunshine again than he began firing questions at me, master to student.

'Tell me what you see,' he commanded, narrowing his eyes at the street, quite as if the image it presented were blurred, not by time, but merely by distance. 'And concentrate only on what your senses tell you. I am not in the least bit interested in what you think I want to hear.'

I turned my attention to the sunlit street. An exhumed water fountain with the face of a beatific god. Temple columns, catching the light. Ancient doors. Ancient windows.

'Remember,' he added severely, 'our powers of deduction rely as much on clues we cannot see as those we can.'

I was at a loss. How the hell was I supposed to form a judgement on something I couldn't even see?

The longer he waited without an answer, the more intimidating his presence became.

'It was technologically accomplished,' I said, taking the jump at last, 'at least for its time.'

D- for effort, judging from the acerbic grunt it elicited.

'And on what do you base that judgement exactly? Merely on the things I have already shown you?'

'No, because of the plumbing,' I said, pointing out the ceramic pipes entering the houses with fresh running water, and the waste-water drains leaving them, the channels running concealed under the streets.

'Why twin pipes?' he snapped.

'One for cold, one for hot?' I blurted, stupid, I know, but it was the only answer I could think of. And it just happened to be right. There were even pipes for winter heating, the water probably tapped from volcanic hot springs nearby.

In some houses, even the windows were still intact, or at least sections of them, bronze frames of small squares or triangles, each holding a pane of hand-blown glass, mica, even seashell.

And then I saw it. The clue that was invisible. The revelation hit me so strongly I almost felt winded by it.

'There are no people,' I said, remembering the kitchen with everything neatly in its place.

Judging from the ironic pat on the shoulder that elicited, my marks had just taken a belated leap for the better.

'That is the mystery in which we find ourselves. Every house is the same. Deserted. Where are the bodies? What happened to the people who once lived here?'

When finally he saw fit to explain, I understood at once. At Pompeii, archaeologists had discovered scores of bodies entombed under the ash, their lava-petrified faces contorted in horror or astonishment. As Vesuvius blew its top, virtually without warning, the inhabitants of the city abandoned their houses in panic, leaving half-eaten meals on tables and pots and pans still bubbling over fires. As they ran for their lives, the sluggish and infirm collapsed in the streets, overcome by the poisonous fumes. Others, their escape routes blocked by lava flows and earthquake fissures, had been embalmed or devoured alive.

Here, it was a different story altogether, the streets and houses bearing no evidence of panic or escape at all.

'And what do you deduce from that?'

I hesitated, reluctant to state the obvious, but then took the plunge anyway. 'They must have been forewarned.'

'By what?'

'The volcano.' Taking in the shattered remains of the crater wall and that immense caldera, 8 miles long, 4 miles wide, I was still struggling to visualise it, towering over the people with its forested slopes and snowy peak, awesome, ominous, beautiful. 'The eruption was slow gathering momentum. Weeks, maybe months. At first, who knows, maybe it was only sending out smoke signals, a column of ash. Then earth tremors, ash falls, lava flows...' I paused, wide-eyed at the realisation. 'They evacuated the island en masse as a precaution. That's why everything's so neatly put away. They expected to return!'

I was feeling quite pleased with myself when he said, almost scathingly: 'Methodical and orderly, is that what you're saying? No need to run for their lives. No reason for blind panic. That's why, under the ash, every street and every house is the same. Pristine. Immaculate. Deserted.'

'It's plausible, isn't it?'

He grunted noncommittally. 'Like all speculative theories, that awaits the proof of confirmation.'

53

On the rubble strewn slopes beyond, we passed a graveyard of broken machinery; conveyor belts, rusting tractors with crooked wheels, excavator buckets, tangled coils of barbed wire. There we ran into Nestor again, this time supervising the cutting of another deep exploratory shaft into the tephra with his so-called 'trench moles', a band of labourers and off-island engineers apparently handpicked for their dependability and experience.

A man of many talents, Nestor Louganis. Maybe that's why Huxley placed such faith in him. No midday retsina under the olive trees for this Arcadian Greek. Methodical, industrious to a fault, chasing time before time chased him. So mechanically-minded he could fashion almost any tool demanded of him, be that out of cannibalised parts, wood, iron, tin or rope, it just didn't matter. As long as there was something practical about it, he could turn his hand to almost anything, and seemed just at home adjusting the monorail field camera, as he was poring over blueprints or operating one of the backhoes.

According to locker room talk, for fifteen years he'd sailed the seven seas, working his way up through the merchant ranks from galley boy to first mate — some explanation, perhaps, for that curious habit of his of addressing Huxley not by name but by his rank — *Kapítán*.

As for his motives for dropping anchor here, the same garrulous mouths were divided. Seduction of the island, said one, Huxley's vision, said another, no, the intoxicating sight of Maria, winked a third, her legendary beauty enough to send man or boy weak at the knees.

Retracing our steps into camp we crossed the dunes. On the wind-ribbed summit he paused, gazing out across his lost city, less in pride this time than in calculation.

'*This* will be the island's legacy, like it or not.'

An allusion to local opposition mounting against him, no doubt. A moment later, I had to wonder.

'Streets, houses, frescoes. You might say those are only the most obvious manifestations of what we disinter from the ash. In a deeper sense, what we are unearthing are secrets of ancient thought and mind. Knowledge that might one day change the course of human history.'

I took that to be ego talking, hardly an exceptional trait among archaeology's brightest lights, even to my limited knowledge. 'What about the locals. Can you count on them?'

'The locals!' He snorted derisively. 'Of what consequence are they in the great scheme of things? Mere drops in the ocean of time. The ancient city exists with or without them, and I am raising it from the dead.'

The harshness of the insult seemed to boom-echo off the quarry walls. Seconds later, labourers were throwing down their shovels and pickaxes, and bolting away, all panic yells and flailing arms. They stampeded past us, Nestor giving chase, baying at them to stop.

Exasperation his second nature, Huxley threw up his arms. '*What now?*'

His foreman came striding up the dune, making short work of it on his long, powerful legs. 'I tried, Kapítán,' he said between gasps, 'I tried to reason with them.'

Huxley clicked his tongue in disgust. 'What is it this time? A gladiator? A charioteer? You would think that, after all the trouble and expense I have gone to, they might at least have the decency to see Minoan rather than Roman ghosts.'

The answer, when it came, was almost apologetic. 'Not this time, Kapítán. They say they saw Benja, over there at the trenches.'

They always called him that. My predecessor. Benjamin Randal. The boy I had come to replace.

8.

'Look at them,' sneered Huxley. 'One fool thinks he's seen a ghost and by the time they've bolted out here, all of them have.'

The labourers were huddled around the mess tent, swigging raki from the bottle and muttering furiously among themselves, eyes still bulging from the shock of whatever they thought they had seen.

Less quick to pass judgement, Nestor said: 'You forget Kapítán; some of these lads have never set foot off the island, not once in thirty years or more. The old ways are still in their blood.'

Huxley grunted disparagingly. 'There is not a man amongst them without a talisman around his neck or a clove of garlic in his pocket. Do you see them dangling there, Mr Pedrosa, amulets fashioned by their mothers, wives or sisters, each containing some kind of magic concoction to ward off evil spirits or the evil eye — human hair, perhaps, an eyelash, a fingernail, the crushed bone of some dead kinsman.'

But I was noticing something else about them; the fierce exchanges, the sudden bursts of bravado that came to nothing, the dangerous pride every bit as stubborn as Huxley's own.

Having received the assent of his comrades, the brawniest of the labourers got to his feet and took several wary paces towards us. He beckoned Nestor to his side with a glance and a stiff jerk of the head.

Some hard bargaining was obviously about to ensue, and Huxley shooed me off to record events, adding curtly that that was what he was paying me to do.

Our labourer was covered in dust from head to foot, the grey ash accentuating his eyebrows and eyelashes.

Like most of the farmers or fishermen who had been persuaded to join the dig, he was a man of few words. 'There are ghosts, no one can deny it. Every day we see them. The old ones, and now a man just buried. A man we worked with every day. A friend. Now made *vrykolakas*. The Devil is about. We cannot go on.'

When I heard those words, spoken with such finality, I expected every last man of them to march for the gates.

Nestor, however, knew better and began talking in slow, measured tones. At first, nothing would budge them. Not beer, not wine, not bonuses, and certainly not appeals to reason.

Our trench digger tossed his head defiantly and clicked his tongue as the Greeks often do to voice their most emphatic 'no'. Then finally it was out in the open. What they really wanted. Probably already knowing how Huxley would react, Nestor winced loudly, exasperated hands streaking back through his hair. But there was nothing for it. We retraced our steps back to the dune, upon whose summit the imperious Huxley still stood, waiting impatiently for news.

'What's a *vrykolakas*?' I asked, wondering about the noun they'd used to describe Benja's apparition. 'I don't know the word. Is it a ghost?'

'Kind of,' Nestor replied grimly. 'The island's famous for them — maybe just because the volcanic soil is so slow to rot the flesh once the body is buried. They're vampires, poltergeists, the undead. Anyway, different from the rest; maybe less because they have a taste for young blood than for all the trouble they cause whenever they appear. Sucking the goats dry of milk. Draining the wine barrels. Assaulting innocent people in the fields. Tossing people out of bed in the middle of the night. Demanding sex even though they're dead. They never accept their fate. They rebel even against death itself.'

'Well?' demanded Huxley abrasively, as we reached the crest. 'What is it this time?'

I really had to admire how unflinching Nestor was in facing the music. 'They're demanding the dead be laid to rest, Kapítán. Benja. The ancient ones. They're demanding a blessing by the Papás. An exorcism.'

News broken, I could see Huxley grinding his teeth in fury, and half expected him to sack the strikers there and then.

'Kapítán, no one is denying the lads have worked themselves into a frenzy, but take heed, they believe what they say; it is not a means to trick you. Do nothing and it will get worse. A *vrykolakas* becomes more powerful if it is left to its own devices, that's what the tradition says. The men know that; they won't need reminding.'

Panting, mopping the sweat away from his eyes, Hadrian came lumbering over from the trenches.

'I hope you will not acquiesce to this nonsense, Huxley,' he said in a shrill, indignant voice. 'Have I seen a ghost? No! Have you, Nestor? Well, have you? No, I thought as much. This is the slippery slope, Huxley, mark my words. Once you let it into camp, we will never be rid of it, never.'

The glance Huxley threw back at him said it all. *Do you think you have to remind me of that, Hadrian?*

'We need a decision, Kapítán. Before the men walk.'

Huxley sighed irritably, apparently trying to weigh up which option was worse, days of labour lost to strike, or the ignominy of being rescued by a man whose religion he so despised.

At last he said through gritted teeth: 'Well, one calls in an exterminator for an infestation; why not a Papás for a poltergeist? Since he supposedly laid Benja to rest less than twenty-four hours ago, perhaps it's still covered by the guarantee.'

His tone was as corrosive as battery acid, but Hadrian still clicked his tongue loudly in disgust, apparently at the way Huxley was prepared to sacrifice logic like that, on the altar of expediency.

The decision, however, had been made and Huxley was already stalking towards the fragments hut in a foul temper, another shouting match with Sam ensuing along the way.

With nothing else to do, I resumed my exploration, and presently found myself wandering down to the cement dock, where a boat was moored. The *Persephone*.

I recognised it immediately. A white caïque with sprit rig and burgundy sails, it had been among the flotilla of boats ferrying us off the *Pegasus* after our storm-tossed voyage from Piraeus.

I knew the skipper by sight as well, now padding about deck in torn work clothes — some blunt-faced, tousle-haired 18-year old from Akrotiri, who had been shouldering one corner of Benja's coffin as the procession wound its way into the cemetery.

Shifting crates on deck, he offered a brash grin as I passed, even if there was something ambivalent about it.

Rounding the great boulder beyond the quay, I ran into the last person I wanted to see. Sam — from the sullen look twisting his face, still fuming after his latest run-in with Huxley, hands thrust deep into his pockets, feet booting beach shingle.

Too late to back away, I swore under my breath.

'What do *you* want?' It was almost a snarl.

'Nothing.' *What the hell had I ever done to him?*

'So he showed you the ancient city.'

'*Uh-huh.* Some of it. He said the rest would come in good time.'

'Of course. His time. His terms.'

He threw me another glance, and I saw then what the lovesick student girls in camp were always mooning about, eyes as blue as the sea.

Maybe they had the benefit of distance. Up close, they seemed as real, as personal as glass.

He moved to the shelter of the rocks, a sun trap cheating the chill breeze. Out of his pocket he fished a tobacco pouch and rolled a cigarette. Every so often, he'd cast a narrow-eyed look over to the *Persephone*, where the boy was still stacking fish crates. The smoke smelled strange, and at first I assumed it was just that acrid Greek tobacco that everyone smoked straight from the sun-drying fields. But soon his pupils had grown as big as saucers, so that was that.

'Maybe he doesn't understand your point of view,' I ventured.

'He does not *want* to understand!' spitting out the words with some loose tobacco and weed. I caught the Parisian accent, boiling over his perfect English for once, like milk left on the stove too long. 'It is always what *he* wants.'

Even to me, it seemed a strangely childish thing to say.

That there was more to the tension between Sam and Huxley than quarrels over Roman ceramics was obvious. It was apparent in the body language, in the looks that clashed at fifty paces.

'Can you imagine?' he was saying. 'All the secrets of the Roman occupation that might still be buried here, a subject we're totally ignorant of. Trashed. Bulldozed.'

'Why is he doing it?'

He drew heavily on whatever sticky weed he was smoking. 'Don't you get it? Nothing can be allowed to get in his way. All he cares about is what lies a hundred feet down. We're just trashing everything along the way because Huxley needs to get there before he's thrown off the island for good.'

'Get where?'

He clicked his tongue. 'Atlantis, of course.'

The laugh dried on my tongue. 'Atlantis was in the Atlantic.'

'Was it?'

'Wasn't it?'

'You are very sure about something you know nothing about.'

'So you're saying Professor Huxley believes he's discovered Atlantis?'

Sam offered a lazy shrug, a knowing smirk on his lips.

I found myself staring into his blue pools of eyes as the implications swept over me. Trying to read the truth from them. Those eyes, I thought. It would be wrong to call them cold. There is something missing in them, but what?

For a second or two, I was tempted to doubt everything he said. But then Huxley's boast rang through my head, about his excavations changing the world, about him raising this miracle from the dead.

9.

I wandered off along the shore, my thoughts less like the lucid blue sky above than children lost in the fog.

Threading my way between the trenches I came across the Italian pottery specialist, Anna, sitting on an ancient stone wall, an intact water jug in terracotta and blue exhumed at her feet.

'So Sam has been quarrelling with Marcus again,' she said, still absorbed by the pencil sketches on her lap.

She was the only one, I realised, to call Huxley by his given name; maybe she wasn't quite so harried or intimidated by him as the others, the great man around whom all events here seem to revolve.

'Why, is the fur always flying like that?'

'Cat and dog.' She looked about to laugh her champagne laugh at the mental caricature that evoked but something caught it, dragged it back. And I already knew what it was. The thought of Benja, still haunting her, even without the stupid labourers imagining things, seeing his ghost quiver out of the trenches at them. The funeral. The hurtful things said by the dead boy's wife, Jenna.

'Is it true?' I blurted. 'Are we really excavating Atlantis?'

She looked up sharply, saw my face, and this time couldn't help it, the cork popping, the bubbles fizzing.

'Who told you that?' she gasped, amid gales of laughter.

'Sam,' I replied through gritted teeth, feeling angry and stupid all at the same time. 'Does he hate everybody in camp?'

'Of course not.'

'Well he hates Professor Huxley, doesn't he?'

'Marcus is a demanding man, Nico, you will learn that for yourself soon enough. He gave Sam his chance, told him at the Sorbonne, barely a month after graduating from Cambridge: stay here and become a teaching assistant, teaching dusty history to dusty minds. Or come with me, help me lift this Minoan city from the ash with your own bare hands. You will be my apprentice, you will be my protégé, but you will listen, you will learn and you will obey.'

So that was it. Already despising the establishment that might one day have lifted him onto its shoulders, bright spark Sam had dropped out altogether, lured out here by one man's irrepressible dream. Perhaps it was just his rebellious streak but, somehow or other, he had failed to live up to Huxley's lofty expectations.

'So when Sam played that trick on you, well, it was just his way of getting back at you, that's all.'

'Getting back at me for what?'

'For taking what was once his, of course. His job.'

'But that wasn't the job I took,' I said in dismay.

'It was. You just didn't realise it.'

Then it struck me, and I said, trying to make my voice sound more resolute than it really wanted to be, 'What about Benjamin Randal. Was he Professor Huxley's apprentice too?'

Her voice turned wistful — or was it guarded? 'Yes. He was the first to replace Sam.'

What must the tension have been like between them, I wondered, Sam and the new boy, with the wound still red raw. The jealousy that must have consumed him, the spiteful pranks he must have played.

I swallowed hard. Suddenly, I was thinking about the accident and Jenna's accusations of foul play, and I didn't want to be thinking about them at all. 'How did it happen — his death, I mean?'

Again, at the mere mention of his name, I saw the shadow darkening her eyes. Reluctantly, she motioned towards higher ground and a three-storey house silhouetted against the blue sky. House 16. The house Huxley and I had passed that very morning, Nestor up on the highest scaffold, hurriedly hammering home nails, lashing together the supports.

She shook her head in disbelief. 'In the blink of an eye. Living, then dead, one second to the next! Everyone going about their daily routine, in the trenches, in the sheds, in the houses. Suddenly there's a splintering of wood, an ear-splitting crash, a great cloud of dust. I think I even saw the scaffolding give way — and Benja, falling. We were frozen in shock, it felt like time had forgotten to move...'

'And then?'

'Chaos. Everybody running. But there was nothing we could do, *nothing*. The men cleared away the wood and rubble, and there he was, like some broken puppet, his neck and limbs all twisted, his lifeless eyes staring up at the sky. But there was that look in them... I don't know, I can't describe it...' She bit hard into her lips, eyes brimming with tears.

'What about Professor Huxley — how did he react?'

Sniffling, she forced a smile. 'Intense annoyance — at least, until he realised what was happening. Then he just stood there, paralysed, watching the others in their desperate, futile effort to bring Benja back to life. Like so many men of his intellectual intensity, Marcus is totally hopeless when it comes to practicalities or sudden emergencies. He expects the mind alone to solve all problems because, for him, everything of value occurs within the mind.'

'What was he like?' I said, suddenly feeling the need to know more about the boy I had supposedly come to replace.

Glad to have a kinder memory to talk about, she gushed: 'Oh, Benja was wonderful, Nico. An inspiration, yes that's it. Full of life. Everyone loved him.'

'Except Sam,' I pointed out. 'How old was he?'

'About your age. And already married with a child he'd never seen.'

'Never seen?'

'Well, sometimes it's difficult to get away, isn't it, when you're stuck on a rock like this in the middle of the sea, totally absorbed by the demands of the job.'

She caught my look. 'Yes. He had his problems coping with Marcus, but where the dig was concerned, wild horses wouldn't have dragged him away. He lived and breathed for it.'

And died for it too, I thought.

Now we were there, I had to ask. 'Why did his wife say those things? About Benja being killed?'

'Look, we all say things when we're upset, things we don't really mean.'

'But why did she have him buried here? Why didn't she take the body home with her?'

It was as if our conversation had just hit a pothole.

She sighed with irritation. 'I think Jenna believed his soul had been lost to her long before, that's all.'

'So it's just gossip. About it not being an accident, I mean.'

She clicked her tongue in annoyance. 'Those two village policemen, playing detective! Manolis and the fat one, Chondro. Well, they have their own axe to grind. Every night you'll find them drinking with the men who own land on the peninsula, men who once thought they had

63

a plot of dust hardly worth tending, save for the odd vineyard or carob tree. Now they see the ancient city rising, and some people are already smelling money.'

Things were obviously far more complicated than I imagined.

Thinking there was some kind of bond between us now, I thought what the hell, tell her, and so I did, how I'd found my luggage broken into, my stuff ransacked.

I don't know why but the suspicion, unspoken, unintended, nevertheless hung in the air, and suddenly I regretted having said anything at all. The last thing I expected was for her to rush to Huxley's defence, least of all with such conviction, such vehemence. 'He would never do such a thing! Never!'

I heard the door to the fragments hut slam loudly and then the crunching of pumice underfoot. I noticed how Anna's look drifted towards him, and how an ambiguous expression momentarily entered her eyes. What was it — indulgence? Forbearance? Irritation?

With a tremor, I found myself wondering whether he had overheard us, the quarry walls, the shells of houses, almost uncanny in their ability to carry and amplify sound.

He threw a sardonic glance at the black notebook stuffed under my arm. Again, his voice carried the distant threat of thunder.

'Well, have you begun to understand, Mr Pedrosa — how we must never take anything at face value? How the truth is forever playing hide and seek with us? How nothing is what it appears to be?'

I flinched as that great paw of a hand closed around the nape of my neck.

'Write it!' he boomed. 'Write down everything you see, everything you hear. No matter how inconsequential it seems at the time; no matter what secrets you think you're trespassing into, no matter how much it hurts, how much it seduces, how much it shocks. Whatever is out there, believe me, we will have the truth of it, come hell or high water!'

I scrambled to find my pen, first in my jacket pockets, then in my bag.

He was still talking as I rummaged desperately through its compartments.

'You will work hard to earn your keep, make no mistake about it. You will learn everything there is to learn about our science. The wonders of photography and darkroom technique from Nestor…

Stratigraphy and cataloguing finds from Hadrian, wall painting stabilisation from Sam, pottery restoration from Anna, epigraphy from me, digging trenches with the labourers, burrowing through the tephra with the moles, excavating a Minoan storehouse with Galatea and her students, improving your Greek with the Greeks... And along the way, you will also keep the logbook record...'

I seized my pen, uncapped it with my teeth.

'Remember, historians of the future may well come to depend on you for an accurate record of events that took place here.'

I dutifully scribbled a few words in my notebook, all the while wondering about the psyche of a man who could so lucidly picture his legacy to the future.

Though my job description had finally become apparent, I was more confused than ever.

Why entrust such a sensitive task to me, a complete stranger? Why not Anna? Why not Hadrian? Why not even mend his fences with Sam? At least they knew the lay of the land, at least they knew what to do when they jumped into a trench armed only with a trowel and brush.

Anna must have been thinking the selfsame thing because, looking up from her stone wall, shielding her eyes from the sun, she said matter-of-factly: 'He's so young, Marcus. Can't you leave well alone this time?'

I hardly knew whether to be grateful or insulted.

'Not everyone can live up to your own impossible expectations.'

I admired her fearlessness, but braced myself for the blast all the same. The thunder, however, failed to boom. Cutting, trenchant, he may have been, yet for all that I could sense in him an indulgence for Anna he rarely showed anyone else.

He said with a glare: '*Why not?* At his age, Alexander the Great had conquered half the known world. I will not have mediocrity in my camp, particularly if I'm the one paying for it. I will not have people around me who will do nothing to lift themselves above their own crippling limitations.'

Discussion closed, he turned his attentions back to me.

'Well, it seems that you are to inherit the Morris Minor, Mr Pedrosa, since it has lost its former owner.' He jangled the keys, then tossed them at me. 'It may be an old boneshaker but, in any event, it will get you from A to B.'

Shocked at his callousness, I just stood there, gaping like a freshly-landed fish.

I left work with the others, climbing aboard the bus in the gathering dusk, just catching a glimpse of the pale blue Morris sitting there in the compound, looking strangely forlorn, like something orphaned. I wasn't going to get in to it today, whatever anyone thought of me.

By the time I got to my lodgings, it was already dark. The day's events were blitzing though my head like a lightning storm. Flashes. Thunderclaps. Discharges streaking across the sky.

To give my mind something else to think about, I made up a feta and olive sandwich from the stuff I'd picked up from the mess tent. Then cracked open a bottle of island red, as dark as the volcanic soil it grew from.

By the second glass, the shock was beginning to wear off. With some semblance of logic returning to my head in lieu of ghosts or other things that go bump in the night, I was seeing things with the acuity they deserved.

The labourers were stupid, craven, and superstitious, just as Huxley so vehemently insisted.

Jenna had lost the love of her life; who could blame her for lashing out at the man who was ultimately responsible for safety in camp, Marcus Huxley?

As for us digging up Atlantis, that was just an infantile trick of Sam's, out to get me from the start.

Despite the red face it had earned me, in my defence it seemed pretty reasonable when you thought about it: Atlantis, torn apart, sinking beneath the waves; this ancient island and its luminous civilisation, torn apart, sinking beneath the waves.

Suddenly, I was sitting bolt upright, my feet clattering onto the cement floor. But wait... *Wait a minute.* I poured another glass of wine and drank it in three gulps. What if it wasn't a sadistic little prank at all. What if Sam had been betraying Huxley's great secret instead, high on weed and resentment? *What if this was Atlantis?*

10.

Day 2 in my brand new job. They came streaking down the mountain track, dust churning behind them. A grim-faced Nestor Louganis at the wheel with the Papás at his side, the old man clutching his chimneypot hat with both hands lest it be blown away or crushed under the wheels.

Once through the gates and into the compound, the jeep ground to a halt. Struggling out, the priest brushed off his dust-smothered robes, straightened his hat, and let the labourers converge upon him like sheep to a saltlick. As they did so, bleating and signing the cross over their hearts, a flicker of emotion illuminated his otherwise habitually austere eyes.

In the crook of his arm, amid the ample folds of his black robe, lay a grey-speckled cockerel with a quivering red comb and blink-glazed eyes. He must have been on his way home from market when Nestor crossed his path.

The men were lining up at the trenches, shuffling along with that peculiar blend of anxious submission, touching hands, moving only at the warbling encouragement of their Papás.

His gaze swept over the peninsula, its rust cliffs plunging into the sea, turning Lucifer-red in the afternoon sun. When, in the far distance, his eyes caught the outlines of the ancient houses climbing the hill, and the skeletal columns of the temple, he scowled, shaking his head.

Nestor came scrambling over to us, his face all dust- and sweat-streaked. Probably already fearing the worst, Huxley shut his eyes in angry despair.

'He is telling them it's fate, Kapítán, the hand of God. That this is what comes of our meddling, digging up this cursed city that God in his wisdom saw fit to punish and destroy so long ago.'

Huxley glowered, turned on his foreman, spitting the words through his teeth. 'Then make it known, Mr Louganis. My own Commandment. From tomorrow on, I will sack anyone who so much as breathes the word "fate" in my hearing.'

Little by little, other people began wandering up to watch, students, teachers, members of the crew. I saw Maria arrive from the site office, where she valiantly tried to keep up with Huxley's chaotic paper chase, permits, contracts, invoices, accounts.

Someone sidled up beside me. Sam.

'So I hear you've been checking it out already,' he said at last, squinting at the labourers lining up between the grave-like trenches. 'Our own little crime scene.'

'I've taken the tour,' I said warily. 'I've seen the house where he fell.'

'Well, you really had to be there to appreciate the finer moments.'

'I take it you and Benjamin were never friends.'

'*Benjamin*,' he mimicked, ridiculing both the dead man and my pronunciation of his name in the same breath.

I stared straight ahead at the unfolding drama among the trenches, trying hard to ignore the provocation.

'It has you spooked, hasn't it? All this talk about ghosts, death, dying. But if you're scared of dying, Nicky, you really shouldn't be here at all —'

He bit his tongue, his whole body tensing as Huxley appeared beside us.

'Ready for church, Mr Pedrosa?' Had it been liquid, the voice would have acid-burned anything in its path. 'I suspect you never imagined for a moment that your new job would also offer you a religious education.'

A few heads down, the boy from the caïque was pushing awkwardly into the line, and looking very hangdog about it. Aris something; I never did learn his family name.

Now captain of his father's boat while the old man sat at home nursing resentment and his dynamited stumps of hands. The way Nestor told it, he hated everything about the foreigners; hated his neighbours who were on the payroll, uttered a dark bitter laugh whenever the ghosts made them run for their lives. But what choice did young Aris have? The second those fizzling sticks went bang, the boy found himself thrown in at the deep end, no longer his father's casual apprentice who needed a yelling to do things right or do anything at all, but the sole breadwinner of the family. Had his father not lost his hands to fate, he would surely have boxed the boy's ears black and blue, but still Aris snatched the lifeline Nestor threw him; from now on, we'd buy every fish he could land for the swelling chow line at camp. For good measure, we'd also charter his boat to ferry in supplies, saving countless expeditions along a rutted dust track.

As the Papás fixed the boy in a withering glare, the message was unmistakeable even to me. *How could you betray your crippled father, betray your island with the job these* xeni *have thrown you like scraps to a stray dog, these foreigners who don't belong here? These labourers and trench diggers are bad enough, but you, right in the middle of them!*

Hadrian had come barrelling over from the sheds, and now thrust his way between us, exclaiming: 'I would not miss this for the world!'

'I thought you despised the very idea,' Anna rebuked him, the bulk force of his arrival almost toppling her like a bowling pin.

'I despise every sing-song prayer of it,' he affirmed, putting out a hand to steady her. 'But at least in defeat of logic I shall enjoy the spectacle of people making utter fools of themselves.'

'Ah, Maria,' he added, glancing left to take in Nestor's sweet betrothed. 'Our sweet bird of youth!'

A weak smile fluttered back at him, the tense fingers that had just signed the cross over her heart and silver amulet missing detection by a shadow.

The priest was moving along the trenches now, sprinkling holy water over the heads of the labourers with his sprig of bay laurel, chanting his incantations. Half-sung, half-spoken, I found the voice unexpectedly mellifluous, and strangely hypnotic. Every so often his eyes, like fire in the mist, would stray from the ragged line before him to find Huxley's seething look upon him. A look that was also unmistakeable. *What business does this Christian priest have among the ancient dead? This backward village papás, perpetuating these medieval superstitions? And these fools that listen to him, drinking my precious time like profligate drunks.*

Elderly he may have been but, to my eyes, the priest looked more than a match for the professor. Reciting the rites of exorcism with the deliberateness of a metronome, I wonder who among us could have escaped the obvious: that rather than the ghosts, it was Huxley himself he had foremost in mind, not to mention us, the archaeologist's own band of pagans.

Every so often, Huxley would mutter some cutting remark about gullibility or superstition, to which Hadrian would chime in with some equally acerbic comment of his own. Those caustic words of reason somehow possessed a magic of their own, diminishing by several degrees at least, the eerie strangeness of the ceremony itself.

I remarked as much to Anna, standing behind me at my left shoulder.

But it was from the right that the answer came, as quick as a knife blade.

'Huxley doesn't have a superstitious bone in his body,' whispered Sam, so powerfully I could feel the force of his breath on my ear, 'is that what you think? Then just ask him about the ancient silver drachma that's always jangling around with the loose change in his pocket. Ask him what it's for!'

Nestor threaded his way up the line towards us until he was standing at Huxley's shoulder. For an unlikely moment, fighting the singsong from the trenches, it almost sounded as if he were remonstrating with his 'Kapítán'.

I shuffled sideways, until I could just catch what he was saying.

'It cannot go on like this. You must see that, Kapítán. There is too much opposition. Too much hostility.'

'What would you have me do?' growled Huxley. 'Haven't I bent over backwards for these people? Haven't I given them jobs? Haven't I put food on their tables?'

'You must give them something else, Kapítán. Something they will never forget. Something that will make them proud.'

The next thing I knew I was gaping in shock at the trenches. The Papás had the cockerel by the neck, and from the slit throat the blood was spurting into the dust.

I heard Sam say: 'Blood: the first and last to be spilt.'

I heard Anna murmur: 'Too late for that.'

Hadrian caught my shocked goldfish look. 'You think Christianity was virgin born, Pedrosa? That the people who flocked to it came with virgin minds, virgin hearts? Well, think again.'

The ritual worked its curious magic. Ceremony over, the men were treated to wine, charcoal grilled fish and huge chunks of fresh bread. They seemed calmer now. Once the flagon had been sucked dry, there was even a chance they would return to the dig.

I was less surprised to find the Papás himself imbibing a glass than to see Huxley at his side. As I passed, he grabbed me by the shoulder and swung me about-face.

'Make yourself known, Mr Pedrosa.'

'A new face,' observed the priest, nodding.

The civility was skin deep, Huxley probably mindful of the warning

Nestor had dished out about making enemies.

'This is Father Constantine Nannos,' said Huxley, his forced politeness, I could tell, about as tolerable to him as bamboo splinters under the fingernails.

I found myself shaking hands, and was conscious of the old priest's slender bony fingers that somehow reminded me of the relics of a saint I had once seen in Catalonia.

'Can you tell me, Huxley, what you expect to find buried here?' Vaguely, Father Nannos shook his stick at the trenches, at the distant buildings on the hill. 'The ruins of a civilisation dead and buried, is that all you will have to show for it in the end, after all this toil?'

'Oh no, Papás, it is not the dead that I would know, but the cause of death.'

The Papás glanced sharply at him and I could see it in the looks that crossed like blades, a mutual recognition that both had been speaking in metaphor.

Seconds later the revelation hit me, I don't know why. My stomach fell through a trapdoor. I could feel the blood draining from my face.

The only thing I couldn't understand was why I hadn't realised it before. Benja, my predecessor. He was still alive when I was given his job. That could mean only one thing. They were planning to give him the push — from the job, from the scaffolding, or both. It was premeditated. Is that what Jenna meant, hurling that livid accusation at him between the tombs?

11.

'Hello, Nicholas. Are you settling in?' It was Maria, with a big bright smile like the dawn sun, light triumphing over the dark.

I shrugged, forced a grin, not wanting to sound sorry for myself.

Far from settling in, I felt strangely out of place, stranded between somewhere and nowhere.

Pensively, I walked around the Morris, peering in through the windows, kicking the tyres, but still couldn't quite bring myself to get inside.

If there was one thing I needed, it was a night's unbroken sleep. Just to clear my head. Just to put things into perspective.

It was not to be.

When Huxley expected your company, it didn't matter what time of day or night it was. You were always on the clock. It was part of the job description, unwritten, unspoken, but there nonetheless. No apologies. No excuses.

And so that night the work went on, not in the trenches or the sheds, but in the taverna of Alexis Pangalos, Huxley apparently taking a shine to the place for no other a reason than their mutual scorn for the Papás and his bleating flock.

A great bull of a man with oxtail eyebrows, Pangalos was a diehard communist and proud of it. Unlike some Greeks of that persuasion, he was also a devout atheist, the kind of man who'll let nothing in the whole wide world stare him down, least of all things that are invisible.

It was a strange place. A great smoke-filled room as frigid as the stone, tile and glass it was made of, the ceilings so high you normally never even saw them. Straw-seated chairs that dug into your backside. Wobbly tables too small for the people that were supposed to sit at them. Stubble-faced men in overcoats playing *tavli* under harsh fluorescent lights, the counters crashing down on the chequered boards, accompanied by shouts of triumph or protest. Behind the glass and enamel refrigerator display, the kitchen with its charcoal grill, the sparks cracking all over the floor, and beyond, the dirty footprint toilet that would flood your ankles if you didn't leap back in time. On the walls, damp-buckling portraits of Lenin, Che Guevara, and an incongruous Einstein, the physicist looking vaguely surprised by the company he was keeping.

Yet for all that my boss far preferred Pangalos' to the dingy hangout a few doors down that claimed to be Orthodox and democratic, but in political terms was probably closer to the barracks than the ballot box. The fact that taverna Elefteros was frequented by the police and their informers did little for its broader popularity.

Huxley poured wine from the tin carafe, deep earth red wine straight from the barrel. Alexis Pangalos barged his way between the tables, ferrying plates of Greek *mezedakia*. Octopus tentacles, a burnt offering from the grill. A plate of raw, shell-cracked sea urchins. A bowl of *horta* — bitter weeds from the fields, smothered in dusky green olive oil and lemon juice.

It was almost harder to get used to the food than the tomb damp cold.

Having heard all about the exorcism of the dig long before we walked in, Pangalos said in mock sympathy: 'You have to make allowances for our Papás, Huxley. Here was a village boy who, having no other talents to pursue, was taken under the wing of his mentor, another village priest! It is how ignorance achieves its sublime immortality!'

Clearly bruised by the day's events, Huxley was in a determined mood, drawing up lists, plotting strategy, firing questions at his inner circle, Hadrian, Anna, Nestor, even Sam when necessity dictated. He was pushing them, demanding the impossible, only too conscious of the fact that his enemies were gaining in strength and number.

Pangalos reappeared with a plate of battered *gavros*, greasy sprats you were required to swallow head, tail and all. Under his breath, he added: 'Do not forget. The bishops are hand-in-glove with the tyrants. Cross one and you may find yourself answering to the other.'

He splashed wine into his own glass, raised it aloft, shouted '*Stin ijá sas!*', drained it in a single draught, and promptly vanished again.

'Pangalos is right, Kapítán,' said Nestor, who could read a brewing storm before it even knew its own mind.

'You must do something, Huxley,' piped Hadrian, only half in jest. 'It's getting so as I dread even setting foot outside my own front door lest the neighbours spit at me.'

'Can't the Foundation help, Marcus? I know they're in Paris, but —'

'No!' said Huxley, his brusqueness killing the idea at birth. 'We cannot drag the Foundation into this. You know the Comte. He insists on hearing only the good news, never the bad.'

The Comte Guillaume d'Adhémar, and his Orpheus Foundation. Huxley's wealthy benefactor, his bank drafts from Paris apparently paying for everything. Even me.

I watched, learned, and spoke as little as I could get away with. I suppose that's why the moment stands out so vividly in my memory. Watching Huxley light his pipe, the flaring match illuminating one side of his face while casting the other into shadow. It was a strange, if fleeting, sensation, as if two identities had suddenly materialised before me.

Just when I thought, that's it, we'll be here till daybreak, Huxley abruptly snapped shut his notebook, downed the last of his wine, and stood.

Outside we said goodnight, and I began walking back to my lodgings through the warren of streets above. I could hear their disembodied voices fading into the night, still debating work and all the problems and challenges we faced. Mingling with them came the sighing of the wind again, like plaintive voices crying through the wires.

I quickened my pace to get home, the lament of the wind seeming to echo through me as I reached the town's highest point. Just at the sound of it, those stupid village folk tales came welling into my mind again, the ones saying this wasn't the wind at all, but the songs of ghosts.

As I fell into bed with four hours' sleep ahead of me, I couldn't help thinking, this isn't the job or the Aegean island your imagination painted for you back home, is it, all blue on the edge of the world.

If not for the alarm clock jangling its head off, I would have overslept. As I fumbled for it over the floor, my first thought was that it must have gone haywire because there was no wash of dawn in the sky. It was still pitch black outside. And it was only after poking my head around the front door that I realised why: the streets and houses had vanished, swallowed by dense cloud and sea fog.

And that's how it stayed. Day after day, night after night, the only thing to thin or diminish: our patience, first with the weather, then with each other.

As the week wore on, I began to wonder if we would ever see the sun again, ever find our way out of the fog. The sense of isolation and claustrophobia it brought about reached the brink of unbearable.

There was no horizon. The world seemed to stop at the cliff's edge.

By day, we were in the unheated sheds, or out among the trenches, what we could see of them through the fog.

Even at night, it seemed impossible to find anywhere warm to sit. Imported firewood was in short supply and the smoky paraffin stoves in some places would drive you outside with the stink. Huxley didn't seem to care, and simply had our table moved nearer the raining sparks of Pangalos' grill.

It was hard to believe just how cold and clammy everything had become to the touch, the clothes in the cupboard, the clothes you stood up in, pillows, bed sheets, blankets. The briny dampness seemed to infiltrate everything, and the longer you spent in it the more bone chilling it became.

I began to wonder how I was even going to make it through the next twenty-four hours without throwing in the towel, packing my bags. I was craving the lost blue sky as a means of finding clarity and understanding within my own mind. What it was I was doing here. What was expected of me. What was going on.

A week into the fog, and I was finding it harder than ever to settle in, the grey ash landscape against the grey sky, and the grey faces in the trenches giving me a dose of something I never expected, not for a moment. Homesickness.

Worst of all was the fog's echoing isolation, the sense of being cut off from everything you once knew. The *Pegasus*, even in good weather, would only call in once a week, the day and the hour anybody's guess. English newspapers were rare and usually weeks old even if you ever did manage to lay your hands on one.

Hoping there might be news from home, I waited eagerly for the next mail call in camp, only to be told brusquely by my boss to forget it; letters here take weeks, sometimes months, to arrive.

There were black-and-white televisions in some of the tavernas, a crackling old radio in one of the workshops in camp, but who could trust the news in a military dictatorship, even if they were all avuncular smiles for the tourists? What remained was something as ancient as myth itself — whisper, rumour, fragments of stories, travelling by word of mouth along the village streets. By the time it reached your own ears, you didn't know what to make of it, disasters abroad, arrests of anarchists in Athens, a moon landing, an atomic test, getting all muddled up with the lucky escape of some teenager from a *vrykolakas* in the fog, the failing health of someone's donkey, or Mad Yanni the gravedigger threatening to exhume bodies in the cemetery again.

It became impossible to tell what was real and what was not. Facts could no longer be trusted. Gut instincts could no longer be relied upon. The things people said could no longer be taken at face value. Answers could no longer be drawn even from observable events.

Like the quake-prone island upon which we stood, the bedrock truth had a habit of buckling, lurching or giving way underfoot just when you least expected it.

At my most paranoid, I even began to wonder if this was some clever, manipulative way of Huxley's to prove the point he always insisted upon, that appearances are inherently deceptive. It was the one point we might have agreed upon, had conversation between us ever been more than oblique.

'What is the greatest challenge that confronts us, Mr Pedrosa?'

My eyes swept over the desolate moonscape, pockmarked with trenches and mineshafts, houses still wallowing in ash. I shrugged, 'To shift all this tephra.'

'No! It is to understand the nature of reality. Theirs, ours. There is no greater challenge in the universe and no higher calling.'

Ten days in, and I had decided I didn't like him at all.

He was intimidating, autocratic, manipulative. Everything revolved around him, including us, diminutive moons caught in his relentless gravitational field.

In fact I could hardly count up the things I didn't like about him, trivial or profound.

The callousness with which he treated the memory of his own dead protégé. The huge charcoal-burning samovar in his field tent in which he insisted on boiling up his bitter Russian tea. The careless contempt with which he treated customs and opinions that differed from his own, for all his pretensions about an ancient golden age of philosophical debate, great minds contemplating the universe in search of truth. His atheism, so rabid it shocked even me, Nicholas Pedrosa, whose grandparents had attended Sunday service to be seen by the neighbours, not by God.

That uncanny ability he had of reading the mind, reading the mood. And worst of all, the way I would have to struggle to meet those hypnotic mosaic eyes. Perhaps I already sensed something inside; that he wanted something from me, something that could not be spoken out loud.

'You take Marcus far too seriously,' Anna scolded me, an ancient window emerging before her in the face of the trench. 'You have to stick it out, give it a chance.'

'Is it true?' I asked, keen for a denial even if it meant being made a fool of again by Sam. 'That he put the silver drachma in Benja's mouth — to pay the Ferryman?'

She glanced up with a wince of a smile. 'It was a gesture for old time's sake, that's all.' But even she sounded unconvinced, as though she had caught herself defending Huxley out of loyalty rather than conviction.

I fought tooth and nail, but still could not shake the feeling that I had made some terrible mistake in coming here.

I felt my eyes roaming over the tortured landscape too jerkily, too tentatively, knowing something was wrong.

'Benja and Sam, they were like jealous children,' sighed Maria, with a slow sultry blink of those wide almond eyes.

'Jealous of what?'

'Attention.'

'Whose?'

'Professor Huxley's, of course.'

'*Why?*' uncertain whether that was bewilderment or premonition thinning my voice.

Whenever I saw her, I could hardly breathe, hardly string two words together. A schoolboy crush, I suppose. Except I wasn't supposed to be a schoolboy anymore.

I imagined how she slept. How it would be to fit the curve of her back, the arch of her legs. Twice that week I woke up in the dead of night, the spattered sheets all wet and cold.

Just when I'd given up all hope of ever understanding anything again, there it was.

Bright blue brilliant sky. Between streamers of rose-coloured mist.

As for the tense morose faces in camp, they had vanished, along with the clinging fog. From one moment to the next, it was hard to find anyone without a smile or a sympathetic look in their eye.

Except Huxley.

Without looking up from the fragments at his fingertips, he brusquely ordered me to take the day off work — my first in the fortnight I had been here.

12.

I got behind the wheel of the Morris, trying hard not to think about the dead boy who had once owned it, and whose fingerprints were now touching mine.

Once beyond the hairpins, I began exploring the island's unmarked roads and dust tracks, with each twist and turn gaining a better understanding of the lay of the land, and something of its tortured history.

Following the cataclysmic eruption that tore the Minoan island apart, it must have taken centuries for people to resettle the crescent-shaped crater rim that remained. They would have fished the sea and tilled these very fields, the remnants of the volcano sloping down towards its eastern shores, and miles of black sand.

Between subsequent convulsions, that shook the earth and spewed molten rock and poisonous ash, came Egyptians, Phoenicians, Dorians.

After the Romans had abandoned their outpost to the snowing ash, it took another hundred years or more for the next wave of farmers or fishers to colonise the island, refugees from the Empire's gathering turmoil. Christians, raising churches and shrines to pacify the pagan gods that still haunted the island from every vent and fissure, apparently undaunted by the Bible or the Cross.

Making my way over the island's scaly spine, I caught the sting of sulphur in my nose, heard the bubbling of a hot spring, and began to understand. Santorini was a sleeping dragon of an island, its nostril vents exhaling hot fumes, its rock veins oozing lava in lieu of blood.

Little by little, I began to settle in.

Faces in the street, once anonymous, became familiar to me. Neighbours would engage me in conversation, offer me a glass of sweet wine, press vegetables or fruits into my hands from their own gardens, sometimes an egg if the hens were laying.

Angeliki, the little handicapped girl from along the way, came to my door with a bunch of winter flowers, and a bright smile. Apparently, I was home.

Hospitality to strangers — it could trace itself back to Homeric legend, I knew that, but still it took me by surprise. Most of these people hardly had two drachmas to rub together.

They lived off their fields, vineyards and hemp nets, or waited for whatever could be spared from the wage packets of their sons or husbands, working the docks in Piraeus or the ferries and freighters that plied the Aegean. There was a quiet dignity about them, in hardship, in poverty, in a stubborn determination to endure. I began to think Huxley was making far too much of their submissive attitudes towards fate, a trait that never ceased to enrage him.

On the way to work at the crack of dawn, or coming home at night, I would often see the same faces along the whitewashed streets.

Panayiotis and his wife Elpeda at the bakery, paddling loaves into the glowing *fourno*. Orestes the postman, riding his motorbike from one village to another, a tin trumpet slung from his belt to summon the villagers into the dusty street. Mad Yanni the gravedigger, grumbling about where he's going to put the next body, the small cemetery so chock-a-block that whenever he breaks soil for a fresh grave, he ends up exhuming an arm or a foot.

My Greek teacher never coached me for this, I thought, struggling with the language, the dialect, the subtleties and hidden meanings populating sentences like stones in a field. The more familiar I became to my neighbours, the more talk they would throw at me.

I began to wonder if this hadn't been Huxley's intention all along, tossing me in at the village deep end so that he would have his bellwether to gauge the local mood.

If so, it was working, and it wasn't long before I could identify his friends and enemies by sight; those who wished to undermine or sabotage the excavations, and those who gained financially from them.

By the third week, I was seeing my colleagues in a new light — not merely as archaeologists but, as Huxley himself liked to boast, forensic scientists hunting for clues at the scene of a crime. Piecing together the evidence at their fingertips, reconstructing events in the hours and days before this civilisation met its doom.

Hearing him say it so matter-of-factly, I was struck by the irony of finding myself in the middle of two great mysteries, one ancient, the other numbered in days. For while Huxley was digging up the ancient past, his enemies were busy digging the dirt on Huxley himself, still hoping to implicate him in Benja's death.

The police continued to make their blundering appearances in camp, the effect being to diminish rather than amplify the seriousness of the allegations against him. They'd come wobbling up to the camp gates on their sputtering grey Triumph, Chondro at the handlebars, Manolis riding pillion, the prodigious rump up front threatening to eject him at every bump and pothole. Confronting Huxley across the trenches, they'd rant and rave about having him charged with manslaughter, murder, smuggling, offending the morals of the nation, virtually anything that sprang to mind.

'You will be arrested and thrown off our island!' boasted Manolis on several occasions, though nothing seemed to come of it.

Catching Anna brush-dusting an exhumed amphora, Chondro's face creased with suspicion and he demanded: 'Why are you looking for fingerprints?'

At the back of my mind, I couldn't help wondering if it wasn't so much the evidence that was missing as the wits to recover it.

Yet as I began to find my feet, my own suspicions about Huxley and his camp began to fade, until finally I could convince myself that the long journey from England had been to blame — that and landing on an island as outlandish as the moon.

'Tomorrow is Sunday,' remarked Huxley, the light of the magnifying glass flooding back into his face, his enlarged fingers examining a translucent fragment of pottery.

'It is?' How easy it is to lose track of the days here, I thought, the colours of them running into one another, like Aegean blue into heaven, like sunset into volcanic rock.

'And you have not yet been to my house at Monolithos.'

'No.'

'Then you shall come to dinner. And be sure to arrive well before dusk. You won't want to lose your way in the dark.'

Why does he have to be so damned mysterious about everything? I thought. No wonder the most poison-tongued of his enemies had him up on temple hill at the witching hour, a hooded figure surrounded by his chanting acolytes, we the Devil's apprentices, the young girls and boys from the student tents our juiced up sacrifices.

I decided to try my luck with Anna instead, and stuck my head around the pottery hut door.

'Symposium,' she murmured, her eyes focusing hard on the handle of a small water jug as she cemented and tweezed it into place; another exquisite piece of Bronze Age pottery, this one depicting a mountain cascade.

So that was it. I was finally considered worthy enough to attend one his mysterious philosophical gatherings, the rites and rituals of which the uninitiated could only guess at, so tight-lipped were those who had ever attended them. Hadrian, Anna, Sam. His Greek friends. Contemplating the universe in the company of some pretty young things and a barrel of wine. At least, that was the talk about camp, issuing as usual from the knowing mouths of those who had never been invited.

'You will need a topic of conversation,' said Anna. 'That is the rule. The more provocative the better. And I hope you can drink and think at the same time.'

'Why me, what about the others?'

'The initiate brings the subject, that is the rule. And you may not discuss it with anyone beforehand. No one may be primed. That is the rule.'

'There are a lot of rules, aren't there. What am I supposed to talk about?'

'Islands.'

'What kind of islands? Greek islands? Hawaiian islands? Polynesian islands?'

She glanced up, blowing the stray red hair out of her eyes. 'Islands anywhere. Mythical, legendary, real, it doesn't matter. In the sea or the imagination, in archaeological history or a poet's mind. We must have visited hundreds by now. Atolls, archipelagos, island chains. Benja, too, before he was taken from us.'

Suddenly, I was getting cold feet. 'I don't know anything about islands. Even the British Isles for that matter.'

I waited, hoping she'd offer to get me off the hook. 'Well, you have twenty-four hours to come up with something. We'll all be waiting. With bated breath.'

Fuck.

The screen door creaked open and there stood Hadrian, plump and pompous. 'Symposium, did I hear Symposium?'

'There's a lot of talk about them in camp,' I said pointedly. 'About what they're for.'

'Of that I have no doubt at all. They are for edification, Master Pedrosa. Of the mind. Of the imagination. Of the taste buds.'

'*Taste buds?*'

'Why must everyone make an intrigue out of everything? Truth be told, the only singularly exceptional thing about a symposium at

Monolithos is Myroula's *cuisine*,' he said, almost kissing the word. Kneading his fingers together in gleeful anticipation, he gushed: 'Sharp, crumbling goat's cheese with wild berries and a drizzle of honey. Garlic baked mushrooms in phyllo pastry with wild greens... You can't imagine the taste!'

'Sounds like you're more interested in the food than the philosophy.' Anna giggled.

'Certainly not,' he replied with bruised dignity. 'No one appreciates the ancient concept more than I... Evoking for our fellow travellers the most enchanting, the most seductive, the most terrifying islands on or off the map. Bringing impossible ideas to the dinner table, all designed to exercise the mind until it sweats... Well, helmsman? Do you know your compass bearing? Have you set the course?'

'He has no idea.'

Hadrian threw up his hands in exasperation, as if I were personally in danger of scuttling the whole ship, wine, dine, philosophy and all. 'Then make hay, Pedrosa, make hay!'

I threw him a great big thank you and went to clock-out.

Just as I drove the Morris out of camp, it hit me. The compass heading. Of course. I knew exactly where to take us. And I wanted to see Huxley's face as I did so. I wanted to see Sam's face. If they wanted an island mythical, legendary or real, I would give them the most legendary one of all.

13.

Mindful of his warning about getting caught out by the dark, I set off with the afternoon sun still flooding the caldera, the light creating a pacifying orange blur over the mud-spattered windscreen.

The Morris' bull nose dipped sharply to follow the track at the foot of the mountain, and then we were coasting down towards the remote eastern shores, passing the odd wiry fig or carob along the way, and fields of nest-shaped vines, like the dust-blown relics of prehistoric birds.

Finally, after getting lost half a dozen times on the criss-crossing vineyard tracks, turning back, ending up where I started, there it was. Unmistakable.

Rather like the man himself, Marcus Huxley's house was solitary, imposing, and more than a little mad. The traditional Cycladic architecture had obviously experienced the subversive hand of an individualist, the white cubist model infiltrated here and there by raw stone, curves and arches.

Grating into gear again, I drove on through the open gates, parked, then took the steps down to the house.

Beyond the meandering stucco walls that hid it from view, I found myself in a garden of petal, leaf and stone, honeysuckle, jasmine, a grove of watered olives.

Twenty yards on, the path ended in a vertical drop at the cliff face, a certain death-trap for any unsuspecting visitor in the dark. At least I had been forewarned.

Obviously despising the straightest route, the stone flags then went snaking back towards the house, and I was almost at the steps to the front door when I hesitated, turned, my attention drawn to a secluded corner overgrown by wild grasses and camomile.

The moment I set eyes on them, I had to think again of the trafficking rumours that wouldn't leave him alone. Dismembered Hellenistic statues, broken marble columns, a temple frieze. Materialising from the camomile like dead men rising from their own graves, a pair of marble cadavers, their enquiring heads and opaque eyes turned up to the sky as if struck blind by whatever they had once dared to see. Staring out from the crevice of an olive tree, a mystical face carved from Nile sandstone, its eastern features almost worn smooth now by the relentless streams of time. Did he even have the paperwork to prove the legality and provenance of these antiquities? Where did they come from? To whom did they belong?

I rapped at the front door, the heavy brass knocker staring back at me with the ecstatic, inebriated face of Bacchus.

Upstairs, I thought I saw the curtains twitch, then a shadow fall across the next window. In the raw tension it evoked, it was suddenly hard to shake the feeling that every moment since my arrival at the gates had been devoured by greedy, voyeuristic eyes.

The door heaved open. Looming over me was a great barge of a woman in an apron the size of a parachute, with shrewd, no nonsense eyes, up to her elbows in flour and dough. She was busy in the kitchen, she screeched, did I think she had time to waste answering doors every five minutes? Huxley's housekeeper Myroula.

Clucking and clacking, she shooed me into the kitchen, where the countertops and the great wooden table betrayed the wonderful chaos of Myroula's poetry in motion, pots bubbling, wood oven billowing flame, charcoal grill showering sparks, tabletop decked in sheets of phyllo pastry.

I was confused. After scolding me in that shrill indignant voice of hers, Myroula was now cooing at me as if I were her favourite nephew, plying me with mouth-gumming honey cakes.

Around the corner, Hadrian was bumbling around like a pollen drunk bee, his eyes feasting in wonder at the dizzying array of dishes and *mezedakia* lining the countertop at the windows. 'No, my eyes will not believe my taste buds, nor my taste buds my eyes!' he cried, picking and tasting as he went. 'You have outdone even yourself, Myroula-mu. Charcoal grilled sea bream stuffed with herbs and wild garlic... Octopus and tomato pie, the morsels so tender they melt in the mouth... Artichoke hearts in lemon and dill... Fresh mussels steamed in white wine! Whoever said there can be no heaven on Earth?'

He managed to snatch one last morsel before Myroula chased us both out of the kitchen, screeching.

Out through the back door, we found ourselves on a crow's nest terrace carved out of the rock face, so close to the brink it appeared to be levitating over the drop to the sea. There, gathered around the stone table, sitting on the retaining wall, or leaning up against the pergola with its budding grapevine, were our fellow symposiasts. Huxley's Greek island friends, most of whom I already knew by sight.

Stavros Sanassis, the town's only doctor. Brisk, precise, grumbling in his good-natured way about the patients who could only pay him in kind, a rabbit, a chicken, a leg of goat, a slab of feta. Or even worse, the patients who were not even human at all but were all hide, fur or feathers, padding, trotting, flapping into surgery with their owners.

The postmaster, Vassilis Nafpliotis, cultured, urbane, rarely with a single silver hair out of place, who dreamed of a time when Aegean islands had been seats of learning and invention, not rough and ready places like this, he'd say, no more civilised than a seagull rookery.

Nondas Maharis, the affable barber who cut Huxley's hair and sometimes shaved his three-day stubble, talking animatedly into the mirror on just about anything that sprang to mind, ancient glories, modern follies.

Alexander Vouris, the ghost-pale schoolmaster, with whom Huxley practised his French. A bespectacled and faint-hearted man, a sense of failure clinging to his clothes like mildew. My neighbours swore blind it was his long-dead father, haunting him from beyond the grave, but that was probably just their way of saying that the father had expected more of him than this, a village schoolmaster with not enough of anything to go around, desks, books, slates or chalk.

And last but not least, diehard communist Alexis Pangalos, who tonight had left the taverna in the capable hands of his wife and bright, 11-year old son.

Sam, then Aris, appeared at the arching doorway to the cellar, each carrying a large flagon of wine tapped from the barrels.

At the far edge of the terrace, Huxley was in animated conversation with Dr Sanassis and the schoolmaster.

They sounded worried. I tried to eavesdrop as Maria chose that moment to arrive, looking about as sultry as a tropical volcano, a white blossom behind her ear.

'Nestor is right, Marcus,' the Doctor was saying. 'Papadaikis is on the ropes. He can't hold out.'

Giannis Papadaikis, Junta-approved mayor and island demagogue. That barrel round man with the mangy comb-over I had encountered

85

on my first night in the wine cellar, going six rounds with his sworn enemy, the Chief of Police. As mayor, Papadaikis led the island council, a gaggle of fractious local officials whose dealings variously earned the approval, derision or indifference of everyone else.

'There's only so much I can do, Stavros. Papadaikis is still for us, isn't he? God knows he has no conception of the culture, just the money, but still he greased the wheels.'

'But for how long?' put in the Schoolmaster in faint voice. 'As our enemies grow in number, so do his. If the men in uniform decide he is a risk or a liability, he will crumble.'

Huxley scowled as that ominous thought was left dangling in the air.

'Those who cannot imagine the possibilities that lie in wait for the island, Alexander. What should I do, steal into their minds, colour their thoughts with the vivid palette of the frescoes themselves...?'

While the Schoolmaster pondered that with pursed lips, Dr Sanassis grinned. 'Isn't that what the greatest philosophers have always done, Marcus? Putting their genius in alchemy to good effect, transforming minds, transforming opinions, base metal into gold.'

Over the ridge the sun was setting, the redness of it infusing the sky like a fan. The emerging stars brought a chillness to the air and at Huxley's urging we retreated to the living room where, over the long dining table at the windows, Myroula's sumptuous feast had been laid. At the fireplace, the flames were leaping high.

After all the gossip I had endured in camp, I was half-expecting us to be lolling around on couches, Roman-style. What with the ragtag collection of chairs awaiting us, however, that was one picture that thankfully went right out of the window. Apart from Maria, now reading coffee grounds with Myroula in the kitchen, oblivious to what the lord and master might think of them, there were no pretty young things, either; unless anyone was of a mind to count the perpetually brooding Sam.

I was wondering when the Symposium would begin, or if it already had, when the postmaster said: 'Friends, how many times have we gathered here, dreaming of a time when love of wisdom would be king? Stepping aboard our metaphysical ship, its sails catching the streams of time and possibility, journeying to islands at the four corners of the Earth and beyond. Imagine the tremor that ran down my spine, then, when on a brilliant morning last week I first set my eyes upon the frescoes of the spring. The swallows. The saffron gatherers. The flotilla of boats. The leaping dolphins! Such was my astonishment, I thought for one moment that our metaphysical ship *had* carried me away! Returning to the present, I almost expected to feel a sense of bereavement for that heavenly world now lost to us, bitterness, emptiness, regret. And yet I returned to the post office with a spring in my step — *why?* Because to behold the achievements of our ancient civilisation is to understand with utter clarity that the idyll is not an empty dream; love of wisdom *can* be king!'

Pangalos uttered a raucous *hear! hear!*

'Fine sentiments indeed, Postmaster,' Hadrian cut in, 'but at some point our metaphysical ship hits land, if not the shoals or the rocks beforehand. Call it reality. Its immutability to change.'

To which Dr Sanassis raised his own objection. 'You say that, Hadrian, and yet while all was Bronze Age darkness and superstition, warlike Mycenae to the north, cruel querulous tribes to the east, here was a beacon of pure light, free, inventive, sensual, spiritual... Even the women in the frescoes depict that: they are not closeted in their houses, veiled in the streets. They are confident, elegant, free, from the priestess in the temple, to the saffron gatherers on the hill...'

'And how might we compare today,' lamented the barber, Nondas Maharis. 'Marooned on this broken rock? With its own awesome beauty to be sure, but where is the imagination, where is the invention, where is the civilisation? A thousand churches and not a single library...'

'A billion stars above our heads and not a single telescope!' added the Schoolmaster, the wine finally bringing some backbone to his voice. It made you wonder how he ever managed in class. 'As for logic, philosophy, every free thought is smothered by the Church or the Colonels. I dare not even teach Plato except as something ancient, something dead, every line superseded by the infallible Word of God: the priests and bishops!'

'The teachings of Socrates,' Huxley grunted caustically. 'Still corrupting the minds of the young!'

'That scrawny whore of a police chief plots to have us all thrown off the island or thrown into jail,' growled Pangalos. 'Maybe it's time to turn the tables!'

The postmaster's eyes widened in alarm, straying first to the window, then to the door. 'You would do well to remember, Alexis, walls have ears!' He paused in sudden regret and said: 'But yes, I understand the sentiment, Friend. For why shouldn't we dream of an island of ingenuity, culture and invention? If not for the dream how would ever we get there?'

We were already through the second flagon of wine by the time Dr Sanassis, the night's master of ceremonies, chimed the rim of his glass and said: 'Our dear Benja. You knew him well. Lost yourselves to the seas and islands he evoked for us in this very room. Islands made of ice, stone or fire, islands made of thought, on this side of the sunset or the other. His was the spirit of a navigator crossing unknown seas. However daunting the journey, or turbulent the emotions it might provoke within, euphoria or despair, daring or trepidation, we knew better even than he, perhaps, that the helm was in good hands...'

Murmurs of approval swept through the room. Anna's eyes had brimmed with tears. She was biting her lips. As I took it all in, an unexpected thought occurred to me: if this was the eulogy, what had the reality been like?

14.

Aris appeared with two more flagons of that fierce volcanic red. Somehow or other I'd have to pace myself but it was getting harder and harder. I needed a clear head to pull off my plan but, as the moment of truth edged ever closer, I also found myself needing its kick more than ever.

Another toast, glasses chiming over the candles, and the formalities were over. I was now officially a symposiast, albeit on probation.

I was asked to take the helm. That vacant seat at the head of the table, last occupied by Benja himself, apparently, on some voyage beyond sunset. Despite the sudden attack of stage fright, I pushed back my chair, determined to see it through.

I laid my crib notes on the table, where they'd seem a little less obvious secreted between the wine and the *mezedakia*. Whatever their colour or intensity I was aware of every pair of eyes on me, eager, quixotic, sceptical, sardonic, and I don't know what else.

'At the risk that you have made landfall there before,' I began, my voice trembling like a sail before it catches the wind, 'even with my predecessor at the helm, I have chosen to set a course for what must be the most legendary of all islands...' I snatched up my wine, downing what was left of it in a slow gulp, just so as to measure the reaction on each face as I finally spoke its name. '...Plato's Atlantis. The Lost Isle.'

I caught the thunder in Huxley's eyes. The smirk in Sam's. The pompous disdain in Hadrian's. The brief effervescence in Anna's.

I pressed on, already knowing I was about to hit high seas.

'Why not, indeed?' said Dr Sanassis, beaming. 'As legends go, it has surely proven the most eternal, the most mesmerising of them all.'

Huxley said: 'Then I hope you will explain Atlantis to us, Mr Pedrosa; where it is and, more importantly, what it is.'

'An island of incomparable beauty beyond the Pillars of Hercules,' I said. 'A lost island paradise.'

'Is that so?' Was that a sarcastic or defensive edge to his voice? I couldn't tell. 'Then it was written in the naivety of youth, was it?'

'No, in old age. They were Plato's last great dialogues, the Critias and the Timaeus.'

As Pangalos rapped the table loudly in appreciation, Huxley declared, 'Then set the stage for us, Mr Pedrosa. Paint the picture for our mind's eye. It is Athens, 350 something BC. We can see the forested slopes of Mt. Hymettos, known for its springs, temples and thyme honey. Beyond and between the houses, pasture, olive and citrus groves. We can see the Eridanos stream flowing through the agora; beyond, with their reeds and kingfishers, the rivers Ilissos and Cephissus whose beauty earned the songs of poets. We can see pilgrims along the Sacred Way, making for Eleusis and the Mysteries. Where is Plato? Where is Socrates?'

That's when I realised: Oh God this was a big mistake. I was so far out of my depth the water was up to my nostrils.

Making matters worse, I could already hear the slight slur in my voice. Obviously the others had far more practice than I, and could probably drink and talk me under the table all at the same time.

'Plato finds Socrates in a walled garden in the shadow of the Parthenon,' I said. 'He's just left the agora. It's a late afternoon in summer.'

'Who are the other characters?' boomed Pangalos, affably. 'I don't see them! I don't hear them!'

'Timaeus, the Pythagorean philosopher. Hermocrates, the soldier and statesman. And Critias, of course, after whom the dialogue is named. In his youth, a devoted follower of Socrates —'

'Wait, I've heard of this Critias fellow before...'

'Every Greek child should have,' said the Schoolmaster in mild rebuke.

'Not the best of disciples,' remarked the Doctor mordantly. 'Critias went on to become the most hated and bloodthirsty of the Thirty Tyrants ruling Athens, his reign of terror destroying the very foundations of democracy laid by Solon — poet, visionary, one of the Seven Sages of the Land. The man who freed the poor from the shackles of the rich, who rescued them from being sold into slavery abroad when they could no longer pay their debts. Who confronted the oligarchs with those immortal words: *Equality does not create sedition.*'

'Solon was there too,' I said. 'In spirit at least.'

'Let the boy speak,' growled Pangalos. 'At this rate we shall never even leave port!'

'Socrates is asking the others what might constitute the perfect society, the ideal republic. And Critias recalls that, many years earlier,

Solon had returned from a journey to Egypt with a strange and wonderful tale, all about an idyllic island in the far west.'

'Where in Egypt?' garbled Hadrian, his tongue burning from one of Myroula's red hot pepper concoctions. 'The Pyramids? The Sphinx? Alexandria?'

'Solon was visiting a temple in Sais on the Nile Delta, where a venerable Egyptian priest related the legend to him. According to the priest —'

'You mean according to Plato, according to Critias, according to Solon, according to the priest —'

'Let him speak!' cried Pangalos.

'According to the priest, the record of Atlantis' existence was still preserved in the temple archives. He spoke of its high mountains, lakes and rivers, its bountiful fields and meadows, its trees of exquisite height and beauty, its sacred groves and temples. The Atlanteans were a people of grace, wisdom and honour. Their great works of art, science and engineering startled the eye of any who beheld them, from their gorge-spanning aqueducts and bridges, to the concentric rings of canals running through the island like ripples through a pond. But the glory days were not to last, the priest tells Solon. The island became wicked and impious, obsessed by war and wealth.'

I brought them back to the present, that walled leafy garden in ancient Athens, five friends drinking wine with the ghost of Solon.

'Critias tells them: "for many generations, as long as the divine nature lasted within them, they were obedient to the laws, and well-affectioned towards the god, whose seed they were; for they possessed true and in every way great spirits, uniting gentleness with wisdom... They despised everything but virtue, thinking lightly of the possession of gold and other property, which seemed only a burden to them... But when the divine portion began to fade away, and became diluted too often and too much with the mortal admixture, and the human nature got the upper hand, they then, being unable to bear their fortune, behaved unseemly, and to him who had an eye to see grew visibly debased, for they were losing the fairest of their precious gifts; but to those who had no eye to see the true happiness, they appeared glorious and blessed at the very time when they were full of avarice and unrighteous power."'

Silence. The moment of truth.

'Angered beyond endurance, a wrathful Zeus summons the gods of Olympus to hear his judgement.'

'And then?' rasped Pangalos. 'What then? I'll bet you he wiped it off the face of the Earth.'

'The dialogue breaks off in the middle of a sentence...'

'What? Why? How is that possible?'

'Nobody knows. Maybe the ending was lost. Maybe it was never finished. It is only through Timaeus that we learn of Atlantis' fate. Torn apart, sinking beneath the waves, the island meeting its doom in an earth-shaking apocalypse of fire and flood.'

Silence for a good ten seconds. No one was giving anything away, unless silence alone could be incriminating.

But then Huxley raised himself up, took another deep draught of dusky red wine and said: 'So that is the question. The great baffling imponderable question. Mr Pedrosa here has had his head buried in the reference books all morning just to get to the bottom of it for us. And yes, credit where credit's due, entirely undaunted by the fact that argument has raged over Plato's motives ever since Plato committed stylus to wax in the fourth century BC, and the so-called Lost Isle insinuated its way into the popular imagination like a virus...'

Before I knew it, we were facing the full force of the waves, dark and trenchant. 'Atlantis: the island that has seduced, perplexed and obsessed human minds for more than two millennia. That has spawned more theories than fleas on a slum cat or bloated ticks on a pye-dog...'

The wine's gone to his head, I thought. He's trying too hard to cover his tracks. Sam grins that devious grin of his. There's a puzzled look crossing Anna's face; an indulgent glance from Stavros Sanassis. Even Hadrian's eyes have widened at Huxley's odd vehemence.

Why don't you just fucking admit it, I was thinking. That's your secret. Who knows, maybe it's even why Benja went flying off the scaffolding.

'But what, exactly, is Atlantis,' demanded Huxley. 'Does anyone even know? History or fable? Myth or legend?'

'But there is so much detail provided,' objected Anna. 'The architecture and customs. The landscape. The political system.'

When someone expressed their scepticism about Huxley's own motives, he replied, 'Then let me ask each of you in turn to render your own judgement. *What is Atlantis?*'

'We should be asking where it is, not what it is,' insisted Nondas the barber.

'True,' said the postmaster. 'Plato was an honourable man, a good man. Would a man in search of the eternal truth deliberately foist a blatant lie upon humanity? I think not.'

Panaglos nodded. 'It was real, mark my words. A lost history of a noble people...'

With a provocative glint in his eye, Hadrian said: 'I would submit that all this has less to do with human gullibility than Plato's own. The cast of characters is clearly a literary contrivance. In all likelihood he overheard that fishy tale from some itinerant in the agora; you know as well as I the streets were teeming with travellers; would-be philosophers, demagogues, priests, medicine men, mariners, all as garrulous as a fishwife. Between the pretty boys in the Gymnasium, the political intrigue among the elite; the chattering classes, and the callings of the universe, how was poor Plato supposed to keep track?'

'Archetypal Greek tragedy,' said Anna. 'How can one escape it? This distant island utopia, blessed by the gods, whose hubris ultimately brings about its own apocalyptic destruction.'

'*Fate! Hubris!*' growled Huxley, the distaste turning to acid on his tongue. 'It appears that in his dotage Plato became hopelessly lost to his own moralising.'

Still fussing over which of Myroula's delicacies would meet his taste buds next, Hadrian cast him an incredulous glance. 'I thought you lived and breathed for Plato, Huxley.'

'After the scintillating logic of his earlier dialogues, what can be more disenchanting than to witness the decline of a brilliant mind into wretched superstition. Apparently Plato forgot that enlightenment requires knowledge and knowledge cannot be found prostrating oneself to anything, much less to fate or to God. It is a moralising fallacy, a weakness, an impediment to knowledge. Enlightenment is found because we seek it, we demand it and for no other reason. As for Atlantis' myth or reality, lie or legend, it is doubtful we shall ever know, such is the morass of human credulity in which it wallows...'

'What about you?' I said bluntly. 'You've barely said a word all evening.' Sam. He had been trying to outstare me for the past five minutes, with that look that's as ambiguous as everything else about him. If he's drunk enough, he might even blurt it out again, and to hell with the consequences. It was just inconceivable that no one even remarked upon the parallels between Thera and Atlantis, not even the Doctor or the Schoolmaster.

'What if it's none of these things,' he began hesitantly, the wine accentuating the Parisian in his voice for once. 'What if it is neither fact nor fiction, truth nor lie... but a riddle nobody has understood.'

'A riddle?'

'A conundrum...'

'What kind of conundrum?'

He shrugged. 'One contained within the dialogue, unwritten, unspoken, but there just the same: *What is Atlantis?*'

Suddenly they were hanging on his every word and Huxley's face had darkened to a bruise black storm. As for Sam, there it was again, that same look of thirsty revenge.

'In the boulevard Saint-Michel there's an antiquarian bookshop called *Le petit Phoenix.* I was twenty-one, back from Cambridge, a postgrad at the Sorbonne.'

'That's enough, Sam!' said Huxley dangerously. 'We don't need to know.'

'Why not?' said the Doctor breezily. 'Let Sam have his say. Those are rules, Marcus, like it or not. Every soul will have their say.'

'It was a bright day in October, but suddenly it began pissing rain, so I dived into the shop until the worst was over. I was browsing the shelves, just to pass the time, when the pretty girl behind the desk said I'd be sure to be interested in this, it had just come in that morning. She slid it across the counter with a smile in her eye. Charcoal cover, gold-embossed lettering, published by some obscure academic press in Leiden. *Travels in Elysium*, read the title. It must have been thirty, forty years old, nothing exceptional by antiquarian standards. I turned to the first page and it struck me almost from the start, the style I mean. It had a strange, almost lyrical quality to it, and yet... within that passion, within that naivety, something dark, something...' He shook his head, struggling for words, '...Maybe corrupt or contaminated...'

'Who was the author?' enquired the Schoolmaster. 'Do we know him? Have we heard of him?'

'There was no author...'

'No author?'

'Anonymous,' said the postmaster sagely. 'To protect the author's own name or another's — that can be the only explanation.'

'Whoever it was,' said Sam, seemingly oblivious to Huxley's murderous looks, 'at least half the book must have been devoted to just that: *what is Atlantis?* The same doubts, the same impossible questions that have tormented minds since Plato's day, no matter if they believe in Atlantis or not. Atlantis is history, mummified in Egyptian legend. No, it's an allegory of ancient Athens, torn between freedom and tyranny. It's fable, parable, noble lie, no, it's just a deliberate hoax on human gullibility... But then our mysterious writer, he spots something else, something in all the people Atlantis has ever touched, whose lives it has entered, whose minds or emotions it has shaped. Doesn't matter who. Archaeologists, philosophers. Treasure hunters, tomb robbers. Swindlers, thieves. Driven men hunting a prize as tantalising as the Holy Grail or the True Cross: the discovery of Lost Atlantis...'

He paused to take a shot of wine, playing the audience, knowing he had us in the palm of his hand. *'Not that the great event hasn't already been proclaimed with bewildering regularity,* sneers our anonymous author. Ruined underwater cities, or at least, intriguing rock formations smothered in seaweed, have made their splash from the Canary Islands to Polynesia, from Ceylon to the Bahamas — discoveries usually less compelling for the proof they offer, than for their ever promising ambiguity.'

'So what is he saying?' slurred Pangalos. 'What's he on about?'

'He's saying there's something far deeper to its construction,' said Dr Sanassis. 'Something metaphysical. Perhaps the reflection of a universal law or something.'

'Do you want to know what he said? I still know it off by heart, so striking was the impression it made on me on that rainy day in Saint-Michel.' He could barely restrain hurling a glance at Huxley, now doing an admirable job of disguising his fury, wrenching apart the unshelled prawns on his plate.

'Of course,' growled Pangalos, 'spit it out!'

And with that Sam began reciting the passage like a poem, his eyes growing so distant you might even have imagined the falling rain reflected in them, the autumn leaves, the wet cobblestones.

'For an island paradise, a vision of utopia, Atlantis has attracted more than its fair share of madness and obsession, hasn't it.

It has known hubris and enslavement, cruelty and even murder with stark brutal intimacy.

What tragic irony! That through its eternal fame and infamy, Plato's golden legend has become riddled with the same kind of sleaze and corruption, the same kind of gullibility and saw-toothed ambition, the same kind of ruthless exploitation of the innocent that so infamously brought about the island's destruction in the first place!

...But wait... Wait a minute... What better way to demonstrate the Platonic theory that ideas do have lives of their own? What better way to demonstrate how the light of the perfect idea dilutes, dissipates, the further we are away from it?

Is that what our metaphysical genius has been up to all along?'

15.

The days went by in a blur and the next thing I knew, the island was drifting into spring. Showers swept in from the sea, drenching the dark earth, turning paths into spontaneous streams and torrents, ancient steps into cascades.

As the sun returned, the transformation was just miraculous, that's all. On the Lucifer-red volcanic slopes, previously as dead as the Martian plains, lush green grass materialised. Elsewhere, the grey dust all but disappeared under blazing fields of wildflowers, in every colour and shade imaginable.

I was supposed to be learning camera techniques with Nestor, then stratigraphy with Hadrian, but as the others struggled into their overalls Huxley threw me a glance and said: 'Mr Pedrosa, you are with me.'

We threaded our way through camp, along the fringes of the eastern sector.

The Professor whose students had nicknamed her Galatea-the-Ghost because of her ash-powdered hair and eyebrows, raised herself up on her elbows, called out. 'Marcus, wait!' Her two favourites bobbed up beside her, wearing brighter variations of the same frustration, Christos and Helia.

Evidently there were rumblings of discontent throughout the sector. Lack of progress. Nothing to find. So far, just an empty storeroom, and these burnt-out shells of houses; an amphora that had probably been broken even before the eruption. That the other zones in the east had fared little better in unearthing a dream fresco, a piece of jewellery or a mummified body had only served to spike the rivalry between them, as friendly as that was face to face, and as snide when backs were turned.

Huxley ground his teeth, cast a jaundiced look over the bleak grey ruin of the storeroom.

'Keep trying, expand further east,' he said at last. 'Remember, it was two years before we hit the first houses on temple hill, and even that was mere fluke, a fragment of Minoan pottery scooped out while they were quarrying tephra up there. Keep that in mind whenever you get demoralised, Galatea.' I had never heard him give pep talks before, and it struck me how out of character it was for him, the man whose habit it was to demand rather than request, push rather than coax.

House 16 loomed up before us but he pressed on without so much as a murmur or a glance at the scaffolding. Why? Had Benja failed him in some way, was that it, just as Sam had before him? It made you wonder about the nature of their relationship, what it was, how far it went. More than mentor to apprentice, that's for sure. Whenever Benja's name entered the conversation, Huxley's face assumed that same stony mien, as inhospitable as the mountain up there. Hardly the look of someone who had lost a friend, was it.

We walked on, past the deserted shop fronts, then on to the first houses climbing the hill.

Between them, the rains had turned the plots of wasteland into flower-dappled grassland and there the sea breeze played, lending a peculiar animation to a city that was supposed to be stone dead. Wild-flowers lifted their vivid heads even between the geometric stonework, seemingly growing out of bare rock. Butterflies flitted about the water fountain, still brimful from the rains.

We resumed our climb towards the temple, its mathematical columns silhouetted across the sky.

Broad marble steps ran beneath them east to west; according to Huxley's confident deduction, in veneration of dawn and sunset. As night fell, the minutely aligned columns would follow the emerging constellations.

He passed under their shadows to the western steps, then crouching, carelessly swept away a film of fine dust to reveal the find beneath that had so recently claimed the headlines. Obsidian hieroglyphs inlaid into the rippling stonework, along with other geometric symbols, spheres, ellipses, spirals…

'Who knows,' he murmured, 'perhaps one day we shall finally decipher this language, and these few hieroglyphs will explain everything.'

Fifty yards on we entered a great square, bound by three-storey houses with sky terraces, half of them still wallowing in ash. On the western edge, still in the perpendicular stripes of shadow and light thrown by the temple columns, stood another partially exhumed house, a mineshaft-like tunnel burrowing into it through the lava crust. The number '34' had been chalked onto its rough plank wood door.

The building was long and narrow, and different from the others, even at a glance. I asked him what it was. He grunted. 'There are no frescoes, just a series of stone arches running through a single hall. Given its proximity to the temple it might have had some kind of religious function, but there's nothing inside that would prove it one way or the other.'

I was still trying hard to visualise what it must have looked like in its heyday, the way the temple heights and its sacred grove broadened into this great square with a criss-crossing of streets, and beautiful geometric stonework underfoot.

'The agora,' Huxley declared. 'The marketplace. We have found the remains of foodstuffs in sealed containers — olive oil, grain, salted fish, wine — but not a single coin.'

To my blank look he added: 'Do you know what that means — for a civilisation as advanced as this to have no concept of money?'

He was testing me, I was sure of it, but how far did I have to go to prove my loyalty. Had Benja proven his?

Probably mistaking my pensiveness for daydreaming, he said with a glare: 'Don't you realise what's going on here? We have been digging for five years and have yet to unearth a single arrow, spear or catapult stone, a single fortification... Do you not understand the significance of that?'

Now I was sure of it. I *was* supposed to be following the tenuous clues scattered for me. I remembered the passage by heart: *They possessed true and in every way great spirits, uniting gentleness with wisdom...*

If this was his great big secret, I wanted to be trusted enough to hear it, even if I was the new boy on the block, even if he did have enemies in camp.

Still finding my way among the unfamiliar landmarks, the shells of buildings, the interweaving streets, I was mildly surprised to find us passing Nestor's graveyard of broken machinery below house 34. Even if all this was still a work in progress, what with the tangled loops of barbed wire and rusting hulks, it still seemed a crude blot on the landscape.

'What *is* in there?' I asked, peering down from the temple heights, the burrowing machines whirring in the distance. Nestor and his moles had been cutting exploratory shafts into the tephra in there for the better part of a fortnight.

'Nothing!' he snapped, annoyed at the distraction, and quickening his pace. 'As you can see with your own two eyes, it's just a scrapyard. Do you think I have time to excavate every square inch of this broken volcano?'

Preoccupied as ever with his reconstruction of events, he again crossed the square, apparently intent on surveying the excavations from every conceivable angle. True to forensic method, he was interrogating thin air, seeking the invisible, willing the evidence to emerge from its camouflage.

'And so this is where we find ourselves,' he said at last, the frustration grinding the words between his teeth, his eyes sweeping over the tall deserted houses. 'On a ghost ship of an island. *Where are the bodies?* Failing that, where is the evidence that the people abandoned the island en masse?'

'You said the eruption was five times the magnitude of Krakatoa —'

'So the vulcanologists tell us.'

'But then if it shook the ancient world to its core like that, shouldn't there have been some kind of record of it, I don't know, in Minoan Crete, in Egypt...'

Screwing up his eyes, he replied, 'True enough. An event of that magnitude should have inspired a rich vein of apocalyptic myth and folklore... And perhaps it did. Deucalion's Flood, for one... Given the tidal waves, even the predicted impact on the climate, the torrential rains and floods, it can't be ruled out.'

The door was open, and I leapt through it. 'Or Atlantis.'

The thunderclap boomed back at me. 'Atlantis is a morality tale, nothing more! Who's been feeding you this garbage — Sam I suppose?'

Something beyond the menace in his voice made me stand my ground. 'But the parallels,' I said. 'You must see them —'

'What parallels?' he barked, a little too unconvincingly. 'Atlantis lay beyond the Pillars of Hercules.'

'But the legend may have become corrupted over time. You said so yourself. Today's realities become tomorrow's histories, then their legends, then their myths. It would be another 1000 years until Plato wrote the Critias. What if the eruption wiped out virtually any trace of Atlantis' existence, including its original name? Even Sais itself no longer exists, does it? So why couldn't this be Atlantis?'

I braced myself for the blast.

Instead he levelled a curious stare at me, taking several shallow breaths, probably deciding how much to admit or deny. 'Atlantis,' he murmured at last, with a wince of a smile. 'Is that what you would have me say?'

We came to a stone bridge, arching over a deep cleft in the ash crust. I peered over, but it just disappeared into the blackness, seemingly bottomless. 'A fissure...'

'An ancient watercourse. Rivers, streams, torrents. We know they existed because they are depicted in the frescoes. We have geologists looking for larger riverbeds, rivers that might have carried boats, people, produce.'

He silenced me with an abrupt gesture. I was to listen now, not speak, see, not look, abandon myself to the moment, not think. 'Water. One word that should transform everything you see.' His voice seemed to resonate between the houses, the swaying grassland and the wildflowers catching the wind.

'Do you begin to visualise the island now? Do you see how it stretches out into the distance, ten times greater than it is today? Do you see the great volcano capped with snow? Do you see the streams and rivers, the forests and gardens, the farming villages scattered over the green hills? Do you see the city laid out before you, with its fine harbour and its ships setting sail?'

He had no trouble doing so, I felt sure. It was probably second nature to him by now, these spells of hypnotic abstraction that shallow fools must have attributed to absentmindedness.

He could probably form a mental picture of its busy streets, even the sophisticated pursuits of its inhabitants. See its engineers and artisans at work, farmers in the fields, winnowing wheat, young women on the hillsides gathering saffron. A donkey trudging over a stone threshing circle overlooking the sea, the chaff golden in the wind. Fishers exchanging a shout as they cast off from the harbour. The marketplace, teeming with colour. An academy in the grove, its teachers trying to get young minds to focus on science, philosophy, engineering, not the blue summer's day outside. All I saw was a ruined city, however well embalmed by the ash, and beyond, the forbidding face of a shattered mountain.

But then as he spoke those mellifluous words, something strange began to happen, I don't know, almost as if they had the capacity to colour in the bleak ruined shells around us. Bringing a wash of blue and ochre to their baked stone walls, bringing the scent of splashing water and blossom to the air.

I caught myself wondering if that was his voice, going to my head. If that really was the colour of the sky up there, delirious blue.

And the light. I had seen it glow before but never quite like this.

Seconds later I felt the force of it on my skin, like an invisible wave pulsing through air. The sky seemed to quiver, and I had the strangest sensation of being separated from my own body. I heard a tuning fork whine on my eardrums; then the murmur of distant voices, chanting, melodious. The rush of a river, tumbling down the mountain. The fluttering of leaves.

It's just the wind playing tricks, comes a cautionary thought, the way it does sometimes.

But then it just sweeps over me, I don't know what. A kind of tranquillity. A kind of timelessness. I experience the strange, almost irresistible impulse to laugh — as if the universe, too small, too narrow to breathe in before has in some sheer instant made of light just grown a thousandfold.

The vision, if that's what it was, burst as abruptly as a child's soap bubble. As it did so, I was left with the strangest impression that I really had just seen a tree-shaded avenue dipping down towards the sea. Silver thread rivers. Lakes. The snaking contours of a mountain range, silhouetted against the sun.

In the haze in which the moment had abandoned me, I experienced a moment of panic, like a poor swimmer who realises he's drifted far out of his depth.

When I came to a moment later, I needed the stone wall at my back just to steady myself.

I found Huxley's eyes swimming into mine. Green prism irises like the flecks and fragments of a child's kaleidoscope.

'What's wrong with you?' he demanded, taking me roughly by the shoulder. 'Have you eaten anything today? Have you drunk enough?'

I shook my head.

He peered at me curiously, and seemed on the verge of demanding details of what I thought I had seen. If so, he quickly thought better of it, and said brusquely, 'The sun is stronger than ever, can't you feel it?'

Nearby, a silver rain torrent was splashing over the ancient stones, and we lingered by it, perhaps all too conscious of its ephemerality.

That's when he said, almost absently: 'Could it ever be done, do you think? Could an island like this ever be recreated in the present? Do we have the mind for it, the soul for it?'

Coming so soon after my hallucination, the words caught me off guard. I stuttered over their meaning, seeing a great open air museum, restored streets and houses, a stone amphitheatre, trees replanted on the hill, the river splashing between them, and I don't know what else.

In the wake of that out-of-body experience, whatever it was made of, anything seemed possible.

It was just that the sentiment didn't fit.

No one in their right minds would have called Marcus James Huxley an idealist or a romantic, whatever madly quixotic ideas his Greek friends brought to the dinner table. He was far too cynical, far too hard-nosed for that, wasn't he, the kind of man for whom everything was either an obstacle or an opportunity.

16.

What are you hiding? What is it that you don't want me to know?

I was standing over his shoulder, his hands in the bright illumination of the lights above, his face in partial eclipse.

He was snatching up orphaned fragments, placing them in relational patterns across the tabletop. I asked if he could begin to see the picture that impossible jigsaw was hiding from him.

He grunted disconsolately. 'The fragments always seem to be on the verge of forming a different picture. One struggling to emerge, like the ancient face you see in a twisted olive tree, a wood grain, a drifting cloud.'

He rose from his chair with a grunt of frustration, then crossed over to the door.

'We won't get any more work out of them today,' he muttered, glaring at the labourers outside the mess tent, leaning on their shovels, smoking, drinking frosted beer.

He sighed irritably. 'I suggest we pack up and go home, start afresh tomorrow.' The men, he knew, would be keen enough to draw double time on a Sunday morning after church, notwithstanding the messianic wrath of the Papás.

We were almost out of the gates when our plans abruptly changed, and about as inexplicably as they always do in Greece.

'We're crossing the whole island, just to see the sunset? But we can see it from here. At least, we can see it going down over Thirassia.'

'Never underestimate the power of sunset, Mr Pedrosa. The sight of Helios plunging into the open sea. Thus, after all, begins his nocturnal journey along the River Ocean, passing Hades as he goes.'

Times like this, you could never tell whether he was showing off his erudition or his searing irony.

And so we piled into our cars, Anna, Huxley, Sam, Hadrian and I, and drove out to Oia, that shabby little village on the other end of the crater rim. Ten years earlier, an earthquake had struck without mercy, wrenching the houses from their foundations and tossing them into the sea, along with their sleeping families. Oia had become a ghost town overnight.

Given her day job I found it strange that Anna lived out here at all, and even stranger as we began threading our way along the overgrown footpaths to her front door. Abandoned shells of houses that must have taken the brunt of the shockwave, making the cliff face look as if it were riddled with caves. Solitary gateways opening onto nothing but the fall to the sea. Stairways ending brokenly in a sheer drop. Crumbling facades with nothing beyond them but thin air, the house number still painted hopefully over the door. A freshly whitewashed church with a caved-in dome. A village shop between houses reduced to rubble. The occasional inhabitant doing vanishing tricks among the crumbling walls.

Finally, there it was, the place she called home, a barrel-vaulted house, burrowing back into the lava red rock face. Leading up to its front door, a long terrace clinging to the precipice, and inevitably, another thousand foot drop to the sea. Within shouting distance, the jagged island of Thirassia, once part of the same crater rim.

We dragged chairs out into the sun, Sam taking the table, lifting it over his head, placing it next to the retaining wall so he could sit there, one foot dangling over the edge.

It was mid-afternoon and, apart from the muted voices from the kitchen or the sea breeze that occasionally sounded a tentative note through the wires, utterly quiet. Time seemed to hesitate, as if catching the faint echo of its own voice.

My boss was staring out across the silver sea, the sea and Thirassia beyond reflected back into his sunglasses.

For an hour or more, no one said a word about the dig or about the troubles it faced, bureaucratic, archaeological or otherwise.

Then suddenly Benja's name appeared over the table, like a ghost walking through the walls of the words.

'You should have known him, Nico,' Anna was saying wistfully. I felt my stomach tighten. 'He had the courage of a warrior, the pure heart of a child.'

Sam blew a disparaging cloud of smoke into the air.

'He loved the island and loved the people and loved everything about the dig,' she went on. 'You should have seen him, standing there covered in ash, the first Minoan house finally free of the tephra. His eyes were on fire, even if he could have slept for a week. I still can't believe it. I can't believe he's gone.'

'Such is the nature of death,' said Huxley, with the sensitivity I had come to expect of him. 'It is the one subject that forever defies our pursuit of knowledge. Ten thousand years of civilisation and of the one event that will inevitably confront each and every one of us without exception, what have we got to show for it? Nothing. We have myths, folklore, superstition, but knowledge? No, not one scintilla. As to what death is or what it might mean, we know nothing at all.'

'That,' said Hadrian trenchantly, 'is because there is nothing to know. It is the most accurate reflection of what awaits us: nothing.'

He stood over the table, drizzling olive oil onto the salad with the flourish of a chef. Somehow, I had lost my appetite.

'Are we to assume you share the same opinion?' demanded Huxley, a penetrating glance striking me right between the eyes.

Anna said crossly: 'Don't Marcus. Not with Benja barely cold in his grave.'

'We are waist-deep in death every day, Anna. Every fragment we tweeze out of the earth, every building we exhume from the dust.'

'There are just some things that make no sense to talk about, that's all.'

'Well, there you have it,' said Huxley cuttingly. 'Our ten thousand-year ignorance in a nutshell. As to the meaning of death, do not ponder. As to what awaits us when we die, do not ask.'

'Life after death Marcus?' she said wearily, twisting the napkin anxiously between her fingers.

'Perhaps you are forgetting the people who have been to death and back,' replied Huxley, his voice even, his mood unreadable, as my eyes darted towards him. 'Men, women, children, who were pronounced clinically dead, and yet somehow lived to tell the tale. And what a tale… A white light in the far distance, apparently irresistible. They float towards it. At first, it is like a single distant star, then a sun, then a luminous nebula that seems to know them inside out.'

'A trick of the dying brain, Huxley, no more.'

'You may well be right, Hadrian, but regrettably you have no more evidence to prove it than has the Papás for his faith in heaven and hell.'

Hadrian squirmed in his seat, as he always did when Huxley harnessed science and drove it recklessly into the unknown. 'As futile as a fish trying to escape the sea,' he opined and left it at that.

Despite the dark impenetrable glasses, I became aware of Huxley's look moving from one face to the other, lingering over each of us. Almost as if he were testing us, or assessing our reactions, *but why?*

For a second, as his invisible gaze fell on me, I had to wonder if the whole conversation was being staged, and if so, for whose benefit. Welling-up behind came a nauseous feeling right from the gut: that even if I didn't know one word of the script, I was still a part of the cast and not the audience.

'Then where is he now?' said Anna. 'Our dear Benja.'

Hadrian clicked his tongue. 'Six feet under, Anna, where do you think? Or knowing Mad Yanni the gravedigger, three feet under.'

'Perhaps Marcus is right,' she objected. 'Perhaps we should have an open mind.'

'An open mind, yes, Anna, but as my dear father always used to say, not so open that anyone can use it as a rubbish tip.'

'What do you think, Sam?' It was an effort for Huxley to ask, I could tell.

Sam blew another disparaging smoke ring. 'I wonder why you all think the metaphysical must conform to physical laws, that's what I think.'

'Yes,' muttered Hadrian, 'spoken by someone who's truly metaphysical any hour of the day or night.'

Irritably, he fanned away the pungent smoke wafting towards him.

I wondered why Huxley didn't say anything. It was one thing for Sam to smoke his weed in secret, quite another to do it out in the open like that in front of everyone. If the police busted him, there'd be hell to pay. Sam would be dragged off the island in chains, probably rot in jail. Even Huxley himself could be implicated; he was the boss after all.

Sam raised himself up with a scowl and said with a reckless edge: 'All right then, if you want to know. If golden boy's still on his travels, he will have crossed the Styx and Acheron by now. Charon must have been well pleased with your generosity Huxley, a silver drachma where the traditional obol might have done just as well...'

Behind those black glasses, Huxley was... *what?* encouraging him, glaring at him, regretting it wasn't Sam who was dead.

'Then when he passes through Hades, if the Orphic tradition holds true, he must take care, he must remember: whatever you do, don't drink from the Lethe, the river of Forgetfulness. He has to say to the guards: "I am the son of Earth and Starry Heaven. I am thirsty, please give me something to drink from the Mnemosyne, the river of Memory."'

Silence, just the song of the aeolian wind, the dove from the ruin of the church. Our eyes were drawn to the molten silver sea, turning gold, then bronze, the ancient crater rim and the Burnt Islands cast into deep silhouette.

'Look,' said Huxley, in that treacle-deep resonance his voice could sometimes assume. 'Can you see what is happening?'

I squinted, trying to understand.

Blood orange, the sun's about to plunge into the sea.

'There,' he says, that mellifluous voice still drawing me in. 'Levitating over the horizon.'

No reason to resist, not like this, when I am walking on air, my eyes drinking in the sunset, a sketch of clouds as dark as charcoal.

'Do you see it? Do you see it now?'

As if my fuzzy eyesight has just snapped into focus, there it is, unmistakeable.

A luminous sea, painted onto the sky, and upon that sea, a scattering of islands. Curving bays, inlets striking deep inland. Silver rivers tumbling down undulating, silhouette mountains. Wind-pattern lakes nestled among the forested hills.

An optical illusion, a trick of the light... it has to be. Screwing up my eyes, I try to blink it away. Clouds kneaded into any form the imagination allows. You expect them to change shape or fall apart, the wind and the sun making short work of them.

But not today. Though the clouds flowed, it was with a liquid motion almost undetectable, so that, rather than the picture being destroyed, it was as if we were continually seeing the same archipelago from a different vantage point.

And there the illusion remained, apparently immune to logic or common sense.

I wondered what it was that was making my head swim — the wine, the wafts of resinous smoke, the sheer drop, the molten sea, Huxley's voice, something in the food.

'Anna?'

'Yes, I see it now,' she replied in a rapt whisper.

'The Isles beyond Sunset,' added Sam, his sullenness abandoning him for once.

I glanced sharply at Huxley, certain now that I had boarded his metaphysical ship again, but this time without even realising it; the tiller firmly in his hands; the wind pulling taut the sails.

I shifted uneasily in my chair as it occurred to me that the illusion might have been his doing as well. Not that he had conjured islands out of cloud, of course not, but that he had somehow shaped them out of our own thoughts.

'I see clouds and charred rock, light bouncing off water, that's what I see,' mocked Hadrian, playing the role expected of him to perfection.

It was enough to break the spell. When I blinked and looked again, there was nothing, just ragged tufts of cloud.

Huxley: 'You lack the poetry of the soul, Hadrian. For as Benja came to realise, it's only in that lyrical streaming that one can truly find the Isles, wherever they are — mythical, legendary, real, home to the living or the dead.'

Hadrian, disapprovingly: 'Philosophy is one thing, Huxley. Obsession quite another.'

Anna: 'And it was your obsession, Marcus. Long before it became Benja's —'

Huxley: 'Islands have obsessed us since the dawn of time, all the more so those capable of seducing the heart, hypnotising the mind, captivating the soul. By their very existence, they demand intensity. Benja knew that. Sam knows. You would know it too, Hadrian, if you spent more time taking in the view than the mezedakia.'

Anna, sighing: 'I hope he's seen the Isles, I hope he's walking on them now whatever anybody says, past the waterfalls, between the lakes...'

'Isles of the Blest!' Hadrian scoffed. 'I ask you, how much more gullible can people get, creating islands out of cloud?'

'Is that what they are created out of, Hadrian?' Huxley rebuked him. 'Plato, I venture, would have said that they are merely reflected in the sunset, since as a universal law thought must always precede matter.'

'The transcendent realm,' chimed Anna. 'A place beyond time or space, where every object in the universe exists in a pure, perfect form.'

Hadrian grunted disdainfully. 'Yes, Plato, the great philosopher, the one who even swallowed that fishy tale about Atlantis, hook, line and sinker!'

'A momentary lapse,' muttered Huxley with clenched jaw, as if even to speak the island's name out loud was as excruciating as a fingernail to a blackboard.

'Was it? Or was the Great Thinker a fraud, Huxley, even fooling himself into the bargain? Can't you see, in the intricate constructs of his philosophy, what it is he's using to weld together his ideas? Wishful thinking. Nothing deeper than that. The stupidity and brutality of the world offends him and so he creates another in his own mind — the folly of every idealist known to our species. As for the so-called transcendent realm, it was a crutch so that poor Plato's ideals, otherwise crippled by human nature, could at least hobble around in public.'

Human nature. Divine nature. It was the heart and soul, blood and spirit of the Atlantis legend, I knew that, but what kind of convoluted game was it playing here?

I glanced at Sam, held my breath, wondering if he would dare breathe the word 'Conundrum' again in Huxley's presence.

I sank lower into my chair, trying to keep my troubled thoughts to myself, if only because I could imagine them being used against me somehow.

I had to think. Face facts.

The trouble was, I had precious few to go on that were not open to doubt or interpretation; I could almost count them off on the fingers of one hand. The job in which I now found myself, advertised before my predecessor's death. My belongings, ransacked on my first day. Huxley's apparent recklessness in digging down through the tephra. His incandescent ego, that appeared to demand homage from anyone in sight. And the power he appeared to wield over people — psychic, hypnotic, I didn't know what to call it.

And in terms of objective fact, that was all I had to go on.

The night deepened, my companions becoming silhouettes against a sky so dense with stars it seemed possible to reach out and thrust our hands between them.

And then it struck me. Something that nearly got away disguised as coincidence. The only tangible link between events that appeared to exist.

Plato's legend of Atlantis, breaking off in the middle of a sentence… Just like the lives of those doomed people in the ancient city as the volcano exploded. Just like Benja, as he went flying off the scaffolding. Lives, legends, strands of time, breaking-off in the middle of a sentence. What the fuck was going on?

17.

The telegram, dictated in that abrupt, staccato style that normally announces a mortal illness or a death, left Huxley in no doubt. He was under investigation. Not for murder. Not for manslaughter. Not even for looting antiquities. In fact, there was *no* formal accusation against him as such, just the suspicion, hanging there in the smudgy air between the lines. Certain irregularities reported at the dig. His methods and results would be audited.

To that end, the state Archaeological Service was despatching its Inspector General to the island, one Sophoklis Sarrides. He would be accompanied by the eminent archaeologist Claude Guirand, a Minoan expert. Huxley was expected to grant them unfettered access to the site, including all finds and inventories. Signed, Sotirios Kenteris, Director of the Archaeological Service.

I saw his brows knitting as he read, his eyes leaping from word to word, trying to make sense out of them. I saw the thunder appear. He crushed the telegram in his fist and tossed it into the dirt. Hadrian scrambled after it, squealing in protest.

Fit to explode, Huxley was already marching towards his Land Rover, kicking pumice as he went. Hadrian waddled after him, pelting him with questions, each more agitated than the last.

'We are shipshape, Huxley... aren't we?' I knew what he was thinking; I could see it in the small beleaguered eyes. What would they say about the Roman and Byzantine remains? What would they say about the conveyor belts, the bulldozers?

'Sotirios Kenteris!' spat Huxley. 'The man knows nothing about archaeology, Hadrian. He's a political appointee. He probably doesn't even know what he put his name to!'

'But that is even worse! At least if everything were above board at the Service we might enter an inspection with some degree of confidence. But like this...!'

All hell then broke loose in camp, Huxley demanding inventories, demanding paperwork checks, ordering the Roman ceramic dump be given a shallow grave.

Sunday morning, two days later, and I was on lookout duty, posted at the top of the serpentines in Phíra to await the arrival of the mule train.

Laying a white steam cloud across the sky, the *Pegasus* had already entered the caldera an hour ago; I had seen the rowers making for her, then the caïques.

By now, I was sweating, and it wasn't the dazzling early sun that was to blame: Huxley was late. I cast anxious glances up and down the street, but there was still no sign of him. Just the village women in procession, bringing their Sunday roasts to the baker's oven, a few drachmae jangling in their apron pockets.

At any moment, the first mules would come clip-clopping up the steps. If I was still alone then, what would I do, what would I say?

'Say good morning,' Huxley had said in that sardonic way of his, 'and then bring them here.'

Thinking about it now, he'd probably never had any intention of turning up to greet them at all. It was all about mind games, all about brinkmanship.

There was no mistaking them when they did arrive, clinging to their dignity and their crude wooden saddles.

Sophoklis Sarrides, disparagingly called 'the Beak' because of his raptor's nose and buzzard eyes. Dressed with authority uppermost in mind, even aboard a sooty ship or among the dirt trenches, in a creased black suit and waistcoat. By the look of it, made to measure by some backstreet Athens tailor who has some trouble with numbers.

The instant Professor Claude Guirand lurched into view behind him, I uttered a silent gasp, the shock paralysing me where I stood. Of course. The rude, insistent Frenchman on the First Class passenger deck, who had been so eager to engage me in conversation. Bleak yellowing eyes, parchment skin stretched over a bony frame, subsiding at the cheeks.

So this was Huxley's nemesis. According to the feverish whispers about camp, all this, the audit demand, the surprise inspection, the shock telegram, could all be laid at his door.

An archaeologist of some repute, if less for his discoveries than his blue-blooded ancestry and his mercurial temper. Recipient of the *Légion d'honneur*. A sitting member of the board of governors of the French Archaeological Institute in Paris, and their schools in Athens and Rome.

Before falling on hard times, the Guirand ancestral home had been one of those magical follies poised over the Loire, all steeples, towers and turrets, surrounded by orchards and terraced vineyards.

So at least the manner in which he had addressed me on deck, master to servant, now made some kind of warped sense.

He was still wearing his favourite outfit, the colonial explorer white suit, the same straw hat, probably traded for a pith helmet south of the equator.

Stiffly, the men dismounted. In expectation of a few drachmae, the muleteers helped them down, offering their shoulders, forming stirrups with their hands.

Bringing up the rear came two youngish subordinates, one apparently in charge of papers, the other, luggage and archaeological paraphernalia. Their faces wore the same dour expression as Sarrides himself, quite as if their employment would have been in doubt without it.

Guirand was dusting himself down with his panama, distancing himself from the frothing nostrils of his mule. Then, in that imperious way of his, he motioned the others towards the *kafeneion* on the corner.

The impish little man with the twitching moustache and bright, darting eyes was already there at the open door, swaying sideways expectantly, the loose change jangling in his pocket.

Leading the way, Guirand swept past him, taking a table at the windows where the world just fell away to the Burnt Islands far below. Flustered, the little man scurried after them, hawking the same things he always did, mountain tea and muddy coffee, ouzo, raki, *gazoza*.

Guirand could look down his nose at almost anyone but there was something especially disdainful in the way he treated the little man in the white waiter's coat. It was not as a nobleman might treat the most menial of servants, but as a nobleman obliged to soil his hands with despicable, but necessary, things.

Of course. The ransacking of my bags and suitcases. One of his informants rummaging through them, maybe his own valet, as the little man cast worried glances up and down the street.

As I peered in through the grimy street window, they took their places, chair legs scraping over tile.

The little man brought tea, and glasses of cistern-cool water. They always did that on the island; it was just one of those unspoken deeds from the ancient past, hospitality to strangers, even if water was scarcer than wine.

After another fruitless half hour waiting for Huxley, I realised there was nothing for it, and took the plunge.

As Guirand's jaundiced eyes found mine I braced myself for the flicker of recognition, the inevitable interrogation. There was none.

We headed towards Akrotiri under a pall of silence, Guirand up front with me, skull-headed cane clutched between his knees, his eyes drawing in the road beyond the Morris' bull nose like black holes sucking in stars, devouring light.

The instant we drew into camp, I dived out of the car, just glad to get away from them. Seeing Huxley lumbering up to us, his face fighting a scowl, I beat a hasty retreat towards the trenches where Hadrian, Anna, Sam and a few hand-picked students were doing a passable job of pretending to work. In-between brush and trowel strokes, they stole wary glances at the new arrivals.

Huxley made a point of greeting Sophoklis Sarrides, and even his underlings, before acknowledging the presence of the old Frenchman with the dead book complexion. But finally they shook hands, wincing as they did so, as if the skin of one were rebelling against the touch of the other.

And thus the inspection began, Guirand, Sarrides and the two clerks crowding into the site office, rifling through official records and inventories. By the time they had finished, poor Maria could hardly be seen for the ring binders, archive boxes and folders stacked up all around her.

It was a deliberately provocative first move, one that might have anticipated Huxley losing his temper from the start, his violent reaction incriminating him even if the evidence didn't.

Hour after hour, day after day, they scoured the site, sifting through crates and boxes in the storage sheds and fragments hut. They checked the trenches and the conveyor belts, looking for evidence of damage. They inspected the work of the students, postgrads and teachers, looking for proof of negligence or ineptitude, even theft or petty pilfering. They spent hours in the ancient city, examining frescoes and hieroglyphic stones.

'What are they looking for?' exclaimed Anna indignantly. 'No one inspects an archaeological site like that. No one!'

Finally refusing to wait it out in impotent torment, Huxley hit town instead, dispatching telegrams at the post office, working the telephones, calling his supporters in God knows where, Paris, London, Athens.

Every day, the same game of cat and mouse. The same provocations. The same thirst for justice or revenge.

Having already convicted Huxley in his own mind, Sarrides had his minions mount a forensic audit of the camp paperwork, line by line, item by item. Twice I saw him grind his teeth and wince in frustration, as if the cataloguing and inventories, the reams of paper, had been purposely contrived to muddle the trail rather than illuminate it.

Perhaps even more than the Beak himself, Claude Guirand brought to the inspection an excruciating attention to detail.

Rain, wind or shine, he would be up there on temple hill with his kit, poking his nose into every nook and cranny. Whenever Huxley came within range, it was almost as if Guirand were deliberately provoking him, less to incite anger, perhaps, than to gauge whether he was veering hot or cold in his search.

Keeping them in my sights, I happened to glance over at Nestor's scrapyard on the southern slope. Somewhere among the rusting metal hulks in there his trusted moles had been cutting deep exploratory shafts into the tephra, but there was no sign of them now, just more heaps of rubble, more unruly coils of wire.

By midweek, the Beak was dosing himself on local firewater until the small hours, and by Sunday, the raptor's desolate cry could be heard echoing through the paper thin walls into the hotel corridor, every cry a cry of frustration or contempt. Huxley and his naive Greek helpers; the bureaucracy in Athens, riddled with corruption, even the island itself, with its twisted landscape, twisted politics and twisted superstitions.

It was lucky Huxley had had the foresight to plant a trusted man in the room next door, equipped only with an old stethoscope, a notepad and pencil. His friend the schoolmaster, Alexander Vouris.

'What is the Englishman doing here at all?' Sarrides was heard to rasp, the lip of the bottle clinking roughly against the rim of his glass. 'Do they imagine it has escaped our attention? The tomb and temple robbing, the looting and smuggling? Crimes organised not by criminal gangs, no, not for the richest spoils, but by foreigners with impeccable reputations, archaeologists, auction houses, metropolitan museums, even embassies and consulates! Ancient shipwrecks on the seabed, their holds spilling treasure to foreign divers. Priceless museum pieces, replaced by fakes at the hands of fake tourists. The loot smuggled out of the country under the noses of our customs officials, corrupt or incompetent, who's to say —'

Alexander caught the sound of chair legs striking tile. Silence. And then Sarrides' voice again, wet with patriotic triumph: 'Yes, just like those venal pre-Junta Ministers and bureaucrats who signed the papers authorising these foreigners to dig here in the first place... Oh yes, the Colonels will demand answers. They will demand heads! Are they not the moral guardians of the state?'

Precisely one week after their arrival the inspectors upped sticks and left, the psychological war still evident in the abruptness of their departure.

18.

Mid-morning I found my boss staring up at the mountain, a frown creasing his face.

He collected a stout walking stick from the fragments hut, and curtly motioned me to follow him.

'Where are we going, what are we looking for?' I asked, as we began our ascent. The pathway rose steeply, zigzagging its broken way towards the mountain face, austere, forbidding.

'I told you. That which hides beyond appearances.'

Boulders. Grey scree slopes that even a careless lizard might turn into a landslide. Shadow cut clefts and fissures, falling into nowhere. A few stunted trees, crippled by the wind. As far as anyone could see, a place fit for the snakes and buzzards, that's all.

The ascent was tough going and he took the opportunity to rest where the path took another demented twist into the sky.

'Remember,' he said, breathing hard, 'knowledge is our great, baffling jigsaw. How can we expect the true picture to emerge before we have collected and assembled its scattered pieces? The same, you might say, goes for the picture we make of the world, and the picture it makes of us.'

He resumed his ascent, his stick fighting for grip.

It might have been the futility of the climb, or the annoying way my soles kept skating over the scree, but I said with a flippant edge: 'Then what if all the pieces are put together in the wrong order?'

Half cocking his head down at me, he retorted: 'And what makes you think they are not?'

I felt the smile withering on my face and immediately regretted I had said anything at all.

On and on we climbed, weaving our way between the great boulders, the sun already darkening our shirts with sweat.

Far below us now, I could see the ancient city, temples and paved streets catching the late morning sun. I could see the marks of the trenches and the stick figure students and teachers filing out of the quarry and into the mess tent. I glanced at my watch, felt the growl in my stomach, and wished I could have been there with the others, with nothing more demanding to talk about than the food or the weather or the dig.

Sensing my discomfort, he pounced. 'How would you describe yourself, Mr Pedrosa? And take care. I have a keen ear for a lie.'

'What do you mean?' thrown by the bluntness of the question.

'Who are you? What are you?' Then, to my blank look, he added: 'Describe yourself.'

Stumbling over the words, I almost lost my footing on the scree into the bargain. *What does he want from you?* I thought. That unspoken thing he demands from every one of his young apprentices, first Sam, then Benja, now me. *I told you there was something wrong about him, I warned you from the start.*

'You don't know who you are?' he demanded, in fake astonishment.

'Of course I do.'

Then, feeling stupid, I just blurted out all the stuff I could remember from my CV, name, sex, date of birth; nationality, religion, education. All the things that best seemed to describe me.

When I had finished, he turned and offered a slow, sarcastic round of applause. 'So that is who you are. Well, never let it be said that man or boy cannot know himself.'

As he resumed his climb, I pulled a face at his back. 'I couldn't think of anything else to say.'

'Try harder.'

'My name is Nicholas Pedrosa. My mother is English, my father Catalan. I'm 22. I was born on the 4th April, in Moreton-in-Marsh, that's in the Cotswolds.'

'Details,' he barked.

'About what?

'About what makes you who you are, or pretend to be.'

'*What?*' Getting no reply, I just hurled myself into the river of my own turbulent thoughts: 'We never visited Spain. It was difficult for my father because of Franco. He hated the Fascists. I went to private school until I was 11. They beat us when our marks weren't good enough. Cane, gym shoe, the blackboard eraser. Anything.'

'And yet you have your schoolmasters to thank for being who and where you are today, isn't that so?'

'*What?*'

'You didn't mention your hobbies. A boy like you must have some; I suppose it's stamp collecting or something equally inspirational.'

'Cycling, I like cycling. I like hiking.'

But not up this mountain with you.

He squinted down at me. 'And after grammar school in Stratford, it was off to college, wasn't it?'

'Aberdeen.'

'A long way from home, way up there, almost in the ice.'

'What's wrong with that? It's all to broaden the mind, isn't it.'

'You had an unusual education. Learning Greek instead of French. Ancient and modern literature instead of economy or one of the sciences. Different than many boys your age.'

'That was my father. He wasn't the conventional type.'

'More.'

'There is no more. There's nothing more to tell.'

He grabbed me roughly by the wrist. 'That's a nice watch,' he said, his eyes devouring the silver Omega, with its green leather strap and radium dial. 'Tell me about it. It must have a story, a fine watch like that.'

'It's just a watch. It doesn't have a story. It was Dad's present for my 21ˢᵗ, that's all.'

I snatched my arm way.

'Well, now we know all about you. Everything there is to tell. And here I was imagining you had something to hide…'

'*What?* I've got nothing to hide.'

'Well, I'm curious, that's all. If your father so ardently wished you to broaden your mind, broaden your horizons, why is it that you do everything you can to cling to your petty provincial ideas? Why the stunted emotions, the stunted imagination? Of all the opinions you express today, or the ideas that enter your head, how many are actually yours, do you even know? But, if they're not yours, then whose were they before they became your hand-me-downs?'

I must have been gaping at him like a shocked fish, wondering what the hell I'd done to deserve being spoken to like that.

But then finally it dawned on me. What it was he was driving at.

Given the philosophy with which he viewed the world, the special apprenticeships, the symposia he hosted at Monolithos, I should have seen it coming.

He was talking about knowing the self, finding the self. The quintessence of Socratic thought, engraved even on the sacred stones at Delphi.

'So that's what all this is about,' I said, with a grin, seeking my confirmation. 'You brought me to the mountain to find myself.'

When all's said and done, why not? — everything we do here is about searching and finding.

I was still breathing my sigh of relief when his answer came, so blunt it almost knocked me off my feet.

'Let the less deserving struggle to find themselves, Mr Pedrosa. I brought you here to do the exact opposite.'

'Look, I don't know what you want from me. Whatever it is, I'm not interested. I don't want to know! It's not part of my job.'

'You think not? You think it is that easy to escape? Look at you. You are not even awake!'

Again, that uncanny ability to read the mind, read the mood, and then make the truth appear like a sunrise in the wrong part of the sky.

'Do you think you have even come close to filling Benja's shoes? Well think again.'

'What is it you want from me?'

'You must give up the past. You must forget the past. Family, friends, everyone. You must be prepared to leave everything behind, and let go, let go...'

Absently, my eyes caught the purple clouds billowing up on the far horizon.

He's hypnotising you again. Can't you feel it? You must resist him. You must fight him.

'You are no use to me otherwise. No use to yourself or anyone else. You are wasting time; resisting it, fighting it, impeding it, every moment of every day. How much longer do you think I am prepared to wait?'

'I don't know what you're talking about!'

'You must lose what you have become.'

'How can anyone lose what they have become?'

'By becoming what they are not.'

The riddles were squirming in my head but then on a wave of blood the realisation crested over me.

He's tunnelling into you the same way he's tunnelling into the tephra, turning the whole peninsula upside down. Those fragments he has in his hands, the ones he's rearranging over the draughtsman's paper, they're pieces of your personality, pieces of your soul.

I should have seen it the moment we set out from camp, the way his tormented eyes swept over the mountainside, not in awe or wonder, but in interrogation. He's still searching, still hunting, even up here, fighting the shadow of his nemesis, Claude Guirand. Something buried between the rocks, perhaps, or deep within the mountain. Some artefact or treasure that has survived this apocalypse. 'It's what you're here for. It's why we chose you. To know what lies beyond your own horizon. To become what you are not.'

'What are you doing?' I yelled, and in my anger experienced a surge of relief, as though it were reasserting my right to be me. 'It's true, isn't it? What they say in camp? That you hypnotise people, that you turn their thoughts against them, steal their sense of self.'

'You may not wish to accept it, but we live in a hypnotic world.'

'Then what is real, what is not?'

'That is a question only you can answer.'

'Like that hallucination on temple hill,' I added scornfully, remembering how stupidly I had been taken in. 'Like those islands we think we saw in the sunset. They were all illusion, weren't they?' I might have added, 'Ones that you engineered,' but held back, if only for fear of provoking the psychopath in him.

His eyes narrowed. 'But why would you assume that the Idea must be inferior to its object, its physical manifestation? If that were the case, wouldn't the poet's ink and words on the paper have a greater implicit value than the inspiration that preceded them?'

Higher and higher we climbed, until we were almost in reach of the light clouds playing the thermals around the Prophet's head.

Gingerly, we edged along its massive limestone wall, the thin thread of the path dropping away at our feet to the skull-cracking rocks below. The stones were like marbles underfoot, and it was hard enough just staying upright. Wary of any sudden movement, maybe the lunging stick in his hand, a rock snatched up as a weapon, I kept a good five paces between us.

'Has there ever been a time in your life, boy, when you could say, *now I am truly, undeniably awake, truly, undeniably alive*. Well, has there?'

From the east, the flash-angry sky came roiling towards us. Massive thunderheads rising up into the heavens, their billowing crowns reflecting the sun, their underbellies as livid as a bruise.

The wind began to gust, driving the sea into frantic crisscrossing patterns. The first raindrops came in a sudden frenzy, pockmarking the dust. It was getting darker by the second.

We entered a narrow cleft where, at the mouth of a shallow cave, a tiny chapel had been built centuries ago, probably in veneration of the freshwater that still drip-echoed off the arching limestone.

It clung to the rock face, a ledge-like platform the only thing between us and thin air.

For the first time, I could feel real fear clawing inside. Something was going to happen. I just knew it. The voice in my head yelled a warning. *He could kill you where you stand and no one would be any the wiser. No one. Like the boy whose shoes you can never fill. An unavoidable accident, a slip of the foot, and a heartbeat later, there you are, plunging towards those jagged boulders, the roiling sea.*

19.

There was a scrambling of feet behind me, and I spun around in alarm. The yell was halfway out of my throat before I even realised. I was staring into thin air.

Somewhere between the incandescent flashes and the blinding darkness that followed, Huxley had vanished. And the storm was about to collide with the mountain.

The wind came shrieking in from the sea, rain and hail spitting into my face. Forking madly out of the clouds, the lightning was almost upon us, thunder ripping the sky.

My eyes swept towards the boulders, then the chapel, then the shallow cave at whose mouth a wiry fig grew upside down from a crevice in the rock, its limbs and leaves frantic in the gusts.

He must be hiding somewhere, I thought angrily, and yelled out at him.

Snatched by the wind, my shout was driven down the broken path, taking my premonition with it, feet skating over scree, a body tumbling headlong onto the splintered rocks far below. Too late to turn back now.

He must have known. He must have seen it coming over the horizon, a blackening stain heaving towards us. Then, rabid opportunist that he was, he would have seized the moment, turning it to his advantage. Doing away with the next apprentice unable to rise to his impossible demands. The storm would do his dirty work for him, death a foot slip, a ripped fingernail away.

Must take shelter quickly, but where? Not the shallow cave that would soon be taking the brunt of the storm. Not between the boulders, the lighting forks about to detonate all over them.

That only left the little chapel clinging to its rock ledge, and I scrambled towards it. When the door failed to budge as I shoved against it, I glanced down, unable to believe what my own hands were telling me amid the sky's livid flashes.

Since when are churches locked? I yelled, already visualising the key between his fingers. Down at camp, there were padlocks everywhere, and more than once I'd seen him fish one out of his pocket.

At least there was no choice, no decision to make now. I had only to face what was coming. And so I huddled into the chapel doorway, taking what little shelter I could.

I had never known anything like it. Not even the gales in Scotland had been like this, not unless you got caught out on Nevis or the Western Isles or something.

I clung to the doorway until my knuckles turned white and my fingers threatened to snap. Any moment now, I thought, you'll be blown away, thrown into the air, tossed over the ledge.

The rain came sweeping across the mountain in oscillating waves. Lightning stabbed the island in a frenzy, the ground shuddering under every strike. The wind rose to a howl and then a scream. I could feel the gusts beginning to lift me off the ground, my grip slipping from the door.

In the terror of the moment, I remember hurling a kind of primal scream into the blackness, into the night, into the storm. If I was going to die out here on the ledge, I was too angry to go out with a whimper. I wanted the whole black world out there to know who had done this to me.

That full-blooded cry. It awoke something within me, something I had never known before. And it was then, as it blew its way out of my lungs, blasted through my throat, that I realised. There, in the few euphoric moments it took me to remember to think. I was not afraid at all. In letting go, I had ceased to be me, the Nicholas Pedrosa who normally faced the world. In his place, I recognised something I never expected: the storm and the thunder and the wild night.

That is just coincidence! I cried, angry that the thought had even occurred to me at all.

The sun was still a dawn ember as I retraced my steps back to camp.

I knew what I had to do. Confront Huxley point blank, preferably in front of witnesses. Then pack my bags and take the next ship out.

By the time I reached the lower ridges of the mountain, Akrotiri was already in full sun. The sight strengthened my resolve.

I could already see him, sitting imperiously at his field tent. He'd be drinking his bitter Russian tea from the samovar, the saffron sun awning bathing him in a benign light he just didn't deserve, his impatient hand already dashing off instructions on the qualities required of his brand new apprentice.

I could already feel the shout and the accusation burning in my throat.

But as soon as his tent sprang into view, I stopped dead in my tracks. His workplace was deserted, the camp table, bare.

By mid-morning half the camp was puzzling over his absence.

The more they debated his motives and whereabouts, the more I found myself tormented by my own conflicting emotions. I wanted to pack my bags, make a run for it, but how could I leave now?

By mid-afternoon even the labourers were becoming restless, and again there were dark whispers about Akrotiri's undead and its ancient curse.

Hadrian, greatly irritated by such talk, drove out to Monolithos to settle the matter once and for all, but found Huxley's rambling old house deserted. Worse, his bed had not been slept in.

In an anxious huddle we gathered at Huxley's tent, wondering what to do next. The voices, I realised, were getting more subdued and everyone, even Nestor, was running out of ideas. Darkness had begun creeping in over the sea and, with a moonless night in prospect, it was too late to send a search party out onto the mountain.

'Who saw him last?' demanded Hadrian, irritated that even that simple inescapable fact could play the Houdini with us.

I felt Anna's eyes on me, sensing that I knew something; that I was holding back.

Reluctantly, I raised a hand. 'Me,' I said over the hubbub, angry at hearing the guilt in my own voice.

Then suddenly they were all pouncing on me, demanding explanations, not to mention their pound of flesh.

'Why didn't you say anything before?' squealed Hadrian. 'You've known for hours but didn't say?'

'Idiot!' muttered Nestor between clenched teeth. 'What were you doing with him up there?'

'That doesn't matter now,' said Anna firmly, and for a second, I had to wonder whom she was protecting, me or Huxley.

'What did you do with the body?' demanded Sam, a stupid smirk on his face, his eyes flashing like a night animal's.

I began to wonder if I would end up being the last person to have seen Huxley alive.

20.

Come first light, our search party was already scouring the mountain-side, fanning out across the Prophet's slanting face.

Struggling between the rocks and the thorny maquis, I still couldn't entirely shake the suspicion that Huxley was safe and sound somewhere, laughing down at us.

Midday came and went, but still there was no sign of him. I began to detect a creeping sense of desperation and incredulity among my fellow searchers. How could a grown man simply vanish without trace?

Conceding that the search over the southern face was getting us nowhere, we headed back to base camp, tired, dispirited, and in much need of sustenance.

While we caught our breath and raided the mess tent, a decision was taken to split the search party up into pairs so as to widen the hunt.

Poring over map scrolls at Huxley's tent, Anna was making the best of organisational skills normally libelled for their Italian anarchy. With Hadrian and Nestor dispensing advice at her shoulder, she divided the mountain into sectors defined, wherever possible, by natural or manmade landmarks — ravines, medieval walls, a Byzantine chapel, a shrine.

Just when I was wondering how twenty-odd labourers, teachers and students were supposed to cover the entire mountain, with all its meandering goat tracks, ridges, boulders and gullies, unlikely rein-forcements arrived on board the *Persephone*.

Crowding the deck, they came cork-bobbing through the swell, mumbling prayers to Aghios Nikolaos, the briny saint of seafarers, his seasick icon swinging back and forth in the wheelhouse.

First down the gangplank, Huxley's symposiasts. The doctor, Stavros Sanassis, with his medical bag in tow, just in case. The spindle-thin schoolmaster, Alexander Vouris, his face as sorry as a cracked teapot. Nondas Maharis, the affable barber with the bald crown and an atoll-like ring of grey. The postmaster, Vassilis Nafpliotis, sporting a pair of checked knickerbockers and stout brogues, ready for the grim task of negotiating the snake-infested rocks. Alexis Pangalos, glaring at the mountain that had the nerve to call itself after some Old Testament prophet.

Aris was slinging a backpack over his shoulders, lacing his boots, as others pushed past him on the aft deck — men and women for whom Huxley was either a curse or a blessing.

Down on the quay, all gyrating arms and whistle blasts, police chief Manolis and his constable Chondro, vainly trying to clear a path through the crowd for those they imagined to be the island's dignitaries. The Mayor, Giannis Papadaikis, wispy strands of hair flying in the wind. Father Nannos, face set in a stony frown, effortlessly conveying the belief, now confirmed from above, that no good would ever come of Huxley and his heathen digging.

Mule drivers from Phíra, farmers with fields on the peninsula, fishermen from Perissa, labourers from the trenches. They were all gathering in the compound now, jabbering their certainties about Huxley's fate and the treachery of the mountain. Our volunteers went weaving between them, handing out glasses of water.

Some, I knew, would secretly be only too pleased to see the archaeologist disappear for good, including half of the council elders.

At the thought that I might somehow be blamed for Huxley's disappearance, even his death, my stomach went into knots. I flinched as the police glared at us, the suspicion in their eyes seeming to single me out from everyone else.

Had he tried to do away with me on the mountain? It just seemed like stupid paranoia now, however sinister his behaviour.

Anna was still pairing us up for the afternoon manhunt and was keen to be done before half the island descended upon her.

'And you, Sam?' She shot him a warning look, clearly in no mood for games, sulks or tantrums.

She was in luck, though the same could hardly be said for me.

'Nicky's with me, going east.' He tossed his head towards me, as full of himself as he was the bhang.

Given his open hostility towards me, the idea of teaming up with Sam, of all people, seemed crazy. My eyes darted towards him and sure enough, there it was, the cold-blooded smirk.

Not for the first time, I had to wonder about his tortured psyche, the cause of it, the extent of it, the possible victims of it. Apparently, I was about to find out in ways far too close for comfort.

I wasted no time in heading for the Morris, half-hoping that my new partner would be too stoned or too lazy to follow. No such luck. Tossing his rucksack into the back, he slipped into the front seat beside me, map propped against the metal dash, our assigned search sector already marked in hazard red.

'Go! *Go!*' he yelled, thumping the dash.

And so with a slipping clutch we kangarooed out of the gates, leaving the mess in the compound behind us.

Navigating between rocks and potholes, I kept my eyes glued to the dirt track, trying all the while to shake the unnerving feeling that there was something fake about everything going on around me.

I know what Huxley would have said. *Look for what you cannot see, not for what you can. Look for the evidence that is missing.*

My sense of unreality was hardly helped by the island itself, still in metamorphosis, struggling from its winter cocoon on wet iridescent wings. In the pumice littered fields now, blossoming almonds. On the volcanic grey slopes, poppy fields. On the breeze, blossoms, sailing away in the rain torrents like little paper boats.

We headed east, over the scaly back of the island.

'Why do you smoke so much of that stuff?' I said, knowing it would be up to me to break the grinding silence between us, and angry that I had to spend any time with him at all.

He threw me a big bloodshot glance. 'Because I like it. Is that a problem for you?'

He planted his feet on the dash. 'At least I can understand Huxley when he talks about the metaphysical, about piercing the nature of reality. I'm probably the only one who can.'

Again, that twisted sense of betrayal, as if first Benja and then I had usurped his rightful place at Huxley's side. The apprentice. That focus of impossible demands, impossible desire.

The experience, or the loss, had bequeathed him the angry, frustrated soul of a poltergeist, hurling inner conflicts around the room in lieu of dishes and candlesticks.

A personality quarrelling with itself, uncertain who it was supposed to be. You could read it in his face, a sullen beauty that cannot quite tolerate itself, and that upwelling ugliness that has its cruel, guilt-ridden job to do. Or the little symbols that, if you noticed them, gave far too much away. Like that black leather choker worn tight around the neck, a single blood-red stone at its centre. Just enough to insinuate a desire for conquest or submission, but who would dare? His was an attraction spoken in a chemical language far too ancient for the mind to argue with. An attraction not of candour, but of lures and snares. Communicated through instinct, scent and colour, yes, but like some pincer-clawed insect to its dinner. No wonder the pretty little student girls preferred to swoon from the distance. They probably already sensed that a step too far there would be tears, and one broken heart leaking its contents into the dirt.

'You think I ever wanted the fucking job?' I yelled, losing my temper. '*I* didn't ask for it. Take it if it means that much to you.'

But you can't can you, because Huxley doesn't want you anymore. He's used you, spent you, had enough of you.

The blue eyes were on me now, staring, absorbing my vehemence as a lens absorbs light.

I had been wrong to call them lifeless, as warm as glass. It was just that there was something missing from them, and it was only now that I realised what it was.

It was him, himself. Missing from his own eyes.

At least his derision for his own past, friends, family, former loved ones, made some sense to me now. As he had so proudly proclaimed at the time, if bitterness can ever be proud, he had obliterated every trace of their existence from his mind.

Why, he would not say but, given our mentor's insistence that we abandon everything we had become, I had to wonder what incendiary role Huxley himself had played in getting Sam to burn his bridges to the past.

Where the dirt track just petered out into scree we abandoned the Morris, and began hiking along goat and donkey tracks.

At first we were crunching over flint-grey rock, weaving between boulders, but rounding the mountain to the east, everything changed. Fields of wild grass and poppy, sweeping down to the sea. Medieval terraces formed by dry stone walls, a few scattered fig and almonds gone wild. The sky had that crystal look about it, so too the prism clouds turning around the peak.

'So what happened up there, Nicky? What are you hiding?'

'Nothing! The storm hit the mountain, that's all. There was a flash of lightning, so white, so brilliant, for several seconds I couldn't see anything at all, just a vanishing silhouette burnt onto the back of my eyes. Then blackness...'

We roamed the mountain, the intensity of the manhunt somehow easing the strain between us.

The hours stretched into days. There was no time to go home to wash, change or rest, and only infrequently did we return to camp to pick up fresh supplies. We lived and slept in our clothes, cooked our meals over driftwood fires, and caught a few hours' sleep, stretched out under the stars.

I could hardly believe it when I heard that half the search party had thrown in the towel and gone home, swearing blind that Huxley must have fallen into some bottomless crevasse, or else had jumped ship altogether, knowing justice was finally catching up with him.

We crisscrossed the mountain, extending our search to the north, vowing never to give up. We wanted the truth, even if it was his dead body.

One night, lying on the edge of the mountain, the campfire just embers at our feet, he shook me awake. My eyes darted open to find a meteor shower streaking over the sea, fire-sputtering reflections caught in the still water. He sprang to his feet, ecstatic, clapping his hands, dancing on the edge of the precipice, his end just a careless footfall away.

★

The sun, deceptively fierce, burnt our faces and shoulders. We moved down towards the Monolithos coast. We stripped off our clothes and threw ourselves into the sea, gasping as the winter currents licked our bare skin. Shivering in the wind, we collapsed laughing onto the blood-warm rocks.

He spoke without lifting his head from the stone. 'It's strange, isn't it?'

'What is?' I asked lazily, disarmed by the gathering summer in my mind.

He struck, as darting as a snake. 'Huxley offering you the job when he did. Benja was still alive. Why would he want you at all — unless of course he already knew Benja was going to die?'

For a minute or more I just lay there, staring wide-eyed into the sky, knowing I had been a fool to bury that chilling suspicion at the back of my mind.

Sitting up on my elbows, I said: 'Benja never mentioned anything to you? About leaving, about going home?'

It was a long shot, I knew that. Why would Benja have confided in Sam, of all people, when Hadrian, Anna, even Nestor had already killed the idea stone dead. Benja had said nothing about leaving. Huxley had said nothing about sacking him.

Sam shrugged. 'Not a word. So where does that leave us, Nicky boy?'

We barely exchanged another word for the rest of the day but, as the sun fell towards the sea and the sky turned gold I began to detect an air of regret or denial about him. Whether that was because he'd been caught telling a lie or telling the truth, who could say. For all I knew, it was just the poltergeist in him.

But taking the rare opportunity it offered, I asked him about that strange book he had found in the Petit Phoenix in Saint-Michel, *Travels in Elysium*. Why had the mere mention of it brought a thunderous look to Huxley's face?

Uncorking a flask of wine between his teeth, he threw me a mocking glance. 'Chance discovery, happy coincidence, is that what you think, Nicky? A day after meeting Huxley at the Sorbonne.'

'So he planted it for you, is that what you're saying? Why not just hand you the damned thing like any normal person and say, read this.'

'How else was he to insinuate the beautiful obsession into our minds? *Islands mythical, legendary, real!*'

'But he denies even knowing the book.'

'He knows it back to front and always has. Every island, every sea. But you only begin to realise after a few months —'

'Realise what?'

'How the islands have been making their tangential appearances in your own life. At Monolithos. In your dreams at night. At the dig. In the frescoes. In the potsherds. In some innocent remark you hear in the street.'

'Wait… you said something about the book's peculiar style, what was it?'

He shook his head. 'It was an impression, that's all. Something beyond the lyrical prose, the farther he travelled, island to island…' Again he struggled for words, just as he had at Monolithos: '…I don't know, something innocent and corrupt, naive and ruthless all at the same time.'

That's when I thought, it's the spitting image of Huxley himself, isn't it. You never quite know what to expect of him. Look at us now, out on the mountain searching for him, while his enemies are still plotting to evict or arrest him. That was his vulnerability, his Achilles heel, these headlong lapses into unreality. No one would ever have caught Claude Guirand talking about visionary islands puffed out of sunset cloud, archipelagos streaming out of some transcendent realm. No, Guirand would be back in Athens or Paris, frequenting academia, walking the corridors of political power, dining with Colonels, ministers and kings. I felt sure he could even be charming, given sufficient rehearsal.

'I tried to get him to admit it,' said Sam. 'That he wrote it, thirty years ago or something. He denied it, of course, and the more I insisted the more incensed he became.'

'Maybe he needs the mystery,' I said. I was trying to straighten out the crooked lines of thought that told me the Isles weren't sinister, at least not at heart. It wasn't as if I couldn't see the poetry or adventure in them, but they were just ancient myths, weren't they, dangerous only to those who took them too seriously. *Fuck.*

'You'll know the seduction, Nicky, sooner or later.'

'Not me. No way.'

The Isles beyond sunset. The Isles of the Blest. Elysium. They were figments of desire, lands of milk and honey, that's all. Given the relentless suffering life threw at the ancient inhabitants of the Aegean, who could blame them. Warriors killed or maimed in battle. Mothers killed in childbirth. Fishers swallowed by the merciless sea. Farmers tilling the stone-choked fields, blessed with bountiful harvests one year, cursed by drought, blight, famine the next. Entire villages killed or sold into slavery. They needed their golden heroes; crossing enchanted seas to islands inhabited by gods, nymphs and demons, climbing down into Hades to rescue the love of their life from the King of Death.

'At first you're not even sure,' Sam was saying, the sunset finding the sea in the blue of his eyes. 'You're there now, aren't you. You feel the curiosity and revulsion all at the same time. The ambivalence. Randal was exactly the same. Then before you know it here it comes, the desire, the craving, the seduction.'

I shook my head. He'd been opening up to me, but now it was just the weed and wine talking.

I tried to bring him down to earth. 'Maybe he denies he wrote it to protect his reputation. Did you ever think of that? *Plato's Conundrum.* Maybe the theory was debunked years ago, and Atlantis is just what Plato said it is.' I added with a twist of sarcasm, 'and not some brilliant metaphysical device that can demonstrate eternity to the future, or the mechanics of the perfect idea as it shifts through time and space.'

'Do you think it's too deep for you to understand, Nicky?'

'How deep is it, how deep can it be?'

'It's travelled two thousand years into the future, hasn't it? We're discussing it now aren't we?'

'What do you mean? So you believe it? You understand it?'

'I didn't say that. I see the glimmer of it, that's all... His distant island Utopia, Atlantis. The purity of it. The corruption of it. I see it entering our lives.'

When the bottle slipped from his grasp I thought he must have passed out or something, but not long afterwards his voice welled out of the darkness.

'*I* wanted to get to the island, you know. It was my right. Not Randal's.'

'What?'

'I wanted to say to the guards: "I am the son of Earth and Starry Heaven. I am thirsty, please give me something to drink from the river of Mnemosyne."'

'What the fuck are you talking about?'

'Atlantis, Nicky, Atlantis, what do you think?' he slurred, collapsing back into the grass, the night sky surging into his eyes.

They were obsessed, all right. And with Huxley at the helm, probably closer to cloud cuckoo island than anywhere else.

At some God-awful hour he slumped down next to me and shook me awake. 'Come on, Nicky, shall I turn you on?'

Expecting him to be splicing together his cigarette papers, I groaned, 'go to sleep!'

'Shall I show you something that will blow your tiny mind?' He leapt up, dragging me to my feet. We scrambled across the terraced hillside, relying more on trust than eyesight in the moonless dark, higher and higher towards the surging stars.

He stopped dead, panting.

'Close your eyes.'

'I can't see anything anyway!'

'*Do it!*'

I caught the wine breath on my face, and knew he was peering at me through the darkness, just to make sure I was obeying him. Then, grabbing me by the arm again, he pulled me stumbling to the edge of the terrace, and spun me around.

'*Now!* Open your eyes!'

I was struggling to understand what I was seeing. Some kind of phosphorescent mist, floating over the lower reaches of temple hill. A white glow through the squid ink darkness, bringing even a faint illumination to the temple columns.

'What is it?' I whispered.

That made him laugh all the more, too stoned, too manic to care.

'It's probably just a volcanic phenomenon,' I said, the only guess I could come up with. I thought he would fall over laughing. 'Or Nestor's moles on double shift, drilling down through the tephra.'

21.

The water-splashed days of April evaporated into May and still there was no trace of him, dead or alive.

Huxley had now been missing for ten whole days.

Spinning the sticky threads of village mythology, there was talk of Benja the *vrykolakas* exacting his revenge; of the Junta doing away with him; of Huxley falling victim to his own smuggling ring in some deal gone sour.

'You cannot vanish into thin air,' said Hadrian, screwing his feet indignantly into the dust. 'You cannot!'

Everyone knew what he meant. That a broken, bloated body would have to turn up sooner or later, lying at the bottom of some ravine. Either that or Huxley really had jumped ship, just as the police now alleged, if only to justify their decision to trade the mountain for the taverna.

More than most, Anna was struggling with impossible emotions, the flood tide commanding her to rise to the challenge; the ebb to crumple into tears of frustration or despair. I began to wonder if there was something deeper to their friendship, maybe even love, but whatever the truth, we watched our words whenever she was in earshot.

Without admitting it out loud, the rest of us had already shifted our attention away from the living, following the stench of animal decay among the rocks or closing in on a flock of crows, picking noisily over something in the fields.

Our worst fears appeared confirmed when, three days later, one of the students stumbled over an upturned shoe in the dust, not far from the chapel where I had last seen him alive.

As soon as Anna, in grim certainty, had identified it as Huxley's, our scattered teams converged upon the scene, summoned with bed-linen flags, shouts and whistles.

Determined to cover every inch of ground on the southwestern slopes, we made our descent in a slanting line, the sea and the ancient city below glowing in the afternoon sun.

After another hundred foot drop we crossed an old mule track. While the others carried on towards camp, Hadrian and I struck out along the rock-strewn trail, heading east along the girth of the mountain. Up ahead, we could see another derelict chapel, teetering precariously over a sheer drop, the mountain plunging into a fathomless cobalt blue sea.

My heart went into free fall. I blinked and blinked again, doubtful that I was even seeing straight... Marcus Huxley, stumbling into view on one shoeless foot. It may have been the sweat in our eyes and the reddening sun on our backs but to my mind and memory, in the abruptness of the moment, he still emerges like an apparition out of thin air. Maybe that's why Hadrian was so incensed, in that it added insult to injury. At my shoulder, I heard him gasp, and his breath quicken. Then, before I knew it, he was marching up to him, venting all the fear and frustration that we had been bottling up inside since day one.

Seizing Huxley by the shoulders, he shook him violently, while the great man himself, his face disguised by a thirteen-day stubble, just stood there, dazed and tottering, his eyes rolling.

'Is this is your idea of a game, Huxley? Do you know what you have put us through? Do you? Who the hell will come to your rescue next time, answer me that, who the hell will turn the island upside down for you. Do you think anyone is going to give a damn. Good riddance, that's what we'll say!'

I pulled Hadrian away. As he wheezed and panted, fighting an impulse to retch, I led Huxley to the retaining wall of the chapel. He looked like a tramp, his hair matted and all over the place, his eyes strangely vacant. Markedly thinner, too, even haggard, though whether it was the look of someone who had just been starved for a fortnight was debatable.

As for the stink, that certainly wasn't fake. Nor the blood-encrusted hands, where several fingernails appear to have been ripped away.

Moments later, Sam, Nestor and Anna appeared over the rise, followed by Aris, Galatea and a gaggle of students.

They may have started off in different places, but the second they set eyes on him their faces went lurching through the same turbulent emotions, shock, doubt, relief, suspicion.

Seconds later they were hurling questions and accusations at him, at each other, the sky, some of them just colliding in mid-air.

Where have you been! Where has he been? He can't say. He won't say!

Anna flung her arms about him. She was crying in fury, in relief. She said through sniffles: 'Oh, Marcus! Where on earth have you been!' He looked down at his hands. 'What day is it?' he asked. A voice so insubstantial it hardly seemed to belong to him at all.

'Sunday. We've been searching for you for thirteen days. *Thirteen days!* Can you understand what I'm saying?'

As for Hadrian, the accusation was written large all over his face. Huxley, for twisted reasons of his own, had been playing us all for fools. He shot me a warning look as if to say, *don't be taken in, not by this charade.*

Wary as I was, suspicious as I was, I couldn't help wondering if Hadrian wasn't too punch-drunk himself to realise how disoriented Huxley was. No one, not even Marcus Huxley, was capable of this, faking sunburnt skin, gaunt face, glazed eyes. Was he?

'Do you know,' Huxley replied at last, glancing up into Anna's anxious, doubtful face. 'I really don't remember.' There was a quiet indifference to his voice, so out of character I felt a tremor run down my spine.

'We have to get him off the mountain,' said Anna, summoning Aris with a brisk wave.

With help he struggled to his feet, Nestor and Aris on either side of him, shouldering his weight. We then made a painfully slow descent to camp.

After some debate it was decided to make up a bed for him in one of the huts behind the site office. The considered opinion was that he was too weak to make the bone-jarring drive to Monolithos, and no one trusted him to remain there unsupervised.

Stavros Sanassis hurried into the hut, his face torn between concern for his good friend and the puzzled look of a physician who cannot quite believe his own eyes.

'So you are back from the dead,' he said teasingly, fishing the stethoscope out of his bag. 'I was almost having to reconcile myself to the fact that I would have no one to discuss impossible ideas with anymore.'

Huxley apparently found it difficult to speak. He tried to say something, croaking a few words. The doctor motioned him to spare his voice.

Sometimes, he appeared to drift off into sleep, at others, through slit-tired eyes, seemed vaguely conscious of the doctor examining him, testing him for concussion, fever, broken bones.

'I can find nothing seriously wrong with him,' he concluded at last.

'*Quelle surprise*,' muttered Hadrian from the doorway.

'A weaker man might have died out there,' remarked Sanassis, prescribing a zinc salve for his sunburnt skin, a linctus for his sore throat, an antiseptic cream for his bloodied fingertips. 'What he needs now is rest and recuperation. Good, nourishing food. *And no third degree.*'

Hadrian's eyes narrowed.

Once the doctor had taken his leave he just couldn't resist taking one last swipe at the man who, for thirteen straight days, had been running him ragged.

'You'd better come up with a more convincing explanation than that, Huxley, after making half the island turn out to hunt for you; after some even put their own lives at risk for you. Otherwise, mark my words, they'll never forgive you.'

Yet of the two, it was Huxley, not Hadrian, who turned out to be a better judge of the Greek soul.

Far from alienating those who had scoured the mountain for him, it was precisely this intangible air of myth and mystery that elicited their sympathy and stoked their imagination.

His great adventure, and the heroic parts they imagined they had played in it, must have been told and retold in a thousand different ways, each a little less credible than the last. By week's end, you could marvel at how all these colourful threads had become woven into the tapestry of island legend, the truth itself impossible to disentangle.

As he lay propped up in bed, recovering his strength, a steady stream of well-wishers brought him the most restorative concoctions they could think of, dishes like fish soup swimming with eel, clams and shrimp, chicken pilaf with lemon blossom, island sweetmeats gumming the mouth with almonds and honey. Just for a second, I had to wonder if those were tears he was fighting back. But how could that be, someone so cruel and manipulative?

I cleared away the clutter at Huxley's bedside, avoiding his eyes.

The storm has changed him, I thought, yet couldn't for the life of me say what it was that was different about him.

What puzzled me most was that he had failed to reappear with a more convincing story, something about losing his way in the storm, perhaps, falling, cracking his head against a stone, losing consciousness. That would have been easy enough for any liar; for him, plain sailing.

Then there was his post-storm behaviour, which did little to shore up his claims of innocence.

Dr Sanassis had ordered a week in bed. Rest, recuperation, plenty of sleep. It was not to be. No sooner had the last of his well-wishers taken their leave than he threw back the bed covers and hurried groggily to the trestle table at the far end of the hut.

Anna's workplace. I watched as he rummaged through her papers and map scrolls. Finding a black notebook under the mess, he clumsily flipped it open with his bandaged fingers and began scouring every line.

'What are you doing?' I protested, mindful of the doctor's orders.

'Reading, what does it look like?'

'Reading what?'

'Anna's log, of course,' he snapped, his eyes skimming text, apparently in search of some buried fact or hidden clue.

The wind whistling around the hut only seemed to amplify his own silence.

He threw me a glance. 'I suppose I should be thankful that you do not harangue me like the others, demanding answers I do not have, do not remember.'

No, I am just watching you instead, waiting for the truth or the lie to incriminate you.

'Why did you do it?' I yelled, all the pent-up fury and frustration suddenly breaking over me. 'Why did you leave me on the mountain like that?'

'I told you. To lose what you have become... to become what you are not.'

So *that* memory too, apparently, his amnesia had spared him. How convenient.

'Even if that were possible,' I shot back, 'why would anyone do such a thing. Throw away their past, their childhood, everything that makes them unique...'

'You are deluded,' he scoffed. 'You are a product, nothing more. There are hundreds of thousands just like you, coming off the production line every day, as unique as anything else exuded from molten plastic.'

'If I'm so useless,' I snarled, 'why hire me in the first place? Why give me his job?'

'Why?' There was a hard, unrepentant edge to his voice. 'Because, like Benja before you, you have potential. Nothing more. It is largely up to you to decide whether you will live up to it or not.'

'In whose judgement? Yours I suppose.'

'I very much doubt I shall be the one remembering this day twenty, thirty, fifty years' hence. The day you come face to face with yourself — what you were, what you are, what you might have become. Will you finally have come to terms with the torments of your childhood? Will you have come to terms with life? With death?'

'*Death?*' I mocked. 'Don't you have anything else to think about or talk about?'

'You think you are in the land of the living?' he retorted. 'Well think again. Death is everywhere, death is all around us.'

'Nobody wants to think about it, of course they don't!'

'No, they don't. Death is the unseen predator that will snatch them or their loved ones when they least expect it, that's the terror they hold inside. And so they lock and bar the door, light a devotional lamp to drive out the darkness where it hides, and pretend it isn't out there, prowling the night, stalking them, waiting.'

I made a beeline for the door.

'Benja's pretty young wife was the same,' he taunted. 'Such was her denial that no sooner had she landed on the island than she began disposing of his clothes, burning the bed sheets, scrubbing the house clean, disinfecting any traces of him that might have remained. It was her way of coping — not with loss, no, but with death breaking into the home.'

'Why are you telling me all this? That's not part of my job!'

'It is a part of your *life!*'

140

22.

No one could keep him confined to bed for long, not even Dr Sanassis, checking up on his patient bright and early the following morning. Having extracted an irritable and entirely unconvincing promise about taking his medicine and not exerting himself, Stavros threw up his hands in defeat. Stowing away his stethoscope, he said: 'Then I'll expect you for Easter, Marcus. Feasting with the family — uncles, aunts, nephews, cousins, and half the street for good measure. At least I shall be able to keep an eye on you.'

The narrow streets, freshly-whitewashed, were festooned with flowers. Honeysuckle drenched the air. Over the rooftops, in a cerulean blue sky, swallows in full flight, diving, soaring.

'I've seen them somewhere before, just like this, but where?' The words were hardly out of my mouth when it hit me. In the ancient city, of course, in the frescoes of the spring, the artists appearing to capture this very moment in eternity, swallows soaring, impossibly reckless, impossibly graceful.

'Where are we going?' I asked suspiciously, as the doctor's house disappeared behind us and we joined a path engulfed by wildflowers undulating over the crater wall.

'To Stavros', of course. We are spending Easter Sunday in the fields. Have you learnt nothing yet about pagan tradition?' According to Huxley, even Easter was just an ancient full moon ritual now in the indignity of Christian disguise.

We came to a tiny daredevil chapel, crippled by its own foolhardiness, clinging to crumbling rock and thin air, a jagged crack gashing its dome.

Oblivious to the danger, he heaved open the tired old door and stepped inside. Against my better judgement, I followed, our unexpected movement startling a pair of swallows, busy making their nest among the painted constellations that still shone dimly from the vaulted dome. A rampant fig tree had thrust its searching boughs through the fractured stonework and had burst into leaf, casting a dappled light over the walls. Across the alter screen hung a row of icons, obscure island saints fading into the darkening wood, taking their battles with demons and dragons with them.

Above, the swallows went on about their business, diving through the crack in the universe.

So transfixed had Huxley become, I began to wonder if it was the crumbling floor that was belatedly worrying him, some sudden movement that might send us all toppling over the edge.

But when at last he turned to leave, I realised I had never seen his eyes quite like that before, so open, so disarmed.

As we tiptoed out, he murmured: 'This is the true church, Mr Pedrosa. Don't let anyone tell you differently.'

What did he mean? That it was in ruins? That it had no priest? That it was more pagan than Christian? That it was half in this world, half in the next?

'I thought you hated everything about the Church,' I said. 'I thought you didn't believe in God. I thought you despised people who did.' He did not reply.

I glanced sharply at him, wondering, how can you be like that, unforgivably callous one minute, compassionate the next?

He paused to take in the silver blueness of the caldera, the curve of the crater wall and the Burnt Islands far below.

'Whatever your impressions of our island and our work thus far, Nicholas, be careful not to confuse mystical experience with superstition. One does not necessarily equal the other... Or are you one of those people who assumes we cannot bring the power of logic to the soul?'

Spiritual revelation, as ordinary to everyday life as a tree to a landscape. That's what it sounded like. Thinking it must be his black humour, I was about to laugh out loud, and only resisted the impulse to do so because it was the first time he had ever called me by my given name.

Ten minutes later we were pushing open the gate of Dr Sanassis' white-walled garden. The doctor's two young daughters pressed glasses of stone-chilled water into our hands.

Under the trellised vines a feast fit for a king had been laid along the length of the table. People were milling about everywhere — women fussing over the *mezedakia*, men tapping wine into flagons at the oak barrels, little children playing tag between the trees. At the far end of the garden, against a jasmine-smothered wall, the lute and fiddle players were already tuning their instruments, making a feint into some popular folk song, then snatching up their wine, plucking and tuning. The feast would go on for hours and, by nightfall, half the barrels drunk, the goat and lamb devoured, everyone would be dancing.

Down at the fire, the men were disentangling the *kokoretsi* from the spit — supposedly a delicacy of roast goat entrails. Beaming, Dr Sanassis' wife Despina was making a beeline straight for me with a generous helping of the stuff, and I just managed to duck out of the side gate without looking too obvious about it when I ran right into Huxley and his Greek symposiasts.

'I'm just saying,' said Pangalos, 'Easter is the sun and moon, the alpha and omega of the Orthodox calendar, it calls for reconciliation, but don't expect the truce to last.'

Catching my approach, Alexander Vouris cautioned him with a worried look, and they abruptly fell silent.

With a fleeting glance at Huxley, Dr Sanassis said, 'That's all right, Alex. Nico's one of us now, aren't you Nico? One of the travellers.'

'We were just talking about the island,' said Huxley pointedly. 'What it was. What it is. What it has the capacity to become.'

Sanassis sloshed white muscat into a glass and handed it to me. 'Look, Nico,' his eyes sweeping over the neat, cistern-irrigated terraces below, where a hundred green saplings had been planted, fir, pine, even platanos. 'You and Marcus missed the planting ceremony. Alas, the saplings couldn't wait.'

'First small steps,' affirmed Nondas the barber, with a faraway smile, 'for a civilisation.'

'We shall forest the mountain,' boomed Pangalos, 'turn dust into soil, desert into leaf and flower!'

'To the saplings,' toasted the postmaster, his eyes shining bright. 'May you, too, children, rise a hundred feet tall!'

Huxley has inspired all this, I thought, somewhat incredulously. *Is that what he's been driving at, with all those oblique coded words... testing before trusting you.*

Change. Transformation. A revolution in ideas.

Can I have been so wrong about him?

23.

The audit his sword of Damocles, Huxley returned to the excavations like a man possessed. He knew it was only a matter of days, weeks at most, before the Service rendered judgement. He barked orders at his inner circle, students and trench moles, flying into a rage whenever the dig progressed by inches instead of yards. He pored over stratigraphy maps, marched up and down temple hill, sat hunched over his jigsaw fragments until his brain boiled, and even swung the pick with his own hand when his patience hit breaking point.

What with his irascibility and impossible demands, there can hardly have been a man in camp who didn't feel some nostalgia for those 13 glorious days he had gone missing on the mountain.

Even in his rare absences there was no let up. Rumours went seething through camp, as virulent, as infectious as a dose of island flu. Our days were numbered. Guirand had been invited to make his case to the Colonels. Sarrides was dotting the i's and crossing the t's of his damning report. Sometimes, it was hard to tell if the rumours originated with Huxley's friends or his enemies.

There were more sightings of Benja the *vrykolakas*. More wildcat strikes as labourers threw down their tools and took to their heels, the fear of God pumping their hearts and legs into a frenzy.

I glanced down at my watch and winced. Three o'clock in the morning. Should have known. Dinner with Christos and Helia and the other Greek students always stretched long into the night, the table a bedlam of plates and spent raki bottles. Huxley would hit the roof and probably dock my pay if I was late for work; that meant two hours sleep, tops.

I was already on the hairpins when I caught the brief flare streaking across the mirror. Thinking it must be the headlights of another car, I slowed.

There it was again, a white light, welling brighter, then ebbing away.

I piled on the brakes. Got out of the car. Waited with bated breath, eyes boring into the grey shadowlands of the western sector.

Until — yes, *there!* a brief pulse of light, settling now into a kind of white phosphorescence. I remembered our last encounter on the mountain, Sam doing his death dance across the crumbling cliff face just at the ecstatic sight of it.

Why? Did he know what it was?

Rash decisions are made out of moments like this, the vapour of the raki, the frustration at being kept in the dark, the resentment of other people's secrets squatting in your own living space. Executing a reckless three point turn between ditch and drop off, and I was on my way, still tracking its presence hairpin to hairpin.

On the final run up to the gates, it had become a faint nimbus just tingeing the outline of the hill. Intentionally or not, well camouflaged from the student encampment and the eastern excavations.

I hurried through the enveloping darkness, the penumbral outlines of trenches, tephra shafts, then ghost houses looming up left and right. The moon had slipped over the horizon, and the stars were so dense they appeared in danger of colliding.

I joined the ancient path, telling myself, no, don't turn on the torch. You're safer in the dark. It's as much your camouflage as it is theirs, whoever they are. Insinuating your way through the darkness like a breeze. Between the houses with sky terraces, stone floors and staircases, almost expecting to hear the sound of sleeping breaths, sense the presence of ancient dreams in the air, past the bakery and the scent of fresh bread.

The phosphorescence seems to be leaking out of the earth, maybe through the tunnel entrances and exploratory shafts. That can be the only explanation for it catching the temple columns like that, an insinuation of light that could equally be manmade, or some kind of optical resonance from that ocean of stars up there.

Each step more unnerving than the last, I kept having to tell myself, you have to see it through. You have to. Wondering what the hell I would find up there, that atavistic fear of the night so effortlessly mocking the rational vanity of the mind that clings to broad daylight. Huxley at the altar stones, his hands bathed in blood, invoking Lucifer as the Morning Star dawns over the sea, a stone-chalked pentagram at his feet.

A gang of traffickers, looting antiquities, manhandling the crates down the hill, into the hold of some fast launch or fishing caïque.

Who knows, maybe even Benja himself, on the lookout for young blood or a flagon of wine.

I quickened my pace.

No, it must be Nestor and his moles, burrowing ever deeper into the tephra with their new tunnelling machine. The only thing is, it's utterly silent. I struggled over the heaps of ash, between the coils of barbed wire, into his junkyard of broken, rusting machines. Not even Guirand had bothered with it. Why should he, it was just a metal graveyard, and in the unlikely event that it ever did make an appearance in the audit, Huxley would probably be accused of sullying the landscape, polluting the integrity of the site.

A rusting strand of barbed wire snagged my shirt, then skin, drawing blood. Wincing, I staunched the cut with my sleeve, then sank onto the nearest ash dune, watching, waiting.

The light was changing, and with a subtlety that escaped me for a good thirty seconds. Ebbing, fading away, the temple columns losing their sheen, the curve of the hill losing its faint firefly aura.

Realising why, I jumped to my feet. The light was moving, and with a fluid, floating motion. Between the restored houses, between the ruins, down the slanting path towards the cliffs and the sea. Meeting the cliff edge, it was abruptly extinguished.

Could there be a boat down there? Impossible to say. The angle wasn't right, I was too far from the water.

As I hurried back towards camp, thinking to check out the dock, I caught a movement, so subtle a single blink might have missed it. A human silhouette, moving against the star crushed sky. I held it in my field of vision, focusing so hard my eyes hurt. Tracking his movement now. Down the hill. Over the river bridge. Several times I lost sight of him altogether as he stole darkness from the wall or the ruin he was passing. Lingering now at house 16, under the scaffolding. A match is struck, the flare, the gleam of the cigarette, seeming to capture the contours of the young face, the blond hair.

I stared. Willing him to reveal himself. Praying for some careless torch beam to strike him in the face, destroying that impossible resemblance in an instant. Trying to forget about those stupid labourers with their stupid superstitions about Benja the *vrykolakas*.

Gone to the evil. Out to haunt them. Trick them. Steal their raki while they're not looking. Ambush their women. A danger even after a barrelful of wine, these *vrykolakes*, their lips stained purple, their erections mocking everyone in sight.

A lamp flared among the student tents, a ball of light glowing dimly through green canvas. I waded through the darkness towards it, past the large 6-man army tents, on towards the smaller pup tents.

Fuck. What's going on? Suddenly, my heart's in my mouth, thrumming through the roof of my head. The tent's shaking on its poles, like it's fucking possessed or something, guy ropes twanging, canvas flapping, faster and faster, then thud, thud, thud.

A longing moan, a grunt, and it's all over. The tent falling still after its unearthly excitement.

I caught the girl's face in the lamplight, the dishevelled hair, the sleepy look, the nipples sucked red. The boy, crawling out between the flaps now, his cock still wet and swollen.

Just Christos and Helia, that's all, going at it full tilt.

Red-faced, I began edging away before I had a lot of awkward questions to answer. Swore under my breath, feeling like an idiot; then, just as I turned, lights came on in the fragments hut, betrayed only by those narrow windows under the eves. I made haste, the ash muffling my footsteps.

I was still wondering if I should raise the alarm when the handle jerked out of my grip and the door almost hit me in the face.

Huxley.

'What are you doing here?' he glowered. 'Get inside. You'll wake the whole camp.'

He closed the door firmly behind him, crossed over to the trestle table.

'It's four-thirty in the morning,' I said. 'I saw a light.'

As his eyes bored into mine, I realised my mistake. 'In the hut I mean.'

Everyone knew he was an insomniac, he claimed it came with the territory, but what was he doing up on temple hill in the dead of night? And who were the others?

'I thought it was an intruder.'

He squinted at me, apparently weighing the words for their veracity. 'Come here boy, and sit down.'

I did so, casting an eye over the arrangement of potsherds across the tabletop. A mountain lake, its face reflecting the bright eyes of a water nymph. A young fisherman casting off from the dock. Antelopes on the curve of a green hill.

'Pay attention,' he said, his eyes straying first to the door. 'Our enemies are gaining in number. There will be trouble, you can bank on it. The lust is too strong, the prize too great.'

147

'The prize?'

'I want you to swear. I want your solemn word. That you will respect the absolute confidentiality of the dig, its aims, methods, results. That you will divulge nothing to third parties without my express permission, and mine alone. Is that understood?

'Yes... No! Not really.'

'You think our enemies have no informers in camp?' he went on, almost accusingly. 'That their eyes and ears aren't primed to catch every careless remark, every blabbing tongue? That they would have even the slightest compunction about tricking you, drugging you, stealing your notebooks...'

I was almost on the verge of believing him when the obvious knocked some sense into me. 'Nobody's going to be shouting "eureka" from the rooftops from anything I have to say, are they. Nobody's kept more in the dark than I am.'

'What matters is whether they understand it, not you. The information you learn here is privileged. You will share it with no one else. *Understood?*'

'What about the others?' thinking he could hardly mean his closest colleagues, our inner circle, Anna, Hadrian, Sam.

'To no one,' he replied, bringing an implacable force to the words.

I was in a corner, and knew it. Exhaling hard, I played for time.

'What about Benja? What about Sam? Did they swear?'

'Of course,' he replied with unflinching eyes. 'Why do you think I have such trouble with Sam? Do you know how close he comes to breaking his word, just to taunt me? Throwing out lies and half-truths, yet ones he knows full well could inspire intelligent, enquiring minds to prise open the truth beyond.'

So there it was at last, the implicit admission that here was the anonymous author of the *Travels*.

'You said your discovery would shake the world awake,' I pressed him. 'What will? How am I supposed to keep the secret if I don't even know what it is!'

He bit his lips and frowned, probably debating which of his secrets he could afford to give away. The more he procrastinated, the more exasperated I became.

'I want the truth!'

'The truth!' he snorted, the words oozing contempt. 'As though you or anyone else has earned the right to it simply by squelching out of your mother's womb, by the smack on your buttocks, by the blood and slime you've smeared over the bed sheets.... Well, let me tell you, no one has the preordained right to know or to understand anything. Nobody has the right to be told the truth. Instead, we have the right to demand it, the right to seek it, nothing more!'

I threw up my arms, part in fury, part in defeat, and made to leave.

'All right,' he conceded, calling me back, and with the air of a man who knows he will come to regret what he is about to say. 'All right. I shall tell you.'

His face in partial eclipse over the fragments table, I stared back at him, half dreading, half relishing the revelation about to come my way.

'You were right,' he said, threading his way between the words. 'I commend whatever it was that made you see it — foresight, instinct, logic, even luck.'

'About what?'

'That we are entering Plato's Atlantis, of course. Every day, inch by inch, yard by yard, we are closing in on the heart of the city.'

'Atlantis?' I said, slipping back onto the chair again, the urge to jump at the explanation thinning away into disbelief. 'After all the scorn you heaped upon it! After the way you laid into Sam?'

'It is sometimes a necessary evil to dissemble.'

I shook my head.

'The parallels are stark enough, aren't they?' he growled. 'You said so yourself. You couldn't believe how no one else had even remarked upon them.' He added with a scowl, 'except Sam, of course.'

'And why didn't they?'

'Why? Because the Atlantic leads them astray, that's why, way beyond the Pillars of Hercules. They are literalists. What they don't see, what they don't appreciate is how immense a catastrophe it was when the island blew apart with the force of an atomic war. If anything, it would be strange if the event recorded by the temple priests of Sais had *not* become garbled, history twisting swiftly into legend.'

Folding my arms, I glanced sharply at him, wondering if it was the truth or the lie that had just been thrown at me to swallow, hook, line and sinker.

'What is Atlantis?' he challenged me, his voice hardening.

'I don't know.'

'You knew at the symposium.'

'I knew at the start. Not the finish.'

'And at the start. What *is* Atlantis?'

'An idyllic island... Socrates has asked the symposiasts to consider what might constitute the perfect society, the ideal republic...'

His eyes were shining now, urging, coaxing me to see the truth that had just opened up like one of those paper flower buds, tossed into water.

'So Atlantis is what?' he demanded ruthlessly.

I closed my eyes. 'Atlantis is *what*?' he repeated.

'A metaphor. A code word.'

'Yes,' he said in grim satisfaction, his eyes narrowing. 'That is exactly what it is.'

I swallowed hard as the implications swept over me.

Everyone knew the symposiasts had gloriously improbable dreams for the island. It wasn't just talk. They planted trees. Taught philosophy to the children of poor fishermen and farmers. Gave homes to stray dogs. Treated the sick, all hours of the day and night, no matter how poor or penniless. They dreamed of stone amphitheatres, academies, windmills, and where the regime in Athens was concerned, something else. Sedition. Revolution.

'You must keep the secret from the others,' he cautioned me, 'that is what I meant. At least for now. They would not understand, and we cannot afford to let the discovery of Atlantis slip to the public. Not yet.'

'Of course,' I mumbled.

'Then you begin to see. That there is far more to be lost here than a dream, a career, a job, even liberty. Lives are at stake. Remember that. Yes, including our own. Do you understand?'

I nodded.

'So you swear.'

'I swear.'

I stepped out of the hut and into the compound, and felt it sweeping over me with nauseous intimacy, a loneliness as deep and frigid as the fading universe up there. With that oath, I had become a stranger to everyone, even my own friends.

24.

The students were wriggling out of their tents, throwing on clothes, showering at the wash house cisterns. Picking up a coffee at the mess, I found a quiet corner to sit, my head still ringing from everything I had seen and heard. Lies, truths, moments of candour or cunning, who could tell. I saw contradictions everywhere. At the dig. In the things he told me. In the volatile moods that took him.

A man of high principles all right, even if nobody knew what they were, or what god or demon they served.

Dawn appeared in a delirious vermillion sky, throwing the mountain into stark silhouette. Bathed in that lurid glow, it struck me and struck me hard.

Who is Marcus James Huxley anyway? Finally confronted point blank, I really had to admit. I had no idea.

I knew nothing about him. Nothing about his personal life. Nothing about his previous digs or discoveries.

I swore at my own stupid recklessness, the way I had lunged at the job with both desperate hands. Swore at the florid image of Heaven, bobbing in front of my eyes, spluttering his pious admonishments about accepting jobs from strangers: 'You'll come unstuck, my lad, you just see if you don't!'

There had been that unearthly rush to get me onto the night train to Dover. No time to get to the reference library in Stratford, just to double-check, just to be sure. Just as Svetlana Bé had so patronizingly announced at the Garden House Hotel, the few words laying it on as thick as Cornish cream, a well-funded international dig, archaeologists with impeccable credentials.

Barely enough time to pick up the phone, call Aberdeen, find Ms. Summers in the staff room, in a fluster to get to class, warbling her congratulations... *Yes, but you do know him, you have heard of him?* She's conferring with a colleague in the jam-packed corridor. Yes, they know him, they know the name...

Or maybe they think they should... Fuck.

Well, we would see about that, I thought grimly, crossing the compound. It was time to act.

Making an early start, I collected my gear from the lock-ups and began my rounds, fact-finding for the daily log. Visiting the teachers and students in the trenches or among the half-excavated shells of houses, it was easy to pretend I was just passing the time of day. I'd toss them some casual remark about Huxley's time at Cambridge, or about his accent that nobody could quite place, thinking they'd soon be spilling everything they knew about him. All I would have to do is connect the dots.

But by the mid-morning coffee break, I had to face the fact that I was getting nowhere. Huxley's workforce either knew as little as I, or had mouths as tight as winter clams. Collecting their hardhats and other gear from the lock-ups, Nestor's moles wouldn't even talk about their progress drilling shafts into the tephra, much less betray any insight into the big boss himself.

During the lunch break, I slipped into the study hut and began trawling through the rows of reference books and classical encyclopaedias lining the back wall. Pulled out the Archaeological Biographies directory, turned to 'H'. Nothing. Not a single line.

For a life already half a century old, it seemed odd, and scarcely credible, that my boss had barely left a mark. If I was to believe the emptiness where the answers should have been, he had no family ties, no home town and no clutter of possessions to cling to. Even the house at Monolithos had apparently been rented from a local, now an émigré in Astoria, New York.

Hadrian recited a few academic papers Huxley had written, implying, I don't know why, that I was taking things far too seriously. It was high time I took everything about Huxley with a large grain of salt, he added, just like the rest of us. He lives to flummox the mind, to make it run the steeplechase of provocative ideas, to make it sweat, haven't I told you that already?

You have to be more discreet, I chided myself, casting a wary glance at the fragments hut while moving on to my next best candidate, Anna. Supposedly Huxley's friend, and maybe more, for the better part of fifteen years. She would be sure to know something of his past.

I found her in the site office with Maria, trying to make sense out of Huxley's muddled accounting, invoices, receipts, taxes, credits, debits.

'He is the most impractical man I have ever met!' she exclaimed to the ceiling in sudden exasperation. 'Even a child would have a better head for figures!'

Maria was slitting open envelopes, airmail mostly, and cheques, banknotes, sometimes even coins were spilling out over the trestle tables.

'Look at all this money!' she cried. 'What am I to do with it?'

'Bank it,' Anna replied firmly. 'If people wanted to make a donation, they should have sent it to the Foundation in Paris, not here.'

She uttered another exasperated sigh.

'Perhaps that's how he was brought up,' I ventured. 'With the classics uppermost in mind, I mean, not maths, not bookkeeping, that sort of thing.'

I half expected them to chase me out of the office, but instead became a convenient distraction from their own purgatory.

'I suppose you could say he swept me off my feet,' said Anna, gurgling on the dregs of an iced coffee through a paper straw. She caught my look. 'No, Nico, not like that! A different kind of passion altogether. The way he could make dusty ruins and relics come alive; it was the first time I had experienced anything like it. Almost as if those places, and the people and trees and animals that populated them, had always been living there, beyond our capacity to sense them. Somehow, he lifted the fog from my eyes.'

That's right, I thought, he puts the colours, sounds, scents into your head. Makes the temple priestess, the saffron pickers, the fishermen come alive. How benign she makes it sound. Moments that catch you off guard, plunge you into the vivid evocation he offers of a life that should be dead. A few short delirious seconds plunging you into another world.

'You joined him on a dig, but you knew nothing about him.'

A curious glance. 'I did. Do you expect to know a friend before they become a friend? Of course not.'

'But he never says anything about himself,' I objected. 'Nothing about his past.'

'Marcus might say you're demanding his history because you're too afraid of losing your own...'

I stood my ground. 'If personal history is so unimportant to him, then why was I prodded and probed for every last shred of mine during my interview, tell me that.'

Obviously lost for an answer, she flipped the accusation back in my face. 'Why shouldn't he live without a history if that is what he wants? Why shouldn't he liberate himself from the past?'

'What about you? Is that what you have done?'

She considered the question with a frown, then said: 'Weeks into our new dig, I realised something, something about myself. *Do you see it, Anna? I said. You are becoming flesh and blood again. For longer than you can remember you've been alive only in name, your heart ticking like a hollow clock. It's years since you've seen beauty like this, no, years since you let it enter you, let it take you...*'

'You were already here then, breaking ground on the dig?'

'No. That was thirteen years ago. Not long after Marcus and I first met at a roadside coffee shop in Alexandria, hardly able to hear ourselves think over the traffic and the street hawkers and the beggars.'

'Egypt? You were in Egypt together? Where was the dig?'

'The Nile Delta. Sais. Looking for the grave and temple of Osiris.'

'That's the temple that Solon visited, isn't it?' I said, feeling the blood thrumming in my throat. 'That's where he met the priest, the one who told him about Atlantis.... Did you find it?'

'No. Smugglers and traffickers had been there long before us. Even the older mud brick buildings had been torn apart by farmers, crumbled and scattered over the land as fertiliser.'

'Who was Osiris?' piped Maria.

'God of the Dead,' said Anna, and as she caught Maria's shiver of disgust, added: 'But not only. As ruler of the Underworld, it was his radiant power that granted all life to the world above, bringing the annual flood of the Nile, the greening vegetation, the flowers, the migrating birds. I suppose you could say he was the god of life *and* death.'

By the time I clocked out, I grudgingly had to admire the efficiency with which Huxley had covered his tracks, having successfully convinced everyone that his personal history was either none of their business or the pursuit of fools intent on smothering their own potential.

I was just about to head home when I caught sight of Nestor in the student camp, distributing letters and parcels from the tailgate of the jeep out of a huge postal sack. Mail call. The sight set my teeth on edge immediately. Almost three months and still no letters from home.

'Anything for me?' I yelled, to which Nestor tossed his head in his best fatalistic 'no'.

I couldn't believe it and spent the next 5 minutes calling the Hellenic Postal Service every fucking name under the sun.

Enough was enough. I couldn't wait any longer.

And so on my way home I dropped in at the telephone exchange, and after waiting half an hour in the sweat and smoke and one-way conversations bellowed over the sea, squeezed into the single booth at the end of the counter. Dialled half the number. Got an engaged tone. Dialled the number again, almost getting to the last digit before the line went beep-beeping engaged again; who knows where, Syros, Athens, Morteon-in-Marsh or just the exchange with its octopus tentacle plugs behind the counter, the eccentric Toula shrieking into the mouthpiece to get people on the phone, off the phone, patching them in, cutting them off, eavesdropping intently on any gossip that takes her fancy.

Finally, it's ringing. *Ring ring. Ring ring.* Nobody home. *Ring ring.* Then a click. 'Hello?'

'*Sofi?*'

'Nico!' The voice is urgent, relieved, angry, and so faint, so distant it really is like we're yelling across the sea.

'Where have you been? What are you doing? We've been worried sick. We must have written a dozen times!'

'What?' Silence, just sea static as the waves swept over me. 'But my letters. What about mine. I wrote every week.'

'We didn't get one letter, Nico. Not one. Mum's going to kill you. If you don't kill her with worry first. She even wanted to call the Foreign Office!'

You must forget the past and everything it has made of you. You must be prepared to leave everything behind and let go, let go.

I was bent over double in the *plateia* outside, gasping for breath, fighting the cramps in my stomach, thinking I'm going to vomit blood. Nondas the barber called out to me from his shop along the street. 'Nico. What's up? Are you all right? Come inside, sit down. I've got no customers.'

Vigorously, I shook my head. 'I'm all right.'

He nodded uncertainly, and I could see the look imprinted there. Maybe he should tell his good friend, Marcus.

And that's where I was now. Cornered. Trapped. Eight hours ago I had been the loneliest guy in camp because I'd sworn that solemn oath to Huxley that I'd keep everything to myself, I wouldn't confide in another living soul. Now I was the loneliest guy in camp because there was no one I *could* confide in, no one I *could* trust.

I mean even if his secret was true, even if it was the biggest, brashest, most golden Holy Grail of a secret in the whole wide world, even if he was guarding it with his life, and expected me to do so as well, was this justifiable behaviour. Was it?

Half an hour later I was stuffed into the phone cabin again, smoothing things over with Mum, until finally the incompetent, indolent, corrupt Hellenic Post had become our bloodied scapegoat.

'Wait,' I said, just as we were about to hang up. 'Put Sofi on again.'

Making me promise to call every Sunday, there was a rustling as she passed the receiver.

'Sofi? You wouldn't like a trip up to London would you?'

No need to explain. Sofi had been reading between the lines from the beginning. We had been finishing each other's thoughts and sentences since we were kids.

'You want to know more about him, don't you. Biography, background, that sort of thing.'

'I should have —'

'Done it before leaving. You were always too impetuous for your own good, Nico. Too trusting.'

'I'll call you in a week,' I said.

'All right.' Pausing just to say, 'Just be careful, Nico.'

I was glad to get home without meeting anyone I knew.

My head was like a grey storm-tossed sea. Waves breaking over my head. Visibility zero.

Just before I fell asleep flat on my face, the image came welling into my mind, I don't know why. Benja, that silver drachma on his tongue to pay the Ferryman. Extravagant, said Sam, in that dangerous, taunting way of his. Charon must have been well pleased with your generosity, Huxley, when a bronze obol would have done just as well...

What did he mean by that? I don't know. *Think! What happened to the people who couldn't afford the crossing, those who died where they fell, without the proper rites?* They were left on the nearside shore, neither dead nor alive. *But that wasn't Benja, was it.*

I sprang awake at the crack of dawn, dream silhouettes still leaving their ghost trails in my eyes. The stinking river Styx, its cackling reeds whispering the names of the dead. Charon punting his way towards me through the swirling mist, his black cowl like the mouth of a bottomless cavern where all light and life must be devoured.

I staggered into the kitchen for coffee. No milk. No bread. Nothing! Fuck! I ploughed everything off the table, books, letter paper, envelopes, coffee mug, crashing to the floor. Now after my stupid fit of rage, I didn't have a coffee mug either.

I took a deep breath instead, thinking of Sofi, thinking of the plan. I would get to the bottom of it. I would.

Head still in a fog, I set off for work, dashing out of the front door — only to go sprawling headlong into the street, thrown by a teetering stack of books and paper.

I spotted a handwritten note, and reached for it. 'For perusal at your leisure, Mr Pedrosa.'

In a nervous daze, I gathered up the scattered paper — all of which, I quickly realised, had only one real subject. Him, himself. Standard scientific tracts in obscure academic journals, personal reminiscences mimeographed onto sheets of foolscap, thin monographs on epigraphic interpretation of arcane ancient inscriptions, brief columns in the popular press — each and every item bore some relation to the great archaeologist himself, his life, his opinions, his career.

The discovery filled me with sudden dread. So, too, the mental image of him stealing up to my door in the dead of night. I broke into a cold sweat and could feel the blood surging in my ears. There could be no doubt as to the motive, nor the deeper implications.

'Does he have everyone in his pocket?' I ranted, throwing his paper life onto the kitchen floor. 'Everyone on this whole stinking island? Is no one beyond reach?'

25.

As their faces ebbed and flowed through my mind, I realised the hideous truth of it. They were all under his spell in one way or another. All of them. Even Sam in his sulky rebellion. Even Hadrian, in his cast iron conviction that nothing exists beyond that which can be seen and measured. Anna, in her magic carpet way of seeing the best in everyone. The symposiasts, blithely swimming in the blue bubbling waters of his charisma. That island he holds out to them like a vision in the sky, devoted to philosophy, to invention, to the goodness of the human heart.

Over his ritual morning coffee with the postmaster, broaching the disagreeable subject with a wince, letters going astray in the mail, *for the cause Vassilis, you understand, our enemies are at the gates.*

I threw what was left of my coffee mug at the wall. Fucker.

As far as manipulation went, he was obviously a master of the dark arts. Friend or foe, Huxley had virtually everyone exactly where he wanted them, pieces moving across the chess board according to the strategy of the game he himself had devised.

Even the Papás, with his uncompromising opposition to everything Huxley did and stood for. What did it matter, when half the island or more relied on Huxley to put food on the table, muleteers, shopkeepers, the crews of the freight caïques, the labourers who shifted his moon dust? Even the chief of police and his constable, blundering about and making fools of themselves, thereby reinforcing his own innocence. Check and checkmate.

Coming on a nauseous wave, I realised I was no different. I, too, had become a sightless pawn in his mysterious game, falling into the same squares as Benja before me, like it or not.

I began throwing my things into a suitcase. The *Pegasus* would sail for Piraeus at dawn, and I intended to be on it.

I imagined myself on board, cutting a dawn orange wake towards the north, leaving behind forever that viscous air of myth that permeated everything here, as though objective truth had yet to be invented.

But that, I realised, is exactly where he hid, in the tremulous space between fact and unreality. Like other human frailties that he so skilfully manipulated, leaving barely a fingerprint to incriminate himself, superstition, fear of the unknown, aided and abetted him.

Ghosts. Ancient apparitions. Peasants kissing their blue eye amulets, and spitting in the eye of the Devil that wore Huxley's face. If not contaminating the evidence against him with absurdity, the same atavistic terror was probably a better deterrent to would-be tomb robbers than buckshot or razor wire. Who knows, possibly rivals in his own criminal racket. It was no wonder Sarrides and Guirand were having such a hard time making charges stick.

But that, in turn, raised its own question, the biggest one of all. What had driven him to create or exploit these multiple layers of deception? What was he too afraid for us to see? That he was a fraud and a charlatan? That he was so deeply involved in Benja's death he could hear the eternal echo of the prison door slamming shut?

In passing, I shuffled through the articles and cuttings littering the floor, the sneer already there on my face to greet his privileged upbringing in Cambridge, glowing tributes to a distinguished academic career, records of accomplishments on this or that archaeological dig.

Yet the more I flicked through the pages in front of me, the more obvious it became that Huxley was none of the things I had imagined him to be.

Rather than accomplishment and fame, his professional life had been dogged by obscurity, failure and controversy in equal measure.

One cutting, already two decades old, described him as an archaeologist of fading promise who would probably never fulfil his potential. Others portrayed him as a maverick, too keen to take risks, too liable to make rash assumptions.

Relentless pursuit of what lesser mortals might consider mere hunch, countered another, is the hallmark of archaeological greatness. Amongst the brightest luminaries it is precisely this ruinous single-mindedness, this incandescent vision, that ultimately unearths ancient cities and civilisations, treasures that have lain buried for thousands of years. The timid and the fainthearted need not apply... Success alone, apparently, would turn these insufferable egoists into heroes.

The photograph accompanying the piece showed Huxley on some sandy windswept dig, the jaw just as defiant as it was today, though without the lines and the grey. He looked almost youthful.

All in all, the judgment against him was damning, and I could hardly believe he had been able to restrain his notorious pride enough to thrust this stuff under my nose like this.

Though I hardly realised it, I was now sitting on the painted cement floor, Huxley's bared life scattered all around me.

Scrapbook photographs, the sepia tones betraying their age. Reminiscences penned in the hand of a child, the letters still bearing the same hopeful, demanding loops his handwriting showed today.

At first, the photograph threw me. I could see the resemblance in the eyes, in the jutting jaw. The figure appeared to be Huxley himself, standing on a dilapidated loggia between Indian rattan furniture, waiting irritably for the camera. But then I realised: this must have been taken forty years ago. The man in the threadbare jacket was not Huxley at all. It was his father. Had it not been for that curious trick of time, I might have missed something altogether more astonishing: the dog collar around his neck.

I riffled through the other photographs, and the captions and diary entries that accompanied them, some barely legible.

The boy had been dragged along in his father's footsteps to some of the most remote and untamed reaches on earth. Jungle tribes in southeast Asia, desert nomads on the Horn of Africa, poverty stricken slum-dwellers scattered across the Indian subcontinent. At one time or another, they had all born witness to this thickset missionary stumbling into their lives with a book of psalms in his hand, a glazed look in his eye, and a bewildered little boy at his heels.

Even the son, apparently, could offer no convincing explanation for the father's decision to relinquish his Devon parish, desert his wife of 15 years and head into the wilderness, intent on bringing salvation to the lost tribes.

A Calling, the father maintained, the crystal vision of it visiting him in a dream.

It was the last that Huxley ever saw of his mother.

If he grieved over her death, or pondered the psychology that hastened it as surely as a razorblade to a vein, he made no mention of it. But even in my inexpert way of reading between the lines, it was difficult to escape the impression that this was less a journey of edification imposed upon the boy than a kidnapping.

No wonder Huxley the Younger had come to despise the Church, I thought, its God having substituted in his father's once reassuringly parochial figure, a complete stranger.

He attended school in India, but travelled widely through the sub-continent. He was pictured wearing khaki fatigues and a pith helmet in the jungles of Borneo. Another captured him in the streets of Mandalay, standing among a fleet of bicycles, a golden stupa at his back.

He was barely 16 when he escaped his father's clutches, and in circumstances conspicuous for their absence on paper.

He made his way north, up from the desert shores of Tamil Nadu, into Kerala.

Every tortuous, sweat-caked mile on the road was another mile separating him from his past. The past, he writes, that must cease to exist if the future is to be born.

To the boy's mind, it possessed a magic every bit as dark as the spells and curses that shamans concocted in the jungle villages he passed through. It didn't even matter if this sorcery was objectively real or not, he realised. To succeed, it required only belief, the submission of the victim's mind to a state of unreality. Which begs the question, writes the boy, the words dashing onto the paper in a scrawl lest the realisation desert him midway between thought and ink, what state of unreality does my mind now unquestioningly obey? What is it that lies beyond this state of morbid trance? Knowing that it is ever present, what is to stop us lifting ourselves above it, breaking the spell? To emerge from the primeval mud in which we still wallow, our actions dictated not by the power of logic as our vanity would have us believe, but by unconscious impulses, emotions, shadows of the past.

Among the ancient ruins at Hyderabad, Huxley found his mentor, a young, bespectacled archaeologist of Swedish descent, Lars Petersen.

Huxley divulges little about the man or his curious family, perhaps because he was still stumbling out of the ruins of his own past, along with the idea that falsehoods can only be perpetrated against a mind that is not free of attachment.

Petersen appears to have treated him like a son nonetheless, his Hindu wife too, and of the loose snapshots wedged into the scrapbook spine, the one that is most striking of all shows Huxley at the dinner table with his six newfound siblings, kids with wide eyes, chocolate skin and straw blond hair.

As any archaeologist must who is worth his salt, Petersen prided himself as a free thinker, a nonconformist, and in that potted description of the man, I could at least detect something of his that had made its mark on Huxley. His own sons and daughters evincing neither the enthusiasm nor the aptitude for anything more ancient than yesterday, he took the young Huxley under his wing, teaching him everything he knew on the Ganges dig.

Six years later, having won a scholarship to King's, that tutelage saw him board a steamer for Portsmouth. He was on his way, apparently destined for great things.

Huxley, craving fame, craving recognition — is that what all this was about? Satisfying an all-devouring ego?

At least it added up. In a way, it was what we were all working for when you thought about it, his labourers shifting ash, his archaeologists in the trenches, me with my black book keeping the record of events. Lifting the legend that would make his name.

Any obstacle to that life-and-death ambition, ruthlessly swept aside. People who had outlived their usefulness, forgotten. Like his father. Like the Petersens. Like the dead or murdered Benja.

I ran down to Katina's for my ticket, the corner shop next to the church, a grocer's, ironmonger's, chandler's, shoe shop and more, all rolled into one. Sacks of dry beans and grain lining the floor, along with farm tools, fishing tackle, boat anchors, mops and buckets. Salted fish impaled on a line of hooks, fly paper coiling down beside them, still beaded with last summer's vile catch.

A huge ledger at her fingertips, Katina stood behind the counter in her grubby smock, totting up debts, interest and repayments due in her money-lending scheme, the familiar look of weary suffering in her eyes.

She tossed her head, clicked her tongue, the Pan-Hellenic sign language for *no*. 'No ship, Nikos,' she said. 'Ship broken. Maybe ship next week.'

It was not until six the next morning that I realised the extent of their deceit. Still half asleep, I happened to glance out of the window as I put the kettle on the stove. And there she was; the *Pegasus*, steaming north, laying a streamer of cloud across the dawn sky.

I could hardly believe it. *He is keeping you here against your will!* I shouted to myself, my fist punching the wall, breaking skin, leaking blood. Despite a wild urge to fight it out with him, I bit my tongue, knowing that this latest accusation, like all the others, sounded even less plausible when spoken out loud.

For seven more days until the *Pegasus* returned, I would watch and wait. I would play him at his own game, challenging every claim and every assumption. I would turn detective myself since there was no one else even remotely competent to do so. Instead of ancient potsherds, I'd be piecing together fragments of evidence, piece by piece.

Murder, smuggling, fraud. Whatever he was up to. Given half the chance, I would make him pay, I would prove his guilt.

26.

I reported for work as usual, just hoping to keep my cool.

Summer was almost upon us. Above our heads, the arid sky held a premonition of drought. From the parched fields and the wiry trees, the cicadas had already commenced their ratcheting chorus. Of the grass and wildflowers born of the spring rains, nothing much remained, just a few thistle-dry leaves shrinking into the dust.

As the scrap metal gates swung open, I saw Huxley disappear into the fragments hut, the absorbed look on his face now seen for exactly what it was: lust for the recognition and acclaim that had so long eluded him. Living with that sense of failure year after year, perhaps he didn't even notice the rancid stench of it anymore, like old sweat.

I slammed the steering wheel in triumph.

Of course! That's why he talked about death all the time. Not just because, as he liked to pretend, archaeology can never escape the tomb, nor the passing of civilisations. As the unmasked author of the *Travels*, he knew better than that.

If anything, the answer lay in the book's obsession with immortality, with afterlife. That mania for islands of timeless legend, Atlantis, the Elysian archipelago, islands levitating over the sunset. It was all about thought transcending matter, ideas cheating death. It was all about Huxley himself gaining immortality, not for his soul or his body, but for his mind. That one great discovery that children would be learning about a thousand years from now. A sepulchre where devotees would still bring flowers. A pigeon-spattered statue in a London park.

Starting my rounds I headed for the ridge, where Anna, Hadrian and Sam were working in the shadow of house 16, fussing over an elaborate array of clay water channels, feeding the buried streets beyond.

With the prime suspect nowhere in sight, I began my investigation, approaching them one at a time as I always did, crouching down at eye level, sometimes even sliding down into the trench beside them. The clipboard forms and logbook were useful props, allowing me to take notes and formulate questions even as I followed the usual drill.

'The scaffolding lurched away from the wall,' Anna recalled, adjusting her headscarf and wiping the sweat from her brow. 'There was a splintering of wood, a crash, then a great cloud of dust.'

At least the intervening months had healed the rawness of the wound, I reflected. When I'd asked the same question back in March, the pain, the trauma, the reluctance to talk, had been all too obvious.

'You said there was an odd look on his face as he fell,' I reminded her. 'I suppose it must have been fear, alarm, the sudden shock of falling.'

Casting a wistful look up at the lava-scorched walls and repaired scaffolding, she said at length, 'No. Something else. I saw it only for an instant, but...'

'But what?'

'It was the way he flew out from the scaffolding... Not like someone who stumbles and falls, but rather, like someone who takes a leap.'

Astonished by the implication, I said: 'You're saying he jumped?'

'I don't know, Nico. Even after seeing the scene replay a thousand times in my head, I still can't grasp it. The thing that haunts me most was the look in his eyes as they pulled the boards and scaffolding off him. I don't know... something like serenity, something like... *deliverance*.'

Deliverance from what? Or from whom.

'I know what you're thinking,' she put in quickly. 'That perhaps he had a death wish. Well, to the best of my knowledge, he did not. What I can say is that death was on his mind, maybe more than it should have been — what do you expect when he was Marcus' shadow day and night?'

So Anna's implying it was suicide, I thought, but without really wanting to say so outright. Why the reluctance? A throwback to her upbringing in rural Italy, perhaps, where suicide is not so much a tragedy as a mortal sin. Or maybe because it would reflect badly on those closest to him, those who might have saved him.

'An interesting theory, Master Pedrosa,' said Hadrian, in that pompous way of his, his florid face appearing over the lip of a neighbouring trench. 'As long as one refuses to countenance the alternative — that he jumped not to *kill* but to *save* himself as the scaffolding gave way.'

One trench over, Sam heaved himself up on dust- and sweat-plastered arms. 'Why not ask who can account for their movements,

Nicky? Who has their alibi?' The devilish look said it all.

I saw Anna stiffen, her mouth forming a thin, cross line. 'That's enough, Sam.'

When the fragments hut door slammed, my heart leapt into my mouth. Luckily, it was only Maria, on some errand for Huxley, but the shock served as a timely reminder of the risks I was running.

Worse still, this was not what I had intended at all, the exchanges becoming too blunt, too loud, all pretence at casualness already blown to pieces.

Still, what choice did I have. There would never be an opportunity like this again.

'But you said Huxley was furious, that he came striding over even before the dust had settled, more worried by the disruption than the casualties.'

'Yes, of course,' said Anna, and I could tell by her sudden eagerness that, to her mind, the shock and bluster were proof of innocence.

'Why can't you just admit that Huxley was standing right there on the scaffold,' taunted Sam. 'Right behind Benja, moments before he fell.'

If looks could kill, Sam would surely have fallen dead on the spot. We had obviously reached the limits of Hadrian's willingness to exercise the mind.

'That's a careless insinuation,' he spluttered. 'He might have been there, five or ten minutes before the fall. There is nothing suspicious about that. Nothing at all.'

'How would you know?' came the insolent reply. 'You weren't even here. You were in Athens, then on the boat — as it happens, with golden boy's brand new replacement here —'

'If anything,' said Hadrian, forcing his words between Sam's, 'it was negligence. You know how he has the labourers racing the clock. More likely than not, the scaffolding had never been erected properly. Mark my words, it was an accident waiting to happen.'

But that too was a careless insinuation, Hadrian not even realising that Huxley's site foreman was within earshot at the nearest wall. Nestor Louganis, the man who prided himself on solving any engineering challenge the camp could throw at him.

'There was nothing wrong with the scaffold,' he bristled. 'I saw to it myself. If you believe the sun will come up tomorrow morning, believe that.'

How different he is to the others, I thought, all manual labour and practicality, technical schematics, pulleys and buzz saws, not trowels and tweezers, not ancient riddles.

As he stepped forward, hands thrust deep into his pockets, his elongated-shadow darted over us in the trenches. 'Better ask why he was at the doctor's every other week,' he added grimly, 'getting his tablets. Didn't you know he'd been complaining of dizzy spells for weeks? No, I thought as much.'

By the midmorning coffee break, my head was spinning. So contradictory were their recollections of events, it seemed scarcely credible that they had been in the same place at the same time.

Benja had been murdered, the scaffolding sabotaged. He had taken his own life, diving off the platform in a moment of light devouring despair. He had tumbled to his death, not the victim of a freak accident, but of negligence. He had been cheated out of life by illness, vertigo striking just at the wrong moment, the weight of his falling body pulling down the scaffold with him.

Everyone had a different story, a different interpretation of events. Even Maria, drinking me in with those sultry eyes in the site office, saying something about Benja befriending Aris, about the young fisherman's stump-armed father with the gunpowder temper, and his rabid hatred of the foreigners who were running all over the island, buying the Greek soul with coin. Alone with Maria, I always found it difficult to concentrate, if you know what I mean, my imagination running away with her.

How can everyone have seen something different? I thought, on the verge of tearing my hair out by the roots. It's as if the facts are only as objective as their inconsistencies and contradictions allow.

But then it struck me. It was all smoke and mirrors, and was meant to be, even if the others didn't realise it.

It can hardly have been coincidence, can it, that the reports of my eyewitnesses were the spitting image of Huxley himself and his own contradictions. Contradictions that would spell madness to anyone in their right mind.

How else would you describe a man who despises fate yet believes himself destined for great things? Who speaks of freewill while enslaving others to his dreams. Who demands the truth beyond appearances while using every means to disguise, distort and hide it from the rest of us. Was this the psychology of a sane man?

27.

Knowing I would have to face him sooner or later, I nudged open the fragments hut door.

Face in partial eclipse, his floodlit hands fussed over the mind-boggling jigsaw littering the tabletop... Fragments of gods and animals, mountains and busy market streets, philosophers, artisans, fishermen.

He glanced up as I approached, his face as inert as stone. Not one word or giveaway look about the cuttings dumped on my doorstep, about the letters intercepted in the post, about the dirty little trick to keep me here.

Waiting in ambush, the words leapt out of the shadows. 'It's time we turned detective, Mr Pedrosa, wouldn't you say?'

A tremor ran through me, cold, electric.

It's almost as if he realises everything before it happens. Reading the mind, reading the mood, effortlessly pre-empting anyone who might act against him.

I stifled a sigh of relief, the panic in my gut doubling back on itself. *No. He's talking about his forensic investigation, that's all. The unexplained hours before the holocaust.*

Abruptly, he stood, slamming the table with his fist so hard that the fragments jumped. Exasperated, he swept them aside with his arm, instantly destroying any semblance of order his jigsaw-building might have accomplished.

'Where are we going?' I called after him. But he was already marching through the compound, and I was scrambling to catch up, curious and rattled in equal measure.

'I want your eyes, your ears, any vestigial sixth sense you might still possess.'

If not for the flint in his voice, I might have taken it for sarcasm. But this much I did know: it was always on his mind, an obsession bordering on fixation. His conviction that the missing fragment is there, right in front of your nose, unseen, invisible, stealing camouflage from the things around it; sometimes, even from the assumptions in your own head.

We came to Huxley's field tent with its gleaming samovar and saffron awning, but kept on walking. We threaded our way between the dunes until even the droning conveyor belts fell silent.

'You haven't told me anything about Benja,' I said, as we passed under the scaffolding of house 16.

'There is nothing to tell,' he snapped.

'He was your apprentice. Did he fail you in some way, is that it? Like Sam…'

'It was I who showed Benja he could lift himself above the fog,' he replied, the boast all the more offensive because its focus was dead. 'It was I who made him realise he could become more than he was or what the world wanted him to be.'

'And did he?'

'Only so far,' he conceded through clenched teeth. 'In the end, you might say he had no head for heights.'

Flooded by afternoon light, the houses on temple hill were looming up before us like some apparition from the sky.

I couldn't help thinking, soon we'd be out of earshot and no one would come running however loud the cry for help. At least I was a match for him physically, but mentally…

Onto the pathway, our feet touching ancient milled stone. Past the petrified tree stumps, over the river bridge, to the first of the shopfronts. I was fighting him every step of the way, the silent tension between us seemingly raw enough to tear muscle, snap bone. I was aware of his eyes upon me, remorseless, hypnotic.

Any second now it would come welling out of blue air, I was sure of it, first that tuning fork whine on my eardrums, then the trees in the wind, the birdsong, the splashing water, the voices walking through us. And then in their gathering wake, that impossibly beguiling sensation of mind existing beyond the physical confines of the body. Of time, obeying other laws than we are accustomed to.

I gritted my teeth, scowled. Somehow, he was making me feel these things. He was making them happen, I just knew it.

The summer sun wasn't helping either, dazzling the eyes, melting thoughts, burning deliriously into the skin.

What's that? The sound of flowing water over the shallows, almost musical… There it is again, unmistakable, the fitful breeze amplifying the notes like a wind chime. Now I pause mid-stride, trying to catch it above my own thumping heartbeat. Eyes sweeping over the hill, over the medieval terraced fields, down the escarpment towards the cliffs. Where's it coming from?

There!

A flock of goats, that's all, crossing a distant stony ridge, their faint tinkling bells imitating water.

I heaved a sigh of relief, and was only puzzled by the hollow emotion that was left high and dry in its wake... something like *disappointment*.

Rounding the western edge of temple hill, we passed Nestor's graveyard of broken machinery. Rubble-littered slopes giving way underfoot and almost impossible to climb, conveyor belts, rusting tractors with crooked wheels and bug-eyed headlamps. Teetering stacks of corrugated iron, and wooden packing crates.

'Nestor's moles have been in there for weeks, haven't they?' I blurted, impetuosity getting the better of me. 'Digging by day. Digging by night. Covering their tracks when Sarrides and Guirand were here. What's in there. What are you hiding?' I was pushing my luck, I know.

Abruptly, he scrambled down the slope, and was soon picking his way between the barbed wire.

We edged along a steep shaft cut through the tephra, its friable walls leading to the exposed top floor window of another townhouse.

He fished a torch out of his pocket, stooping gingerly as he ducked under the supporting timbers. Chutes of dust cascaded down over our shoulders. Mindful of the risk, he then darted through into the relative safety of the house itself. I jumped after him, instantly finding myself in the pitch dark. I heard him shaking the torch, its feeble beam struggling against the blackness with all the power of a candle against the stars.

The air so musty, so ancient it crosses your mind to ask if it still remembers the day the world ended.

Huxley whacked the torch against his hand and it obediently brightened. As he did so, the frescoes leapt out at us, the torch's silver reflector casting odd ribs of animating light and shadow.

Too shocked to blink, I just stood there mute and staring, my racing pulse in a turmoil of adolescent emotions.

'Analysis, Mr Pedrosa.'

Fighting the dryness on my tongue, I said, 'It's obvious isn't it?'

Two young fishermen at the water's edge, stark naked, arms draped lazily over each other's shoulders.

A doe-eyed girl at the village fountain, meadow wildflowers at her summer bare breasts.

Fisher boy and doe-eyed girl under the waterfall, lips, fingers exploring the drenched sensuality of each other's glistening bare skin. It went on like that, wall to wall, room to room. In every possible mind-bending, body-contorting combination. Boys and girls in sexual awakening. Alone, together. Girl with boy and boy with boy with girl. Who could keep track? Licking, tasting, taking each other in the mouth, between the legs, anywhere. If anything had been left to the imagination, I wasn't aware of it, that's for sure.

Hanging from one of the struts at the doorway he found a gas lantern, and lit it.

'So that is all you see?' he demanded scathingly, as the mantle hissed and bathed us in its trembling glow. 'Only that which offends you?'

'It doesn't offend me.'

It was something else. Something that doesn't even share the same language or reality. Hiding in that sense of claustrophobia, of sweet entrapment, almost overwhelming.

'Well?' demanded my tormentor. 'Then what is it that your logic tells you?'

'There's something about them...' I began, struggling for the form beyond the image. 'At first they seem erotic, pornographic even, it's true, but then —'

'But then you perceive something beyond the pigment or the composition. It is the mind of the fresco painter himself, speaking to you.'

'No. It's something before him.'

'His inspiration, then, his muse... Then what is it that belies the carnal image? What aspect of soul or psyche has the wet pigment and plaster preserved?'

My eyes drifted to the young lovers on the mountaintop, where some ethereal essence of soul, or being, seemed to be flowing out into the firmament; or was it the other way around? I couldn't tell.

'There is a purity, an innocence, a naivety about them. The fresco painter wants to say... he wants to say love like this can become so pure it can achieve spiritual awakening.'

He grunted his approval, adding: 'And you wanted me to hand over these frescoes to the likes of Guirand and Sarrides? People who still believe Atlantis is myth, a sop for the gullible. Sarrides can count himself lucky he didn't have to explain them away to the Colonels, or the Bishops for that matter. They would have his head on a stick.'

Suddenly, he laughed out loud. 'Wouldn't you say that the lad over here bears a passing resemblance to our young ferryman, Aris?'

Caught by the hissing lamp and its magnifying ribs of light, the young fisherman seemed to spring out of the wall at us. Cast net slung over his shoulder, his lust for the girl at the well already in his eye, not to mention between his legs.

I mumbled something, neither here nor there, but secretly had to admit that there was a likeness, all the more troubling for my inability to explain it.

'And there, look!' he cried, evidently finding it very funny indeed. 'Isn't that Sam with the other fisher boy? And our very own Maria, finding love at the riverbank?'

It was getting unnerving. The more I stared, the more people I seemed to recognise in one way or another. Faces I had seen about camp, a look or facial expression that reminded me of someone from Moreton-in-Marsh, from college, even from the ship coming in.

Seeing Maria arched back like that over the warm stones, the water cascading all around her, I began to feel it in the swelling hardness between my legs, in the thirst of my tongue. The way that boy had her impaled on his thrusting cock like that, it's just…

'It's just a trick of the eye, that's all,' I snapped, retreating a few steps. 'Like seeing faces or animals in the clouds.'

He didn't reply, leaving the uncertainty hanging there in the breathless ancient air, no doubt deliberately. Abruptly, he ducked out of the house and into the dazzling sunlight. Alarmed at the shroud of darkness falling in his wake, I scrambled after him, experiencing a moment of sheer panic as I felt my way along the shaft.

Rubbing the dust out of my hair, I followed him down to the river bridge. There was an absent look in his eye, and for all I knew he was seeing the water cascade over the stones, fisher boy and doe-eyed girl walking barefoot through the leafy coolness of the riverbank trees.

'So now you begin to understand,' he said at last, in that voice as deep, as rich as honey. 'The discovery that will change our reality, shake the world awake.'

I shook my head uncertainly. 'No. Not really. At least…'

His voice tightened a notch. 'I will need your help if we are to accomplish this, Nicholas. Do you understand?'

I nodded. 'I suppose.'

He's lying to you, he doesn't even know what truth is!

But if it is true, if this is Atlantis, you'll be there, won't you. You'll be a part of its discovery...

'Now more than ever, I need you to be my eyes and ears in camp. There are people working against us, people who will stop at nothing to sabotage us. Do you understand?'

My eyes swept over the tent village, as though the wish alone might flush out the spies in Guirand's pay. One of the teachers, perhaps, or a student already selling his soul for the sake of his future career.

I nodded again. I could feel myself wavering, thinking he might just be telling the truth after all. *Fight him*, an inner voice shouted. *Do not let him get away with this!*

Silently, we made our way back to camp, passing the dock and the moored *Persephone* along the way. At the sight of Aris, sprawled lazily on deck, barely a stitch of clothing to his name, I swore under my breath.

After having his ancient likeness thrust into my face, doing things to girls and to boys that really belonged in the dark, if anywhere at all, I knew I'd never see him in quite the same way ever again.

28.

I was still living out of my suitcases as the days tumbled into July, all blue and sun-drenched. By rights I should have been feeling as carefree as the village kids splashing about in the sea, but couldn't shake the feeling that something bad was going to happen.

When on a Friday morning Huxley insisted that we abandon trench work for the beach, I knew there had to be an ulterior motive.

For one thing, Huxley never took days off. Even if he sometimes appeared to do so, his thoughts were always on duty, probing, intimidating the shadows, seeking advantage.

For another, what about his head-thumping deadlines at the dig? What about his earth-shattering discovery? After almost tearing out his hair over the missing fragments of evidence, absconding to the beach just didn't make any sense.

My suspicions spiked the moment I caught sight of the giant picnic basket loaded into the back of Huxley's white Land Rover. This was no spur of the moment thing, even if he would have preferred us to think so.

When no one was looking, I stole a glimpse into the hamper. Myroula had been busy. It was a feast fit for a king and made me wonder if he was already celebrating.

We jammed into the Land Rover, all seven us, Nestor and Maria included. Then set off for the black volcanic sands on the east coast, cicadas echoing hypnotically from the scrawny roadside trees, heat mirages forming over the dusty fields.

Along the way, we passed another of those garish billboards saluting the coup, this time with two real-life soldiers playing sentry against the phoenix rising. I couldn't help noticing both had fixed bayonets on their rifles, just as their billboard silhouette demanded.

'I trust the symposiasts are watching their tongues,' muttered Hadrian, as the soldiers followed us with listless eyes. 'It seems we are living in uncertain times.'

I caught Huxley's piercing glance in the rearview mirror, as though I alone were sharing his great coded secret. 'Oh, Papadopoulos and his henchmen will be gone by Christmas, Hadrian. Either that or they will learn to live by civilised standards. Tourists want to swim and sunbathe under eternal Greek skies, not under a military dictatorship.'

'How I admire your eternal optimism Huxley, when there could just as easily be civil war!'

'Can we please just enjoy the day!' protested Anna.

'The black sands will be a religious experience,' said Hadrian archly. 'Like walking over burning coals. Whose idea was it to go to the beach at this hour anyway, the sun beating down on our heads?' As if anyone had to ask.

Huxley said nothing but at the last minute veered north along the coast, bypassing the deserted, treeless beach below. I had to wonder how this change of plan would affect whatever little scheme he had cooked up for us.

A whirlwind of dust spinning up the coast behind us, on we drove, the track cutting through powdery fields of nest-shaped vines. Several twists and turns later, we drew up, brakes squealing. We were there.

I had only ever seen them from afar before, the white crystalline rock beds that undulate into the sea like petrified waves.

For once, everyone seemed satisfied, a not insignificant feat given the personalities involved. For the pale faces, a fortuitous brine tree had somehow managed to find purchase in a narrow crevice, spreading its weeping branches over the surrounding rock. For those who preferred the thrill of the somersault or the high dive, the three towering rock spires twisting into the air would doubtless prove too tempting to resist. Less adventurous souls could drift towards the edge of the rock beds themselves, where the lucent white waves turned from limestone into water. And there they could just slip into the sea, like two liquids intermingling with one another.

Huxley settled under the tamarisk, where the hamper had also found shade.

I changed into my swimming trunks, then found a place for my beach towel, close enough to keep him on watch, far enough away to escape his attentions.

Huxley lay back in the shadows, eyes so narrowed against the glare that sometimes I couldn't even tell what he was looking at, the week-old copy of *The Times* on his lap, or the formless horizon on the edge of the world where his ambitions lay.

Sometimes, I almost found it difficult to breathe, unable to evict the idea from my head that I was about to be trapped. *What was he doing?*

Another 15 minutes must have passed before I realised the truth. Behind those slit eyelids, he was studying the others intently, every move, reaction and interplay. Maria emerging from the sea like a glistening mermaid, Nestor in his sharp, almost splashless crawl across the bay, Sam in his daredevil jumps off the limestone spires, Anna swimming between ribs of light on the seabed. Hadrian, pottering along the shoreline, inspecting rock pools, his milky English skin already reddening under the fierce sun.

I wanted to shout at him. *Why aren't we digging, cataloguing, mapping, sorting?* But I bit my tongue, already knowing how useless it would be to confront him.

Instead, I lay back to catch the stray tamarisk shadows, watching the watcher.

Trying to beat him at his own game was far harder than I imagined. Facets and prisms of light scattering hypnotically over the water hardly helped matters and, in the end, I think I must have dozed off.

When I came to, it was to see a white caïque with sprit rig and burgundy sails come drifting towards us. Aris. Nearing the rock beds, he swung the tiller sharply with his bare foot. While the breathless sails flapped, the *Persephone* veered obediently to starboard, gliding into a narrow, cleft-like inlet as white and crystalline as sea salt.

Jumping away from the tiller, he tossed the anchor overboard, then darted to the mast, wrenching down the sails, his fingers working canvas and rope with a deft impatience.

Fairer than most Cycladic Greeks, his hair had become sun-bleached with the summer, a fact that didn't escape Huxley's attention.

'Golden, like the warriors of old,' he mused. 'Who knows, perhaps, against all the Balkan odds, some of the ancient blood still courses through his veins.'

'Like an ancient statue come to life,' said Maria, the stifled giggle doing little to disguise her appreciation of the fisher boy's summer bronze skin and rippling muscles.

I experienced a twinge of jealousy, but couldn't help noticing that Nestor was safely out of earshot.

Three pairs of eyes fell on Aris, stripping off his clothes on deck and somersaulting into the sea.

Darting back to the surface, he moved with powerful strokes along the cliff face, his self-taught crawl not exactly elegant but effective enough, I suppose. Just as he rounded the point, Sam came plummeting down the rock face, a reckless act that was typical of someone who dares life to kill him at every conceivable opportunity.

Once the shock and spray had subsided they lolled about in the water, laughing. Seconds later, they were splashing each other in the face, ducking each other under by the shoulders, diving around each other's feet, corking to the surface through the bubble stream.

Nothing strange or exceptional about it. Just guys larking about as they do every summer's day on thousands of coasts just like this.

It was only as they emerged from the water that it struck me. The uncanny resemblance they bore to the boys in Huxley's ancient frescoes. Standing there stark naked on the crystalline waves, Sam's arm slung lazily over the fisher boy's bead-glistening shoulders.

Fleetingly, I caught Maria's profile, almost Levantine in appearance, the wide eyes pronounced with kohl, the lips set in a knowing smile, bronze ankle bracelets jangling as she dips her feet into the sea.

I could feel the sticky dryness in my throat as I tried to swallow. Caught the tuning fork whine on my eardrums. My own hollow thumping heartbeat.

They saunter towards us over the petrified waves, Aris' glance plunging into me as they come.

Those eyes. Somehow, they're different than I remember. Too wide, too bright, and too much like the sea catching the summer blue.

Capable of disarming without a struggle, almost as if they have nothing to hide or dissemble. Save for that image in the half-buried house, I have never seen eyes like that before, not even a child's...

I sat up sharply, trying to catch my breath. After months playing hide-and-seek with him, it seemed I was still no better at anticipating Huxley's mind games or his motives.

I felt a surge of unrestrained hatred towards him, just at the idea that he could manipulate us like this, making us act in his stupid theatre, never knowing the script or the plot.

My eyes darted towards him, already sensing the penetrating look awaiting me. But I was wrong, or too late. Huxley's gaze was fixed intently on that spitting image from the frescoes, and it was up to me to decipher the cryptic look on his face.

Moments later the boys drifted apart, the tension in the air vanishing like a magic trick that had never happened.

Almost imperceptibly, Huxley's attention flickered towards Anna and Maria, flapping out a threadbare tablecloth for Myroula's feast.

Maria in a turquoise bikini, one delicious size too small, stooping over the rocks towards me, laying out plates and bowls full of succulent fruit, her breasts almost... I rolled over on my belly, suddenly alarmed that, in my tight swimming trunks, I was giving myself away to everyone.

Behind those slit lids his eyes were darting between us, I could tell. Watching us, analysing every expression, reading every thought open enough to be read.

The answer was all there in the look, I just knew it. One way or another, I had been under that searing gaze since day one. At Benja's funeral, when first I set eyes on the dead face in the casket. On the mountain, climbing into the storm. In the ancient city, taking the winding path up temple hill, ancient voices, trees, torrents on the edge of the wind. In the half-buried house, so innocently remarking our likenesses to the dead, the vanished. Every scene contrived to shock with pleasure or pain, euphoria or fear.

But why? Save for madness or perversion, sexual or otherwise, I still had no convincing answer.

If there was one tenuous link to past events, it was how incredibly thirsty I was. I snatched up a water flask and, lifting it to my lips, could feel the beautiful coolness cascading over my tongue.

A little while later, Aris returned from the boat with a brace of sea bream and red mullet, and laid a driftwood fire to grill them.

'You had a good catch, Ari,' said Sam, crouching down to help him.

'Did you see the light over the sea last night?'

Sam shook his head. Unable to disguise his curiosity this time, Huxley stirred, his head almost twitching towards them.

'Like a white mist over the swell,' Aris was saying, 'but strong, strong enough to draw shoals of fish to the nets.'

'Weren't you scared?' He traced his forefinger along the fisher boy's upper arm, following the ribs of salt and sand that had dried there.

Unable to stand it a moment longer, I crawled under the tamarisk, intent on confronting the man who obviously knew the script back to front.

'What's going on?' I said, the words sounding so hollow to my own ears I wondered if I was still sleeping, or if the line had already been written for me.

I was treated to a questioning look, clearly fake.

'What are we doing out here?' I added in an furious whisper.

'I thought you said time was against us. I thought you said we were excavating Atlantis.'

'And are we not doing so?' he replied, replete with all those buried ambiguities you could never be sure of.

With a caustic glance over his newspaper he added: 'Let me guess. It's come as a big shock to you that Sam likes boys, that he's queer.'

'That's not the word I would have used, but I didn't know —'

'*That* which you do not know, Mr Pedrosa, would doubtless fill an entire universe,' the put-down so biting it almost made you look for teeth marks.

'I suppose that should serve as a lesson to us all,' he added, apparently addressing the far more perceptive tamarisk now. 'How easy it is to take the boy out of the provinces; how hard it is to take the provinces out of the boy...'

'Look, I don't care. I just didn't know, that's all. The first time I saw him he was all over the girls, now it's the boys, so what's up?' *Just admit it, you liar! You're the stage manager, you're the one making the frescoes come to life.*

'Why does it concern you?'

'Because it doesn't make sense, that's why. Two days ago, I thought he was going to stick his tongue down my throat or something.'

Now I had blurted it out there was no turning back, but how much to admit or deny without incriminating myself? That stupid encounter between the tents I far preferred to forget, Sam luring me into his trap by pretending he had new leads on Benja's death.

'And felt me up... you know, between the legs.'

I could swear he was now fighting off a laugh.

'Did you kiss him back?'

'No! I don't know. It's complicated!'

'I assume you duly recorded the momentous event in your notebook?'

'Of course not!'

'Why not?' he glared, as though now I had been negligent in my duties. 'Is it not important?'

'Yes...! No...! *I don't know!*'

Fuck. I was looking like a complete idiot.

'Why do you keep painting me as some kind of country bumpkin. I'm not. I have an open mind.'

'Is that so? Well, that we shall see.'

He shook the newspaper as though I had interrupted his reading, but then said: 'He's fallen in love with you, is that what you think? A good-looking boy like you, who could blame him.'

'No, of course not.'

'Well, then, set your mind at rest, because that's Sam all over. He wants what he can't have and loses interest in what he can. He must shock, provoke, demand the world prove he's alive. Without it, he's always wading through the fog, always in danger of mediocrity's clammy grasp. I suppose that's what drew me to him in the beginning — that, and a certain innocence with which he viewed the world.'

Innocence? I thought, incredulously. That's a strange thing to say about someone as bloody-minded as Sam.

We settled around the tablecloth. Icy wine splashed into our beading glasses, the glasses chiming like mountain bells as Hadrian offered the only toast he could imagine everyone might agree upon, the beauty of a summer's day. At the rock pools nearby, Aris was cracking open sea urchins for anyone odd enough to think the quivering morsel inside a delicacy to be splashed with lemon juice and slurped raw into the mouth. He leaned forward to offer me one of the spiky shells, and it was only as he glanced up that it hit me, the hollow echo in my own chest seemingly loud enough for the whole ragged circle to have overhead.

Those eyes. If ever they had been that ancient cornflower blue even Huxley had remarked upon, they weren't any longer. They were as brown as the lava cliffs themselves.

Even Huxley cannot have engineered such a phenomenon — unless, of course, blue coloured the thought he planted in your mind.

Once the feast was over Huxley retreated to the tamarisk again, the newspaper propped up on his knees.

I thought he had dozed off until a voice spoke, sending a tremor through me. 'Is that where you expect to find the truth, Nicholas? Wallowing through the primeval sludge of your own psyche?'

'What do you mean?' I could feel every muscle tensing. 'You can't tell me nothing strange is going on here, you can't!'

His silence almost seemed like an admission, and I clutched at it with both desperate hands if only to still the darting premonitions of my own madness.

He watched the others splashing about in the sea, all blue and silver. I had begun to think he wouldn't reply at all when at last he demanded:

'Why are we here?'

'To raise the lost city.'

'No! I told you on your first day. It is the truth we demand, ours, theirs, beyond reality's relentless capacity for deception and trance. That is how we apply our insight, our logic, our rationality.'

Logic? I thought, wondering if I had just caught an inkling of his curious power, that could so effortlessly turn your whole world upside down. Because logic means something different to a man who believes the universe is woven out of thought, doesn't it, than to someone who sees only physical matter, only elements and compounds.

'So what would you have me do?' I snarled. 'Pretend the lies are truths, the illusions are reality?'

'I told you. You wade through the swamp of your own fears, your own emotions, your likes and dislikes, your desires and aversions, your passion for this, your suspicion of that. I ask you again. Is that where you expect to find the truth?'

Seeing my blank look, he forced the words through gritted teeth. 'Climb out of yourself! Even for a few brief moments. Experience what it is like to escape the gravity of your own world.' Adding with a mordant chuckle: 'Yes! Call it an out-of-body experience.'

I felt a squirming in the pit of my stomach and for a moment thought I would have to run away to hurl its contents between the boulders.

Aris was hoisting the sail on the *Persephone*, heading home. The others were frolicking about in the waves, laughing, giggling, splashing each other, all as if nothing had happened. But it had, and things would never be the same again, I knew that.

29.

It was after dark by the time I headed home, the Morris labouring up the hairpins. Almost at the cliff top, I hit the brakes, catching the same luminosity in the wing mirror, tingeing the western slopes.

The only thing I couldn't explain was running into Nestor and his moles at Alexis' taverna half an hour later, already on their fourth round of raki and yelling for more.

If Nestor's crew wasn't digging, who was?

Clocking in early, I reported to Huxley's field tent, on the lookout for answers.

Too absorbed to look up, he acknowledged my arrival with a grunt, his propelling pencil dashing over the site map, annotating its various landmarks with scribbled comments, interconnecting arrows, question and exclamation marks. Grudgingly, I had to admit that there was at least method to his madness.

Reading his abrupt toss of the head correctly, I poured him more tea from the samovar, casually reporting my sighting as I did so.

If only for a fraction of a second his hand froze, his lips betraying the first twitch of a scowl before finding refuge in his tea mug.

Gathering up his papers, in next to no time we were marching up to the bakery and the first of the workshops, where Nestor was busy setting up the monorail camera, a little worse for wear after the raki blowout with the men, but refusing to show it.

Motioning towards me, Huxley said in an undertone: 'Mr Pedrosa thinks he has seen the glow of lights, up on the hill.'

Nestor threw me a frown. 'Probably just the stars in the marble Kapítan, you know how bright they are. I have handpicked men patrolling dusk to dawn, and even when we were digging, the tephra was muffling the noise. You couldn't hear a thing, not on the surface. There have been prowlers, of course, but nothing we couldn't handle.'

Huxley found a perch on the steps, and unfurled the site map over the rippling ancient stones.

The ends scrolling disobediently back into his fist, he stabbed the scrapyard with his forefinger. 'Then take half the crew and tunnel west from the exploratory shaft.' Adding to his foreman's nod: 'No need to remind you we work by night…'

'What are we looking for?' I said as we retraced our steps, past the windows of the ghost houses that seemed to hum in the wind and the silence.

'What we are always looking for. Bodies, of course.'

'But I thought you said the volcano must have given people ample warning — that's why there aren't any bodies.'

'You forget,' he snapped. 'Absence of evidence does not mean that the evidence is absent.'

Yes, I thought grimly, you're right, my thoughts lurching back to my faltering investigation into Benja's death.

'How can you play detective if you will not think?' he rebuked me, tapping his forehead. 'If you will not use the grey matter that God has given you, to reason, to deduce?' I don't know which threw me more, his mocking reference to my amateur detective work, or his reference to God. 'Assuming the vulcanologists are right, the inhabitants may have had days, but it doesn't make sense that a wisp of smoke from the cone or even a smoky belch or two convinced them to evacuate the island en masse. At some point, the ash fall must have looked like a snowstorm. Imagine it. Incandescent lava flows streaming down the mountain, consuming everything in their path. Earthquakes shaking the city to its core, ripping open fissures and chasms. Poisonous gas choking the life out of anything that breathes. In the inevitable panic, do you really think there'd be no casualties, not even a single child or a weakling falling underfoot in the stampede?'

'Maybe they were lucky.'

He looked at me as if I were feeble-minded. 'There is nothing at all, not a donkey, not a goat, not even a chicken's wishbone anywhere along these streets. Explain that if you can.'

'Maybe they took all their animals with them.'

'So I suppose no one died throughout the entire history of this civilisation?' he demanded, and in that especially acerbic way of his. 'No… There must be a burial ground somewhere. And within the tombs, finds that will blow the cynics to kingdom come.'

Determined to resume my own investigation, I was one of the first on site the following morning.

With the sun rising behind the mountain, half the peninsula was still in shadow. All too conscious of the mythology surrounding it, I found myself standing in front of the tall house on the ridge from which Benja had taken his fatal plunge. Its windows like empty eyes. The number 16 chalked onto its lava-charred wall as though waiting for the postman to call.

I glanced up at the serpentines. Still no dust cloud from the convoy or from Huxley's Land Rover. He was late.

First, check the perimeter, starting with the half-exhumed rear of the house. I scrambled up the ash mound, using the wall for purchase.

Entering from the back I climbed in through a second-storey window, then made my way out towards the scaffolding, gripping the exposed stones with my fingertips just in case. True to Nestor's word, it was rock solid, or at least it was now. My attention was drawn to the compound, where a few people were just appearing, students carrying buckets of water to their tents from the cisterns, or hanging about outside the mess, waiting for it to open. Up on the hairpins, the dust cloud had finally appeared and was now speeding down to camp. Getting caught up here was the last thing I wanted but, just as I turned to leave, something else caught my attention. The incredible view it commanded over the peninsula, the houses and temples on the hill already bathed in sun, an island of light in a sea of shadows.

So this is the last thing that Benja saw.

I hurried back, feeling my way through the rooms where they were darkest. Back through the rear window, down the ash mound in a slide. Then, in a reckless gamble against the approaching convoy, vaulting in through a first floor window. Before even landing on my feet, I wished to God I hadn't.

The stench of putrefaction was suffocating, eating what little was left of the stale air.

I remember thinking, some unfortunate creature must have crawled into these ancient rooms to die.

Dry-retching half a dozen times before regaining some kind of self-control, I peered into one of the side rooms, eyes still streaming, arm stuffed against my nose.

That's when I saw it... what looked like a body with rigid, twisted limbs. Huxley's obsession in my head, for one stuttering second I had to wonder if it might be the petrified remains of some ancient corpse. But of course I knew that couldn't be true. For one thing, it was still dressed in tattered clothes. For another, it was still rotting.

The next thing I knew I was outside under the scaffolding, vomiting uncontrollably into the dust, and Huxley was yelling at me, demanding to know what was going on. Getting no sense out of me, he went to look for himself. Hardly a minute later, he was raving at his foreman. I thought I was hearing things, and by the stupefied look on his face so did Nestor Louganis as he received the order to have Benja's body removed from house 16.

'And not a word!' he rasped, as the bus chose that moment to whine and grate its way into the compound. But even Huxley couldn't keep something like that secret for long, not with the stench leaking out of the house in the midsummer heat, or the sheet-covered corpse that Nestor and Mad Yanni the gravedigger carried up to the jeep when they thought no one was looking.

Getting wind of it, half the labourers downed tools where they stood, and scurried back to the bus, imagining all the other dead things that might be breaking out of their graves.

Still reeling from the shock, I sat outside the mess tent, head in my hands, and only started to recover at all after Anna appeared with two glasses, a bucket of ice, and a bottle of raki to split between us. 'Drink,' she said firmly, the bottle clinking nervously against the glass as she poured.

★

Just how Benja's mangled corpse came to be in house 16, and who had put it there, captivated the island for weeks. It was on everyone's mind, everyone's lips. Who can have done such a thing? And why?

According to the tephra diggers, it was obvious to any fool. Benja the *vrykolakas* was breaking out of his grave whenever the fancy took him. *Did you see his skin,* they cried, *did you see his straw blond hair as they carried his body away? As unblemished as the day he died!*

Pensively, Nestor rubbed the stubble on his chin, and said: 'I'm thinking maybe one of those fools dug up the body, Kapítán, planning to row it over to Thirassia, with or without the Papás' blessing. Cut out the heart, burn the corpse on the shore. You know they say it's the only way to be rid of them; a *vrykolakas* can't cross water.'

I thought Huxley would explode. 'Why bring it here?'

'They could hardly carry it through town, Kapítán, all the way down the serpentines, in full view of everyone.'

'Most of them jump at the sight of their own shadow,' objected Huxley. 'I can't imagine even one of them having the guts to do it.'

'A malicious act of sabotage, mark my words,' said Hadrian, blinking at the chaos that had descended upon camp. 'If you can think of a better way of disrupting the excavations, I'd like to hear it.'

Before the morning was out police chief Manolis and his deputy Chondro had descended on camp, equipped as usual with that peculiar brand of ineptitude and officiousness that was their stock-in-trade.

Once on site, they made a point of walking down every path transecting the excavations this side of the ridge, but paled at the suggestion that they venture into the ancient city itself, let alone enter the crime scene at house 16. Humiliated by the catcalls of the few stubborn labourers still lingering outside the mess tent, they eventually plucked up the courage to do so, croaking a weak hymn as they went to keep the phantasmata at bay.

After they had returned, none the wiser but at least in one piece, Manolis made a point of interrogating everyone in sight, playing up to the audience that had gathered around him. Every man and woman in Huxley's employ, he proclaimed loudly, was now officially under suspicion.

Huxley was in a bloodcurdling mood. No one dared speak to him.

He looked tired, even haggard, but now more than ever knew that his enemies were no longer merely at the gates, but among us. And it seemed they were capable of anything.

We may have been too shell-shocked to realise it at first, but the psychological impact went far deeper than anyone can have guessed, perhaps even the perpetrators themselves.

But it was Anna's reaction that threw me. I suppose I had been half-expecting to see her in a tearful storm like Maria. Instead, mid-morning four days later I found her at the perimeter of the site, fingers entwined around the wire mesh fencing.

'Do you *still* think it's Marcus?' she demanded, with a bitter swipe. 'That he is responsible for everything?'

'Does finding Benja's body in house 16 prove he's innocent?' I had spoken too defensively, I know, but I was more rattled than ever. The shock of finding the corpse had hit hard and hit deep, along with all the stress I'd been under for weeks. The psychological tricks. The lies. The tantalising dreams. The impossible demands.

'I've been manipulated since day one,' I added in sudden fury. 'And somehow, he always manages to do it. The more I struggle against him, the more I find myself acting the role he has created for me.'

She threw back her head and laughed, her eyes all crinkling up. But it wasn't the champagne laugh I was so used to.

'Oh Nico!' she gushed, turning, grabbing my arm. 'Don't you see? We are all characters in Marcus Huxley's epic drama. We shuffle on or off the stage according to his directions, speak the lines written for us as if we were the mere figments of his imagination, and the question we are always left with is, can mere actors ever change the script once they are up on stage?'

For several seconds I just stood there, dumbstruck. Somehow, I'd been half-expecting her to rise to Huxley's defence again, explaining everything away with references to his charisma and magnetism and brilliance. His was not a mind that could hypnotise or control, she'd say, merely evoke or inspire.

'You can't be serious,' I stammered, stung at having my own apprehensions dragged into the realms of farce. As I pulled back, I caught the whiff of aniseed on her breath, noticed her puffy eyes for the first time. She had been drinking. This time, not just for the shock but for the comfort.

That explained a lot, but not nearly enough. Did she suspect Huxley or not?

Just a few more days, I told myself. To see this thing through. To understand what is happening.

30.

On the other side of the ridge, an old farmer on a pearl speckled mule came plodding out of the parched fields. Lean-faced, as dark as a raisin, he pulled up on the verge as I came lurching through the potholes like a boat through waves. Finding my face at last through the dust-caked windscreen, he waved me down. The brakes were still squealing as I thrust my head out of the window.

'Giasou.' Said as phlegmatically as the fishers and farmers always do here. You never know what's going on inside their heads.

I studied the man's face, his shrewd, guarded eyes. I thought I had seen him somewhere before but couldn't place him.

'Kostas,' he said, obligingly, with a vague flick of the thumb to his own chest. *Great. Another one. How was one supposed to keep track?*

Then silence. Just the Meltemi sweeping across the terraced fields, rustling the sun-dried thistles at the roadside. It was often like that. You never knew if they were going to say anything or not, or what they had stopped you for in the first place. I was just grating the Morris into gear when he said through cracked lips: 'The dead boy.'

He has to be talking about Benja, I realised, almost slipping and falling between the words.

'I saw him,' he went on, tearing into a purple-hearted fig. 'That day he died.'

Thinking it had to be another *vrykolakas* sighting, I tried to catch the whiff of wine or raki on his breath.

He motioned towards the sea, down past the bird's nest vines, onto the black sand beach and a jutting promontory of lava.

'A fisherman who catches no fish, that's what he was.' More riddles, I groaned, wondering how to escape. But seconds later I realised my mistake. He wasn't talking in riddles at all, just plain village Greek.

I caught the wince of a smile, humour going as dry as the cracked skin under this blazing sun. 'He would sit out there on the rocks, casting his line into the sea. *Giati?* Why? Hour after hour, his hook catching seaweed, not a single fish. Even in the dark, there he was, a shadow against the sea. Why would any man do that?'

Only one reason I could think of. To get away from Huxley. To be alone, to think. As taciturn as he was, the old man had obviously been concerned enough to offer Benja the use of his grape harvest *kalivi* in the fields.

'His odds and ends are still there, scattered about. One of these days, I'll bring them down.'

'No, don't do that,' I said, a little too abruptly. 'At least, not yet.'

Thinking it might just be the break I had been looking for, I was eager to see the farmer's hut with my own eyes. I pulled the Morris off the road, taking advantage of a dry stone wall to hide it from passers-by. Then I was on my way, following the old man's directions through the vineyards.

Soon I was zigzagging back and forth along the shore, buffeted by the wind, feet sinking into ankle-deep volcanic sand, wondering where the hell it could be.

Just when I was beginning to wonder if the *kalivi* existed at all, there it was, higher up across a gully of splintered rock.

I must have passed it half a dozen times, and now I realised why. The wall that showed its face to the shore was almost indistinguishable from the volcanic stone that surrounded it, and from which it had probably been carved centuries ago. No wonder Benja had jumped at the chance of renting it from Kostas the farmer. With a few drachmae more to tie the old man's tongue, who would have ever found him here? Maybe not even Huxley himself, for whom knowledge was power.

I scrambled up the gully, my hands tearing out dry weeds by the roots. The *kalivi* had clearly seen better days. Flaking blue paint, a sagging trellis bearing the weight of a rampant vine, a grimy window with a cracked pane.

At my touch, the door creaked open an inch before sagging on its hinges. I pushed harder, putting my weight behind it, and at last it scraped over the crude packed-earth floor. I lingered on the threshold while my eyes adjusted to the gloom, a feeble shaft of daylight from the square window highlighting dust.

For the first few minutes, I tried to interpret the scene as methodically as I could, remembering Huxley's famous dictum about looking for things that cannot be seen. At least I had learnt something from him.

Crude it may have been, but Benja had made something of the

place anyway once the mule had been sent packing. In one corner, a simple iron bed with a straw mattress, sheets frayed and crumpled. On an adjacent wall, a rickety old table, a couple of straw-seated chairs, a cupboard. On the plaster mantel of the *tzaki*, an antique postcard from a friend in England; bathing belles on the beach at Brighton. A sink made of stone, the water from the cast iron hand-pump draining through a small hole under the window frame onto some grateful weeds outside. An oil lamp, a couple of candle stubs. A shopping list, lying forgotten or discarded on the bleached wood table.

And something more. A ticket for Piraeus, dated for the looming Sunday he would never see.

I turned to the shelf over the bed and the dog-eared books already spilling their guts to the summer heat. Carelessly lodged between the cheap novels, something distinctly out of place. A black notebook, much like mine. I began leafing through it, half expecting an excavation record as dry as the ash they had been shifting. But as my quickening pulse told me moments later, this was a diary, not a missing site log.

The entries were inconsistent, even sporadic, in full flow one day, terse or missing the next. Jottings. Impressions. Private thoughts that should have been in Huxley's possession. But they were not. They were here, along with other things that Benja had wanted to keep just for himself, elements of identity, of self, of past, that his master insisted he abandon forever.

The words almost make him flesh and blood, I thought, my fingers running through the weeks and months. They seem to colour him in with light and shadow, that ink outline that I have been carrying around with me for months.

Like a branch thwacking back into my face, the obvious struck me almost from line one. Benja's raw ambivalence towards the man who had lured him here. If not for the mute ink preserving it, or the eardrums that cannot quite find its frequency, I imagined you might still hear it in the air, a lingering cry that wells and diminishes like the wind through the wires.

The signs are there almost from the start, Benja missing his young wife, Jenna. It's midwinter, and he can't get used to the tortured landscape or the tomb damp cold that infests everything. He still remembers the almond icing wedding cake. The showers of rice. The bright smiling faces. At home, there's a baby on the way, and he tells himself the pay packet's everything now. He has to stick it out.

'According to Huxley, an archaeological dig is not a holiday camp for missing wives, husbands, lovers. I have been here four months already, but still he refuses to allow me home on leave. He won't say so outright, but the implication is clear: if I do go, my job won't be here waiting for me when I get back. What can I do? Without it, I'll be nowhere. He knows that. Digs like this come by once in a blue moon. Jenna has to understand that.'

March: Huxley is already burrowing into his soul, as though a ruined city were buried there beneath the surface. 'Desire. Like some fake Buddhist mystic, Huxley claims I must rise above it, cling to nothing. But who on this godforsaken rock of a planet is more ravenous than he, whose desire burns like phosphorous, hissing and sparking? We can lust after women or wine, dream of building a home, or a family, and at least the dream is somehow solid to the touch. But Huxley's? No, he craves something no one can even see. Islands beyond the next horizon. Islands hiding behind the sunset. An echo of the Perfect Form. He drives us, if not to drink or weed, then to an addiction of quite a different sort. Truth beyond the ever-present lie, reality beyond the conjuror's illusion, a state of being beyond the impossible. Damn you, how can it be done?'

April: 'No. He's right. Admit it. It's not as though it never occurred to me before. The world reeking of lies. Reality as honest as a fairground mirror. I probably knew it all along. Sensed it as a child, then as a college kid, raging at the fools and thieves in power. Angry at the masks people wear to hide the faces they are ashamed of, often with good cause, often not. I wanted to tear the masks away from their faces, just to make them stop parroting their pathetic lies. Jenna calmed me down, I suppose, even if I did take it out on her every way I knew how. Sometimes, I'm shocked she fell in love with me at all. If only I could remember what it's like, her touch, her kiss, her lips on mine.'

September: 'Islands, islands. On a blue arc that finds infinity. Time slips away. Almost into insignificance. I begin to lose track of the days. They run into each other like pigments bleeding into moist plaster. There where they touch, a new colour, a new island comes into being. Has no one noticed?'

March: 'When first we peeled that exquisite fresco from the wall, the eyes of the saffron gatherers gazing down upon us, I sensed some-

191

thing, something almost too strange to put into words: that the things we are raising from the ash have some hidden portent for our own lives we have not even begun to grasp.'

'Anna sometimes looks up from her trench as I pass by, and she'll call out. *Did you get the mail call? Did you get anything from home?* I know what she's thinking. That I'm slipping away over the next horizon. That I can hardly remember Jenna's face. But as I walk up temple hill, I can feel it entering me, as irresistible as a siren song. Sweeter than the music of the lyre...'

The hollow echo of my own heartbeat startled me. All the while I had been drawing strength from the similarity of our experiences, Benja's and mine, because it proved Huxley's complicity. But now I was getting scared.

Less than a week before Benja's death, and Huxley is having another of his bad days.

'*We are getting nowhere!* he rages. *You are no longer an asset, but a liability!* I protest that we are raising this idyll from the dead, houses, workshops, temples, but he isn't satisfied. Of course not. He never is. For him, these things are doorways, leading to somewhere else, not here. He accuses me of squandering my potential, of indulging myself in irrational sentiment, worthless emotion. That may have been true once, but not now. If anything, all this has made me stronger, his intimidation, his mind games, even his casual disregard for what I now have to say. Through the tunnel darkness I perceive the light. Things I never understood before fall into place with an almost mathematical elegance, and I have to wonder if

I turned the page. There was nothing there. Not a single word. Just a serrated edge where the paper had been carelessly torn away.

My first thought was that Huxley himself must have beaten me to it, but that didn't make sense. No more so, in fact, than Benja being suicidal, on the verge of throwing himself off the scaffolding. Given his rages, even his implied threats, Benja's determined state of mind looked bad for Huxley.

According to his final entry, Benja had visited the *kalivi* on the windy, rain-spattered night before he died. But what else was the past telling us?

Trying to visualise it, I subsided back onto the bed, willing events to fall into place.

At first, I barely noticed. A subtle fading of colours that I put down to the changing daylight outside. Perpendicular lines assuming an almost imperceptible curve. Things that do not belong in the scene, like me, losing their shadows and reflections.

The door creaks open on its sagging hinges, dragging over the packed-earth floor. Dusk sweeps into the room chased by a reckless sea gust. Benja hurries in, tears off his waterlogged jacket, shakes the rain out of his straw blond hair, still dark from the drenching outside.

He crosses over to the table and lights two candles with a single match, the sulphur head just catching on the third strike because the matchbook has gone soft and damp in his pocket. He pulls his notebook off the shelf, slumps down at the bleached wood table and begins writing in a fury, as though something or someone might stop him.

Then, just as abruptly, he stops, looks around uncertainly. Reaches across the table, picks up the stub of a pencil, tears a blank page from the spine. I recognise it at once. It's the shopping list. I experience a plunge of disappointment, willing him to do the impossible, to get back to the diary, to complete the sentence he will never finish.

The rain lashes against the door and window pane with a sudden eerie ferocity, as if begging me to see the obvious.

Hesitantly, he begins to scribble, just a few letters at a time.

What's the matter? You seem to be taking a hell of a long time just to write some stupid shopping list. You're distracted, that's it, still thinking about your unfinished line in the notebook.

For an hour or more he just sits there, brows furrowed, eyes sometimes straying to the window or the other stuff cluttering the table, the folded site map, the tobacco pouch and maize cigarette papers. At last he sets the list and chewed pencil aside, prepares to turn in for the night. Moving my way, his face suddenly magnifies in globules of candlelight, revealing things that might normally go unnoticed. Anxiety, trying to restrain something else, something obvious now... a kind of lucid euphoria that comes scattering out of the irises. He knows it, I think. He knows the secret. But what? The answer is almost on the tip of my tongue, just creeping into the light, when he snuffs out the candles, plunging us into darkness. It's strange to think that tomorrow he'll be dead.

I came to with a start, realising I must have fallen asleep on the bed. Outside, the wind was still gusting, rattling the loose windowpanes. It was almost dark.

I could feel the mystery defeating me. Even if I had always harboured doubts about my ability to solve it, suddenly I knew what it was like to be crushed by disappointment. I crossed over to the table and, like Benja before me, slumped down onto the tattered, straw-seated chair.

My attention wandered to the shopping list.

It seemed unremarkable enough. Bread, cheese, wine, tins of fish. A few things from the hardware shelves, rope, hooks and line, candles, matches.

But then my eyes strayed to the figures appending each item, and I knew it at once. They didn't make any sense, not as quantities.

Two tins of sardines, yes, that's plausible enough, but 18 feta, 22 ropes, 115 candles?

I shoved the list into my back pocket, the notebook into my dispatch bag.

I had my first real clues, even if I had no idea what they meant. A shopping list with impossible numbers. Another text whose eureka moment breaks off in the middle of a sentence. Like Sam, like me, he must have known that last passage of the Critias off by heart. What was he thinking, as the inspiration driving the words flew headlong into thin air?

31.

Knowing I couldn't avoid him all day, I poked my head around the fragments hut door. It was only ten but I could already feel the heat wave blasting back off the mountain.

The days were melting into one another, blue and formless. By midmorning, my thoughts would be melting too and, if only for that reason, I needed no reminding. I had to be on my guard as never before; alert, as anyone ever could be, to those Rasputian mind games and that sixth sense of his. One way or the other, I had to give him enough rope to hang himself.

'Do you see?' he murmured, fingers fussing over the shattered fragments cluttering the tabletop. 'How close we are coming. How very close?' One cluster, I could see, was beginning to resemble something coherent, water currents between banks of reeds, the blunt prow of a river punt.

'Don't you even care that people think you did away with him?' I blurted. 'Benja, I mean.'

'And am I the most likely suspect?' he enquired, with cutting non-chalance.

'Well, aren't you? Who else even had motive?'

If I'd been expecting him to duck for cover under the suicide theory, I was sadly mistaken.

'Well, what about Sam, for one?'

'Sam?' Not that I couldn't see the logic in it. I could. It was just hearing it from Huxley, my prime suspect, that threw me.

Great. So now they had implicated each other in the crime and, for all the clinching proof I had of anything, I was back at square one.

'If I were a satisfactory culprit,' Huxley was reasoning, 'then surely Sam would be dead as well?'

'Maybe he wasn't threatening to leave,' I flared, irritated by his insouciance, almost mocking. 'Maybe it hadn't even dawned on him then, the way things keep breaking off in the middle of a sentence.'

I had said too much and bit my lips. He threw me a puzzled look, and was about to utter some riposte when there was a squeal of brakes outside.

A blue Land Rover had pulled up, disgorging several young geologists from Adelaide. They looked as if they had been sleeping rough for a week, and probably had, camping out in the southern sector where they had been trying to plot the sub-tephra topography.

Huxley called from the doorway: 'Anything? Anything yet?'

The brashest of them, a man in his late twenties with wild hair, and a five-day stubble, nodded vigorously, arms akimbo. 'Yeah. A riverbed for sure.'

'Deep enough for a boat?'

'Looks like it. At a guess, wide enough for a pair of those Minoan galleys to pass.'

Huxley favoured them with a smile, almost triumphant. Nodding their goodbyes they hurried down to the mess tent to break open the frosted beer.

The better to take in the lay of the land we climbed up to house 16, and were almost on the ridge when I spotted two of Nestor's moles, hiking towards the mountain, potholing gear strapped to their backs. Climbing ropes, safety harnesses, helmets with lamps.

'Where are they going?' I said, my suspicions spiking.

No answer. Nor even any recognition that I had spoken at all.

I said in mouth numbing anger: 'I'm walking off this site and never coming back, do you hear me. I want to know what they're doing and where they're going!'

Roughly, he dragged me aside, pushing me up against the scorched walls of 16. He looked about to explode in my face but then relented. 'All right. I ask a lot of you, I know. But if you do not rebel against the darkness, how will you seek the light?'

As I shoved him away, he said: 'That day on the mountain, when we ran into the storm —'

'Don't tell me. The amnesia was just a fake.'

'Yes. And no. There is little I remember, but I remember this. It was dark. The rain was pelting down. Fumbling my way around the peak, a bolt of lightning struck, so white, so dazzling, I lost my footing on the slick black rocks. Before I knew it, I was tumbling through the darkness, my head cracking against the rocks, my fingernails being torn out. I must have fallen a good 20 feet. When I came to, it was to find myself at the bottom of some fissure, with no way out on top. Fishing out my pocket torch, I realised: no, this was no fissure, but a cave, with several coiling shafts leading off from the main chamber, plunging ever deeper into the mountain. Dazed as I was, I entered the first shaft, quickly finding myself in a warren of tunnels. The torch was giving out, and by the end I was feeling my way along. Resting, sleeping, waking, crawling, losing all track of time.'

'You're sending in the moles to explore them?'

'They have to find them first. You know what it's like up there.'

I was about to ask why it could be so important to him, when it dawned on me. 'You think there might be catacombs in there. Tombs. Bodies.'

He grunted. 'That or an ancient network of caves and tunnels that might run into the city itself. If so, we have to map them.'

Why should you believe him now? After all the lies he's told, the things he's done?

'Do you know what I think, Nicholas?' His gaze roamed over the southern horizon. 'I think we are just weeks away from finding the circular waterways that swept into the heart of Atlantis from the open sea. Do you remember?'

I shook my head, trying to dislodge the echo sweet sounds so faintly entering my mind. Sounds Benja also heard, at least that I knew for certain now. Cascading water. Leaves in the wind. Voices, ebbing and flowing.

'You will have your part to play in this, Nicholas. I am depending on you. We cannot give up now, not when we have come this far. You know that, don't you?'

It was almost as if Guirand and Sarrides could read his intentions.

32.

'They have been in séance every night,' said Nondas, throwing a white apron over Huxley's chest, and a worried glance into the mirror. What with the view his barber's shop commanded across the *plateia* or the gossip reported by his customers, nothing much escaped his attention. 'The Mayor. The Councillors. The Papás. The doors locked, the shutters closed tight. Yes, even on a hot summer's night like that! They mean to move against you. Toula's husband Nikos told me so himself...'

Toula at the telephone exchange, eavesdropping on conversations to while away the time.

'Giannis Papadaikis,' said Huxley with distaste. 'We should have known better than to trust a Junta-appointee with a weakness for baksheesh.'

Nondas threw a sardonic glance into the mirror, as he brought the shaving brush to lather Huxley's three-day stubble. 'Of the three P's, Marcus, forget about principle; our beloved Mayor recognises only preservation and profit. He's been on the telephone with the Frenchman every other day for a week, shouting himself hoarse across the sea, the Councillors and notables huddled around his desk, weighing trouble, weighing advantage. Toula heard every word. Promises that will pave the streets with gold, turn hovels into palaces. Promises only a dunce or a scoundrel would fall for.' He shook his head in disbelief. 'But I suppose they always sound that much more convincing after a well placed threat or two — the Frenchman not above namedropping his good friends the Colonels, *if only they could be restrained from their unhealthy obsession of weeding out corruption!* One minute they're seeing themselves up before the judge, thrown into jail, ruined, and the next, what do you know, money's falling out of the sky like manna from heaven. By the end, poor Toula could hardly hold back from shrieking "liars!" down the mouthpiece, and cutting them off, you know how she is.'

I cast a worried glance across the *plateia*, where a glowering Chief of Police was pacing back and forth, waiting impatiently for orders and reinforcements from Syros.

Under the saffron awning of Huxley's field tent, the faces of the others looked oddly numb and drawn as he broke the news, making little effort to sugar-coat the truth.

'They have us by the throat,' said Hadrian, his eyes small and beleaguered. 'Sarrides climbs the greasy pole, hand over fist, and would rather sacrifice his own mother than his career. Sotirios Kenteris is a hangover from before the coup, and didn't survive in his post without knowing how to flatter a liar or stab an honest man in the back. Mark my words, they'll all be trying to prove their loyalty to the Colonels now, each and every one of them.' He wrung his hands in anguish. 'What are we to do?'

In the sledgehammer heat it was difficult to breathe, difficult even to find a straight thought.

'Fight, Hadrian, as we always have,' replied Huxley impassively.

Hadrian threw up his hands in dismay. 'Fight a dictatorship? Have you taken leave of your senses?'

'Hadrian's right, Marcus,' Anna scolded. 'You make too many enemies. Here on the island. In Athens at the Service. Even in Paris.'

'You want to make friends out of enemies, Anna, is that what you want? I think you better be careful what you wish for.'

A day later, the first blow was struck.

A letter bearing all kinds of official stamps was delivered straight to Huxley's tent from the *Pegasus*. A moment's pause to compose himself and he tore it open. It was an eviction order.

A faint, scornful smile crossed his face. Here and there, he noted, the typewriter keys, hit in anger, had punched holes straight through the paper.

Sarrides' handiwork, no doubt, even though the letter itself bore the pompous signature of Sotirios Kenteris, director of the Service. A single paragraph, terse enough to bruise, advised Huxley that all previous permits had been rescinded. He was ordered to suspend excavations until further notice, and vacate the site forthwith.

'You see,' he said, seizing reason for hope where we saw none at all. 'No mention is even made of the audit, nor of any evidence against us. Why? Because they have no evidence, that's why.'

'Since when has a dictatorship needed evidence,' squealed Hadrian.

'What now?' said Sam, barely able to restrain a grin.

'Fireworks,' replied Huxley, turning on his heel. 'Light the blue touchpaper and stand well back.'

Baffled, we stared at his receding back as he headed for the Land

Rover. If anything, it was the news from Athens that went stuttering through camp like a giant firecracker. Everyone in shock, walking about with dazed heads and ringing ears.

Impatient for results, the island Council descended upon camp the following morning, their mode of transport a bent and battered lime green minivan that did little for their gravitas.

Katina at the hula-hoop steering wheel, the Papás at her side, chimneypot hat crunching up against the roof. Relegated to the second row and not liking it one bit, the Mayor, Giannis Papadaikis, squashed in with two other councilmen.

They came rattling down the mountain track, escorted by the police on their old grey Triumph, backfiring loudly on the bends.

Once through the gates and into the compound, they made a beeline for the site office where Maria, with great poise, asked them if they had an appointment. No? Well, the Professor was somewhere about camp, but doubtless would be making an appearance sooner or later.

Huxley was making them stew. He'd already heard about their bickering in the Mayor's office, like quarrelsome magpies picking over the promises Guirand had tossed them.

Now, while they were still at their jittery best, he wanted them to doubt and second-guess each other, the wait perhaps even provoking another quarrel.

Five minutes dragged into ten and then stretched to twenty. The delegation first declined and then reminded Maria of her offer to serve coffee. An hour passed, then two.

When Huxley at last considered them suitably stewed, he appeared in the compound, a preoccupied look on his face. Pretending to consult the site map in his hand, he collared a passing student, motioning him towards the new trenches in the east.

At Katina's urging, the Mayor rose to his feet, his thickset eyes struggling to understand. Then they tumbled out of the site office to intercept him, the police officers advancing from the rear.

With bruised dignity, Papadaikis declared: 'Professor Huxley, you must know that the authorities in Athens have revoked your permit. You have no right to be here. You must close the site immediately.'

'And you must leave Greece within 24 hours,' added Manolis, with a sunken-cheeked glower.

'And the island as well,' put in Chondro for good measure, oblivious to the scowls it earned him.

'If you do not obey, you will be arrested,' blustered Manolis.

The thunder appeared in Huxley's eyes, roiling clouds turning blacker with every word.

At his command, Maria appeared from the site office with a large Manila file, which he then made a great show of opening, all the better to feast on their widening eyes. Unmistakeable official seals and letterheads, adorning virtually every document within. And not just the ink pad stamps of a local council or a police station, either, but the red wax seals of Ministers. Culture and Sciences, Public Order, Foreign Affairs.

'Let me understand you correctly,' he said, his voice as dry and abrasive as a sandstorm. 'You are saying that the order of a petty functionary from the Archaeological Service supersedes all these?'

He went on, letter after letter, and didn't stop until he had reached the Prime Minister's office and the Royal Palace.

If the others were gaping at him, part in awe, part in incredulity, so was I. I had no idea he had friends in such high places. It had to be because of the Comte d'Adhémar, our mysterious benefactor in Paris.

Manolis was fuming, already spluttering about forgeries. The Papás silenced him with a look that would have withered thistle.

It was supposed to be their day of triumph but the weather had turned, seemingly without warning. Moments later, they were in the thick of it, probably wondering what fool had convinced them it was possible to enforce the eviction order without inciting a riot.

Seeing the alarm in their eyes, I glanced over my shoulder, and suddenly realised that virtually the entire camp had now converged upon the scene.

Labourers and trench moles covered in dust from head to foot. Machine operators. Students and teachers. Even the canteen staff.

Tempers quickly began to fray.

'Can't you see what the Frenchman is doing?' Huxley demanded, searching each of their faces in turn. 'He and Sarrides, a man whom even his friends call *the Raptor*?'

'Oh yes, Huxley, we see,' retorted Papadaikis, furious that anyone, least of all a foreigner, should impugn the imagined dignity of his office. 'He is our friend, our ally. He will serve our interests far better than you have ever done.'

Huxley spun around to his labourers and trench moles. 'Do you hear what your Mayor says?' he shouted at them. 'Well? Has the

Frenchman made his promises to you as well — you Nikos, you Kostas, you Panayiotis?'

I was surprised he even remembered their names.

Sullenly, they tossed their heads or barked a resounding *Oxi! No!* back at him, aiming murderous looks at Papadaikis.

He turned back to the councillors.

'And what will you do when Sarrides orders that the ancient treasures be dismantled piece by piece, shipped off to Athens to adorn some museum or other, an act for which he and the Frenchman will claim credit and worldwide acclaim?'

The shock seemed to ripple through the crowd.

'You mean to tell us it has never occurred to you before?' he accused them, rabble-rousing quite shamelessly now. 'You mean to tell us you know nothing of the Raptor's plans to evacuate the treasures, saving them from the robbers he sees amongst you?'

Now he was rubbing salt into their fresh wounds, and it stung.

'And you, Papás. Will you finally be content that these pagan relics no longer pollute your Christian island?'

I would never have believed it possible had I not seen it with my own eyes. People in the crowd who had never spared a thought for the ancient city, suddenly thinking it was theirs and about to be snatched from them in broad daylight.

A troubled look crossed the Papás' face. I could lip-read his question at twenty paces. 'Is this true?' he demanded of Papadaikis.

To which the Mayor tossed his head in an angry gesture of defiance, half buried eyes probably still clinging to the sticky dreams Guirand had been spinning him for months.

Whistles and catcalls from the crowd, cries of 'vandalism!' and 'thieves!' from among the students.

Having sensed which way the wind was blowing, Katina struck an indignant pose, fists digging into ample hips. 'And what right does this Frenchman have anyway, sticking his nose into our affairs, that's what I would like to know!'

More colourful epithets were aimed at Papadaikis, mainly relating to the bribes he had obviously pocketed for his treachery, and his collusion with tyrants. Glaring into the crowd, Manolis was scribbling down the names of the worst offenders, each rash tongue risking jail for besmirching the good name of the Junta.

Before he knew it, his notebook had been trampled into the dirt, the hotheads shoving bodies to get to the Mayor, fists punching air.

The Councillors were tottering on their feet, Manolis and Chondro straining to push back the buckling line, their uniforms twisted out of shape. Fearing the worst, they beat a hasty retreat to their lime green rust bucket, the angry mob chasing them along the track like a cloud of angry hornets. Cheers echoed over the peninsula as the van finally disappeared over the ridge.

Huxley didn't wait to see them go. He thrust his way through the crowd, ignoring the laudatory claps on the shoulder from those who had elevated him to hero of the moment.

I was thrown by his reaction, puzzled that he obviously saw no cause for celebration.

'There is less time than ever,' he snapped, stuffing papers into his briefcase. 'They will be back. We have won a temporary reprieve, nothing more. The order has been served.'

'But those permits...'

'They have been out of date for months. Half the ministers who issued them have probably fled abroad, and the rest will be too busy shredding documents if the Junta *has* delivered its verdict.'

33.

July was melting into August. It was 97 degrees in the shade, and the mercury was still rising. People hid away in whatever shelter they could find. Groaning, they lay in darkened rooms, wrapping themselves in water-soaked sheets. Scarcely a coherent word could be heard from anyone, the white heat bringing about its own stubborn delirium. Every day the sun rose as a molten globule, squashed by its own weight, then climbed into a whitening metallic sky.

At night, we tossed and turned in our beds, gasping for air, swatting at the mosquitoes whining in our ears, eventually falling into a sticky, delirious sleep.

Tuesday morning. The mercury nudging a 110. Not a breath of wind. The air seemed denser, staler, than ever, the bleached-bone mountain radiating heat like a stove.

Too hot to dig, write, even think, we were drinking iced tea under the white sail awning strung over Huxley's tent, which at least offered some respite from the worst of the sun.

'Where is he?' fretted Hadrian. 'We've not seen hide nor hair of him in a week.' He added with sudden asperity: 'Is he even *on* the island?' Though spitting sarcasm, the implication was clear enough: Huxley wasn't the kind of captain to go down with his ship, having selflessly seen all hands safely to the lifeboats.

'He's at Monolithos,' I said, in the know for once because I'd been ferrying him supplies every day, everything from logbooks to typewriter ribbon.

'Doing what?'

'Writing.'

'Writing what? His memoirs? Letters home? A stage play?'

'Perhaps he will still pull something off,' said Anna gloomily.

'It's over. Get used to it,' retorted Hadrian, his face drenched in sweat, the hair plastered to his forehead. '*Talk of the devil*,' he muttered, squinting into the distance as Huxley chose that moment to advance across the compound, almost like a liquid mirage himself until he entered the shadow of the sail.

'Well?' he demanded peremptorily, settling into one of the canvas chairs, a hefty Manila file under his arm. 'Have I missed anything?' He stretched across the camp table, splashing iced tea into a glass.

'We were talking about Atlantis,' said Sam, with a bloody-minded grin.

Huxley replied stonily: 'I am gratified to hear it, because it is high time we presented the evidence.'

'In this heat?' groaned Hadrian, apparently still convinced that Huxley's only intention was to put minds on the philosophical treadmill again.

'Time waits for no man, Hadrian,' came the terse reply. 'You of all people should know that, after sacrificing 25 years of your life grubbing about in the dirt bequeathed to you by the dead.'

It was enough to freeze the moist pink smile into a grimace. 'What do you mean?' he asked weakly.

Thrusting his hand into the manila envelope, Huxley retrieved a sheaf of neatly typed pages, the first bearing a title in block capitals I could just decipher over his elbow: *PLATO'S ATLANTIS. THE LOST ISLE, DISCOVERED.*

Across the table the others were still squinting hard at the inverted lettering as he flicked over the page. Snatching a defiant breath, he began outlining his theory, deftly interweaving elements of Plato's legend with our finds on the peninsula, splicing in every discipline of science from vulcanology to botany.

Well into his stride now, he was counting off the points of his argument one by one as if they were court exhibits, from the lofty trees and flowing rivers, to the ingenious feats of architectural engineering; from the keen knowledge of astronomy, to the vivid scenes of spiritual and aesthetic devotion depicted in the frescoes, the sheer glorification of life.

Peering over his half-moon reading glasses, he paused to make eye contact with each of us, just as a lawyer might the members of a jury.

'When the volcano exploded, the shock wave was greater than a hundred thousand Hiroshimas. The blast was heard across a quarter of the world. Ash, churning into the sky, turning day into night. Volcanic bombs raining down over the eastern Mediterranean, torching fields and villages, hurling debris as far away as Egypt and Asia Minor... The resulting tidal wave, 500 feet high, swept across the Aegean, drowning all but the mountains of Minoan Crete in less than an hour. Asphyxiated by toxic gas, suffocated by mud and ash, drowned by flood waves, people perished en masse. Ash and other debris remained in the upper atmosphere for years. Temperatures plummeted and, in all likelihood, weather patterns were disrupted over the whole region. Floods, droughts and plant-withering frosts would have become commonplace for years. Worn away by pestilence and starvation, survivors closest to the epicentre might well have envied the dead...'

We were hanging on his every word. And how compelling it sounded when all the facts were glued together like that, one reinforcing the other.

I was startled by a slow, mocking handclap: Hadrian's.

'I commend you, Huxley. Especially for the atomic analogy. How well it suits the times. The blast at ground zero. The rivers of fire. The fallout, exterminating an entire people. The ash clogging the sky, creating an atomic winter. Why,' he added, his sarcasm like a whiplash, 'one can almost picture Almighty Zeus himself, peering out of the Olympian clouds, hurling his bolts of radioactive lightning —'

'You don't find the theory plausible, Hadrian?' said Anna, crossly.

'A theory?' cried Hadrian indignantly. 'Is that what it is? And what do you make of it — you, Sam, you Pedrosa?'

'It is... intriguing,' replied Sam guardedly, the blue prisms apparently regarding their former mentor in a curious new light.

'There are so many pieces of evidence,' I said. 'The theory sounds compelling, yes.'

Hadrian threw up his hands in disbelief. 'You see? Proof positive, if any were ever needed, that science should be left for trained minds, not the idly curious, not the ignorant —'

'What do you mean?' I said, stung by the insult.

'Truth is not what we want to believe, Pedrosa. Science is not what is most convenient to us at any given moment in time. Theories are meant to transcend subjective desire or personality, not become the products of them.'

'Then why are your own theories so petty and bourgeois?' scowled Sam.

'Don't you see?' demanded Hadrian, ignoring the barb. 'Huxley should be trying to prove himself wrong, not right. That is the measure of any scientist worthy of the name.'

With distaste, he turned to the object of his indignation.

'Well, isn't that so, Huxley? In fact, wasn't it you yourself who always insisted that facts should form the theory and not the other way around?'

Huxley offered a curt nod: 'Examine the evidence. That is all I ask.'

'Yes, by all means, what *about* the evidence?' demanded Hadrian, his voice, sharp with impatience, gaining an octave. 'More to the point, what about the evidence that is all the more glaring for its absence?'

The evidence that is invisible. My eyes were darting around the table, one face to the other. I think I had forgotten to breathe.

'Your hypothesis is a house of cards, Huxley,' Hadrian went on. 'A rusty bucket full of holes. And what I find most troubling of all is that it is inconceivable that you don't know it yourself. Almost as the basis of your so-called theory you reason that every ancient myth is rooted in fact. You speak of Mycenae, Atlantis, the Labyrinth of the Minotaur, even the Valley of the Kings in the same breath. You assign significance to every find, fact or supposition, linking it to the legend, highlighting coincidences, ignoring contradictions.'

'You are mistaken,' replied Huxley, in a deceptively mild voice.

'Am I? Then kindly explain the most fatal contradiction of all... If this is Atlantis, if this is Plato's legend incarnate, then where pray tell is the evidence of its evil decline? Where is the evidence of an honourable, spiritually-enlightened people falling from grace, becoming unprincipled, warlike, filled with avarice? Where are the spears and broadswords, the catapult stones? Where is the corruption and decay? Where is the evil, the bloodlust. Where is the hell on earth?'

So that's what you've been turning the peninsula upside down for, I thought, with a sudden thud of realisation. *Not just bodies and tombs, but evidence of war, murder, greed.*

'Everyone is entitled to their own interpretation of the evidence, Hadrian. I have made mine. And now we shall see what the world makes of it.'

'You can't be serious,' spluttered Hadrian, reluctant even now to think the worst.

'The news will be breaking even as we speak,' said Huxley, stony-faced, glancing at his watch. 'The press communiqué has been distributed through Paris. The abstract of the paper submitted via the Secretariat itself.'

We had been cut out of the loop, sidelined. From what he was saying, the Comte's Orpheus Foundation was now handling the press-work from the ground up, working the phones, dispatching telegrams and telexes. London, New York, Tokyo. Paris, Rome, Athens. Within a few short hours, no one would be in any doubt at all about Professor Unknown staking his claim to Atlantis, the most immortal legend of all.

My eyes strayed to the others. Like me, they were slowly coming to, recovering from the blast.

Hadrian, livid, shell-shocked, the words still ringing in his ears. Nestor, calculating Huxley's motives and actions like an engineer pondering an unfamiliar blueprint. Sam, his face flushed with renewed admiration for the mentor he imagined had betrayed him. Playing chicken with the Junta, taking the brinkmanship with Guirand and Sarrides right down to the wire, as exhilarating as dancing along a crumbling cliff edge.

'It's one thing to debate such matters around the dinner table, Huxley,' rasped Hadrian, 'where I almost expect you to take an indefensible line — but this! It will ruin us.'

'You might have consulted us first, Marcus,' said Anna, resentfully. 'Before our names are plastered all over the papers.'

Suddenly, Hadrian seemed to be on the verge of heat stroke, wheezing, trying to catch his breath. Anna hurriedly refilled his glass with iced water, then drenched a tea towel for his forehead. Hadrian snatched it up, burying his face, as the implications broke over him like some immense tidal wave.

'How dare you!' he croaked at last, his oval face emerging from the towel, glasses skewed over his nose. 'How dare you gamble with our lives and our careers like this!'

'It may not be as bad as you think, Hadrian,' soothed Anna unconvincingly, but he roughly brushed her aside.

'You think archaeologists can live off headlines, Huxley? Well think again. Once the press gets hold of this, we'll be a laughing stock. Pilloried! Ruined!'

'How little you know of human nature, Hadrian,' said Huxley remorselessly.

'And how little you know of our profession! The genteel thuggery. The petty reprisals for slights real or imagined. The barefaced egotism masquerading as scintillating logic. When they hear about this at Oxford, Cambridge, Boston, wherever, they'll never let us live it down. Never. Overnight, we shall all be tarred with the same brush — crook, crank, charlatan — the perfect company in fact for all those other spiritualists, mediums and con men who have exploited Atlantis for fame, gain or glory for two thousand years. Either way, we can kiss our careers goodbye. No one on any self-respecting dig will touch us again with a ten foot bargepole.'

'He warned you yesterday, Hadrian,' said Sam, his eyes bright, his lips fighting a grin. 'Be careful what you wish for —'

'Oh, go back to your weed, Sam — you deserve each other! As for you, Huxley, there are no words to describe my contempt for you or for what you have done.'

'Where are you going?' said Anna, as Huxley pushed back his chair. She added forcefully: 'You can't leave it like this Marcus!'

'Where's he going?' she trailed-off, as he disappeared between the sheds.

'To meet Papadaikis and his cronies, of course,' said Nestor, as though that should have been transparent even to a child.

'And here was I thinking he'd gone in search of Atlantis' evil decline,' said Hadrian, the words spitting venom. 'Fitting, you have to admit, for someone who has just sold his soul to the Devil.'

34.

It wasn't even daylight when the phones started ringing. At first, a discreet trilling. By midmorning, a jangling peal. By midday, a chorus every bit as grating and insistent as the midsummer cicadas. And that was only Athens and Thessalonica calling.

When the *Pegasus* landed on Friday morning, three-day old newspapers were carried from house to house like the sacred Easter flame, their front page splash about Atlantis, about the island, about Huxley, probably eliciting more amazement here than anywhere else.

Suddenly, everywhere you went, you'd hear people expounding authoritatively upon the legend. Fishermen stitching their nets, kids playing hoops, street hawkers jabbering over the floppy ears of their donkeys. Recalling Homer, Aristotle, Alexander the Great, their own great grandmothers, occasionally, even Plato himself.

You heard the knowing voices in the street, in the corner shop, in the *plateia*, or from the passing mule train. About Huxley, the good and learned man, whom providence had sent into their lives. About the certainty of the legend's home here, because it was right and just.

Hearing that, I couldn't help remembering the accusation the 'good man' had hurled at Hadrian, about him knowing so little about human nature.

Then all of a sudden, the rest of the world woke up.

At the telephone exchange poor Toula was at her wit's end, a barrage of calls hitting her in languages she never knew even existed.

The machine with the octopus tentacles that had intermittently croaked into life had gone crazy, people with faint, unintelligible voices wanting this, that, the other, she couldn't say what. She sat there tugging and plugging the patch cords, shrieking about her aching arms to anyone on the other end of the line, it didn't matter if it was the Mayor down the street or the news desk of the New York Times.

When the language defeated her, she patched the calls through to any number that was still free, so that a puzzled Papás, Chondro or Mad Yanni the Gravedigger would suddenly find themselves talking unintelligibly to Tokyo, Los Angeles or London.

In the Mayor's office, the phone was ringing off the hook, day and night, a bewildered Giannis Papadaikis right in the thick of it, fielding intimidating questions from Junta officials in Athens, livid demands from Guirand or Sarrides, and enquiries from reporters in places where it was apparently morning in the middle of the night.

New York, Melbourne, Hong Kong. They were all on the phone. Sometimes, they were even on their way, broadsheets, tabloids, glossy magazines. Radio and television stations were assigning crews, fighting paperwork to get their gear through customs, snatching up the last vacant cabins on the *Pegasus*. Within days, the ship was having to adjust its route and timetable just to meet demand.

'Why? *Giatí?*' Papadaikis was heard to ask, bewildered by all the commotion ringing in his ears.

'Atlantis, the discovery of the century?' came the incredulous reply, tossed and buffeted across the oceans.

Sunday afternoon, the Councillors and notables beat a path to Huxley's door, bearing gifts, heat wave shines to their cheeks, bright broad smiles stretching their lips.

Giannis Papadaikis, with a sticky gloss comb-over, leading the huddling little procession between the dismembered statues in Huxley's garden, climbing the steps, tapping the door, a glass flagon of the island's finest wine cradled in the crook of his arm.

His wife Stavroula, the power behind the throne, hair rinsed and set just for the occasion, a ribbon-tied box of island sweetmeats in her hand.

Katina at her shoulder, pushing forward, a huge bouquet of flowers tickling her nose. Trailing down the steps, the rest of the Council, then something even stranger. Manolis and Chondro, fumbling with the buttons of their uniforms, their ears still ringing from the dressing-down they'd received from the superintendent in Athens. Only Father Nannos was conspicuous by his absence.

Standing behind him as he wrenched open the door, I almost expected Huxley to turn them away with a flea in their ear; he probably had every right to.

Instead, he welcomed them out onto the terrace under the grape-heavy vines, cleared the table and, with Myroula's help in the kitchen, conjured up a feast, indulging his guests in a hospitality that even the ancients might have smiled upon. More tables and chairs were carried out from the storeroom. More *mezedakia* from the kitchen, Myroula beating eggs, dicing hot peppers, frying feta, scolding him about the chaos, but not really meaning it.

Soon, half the island was there, including the bouzouki and violí players from the village.

I could hardly believe it. Just days ago we had been pariahs, about to be booted off the island for good, goodbye and good riddance. And now look. We had become heroes of the hour, every last man and woman in camp, it didn't matter if it was Huxley himself, the teachers and students, or one of the trench moles.

I saw Stavros Sanassis arrive, and caught the amused, penetrating look he threw his friend, as if to say, *so we are on our way then.* Then the postmaster, Vassilis Nafpliotis, nodding in his dignified way to this face or that as he threaded his way to the head of the table.

They had hardly taken their seats before the band struck up, diving into one of those traditional Aegean ballads that every Greek knows by heart, be they eight or eighty. The first dancers were drawn into the circle between the tables, moving with that raw grace that sings not of cities, but of sea, ridges and mountains.

Between songs, the postmaster rose to offer a toast, in one urbane breath commending both Huxley and the slack-jawed Papadaikis for their vision. In the euphoria of the moment, the heady fumes of the wine, even his romantic evocations about amphitheatres and windmills, academies and forests, met with delirious applause.

I saw Hadrian arrive, blundering onto the terrace in a kind of stupor, unable to believe his eyes. He sank into the nearest vacant chair, pouring himself several glasses of wine and downing them in quick succession. He gaped at the dancers in the daisy chain, Anna, Nestor, Maria, Aris, Alexis Pangalos, the councillors. He gawped at Huxley playing the gracious host, explaining Atlantis to Giannis Papadaikis in ways that would have suited a child's picture book. *Never mind about the inconvenient facts. Just look at the pretty pictures.*

'Expediency of the worst kind!' he seethed, spurning even Myroula's finger-licking mezedakia. 'Huxley's barefaced cynicism will end up costing us our careers, quite possibly even our liberty, you just see if it doesn't. Solemn archaeology, with its bickering and backstabbing, will see to that. While these village fools are dancing their socks off, Claude Guirand will be running from ministry to ministry, thrusting the offending headlines into the faces of officials, demanding our expulsion, if not our heads — you can bank on it.'

Watching Hadrian grumble and sweat, I had no trouble picturing it. Guirand in the asphalt-melting streets, trying to find some minister who wasn't on the beach, some functionary prepared to take his myth-poisoning accusations seriously.

Snapping at his driver to run the lights, rapping the front passenger seat with his skull-headed cane, too self-obsessed to realise what was happening under his very nose: human nature, picking off his allies one by one. They were all falling under the legend's hypnotic spell, gone before Guirand could even beat the traffic to prevent it.

First the dazzle-eyed desk clerks drinking in the morning headlines with their muddy Greek coffee and sesame rings. Then up the stairs to the mid-level staffers, two days into the sensation and already thinking Atlantis as true to Hellas as Alexander the Great. Then all along the parquet corridors to the upholstered doors of the permanent secretaries themselves, forever fretting over scandal and insulating themselves from liability. Taking in the rapturous headlines, and thinking, there's just no denying how popular, how irresistible this thing is becoming, why put a stop to it now? Deskbound or lolling under a beach umbrella, who could fail to see that? *Atlantis*. At worst, just a harmless summer craze, something that will die off with the mosquitoes in autumn.

Then on to the Junta-appointed ministers and their deputies, caught off guard at first by the questions fired at them from the sudden press scrums on the pavement, the microphones thrust into their faces, the sizzling flash bulbs going off in their eyes. How long did it take them to realise it — days, hours, minutes? That there is far more to this than meets the eye, far more than a midsummer madness. There's opportunity, advantage, profit.

Just look at how the headlines are deflecting attention away from other things; officials on the take, exiles clamouring for justice and revenge, political prisoners on hunger strike, democracy being murdered. Look at the press, turning this foreigner into a popular hero. Look at Hellas, suddenly on everyone's lips for all the right reasons for a change, making its blue and white splash in the capitals of the world. Enough to bring an avuncular smile even to the lips of the Colonels themselves. How can the regime move against this Huxley character now, whatever black marks have been put beside his name? — as likely as not, out of envy or jealousy, you know how it is sometimes in this country, every man trying to get ahead by killing his neighbour's goat. There would be money in this, anyone could see it. Even a simpleton could see it. It was just human nature. There would be political capital. There would be fame and fortune beyond reckoning.

35.

The August sun was hissing and boiling into the sea by the time they returned from the temple heights, hurrying now before the pagan darkness could surround their Christian souls. Less a gesture of homage than the staking of a land claim but, even so, Huxley took it in his stride. Bright with chatter, the notables billowed past us, still gushing about the frescoes of the dolphins and saffron gatherers, the Atlantean plumbing which had to be seen to be believed. *Toilets, with running water, right inside the house! Baths, you could almost swim in!*

'Let the green-eyed haggling commence,' said Hadrian scathingly, glad to see the back of them.

'But they represent the local community,' I said. 'They'll do their best to make sure everyone benefits, won't they.'

'Yes, Pedrosa. That's exactly what they're going to do. And we'll all live happily ever after.'

'You're forgetting about the symposiasts,' I snapped, clicking my tongue at him. 'They have the vision, the idealism, to make it happen.' Adding under my breath: 'That's what Atlantis is, isn't it. A lost island idyll, the code word for the perfect society.'

He threw his arms into the air with a disparaging groan.

Let Hadrian complain all he likes, I thought, lagging behind as the others disappeared into the twilight. At least Huxley is trying to get us off the hook. Enemies turned into friends, just like he said. The notables, beating a path to his door. The police, fawning all over him, wagging their tails. Guirand and Sarrides, chased back to the damp cave they'd flown out of. The Colonels, not even suspecting for a moment this Trojan Horse of an idea they had just wheeled into their own midst.

If anyone could pull this off, Huxley could.

If ever I had feared the power of his mind, or those soaring moments that could meld colours, bend reality, evoke eternity, I didn't any longer. He could make the impossible happen. I had seen it with my own eyes.

The sun was spilling the last of its liquid light into the sea, drop by drop. I watched the shadows deepen, the watermelon light lingering over the horizon. A breeze was rising. Clouds were fluffing up in the darkest part of the sky. The brightest stars were appearing between the temple columns.

The more I thought about it, the more I began to wonder if I hadn't misjudged him all along.

Even that accusation he'd hurled at me out on the rock beds seemed all too reasonable now — about expecting to find truth wallowing in the primeval sludge. Things that hypnotise, attract or repel, that evoke loathing or desire. Is that really where I expected to find the truth?

At the time, I'd resented even hearing it, but now found it increasingly hard to deny. What pure, unadulterated facts did I have to go on to prove his guilt about anything, when all was said and done? Suddenly, I was hard-pressed to find even a single accusation that had not been spawned in the mud, mine or somebody else's.

In the deepening shadows, Huxley's approach seemed hardly more tangible than the wind rustling the dry thistles among the ruins.

'So we are not to be thrown off the island after all,' I said, eager for news.

'We are not out of the woods yet,' he cautioned me, 'not by a long chalk.'

He shuffled his feet and frowned, gazing off into the dusk, as if trying to make up his mind about something.

At last he said: 'Tomorrow I want you to go to Athens. The paper is ready and I can't trust the mail to deliver it for me. You must take it to the Academy on Syngrou and deliver it by hand. It is time they saw that there is hard science to all this, in spite of what Hadrian thinks. I want you to meet with our supporters, with the press. I would go myself, but can't afford days away from the dig, much less a week.'

I nodded, the gravity of what he was asking me to do making my head swim. He was trusting me, depending on me. I had finally taken Benja's place.

Sensing the jitters in me, he added: 'You know the excavations inside out. If there are any technical questions you cannot answer, then don't. If anyone talks politics at you, shrug and say, you have no politics, your mind is 3,500 years away. I trust you to watch your tongue. You know what is at stake. For all of us.'

36.

Just as the day dawned a livid pink I boarded the *Pegasus*, an overnight bag in one hand and Huxley's own leather briefcase in the other.

Suddenly, looks, impressions, appearances were everything, a fact I found hard to adjust to after having the opposite drummed into my head for months on end.

At Huxley's insistence, a room had been reserved for me at the *Grande Bretagne* on Syntagma square, whose understated opulence and old world charm would doubtless impress anyone who might find me there. Anyone except me, that is, who began to feel like an imposter the moment he set eyes on the Rolls-Royces and Bentleys drawing up outside, the concierge in his impeccable gold braid uniform, the crystal chandeliers.

Ragged thunderstorms had broken the heat wave during the night, and the streets were still wet with rain. Under the returning sun, the tarmac steamed, the tyres singing. I tried to flag down a taxi on the corner but the noon rush hour had already beaten me to it. So I caught a trolley bus down to the Academy instead, huddled under the 'no-spitting' signs with the other straphangers. At almost every stop there was a kiosk, the newspapers and magazines pegged up outside still hailing the discovery of the century.

Climbing the broad marble stairway to the Academy, I presented myself at the reception desk. To my surprise the Director appeared almost immediately, taking possession of Huxley's precious paper in person, a transaction duly recorded with a flourish of signatures and rubber stamps.

On my way out, my luck took a turn for the worse as I ran into the last man in the world I wanted to see. Sophoklis Sarrides, swooping past the flustered doorkeeper, no doubt to remonstrate with the Director himself to prevent publication. There was no mistaking the claw hands, the black smoothed-down hair with the rebellious feather tuft on the crown, the raptor's hooked nose.

Recognising me, he cast me a look that, in another life, might have torn flesh, talons and beak ripping skin.

I hurried back to the hotel, the encounter unnerving me more than I cared to admit, what with the random police checkpoints in the streets, the armoured cars guarding government buildings, the tanks deployed outside the radio and television station.

I tried to focus on the job at hand, the noise, filth and chaos of the city making it harder than I ever imagined.

Soon, I was finding it difficult to sleep, and even more difficult to shake a few clear thoughts out of the smog as I watched the sun rise over the grimy streets sprawling away from the Acropolis.

When word began to spread through the city that I had come armed with new evidence to bolster the Atlantis hypothesis, including spectacular new finds in the western sector, the telephone hardly stopped ringing. The frescoes of the river, with the palm trees and the water birds. The young priestess with her devotional lamp at the mountain temple. The leaping dolphins. Finds that Huxley had purposely left for just this moment, all the more to stoke the media frenzy.

I met with the foreign press corps; with the British Consul; with government officials, some in suits and ties, others in military uniform. For all the butterflies in my stomach, a squint of suspicion here, a calculating look there, it seemed the headlines were working their magic, at least where it mattered most, among the Colonels.

I called home, Sofi's breathless voice answering on the second ring. 'Nico! We just saw you on the news! Mum's over the moon, she can't stop talking about it. *Atlantis*, Nico! *You must be doing somersaults!*'

As the week wore on, I even began to think that I had become a match for anything Athens could throw at me. I should have known better. But then perhaps nothing could have quite prepared me for the moment Claude Guirand blew into the Grande Bretagne on the squall of his own outrage, flew up the stairs and began hammering on my door.

'For how long does he imagine the world will tolerate this fraud, these barefaced lies?' he bawled, barging past me into the room.

I closed the heavy door behind him, hoping it might at least prevent the Frenchman's rant from reaching curious ears all the way down to the lobby.

'Did it never occur to you, young man, that your master is a liar who thinks nothing of exploiting you to deceive the world? Did it never so much as enter that vacuous head of yours that he is looting the site under your very nose?'

And it went on like that for the next twenty minutes, his poison-spitting tirade sparing no one — the cynicism of the press, the gullibility of the public, the spineless opportunism of the regime, the greed of profiteers.

'*Atlantis!*' he seethed, as though the word were too excruciating even to speak out loud. 'He has made monkeys out of you all, *monkeys!* Has it never even occurred to your simian brains that all this is fake and fabrication?'

'All he asks is that the evidence be examined and independently assessed,' I hit back. 'Is that not the correct way?'

With a click of disgust, he slumped onto the sofa, bleak, rheumy eyes straying to the open briefcase on the coffee table. Wheezing, he jabbed the contents contemptuously with the tip of his stick, the careless movement dislodging a single photograph from the pile. Seeing it, he winced, recoiling as if stung. Why, who could tell. It was just the macro of that potsherd I had last seen between Huxley's fingertips, the one depicting a flowing river, reeds, the prow of a punt.

For a full thirty seconds he just sat there, staring, thin lips compressed and almost invisible, parchment cheeks caving in on themselves, gaunt head turning inexorably into a skull. The ferocious cynicism he had barged in with was gone, and what remained was almost spectral.

Struggling to his feet at last, he hobbled towards the window, surveying the mad traffic circling Syntagma below. Hands clasped behind his back, he was trying to catch his breath, coming now in hollow wheezing gasps. For a second, I even contemplated calling down for a doctor.

When finally he spoke again, it was in a venomous hiss. 'You may convey to your master that I am neither impressed by his thoughts nor intimidated by his actions. He has spent years on site and yet what does he have to show for it — a few pretty frescoes, that's all, a few ambiguous fragments.'

The injustice of the accusation smacked so blatantly of envy it seemed inconceivable that anyone would believe him now.

'You have already tried, and failed, to seize control of the excavations,' I said, standing my ground. 'Local people won't stand for it.'

'There is more than one way to skin a cat, young man. The public's infatuation will wane and the tinpots will soon find some other shiny trinket in which to admire their own reflections!'

Our eyes clashed. If Huxley's nemesis had been at death's door a moment earlier, he wasn't any longer. He may have looked like some dazed Lazarus being raised from the tomb, the soil still clogging his hair, the mould still growing on his skin, yet even one glance into that gaunt face was to know firsthand the power of mind over matter.

I realised then, my stomach twisting in apprehension. Staring death in the face or not, this man would go to any lengths, use any means at his disposal, to defeat us. Mad with jealousy, he was capable of anything — even of commissioning Benja's murder, maybe in some thwarted attempt to buy or corrupt him.

As soon as I'd shown Guirand the door I collapsed onto the bed, so sapped of energy it left me wondering about the source of the old man's power, and why he should be walking out of the room reinvigorated, while I was lying there as sick as a dog.

When the phone rang moments later, I couldn't bring myself to answer it. I knew it would be Huxley checking up on me, because he always called at noon. I let it ring, stuffing the pillow to my ears.

I stayed in my room for the rest of the day trying, and failing, not to think about the mess we were in. When finally I ventured downstairs in search of a beer and a sandwich I found the hotel lobby swarming with people, some still coming in through the revolving doors, others emerging from the brasserie or the atrium.

Academics in threadbare jackets and beige slacks. Elegant young women in outfits straight off the catwalk. Old ladies with stretched skin and candyfloss hair, trying to look half their age. Young men in budget summer suits, probably on their way to some cultural event at the Herodion amphitheatre. A group of youths in tracksuits, probably attending an international meet at the stadium. Boys in ragged jeans and tee-shirts, hair tumbling onto their shoulders. Girls in colourful kaftans, all bells, beads and bangles, who looked as if they'd just returned from trekking in the Himalayas, or at least, the tea and resin shops in Kathmandu.

An odd mix, even for a place like this, its foyer an international crossroads.

Passing the auditorium, I ran into one of the blue-rinse ladies returning from the powder room. Her bird-like eyes brightened.

'Aren't you joining us, young man?' she quavered, clutching my arm.

I remembered her from Huxley's interview list, and our rendezvous at the atrium coffee shop, where she had plied me with cream cakes and Viennese coffee, all the while wittering on about the Cycladic light, the sunsets of Atlantis, the spirit of her dear departed husband travelling with her island to island; anything that had come butterflying to mind.

The milling bodies parted like the Red Sea, as some debonair, silver-haired VIP was ushered through the marble foyer with an obsequiousness that obviously owed itself to far more than money, old or new. At his devoted side, a lady exuding the same bedazzling self-importance, repudiating her seventies in a blond wig and impeccable haute couture.

As theatrically as the scene itself, the hubbub, the chatter, the clinking champagne flutes, the laughter, fell like a curtain.

'Who are they?' I asked. Like everyone else, I must have been staring.

An adoring look entered her eyes. 'They are the Comte et Comtesse Guillaume d'Adhémar, you silly boy!'

Silly boy indeed. They were the architects of the Orpheus Foundation. My überbosses. The people paying my wages. Why hadn't Huxley told me, why hadn't he warned me? He must have known. Here and there the Comte et Comtesse paused to greet their supporters, the so-called Friends of Orpheus, indulgent, aloof, sanctimonious to a fault.

I glanced across at the notice board at the elevators, where the pin-on letters said it all. *Atlantis Discovered. An International Seminar, by Invitation Only.*

Dangling from a silver thread, an elegant flyer announced a weekend retreat to the Lost Isle itself, and an exclusive guided tour by the man of the moment, Marcus James Huxley.

I noted the curious wing and lyre emblem of the Orpheus Foundation, and a Latin motto that I could hardly decipher at all, something about the soul in knowledge of the light.

The retinue billowed past like a shoal of fish. Somewhere midstream came a girl and boy, barely seventeen at a guess, in black jeans and dazzling white shirts, almost breathtaking for their looks, their wide eyes and radiant skin. If not for the lack of any familial resemblance I might have taken them for the grandchildren, but that wasn't it. The Comte et Comtesse, so accustomed to according lesser mortals their rightful place in the great scheme of things, were indulgent, no, almost deferential, towards them — but why?

221

The entourage buckled as the Comte paused to shake hands with an imposing man in a stiff new suit, with a chain smoker's gravely voice and an extravagant smile.

'The Minister of Culture,' came an obliging deadpan voice behind me. 'The Colonels can obviously use the public relations. Atlantis — what a gift!'

Or a Trojan Horse, I thought, biting down on my lips.

The Friends of Orpheus were streaming in through the auditorium's double doors, taking places in the tiered seating fanning out from the stage. This baffling mix of humanity, all thronging into one room.

Suddenly, something else caught my attention. Or rather *someone*, down on the stage, adjusting the lectern microphone. The sight did a better job of snatching my breath away than the smog. Svetlana Bé, still dressed in black from head to toe, albeit in chiffon this time instead of winter wool.

I caught the ice splintering look; she had spotted me. Sooner or later, it said. There would be no escape.

My eyes strayed to the elaborate decorations around the auditorium, banners, wall hangings, exhibition-size posters.

I should have known.

Islands, straight out of Huxley's all-consuming obsession. In arcane ancient script, in pigments and poetry, in mosaic, stone and clay. Atlantis, with its volcano-like mountain and circular waterways. The Isles of the Blest in the path of the setting sun. Islands I once supposed were mythical only to end up in the haze of legend; islands I imagined were real only to turn into a metaphor for some other reality.

As the Comte took to the lectern, the lights dimmed. *Was that Huxley's book in his hands?* It had to be. It was just as Sam had described it, with its unassuming charcoal cover and gold embossed lettering: *Travels in Elysium*.

'Friends of Orpheus...' he began, his voice as rich as chocolate as it resonated out across the tiered wooden seating. 'Why deny it? Why pretend? We are obsessed by islands — mythical, legendary, real, home to the living or the dead... *Why?* Because they have always meant far more to us than the dictionary definition would allow: *island*, noun, an area of land completely surrounded by water. — *No, no, no, that will not do at all!*'

My eyes widened at the playful groans and laughter now rippling through the spangled darkness.

'And thus August finds us, not on some Caribbean isle or Pacific atoll, but a stone's throw from Plato's Academy, here to honour the discovery of the most eternal island legend of them all.'

Applause broke through the auditorium like pelting rain; there was something almost ecstatic about it. The Comte raised both hands to quell the bedlam: 'And yet... what *is* Atlantis, does anybody know?'

Navigating my way by the floor lighting, I fumbled into a vacant chair. I had heard them all, a dozen times or more, these motives that cling to Plato's Atlantis as tenaciously as limpets to a sunken rock. Myth, legend, hoax, metaphor, the mummified remains of history. Knowing he would never so much as breathe the words Trojan Horse in public, I was just waiting for the Conundrum to make its mind-bending appearance, when the Comte threw something altogether more startling into the mix: '...Or is it that in the charred remains of our Atlantis, an island that has known life and annihilation, glory and infamy, we are seeing the raw essence of all metaphysical knowledge: that which concerns itself with last things, the end of days, life and death?'

That made me sit up, I admit, and by the time my roiling thoughts had subsided, our blue-blooded Captain was navigating among some of the most mythical islands ever to grace the Aegean sunset.

A murmur, strangely melodic, rippled through the auditorium. Whoever all these people were, in ripped jeans or impeccable suits, they were hanging on his every word, leaning forward in their seats, eyes glittering in the reflected footlights from the stage.

'Where do they lie, the Isles of the Blest?' mused the Comte, pitching his rhetorical question high into the auditorium.

Where do they lie? *Where do they lie?* Up in the tiered seating like that, hands screwed into fists, it made me want to yell it out loud just to puncture their over-inflated, child's balloon of a fixation. Didn't they get it? The Isles of the Blest were just figments of ancient Aegean minds, that's all, peasants dreaming of deliverance from whatever hardship or tyranny had them in its grip. It was just the pure simple logic of it.

'In Greek myth, in make believe, in fairy tales, just as the sceptics' dismal chorus would have us believe?' Murmurs of protest billowed across the tiered rows.

'And if that's what you think,' said the Comte, a pre-emptive glare seeming to cull me from the herd, a single heretic amongst the faithful, 'then your bread-and-butter logic would deceive you, for the Isles of the Blest, or their myriad variations, appear in folklore throughout the Seven Seas. Look to the Biblical lands, and the Isles become Gnostic renditions of Heaven, reached across a resplendent sea. Look to the east, and in Taoist theories of immortality they become known as the five islands of P'eng-lai... As the seas pass beneath us, they become the Fortunate Isles, the Hesperides, the Western Isles, the Buddhist Pure Lands, Mag Mell, Tir na nÓg, a thousand others... Delve deep enough, and you will find these island other-worlds populating cultures from the Hindu to the Hopi, from Tibet to Timbuktu, Portugal to Polynesia.'

So? Maybe they were all dreaming of lands of milk and honey, did you ever think of that? Except... *Except what?* Why should the natives of the bounteous South Seas be seeing the same island visions as Peloponnesian goat herders or Tibetan monks. *Why should every island lie west? Beyond sunset. Fuck. It didn't make any sense at all.*

'Emperors and knights. Warriors and poets. Shamans, mystics, adventurers... Driven or inspired, over the millennia men and women have set sail for them in outrigger canoes, in triremes, junks and brigantines. They have scaled mountains and crossed glaciers for them at the summit of the world. A good many, it has to be said, never returned, bequeathing their bodies to the deep; their minds to the ether. Of those that survived, some found themselves marooned on less fortunate shores somewhere between here and sunset, broken, disillusioned, certain now that the isles were but a cynical illusion after all, lying only in the credulous seas of human desire.'

While he paused to take a sip of water, there was not a single murmur, cough or fidget to be heard.

'Wiser souls, of course, always knew that the journey lay beyond the physical limits of ship and sail... And yet before we ponder the how, let us begin here, in this island sown sea — the Aegean, as full-bloodied as red grape wine... In this part of the ancient world, eschatology tells us, every journey to Elysium begins with the Underworld, the Kingdom of Hades, the abode of the Dead. It begins with the river crossing, and a bronze obol placed on the tongue to pay the Ferryman...' The Comte bared his hands in mock entreaty. *'But then who am I to describe the river myth to those who have already made the crossing at least once before!'*

Applause swept through the auditorium like rolling thunder. Half of the audience were on their feet in rapture, and there were even sporadic taxicab whistles from the youths. The Friends of Orpheus. They adored him. And even if it was something his nobility would never have permitted him to admit, a secret taken to his deathbed, it was plain enough the Comte adored being adored.

Beating the crush, I slipped out through the swing doors, my thoughts still running the gauntlet of my own doubts.

Five minutes later I was sitting at a corner of the hotel bar, ordering my second beer, but still couldn't get that baffling image out of my head: Huxley, placing that ancient silver drachma on Benja's tongue. Why, when a bronze obol, the Ferryman's standard fare, would have done just as well? What had he meant by it? What was the symbolism of it?

A tip for the ride, something to say thank you. But no, that's not it.

Rising from the crypt of memory, one of those useless facts picked up in the college library came bursting out of the fog at me, sending half my beer spilling over the bar.

It was a bribe. *The silver drachma was a bribe.*

Because some trespassing heroes didn't pothole their way out of Hades as they made their escape, did they; they followed a different route altogether. They returned by boat — the Ferryman's, his act of treachery against the King of Death bought and paid for.

37.

The dawn chorus woke me at five. Athens' version of it, that is, cars, trucks, buses, motorbikes racing the clock, chasing the sunrise. The sky already had that nicotine stain to it. It was difficult to breathe. Impossible to sleep. Everyone was trying to get into the city before the heat wave began melting the asphalt.

Up on the hill, the Parthenon was trembling in the sun's orange heat haze, its dead bones silhouetted against the skyline like some mute omen to the future. Whatever Atlantis is or was, I was thinking, maybe the secret died with Plato. Maybe we would never know.

Killing time until the *Pegasus* sailed, I walked down to the lower end of Syntagma, watching the taxis and the battered trolley buses gobbling up and disgorging their prey. Bought a *Herald Tribune* at the kiosk, a sesame ring from a street pedlar, then wandered over to one of the open air cafés on the pavement.

Another breathless splash about Marcus James Huxley and his Atlantis, I remarked, quickly turning the page. I didn't want to read it, if only because the more I learnt the less I seemed to know.

Buried in the sports pages, I hardly even noticed when my coffee arrived, much less when someone sank into the chair at the next table, so close we were almost touching elbows.

'The single most potent weapon in human history,' said the voice. 'You must surely know what it is by now.'

I recognised its owner without even looking.

Svetlana Bé. The slender nose like carved ice. A desolate beauty more at home among the ice mountains of Antarctica than here in the sledgehammer heat of Attica.

'Belief,' she went on. 'The ability to conquer minds, rule opinion, and yes, where circumstances dictate, to deceive or delude. There is no escape. If you find that unlikely, just cast your eyes around the square.' Her ice-water look carried me to the garish advertising bill-boards shouting down at us from the building facades; to the headlines blaring out from the kiosk; to the television set beyond the plate glass window lurching through the morning news, a grin-and-bear-it Comte d'Adhémar shaking hands with Junta leader George Papadopoulos, amid a frenzy of popping flashbulbs.

'Sometimes the truth is elusive, to say the least.'

'You think I don't know that?'

'So the boy is finally becoming a man; Marcus has taught you something, at least.'

She summoned the waiter with a brisk wave and ordered a frappé. 'The world is overrun with lies and deception, Nicholas Pedrosa. If they are the weapons used against us, should we not defend ourselves by taking up arms as well?'

'Some people are conscientious objectors,' I said. 'Some people carry signs saying "ban the bomb".'

She threw me a sideways glance, probably wondering what lay beyond the words, childish naivety or a metaphor too clever for me by half.

'So Huxley called you in again. Is that why you're here? To handle things in Athens. To make sure they don't run out of control?'

'I have never worked for Marcus,' she replied, springing another surprise. 'True, I have acted on his behalf, as I did in Cambridge, inter-viewing you and the others. He needed to know that the candidates would be properly vetted, that there would be no mistakes made in the selection.'

'Like there were before?'

'A psychological evaluation was not conducted with the others. With hindsight, that may have been a mistake.'

Her frappé arrived. She lit a cigarette, probably debating how much I deserved to know.

'Then you work for the Orpheus Foundation, for the Comte,' I said. 'Funny, I hadn't thought of you as the tour guide type.'

'I shall not be accompanying them to Thera,' she replied, so coldly you could almost hear the ice cracking. 'Marcus and I find it trying to be in each other's company.'

To my puzzled look, she added, 'I see no one has told you. Fifteen years ago we were husband and wife — albeit only briefly.'

At first I thought it must be another lie, so farfetched did it seem. I could not imagine either of them in love with anyone, except maybe themselves. That left only convenience as a explanation.

'The Friends of Orpheus,' I said, casting my line into the murk. 'They seem an odd mix… and passionate with it.' *Or fanatical. Obsessed.*

'You should have stayed. You might have learnt something.'

'You forget. I am at the dig every day.'

She puffed at her cigarette in sudden exasperation. 'And still you do not even know what you are digging for!'

'Atlantis. Evidence of the decline. The fall into darkness.'

'Your naivety has not deserted you, I see. Obviously I chose you well.'

The bitterness and self-congratulation threw me for a second, but then I saw the insinuation, as grating as a tumble across the asphalt.

I was here in Athens playing the role I had been rehearsing for months without even knowing it. The lead actor in Marcus Huxley's elaborate theatre of deception.

I was gripping the arms of my chair, fingernails digging into the red plastic cord. If I bit any harder into my lips, there would be blood.

'Guirand was right,' I mumbled, the God-awful truth of it finally breaking over me like a tidal wave. 'Atlantis *is* a fraud.'

'Atlantis!' retorted Svetlana, and in that specially condescending way only she could manage, the pencil eyebrows arching up, the ice water eyes glittering as if from a polar sun. '*So* tantalising, *so* mysterious. And how beautifully it occupies people's minds. It doesn't matter if they're a schoolboy or a Colonel, a bishop or a hack. It doesn't matter if they detest the idea or have become hopelessly enraptured by it; if they profit from it, or can't even decide what to make of it... Well, Nicholas Pedrosa, which one are you?'

'You lied to everyone. The whole fucking world.'

'People ask to be lied to. More often than not, they far prefer it to the truth. As for you, you were warned repeatedly not to take anything at face value, and still you do, even now. You were supposed to seek, demand, not have knowledge thrown at your feet.'

'I thought it was a code word, a Trojan Horse... I thought...' A pitying look.

The traffic had become a blur of taxis, buses, motorbikes. People were jostling by us on the sidewalk.

People, deserving the lies they are told. Needing them. Craving them. However crowing, however outrageous, I could see the truth of it in myself only too well. Huxley's lies and our own gullibility. They were the perfect partners in crime.

A surge of panic hit me at the thought of all the lies I had been telling to the press, to the authorities, half of them in uniform. My name there in the newspapers in black and white. I saw myself running down the street, weaving between swerving cars, the police giving chase, lights flashing, sirens wailing, the air torn by gunfire.

Seconds later, anger hit me like a blast wave.

'It is a fraud. You lied about everything.'

'Grow up, you silly little boy.' The words hissed over the thrum of the traffic. 'It is a masterstroke. A red herring so indescribably perfect it could rival even Plato's Conundrum itself.'

That stupid, arrogant boast. That sneering contempt. It was almost as if they had failed to catch its faint, telltale signature in the margins of their lives, or else considered themselves far too clever to be taken in by it.

But Sam's right, it has entered our lives, hasn't it, it's entwining us all. Weaving itself about our thoughts and actions, colouring and shaping our words, even bringing an indefinable something to the landscapes in which we move. It's in the Comte d'Adhémar, and his adoring followers at the Grande Bretagne. In Claude Guirand as he raps on every door he can think of to have us arrested or expelled. In the Colonels, so desperate for international credibility and foreign exchange the ringleaders have already swapped their medal-bedecked uniforms for those universal hallmarks of respectability, the made-to-measure suit and the silk tie. It's even in Svetlana Bé, feasting now on her own impeccable derision.

She clicked her fingers at the waiter, retrieving a crisply folded 50 drachma note from her purse.

'You said I didn't even know what we are digging for,' I demanded. 'Well, what is it?'

She was brisk, impatient. 'If you had paid more attention to your lessons, you wouldn't need to ask. How many times has he drummed it into your thick head: look for the evidence that hides in its own transparency!'

She blew another exasperated smoke cloud. 'Bodies. Graves. Rivers. What does that tell you? The *Necromanteion*, of course!'

'Necro- *what?*'

'Necro — "dead"; manteia — "divination".'

Seeing my blank look she fumed, 'The Oracle of the Dead. The five rivers of the Underworld. Didn't they teach you anything at Aberdeen?'

Rifling through her glossy black handbag, she placed it on the table in front of me. The *Travels*. A mint-condition copy. 'Not that you have earned it.'

The arrogance almost blew me away. She, recommending Huxley's own mad book. Of course. And now I was deemed ready to lap up its remaining delusions, no doubt as avidly as had Benja and Sam before me.

'In its heyday,' she went on, glaring at the traffic, 'more powerful even than the Oracle of Delphi itself at the navel of the Earth.'

Except it wasn't in this life that the Necromanteion cast the future of its pilgrims. It was in the next.

Irritated by the black dubious look on my face, she flared: 'Why else would he be turning the whole island upside down, if not to find it?'

I shook my head in disbelief, even as the nauseous image of him tunnelling for bodies and burial grounds lunged out at me.

'To be more specific,' she added, 'he is looking for its marker, the figure who guarded the entrance to its subterranean rivers. I assume you know of whom I am talking.'

'The Ferryman,' I mumbled. It was hard just to spit up the words.

'It begins with the river crossing,' says the Comte, his voice resonating through the auditorium, 'and a bronze obol placed on the tongue to pay the Ferryman… But then who am I to describe the river myth to those who have already made the crossing at least once before!'

Bracing myself for the worst, I fired the question at her point blank. *Who are the Friends of Orpheus? What do they want?*

'You are right,' she replied, almost smugly. 'Our Friends of Orpheus, they *are* an eclectic mix — far more so, in fact, than one might normally expect to find gathered under one roof.'

As her eyes held mine, I imagined I could feel the blue ice crystals beginning to frost the blood in my veins.

'But they also have one thing in common,' she went on. 'They have all died.'

I laughed out loud, the sharpness of it drawing the curious stares of passers-by.

Her voice hardened. 'That is to say, they have all been to death and back. They have all had what we call a *near-death experience* — the heart ceasing to beat, the brain fading. Though it was not our intention at first, the Foundation brought them together through its research programme. The Comte was most insistent, it being the natural complement to his own life's work, the study of eschatology in any culture and any land.'

As she spoke, I was seeing them again in my mind's eye, milling about the marble foyer, knowing even then that there was something different about them, something impossible to put into words.

'With the Foundation acting as their focal point, they discovered something they never expected: a certain unifying thread to their experiences, no matter how they died. The way they saw themselves rising from their own bodies. The way their own lives revisited them, years seemingly condensed into heartbeats. The way the white light would draw them across the Void, tantalising, irresistible...'

Head in my hands, I was staring into the maddening traffic, cars, buses, motorbikes, pedestrians, reeling through me.

'Then our survivors began to realise another trait they now shared. Death no longer held any fear for them — this despite the fact that not even one of them can say what it is or why it is. That is what draws them now. They want to know what it is they experienced. They want to know if it was real or merely a last vanity of the expiring mind. They want to know the truth.'

'The truth? *The truth?* You must be mad. All of you.'

Her silence at that moment was louder even than the raucous din of the traffic or the people barging past us on the pavement.

'And Benja? What about Benja?'

'I told you. Mistakes were made. His flaws did not initially come to light. He did not have the measure of what confronts us.'

'Is that so?' Just one more molecule of anger added to the load and I'd blurt it out, and fuck the consequences; demanding to know how come this young man with the fatal flaws had apparently found answers Huxley the Great was still plundering the island for.

'Some people ask to be pushed,' she added, sipping mercilessly on her frappé, and letting me decide whether I should interpret that as unadorned fact, metaphor, or a cynicism as corrosive as the waters of the Styx.

In their boundless arrogance, they probably thought me too gutless to report them. Well, we would see about that.

Just as soon as Svetlana had clicked her stilettos back to the hotel, I'd run to the Embassy, demand a meeting with the Consul, tell him everything I knew. At least they might protect me from the Colonels' secret police. If there was any justice in the world, within a week Huxley would be behind bars, Svetlana too. Maybe even the Comte d'Adhémar.

The sudden plunging sensation in my gut, however, suggested otherwise, and I knew why without even thinking: what they would make of my story, as the interview veered inevitably into an interrogation. The twisted motives they would ascribe to my own contradictory evidence, and worse, my seesaw ambivalence towards him, the man I had extolled as a visionary and condemned as a cold-blooded killer, a master hypnotist, a sexual deviant, a crook.

The more I blabbed, the more I would incriminate myself.

No wonder he was so insistent about you writing the log every day, I realised with bleak finality. In the end, your notebooks can be presented in court, each dead-end lead, each uncertainty, rumour or contradiction reinforcing the inevitable acquittal his lawyers would demand.

Oh yes, I was Marcus Huxley's most faithful alibi.

At that moment, I knew what real hate was.

I shoved back my chair, got to my feet.

Svetlana glanced up sharply, her eyes roaming over me, head to toe. 'He does need you, you know. And not for the reasons you think.'

'You know nothing about me!' I rasped. 'Nothing!'

'I know you will not abandon your friends.'

Before I could blink, I was shoving my way through the crowds, just trying to control my blind, blistering anger, the crowds, the traffic, the buildings, blurring through me. There were soldiers or police on almost every street corner, oblivious tourists thronging the pavements, buying postcards, licking away at ice cream cones, consulting street maps with clueless faces, this sea of humanity churning by them on all sides. All I knew at that moment was that I had to walk, it didn't matter where, I had to get away from all these people. *I was drowning.*

Dodging taxis and trolley buses, I made it across Stadiou by the skin of my teeth. Then fought the traffic and the sweating crowds up Nikis Street.

With every step and thumping heartbeat I could feel it tearing me apart inside, *save yourself, warn the others.* The bursts of angry bravado, the paralysing fear.

As a patrol car careened around the corner with wailing siren and flashing lights, I hid my face in a shop window until the coast was clear.

Then quickened my pace, still fighting Svetlana's smug prognosis that I could no more run out on my friends than betray them by blabbing to the police.

One way or another, we were all lost to Huxley's twisting labyrinthine mind. All of us. Even Galatea and her students, working the eastern sector with a passion that bordered on dementia. Even the Symposiasts, convinced that Huxley's Atlantis would nudge the seagull rookery ever closer to their quixotic island idyll. They had no idea, no inkling of the hurricane sweeping towards them. *You have to go back, you know that, you have to confront your fears.*

38.

The last late passengers came scurrying up the gangway. I had never seen the *Pegasus* so full. Every couch, seat and stool in the saloon bar already taken, every cabin and bunk booked solid days in advance. It was no different out here on deck, a body sun-glued to every plastic chair and life jacket chest. They were even sprawled out on sleeping bags, straw mats, rubber lilos.

At last she was firing up her boilers and huffing out of the oil slick harbour, through the stench of rotting fish.

Just like this red herring, I thought, *reeking from head to tail.*

Despite what was awaiting me, I was glad to see the back of the city as we ploughed into the blue. Perhaps, at the back of my mind, I even hoped to leave all the lies behind me, along with the belching smokestacks and the stinking sky.

Not that there was any chance of that. Not when everything I set eyes on reminded me of the part I had played in making the lie as big as it was. Goggle-eyed tourists flocking to Atlantis, this archaeological sensation, this golden legend raised from the dead. The newspapers and glossy magazines on their laps, reinforcing the lie with every word, every picture. Reporters and cameramen, working on angles, devising questions for the great man himself. And last but not least, just in case I was in danger of forgetting them, the Friends of Orpheus, making their own pilgrimage to the Lost Isle.

Seekers of the white light, Svetlana had called them. People who had apparently met death in person, yet had lived to tell the tale. Accident or heart attack victims dragged back to their bodies through some emergency procedure or other, paddles to the heart, an adrenaline fix, the kiss of life.

Who knows what other lies the troika had been peddling, or what better natures they had exploited for cash, but if Svetlana was to be believed, these people were deluded enough to think that the Orpheus Foundation and its 'science' would ultimately reveal the Holy Grail of all knowledge: the meaning of the white light, the meaning of death itself.

Obviously there was no fraud too blatant or too sordid for the principled Huxley to be involved in.

Maybe the reporters will expose him, I thought hopefully, though after hearing their rehearsed questions on deck, I seriously began to doubt it. *What does it feel like, Professor, to have discovered Atlantis? Will it change your life in any way? What next, Professor, for the man who has made a legend live?*

My agitation wouldn't allow me to sit still and so I roamed aimlessly about deck, stepping over sprawled bodies.

That was almost worst of all. No one else on this rusting tub seemed to have a care in the world. Drinking in the emerging blue, they turned their faces like sunflowers towards the sun and didn't stop until it plunged into the sea. They watched the first stars emerge over the masthead. Made picnics on deck. Bought bad retsina from the saloon bar that they would only begin to regret at first light, still confusing the throb of the engines with the pounding in their heads.

Belatedly, I was in the mood to face facts, however ugly they were, too angry, too incensed, to care about the consequences.

An incident from the past would suddenly leap out at me, like a child running out into the traffic. You swerve, slam on the brakes, already knowing it's too late. At least, that's how it seemed to me. My life in collision, blood all over the windscreen.

Events and incidents that with hindsight seemed so humiliatingly obvious now.

Huxley, standing over the trenches at that stupid exorcism ceremony in March, and Nestor muttering in his ear that he had to do something to quell the rising discontent among the locals: 'You must give them something else, Kapítán! Something they will never forget. Something that will make them proud.'

Or that incident back in May when, at some ungodly hour, Huxley had seen fit to dump a stack of newspaper cuttings on my doorstep. All about him, of course, the child and his twinkle star ambition; later to become a young man on fire, and later still, according to the critics, a meteor in burnout, one failing dig after another to his name.

Somehow, Marcus James Huxley didn't seem quite so formidable anymore. Just an insecure little man driven by past failure and buried feelings of inferiority.

That's when another memory ran out in front of me, the impact juddering through me, cracking glass, buckling metal, skin and bone scraping across the tarmac.

It's April, I'm watching the sun go down over the caldera, the sea turning silver, turning gold. Islands thrown up into the sunset sky, mountain ranges in snaking silhouette, achieving their uncanny rendition of forests, rivers and lakes. An optical illusion, of course. A stupid trick of the light. Imagination running away with us.

But then the Comte's impassioned words came welling out of the Athenian skyline at me. All about those explorers and adventurers of old who believed that the Isles they saw levitating above the sunset were real — not figments, not clouds twisted into funny shapes.

Climbing uncharted mountain ranges at the top of the world. Crossing the ocean horizon in almost anything that could float. Finding some means to perceive the mind beyond matter, the time-lessness beyond time.

I grasped the ship's railings, my fists turning white as the implications swept over me.

Huxley. He's one of them. He's searching for the Isles. Not with ships or pack ponies, but with shovels. That's what he's been digging for all along. He thinks he can reach the dead.

Ransacking my bag for Svetlana's copy of the *Travels*, I went thumbing recklessly through its pages... Islands on the far curve of the world, beyond the setting sun, Atlantis to Tir na nÓg, Avalon to P'eng-lai... they were all there, almost as if its anonymous author were still travelling between them, reality to legend, legend to myth and back again. I had almost flicked to the back when there it was, in black and white. *Necromanteion.*

As nebulous as archaeological rumour can ever be, the Oracle's location, even proof of its physical existence, had defied academics and explorers for generations. Despite the usual embellishments in later antiquity, the only primary evidence was an ancient papyrus from the temple at Sais, missing for the better part of fifteen hundred years.

So that's why Huxley spent six months exploring that sand and mud-caked site, dragging along an impressionable young Anna in his wake. Nothing much to show for it, either, save for the odd scattered bones of some temple or palace, now propping up a peasant's stable. Virtually every trace of this ancient capital lost to Nile floods and looting.

And that would have been an end to it, if not for some obscure inventory fragment listing the Sais papyrus among the rarest possessions of the Alexandrian Library, the seat of all temporal and spiritual knowledge in the ancient world.

A landmark discovery, a triumphant hot air balloon of a moment — had it not come several hundred years too late. By 361 AD there was a new god on the block and his foot soldiers were already battering down the Library's gates, baying for pagan blood and repentance, toppling statues, torching buildings.

"The Fire becomes an inferno, sweeping through the great halls, devouring everything in its path; it doesn't matter to the flames, mathematics or astrology, poetry or satire, erotica or occult lore.

Charcoal figures dart between the tongues of flame and smoke, snatching whatever treasures they can from the pyre. Parchments and papyri that might have scattered to the four winds, if not for those Christian heretics who found God more at home among mountain peaks or in the star sown sky, than in the jealous scriptures of men.

If the whispers are to be believed, the charred remains of the Sais papyrus were spirited away, probably leaving the city that very night, an escape that took our fleeing heretics south along the Nile, their enemies in hot pursuit. On towards the bleached bone mountains on mule and donkey back, finding refuge at last on the Nile island of Tabennisi. A monastery in the making, in whose ramshackle library monks and copyists pored over their Gnostic heresies and apocrypha, mystical writings that speak of revelation.

Had his first impulse been to toss these brittle remnants away, something must have stayed the precentor's hand. A few broken words, perhaps, in whose light and shadow the monastery's keeper of books might have witnessed something exceptional. Papyrus fragments, as light as a butterfly's wing, carried to the makeshift scriptorium and lifted to the writing desk. The best calligrapher amongst his novices summoned with a look as deep as sea.

Fragments of words and verses copied laboriously onto parchment in the black warning ink of the scuttling squid.

Fragments that racked the mind, body and soul of all those who ever came into contact with them.

It is said that men went blind trying to decipher them, that others went mad and never again emerged into the daylight, their darting eyes still pursuing keys and ciphers through the scorched papyrus scrolls.

And there the trail goes dead, every last lead petering out into desert, every expedition returning in defeat.

Despite the deafening silence, only one plausible explanation remains: every last trace of the Sais papyrus was obliterated, and at the very hands of those that had once tried to breathe life into its dying corpse.

Why so much effort to see it destroyed, I hear you ask? Why so much intrigue to see it preserved?

But perhaps you remember our own travels across the metaphysical seas and archipelagos of this lonely blue world. Among them, islands said to exist beyond the far horizon. Islands, you'll recall, that through the timeless ages have inspired many a wandering soul to set sail for sunset.

It is said, of course, that these expeditions were mere follies, and that if even one man ever set foot upon those worlds from this one, then, by implication, he could never return...

Those papyrus fragments, it is said, speak otherwise."

The sea was as calm as a millpond, so anyone coming into the toilets minutes later would probably have been surprised to find me there, gripping my stomach, retching violently into the wash basin.

39.

A klaxon blast almost made me jump out of my skin.

I got to my feet, groaning about my stiff neck and splitting head, wishing to God I hadn't tried to drink myself into oblivion on cheap retsina from the saloon bar.

We were entering the caldera, passengers crowding the railings to take in the sights, the crater wall towering over us, blacker than night, and beyond, shafts of resplendent daylight splaying into the eastern sky. There were *oohs* and *aahs* all along the line.

Down the crazy hairpins, back into camp. The scrap metal gates swinging open for me at the hands of our newly posted guard, Tassos, a lumbering village youth with thickset eyes.

When I saw the ancient city at the far end of the peninsula, quivering in its mirage heat haze, I felt a kind of nauseous emptiness inside, like angry thunder too weak to boom.

There were journalists everywhere, cameramen, sound men, broadcasters, correspondents, stringers. Stumbling about under the weight of their cameras and tripods. Setting up shots amid the trenches, the students and their nervous teachers wondering what to make of it all, torn between the limelight and the notoriety.

It was Huxley's hour of fame alright, and I was dying to see him appear in the compound. I wanted him to emerge from the fragments hut, a thunderous look in his eye, his bark making the wilfully disobedient *touristas* cower in their flip-flops and shorts. I wanted to see the reporters and cameramen converge on him, flashes popping, microphones and lenses thrust into his face. And I wanted to see it in his eyes, as he fielded their questions. The glower. The great pretence that the acclaim meant nothing to him, that the recognition he had been craving for forty years was of no consequence whatsoever, this discovery made with his bare hands, greater than Troy, greater even than the Seven Wonders of the World.

I only realised what I was doing as the hours ticked away and Marcus James Huxley failed to appear at all.

'Where is he?' I asked Maria.

'Where do you think?' she retorted, tossing her head and looking more sultry than ever in her anger. 'At Monolithos, of course, leaving us to clean up the mess behind him. He's far too important for all this!'

I realised then. I had been willing him to do it because it would prove Svetlana a liar, and Huxley wouldn't be doing this thing, burrowing ever deeper into the ash, trying to find a way into Hades, the abode of the dead.

40.

Knowing I had to confront him before my anger fizzled out into one big long depression, I jumped into the Morris and headed out to Monolithos, skidding and kangarooing over the dust tracks.

As I drew up at the main gates, two local boys sprang into view, eyes boring through the dust-spattered windscreen. One of them even had a shotgun braced between his shoulders — Huxley's inimitable way of dealing with the press.

Expecting an argument, I wound down the window, but was waved through without a word. Apparently, I was already expected.

I didn't have far to look. Huxley was upstairs in his study, poring over site logs and survey maps. I entered from the landing, the floorboards creaking loudly underfoot.

Faltering midstream, making a muddle out of accusations I had been rehearsing in my head for three straight days — in the end, I needn't have worried. By the time I hit my stride, I was probably even shouting, everything coming back to me in a sudden furious torrent.

When finally I ran out of steam, he sat back in his chair, thumping the bowl of his pipe loudly against the stone ashtray.

'And how else were you to deliver a performance convincing enough?' he replied, with a brazen look. 'To achieve that, one must live the part, not merely tread the boards.'

'I would never have done it if I had known, *never in a million years!*'

When he spoke again, the disdain was unmistakable. 'I give Atlantis to those who need toys to play with, Mr Pedrosa. A little vision in terracotta and stone. What do I care what name this city once took for itself, or what fiction it assumed in human mythology, when all my life I have struggled only for one thing: to break free of myth, illusion, deception. Try to keep up, or you'll get left so far behind you'll never find your way home again.'

'So Guirand was right,' I said, my anger still raining sparks. 'Atlantis is a fraud, just a barefaced lie.'

'Wake up!' the voice boomed back at me like trapped thunder. 'From the outset, I gave you whatever leeway you required to find your own path. I allowed you to persist in your adolescent detective work into Benja's death. Time and again I warned you, appearances are deceptive, take nothing at face value, and yet here you are, wailing about Atlantis not being all that it seems. Well Atlantis never was, and whatever Plato intended it to be, it is nothing compared to the discovery we are on the verge of, nothing!'

I made to leave, my feet clattering loudly over the floorboards. 'You think I haven't heard enough lies for a fucking lifetime.'

His voice rose. 'Do you want to know what Claude Guirand has really been battling me for, for forty years? Do you?'

Sensing he was about to surrender some personal secret, an event rarer than striking Minoan gold, I couldn't help it, I glanced back from the door. 'You think I'm going to believe anything you say?'

With a curt and unrepentant toss of the head, he motioned me towards a row of faded sepia photographs between the bookshelves.

Sharp, inhospitable mountains and sand dunes. A fortress monastery among bleak rocks and sandstone, with sagging wooden galleries and an almost concealed cupola. And in the lowest, more grainy and blurred than the rest, a group of six men huddled at the far corner of a great cedar wood table. Several pairs of eyes caught out by the exploding flash, others still absorbed by the giant parchment-bound volumes lying open in front of them.

'Look at them,' he commanded.

Pale, western faces, some bearing the gaunt, haunted look of men so obsessed with dreams they forget to eat or sleep. Academics in search of secrets that will pave their streets with gold. Grave-robber archaeologists, whose kit was as likely to contain a revolver as it was a brush or trowel.

'Look carefully!'

My nose almost touching glass, I studied them one by one.

At the head of the table, what I took to be the expedition leader, with a burrowing animal kind of face and bushy black whiskers.

Several places down, between the bookish American and the dashing Istanbul Turk, a boy still in his teens.

Almost unrecognisable, were it not for those flint-spark eyes that would grow hungrier by the year, or the square set jaw that would grow ever more defiant. Marcus James Huxley. Of course.

To his left, a man in his mid-thirties with wispy earth-blonde hair, his angular features partially hidden from the camera lens.

'Guirand...' the numbing that recognition brought about almost robbing me of words.

It wasn't just the sight of them, forty years younger, or even the way age had taken its toll upon them, snatching something else, something indefinable, from their faces. No, it was the undeniable realisation that their long bitter feud began here, amid these creaking galleries and towering shelves.

'This is Tabennisi,' I said. 'The scriptorium and library...'

'No. A different monastery altogether. So off the beaten track it took days to get there by Nile dhow and camel train. The Eastern Desert. The mountains of the Red Sea.'

I glanced back at him in irritation. 'A team player I have never been,' he went on, fighting an instinctive reluctance to come clean about anything. 'Not even as a boy. I sat still for the flash, but slipped away as quickly as I could without being seen. I lingered by the shelves under the stairwell, long enough to allay the suspicions of the doddering old monk who had been assigned to watch over us. He might have been able to recite the Bible backwards, yet these treasures of knowledge that lay unopened and unexplored all around him held nothing but the veiled threat of sin, dark spells and magick, that must forever be kept under lock and key lest some evil escape into the world. What a far, desolate, cry from those early Gnostics who founded the refuge at Tabennisi! Men who had so assiduously collected the rarest mystical texts, in certain knowledge that apocalypse, revelation, will come only to those who intimately seek the truth!'

'You found it,' I said. It was hard to force out the words, I don't know why. 'The Sais Codex.' Even if he did have it, even if he knew it back to front, so what? It was all ancient mumbo jumbo, that made no sense to our modern world. Oracle of the Dead. Isles of the Blest. Resplendent sea. What did it matter?

Except that myths and lies have their own way of bending and twisting reality. That much was obvious from the photographic image that had pickled these two men in sepia 40 years ago, the pointy-faced Claude Guirand, and Marcus James Huxley, his eyes on fire. A pursuit of knowledge so single-minded, so obsessive, it would devour anything in its path.

'He knew,' I said, suddenly feeling the dirt of it contaminating me, even across the years that had never known me. 'Guirand. He caught you. Stealing it...'

'The galleries were sagging cedar wood affairs with shelves towering up into the vaulted roofs like ladders to heaven, rung upon rung of books and codices and papyri, the oldest of which probably hadn't even lain in human hands for a thousand years. As our watchman slept, his face squashed up against a rare illumination of Christ rising from the tomb, I ventured ever deeper, ever higher. Time was running against me, and ever more desperately I slid them back off the shelves, one book, one codex after the other. Perhaps the legend was true. Perhaps the monks had put it to the fire, seeing the mad obsession that had consumed their brethren. The dream was dead, I was sure of it. But then my fingers closed around its spine: the Sais Codex, its somewhat unremarkable exterior the perfect camouflage for the remarkable things within. I needed only to turn a single leaf to see that.'

'What did you do, stuff it under your shirt?' The jibe darted past him, apparently unnoticed.

'Any moment now the noonday bell would ring us to the refectory. Hurriedly, I retraced my steps along the galleries. Then down the coiling stairway, wincing at every groan or creak, reaching the last step just as the refectory bell began to chime, stirring our dozing watchman. Impetuous as I was, I could barely restrain my own sense of euphoria at having triumphed.'

'Until Guirand confronted you.'

Abruptly, he nodded. 'The cold-blooded look said it all: share this secret with me or I will betray you. What choice did I have? None. For forty years, the contention between us has had nothing to do with academic interpretation of the Codex. Neither of us had any inclination to submit our findings for publication. We had encountered death legends, sorcery, magic, ancient hocus-pocus a thousand times and a thousand times again, but this was different. There was something about these lines that radiated authenticity.'

And so they spent the next ten years decoding fragments, making sense out of nonsense, and placing the Oracle of the Dead on this, that or the other point on the map. Their rivalry already clashing and sparking, they raced and spent each other into the ground, determined to prove myth as real as history, legend as dependable as stone. Pointless, futile digs. Holes burrowing into the earth with nothing to show for it but calloused hands and bank accounts running on vapour.

While Guirand began pawning the family silver to finance his adventures, Huxley fell in with the Orpheus Foundation in Paris, whose wealthy benefactors, no one needed to remind me, had dedicated their lives to death and death-defying lore.

'Claude was younger then, of course,' Huxley was saying, glancing up at me from his paperwork, and seeking eye contact for the first time. 'He commanded his own excavations. Opened digs in the Nile Delta. In Cilicia. In Milos, Nisyros, Crete. We were racing each other to find the cave, the Ferryman, the five rivers. Every dead-end lead swept us along, consuming our time, our money and our minds. Guirand was still breaking ground at new sites when he was 70.'

Yes, and knowing you as he did, he made sure that your own plans were fed to him as well, didn't he, buying informants, planting spies.

'Thera was different. Just weeks into our dig the facts became indisputable, even if Claude could never quite bring himself to admit defeat. I had found the island, the source of the legend. Almost every artefact we prised from the ash reinforced that conclusion. He must have sensed it as strongly as I. That it was here underfoot: the Oracle of the Dead, whose initiates would come to know the truth beyond existence, that which lies beyond death, beyond themselves.'

I glanced sharply at him. He was talking as if he really believed it. As if the myth were something other than minds in religious delirium. The Oracle, more than just a hole in the ground into which primitive people planted their hopes, dreams, and writhing superstitions.

'That's why he's trying to seize control of the excavations,' I said, as Guirand's spectral image came quivering back into my mind. The traffic droning through Syntagma below, and the withered old man summoning every last ounce of mental strength to force his ailing body to comply. So obvious now, the invisible becoming apparent. 'He thinks he is running out of time. He thinks he will die before he finds it.'

I didn't bother to ask why they didn't join forces, work together. Easier to ask why the Soviets and Americans didn't turn their missiles into ploughshares. Easier to ask why we don't feed the starving.

In the way his mouth tightened around the words, I could sense something of Huxley's frustration, forty years of it. 'Even if it still eludes us,' he was saying, 'Claude knows as well as I that the truth is closer than ever, perhaps no more than a stone's throw away. That within the Oracle of the Dead, beyond the river, the Isles become apparent.'

'I know what you wrote in the *Travels*,' I said sharply. 'I know it back to front.'

'*I?* I did not write the *Travels*.'

The answer almost blew me away. 'Of course you did! You must have!'

Obstinately, he shook his head. 'No. That was Claude.'

It just wasn't possible. That bitter, shrivelled prune of a man, who didn't have a kind word to say about anything or anyone, lost to the poetry of the Isles. His cynicism as dark and caked as old blood.

'Let's just say,' said Huxley solemnly, 'that he is not the same man as he was half a century ago. In the idealism of his youth, Claude travelled to the farthest reaches of the Earth, honing his island obsession into a fine, if solitary art.'

Finding only disbelief plastered to my face, he demanded abrasively: 'Why do you think he was so incensed by our Atlantis hypothesis? Why, because it humiliated him, reminding him of things he would far prefer to forget. Bankrupt dreams. Naiveties that have withered. The childish notion that in Atlantis, the great thinker had sprung some cosmic conundrum upon the world, so elegantly proving his theory that the universe is mind, not matter, and that even ideas have lives and destinies of their own as they make their eternal journey from the Perfect Form. A stark enough contrast, you must admit, to the more prosaic explanation: that Plato had simply been duped by a gaggle of chattering Egyptian priests. Raking up Atlantis again only reminds Claude of how bitter and old he has become, how foolish he was in his youth. He long ago disowned the book. Lucky for him his name never appeared upon it.'

I said in a mocking voice: 'So he made it all up, that's what you're saying. He just created the Conundrum out of nothing, for no reason at all.'

'Look,' the irritation creeping back into his voice, 'no one knows if Plato's Conundrum ever existed. The most frantic minded of the Gnostic scholiasts made much of it, it's true, but living under virtual siege in their dank monasteries, one might say they had always been prone to dark invention and conspiracy. Claude, too, became obsessed with the idea, and if not digging for Atlantis with his bare hands, spent every waking hour trying to crack the code that supposedly ran through the dialogue itself.' He grimaced. 'Of course it humiliates him. Such is the lesson of life; naivety making the noxious acquaintance of reality. Until at last it is death alone he seeks to understand.'

'Then why throw it in his face like that?' I flared. 'It'll just antagonise him all the more, won't it?'

'You misunderstand. And evidently, so did he — I can only assume his powers of deduction must be failing him. There was a time when Claude Guirand would have had no trouble reading between the lines and understanding the message encoded there.'

I thought I would explode. 'Message? What fucking message?'

'That I am close, of course. That without me the Necromanteion will never be found. Close us down, and your life, your blood, your sweat and tears will have been for naught.'

I slumped onto the ottoman under the window, suddenly thrown by a Huxlian mantra becoming perfectly tangible for the first time: that real events are always occurring beyond mere appearances.

And once again, it was my bright, spacious suite in the Grande Bretagne that grabbed me by the scruff of the neck, yanking me back in time.

I, as Huxley's unwitting courier, carrying coded messages that only the two warring principles were meant to understand.

Staring into Guirand's death mask face, still convinced it's rabid envy alone that's casting its Lazarus-like spell upon him, the blood surging into his blue veins, a reflection returning to his eyes.

But no, that's not it. It's the briefcase on the coffee table, the colour print of that pottery fragment I had last seen between Huxley's caressing fingertips. The one depicting the flowing river, the reeds, the square prow of a punt over the pebble blur shallows... And a presence just insinuated there at the broken edge. A shadow that might equally have been made by a smudge of pigment, ingrained dirt, or something far more insubstantial. The Ferryman.

41.

I could hear the blood thrumming in my ears as I finally began to grasp what I was seeing.

The Sais Codex. Not a facsimile, but the parchment original, offered no more security than a locked drawer behind a false panel in his desk.

He had pulled on white cotton librarian's gloves, and had placed it on the desk between us under the snake-neck lamp.

'The monks faithfully transcribed every word and every fragment that could still be deciphered from the charred papyrus scrolls,' Huxley explained, peering over his half-moon reading glasses.

The gazelle-skin parchment made an eerie rustling as he turned the pages, probably just from the dry, frail spine, but I could feel their movement across my skin like a dank human breath.

'Thirteen fragments survive,' he went on, 'anything from an orphaned word to an entire verse. Sometimes, the fractured lines defy interpretation altogether.' A sudden glare, aimed squarely between the eyes. 'Why do you think we have each spent forty years trying to decode it?'

That the reconstruction was still a work in progress, after all this time, was a revelation in itself. Apparently it wasn't the inherent obscurity of the fragments themselves that was to blame, but shadings and nuances in possible interpretation. Sometimes, even the slightest adjustment to a word or line might shift or contradict the meaning of its neighbour, a contamination that could end up corrupting entire verses.

It was a curse the monks at Tabennisi had come to know with searing intimacy, hunched over their writing desks, going mad and going blind as they chased shifting metaphors and broken fragments across the vellum.

As a bloodied dusk fell beyond the windowpanes, he began reciting them one by one, his voice punctuating the spaces where verse or fragment simply plunged into oblivion.

At the risk that others might fall hopelessly under their spell, I commit to paper the fragments I recall. If nothing else, it might serve to illuminate the mania that possessed the two men, and drove them to every ancient volcano or sulphurous pit this side of Etna in search of an ancient mountain spitting fire.

'Fragment 1: And the mountain shall speak to innocence, for that is where the light of knowing emanates. The light that breaks upon the earth to scatter […]

Fragment 6: Deep within the mountain spitting fire stands the god who ferries souls across the River. Above his head, stars that are not stars. At his feet, the River more ancient than them all.

Fragment 8: The Oracle made of light does not ordain what is to be. Learning the truth, it will yet divine the future.

Fragment 9: The pure white light that enters […] the soul […] the moment inexpressible […]

Fragment 10: Losing what they have become, they become what they are not. […] identity other than the metaphor it has assumed […]

Fragment 13: Unto the Isles now, sown into the dusk sea beyond thy forward reflection […].'

Half an hour later, I really had to wonder why I was still sitting there at all, listening to that ancient gibberish, not to mention the tortured interpretations he brought to every fragment or dead space.

But then I began to feel a creeping sense of unease welling up from deep inside, faceless, nameless. When finally I recognised it for what it was, the force was enough to make me sit bolt upright, wondering what else I might have missed.

They were as mad as monks, yes, undeniably so. Yet every fragment of that dead broken thing had entered our lives in one form or another. It might only have been the way the lines had driven and possessed them, but there was probably not a single soul in camp who had not been grazed or lacerated by their jagged edges.

'Where do they lie,' he challenged me, 'the Isles of the Blest?'

'In myth. In superstition. In *imagination*.'

'Try again,' he growled.

'You cannot do it. You cannot cross a mythical sea.'

'I remind you that sceptics once said the same about Troy, the labyrinths of King Minos, the palace of Agamemnon.' He glared across the Codex. 'What is the compass bearing?'

'West. In the sunset, in a water-luminous sky. But that's just allegory, just metaphor.'

'And how does the Scholiast interpret the Codex fragments?' he demanded, his eyes straying to the copious margin notes in ancient

Greek, in a hand so tiny it was scarcely legible to the naked eye.

I forced out the words: 'He says they are metaphor codes.'

'And?'

'Beyond the metaphor horizon worlds unknown to us become apparent.'

'*Deduction!*' he boomed, a jarring reminder of my hard won lessons among the trenches. 'What would Plato have seen?'

'Islands made of pure thought.' *Apparently as solid as rock to the unconscious sea.*

'Then where do they lie, the Isles of the Blest?'

Rebelling against his logic, I screwed shut my eyes. 'In the transcendent realm.'

That tantalising place in the stillness beyond time. And Plato's curious notion that the things around us are but inferior shadows of ideal Forms that exist on a higher plane, their perfection only diminishing the further we stray from them. Doesn't matter what; a stranger's glance that knows you inside out, a white sail upon the sea, a summer blue day that whispers eternity... and yes, every island on the metaphysical map.

'Do you not see the significance?' the accusation bruising air, snatching me away from my thoughts. 'Do you not understand the implications?' He could sense someone's mood even in the dark.

Reaching across the desk, he seized my wrist in a vice grip that almost caused me to yelp. I found myself slipping and falling into his eyes... still, after all this time, with scarcely more strength to resist than a toddler falling into a pond.

'*They had no word for death,*' he said, reciting the Scholiast. '*And none for war. They knew neither the meaning of good, nor of evil. They saw beyond their own horizon...* Can you not imagine what will happen when this sword of Damocles no longer hangs over our heads by a single hair? Can you not imagine the change it will bring about? If we can illuminate a path beyond death, death as it is will cease to exist.'

Finding only incredulity staring back at him, he tightened and twisted his grip, burning skin, adding with asperity: 'Don't you see? Every brick in the great edifice we call civilisation has been laid in fear or defiance of death. The warriors who gloried in battle. The peasants who fell in terror. The shamans and priests who sowed superstition before knowledge. The human dominion we have always sought over the Earth. The buildings that scrape the sky. The landscapes we lay waste… These are the demons that have driven humans for aeons. They have waged our wars, guided our fingers along the prayers we recite, invoked every manner of craven belief. Knowing the truth of what awaits us, everything will change. Everything!'

He added with grim certainty, 'Before this thing is finished, I will prove that death does not exist.'

Angrily, I shook free of his grip, hardly knowing whether to be more shocked by his hubris or his sense of unreality.

'But it's riddled with contradictions!' I protested, tossing a glance of contempt at the Codex.

Yes, just like you, the man of peace who wages war against everything in sight, the scientist who believes in the logic of the soul, the cynic who believes in myths.

'An Oracle that doesn't know the future!' I added, parodying one of its more arcane fragments. 'What can it possibly mean? Nothing!'

'That we shall discover for ourselves.'

'You are supposed to be a scientist!'

'The man of science challenges and demands answers, Nicholas. He does not throw up his hands in surrender at every obstacle that seems insurmountable, particularly those that rely on myth and superstition to exist at all. He demands the truth. He seeks it out, and when it hides from him, it only sharpens his resolve.'

'At first I thought it was harmless, poetic, beautiful in its own way — but now! How many people have fallen under its spell? How many people have been seduced, corrupted or killed by it?'

That's when he said something else, something I really didn't want to hear.

'You think I don't know?' he replied, with a searing look. 'The times it's entered you up on the hill, just as it entered Sam and Benja before you. If you weren't so busy denying it, you would already know the cause… Something in the ancient city defies death. By some means unknown to us, that other reality momentarily materialises into this one… Wherever it once found focus, there lies the Oracle of the Dead.'

When the obvious leapt out at me this time, I felt as though I had just gone flying off a cliff. The past. It was actually making twisted, perverted sense for the first time.

'You knew all along,' I said, the words spitting between my teeth. 'You used us. You exploited us.'

'No. It was deduction, nothing more.'

Almost as if we, his apprentices, were the dumb instruments that would catch the presence of this thing, whatever it was supposed to be. Our instincts and emotions like an oscillating dial, measuring its signal and proximity.

'I suspected, it's true. But if I'd have said anything at the time, if I'd have said, the dead still live among us — would you have believed me? No.'

He had a point, but that's what I hated most about him. Huxley always did, however insane the conversation.

I kept fiddling with my watch; one of those unconscious habits of mine whenever my thoughts have made a run for it without me. Dad's old silver Omega, with the green leather strap and the luminous radium dial.

On my 21st I had found it lying there on the breakfast table, waiting for me. I was back from Aberdeen for good. Two years of college under my belt before realising the hardship Mum and Sofi were going through to put me there, the meals missed, the scrimping and saving, the danger of losing the house. Now Mum had even found the original Omega box, airing out all the mustiness from the cellar. The glass and bezel so polished up I could see my own face in it. 'You look so much like your father, Nico,' Mum said, biting her lips.

In lost moments like this, I'm always wondering what he would do, standing there in my shoes. What would he say, if I could ask him, if I could just pick up the phone.

Huxley lifted his eyes, caught the restless movement of my fingers, and pounced: 'How did he die, Nicholas? Your father.'

'He just died, that's all. When I was a boy.' To the sceptical look that provoked, I snapped: 'I was only six or something.'

'You want to see him again. You want to know.'

'I don't want to know anything.'

'Because you can't accept that he died, can you. Admit it. You can't accept that you'll never see him again. The brutality of it. The injustice of it. The way he was snatched from you. That's it, isn't it?'

Svetlana's parting comment in Syntagma, almost drowned out by the din of the traffic, came sputtering back to me.

It seemed so brazen, so preposterous at the time, I paid it no heed. 'He does need you, you know. And not for the reasons you think.'

I flinched. Of course not. It was not to spread the lie that he needed me, at least, not anymore. It was to find his Oracle of the Dead.

42.

A single torch spilling light at our feet, we crossed the ridge in star-splintered silence, pumice stones cracking underfoot like ancient bones. I felt the houses slipping by us like sleeping shadows, the pottery workshop, the bakery, the apartments with sky terraces. I could already see the temple on the rise and Orion glittering between the columns. Soon we were squeezing through the rusting bales of wire in Nestor's graveyard of broken machinery. Momentarily losing sight of Huxley between the stacks of corrugated iron, I called out in a hoarse whisper: 'Where are we going?' those uncanny likenesses awaiting us below ground already swimming into my head with bewildering ambivalence.

Before the words were even out of my mouth we hit an abrupt incline cut through the ash, and I had to jerk out both hands just to stay on my feet. Wherever we were going, it wasn't into the house of love and awakening.

Walls closing in, darkness devouring torchlight, I found myself fingering my way along the crumbling shaft, heart thumping, dust gritting the eyes, clogging the nose.

At last we hit level ground, the flashlight catching a stone wall, then among the tunnelling gear left by the moles, a pair of gas lamps. Striking a match, he lit them, swinging the first towards me as the mantle flared.

Beyond, where the hissing light succumbed to the darkness, I could make out a branching passage, then another.

Confronted by the raw facts alone, willpower driven through ash, hubris through stone, mind against matter, it was getting ever harder to deny this madness wasn't real.

'How far do they go?' I asked, peering down the first of the tunnels into the grasping blackness.

'They branch and branch again as they run towards the mountain. If it turns into a labyrinth down there, there's no telling how long they'll take to explore, even with the mapped river courses as our guide.' He added with a breathless grunt: 'We must press on. Knowing what we know now there is every reason to believe the Oracle cave survived the great cataclysm.'

Sensing my reluctance to be convinced of anything, truth or lie, his face twisted back in anger. He had taught me well, and was now probably regretting it.

'Fragment 6, did you memorise it?'

'No.'

'*Deep within the mountain stands the god who ferries souls across the River...*'

'What does that mean? Nothing.'

Abruptly, he turned down a side tunnel, so narrow our shoulders were scraping the sheer lava walls. Stepping through an embedded stone arch, we entered the deep vaults of some half-buried house on the hill.

We moved in silence, chamber to chamber, planting our feet with care so as not to wake the dust. I couldn't help thinking, everything about this place is dead, even the thin, stale air.

A brief flight of steps, another stone archway, then suddenly the unrelenting greyness, the bloodless light, gave way to vibrant colour on all sides.

Blues, greens, yellows, reds, streaming through the darkness as far as our lamps could penetrate. Memory, living moments, preserved in pigment.

The river.

Just as it once was, just as the fresco painter might once have seen it with his own eyes, the water cascading down the distant mountain engulfed in cloud, through the sunlit forest, past the vivid spice terraces tracing the contours of the hills, through summer meadows and orchards, as it meanders towards the sea.

As the frescoes went converging into the distance, the far end of this great hall, whatever its ancient purpose, was not even visible to us.

'And now what do you say?' His eyes were incandescent, almost as if some reaction between the ancient air and the delicate mantles of the gas lamps were making his euphoria visible.

What did he want? My belief? My approval? My admiration?

'I was the same as you, the first time I stepped in here,' he remarked. 'Unable to see the wood for the trees.'

Ten yards on, a graceful wooden boat came gliding down on the current between the reeds and the waterfowl, the near side bank under sombre cloud, the far side illuminated by tantalising shafts of light.

'It must be the sacred river,' I said. 'The river of life. The giver of life...'

Thrusting me towards the tall dark figure at the stern, he demanded: 'Then you don't know this man? You don't know his river?'

Violently, I squirmed out of his grasp.

His eyes narrowed at my new-found defiance. 'You should acknowledge the privilege being accorded to you, Mr Pedrosa, as one of the first humans to witness this moment in 3,500 years. You have entered the Underworld. You have found the Ferryman and the Great River Styx.'

The walls were closing in on me, colours melting, words snatching the dead air from my lungs. I had the panic impulse to dash out into the bright starlight, night air as pure, as sweet as honey, and might even have done so had it not been for the irrational fear of getting lost in this maze of buried rooms and tunnels. I was digging fingernails into my own skin, just to give my stampeding nerves something else to think about.

'Charon?' I retorted. 'It's some boatman, that's all. This is the river of life — not death!' And even as I spoke, my eyes were taking in the golden barley, the sunflowers in the fields, the ripe orchard trees, the mesmerising reflections. *What was he talking about?*

If this was Hades I wanted to see the stumbling legions of the dead, trudging towards the bog marshes of the Styx.

I wanted to see Charon, son of Darkness and Night, a grisly old man with skeletal hands, punting dead souls through the putrid mist. Bone fingers slipping into their mouths to retrieve the coin placed there to pay for their passage.

Mute, weak, unprotesting, they'd draw lots for their next incarnation, then drink from the river of oblivion, every last memory of a life lived expunged.

'Look. The young man depicted here is hardly much older than you. Half the village has turned out for him to say goodbye, to wish him well. See how joyously they carry him to the river bank, the bier and the path festooned with wildflowers. See how they scatter blossoms upon the water.'

That must have been the most disturbing thing of all.

Seeing the ecstatic faces of the living for the dead. The lyre and pipe music, the dancers in delirium, the falling petals like confetti at a wedding, the soul reflections playing over the water.

'In a way he has your look, doesn't he. Something about his expression, his eyes, his cheekbones —'

'The ancients loathed and despised death,' I shot back, 'that's what I was taught. That's the literal meaning of the Styx, isn't it — *hateful.*'

'Feared it, despised it, even dreamed of conquering it. But we have followed the river myth back to a source far more ancient than that. To a time, in fact, when the Ferryman was the intermediary between life and death, that's all. The symbol of passage. One world to the next.'

Frescoes depicting the wonder, the embrace of death, I thought derisively, bursting with colour and light.

As he lifted high his lantern, the river seemed to cast its silver reflection over the young man's face, water lapping, rippling. A trick of the light, that's all. A devious echo through this maze of rooms.

'You asked me once, what was this civilisation's greatest achievement — do you remember? Well, now you have your answer: these people discovered the passage between life and death, and illuminated it. The Book of the Dead, the Eleusinian Mysteries, they all began here.'

'So why did it die out? Why did it become extinct?'

Huxley glowered. He didn't like that question. Not one bit.

Seizing my arm in a vice grip, he propelled me another ten yards along the hall, spinning me around until the river again flooded into my eyes. But this time I was within a stone's throw of the water, the wooden boat tied up at the river bank.

'Our young man takes his seat on board, his back to the far shore, his eyes still in yearning for the life he has left behind. The departing procession retraces its steps through the forest, scattering blossoms as it goes. See how turbulent, how luminous the river has become.'

Lamplight leaping, he spun me around to face the opposite wall.

'*Deduction,* Mr Pedrosa!'

The words were numb on my lips, reluctant to be spoken. 'He comes to the two springs, the Lethe and the Mnemosyne…'

'And what will he say to the guardians of Hades if he is to bring an end to the everlasting cycle of birth and rebirth, the transmigration of the soul? What will he say?'

'He will say.'

'*What will he say!*'

'He will say. I am a child of Earth and starry heaven. Please give me something to drink from the river of Mnemosyne.'

'You remember.' A flinch of a smile in which he nods his approval. 'You must drum it into your mind, create the indelible image in your soul.'

This maze of rooms, I was thinking, *this is the start of the labyrinth. Doesn't he realise. Who's to tell how far its tunnels squirm and tangle into the distance, some carved by human hands, others by lava and steam.*

Another side passage, another corner and we were back at the river bank again, the Ferryman punting over the river towards us. The young man, supposedly wearing my face, sitting up in the well of the boat now, eyes transfixed by the asphodel meadows on the far shore, the rounded hills, the silver streams, the mountain blue sky.

Bracing myself for the worst, I raised my lamp to the Ferryman's cowl, waiting for that hideous mask of bone and gristle to leap out at us.

But no. There was just a whitish blur, that's all. Probably damage sustained during the eruption. I edged forward, the lantern swinging in my outstretched hand. A stupid thing to do, the peculiar magnifying properties of the glass making the whole thing spring to life, the Ferryman punting towards us on waves of shadow and light.

I jerked backwards, just as the cowl-hidden face made its pendulum leap at us.

Then I understood.

The fresco hadn't been damaged. It was meant to be like that. A face radiating pure white light.

To my surprise, I saw the arch we had entered by. Without even realising it, we had doubled back on ourselves.

Here the fresco formed a single panorama over three walls.

The mountain had vanished and so had the river.

The young man with my face stood on the high cliffs, eyes transfixed by an emerging constellation of islands on the dusk horizon, undulating mountains, silver thread rivers, and hill cities just emerging from silhouette.

'And this?' I said, scornfully pre-empting Huxley's inevitable interrogation. 'I can answer that for myself, *Professor*. The Isles beyond sunset. The resplendent sea.'

'Now don't tell me you don't have the curiosity, Nicholas, the yearning. To know what lies beyond your own death.'

43.

Now that I was getting the hang of facing facts, it was clearer than ever.

We were at the mercy of two devious, manipulative minds, their madness feeding off one another, pushing everything to the brink, including us.

Through the baling wire gates into camp. Difficult to find a place to park, tourist coaches drawing into the compound, air brakes wheezing. Day-trippers getting an early start, swarming along the whitewashed paths, climbing under the ropes, frazzling the nerves of the student tour guides.

So this is the island utopia he expects to recreate, I thought bitterly. A kind of ancient theme park. Tourists leaving footprints on streets virtually untrodden in 3,500 years. Sticky paw prints over the frescoes, the temple stones, the hieroglyphs. How long before there's a ticket booth at the gates, a souvenir boutique and a fast-food joint in the compound?

I found Hadrian up at Huxley's field tent, pouring tea from the samovar, pink, plump and pompous.

'Don't tell me I didn't warn you. *Atlantis:* it's a magnet for every crook, crank and charlatan this side of the astral plane.'

I almost missed it; something lurking in the smug sarcasm of his voice. No, things were not quite what they seemed even in dependable, stick-in the-mud Hadrian, and it was only as he darted away to accost some unsupervised pensioner grubbing about in a nearby trench, that I realised what it was.

Right in the thick of it now, with no prospect of escape, he was secretly hoping the Atlantis lie would succeed, if only to save his own bacon.

It just went to show how some people could claim the moral high ground even if they weren't actually standing on it.

When Anna arrived, with a welcome home kiss for me and a playful *'hot tea! in this heat!'* for Hadrian, I said, throwing her a deep glance: 'Aren't you worried? About the mess we're in? About the precipice he's about to drag us over?'

As she sank into one of the camp chairs, I caught the same unconfessed sense of relief. The relief of people expecting the worst, but escaping ruin by the skin of their teeth.

'Look, we have our critics, but the hypothesis has merit. Ask anyone in camp, ask in the eastern sector, they'll tell you: it's no more possible to disprove this is Atlantis than it is to prove it.'

At least Hadrian had the decency to bury his face in his cup.

'You said you'd never live it down,' I reminded him, with an abrupt sideswipe. 'Your name forever associated with Atlantis. It was the end of your career. The descent into crankdom.'

His face flushing pink again, he replied with a harrumph: 'Well, it appears Huxley's right: I am not quite the astute judge of human nature I once thought. Who can have predicted then that we would be courted by academic journals of international repute; they may be in California rather than London or Paris, but still, prestigious enough to ruffle some stale old feathers in Cambridge.'

'So your name will appear on it, that's what you're saying... Dr Adrian "Hadrian" Hunt, co-discoverer of Atlantis!'

He shot back angrily: 'Look, sometimes it is necessary to adapt to changing circumstances. Perhaps you should examine your own conscience before you start lecturing others on theirs!'

'*You have to stand up to him!*' The words came in a furious rush, and in the end, sounded strident even to my ears.

If it was chaos at camp, it was even worse in town.

New arrivals were going door to door, begging for a spare room, a *kalivi*, anything with a bed, shoestring travellers lugging backpacks and sleeping bags onto the bus, heading for the beaches.

Puzzled, spellbound, the townsfolk peered out of their windows as the *touristas* lingered in the street outside, drinking in the views. They stared at them with unflinching curiosity as they hurried by, their days organised by must-see lists and by-the-hour itineraries. They watched hang-jawed as they emerged from Katina's shop, each visit an apparent spending spree. They gawped as they bought fresh sardines from the fishermen, just to feed the alley cats.

I spotted Angeliki, the little handicapped girl, running up to a startled gaggle of tourists, a bunch of wildflowers and grasses in her hand.

'Nico!'

It was Dr Sanassis, off on his rounds.

'How was Athens?' I threw him a sideways glance, thrown as usual by the irony in his voice. 'You returned with a whole crowd of people.'

'It wasn't my fault.'

I had spoken too defensively, and he clapped me on the back, with a grin.

'How are the trees?' I asked.

'Growing. I hope they are dreaming of forests.'

We squeezed through another babbling crush of sightseers in flip-flops and shorts, narrowly missing a volley of camera shots fired at Costas the greengrocer and his donkey Esmerelda, the old man weighing out peaches on his brass scales, church domes and the blue caldera his ethereal backdrop.

On the veranda of his office in the *plateia*, Giannis Papadaikis had the island Council in session, every face around the blue wooden table a picture of brittle cheer.

'You should have been here, Nico,' remarked Sanassis, casting an ambivalent look at the Mayor and his councillors as we passed. 'They haven't slept for a week, and now that they do, they spend half the night dreaming of paradise, and the other half chasing after the thief who's come to steal it from them.'

'Paradise?' At least that explained the creased faces, the glassy eyes.

'Well. Their rendition of it. Opulent cruise ships anchoring in the caldera. Grand hotels lining the crater wall. Villas with turquoise swimming pools. A funicular running up the cliffs, the troublesome mules finally sent to the knacker's yard... People are dreaming dreams so fantastic it's as if the whole island's drifting into myth.'

'What?' The words struck an unnerving chord, and I could still hear the dissonant echo inside. *Islands, mythical, legendary, real.*

Catching my apprehensive look he added with an uncertain smile: 'We try, Nico. We are ever hopeful. We have to believe that no men are beyond persuasion. That there is another dream. There is another way.'

We turned the corner at the barber's shop, Nondas throwing us a worried glance into the mirror as he snipped and combed. Sanassis poked his head around the door. A few words passed between them, the Doctor wincing, nodding his understanding.

'What is it?' I asked, as he stepped back into the street.

'Nondas' landlord. It seems he wants to double the rent.'

★

That Huxley despised the cameras and microphones quite as much as he despised the people carrying them was obvious. Yet oddly enough, it was precisely this aloofness, this implied resentment that they were distracting him from great and noble archaeological pursuits, that made him all the more compelling to them.

The cameras whirred and clicked and flashed whenever he came within range, questions tossed over the ash dunes, hammering against a slammed hut door.

'*Will you strike Atlantian gold, Professor?*' '*What about the missing people, Professor? Did they ever make it as far as Crete? Did anyone survive?*'

'Why do you pretend you can't sense its presence?' I flared, my eyes jerking over the fragments littering the trestle tables. 'Why do you deny its existence?'

'Because it is a fallacy!' he mocked. '*The human nature, the divine nature!*'

'Even Guirand saw it: Atlantis was a conundrum created by a metaphysical genius — not myth, not legend, not moral fable!'

'Well thankfully, Claude came to his senses years ago.'

'At least he didn't lie, he didn't fabricate it. He wrote it in all innocence.'

'*It was a hymn to innocence!*' he erupted, adding through gritted teeth: 'Or should I say, the requiem to its own passing.'

'So what happened to him, what turned him into *that?*' The monster he had become. Something not even dead, but hidden away like some family mutation in the cellar dungeons of his Chateau on the Loire. '*Why? Why is that?*'

★

I couldn't get the stench of betrayal out of my nose, out of my mouth.

'So Atlantis boy is back!' taunted Sam, as he came splashing back to the dock. It was one of the few places not swarming with tourists, and he was making the most of it.

He squinted up against the light, treading water. 'You look as sick as a dog. Don't tell me you've finally seen it for what it is… Like some virus hatching in our own blood!'

Too unnerved to scowl I nodded abruptly, crouching down on the cement. In the distance, I could see the *Persephone* on another of its cargo runs, making slow progress across the glassy wind still sea.

'You're wondering why Huxley denies it, why he belittles it, why he's too ashamed to admit he wrote the *Travels*.'

'Huxley didn't write the *Travels*. Guirand did.'

His eyes widened. They really were as blue as the sea. With a splash he spun onto his back, letting the buoyant water carry him, all the better to disguise the shock. Of all the secrets littering the trail of his broken apprenticeship with Huxley, this had been the first, the key to everything.

Using one of the mooring rings as a leg up, he clambered out, dripping.

Snatching up his towel, he said almost to himself: 'So it was Guirand who planted the book in le Petit Phoenix. And Huxley could only go along with it because that's the Socratic method we were all taught by. Every question sent to test us, so oblique, so tangential, we don't even know there's a question at all! We're left to sink or swim in a reality that may or may not be real at all.'

He muttered some crude obscenity in French, obviously at his former mentor's expense.

If there was one sin in that book, it was Plato's Atlantis, but even that the opportunist had exploited as Guirand squirmed.

'They despise the Conundrum, sneer at it. Even Huxley, the man who supposedly lives to run the mind into a sweat, contemplating the impossible. Why is that?'

His impatient toss of the head drizzled the air with seawater. 'Can't you guess? Aren't you following the fucking breadcrumbs they scattered for you?' Sufficiently dry now to start splicing together his cigarette papers, he added through gritted teeth: 'Because to accept its existence would be to bankrupt everything they believe in, everything they have worked for, that's why. Ideas are there to serve us. They are there to be owned, exploited, subjugated to the human will — not free to fly some metaphysical dimension we cannot even see or touch, much less control!'

I uttered a torn sigh of frustration. 'Who understands it? The mechanics of it. How it works. No one!'

'Maybe that's the ingenuity of it.'

'It's impossible to understand, is that what you're saying?'

'It's like reality itself. How can we explain it unless we're looking at it from the outside?'

'Well, that is impossible. *Isn't it!*'

I had to get into his head before the resin did, obviously. 'What did the Scholiast see that so impressed Guirand? Something made him cry *eureka!* So what was it?'

He squinted into the milky blue horizon, as if willing the answer to emerge. 'He sensed some curious property in the dialogue's construction, buried between the words, reflected in the characters present. Something indefinable, almost labyrinthine. He found it difficult to explain rationally how people could fall so hopelessly under its spell, how it seduced or tormented the minds of all those who ever came into contact with it, believers, atheists, agnostics, it didn't matter. Difficult to explain how it became one of the most widely read works in history. Difficult to explain why, wherever Atlantis makes its appearance, there it is again, that same almighty clash: tyranny and peace, the purity of the dream and the corruption people resort to to possess it... yeah, that's it, an echo of the Big Bang that sent Atlantis sinking beneath the waves...'

The words bequeathed us a numb silence, just the August sea lapping sleepily against the dock. 'But that doesn't make any sense,' I objected. 'Huxley, Guirand, the Comte. How can they believe in the Isles at all, if they despise Atlantis as some kind of moralising fallacy? How is that even possible?'

A scornful glance. 'Who do you think they were, Nicky, the men who set out to find the Isles. *Saints? Good, righteous men? Men who had dedicated themselves to God?* You're joking. They were warriors, tomb robbers, mercenaries, mystics obsessed with their own immortality, priests with daggers and vials of poison. People who wouldn't think twice about lying, cheating or killing to get one step closer to Elysium.'

They were mad all right. The thought acted like smelling salts, acrid, stripping the nose, but at least brought me to my senses. The worst of it was, there wasn't a single person in camp who could be trusted to tell the truth — even if they didn't know they were lying.

'Why are you helping me anyway?' I said, scrambling to my feet. 'You've had it in for me from the start. Just like Benja. You made his life hell, until —'

He squinted up at me, no doubt wondering where the sudden vehemence was coming from. 'Why did you come back, Nicky? To get your fifteen minutes of fame? To bask in the triumph of discovery?'

'*Of course not!*'

'Revenge, then. To get your own back. To make Huxley pay.'

'No... I...' Catching the awkward look, he laughed out loud: 'To warn us! That was it, wasn't it. You wanted to *rescue your friends!*'

'I just thought…'

He moved in for the kill. 'Yes, that's what you thought, because the lie you tell yourself is always the easiest one to fall for, isn't it?'

'What?'

'Admit it! You're hooked. That's why you came back. Seduction! *Curiosity!* Just in case Huxley's right. Just in case you can get to the Isles.'

Wondering why I expected to get anything sane out of any of them, I threw up my hands and stomped away, only turning back on top of the dune to yell: *'I am not hooked!'*

Hands thrust into my pockets, I crossed the ridge, booting every pumice stone that came within range.

Wary of my own volatile temper, I took a long detour around house 16, where oblivious to Benja's death leap, the tour groups were now posing against the charred walls, his fall still bruising the fabric of time.

I pressed on, going nowhere, needing the distraction. Watched the ancient city rising over the western horizon like some physical manifestation of the Conundrum itself, still moments of tranquillity snatched from the holocaust.

The mere sight of him, issuing his imperious orders to the trench moles, made me see red.

'Why did you lie like that?' I yelled, before I could stop myself. He dismissed the men with a curt toss of the head, but they were probably still all ears as they tramped away to sink another hundred foot shaft into tephra.

'It was all talk, wasn't it. A sham, a fraud, just like everything else.' Maybe it even made him feel good, roaming around some dead philosopher's head, while the whole world was going to hell. 'Jawing about it to anyone stupid or drunk enough to listen! Pretending we could *actually do it* — that an island like this could actually be recreated in the present… All we'd need is the will and the imagination.'

For a second he seemed genuinely taken aback, and winced as he finally grasped what I was saying. 'Is that what you thought? You talk as if such a thing were even possible.'

'No! You did. The symposiasts did.'

'We talk like that to exercise the mind, and thereby to free it.'

'You always said anything was possible. That if the idea's strong enough, nothing can stop it. We could move mountains. That's what you said.'

'Perhaps you are right,' he replied at last, not unkindly. 'But you forget — ideas do not need bodies in which to live.'

44.

'There!' barked Huxley, stabbing the western flank of the Prophet Elias with his forefinger. 'There is the cave, ergo there we must dig.'

We were standing on the crumbling dirt track that gives the mountain its oblique facial scar, Huxley, Nestor and I, the chart spread out across the hood of the Land Rover. The sea gusts, too silly to take us seriously, were trying to tug it out of our hands, and have us run after it like children chasing a runaway kite.

'It could take weeks, Kapítán,' groaned Nestor. He glanced up at the ridge in apprehension, his face blanching even at the prospect of it: shifting tons of ash at yet another site, and on nothing more substantial than some crazy hunch. 'We would have to detail half the crew,' he objected. 'Go ahead if you want to, but you can forget about pushing on through that labyrinth of tunnels.' *Crazy?* I thought. *You don't know the half of it.*

I threw a sidelong glance at Huxley, wondering if he would back down, wondering if he was even aware of the danger he was in, getting trapped in the sticky web of his own lies.

Whenever they heard the rumbling on the peninsula, saw the dust storms and feverish digging with their own eyes, most people saw it for exactly what it wasn't: the great archaeologist fulfilling his life's ambition, raising Atlantis, house by house, street by street.

Others, their tongues loosened by grievance or too much wine, whispered other suspicions: that it was the bruised Huxlian ego that was now in charge of the dig, ransacking the city for proof of the Lost Isle's legendary descent into evil.

Even if they were too polite or too intimidated to say it out loud, every archaeologist and every student in camp knew that to be the Achilles heel of his theory. In fact, most now pretended they had known it all along.

Evidence of war, murder, greed. Evidence of a weapon used in anger — even a weapon at all. Evidence of gold and precious stones and the lust for them. There was nothing. Just more frescoes peeled out of the tephra, their vivid colours capturing a moment of heaven on earth.

Up on the ridge, my eyes strayed to Nestor who for once was daring to question the Kapítán's orders.

True to form, Huxley had shared with his foreman only those minimal facts that were required to accomplish the task at hand. The remains of an ancient cave buried under the ash, still tunnelling deep into the magma warm core. Human bones, in simple graves or more elaborate tombs. A statue or carving of a god.

There was no arguing with him.

Men and machines were moved up the mountainside, both grumbling loudly in their own raucous, smoking way.

Summer was still in full-throated song, the *Pegasus* sailing in every other day just to meet demand.

Self-confessed pilgrims to Atlantis, gaping up at the awesome lava cliffs. Arm-gyrating reporters and camera crews, trying to leap aboard the nearest cork-bobbing caïque without tipping everything into the drink. Eager students of this university or that, dreaming of the rich-veined trenches. Businessmen and speculators, on the lookout for a deal or a steal.

They crowded into the tavernas and *kafeneia*, drinking the wine cellars dry, running the schoolboy waiters off their feet. They commandeered any vehicle they could lay their hands on, even those with four legs, thrusting fistfuls of drachmas at their amazed, doubtful owners.

Suddenly, if you were lucky enough to find a room, the island was *the* place to be. Huxley had put it firmly on the map, and I couldn't help wondering if the ink was now indelible.

Along the little streets, signs were going up everywhere. *Rooms for Rent. Breakfast. Bread Butter Honey. Marmalata.*

Hotel Sea View Atlantis.

Taverna Atlantis Sunset.

'And so it begins,' said Stavros Sanassis, casting an ambivalent eye at candy-plumaged tourists flocking the streets.

'What does?'

'I hear it on my rounds. Patients at their wit's end. Sick with worry. The calls out of the blue, voices on the other end of the line gobbling up the words they're talking so fast... *Who is it? Some stranger, I can't understand what they're saying, no, wait, some cousin on my mother's side, twice removed. Some aunt or uncle nobody's heard of in twenty years. Some uncle's cousin's brother's son.* Sometimes, they're already standing there on the doorstep, all the way from Athens, Melbourne, New York, wherever, arms laden with gifts, bright fulsome smiles painting their faces. "Nana! It's me, it's I, don't you remember? How wonderful to see you again! I can't tell you how much we've missed you!" And it's only halfway through the welcoming feast that it comes out at all, the lip-smacking thoughts hardly able to stand up on their own two feet anymore, so greased are they on wine and pork fat. Words finally flushed into the open by the sheer anxiety of it, knowing that the best bargains are already slipping away under their noses. Rows of tumbledown houses, dirt cheap, with panoramic views over the caldera; an old vineyard with a mile of waterfront sand. "But you must know someone who knows someone! Someone desperate to sell, just to meet their debts or something. Someone old or dying! Turn the screws! Nana, warn them, it's just a craze, it won't last, cut them off at the knees!'"

Some well-heeled travellers brought their own accommodation, yachts and three-masted schooners blowing in on the Meltemi and anchoring off the Burnt Islands. Before the week was out they were joined by a vessel that eclipsed even their opulence, an immaculate white yacht with two steaming funnels, and portholes like jewels. *The Pearl Orient.*

A pair of mahogany motor launches playing shuttle, the yacht's lord and lady promptly descended upon the excavations with their own retinue and bevy of attendants, gushing, starry-eyed, and apparently unannounced.

That left half the camp puzzling over the couple's aristocratic identity and their role in Huxley's affairs, but for once, I already knew the answer.

It was the Comte et Comtesse Guillaume d'Adhémar, fresh from their diplomatic exertions in Athens.

Among the flitting Secretariat dogsbodies, the shipboard attendants in starched white uniforms, the elderly companions with stretched faces and vivid coiffures, two others. A girl, a boy, still in their late teens. As out of place here as they had been in Athens, gliding through the hotel foyer in the Comte's wake. *But who were they?*

There was something about them, something out of place... Not the tumbling golden hair, or the bodies that might have driven a sculptor to God or to drink. Not the wide eyes, with the clarity of Cycladic sky. Not even the dazzling white shirts, bringing that suspicion of ethereality to their complexions.

Whoever they were, they were holding hands now, exchanging a kiss, lips to cheek, while the fogey department fussed over their hats, laces, parasols, the dogs' portable water bowls and God knows what else.

No, they were as fake as everything else in Huxley's theatre of the absurd.

At last they set off, the Comtesse a long-suffering vision in white flowing chiffon, a bevy of yapping Pekinese on tangled leashes at her heels.

Close enough to eavesdrop, far enough away to meld into the background, I followed them up to the ridge, shocked that two and two could actually be making four instead of some mystical number contrived in Huxley's head.

I remembered Anna at her wit's end in the site office, slitting open envelopes, cursing him for his irresponsibility, cheques and cash spilling out over the trestle tables.

And here they were, the very people who had signed those cheques in a devotional flourish, converging now along the paths marked with whitewashed stones: the Friends of Orpheus, who bankrolled the cutting of every trench, the sinking of every shaft. Who flocked to the Foundation's invitation-only seminars and to whatever island logic, luck or ritual demanded, so devoted to the Comte's obsession they lived and breathed for the afterlife.

If that weren't pitiful enough, some were said to harbour even more outlandish expectations — that the Orpheus Foundation would help them commune across the Great Divide with their lost loved ones, an escaped husband, a runaway pet, who knows.

Well, in that Huxley was the perfect fit, wasn't he, the charlatan clairvoyant equipped with all the clever little tricks and mechanisms to make the curtains tremble, or propel gullible fingers over the Ouija board.

No wonder those who had made the ultimate round trip were held in such awe, no matter what side of the tracks they originated. They possessed a secret that had occupied minds since the beginnings of time, if only they could remember what it was.

As their paths collided outside house 16, it was at least easy enough to tell the Foundation's two constituencies apart. One in longing for the legendary white light. The other, apparently still carrying it around within.

And there he was at last, gritting his teeth, standing on the first hand-carved stones marking the threshold of his fake Atlantis.

Marcus Huxley. Watching this frenzied crowd converge upon him like devotees to a patron saint, and detesting every wrenching, futile second of it. Journalists and cameramen. Tourists and day trippers. Amateur archaeologists. Orpheans. And now the Comte himself, leading his wealthy claque past a bemused Anna, past Sam chest deep in a trench, squinting up at their wraith-like shadows flickering across the sun.

He whistled between his teeth, apparently at the sight of the Comte's young favourites, with their golden hair and dazzling white shirts.

Raising himself up on his arms he gazed after them with a lascivious grin. 'So what do you think of Célestine and Johnny?'

'Isn't he too young for you?' A sardonic glance, aimed right between the eyes. 'Who are they anyway,' I added, with irritation. 'The grandkids? Nephew, niece?'

'Célestine and Jean,' said Anna, her troubled look following them up the hill. 'They were in some terrible plane crash when they were kids, one of those single-engined things, their father at the controls. Flying through a bank of fog, then a torn second later, there it is, crashing through the cockpit window, the crest of a hill. It's a wonder they survived at all. Both the parents killed instantly. Célestine was dead herself for several minutes before someone gave her the kiss of life.'

'Imagine giving that Johnny the kiss of life,' said Sam.

Knowing what I knew, I expected Huxley and the Comte to be as thick as thieves.

I was wrong again but, in realising it, suddenly sensed the utility of his marriage of convenience to Svetlana. It was to manage situations like these.

There was something about her, a stoicism, a permafrost detachment that allowed her to indulge the fickle whims and fancies of her Comte et Comtesse without actually needing to contemplate death beyond the purely philosophical.

What with the contrasts of his own personality, Huxley found them difficult masters, even with seas and mountains between them. Now, at close quarters, the tectonic pressures crushing him, even the great master himself had to choke back his frustration, swallow his pride, and muster a congenial smile.

A genius in psychological manipulation he may have been, but this just didn't suit him, delivering pep talks about being in reach, about the answer to everything they had lived and worked for, being just a month, a day or an hour away.

Over the arching river bridge, into the agora. He paused to show them the fountains that had once splashed with mountain water, the dolphin frescoes, the decorated plates and amphorae, the petrified trees. Striking the deferential, if unfamiliar, pose they assumed was expected of them, they craned their necks around ancient doorways, inspected the sunken stone baths, gazed up at the sky terraces, the companions murmuring their dutiful oohs and aahs. Yet the mood was souring, faster than milk left out in a thunderstorm. Progress, perhaps not all that it could or should be. Extravagance in all this new-fangled equipment, when good honest manual labour might have achieved the same ends. Reddening skin exposed to the summer sun's cruel glare. Sore feet in shoes designed for the red carpet or the cat walk, not paths of crumbling ash. They were all part of the rancid-making mix.

As they approached the temple heights, the Comte turned to his retinue with some brisk remark about their company no longer being required. Lest that offend the closest Friends of Orpheus, he encouraged them to take in the sights on the lower slopes. Evidently secrets were about to be shared that were for the principals alone. Evidently that included the two golden youngsters they had adopted as their own.

As Huxley led them past the littered remains of the temple grove, even the lap dogs fell silent. For the first time, in light formed out of the temple columns and their stone-etched hieroglyphs, awe was reflected in their eyes. Nearing the half-buried house designated 34, the Pekinese began rebelling against their leashes, and fell to their stomachs, whimpering.

Huxley, tired of my sullenness, beckoned me from the sidelines with a brisk, impatient gesture and thrust the dogs' leads into my hands.

As he did so, I was conscious of Célestine's gaze, as intense as mountain sky. To my surprise, I found a smile breaking over my face.

Nestor was waiting for us at the perimeter of his fake junk yard; the barbed wire had temporarily been dragged aside and a path cleared between the rusting machines to reach the buried vaults below. Once the lamps had been lit, he guided them through the shaft, down into the house of the death frescoes, the Comtesse evincing alarm at the friable walls closing in around her, the Comte tugging at her hand with a frown.

When finally they reappeared to the mellowing afternoon sun, the sprightly step and adoring eyes said it all. Their faith had not merely been restored. It had undergone a resurrection. They were on cloud nine.

As they retraced their steps into camp, it was in rhapsodic praise for everything they set eyes on, the Cycladic light, the temple columns against the indigo sky, the flour-faced students in the trenches, even the normally irritating servants. Life was just wonderful.

Célestine and Jean seemed the only normal people in sight. How bizarre was that?

The d'Adhémars continued to make their odd, theatrical appearances in the days that followed, cornering Huxley in his tent, kidnapping him for dinner or luncheon aboard the Pearl Orient. They plotted battlefield tactics against their own blue-blooded rival, Claude Guirand, and their diplomatic offensive among the Colonels and the Athens cultural elite.

More distrustful than ever, I kept a watchful eye on their movements. The motor launches shuttling back and forth. The flustered Secretariat dogsbody, a briefcase locked under his arm as though it contained the crown jewels. The helmsman of the tender, accepting a package from Huxley's tent.

And every time, sure enough, there would be Guirand's skull in my mind's eye, ranting about fraud and trafficking.

The Friends of Orpheus, meanwhile, spent the week exploring the island, village to village, shore to shore. Sunset would find them up on temple hill, waiting for whatever the dusk might impart.

It was one thing to run into this baffling mix of humanity in the lobby of the Grande Bretagne, quite another to do so under the teeming stars like that, murmurs and silhouettes between the temple columns. I could hear them like ghosts on the breeze as I passed, reciting Guirand's Travels, island to island, as though the old villain's ancient humiliation was poetry of the soul.

Rich, poor. Young, old. Black, white, yellow or brown, there was just no stopping them. You'd hear the music echoing down from the hill, guitar, flute, sometimes a song. Catch a graceful silhouette tripping the light fantastic over the ancient marble steps. Stumble midsentence into their own island travels, uncertain whether they're sailing the currents of memory, myth or delusion.

Every so often, along would come an open bottle of wine, or a gleaming joint shedding more sparks than a meteor, on its way to some old granny, business executive or soldier.

It was weird. *They* were weird.

That Friday, I received my invitation to 'luncheon' aboard the Pearl Orient, along with Anna, Sam and Hadrian. 'The Comte wishes to express his gratitude,' said Huxley drily.

'What for?' I snapped, hackles rising. 'Why me?'

'Célestine was most insistent… She has taken quite a shine to you.'

'What?'

45.

The *Pegasus* it wasn't. Teak decks. Brass fittings so polished you could catch your face in them. Cabins with king size beds, en suite baths. A glittering crystal chandelier over a dining table that could seat thirty without breaking a sweat. There was not a curtain, a sheaf of paper, a single hair out of place. In their impeccable white uniforms, even the deck hands looked as if they had just come back from the cleaners.

Our perpetually harried functionary from the Secretariat ushered us into a stateroom.

'The Comte et Comtesse will be with you shortly,' he announced with earnest cheer, then promptly disappeared.

A slow amazed whistle sounded from Sam's lips at the glass display cases lining the walls. 'Look at all this *stuff!*'

Antiquities, artefacts, relics. In gold, silver and ebony. In clay, ivory or moonstone. On parchment, papyrus or rice paper.

'This must be one of the earliest surviving copies of Plato's Republic,' said Hadrian, his breath momentarily misting the glass. 'Good God.'

Peering over his shoulder at the illuminated folio, Sam said: 'The legend of *Er*. His comrades, they're about to set the funeral pyre alight when he awakes from his own death, still with the memory of what he has seen on the other side.'

'There are others,' called Anna from the far end of the stateroom. 'Here's a medieval record from a Welsh monastery... An encounter with the white light. A vision of the Isles of the Blest. A city made of light.'

So Svetlana, apparently, had been telling the truth after all. Such as it was. These were the d'Adhémars' latest objects of desire, won at public auction, procured from dealers, stolen from tombs.

Testimonies from beyond the grave or a final heartbeat.

Arcane texts on the Eleusinian mysteries, and on every island rendition from Avalon to P'eng-lai.

Legends that speak of the End of Days, the end of the world, the final judgement.

Prophecies on the ultimate destiny of the human soul, wherever they might be found, some Red Sea cave, Phoenician temple or Ojibwa wigwam.

A queasiness gripped me as I moved from one display to the other, and it was only in catching my own reflection in the glass that I realised. I was thinking about Célestine and Jean. The plane colliding into the mountain. The life leaving Célestine's body. The life's encounter with the light.

Is that why the Comte had saved her, as another exquisite work of art from the other side?

In her youth, in her beauty, in that luminous if inscrutable knowledge held within, she was probably the most immaculate acquisition of all.

'These things are priceless,' breathed Anna, hardly knowing whether to be shocked or spellbound.

'Obviously not,' said Hadrian archly. 'Everything under the sun has a price of sorts. The only question is if one can afford to pay it.'

She murmured: 'At least we know now why they're such hallowed figureheads for the Friends…'

'Yeah, the King and Queen of the Underworld,' slurred Sam, a different kind of acid on his tongue for once.

'But where did it all come from? All this money…'

Hadrian uttered a discreet cough. 'Perhaps one should not enquire.'

Sam sneered: 'Why not? I'll bet even that Buddhist Thangka depicting the Pure Lands would pay your salary for a decade.'

'Inheritance, I daresay,' sniffed Hadrian. 'The family silver as it were.'

'You're a veritable Houdini when the facts are inconvenient aren't you, Hadrian?'

'What the hell do you mean by that?' he puffed, bulbous with indignation.

The voices had grown louder, and must have been echoing down the passageway. Anna shushed them.

Sam said in a forced whisper: 'So you haven't heard about the silver mines in South America then, the gem mines in the Congo? Women, kids who haven't seen daylight for a year. Buried when the tunnels collapse. Climbing up the mud walls of some great quarry, thousands of them scrambling over the ledges like some Dantean image of hell on Earth!'

'That's enough Sam!' said Anna in a furious whisper.

Hadrian adding: 'They're paying your own wages as well, Sam, don't forget that when you're being so holier than thou!'

Just then, they arrived in a swoosh of parting air. The Comtesse with a radiant if painted smile. The Comte, his arms outstretched in greeting: 'Dearest friends!' as though he had known us since childhood. 'How much the world owes you.'

As if fearing germs, the Comtesse planted an air kiss on either side of our cheeks.

Bringing up the rear came Huxley himself, the look in his eye just trespassing into the sardonic.

But where was Célestine?

'I see you have been admiring the latest additions to our collection,' remarked the Comte with long suffering pride.

Everyone nodded obediently, Sam chasing off his own reflex with a scowl.

Fidgeting, Hadrian threw a restless glance into a display case containing an illuminated copy of the Critias in medieval parchment.

'Forgive me for asking,' he stuttered. 'But why Atlantis? Here, among all these cultural representations of the lands hereafter?'

The Comte favoured him with a cocktail of a smile, one measure indulgent, two patronising: 'But what is Atlantis, dear Adrian, if not quintessential eschatology?'

Hadrian arched an eyebrow in surprise. Expressed with such conviction, the idea even seemed to have ambushed Huxley himself.

'Consider the parallels,' the Comte challenged him. 'An island lying to the far west; in that, hardly different from the other isles that lie beyond sunset. An island whose inhabitants, blessed by the gods, knew the divine nature. Whose quest for knowledge spelled an end to their childlike innocence, whose hubris ultimately brought about their own apocalypse by fire and flood.'

'But it lay beyond the Pillars of Hercules,' spluttered Hadrian, before hurriedly realising his blunder. 'At least, that's what the legend says...'

'True. And yet what are the Pillars of Hercules beyond their literal meaning? Given Hercules' descent into Hades, his journey to the Isles and back, might we not surmise that they were also a metaphor for the twin pillars of existence, Life and Death?'

★

I was still searching for her along the deck railings, as I climbed into the second launch with Huxley.

'So where was Célestine?' I said, half-suspecting I had been dragged to luncheon under false pretences, just to lend the impression of team harmony. 'And Jean? The Comte doesn't want to share them, is that it? His prize possessions.' When that failed to elicit anything more than an evasive grunt, I turned the screws: 'So some things are priceless, after all.'

'Sometimes the currency is not money, Nicholas. Sometimes it is love, sometimes it is knowledge.'

'What do you mean?'

'I mean you have to earn your desire.'

I was left to chew on my own fury as we skimmed over the waves.

Amid the frothing of the propeller as we neared the dock, Huxley growled: 'I shall be glad when they are finally out of my hair!'

'Who?'

An irritated glance, as though he had been bottling up the frustration for days. 'The Comte et Comtesse, of course! The Foundation. The Friends of Orpheus.'

We clambered out onto the dock.

'Then why are you in bed with them at all? The money, is that it? The patronage?'

I uttered a derisive laugh. 'They pretend it's their life's mission don't they? To illuminate the hereafter and bring redemption to the whole wide world,' adding through gritted teeth: 'Even if any fool can see they're only interested in the immortality for themselves, their yap-yap lap dogs and possibly one or two of the more dependable servants.'

Studying me through narrowed eyes, he said in a crushing voice: 'Your cynicism is no use to me, Nicholas, no use to anyone, remember that…'

'*Me?* I'm not the one sneering at my own supporters. You think I haven't seen you with that snide look on your face for everything they have to say. Calling them the "White Lighters" or something equally disparaging whenever they're out of earshot. People like Célestine. Why is that? Why are you so patronising towards them? Do you believe their near-death experiences or not?'

The accusation, or perhaps the tone of it, caught him off guard. 'Look, it's just that I find their accounts so irritating!' he said at last, the words crushed between his teeth. 'That hopeful, buoyant vagueness.

That clear-eyed optimism about everything in sight! To go around believing they have been to death and back — well, it is a step too far, too presumptuous, even if some of them were pronounced clinically dead. They have been to death's door, that's all. They have not crossed the threshold. Not one of them has ever consciously seen the other side.'

For a second, I had to wonder if that was really envy lurking in his voice. If so, it explained a lot. It was the nature of the man. The one who must conquer. The one who must be first. If nothing else, the revelation offered my first tangible clue that where his search for the Necromanteion was concerned, these curious souls were as much in the half light as any of us, ironic given their preoccupation.

'Even deep hypnosis has yielded us nothing,' he went on, the strain tightening his voice as we climbed up from the dock. 'They talk about the white light as if that were the only thing about their near-death experience they can remember. Formerly articulate individuals can no longer find words to describe what it was they sensed, saw, heard, as if they were being asked to remember the impossible. What *is* the white light? When pressed, some just manage to characterise it as an intelligence, a sentience, something living, something benevolent. Others, more inarticulate than ever, recall that when the light touched them, a part of them *became* light.'

'But they *have* seen things,' I said, thinking how odd it felt to be challenging him on the facts, when I knew them to be delusions. 'The City of Light…'

'Chimeras,' he growled. 'Prove to me they are not so!'

'*Me?* Why me?'

★

The trees had grown. Though still only saplings, a head taller than me, as they followed the contour of the slope, somehow they already carried the impression, the idea, the vision of forest.

Dr Sanassis clapped me on the shoulder. 'So you're here at last.'

'I would have come before. I was busy.' That's when I saw them. Down on their hands and knees, watering, weeding, digging, planting, and with that special kind of intensity they brought to everything. Célestine. Jean. And by the look of it, half the 'White Lighters' for good measure. Why were they so fucking optimistic about everything?

Distracted, I set to work carrying the new saplings out from the walled garden, Sanassis and the postmaster babbling about reconstructing the windmills on the rise, the stone amphitheatre on the Mesa Vouno. When they thought no one was listening, their conversation veered towards the spiking tensions in town, the confrontations that would blow up but then come to nothing; the police throwing their weight around, before drowning their frustrations in raki; the Councillors plotting what could only sound like sedition to the ears of informers; tourists flocking the idyllic streets, oblivious to their lurking tyranny.

Alexis Pangalos could hardly be counted on to keep his wild emotions in check, fretted Vassilis the postmaster. Standing there among his Aegean blue tables, arms akimbo, growling his fury at the dingy taverna Liberty along the way, keeping open door for the police and the army cadets, portraits of the beloved Colonels lining its walls.

My eyes kept straying to Célestine, but it was her brother Jean who intercepted one of those careless looks.

I was taking another slug of water, the sweat stinging my eyes, when he appeared at my side with about as much warning as an apparition. 'Célestine wants to speak with you.' He smiled.

Again, that inexplicable feeling. That there was something unreal about them — *or was it us?*

Still on edge, I snapped: 'Why? So the big chief has allowed us to talk.'

A widening grin. Blissful, almost beatific. Odd enough for anyone, let alone a boy of his age, seventeen or something. What the hell were they on? He wouldn't be quite so smiley once Sam had fucked him senseless.

We met in the shadow of the garden wall. My heart was drumming in my chest. My palms were sweating.

'I am glad to meet you Nico.' Her voice had the clarity of a Himalayan chime. 'At last.'

I swallowed hard. 'Huxley said you wanted to meet me. *If he put you up to it —*'

Her eyes widened. 'But why would he do that?'

'Because.'

'You are his right hand, I can see that.'

'I am not!' I flared. 'I am nothing of the kind!'

Biting back my anger, I found a place to sit. She flopped down beside me, our backs against the garden wall, a scarlet bougainvillea cascading over us.

'You don't like them much do you?' Her long eyelashes blinked almost imperceptibly towards her companions among the saplings.

'Look, I feel sorry for them, that's all,' I said, instantly breaking my resolve to be careful with my words. 'They're just gullible milch cows for the Foundation, aren't they.'

'I don't think so, Nico. You see that gentleman over there with the silver beard? He's been in Africa, digging village wells since the day he died five years ago. Or that couple over there, they've been working in the slums and shanty towns. They don't have money.'

There it was again, that ethereal quality in her eyes I just couldn't name, a collision of things I couldn't make sense of, something made of light, something made of time or the absence of it.

'So what was it like?' I blurted. 'The Comte. He said that you had seen it. *The City of Light...*'

A wince. Who could blame her. She must have heard the question a million times, and in all variations of hope and derision. 'It is difficult... to find the words.'

'So you can't describe it. You can't tell me what it looks like. You can't tell me what it feels like.'

'The words don't exist! There were trees, waterfalls, hill streets rising into the sky... But they were the souls of these things, I mean the soul beyond the waterfall, beyond the hill...'

When I shook my head in disbelief, she said softly: 'You are a very angry boy, Nico. He said you would be in denial.'

'Who?' I demanded with a start. 'Huxley? I warned you didn't I —'

'No. Johnny.'

'*Johnny?*' I couldn't believe it. 'I am not in denial!'

An awkward silence fell over us and I added with a swipe: 'Don't tell me. He died in the plane crash too, didn't he?'

'I resented it at first. So did Johnny. Being revived, I mean. Being dragged back into my body. Realising I was losing the one place that meant everything to me.'

'So you *hate* being alive.'

A laugh, so carefree it reminded me of swallows on a summer's day. 'I love being alive, Nico. More than I ever did before I died.'

I had the inexplicable urge to kiss her on the lips, to run away, to throw myself flying off the cliff, to dig through the volcanic ash until my hands were raw.

I scrambled to my feet. 'I am not in denial!'

Meanwhile Huxley's excavations on the ridge continued unabated, 18 hours a day, seven days a week. Amid the din of the bulldozers and mechanical diggers, Nestor's brand new dust-blowing machines were set to work, propeller contraptions that looked like giant fans, blasting the loosened tephra off the cliff. By night, you could see the flare in the sky as the men laboured under the phosphorescent carbide lights.

Changing shifts, the labourers would return home from the mountain covered in ash, looking like ghosts, their long faces an eloquent reminder of his own folly. Even after shifting half the ridge to strike native limestone, there was still no sign of Huxley's cave or his mythical Ferryman.

46.

Three sticky days later, the Archaeological Service announced its shock decision, one that had Claude Guirand's fingerprints all over it.

The frescoes, the Order declared, amid a flourish of official stamps and wax seals, were at imminent risk from dust, moisture and ultraviolet light. They were at the mercy of unpredictable seismic events, volcanic activity, even looting by criminals. Using the latest cutting techniques, they would therefore be painstakingly dismantled, house by house, wall by wall, and transported to Athens under armed guard. There they would be preserved under climate-controlled conditions in an appropriate museum setting, eventually being put on public display to the cultural edification of all.

As far as twisted minds went, it was a stroke of genius. Simple, elegant, devastating. Even Huxley might have marvelled at it, had his ego allowed him the room — not least of all the way it slip-wriggled through the contradictory forces that held the Athens bureaucracy in its state of eternal paralysis. Suddenly, it no longer mattered that while one department embraced Huxley's stewardship of the excavations, another was plotting his downfall. Or that the Comte et Comtesse had spent days singing his praises among the Athens elite, while at the same cultural evenings and embassy soirees Claude Guirand was spitting poison over the champagne flutes and canapés. Desperate for credibility, even the Colonels would see the utility of such hard science, the Atlantian frescoes becoming another welcome boon as they entered the capital amid patriotic fanfare and media confetti.

With that one decision Huxley had lost everything. The artefacts he needed to plot his course to the Necromanteion. The freedom to explore the tunnels running towards the mountain. The backing of the locals, without which the camp would simply cease to function.

The blast wave sent the Council reeling.

Under the town hall pergola sat a dazed Giannis Papadaikis, cracking worry beads over his whitened knuckles as other island characters came and went, appealing to reason or revenge, dispensing advice, hurling insults.

Summoned for his magic he may have been, but Huxley was in a sombre, defeated mood as he sank into the chair opposite Papadaikis and his Councillors, every creased sleepless face a picture of earnest entreaty.

'The dream is over, face it,' he told them, with a blunt swipe that made even my ears ring. 'Without the vibrant pigments that lend it heart and soul, your Atlantis will wither and die. And without Atlantis, what is there? Just holes in the ash. Just fields of curling vines that look like ostrich nests. Just black sands that scorch the feet in summer. A jagged cliff, beyond which there is what, nothing, an abyss.'

He shook his head, pursed his lips. 'By the time they have finished, you'll be lucky to have the shells of houses still intact, a few grey stones to show your grandchildren.'

'But there must be something we can do!' cried Katina, pacing up and down, mopping her eyes, twisting the handkerchief between her fingers.

Even the austere Father Nannos appeared to have shrunk into his chair, his complexion suddenly wan, his cheeks all sunken in at the shock.

Finding his voice for once, Alexander Vouris the schoolmaster began rapping the table, talking nineteen to the dozen about lawyers and legal injunctions, until Alexis Pangalos, silenced him with an impatient gesture. 'You are forgetting, Alex, the judges are hand in glove with the criminals in power. We'll find no justice there.' Glaring at Junta-appointee Papadaikis, he smacked his fist into his palm, and added through gritted teeth: 'Those sons of whores, they'll rob the island blind!'

Bluster, turning into defiance.

By noon, half the island was up in arms, and it may have been a measure of simmering revulsion for the Colonels that some hotheads began cleaning their hunting rifles and counting their ammunition.

Sensing trouble, Manolis and Chondro hurriedly bolted the police station shutters and reported the names of the worst offenders to their superiors in Athens. They watched and waited, slit eyes aimed across the *plateia,* dazzling white under the late August sun.

In the firing line between the police station and the town hall sat Hadrian, almost frantic with worry under a *kafeneion* sun umbrella, his teacup rattling nervously in its saucer.

Finally, there we were, flickering between sun and shadow, Hadrian desperate to read our faces. Grimacing, Huxley sank into one of the straw-seated chairs, ordered a frappé, then with evasive eyes began relating the news with the dry detail of a site log.

Hadrian mopped his brow, seemed about to nod his acquiescence to the reality engulfing us, when it burst forth: 'Oh yes, Huxley, I know you, each word like an incendiary device; handled with excruciating care, yet knowing just where to detonate them to maximum effect.'

If Huxley's eyes widened at the accusation, for once he seemed too tired or indifferent to make much pretence of it.

'Have you no compunction?' Hadrian seethed, barely keeping his voice under control. 'By encouraging them in this madness, you're putting people's lives and liberty in peril. Friends, strangers, the students in camp, everyone! If the Colonels so much as snap their fingers, there'll be blood in the streets...'

Clicking his tongue between sips of frappé, Huxley replied: 'They will not be so ready to move against us when we are at the centre of the world's stage.'

'But Guirand has the unequivocal backing of the Service,' squealed Hadrian. 'Not to mention science. Not to mention common sense. How on earth do you propose to win this fight?'

'You would do better to ask how he proposes to defeat us, when the whole island stands as one.'

So that was it.

Huxley and Guirand. They were going head to head, and over something no one else even understood. Who would blink first?

★

The Pearl Orient was raising anchor, Célestine waving down at us through flyaway hair, as golden as chaff in the wind. Jean, the Comte et Comtesse, on the upper deck, waving, the Pekinese yapping.

They are not monsters, Nico, whatever you think, she said.

Our feet were dangling lazily in the sea, its surface so summer still it seemed possible to navigate by the stars found in its own reflection.

'So you're there of your own freewill, you wouldn't escape if you could?' Silence, just the faint murmur of the sea.

'If you ask me what I learned most about being dead, seeing what I saw, siphoned back into my body like a captured cloud, that's what it was — there is no better place to be than here, now.' Tell that to the Comte, I thought, trying to make sense of another impossible conundrum. Tell it to Huxley, spending every living moment, awake or asleep, trying to conquer those isles on the edge of the dusk.

We stretched out on the soft sand, a celestial ocean streaming above our heads. For once, it didn't seem quite so remote or indifferent in its incomprehensible infinity. Without turning, she reached for my hand.

'Will you come back?' I asked, not quite daring to look.

'There is no other place, Nico,' pressing my hand to the rhythm of the words. 'No other time than now.'

And there wasn't. There isn't. A breeze rises. Half in the wet, half in the dry, we lie naked at the water's edge, feeling the summer sea lapping between our legs. Gorge ourselves on the muscat grapes she's filched from the ship's galley, the juice running down our cheeks; laughing like kids, we're licking it from each other's lips, then our throats, then our nipples, bellybuttons, thighs, licking ever deeper, ever harder.

Dawn broke over the sea the colour of spilled wine.

'Look out for me on the island, Nico,' she called, still wriggling into her clothes as her brother Jean appeared on the sand dunes to fetch her home.

I felt my heart lunge at the words, a big wide grin breaking across my face, only thinking to ask as the jeep rattled away down the dust track: '*What island?*'

'They will have their work cut out for them,' mused Huxley, jarring me back to the present.

'Don't tell me they actually like meeting those people, the Colonels and their loyal minions, the lapdog journalists.'

'Life is not about likes and dislikes,' he snapped. 'It is about necessities. And lest you forget, the only reason we are still on the island at all, digging, edging ever closer, is because of Atlantis, because of the press.'

A peppy klaxon blast reaffirming the d'Adhémars restored faith in him, Huxley turned on his heel and returned to camp, the parting smile still freeze-dried to his lips, liberated from one ordeal but already in the bruising shackles of another. Keeping minds focused on the dig. Burrowing ever deeper into the mountain core before the enemy landed.

I couldn't help stealing one last glance at the Pearl Orient as she headed north.

'What are you moping about?' he demanded brusquely.

'Nothing.'

'Lovesick, is that it? You're wondering if your beautiful Célestine will come back to you. Well who knows, maybe she will, if you can provide the reason for the Comte to permit it.'

'I am not lovesick and I am not in denial!'

He glanced sideways at me. 'In denial about what?'

'Nothing!' I yelled and stormed off.

47.

Sam came tearing through camp, vaulting over open trenches.

By the time he had reached Huxley's pitch he was doubled over in pain, and panting so hard he could barely spit up a single intelligible word.

Huxley stiffened, his mood like a falling barometer.

What the hell was he talking about, one ragged gasp at a time? Some find in the southwest, where the streets once flowed out of the city to the ancient waterfront. As the crow flies, barely a mile from where the bulldozers and fans were still working on the mountain flank under Nestor's stoical command.

Huxley leapt out of his chair, sending the camp table flying. In the blink of an eye, he was gone, dashing past both of us, sprinting for the Land Rover. By the time we caught up with him, he was already lurching out of the compound, Sam just making it by the skin of his teeth by throwing himself over the tailgate.

Only partially exhumed, it was still lying face-down in the black earth.

A plunging emptiness in the pit of my stomach already told me what I was seeing. At my side, I could hear Huxley's expectant breath, and knew he knew it too.

Sam rejoined Hadrian in the trench, Christos and Helia scrambling in to help them. They exchanged a few words on method and then set about freeing their discovery from the last of the caked tephra — feet, shoulders, ears, hands.

Mechanically, the rest of us shuffled forward, forming a tight huddle around the open grave.

Anna, biting her lips in apprehension, the whiff of aniseed on her breath again. 'The Ferryman,' she murmured, a tremble in her voice.

My head jerked towards her. *How did she know?* The shocked words were already erupting from my lips, when Aris thrust his way between us, the moment lost. Stripping off his shirt, he was soon waist deep in the trench with the others, glistening with sweat as they manhandled the 6-foot figure this way and that, coaxing it free of the ash. They looped pulley ropes over its head and arms, tightening the slip knot at its chest.

Nothing like the lucent marble sculptures of Greek antiquity, if this was the Ferryman it had the darkness and the sheen of charcoal, and owed that to the stone from which it had been carved, volcanic basalt, born in a flood of primordial magma.

As they twisted and turned, trying to ease it from the trench, the statue's head seemed to jerk towards us of its own accord. The shock jolted through us, cold, electric.

Those eyes.

They were the most piercing blue I had ever seen. Bluer than this island-sown sea, bluer even than the winter iris of the sky.

As the body was hoisted over the lip of the trench, the pulley ropes straining at the load, Huxley could no longer restrain himself. Rudely, he thrust the craning bystanders aside, then sank to his knees, cradling the head as if it were his rescued child.

'Do you see?' he demanded breathlessly. *'Do you see?'* In the blur of the moment, incredible as it was, I could have sworn he was talking to the stone dead effigy itself. But then he jerked his head towards me, saying, 'Do you see how vivid, how striking are the eyes?'

Unconsciously, Anna gripped my arm, digging her nails into my skin.

There was something about the fine-boned face, the broad forehead, the advancing posture, the long braided hair, reminiscent of the earliest Kouroi of Nile Egypt.

Unbidden, unwanted, snatches of the Sais Codex went floating through my head, like some disembodied spirit. *He who guards the Oracle of the Dead, as tall as the river god himself...*

And now here he was, standing within inches of us, as tall as a man, as tall even as Huxley himself. I retreated a few steps, hardly knowing why. Something unnerving, not so much for what this naked volcanic god showed the world, but for what it did not. Something lurking beyond those beguiling, deep water eyes.

Deep within the mountain stands the god who ferries souls across the River. Can thou seest beyond? Across the water to the other shore? Through the Oracle as deep as the prism eye? Who, better than he, shall understand that death is a land not far from here?

I tried to focus on more down-to-earth matters. If this sacred river god once stood in the mountain, what was he doing here, abandoned along the verges of this once busy thoroughfare dipping towards the waterfront?

Four hours later, he was standing upright in the well of the Land Rover, bandaged up like an Egyptian mummy, attracting the curious, suspicious stares of village folk as we crawled along the broken tracks to Monolithos, Huxley wincing at every bump and lurch.

What with Guirand's spies in camp and reporters scavenging for stories, the Ferryman would be safer up there, everyone was agreed.

In the fading twilight we hoisted the Ferryman out of the Land Rover, and with eight pairs of hands manhandled it through the garden and up the stairs into Huxley's book-lined study. Ragged, panting and sweat-drenched, we collapsed onto the rug or the ottoman, the Ferryman standing over us like some serene, unperturbable god, his mesmerising eyes seemingly transfixed now by the moonlit sea and the sinuous coast beyond the window panes.

'He won't bite,' said Hadrian, a jibe at Anna who had retreated to the far end of the room, arms crossed, back against the wall.

'I don't like it,' she said with finality, and in a plain, matter-of-fact voice.

From behind his desk, Huxley threw her a questioning glance over his half-moon reading glasses.

'What do you mean, he's beautiful,' said Sam, as if her aversion for the Ferryman somehow diminished his own achievement in finding it.

'It is merely a sculpture carved from flood basalt,' Hadrian rebuked her. 'It does not live. It does not breathe.'

Tell that to Huxley, I thought. *He's the one who believes this thing is endowed with occult powers. He and the Comte, thinking it will spell 'Open Sesame!' to the world beyond.*

Anna stood her ground. 'No. Look at the curve of the lips, sensuous yet mocking. Look at the eyes, that first appear to convey innocence, then knowledge, then utter ruthlessness, as though life, existence, even the idea of love, is but a cruel trick.'

'Oh, please!' said Hadrian, his voice oozing disdain. 'If the eyes have a piercing aspect, it is a testament to the artist's skill and use of materials — the obsidian that forms the pupils, the irises fashioned from lapis lazuli.'

Poring over island charts at his desk, Huxley ignored them.

His silence was about as reassuring as Hadrian's devout faith that everything in the universe can be explained away by human rationality.

What is that feeling, where can it be coming from? Something unsettling, something indefinably sinister. Not in the room, but beyond it.

Almost as if those electric blue eyes, with the gold flecks like stars, are absorbed by events over the horizon. Things we cannot see.

★

At some unearthly hour I drove Anna home, the bloodless landscape gliding by us with the effortless fluidity of a dream.

'I never expected him to find it,' she said, her revelation like a lunging stab in the darkness. 'The Ferryman, I mean. Not for a moment.'

'*You knew?* You knew all along?'

'It's been lost for three and a half thousand years, Nico! Who can have expected him to find it like that, a needle in a haystack?'

My own stammering emotions hit me like a shock wave, one after the other. 'So you know about the Sais Codex, the Necromanteion?' I could hear the anger creeping into my voice, and wanted to deflect it from innocent victims. That was owed to Huxley alone, the man who sought the glories of truth through his ingenuity for deception. And it was owed to me myself, for swallowing the pictures of reality he painted for me. Absurdly, I even felt pangs of jealousy at being forced to share his exceptional secret, or his lie, with another living soul.

'Alexandria,' she reflected. 'All that street chaos and noise, the taxis blaring their horns, the donkeys braying, the hawkers bellowing at the top of their lungs, the grubby little street children swarming like flies, and Marcus wading his way through, tugging me along by the arm, sharing his fabulous secret as if I were the last person alive in the whole wide world. A means to peer into eternity.'

'You believed him?'

'I was vulnerable just then.'

'*To what?* His charms, his charisma, his lies?'

Was that a tear she had brushed away? 'It was just a romantic impossible dream, that's all, and who was I to wake him? People have a right to dream. They have the right to believe the world a better place than it is. But then it became a mania, an obsession, and he knows how I detest it. Death, immortality, the light beyond the still heartbeat.'

'What about Hadrian? What about Sam? What about Nestor?'

She sighed heavily. 'You know Marcus, how he divides the light and the dark between us.'

I felt another surge of anger. Of course, Huxley's principled mind, insisting that only the most deserving have any right to know the truth, those who dig, demand, insist.

'Sam. Célestine. Even her little brother. They say I'm in denial, can you believe that. *Well? Can you?*'

'Sometimes I think we are all in denial.'

Footsteps ringing off the pathway, I made my way home, the mournful howl of a dog for company. Bolting the door behind me, I collapsed onto the bed, too tired to undress or even pull off my boots.

Tossing, turning, I fell into a frenzied sleep that seemed no sleep at all, just mislaid moments of another time.

A pulse of white light flaring through the window, bursting through the keyhole. Huxley, vowing to break into the Underworld, beckoning me to follow him, down through the trenches like cemetery graves.

Dragging our own bodies to the black, snaking river Styx, the faces of our families, our friends, painted with ecstatic smiles. Mum, Sofi, Célestine, tossing petals into the sky.

A bone- and gristle-faced Charon punting us across the stinking water to the other side, the colourless dust billowing up all around us as we stumble ashore.

Dad? is that you?

But it isn't. It's just Huxley feeding a draught of blood to some other straggly-haired zombie, hoping to revive it just enough to demand directions, the road to Elysium.

48.

Huxley acknowledged my arrival with a fractious glance, as though I were to blame for his sleepless dead-end night.

Except for the stars crossing the sky, nothing had moved. Huxley, still hunched over his books and maps in a flood of lamplight, his face puffy and irritable. The Ferryman, his fathomless eyes now drinking in the morning sun and the restless windswept sea instead of puzzling geometric constellations.

In a sudden exasperated gesture, Huxley swept the papers aside. 'This is hopeless!' He turned on me angrily. 'What the hell is Nestor playing at? Ten days throwing men and machines at the ridge, and still nothing to show for it. Without the cave, we are nowhere. Without the Necromanteion, the Ferryman is nothing!'

Tossing his logbooks onto the desk with a defiant crash, I turned on my heel, made for the door.

'Where are you going?'

'Home. Camp. Back to England. I don't care.'

'No,' he replied adamantly. 'You are coming with me. Now.'

After an ill-tempered layover in the kitchen for coffee and supplies we clattered down the steps to the cove below the house, where a sailing skiff was tied up at the crumbling jetty.

'Where are we going?' I demanded, casting a dubious glance at the boat's sun bleached wood and fraying sails.

'We have an appointment. Get in.'

Obstinately, I squatted down on the jetty, avoiding his eyes as he stowed away our food and water in the forward hold.

'Do you think you will understand death through mythology,' he snapped, 'through nightmares and childish terrors?'

How can he know that? It's almost as if he has seen the shadows of your own dreams.

With a vehement jerk of the head, again he motioned me aboard.

Gingerly, one foot at a time, I obeyed, though the toy of a boat still pitched and rocked, water almost sloshing in over the side.

'Sit,' he ordered.

Perplexed, I glanced about, trying to find somewhere away from the unpredictable boom, the tiller, the mess of oars and rope and fishing tackle.

No sooner had I taken my place than he cast off, and we drifted away from the quay. In the distance I could make out the mountain cliffs of Anafi, plunging several thousand feet into the sea, lingering wisps of cloud still swirling about its summit.

He hoisted the sail, a breath of wind snapping the canvas.

'What did I tell you about the past, Nicholas, do you remember? What did I tell you from the very beginning?'

'Destroy it, erase it, wipe it out. So you'd have a nice clean slate on which to write.'

He shook his head, apparently at my bloody-mindedness. 'That silver Omega of your father's. You never told me why it means so much to you.'

'Why should I?'

'It's not just about the watch, is it. It's what it embodies, what it represents, what it records. Time. The hours churning into the future like some immense tidal wave, and however hard we try we cannot still them, we cannot say, wait, stay awhile, rest, remember the timelessness from whence you came...'

I retrieved the bottle of wine from his rucksack, sank into the well of the skiff.

'You always miss the point don't you, Huxley. I don't fucking care and I never have. Nobody cares!'

He leant against the tiller, the breeze filling the sail like the ballooning cheeks of one of those wind cherubs you sometimes find on old nautical charts. Our heading shifted east towards Anafi, the little chestnut-wood boat skimming across the water now with improbable speed.

A motorised caïque appeared off our stern, bobbing and pitching even in the slight swell, its hull as round as a gourd.

On deck as it swelled past us, I was astonished to see Father Nannos, bracing himself against the mast rigging, his proud, jutting face lost to the ancient monastery up on the cliffs, a blue cupola, a brass bell, an arched window, playing vanishing tricks between swirls of sunlit cloud.

The breeze slackened, our sail flapping feebly like the wing of an exhausted bird. Suddenly becalmed, we drifted into a bank of early autumn sea mist, sun-ray gold, floating over the blue depths that carried us.

I had closed my eyes, so lulled by the wine and the cradle rock of the boat that even his voice had become a harmless echo.

'Tell me, Nicholas, what is it that you are most afraid of.'

Through my eyelids, I was aware of the droplets of light catching the trance of the swell.

'The darkness.' That was easy enough.

'Why is that?'

'Everyone's afraid of the dark, aren't they, admit it, deny it, it's something ancient we carry inside. Why else would we light up our cities like Christmas trees. Praise the dawn. Feel that twinge of regret or foreboding as the sun melts into the dusk.'

'But the dark, it's deeper than the night isn't it?' The voice and the swell were making me feel weightless.

'I am not afraid of the night.'

'Then what? Something hidden in the dark, is that it?'

'It's because of the things we have buried here.'

'And your father, Nicholas — is he buried there too? Is he?'

'Wait, I'm looking,' treading through the gloom of that dust-choked place. It's known me forever, hasn't it, the toddler still learning to walk, the kid still learning to tie his shoelaces, the schoolboy still reciting his lines, reciting his lies. 'No, I can't see him, I can't find him... Just the priest over the grave, mouthing something about ash to ash, dust to dust.' I heard my voice crack.

'Shall we walk together? Yes. I shall keep you company.'

'*No!* This place doesn't belong to you. *Go away!*'

'What is it that time has buried here, Nicholas? What is it you don't want me to see?'

His voice echoed through the entombing sky, sardonic, accusing, as if I were to blame for all this, the dead and the dying.

'What a strange, strange place. Rivers cascade with dust. Little crucifixes mark the path of the forsaken and the damned. A few bitter trees drop fruits that explode into dust spores. On the shore break billows of dust, washing in the bloodless tumbling corpses. The dead, who are yet somehow living, conscious of their fate. Very impressive, Mr Pedrosa. But shouldn't you introduce me to your father? What is his name, Xavier, I believe.'

'We don't talk about him! We do not speak his name!'

'Why? What did he do? What was his crime?'

'Nothing! He died, that's all.'

And then I saw him, as I have always done, a grey hungry shadow with black holes for eyes, one shade lighter than the dust landscape to which eternity had condemned him.

'There he is,' I said. 'Don't you see him?'

'I think I do, though I don't recognise any family resemblance, do you?'

Ignoring him, I walked on, feet stirring up eddies of dust.

'He looks sad,' observed Huxley.

'Wouldn't you be,' I yelled, 'being dead, being imprisoned here in this horrific place…'

His face came looming up before mine. 'But isn't it *you*, Mr Pedrosa? Isn't it you who have buried your father here?'

I tried to run, the dust congealing around my feet.

'Why is it that you never speak about him? Pretend he never existed? You're ashamed of him, is that it? How did he die? When did he die?'

Questions, accusations, like body blows, pummelling, remorseless.

'How did he die? *How?*'

The dust was billowing up all around me. I felt myself tumbling down, falling. There was no earth to catch me.

'You wanted him to die!' he yelled. 'Isn't that the truth of it? Admit it! *You prayed for him to die!*'

49.

I lurched upright, striking my head against the boom, my eyes trying to make sense out of clashing worlds.

We were a stone's throw away from Anafi, just drifting in towards the landing stage and the perilous steps carved out of the cliff face, like a stairway into the sky.

I glared at him, rubbing my head. 'What did you do to me?'

Playing the innocent, he pretended to be busy with the tiller, mumbling something about falling asleep in the sun.

Sick, feverish, I lay back under the sail again, trying to splice together the torn strands of dream, trance, or whatever else they were supposed to be. An old wound, gashed open again with the brutality of jagged steel. Beyond the mind's imaginative efforts to hide it, an ancient truth, a dirty little secret suddenly too bloody to deny.

'Are you ready?' he demanded, as the bow nudged the landing stage.

I gazed up at the switchback stairway disappearing into the mist, the snatches of sunlight ever so briefly illuminating a dwarf, crevice-clutching tree, the blue dome of the cloister church, and Father Nannos struggling up the steps, hoisting himself ever higher, a white-knuckled grip on the iron railing hammered into the rock face.

In the sun bright mist, sounds muffle, then amplify. Waves ripple against the rock face, then echo like bamboo chimes.

We began our ascent, the mist putting its ancient vanishing spell upon us.

The further we laboured up the steps, the angrier he became. A delirious thought wondered where my guard had gone, and who would defend me now.

Cocking his head down to me, he said between gasps, 'It is high time you woke up, boy. Do you hear me? High time you saw through your own reality.'

'What, between all the tricks and the lies —'

'You should be more concerned with your own lies; the lies of others you will never vanquish, for that is the nature of the beast...'

Panting, we hauled ourselves up the steepest flight of steps yet, the last of them cutting through the whitewashed parapet above. We found ourselves in the monastery gardens, a little plateau of undulating land on the cliff top.

'The others were right,' he rasped. 'You are in denial.'

'I am not in denial!'

'You have been in denial for fifteen years. In denial about death, in denial about life!'

Fever bursting into flame, I stumbled backwards, and might even have fallen if not for the stone bench carved into the parapet.

A monk came scuttling towards us along one of the intersecting paths, Father Nannos his dark and imposing shadow.

'*Children!*' the monk entreated, his arms outstretched towards us, his berry-round face creased in consternation. 'Raised voices have no place here.'

The Papás glowered at us. 'Making war again, Huxley, even here, in this holiest of places?'

'Sometimes, Papás,' he replied, scowling at me, 'it is necessary to be cruel in order to be kind.'

'My father said the same,' agreed brother Theo, expertly placing the placatory words between the two enemies, 'and I had the weals over my backside to prove it.' He beamed at us, searching for us in our eyes, probably realising that here at long last was the man who had become the bane of Father Nannos' existence, a pagan, a sorcerer, a demon, or whatever insult sprang to the old man's mind when anger or wine loosened his tongue.

Boyhood friends and rivals in temperament, monk and priest had grown up on the same dusty street. To hear brother Theo tell it, nothing much had changed, except that the years had made off with their hair or painted it grey, and the spiders had drawn webs all over their faces while they slept. According to the bilious old priest, the monk could talk the ears off a donkey.

One by one, we filed into the dimly-lit refectory, a grand name for a room that, at a stretch, might just have hosted the Last Supper. Massive, stone block walls against the besieging summer sun. A stone-flagged floor, melon-cool in August, chilblain-cold in January, and a fireplace the size of a castle's, its granite mantel enclosing two carved seats, facing each other over the flames.

At Theo's bidding, we sat at the cedar wood table, five hundred years old if it was a day. Hands clasped behind his back, Father Nannos lingered at the ramshackle window, gazing out into the monastery gardens, as if out of some lingering reluctance to engage Huxley in conversation.

'You must already have some inkling why I called you here to the monastery, Huxley,' he said at last, his voice thick with distaste. 'The Frenchman has his spies everywhere, some in your pay as well as his, and it would hardly be prudent for me to be seen fraternising with the enemy, while the archbishop remains so committed to his cause.'

So there it was. A tacit admission that he had been in league with Guirand from the start. Plotting and scheming to have us driven off the island, even if it was under duress.

'Why the change of heart, Papás?'

About to vent some bilious reply, he caught the monk's look of entreaty and relented.

Their eyes met for the first time. 'In this life, Huxley, we are often not the lionhearted souls our vanity would have us believe. No. We shrink from doing right not because we are inclined to sin but because the true path is the harder to climb.'

Huxley regarded the priest through narrowed eyes, and bit his tongue.

'Rarely have we seen eye to eye, what use is there in denying it?' growled the priest. 'Yet I will not stand idly by while the island is robbed blind of its heritage. You seem surprised by that — if so, you misjudge me. Servant of the Christ God, I may be, but I am still a Hellene, the ancient world still courses through my veins, and I could no more call for the desecration of our ancient city than I could the grave of my own father.'

His voice rose until it rumbled in indignation around the refectory. 'Nor can my conscience rest while our bishops flirt, fraternise or worse, with the tyrants, play-acting at family values while behind locked doors they abuse and torture. Their ministers and office lackeys, meanwhile, hear not a single word of reason, so loudly are they squealing to push their snouts into the trough.'

Huxley leaned forward intently. 'Then they will move against us, Papás... I knew this truce could not last, even with the Comte's diplomacy.'

Diplomacy? I thought deliriously. *Is that what you call it.*

'Sarrides has been grovelling at the feet of the Colonels since the tanks rolled into Athens,' the Papás glowered. 'If he has yet to wheedle from them the promise to strike, it is only because the tyrants have been far too busy admiring their own visionary faces plastered across the front pages.'

Knowing just who had put them there, he glared daggers at us.

'Of course! They see the utility of it. It has the ring of triumph, and the edict couldn't be clearer: it is our patriotic duty to surrender these ancient treasures to Athens, for that is where they belong, not on some sun-baked island with a fiery heart.' He screwed shut his eyes, as if enduring a sharp spasm of pain. Brother Theo hurried to him with a cup of water.

Recovering his composure, he added: 'I fear we cannot win this battle, however righteous the cause. I fear, too, there will be bloodshed.'

A grim, determined look had entered Huxley's eyes, so potent I almost expected to see Guirand's ancient face reflected there engulfed in flames.

The chapel bell rang for vespers, presumably at the unseen hands of brother Eleftherios, the monastery's only other inhabitant, save for the milch goats and the hens, that is, banished from the far distant Holy Mountain, their sex a profanity, a temptation, God knows what.

Suddenly we were alone, Huxley and I, and the refectory had become far too large for us, echoing with the spitting fire from the chimney and our own angry quarrel as we climbed the cliff face.

Hot and cold shivers were running through my bones, my head reeling. Before I even knew it, I was hurling all my pent-up hatred at him.

'You deserve to be thrown off the island! You deserve everything that's coming to you!'

'Drink your wine, Mr Pedrosa. Use it to forget, to deaden your pain, to escape the truth. It's what you're best at, after all.'

'You deserve to be in jail,' I went on, spitting the words at him. 'You deserve the gallows!'

'If what I told you is untrue, then tell me this: what is it that hurts — here...' As he tapped my chest, it made a hollow thud.

I thrust his hand away. 'I wouldn't be living if it didn't hurt.'

A scornful laugh erupted from his mouth. 'Living? Is that what you think? Go and look in the mirror, boy, and see what you are. A ghost! A *vrykolakas!* The perfect companion for your own dead father.'

The room dissolved into liquefying jelly, and the last thing I remember was the stone floor. About to hit me in the face.

It wasn't until morning that I finally came to, struggling to understand where I was and why.

A patch of luminous blue heaven through a tiny barred window. The dusky icon on an otherwise bare whitewashed wall. A beeswax candle, extinguished, on the stone-flagged floor. The narrow cot on which I was lying, a coarse blanket up to my chin. A monk's cell. Then realisation, trickling into consciousness like a dye through water. Huxley, the enemy in my own head, in my own home, breaking down the doors, forcing open the shutters, ransacking every room.

'Where is he?' he's shouting, pulling the whole place apart, rooms, cupboards, loft, garage. Until finally he catches my eye flinching from the cellar trapdoor, the flight of stairs beyond plunging into the musty gloom.

Dad's name was never mentioned again, not after his death, not after he was buried in the grey earth like an expunged sin. Clothes consigned to the church jumble. Snapshots removed from frames, thrown into cardboard boxes, the boxes piled up against the cellar wall, gathering mildew, gathering dust, a tattered cobweb tomb where the trapdoor closes and no one ventures anymore. Except for that bewildered six year old boy, that is, tottering down the steps when no one's about, into the penumbral light from the grated window at soil level. Who doesn't even know the difference between the living and the dead. Who can't forget. That day at the hospital. Visiting Hours. Hurrying along the green linoleum corridor, breaking into a run.

Dad's waiting.

Propped up in his enamel bed behind the screens.

Tubes sprouting from his body like tentacles, wheezing machines left and right.

Months like this, shrivelling, wasting away. Slime dribbling from his mouth. Eyes like dead glass. Until you have to stare into that face just to recognise someone you once knew.

There's something different about Sofi this morning though, isn't there, even as we set off in the car. Something blistering the composure she's learnt to wear, so grown up now in the face of all this, a young girl evicted from her childhood.

We're both standing there on the puke green linoleum, the hateful mechanical breath rasping in our ears.

Sofi, her hands clutching a useless little handbag, fighting back sobs, biting her lips until a trickle of blood appears. Then her shoes ring out across the linoleum, and the next thing you know her arm's swinging down, her hand's yanking out the plug, and the humming pumping machines are falling silent, his reluctant breath with them.

A bubble of shocked silence envelops us.

They come barging in at a run, nurses, doctors, orderlies, replugging the machines, filling syringes, charging up the paddles for his heart.

Then Mum, rushing in behind them, struggling to understand. A wan figure at the bedside, pressing his hand, smothering her own sobs, and I'm thinking, Dad must have been living inside her all those years, because she looks smaller, shrunken now.

Lying there on my monk's cot, I tried to imagine his soul floating away from him, looking down, seeing us standing there, tried to imagine the white light calling him.

What were these things? Mere illusions as Hadrian insisted, the brain fooled by its own desperate vanity? Or a lighthouse for people lost in the storm, guiding them towards... something, somewhere.

As I collapsed back onto my straw pillow, I finally admitted something else to myself. Huxley was right. I was in denial; I had been in denial for years.

He was right to want to end this tyranny. He was right to want it, dream it, chase it. To destroy the concept of death.

I tumbled out of bed, splashed water into my face from the hand pump in the courtyard. Then made my way to the refectory where Huxley was sitting alone near the window, drinking mountain tea and eating a monk's breakfast. The moment we came into eye contact, I knew something had changed. Not with him, but with me. I didn't flinch inside as I normally did whenever his stare barged its way into my soul.

'Good morning,' he said, as though nothing of consequence had happened the night before. 'I trust you slept soundly in your monk's cot.' An ironic, playful reflection scattering across the iris of his eye, like breeze patterns across the water. He poured tea, nudged a plate of black bread, dried figs and feta across the table, a pot of honeycomb honey.

The memory of Father Nannos making his reluctant pact with the

Devil seemed even stranger in the cool light of morning.

'It's the case of the Devil You Know,' explained Huxley. 'In Guirand, the Papás sees somebody far worse than I. Somebody far more dangerous than an agnostic or an apologist for the pagan gods.'

'So the Papás is our ally now? I thought you detested everything he stood for.'

'The wise man respects his enemies, Mr Pedrosa. The wise man knows it's the enemy, far more than the friend, who'll have the greatest bearing upon their own destiny.'

To my sceptical look, he demanded: 'Do you know who has helped me the most in interpreting the Codex? Benja? Svetlana? The *Comte*?'

His eyes bored into mine, daring me to answer.

'No... *Claude Guirand*. He is the one who has been my constant shadow, who unwittingly inspired me, who pushed me on when I felt like giving up. However much my vanity would have me deny it, the truth compels me to admit that without Claude, I would be nowhere.'

50.

We sensed it before our boat even nudged the quay. Something was wrong.

Save for the odd brainiac, who probably didn't even know what day or year it was, the trenches in the eastern sector were deserted; the huts and sheds, abandoned.

Chaos hit us the moment we entered the student encampment, people pulling down tents, stuffing possessions into bags, dragging them towards the bus, while a band of young hotheads pelted them with insults. 'Deserters! Cowards!' they chanted.

'Guirand,' muttered Huxley, marching towards the site office. 'He lit the fuse.'

As if to prove the point, he collared one of the Italian students, dashing towards the mess. 'What happened?' he barked.

The boy threw up his hands in dismay. 'It is all over camp! Police commandoes. Gunboats. Soldiers. They are on their way!'

'You see?' he said as he let the boy go. 'Whoever's in Guirand's pay knew there would never be a better opportunity to spark a wildfire. Nestor up on the ridge. Me, nowhere in sight. Each little rumour like a match to dry grass, until the whole camp is going up in flames.'

'Aren't you going to stop them?' I said, watching the bus filling with frantic students and teachers. 'Let them go,' he replied wearily. 'Those who wish to stay, will stay. The others we can afford to lose.' He motioned towards Galatea and her Greek students. 'Look — do you think Galatea's taking to her heels? Of course not. Having wasted her breath trying to convince the others to stay, she's now taking the time to do her laundry, pegging up her clothes.'

What with the crush of students, I almost missed them sitting there as I waded through the mess tent in search of coffee.

'Sit,' commanded Anna over the din, as a florid-faced Hadrian went shuffling along the bench to make room for me.

'It's just rumour,' I said. 'To incite panic.'

'And you would know I suppose,' retorted Hadrian. 'The boy who gave us *Atlantis*.'

Earning him a murderous look, Sam laughed out loud.

'I warned you didn't I?' glared Hadrian. 'Guirand and Sarrides: such men gain pleasure from destroying their enemies slowly, painfully, piece by piece.'

'What can they do? What's the worst that can happen?' I shook my head. 'The whole island's against them. There's press everywhere.'

'You'll change your tune soon enough when commandoes come marching up the cliff face armed to the teeth, fanning out through the town, hunting down the ringleaders. *Us included!*'

Seeing my dubious look, his voice rose an octave: 'Do you really have no conception of the tyranny under which we are living? Behind the affable smiles, the summer sun, the shining sea, the clink of the ouzo glass, people disappear, suspected agitators are dragged away in chains. Don't you have eyes in your head? Haven't you seen them, shuffling into the hold of the *Pegasus* in the half-light, jangling as they go? Where did you think they were off to? Holiday camp? The lucky ones will find themselves exiled to some desolate, windswept rock in the middle of the Aegean. As for the less fortunate, the least said the better. Or do you really wish to talk about torturers, about murderers in official uniform?'

'Why? Just because of the frescoes —'

Hadrian clicked his tongue, loud and scornfully. 'You apprentices, you're all the same! Naive as a word wouldn't even do you justice. You actually belong in one of those naive paintings hanging in Huxley's study, in which there is not a single evil intent in the world, just idyllic pastures, and trees and rivers with souls.'

Now it was Sam's turn to glare daggers.

Hadrian buried his head in his hands. 'It's not about the frescoes, you fool, or the Minoan pottery! It's the threat of uprising, sedition — the fear that a few sporadic wildfires like this might turn into a conflagration. As long as it was seen merely as a dispute between rival academics, the Junta didn't much care, however rancorous it became; after all, the Greeks themselves have always been a quarrelsome tribe. But as soon as our mentally defective mayor began planting rebellious ideas in peoples' heads about heritage and the robbing of future generations; as soon as farmers and fishermen began parading around in the *plateia* with their shotguns, well, *connect the dots!*'

'We don't even know what secret charges might have been trumped up against us,' said Anna, her anxious voice struggling against the din.

Hadrian's plump fist slammed the table, making the cutlery trays jangle in complaint. 'If it weren't for the fact that a sudden disappearance might be interpreted as an admission of guilt, or the very real prospect of being apprehended at the border, you wouldn't see me for dust!'

'We should have complied with the order from the beginning, and vacated the site,' said Anna, her vehemence talking through her hands now. 'If the soldiers come bursting through the gates, what about the frescoes, what about the artefacts? Don't tell me they can be kept secure in that kind of chaos, even if there's not so much as a scuffle or a shot fired. Don't tell me pieces aren't going to go missing.'

'Sarrides, the Colonels, they won't want to risk them, will they...' said Sam, in a deadpan voice.

'No... no, I suppose not,' said Anna pensively.

'...Not the treasures of Atlantis.'

Much to their disgust, he uttered a staccato laugh. As my eyes strayed to his, I didn't need to be clairvoyant to know what he was seeing or where the rush was coming from, like some emerging geometric reality drawn in starlight. Plato's ancient Conundrum, that by some improbable means could amplify the purity and corruption of the human soul wherever Atlantis made its appearance. The divine nature, the human nature.

In Phíra, the mood was as brittle as glass.

With Vassilis the postmaster offering his own private office as a war room, Huxley's first order of business was to have a call patched through to the Pearl Orient, an exercise itself fraught with mythological complications, and we sat around waiting, drinking frappés, and biting our nails.

Walking the cliff top paths to worry and kill the time, I was struck as never before by the schizophrenic reality in which we now found ourselves. Oblivious end-of-season tourists drinking in the mesmerising blueness of the caldera as they sip their chilled island wine; a band of trigger-happy youths on lookout duty in the church bell tower, hunting rifles and binoculars trained on the northern channel. Young couples whispering sweet nothings as they amble arm in arm along the promenade, past the garish hoardings saluting the Colonels' phoenix rising from the ashes. Big city speculators, easy enough to distinguish by the nightclub suits pretending to sartorial elegance, the crocodile skin briefcases, the big shiny bracelet watches, the stench of aftershave that could overpower even the vagrants and the mad traffic in Omonia Square.

Nondas was shutting up his shop for the afternoon, flipping over the Closed sign. 'What's up, Nico?

'Waiting.' Too, nervous, too distracted to do anything else.

'Well if you hold on a minute, we can all wait it out together,' still fiddling with the padlock and chain.

'Since when are you locking up like that? Are there thieves about?'

He winced at my unintended irony, casting a stony look across the *plateia*. 'You might say that. It's just so as the landlord won't throw me into the street as soon as my back is turned.'

'He can't do that, can he?'

'Who should I complain to — the police? I have enough black marks against my name as it is, you know that. My landlord and his would-be tenant, they spend half the day in the *kafeneion* over there, just waiting for the chance to pounce. Look.'

And there they were, glaring daggers at us from under their sun umbrella, the dour old curmudgeon who owns the building cracking the worry beads over his knuckles, the slick from Athens in the blue polyester suit greedily eyeing up the spoils — and who could blame him, with that panoramic view over the caldera, that Atlantis sunset made of gold.

Holed up in the police station with the doors and shutters bolted, Manolis and Chondro were awaiting reinforcements with increasing desperation, cut off from the outside world by Toula's resolute refusal to connect calls in or out. Occasionally, a pair of eyes would peer between the slats, only to retreat again at the sight of the hotheads patrolling the square, or standing sentry at the town hall.

We were just crossing back to the post office when a gunshot rang out, tearing the air; people dived for cover, baffled tourists glancing up from their guidebooks. Cocking their rifles the hotheads took aim, squeezed their triggers, and were a hair's breadth away from unleashing a volley of shots when Chondro appeared at the door waving a white handkerchief, head covered in ceiling plaster, ears still ringing to the chief's lurid curses.

And all the while the reporters scribbled, the photographers clicked and flashed; they queued up at the single telephone booth at the exchange, yelling their stories across the sea. It was almost in envy that the Greek contingent waited in line at all, already knowing that under their own names all but the glow of Atlantis and the economic boom it promised would escape the censors.

'Did you get through?' All eyes were on Huxley as he emerged from the post office into the blood evening light.

Squinting against the sun, he nodded abruptly. 'The Comte is still hoping to make them see sense, the Minister, the hardliners. They have accepted an invitation on board the Pearl Orient this evening.'

Hadrian grimaced. 'A lavish affair, no doubt, wining and dining while our own fate hangs by a thread... It's a wonder the Comte doesn't choke.'

'The American Ambassador has lent his support. So too various influential business interests.' Feeling the dubious eyes upon him, he added in a pared voice: 'It is necessary. It is pragmatism, pure and simple.'

'No!' replied Hadrian in disgust. 'It is expediency and always has been. Every move you have ever made has been driven by opportunism, expediency of the worst kind.'

'That's enough,' cried Anna. 'The last thing we need is a war between ourselves.'

Hadrian added vehemently, 'It's a wonder we don't all choke, bringing credibility to this regime.'

'No one dragged you here, Hadrian.'

'Look, while we were merely obscure archaeologists, sifting through the ash, I could always persuade myself it was for the greater good, even if I did have misgivings about working under such a wretched tyranny. But this! It is almost as if we were accomplices. Almost as if our own hands were covered in blood!'

It was almost with revulsion that Huxley retorted: 'Do you have to be so melodramatic?'

We were well into the small hours when the call came through, the shrill ring almost making us jump out of our skins. Huxley scrambled to his feet, snatched up the phone. A few terse words passed between them, Huxley's face grey and bloodless under the harsh fluorescent lights. Replacing the receiver with a murmured goodbye he turned to us, forcing the words from his lips. 'He can't say which way the wind is blowing. Either we are to be saved, or thrown to the dogs. There's nothing more he can do. Not now. He has sailed.'

'Sailed where?' demanded Anna.

'Back to Nice.'

The I-told-you-so look freezing into a grimace on his lips, Hadrian crumpled into a chair.

'What does that mean?' I said.

'It means they are on their way!' he rasped, the dread leaching his face of blood. 'They were on their way even as those vile specimens were wining and dining on Beluga caviar and oysters under the crystal chandeliers! No wonder it was "up anchor, full steam ahead" for the Comte the moment his guests had been ferried ashore. *He was saving himself!*'

I felt the twist in my stomach.

Hadrian added with a vengeful swipe: 'Well it was you who made all this possible in Athens, wasn't it? You've lied to their faces, men in uniform, men who settle arguments with guns, cattle prods and jail. *Atlantis!*'

'Shut up, Hadrian!' yelled Anna.

I slipped into the night, but could already see the lurid flush of dawn in the eastern sky.

51.

The lookouts were dozing at their posts as the silhouette loomed through the gossamer light of dawn, funnels belching smoke.

Panayiotis the baker ran out into the street, his fingers still gummed with dough. Shadows stirred, darted through the *plateia*. A light came on in the police station. There were muffled shouts. Church bells rang out in a sudden frenzy.

We hurried out of the post office in a ragged daze, just in time to see a slate-grey destroyer steam past the Burnt Islands with a deep ominous roar, huge gun turrets fore and aft.

With half the island watching from the cliff tops, a detachment of the crew appeared on deck to man the guns, take up positions... *But no.* The next thing we knew, they were stringing colourful bunting across the destroyer's rigging... Almost as if the captain were preparing for a naval regatta than an armed assault.

'What do you make of that?' breathed Anna.

Puzzled murmurs swept through the crowd, the bright dawn spectacle momentarily pacifying even the most febrile of the hotheads. Tourists beamed, clapped, and slipped away in hopes of breakfast. Reporters scribbled feverishly in their notebooks.

Feet dangling over the precipice wall, Huxley trained his binoculars on the warship, scanning the decks in vain for any sight of his nemeses, Guirand and Sarrides.

Fate, Chance, Murphy's Law, who knows what, chose that moment to throw its own mischief into the mix, as a breathless Nestor Louganis came loping along the pathway. 'Kapítán!'

Reading that face, still smudged with dirt, Huxley scrambled to his feet. They retreated to a church doorway and a volley of words passed between them before Nestor hurried back to his jeep.

As he settled beside me, Huxley murmured: 'Wouldn't you just know it... weeks of futile digging up on the ridge, and Nestor finally strikes gold.'

'*Gold?*'

'The Ferryman's cave. The Necromanteion.'

His eyes swept towards the destroyer with its massive cannons; to the crew readying a shore-bound tender; to the crowds pushing and shoving outside the town hall; to the Councillors being jostled along the street.

His glare held such intensity at that moment I could almost picture the salvo of thoughts in his head. Come what may, the discovery had to remain secret. Guirand was old, almost crumbling into dust, but he could sense a suspicious element in the air as a wolf scents blood on the wind.

Captain Aristides of the destroyer *Lefkas* landed unannounced around noon, accompanied by a pair of ensigns in starched white uniforms. Nothing intimidating in their manner. Far from it. Aristides sat at a blue tin table on the quay, sipping a *kafedaiki*, basking in the mellow autumn sun, while the lads earned their keep by racing each other up the serpentines to deliver his message. The handwritten invitation, courteous to a fault, was for Huxley — *Huxley* — not Giannis Papadaikis, nor any of the other island notables.

'What do you make of that?' murmured Hadrian, discerning a flicker of light emanating from the gloom and hardly daring to breathe lest he puff it away.

'It might be a trap, Marcus,' said Sanassis. And you could tell what he was thinking. That the moment they had Huxley safely aboard he'd be put in irons, thrown into the brig.

'And what is it anyway?' added Hadrian, with his own measure of dismay. 'A hearing, a tribunal, a military court…?'

Pensively, Huxley folded the note and slipped it into his pocket. 'That we shall see. My presence is cordially requested aboard the *Lefkas* tomorrow morning, 10 o'clock sharp.'

That night, Captain Aristides' warship presented little more than an ominous shadow to the town, riding at anchor off the Burnt Islands. Several of the crew were even permitted shore leave, there to sway through the streets on their sea legs, loosen their tongues on raki, and frighten the wits out of the townsfolk by blurting out the secret they had been bursting with for hours. *Just waiting for the signal*, cocky words slurring between shots of raki, *a second destroyer, a frigate, a gunboat, a troop carrier, primed and ready to sail.*

I think Huxley had already guessed that, in Captain Aristides, he was dealing with a shrewd, exceptional man — and a dangerous adversary.

We met up at Alexis Pangalos' taverna for breakfast, shunning the grubby interior for the terrace. Two hours to wait. Huxley was tense, fidgety, fussing over the papers in his briefcase. Over fried eggs and muddy coffee he sprang his surprise, insisting that I accompany him.

'Why me? Why not Hadrian? Anna... Sam?'

'Because they are depending on us, that's why. The Captain might appreciate your air of... *innocence.*'

Trying to hide my shaking hands, I started putting my things in order, notebooks to jog my memory, passport and permits in case they demanded them.

At the appointed hour we made our way to the serpentines at the cliff face, where a crowd had gathered. A detachment of island hotheads with sunken cheeks and feral eyes, burning for a showdown, win or lose. In their crooked shadows, mute onlookers with anxious lips and creased faces.

Panayiotis the baker, flour dusting his hairy ears, arms folded across his massive chest. Orestes the postman, his tin trumpet slung over his shoulder. Nondas the barber, a dull worried shine to his bald pate. Doctor Sanassis, with typical gallows humour, warning Huxley against cluttering his surgery with casualties. Alexander Vouris, the schoolmaster, dry, twitching eyes behind wire-rimmed glasses, higher thought suddenly finding its own dismaying limits next to the bullet and the carbine. And oblivious children darting between our legs, chasing each other, yelling, playing with fire.

Emerging from his paper-strewn office across the *plateia* Giannis Papadaikis began wading through the throng, the Papás at his elbow, muttering his stern counsel, Katina in their wake, her face blotched and tearful. The hotheads clapped him on the back as he went, a gesture of encouragement for his defiance, a salutary reminder of the price of surrender. The Mayor forced a leery, broken-toothed grin, cringing slightly under their touch.

His wife Stavroula jabbed him from behind. Papadaikis stumbled, coughed, raised his voice for the benefit of everyone within earshot, Captain Aristides' snub still a fishbone in his throat.

'The island is depending on you, Professor,' he cried, stuck some-where between plea and admonishment. 'All these people. The lives of infants yet unborn. The fathers and mothers who have seen the bread snatched out of the mouths of their own children... Remember that as you enter the lion's den.'

Scattered whistles, a smattering of applause. Huxley didn't even blink, but as he hauled himself up onto the wooden saddle of his mule, briefcase locked under his arm, the sea of faces let out rousing, hopeful cheer, as if hailing their own champion.

It was a peculiar sight, and one that painted Papadaikis' face with a flushed, indignant scowl.

52.

Dwarfed by the forward gun turret Huxley and Aristides exchanged a firm, prolonged handshake, leaving me to read whatever omens I could from the Captain's face. Bushy eyebrows, salt-and-pepper moustache, cautious eyes that in other circumstances might just have sparkled with affability. But not today. Grave and unflinching, each man held the other's gaze, as if probing the strengths and weaknesses both knew to be reflected there.

Aristides escorted us along deck, two young officers bringing up the rear. Though they kept a respectful distance, both were wearing sidearms.

Hadrian's right, I thought, with a stab of dismay. These aren't talks. This is a military tribunal in all but name.

On the aft deck, an old white sail had been strung between mast and gun turret, providing a makeshift awning for the long trestle table that had been erected there.

Six folding chairs, each one still vacant. On the starched white tablecloth, two pitchers of water and, at each place setting, a glass, a notepad and pencil.

We were invited to sit, and then the tense, silent wait began, the warship riding on its bow anchor in the caldera's streaming currents.

As for small talk, there was none. I caught the Captain's eyes straying to Huxley, then flicker towards the ice white towns on the cliff, a grudging acknowledgment perhaps that here was the man, in popular mythology at least, who had discovered Plato's lost Atlantis, putting this scarred ruin of an island on the map of the world.

Five minutes stretched to ten, then twenty. The Captain, growing irritable, consulted his watch, and cast darkening glances along the deck.

The moment I heard that ominous tapping, cane against steel, I knew exactly what to expect. And I was right. Several agonising seconds later, Claude Guirand came hobbling along the deck, battling infirmity with the same obstinate contempt that he reserved for every other obstacle in his life, people, places, animals, plants, it didn't matter what.

Clutched at his elbow, a leather briefcase. Evidence against Huxley, no doubt, against all of us — if any were actually needed to convict us.

When a young ensign darted forward to offer him the support of his arm, Guirand raised his stick as if meaning to strike; the boy shrank back against the ship's railings, his face stuttering between shock and amusement.

Captain Aristides glowered.

Dragging himself to the table, Guirand crumpled into his canvas chair, blazing eyes barely acknowledging anyone.

I found myself staring into his sunken face, still unable to imagine the monster in his youth, crossing sky piercing mountains, raging torrents, just to visit some snow temple abandoned for a thousand years. Piecing together the Scholiast's commentary in the margins of the Critias. Composing those lyrical travels among islands of the metaphysical seas… Today, that shrunken face wore the fierce, messianic conceit of a man whose beliefs had been cast in stone millennia ago.

Any moment now Sophoklis Sarrides would appear on deck, the merciless raptor's eyes fixing their prey. My stomach tightened as two unfamiliar faces emerged from the shadow of the cannons: a woman with a brisk, confident walk, platinum blonde hair all black at the roots; a man in a checked jacket, with pensive hazel eyes. They were 40 years Guirand's juniors if they were a day.

Taking their seats, at last we learnt their identity, Captain Aristides introducing them as Sarrides' first lieutenants in the Inspector General's office, the most feared department in the Service, arresting smugglers, making or breaking careers. Dr Elena Mitrou, lawyer, and Elias Louca, a specialist in restoration.

As for further explanations or formalities, there were none. Invited to present his case, Claude Guirand unleashed a barrage against his enemy so fierce, so unrelenting, that even the Captain seemed shell-shocked.

'I accuse this man because others are too cowardly, too venal to do so,' he rasped, thrusting his finger across the table like a rapier. 'I accuse him of perpetrating fraud against archaeological science and the public at large. I accuse him of trafficking in antiquities, priceless works of art smuggled abroad and auctioned off to the highest bidder — museums, private collectors, a ring of buyers organised by his own benefactor, the Comte d'Adhémar!'

One charge after another, each of such breathtaking gravity I began to see prison bars on the back of my eyelids.

Spitting saliva like venom, Guirand then levelled his most devastating accusation of all. 'And I accuse him of the coldblooded murder of his own apprentice, Benjamin Randal, an innocent young man who stumbled over the truth and paid the ultimate price for it...'

A murmur of dismay swept around the table. Sarrides' first lieutenants exchanged furtive, disapproving glances, and even seemed comforted by the presence of armed ensigns at the railings.

Captain Aristides raised a hand of caution and said in a gravelly voice: 'Whatever anyone may think of the government of this country, Professor, as long as these proceedings are held on this ship, and under my command, I shall hear no accusation without evidence.'

To which the skull rasped in reply, 'You shall have your evidence!'

Captain Aristides turned to the accused, the sheer weight of Guirand's allegations seeming to pull his face into a scowl. 'Do you have anything to say in your own defence, Professor Huxley?'

Huxley offered a flicker of a smile, laying his palms wide open on the white tablecloth, the gesture of a man with nothing to hide. 'I have to ask,' he began. 'Am I to be judged on facts, or on hearsay, the myths and superstitions that so often pass for truth in island backwaters like this?'

'Is that then your contention, Professor,' said Elena Mitrou, in a sultry sceptical voice, 'that every one of these allegations is tainted by rumour?'

Glancing up from his papers his eyes met, not Mitrou the lawyer's, but Guirand's, and he held the old man's hatred and hostility there mid-table, making sure everyone else would see it.

'Wherever they're from,' he began in a measured voice, 'Cambridge, New York, Rome, even Athens, there is always one thing I tell the students and archaeologists joining my dig. Leave your assumptions about reality at home. Trust neither the instincts nor intellectual conceptions you have grown up with interpreting life in modern metropolises, a world away from here — they will not serve you well. Yet I fear that is exactly what the authorities have been doing. Misreading the island psyche, pursuing a policy that is fundamentally flawed and ultimately self-defeating.'

There were exultant howls of protest from Guirand. I winced. The words had not come out right. They sounded inflammatory, defiant.

Aristides said ominously, 'Nothing stands in our way, Professor, least of all defeat. The excavations will be secured by force as and when we deem it necessary.'

Guirand nodded his satisfaction, gloating lips over porcelain teeth the colour of ancient marble.

'I am certain of it, Captain,' said Huxley, barely able to grab hold of his earlier conciliatory tone by the tip of its tail. 'And yet I feel compelled to ask. What if you are being driven towards this course of action not by objective facts, but by fallacies masquerading as such? What then? Isn't it possible that every subsequent step will be made in error?'

Captain Aristides shifted uneasily in his chair, the implications of Huxley's hypothetical chain reaction seeking passage through his mind. No one had to remind him that misreading the compass by half a degree at dawn could sink a ship by dusk.

'Then you are implying that we might have achieved more through diplomacy than confrontation,' said Elena Mitrou through narrowed eyes.

'Preposterous!' seethed Guirand. 'The excavations must be seized, there is not a moment to lose. We have already wasted months on end flattering and appeasing these people. Greasing their palms. Promising the earth. And for what? Blackmail, betrayal, vandalism. Instead of fretting over the welfare of crooks, Madame, you would do better to worry about the frescoes, which they will surely rather destroy than relinquish voluntarily.'

'You bribed government officials?' Her voice was thick with incredulity, if less at the act itself than the brazen admission of it.

'Is it possible to achieve anything here without doing so?' he replied with swift brutality. 'If so, you are living in a different country than I!'

The clash dissipated, like scuttling storm clouds that growl and spit but come to nothing.

'But the archaeological treasures, Professor Huxley,' said Elias Louca. 'The frescoes. The pottery. What of the islanders' insistence they remain *in situ*, at the mercy of the elements, the harsh sunlight, the brine-ridden sea fog, the trampling tourists, earthquakes, God knows what else… Within a decade they would be destroyed, you must realise that.'

'They don't care about the frescoes,' he replied flatly.

His interrogators were stunned, bewildered. Even I had expected more from him than this.

'Explain yourself, Professor,' said Elena Mitrou, sweeping stray blonde hair out of her eyes, sparks of irritation now joining the smoke in her voice.

'The islanders have no natural affinity with the ancient city. For years they refused even to set foot in it because they believed it haunted, cursed.'

'Then why their intransigence?'

'Because the frescoes have become potent symbols —'

'Of what?' growled Captain Aristides. 'Uprising? Sedition?'

Huxley shook his head, the insinuation of a smile on his lips. 'No, Captain. Of livelihood. Of future. Of hope. Remove the frescoes and there is no Atlantis. Merely ruins, the grey empty shells of a burnt-out city. By this time next year I daresay the flood of tourists, reporters, investors will have dried to a trickle... But you know that of course.'

Captain Aristides knitted his brows. The two inspectors shared a barrage of whispers, mouth to ear.

Lighting another cigarette, Elena Mitrou returned to the attack: 'Then kindly explain why so many serious, criminal charges have been laid against you. Do you expect us to believe that they are all either groundless or contrived? That every source was at best deluded, at worst lying?'

'Do you know *why* I tell my archaeologists to abandon their pre-conceptions about reality when they step off the ship and onto dry land?' he challenged them.

His voice was robust yet resonant, as gliding, as amber as honey. Before they knew it, every pair of eyes bar Guirand's was swimming into his. Beguiled, curious, appalled, they were hanging on his every word.

He told them about the sicknesses attributed to witchcraft, the quivering ghosts that struck terror into the labourers, the priest's exorcism at the trenches, the unfamiliar fish that had been proclaimed a sea devil.

'But the tall tale phenomenon is hardly peculiar to the islands, Professor Huxley,' blinked Elena Mitrou. 'You can find it in any backward village, in the streets of Athens — sometimes even in the Ministry, truth be told. And yet you yourself imply that even the tallest tale, even the most bizarre myth at least begins with a grain of truth. What *were* those grains of truth?'

Seeing Huxley stumble into his own trap, Guirand nodded vigorously.

'I can only deduce. The tragic death of my apprentice, for example. A simple misstep on the scaffolding, his body crushed by the fall. The police are called in as a matter of course. Yet by day's end, the air is thick with rumour, each one more lurid, more distorted than the last. Benjamin Randal stumbled upon criminal activity for which the archaeological excavations were always a cunning subterfuge, and was done away with... Who in their right minds, after all, would spend so much time in the blistering heat or the numbing cold, digging, if not for buried treasure? There were many variations to the theme. We were smugglers. We were spies. We were devil worshippers, and Benja paid the ultimate price for his innocence. The ghosts pushed him, taking revenge against us for desecrating their graves and depriving them of their eternal rest. Even the local police began to entertain such suspicions as possible evidence against us.'

Contempt spitting from his lipless mouth, Guirand cried: 'Can't you see he's lying through his teeth?'

Captain Aristides raised a hand to silence him, as Elena Mitrou pressed on with her interrogation. 'And the discovery of his body, Professor, months later in the excavated house? Is that make-believe? Or empirical fact?'

'Fact,' replied Huxley without hesitation. 'After Benja's ghost had struck terror into them, our hot-headed labourers took matters into their own hands, convinced that he had been improperly buried, a pagan on consecrated ground. After Father Nannos rebuffed their demand that the body be exhumed, one night they took matters into their own hands, consigning Benja to the heathen grave he so richly deserved. Had my apprentice not disturbed them in the act, the perpetrators would have followed the prescribed ritual to the letter, burning and dismembering the body.'

'But why?' asked Elena Mitrou, unconsciously hugging herself.

'Why, Doctor?' he asked, pointedly using her title for the first time. His voice hardened. 'Because they had become convinced that Benja was escaping the grave of his own accord, whenever he chose, that's why. He had become *vrykolakas* — one of the undead.'

318

An involuntary shudder of revulsion ran through her, almost as if she had just glimpsed the old superstitions inside, coursing through their own educated blood like some sleeping hereditary disease. 'And if we were to go ashore, Professor, if we were to question local people, demand the truth?'

'Do it!' hissed Guirand.

'By all means,' said Huxley, 'I *urge* you to do so. Leave the confines of this armoured ship, roam the island village to village. Speak to the farmers who swear on the graves of their own fathers that ghosts came flocking out of the ruptured earth when we first broke ground on the peninsular. Speak to the old crones who at Benja's funeral screamed that they had seen Charontas, the angel of death...'

Elena Mitrou glanced up sharply, a face painted with dismay. 'Is this true, Professor Guirand? Have you relied solely upon local informers and bribe-takers to produce your catalogue of... *evidence?*' No one could have missed the distaste with which the offending word was now pronounced.

Guirand shook his crumpled sheaf of papers at her. 'Here is the evidence, Madame, if only you had the mental wherewithal to recognise it. A catalogue of lies, deceptions, criminality!'

Her eyes narrowed. 'We have all studied the charge sheet, Professor. For months now we have been tormented by the rumours buzzing around us, as thick as flies in August. Knowing the reputation that precedes you, the Service agreed to this hearing in the expectation that you would at last present incontrovertible evidence to support your case. Instead, we find ourselves dragged ever deeper into a morass of superstition, malicious gossip, academic rivalry... Evidence so distorted that the truth is unrecognisable — *like a corpse without a face!*' She thrust her hands into the air in sudden exasperation. 'It is impossible to tell what's what!'

'That, Madame, is because you possess neither the will nor the intellectual capacity to do so. Sarrides was a fool to delegate the mission to those so manifestly ill-equipped for the task.'

'Sarrides!' she exploded. '*Sarrides!*'

Relishing the opportunity, Captain Aristides leapt to her defence, breaking the news with all the restrained euphoria that smashes plates in a Greek dance. 'Sophoklis Sarrides was arrested in a dawn raid yesterday morning. He was frogmarched onto a prison ship at Piraeus, and will no doubt already be familiarising himself with the waterless windswept rock that will be his home for the next decade.'

'May one enquire why?' asked Huxley, after a suitable moment of dead air, his eyes straying to Guirand's mummified face.

'Sarrides was discovered with looted artefacts in his possession,' replied Elena Mitrou, 'including a priceless Minoan vase from your own excavations, Professor. Sarrides has protected his own fiefdom through threat and patronage for years, and it was only through information received from the highest quarters that he was exposed at all. Naturally, our esteemed Director General, Sotirios Kenteris, took swift and decisive action.'

Guirand was scarcely more than a bystander at his own wake, a ghost shouting silence, outraged that they were taking him for dead. An unworthy opponent, despite the formidable legend that clung to him, a wizard's cloak turning inexorably into a shroud.

I glanced sideways, just waiting for Huxley to move in for the kill, delivering the swift final blow that would slay this monster once and for all.

Instead he said: 'If Professor Guirand would do me the honour of accompanying me ashore, I am convinced many of these misunderstandings would be swiftly dispelled. There are places on the island where this curious mingling of myth and reality is particularly evident to the trained eye.'

I jerked my head towards him in disbelief.

Guirand looked up from defeat, a startled light creeping into his small beleaguered eyes. You could almost see the hope sputtering inside him like a devotional lamp in a shrine, its oil reservoir run dry, its wick running on fumes. Hope, almost indistinguishable from life itself, that which animates the soul.

'I would agree to that,' he stumbled, the straw-clutching eagerness of it too obvious by half.

Captain Aristides trained a sceptical eye upon them. 'You have forgotten about the frescoes,' he barked, as if hoping the blunt-edged words would be enough to knock the Frenchman senseless. 'Are we to leave them *in situ*, take them by force? What?'

'Reproductions,' snapped Guirand, his voice flinty with impatience. 'Fakes! Throw the dogs a bone. We can fabricate replicas out of painted plaster. A matter of weeks, no more. Do you think they'll even realise the difference, even if they were told?'

The inspectors brightened, only too glad to see the crisis averted without violence to others or their own careers. There was talk of feasts and fireworks, music and dancing, balloons and kite flying, when Aristides abruptly cut their strings.

'We shall have to see what Mayor Papadaikis has to say about it. As for the worst agitators, they will have to be removed, taken out just as you pluck a diseased animal from a herd.'

The inspectors nodded briskly, if only to spare themselves the ugly details. Guirand sneered. Huxley winced, but could find no words to oppose such martial logic.

We were alone under the rear gun turrets, waiting for the tender, when I asked: 'Was it true, what you said about Benja's body? That the labourers robbed the grave?'

'Of course not!' he retorted, the stress finally flooding over, breaking its banks. '*I* had the body planted in House 16. How else was I to get Claude to incriminate himself, the wretched superstitions of his own informers taking pride of place on his charge sheet? To betray his sinister obsessions to men and women who cling to their brave new rationality like a child clings to its cot?'

'How can you have done such a thing?' I said, aghast at the lengths he'd go to get his own way.

'You will discover soon enough that one's actions in this life are dictated by necessity, not ideals.' He saw my look. 'It was just a body, that's all. You think Benja cares?'

'You lied to their faces! You had Sarrides arrested, thrown into jail! Who planted the Minoan vase on him; his own boss I suppose, courtesy of the Comte?'

'What are you blubbering about? Men are called upon to do far worse in war, trade and politics every day of their lives. Where do you think we are living? *Elysium?*'

We climbed down into the frothing tender, the engine roar disguising our voices. 'Their corruption consumed them, didn't it?' I seethed. 'That's what Plato says. The further they fell, the more convinced they became of their own glory.'

'What is that to me?'

'And here I was thinking only the good and just would find their way to the Isles…'

'As the meek shall inherit the Earth, is that it?' he retorted, with a curl of the lip. 'Well think again, because the Isles are knowledge and knowledge can be achieved only by relentless demand, not prayer, not good deeds squandered on those who will never earn them.'

The exchange was still roiling through my head as we went clip-clopping up the serpentines, the destroyer a dizzying thousand feet below. Twisting back in the saddle, I hurled the words at him: 'So they can lie, cheat, murder their way to the Isles, just as they always have, that's what you're saying. That's just the price that has to be paid.'

'We do what is required of us to reach our destination.'

As if in some bizarre reversal of roles, master to student, I demanded: 'In his margin notes to the Critias, what did the Scholiast write?'

'*What is Atlantis?*' he replied, the smug good humour evaporating on his lips. 'Then all that nonsense about Plato and his Conundrum. What of it?'

Entering the intersection of paths at the summit, we dismounted, the mules snorting.

'Once it awakens within you, you will never escape it. That's what he wrote. *Didn't he!*'

Half the town was already surging along the streets towards us, faces desperate for news. 'How do you know they're not the same?' I insisted. 'The Scholiast who discovered the Conundrum, the Scholiast who interpreted the Sais Codex.'

Shouting over the commotion as the crowds engulfed us, he replied abrasively: 'The handwriting analysis was inconclusive. In all likelihood, they were two different individuals, living at two different times.'

'Like Guirand in his youth, you mean,' I yelled back. 'And Guirand now.'

★

With hangovers of Biblical proportion, the destroyer *Lefkas* thrummed out of the caldera the following day, mission accomplished. Promises, the currency of hope, had all worked their slippery magic.

'So those are the people we have to thank for saving the day!' said Hadrian, his glass striking mine so violently they almost shattered. 'Not science. Not common sense. But speculators and oligarchs.'

Promises of asphalt roads, schools, a hospital. Promises of grand hotels with turquoise swimming pools. Promises of peace, the threat of military reprisals diminishing with every conciliatory word, every chink of the ouzo glass, every *ijá mas!* shouted over the feast table.

322

Promises of brand new frescoes better than the ancient ones they would replace.

'*Kala*, Good — but we want brighter colours than the old ones,' insisted Giannis Papadaikis, slurring the words over the table like a grease stain. 'And in shiny shiny paint!'

'Is that what you would like?' said Huxley, clapping the Mayor on the shoulder, his face beaming, while at his side Claude Guirand grimaced at the horror of it all. A shrunken figure among the revellers drunk on ouzo and wine and their own bursting euphoria, the table a mess of cracked lobster shells and fish bones. Dancing and clapping all around him, plates smashing over the stone floor to the vivid pulse of the lute and violí. Guirand, almost rigid with anticipation, waiting for these tiresome creatures to go on about their inconsequential business, so that he might learn the secrets of infinity.

53.

We painted a white streak through the darkness, Huxley's Land Rover pounding dirt tracks towards the Mesa Vouno.

Hadrian and Sam, fighting the lurches and jolts that were always worst on the rear bench seats.

Guirand, up front with Huxley, peering through the dusty windshield at whatever twisted volcanic shapes the headlamps irradiated up ahead, clutching his skull-headed cane as if it exuded some reluctant spell that kept him alive.

Dog tired, my head kept slumping onto Anna's shoulder, only for the bumps in the road to bring me round again.

Up onto the mountain ridge, the Land Rover seesawing like a boat crossing the Meltemi. The track snaking as it heads for the gash along the mountain, past the bulldozers, on towards the cave where Nestor and his moles have been worming ever deeper into the limestone core.

'There!' cried Guirand, almost cracking the windshield with his cane. 'There, damn you!'

My eyes jerked open and into them flared that white phosphorescence, streaming over the mountain.

My heart leapt against my rib cage and began pounding on my chest to get out. Ducking into my seat, I shot open the window, willing my eyes to understand. *What is it?* Like some looming cloud illuminated from within.

But no... Here and there, it resembles the translucent margins of a nebula, scattered points of light like infant stars and wisps of stellar dust. In-between, I can make out the landscape over which it passes, cliffs, vineyards, beaches, some of which I barely recognise at all, or seem oddly out of place.

Clamouring voices fill the Land Rover in a sudden torrent, impossible to understand. Perhaps not ours at all, they hum and chatter as the light comes flowing over us, its nimbus touching the hood, touching the windshield.

Doors opening left and right, we tumble out, still rolling. Guirand, conveniently forgetting his infirmity, scurrying along the dust track in hot pursuit, shaking his cane at the sky, Huxley scrambling after him.

The rest of us, keeping our distance, feet planted firmly in the twilight. Anna and Hadrian, crouching in the dust and weeds, peering out from behind the rear wheels; Sam, spellbound, standing astride the hood, the light swelling like an aurora into his eyes.

Head thrust back between his shoulder blades, Guirand's turning on his heel, drinking in the sky, willing himself to absorb every last lumen it possesses, demanding the light acknowledge his presence.

A good ten paces away, Huxley's shielding his eyes against the pure whiteness of it, the sudden rush of wind flapping his shirt and trouser legs, his hair flying.

Some unseen force seems to jolt through the old man, head to toe. He staggers sideways, his paralysed face twisting back at us as he goes, eyes blind with terror.

Released from its grip, he lurches backwards, finally collapsing into a patch of desiccated grass. Too stunned to think or move, I'm still following the cloud as it tumbles down the mountainside and plunges into the sea, a shoal of startled fish billowing silver as it vanishes along the cave-riddled cliffs.

'Is he all right?' called Anna, her voice flat and toneless because virtually every emotion had been cauterised by shock.

Thrusting past, Huxley and Sam lay Guirand's limp body onto a blanket in the well of the Land Rover.

I glanced down, half-expecting to flinch again at the same abject terror, glass-shattering the old man's eyes. But that's not what I saw. As far as I could tell, nothing was written onto that face at all. I don't mean that he looked at peace. I mean that he had acquired that curious blank look of dolls and mannequins.

'His heart rate's all over the place, but at least he's still breathing. He may have had a stroke — how the hell should I know? Must I be a physician now on top of everything else?' It was almost comforting to have the old Huxley back again, tetchy, mocking, impatient.

'But what *was* it?' said Anna, her voice struggling for volume.

'Something atmospheric, something volcanic,' said Hadrian, numb mouth mashing the words. 'For God's sake, Huxley, when will you finally act and get a vulcanologist out here to explain it to us?'

We hammered on Dr Sanassis' door until he came hurrying down the staircase, a lurching giant his imperfect shadow.

'Despina is still tucked up in bed,' he explained, loud enough for his wife to hear, 'a foolish superstitious woman who won't answer the door after sunset on a full moon night! Apparently there are *vrykolakes* about!'

We placed Guirand on the infirmary cot in the alcove abutting the kitchen, Sanassis taking his pulse, listening intently to his heartbeat, prising open his eyelids.

The combination of old cooking smells and Guirand's rancid disease was making my stomach turn.

'Well?' demanded Huxley, looking down at the crumpled face. Saliva was breaking through the old man's lips and dribbling onto his chin.

'A seizure of some sort. A stroke, perhaps. If I were the superstitious sort, I might even be tempted to believe something had shocked the life out of him. Just nod if it's true, Marcus, you don't need to tell me the ins and outs.'

'Will he recover?'

Sanassis pulled a doubtful face, eyebrows arching up, mouth tugging down at the corners. 'When he comes to, assuming he will, we'll at least know the extent of his injuries and whether the paralysis is permanent. But what can I do for him here?' He spread his arms wide, exasperated eyes darting around the impoverished little room, its personality torn between surgery and *Kyria* Despina's baking and frying. 'I can splint a broken leg, stitch up a gash, treat a snake bite, deliver a baby. How do you expect me to treat a blood clot on the brain? As soon as we can, we must put him on the ferry, and hope the strain won't kill him.'

Dead on their feet, the others traipsed home. 'Where is your sense of adventure?' Huxley berated them. 'Almost daybreak, and you want to waste it sleeping, *now*, when we have a necromanteion to explore? What will Charon think of you?'

They walked on, ignoring us. 'Curiosity will soon get the better of them,' he murmured. 'You'll see.'

Gunning the engine, we set off for Monolithos, the sun rising through a bank of charcoal cloud.

'So you have made your peace with Guirand?'

'Of course,' he replied, if a little defensively, our shadow and dust wake flickering across the coral pink rock face like careless wraiths. 'Because Claude, for all his faults, at least searched. At least he demanded to know the truth, pushing aside the stars and planets, groping his way through the universe, torch in hand.'

326

'And he was struck down for his efforts. Maybe he deserved it.'

'You sound like Anna,' he replied scornfully. 'Spouting nonsense about hubris and retribution. Claude fell because he was old, because he didn't have the measure of what confronts us, that's all.'

I caught a glimmer of light. 'How come you never speak of him — your own father I mean? Because he's trapped in some kind of traumatic memory, like mine?'

'No,' his voice carrying a dangerous edge.

'Then why?'

'Because unlike you, Mr Pedrosa, I do not mourn my father's passing. If anything, I would have done better to mourn his absence while he was still alive.'

'He must have been a strong-willed man.' I was remembering the grim sepia portrait, the shocking abduction of the young boy from his own mother.

He uttered an abrupt laugh, as dark as old blood. 'To live under the tyranny of the strong is one thing, to live under the tyranny of the weak, quite another.'

'How come you still despise him like that... After everything you said about liberating oneself from the past?'

Irritated to have those words thrown back in his face, he retorted: 'Do you think I owe him my gratitude for being where I am today? No, if that were the case, I would be some missionary doctor trying to cure malaria with quinine, or cholera with swamp leaves. I would be trying to dig a well with a spoon!'

'He didn't love you, is that what you think? Is that why you ran away from him?'

I hardly knew where the words came from. We hit a half-buried stone in the road, probably deliberately, the Land Rover lurching so violently I had to grab hold of the windscreen to save myself from being pitched out.

'Love!' he mocked, wrenching back the steering wheel. 'You think love is going to get us where we need to be? Something so capricious, so bereft of logic?'

Exasperated, I shook my head. 'Then what are we doing, what's it all for? We lose the past simply to spare us memories too traumatic to bear, is that it?'

'No!' came the searing reply. 'To leave your mark in time. To resist fate. To look it square in the eyes and say, you shall have no power or dominion over me. Before you crush me into dust, I shall know the sky beyond the stars!'

'Fate?'

'Yes!' he erupted. 'Fate! Karma, kismet, destiny. Fortune, doom, providence. Call it what the hell you like. That force that would have us become as impotent as dead leaves driven by the wind —'

'I thought you didn't believe in fate... I thought you denied it even existed. I thought you despised the very idea.'

'Then you were wrong! It's our attitudes towards fate that I abhor. The idea that it cannot be understood. The idea that its workings cannot be laid bare. The idea that I should prostrate myself before it like some bone-jangling native to his wooden god.'

Tired of competing with the headwind, he pulled off to the side until we were sitting under a wiry, grey-boned fig tree.

'Maybe it can't be understood,' I said, as he switched off the engine. 'Maybe it's all random chaos, and the connections we think we see, just coincidence.'

My ill-considered words bequeathed us an abrupt silence. He turned away, his eyes roaming bleakly across the broken hillside.

'If only I could believe that,' he said at last, the distance restoring some measure to his words. 'The universe, pointless, meaningless, absurd, be that in its flashes of brilliance or its utter wretchedness and cruelty. But I cannot. Not after everything I have seen. Coincidences far too intricate to have been created by something so senseless. Alignments of events far too meaningful to have occurred by mere chance. I know there is a hidden logic behind it all, even if it is malicious and brutal.'

I had almost forgotten about his triumph up on the ridge. 'The Ferryman's cave,' I said. 'So Nestor found it in the end?'

'No, we have Aris to thank for that,' he replied, gunning the engine, and I just knew from the roiling intensity of the words that he was about to pounce. 'It was a hot day, you remember, and Aris was cooling off under the ridge. He swam into a haze of freshwater so cold it goose-bumped his skin. Nestor knew it then, of course. It had to be the Oracle cave and its subterranean river. So you decide now, Mr Pedrosa — was its discovery chance, or was it fate?'

54.

Huxley was still thudding about the house, packing enough supplies to last a week, when they rolled up at the front door, curiosity ambushing them in their sleep.

Anna wandered absently into his study, first towards the window, then the abandoned, paper-strewn desk, before spinning round in her sandaled feet, astonished eyes probing every corner.

She called out down the stairs, 'Where is it, Marcus? Where is that horrid statue? What have you done with it?'

From the cupboard in the hall, where Huxley was hastily stuffing things into a rucksack, came an ambiguous grunt.

Hadrian waddled in from the kitchen, munching on *spanakopita*, drinking goat's milk. 'What's this I hear?' sagging there in the doorway, until the answer, finally understood, knocked the nonchalance out of him.

'You put it in the mountain,' said Anna, descending the stairs in a kind of slow motion rush that you only see in dreams or people in shock. 'You put it in the cave.'

Nestor, Aris and Mad Yanni the gravedigger, three silhouettes manhandling the Ferryman under the milk-stream stars, while Huxley played his cliff edge brinkmanship with the Colonels.

Sam poked his tousled head around the kitchen door, his grudging admiration for the man exposed to the elements like rusting iron relics.

'Let me get this straight,' spluttered Hadrian, another spear wound to his rationality. 'After expending so much time and effort finding the damned Ferryman and digging it up, you've now buried it again. Why? For what conceivable reason? You surely can't —' His indignation died mid-air, unwilling even to contemplate the implications. He tossed the remainder of his pie into the bin, his appetite suddenly spent.

Snubbing them, Huxley went barging out of the front door, the bloated rucksack over his shoulder. The door slammed behind him, bequeathing the hallway a stuttering silence.

Minutes later we were chasing after him through the vineyards, then along the crater rim, eyes peeled for his white Land Rover or its speeding dust cloud up ahead. Before long we were lurching along the jagged scar cut across the mountain face by Nestor's bulldozers. 'Stay well clear of the edge, Anna!' cried Hadrian in sudden alarm, glancing down at the crumbling verge where the mountain fell away to the midnight blue sea a thousand feet below.

The track reached a dead end among giant limestone boulders, where Huxley must have parked just minutes before, the engine still ticking as it lost heat.

Marching single file we threaded our way between them, then past the heavy machinery, all silent now.

Huxley's defiant figure materialised and vanished as we went, tramping heavily through the caterpillar ruts, Nestor at his side.

Sam whistled between his fingers, but neither turned. We quickened our pace.

Below, the ancient city was turning its face towards the afternoon sun, and even from up here I could make out the temple columns, the market square, the sacred grove with its petrified trees.

Ten yards on, first Nestor then Huxley vanished through a wall of solid lava and obsidian. My heart was still drumming on my rib cage when I realised, it's just the mouth of the cave, that's all, almost perfectly camouflaged from the outside.

One by one, they dived in after them, Sam, Hadrian, Anna.

I held my breath, then jumped myself.

If I have always tried to cheat the darkness, or escape the feeling of walls closing in around me, this time, I was out of luck. Still catching daylight, the first vaulted chamber quickly turned into a narrow, coiling tunnel that air and steam must have cast out of molten stone aeons ago. No time to think: I scrambled after the darting torch beams, my hands exploring the walls like a blind man in search of a face.

Plunging ever deeper along the tubular passage, the stone became blood-warm to the touch. If this was our sleeping dragon of an island, we were now crawling through its fiery, sulphurous guts.

On and on we went, so disoriented now it was impossible to tell whether we were heading uphill or down, standing on our heads or on our feet. I caught Hadrian's anxious face frozen in the torchlight, drenched in sweat. Sam had torn off his shirt and tied it around his waist, and was pressing on for all he was worth.

'Where are we going?' called Hadrian, a disembodied voice echoing back and forth along the tunnel like a draught of wind. 'What do you expect to find, Huxley? The Underworld, the River Styx? Elysium?'

No answer; just a drifting pool of light up ahead.

Abruptly, the forbidding lava walls relinquished their grip, and there we were at last, wide-eyed, amazed, spinning round, struggling to take in the palatial inner chamber, its white luminous limestone so flecked with crystal it was like finding a secret universe in the darkness. Somewhere close by, water splashed.

As the torch beams converged, it leapt into view: Huxley's sacred torrent, bubbling up from some deep aquifer. Here, it had carved a luminous swirling pool out of the white travertine, then made its swift escape towards the sea, cascading over the smooth rocks.

As our eyes grew accustomed to the fake stars above our heads and the wandering torch beams, I saw something that shocked me even more, even if I had been warned to expect it. The Ferryman, that supposedly priceless artefact, now lodged into a tight crevice overlooking the water.

'So it's true,' I began, startled at the way the vaulted cavern was distorting my voice, seeming to parody my newfound desire to believe in him. 'But why…?'

'Because the Ferryman is back where he belongs. Just as the Codex demands.'

Gazing up, the Ferryman's lapis blue eyes seemed more disconcerting, more ambiguous than ever.

'*Deep within the mountain stands the god who ferries souls across the River,*' he recited. '*Above his head, stars that are not stars. At his feet, the River more ancient than them all. Can thou seest beyond? Across the water to the other shore? Through the Oracle as deep as the prism eye? Who, better than he, shall understand that death is a land not far from here?*'

'The Necromanteion,' said Hadrian with a wry snort. 'If history tells us anything, it was all smoke and mirrors.'

My eyes were drawn back to the Ferryman's, vivid, mesmerising, indescribably blue, almost as if illuminated from within. Wherever it was coming from, it wasn't the glittering travertine or the torch beams. Edging closer, I realised: light was entering from the sky, a chimney-like shaft rising up through the limestone, the silver flecks amplifying its intensity.

Heaving himself up, Sam uttered a whistle of amazement as he balanced at the Ferryman's shoulder. 'I can see blue sky. What's it for? Air? Light?'

A disembodied voice called out to us from the shadows; Nestor, his helmet light flaring. 'The tunnels, Kapítan. I can hear the men on the other side. *Listen!*'

It was hard to distinguish the welling murmur from the echo of the torrent, or the wafting breeze that tasted sometimes of brimstone, sometimes of water or blossom. 'If I'm right, that warren of tunnels ends up here. All the way from temple hill!'

My heart was in my mouth as we retraced our steps along the dragon's gut. Despite the undeniable splendour of the inner chamber, there was something brooding, ancient and malignant about it. Even with Hadrian's unintended help, I couldn't quite convince myself that it was just a trick of the mind itself, finding an unnerving resemblance between these dark volcanic tunnels and the labyrinths of its own unconscious. Standing under that glittering firmament of stars, which achieves the perfect illusion of infinity, the thought had leapt out at me: *we have no idea where the self begins or where it ends.*

55.

'What's he doing up there?' demanded Hadrian, wringing the sarcasm out of his words like a wet towel. 'Interrogating the sky? Awaiting revelation? Communing with the Dead?' Save for Nestor's milk runs up to the ridge to deliver supplies, no one had seen hide or hair of him in a week.

We were on our afternoon tea break, four o'clock sharp, Russian tea and mess tent baklava under the awning of Huxley's field tent, Hadrian determined to maintain at least some semblance of normality in camp.

I found myself gazing up at the mountain, trying to pinpoint the Ferryman's cave, a little game that always defeated me even in the harsh glare of the afternoon sun, so pock-marked was its limestone face. I tried to visualise the river as it once was, before the island blew apart. Tried to imagine how the Oracle might have functioned, even if it was just light and mirrors.

'The worst of it is,' said Anna, grimacing at the bitterness of the Russian tea or maybe just the mental image of Huxley reciting fragments under the prismatic gaze of the Ferryman, 'I can't trust Marcus anymore. It's as if I have never known him... I have no idea where the lies end or the truth begins!'

I saw her face go numb, her fingers stiffen around the mug. Again, I caught the anise on her breath, the shadow-darting look in her eyes.

'He is not fit to lead us,' Hadrian fulminated. 'Who would have believed him capable of such wretched superstition, meddling in the occult like that? *Guirand. Huxley.* They're two sides to the same coin!'

'That's not fair, and you know it,' I snapped, surprising even myself as I leapt to Huxley's defence.

'What, you're defending him now?' Hadrian's incredulity coming like a sharp pain. 'After everything he's put us through? If it weren't for the fact that we're already besieged by medieval superstition on all sides, I'd be tempted to believe he *had* stolen your soul — *the sorcerer's apprentice!*'

'Look, he's helped me, that's all. More than anyone else ever has.'

A probing glance from Hadrian, too gummed up on English

reserve to demand details. 'So the apprentice has had his epiphany,' he concluded with a sneer.

'I'm not expecting the Isles to materialise out of thin air, if that's what you mean.'

Anna said with quiet ferocity: 'You should call your mother, your sister, your friends — or have you forgotten them already?'

'I'm not Benja,' I retorted. 'I'm not Sam!'

'You think Sam was always like that? *Do you?*'

'Don't tell me. He was idealistic once, he was innocent, he was naive.'

She said with revulsion: 'You make it sound like a disease.'

But it wasn't that. It was just so hard to believe.

As they left the tent in a huff I shouted after them: 'I'd be with him on the mountain if I had my way, and you know what. *So would Sam!*'

But still I twisted and squirmed, Anna's accusation hitting a raw nerve, what with my weekly phone calls home becoming ever more infrequent. But that's just life, isn't it, I told myself, deadlines chasing us, events swallowing us whole, not because I've strayed ever further along Huxley's metaphysical mind map. In fierce concentration, I shut my eyes, struggling for the lucid image that once was second nature to me, the bus stop, the tall gabled house, the garden path, the lilac tree, my mother's, my sister's face at the bay window. Blurring. Losing their light; becoming mere words.

Ten days later, Huxley descended the mountain in defeat, fuming like the crater that had begun to smoke and bubble out on the Burnt Islands.

Eager for news, I headed out to Monolithos through the gathering dusk.

Muffled by the garden walls, angry voices greeted me the moment I stepped out of the Morris, growing ever louder as I threaded my way between the fallen marble statues. By the time I reached the steps to the terrace, I could hear every blistering word.

'It's a mania, an *illness, a psychosis!*' cried Anna, the yellowing vine leaves tumbling down behind her. 'Everyone ponders mortality at some point in their lives, of course they do. But they don't spend every waking minute demanding answers! They don't spend fortunes amassing art collections glorifying death! They don't turn into ghouls!'

The next thing I knew I had been dragged into the fight myself, along with Sam and Benja. It was her fiercest assault yet. 'You taught them to lose their identity, lose their history, forget their friends and family, and for what? So you could fill the vacuum that remained, so you could possess a vacant soul. Why Marcus, why is that? Have you lost your own somewhere along the way?'

At his trenchant best, he took her argument and rung it by the neck. 'But wasn't it you, Anna, who said you could imagine nothing more sublime than losing yourself to eternity? What was it you said... becoming something of the wind that sings through the wires...'

The moment jumps like a skipped heartbeat, just as Anna tries to grasp the sudden twist in meaning.

'Yes, but in death, not now!' she cries at last. 'To totality, not to one dark, grasping ego that wants to devour my identity.'

'Make up your mind, Anna. What's it to be? A sense of self or a sense of totality? You can't have it both ways.'

Catching my careless movement below, Anna scowled: 'What are you doing here? It doesn't matter. Come here. Sit down!' Not long after, Sam appeared, and everyone must have known it was for the same reason, the same unquenchable curiosity.

Huxley growled something incomprehensible, his failure on the mountain eating away at him.

'The Isles!' snorted Hadrian, appealing to the rest of us, all the better to belittle Huxley's beliefs in the third person. 'No doubt he imagines himself on their light drenched shores, among the greatest minds this poor spinning planet has ever had the grace or the misfortune to know. And yet what he singularly fails to realise is that, by implication, the enlightened are forever condemned to live in medieval times. Every free-thinking mind must always be living there. That is the sad eternal irony of it, even he can never bring himself to accept it.'

'And you, Hadrian? For how long are you going to remain in your cosy state of self-denial? You keep up the pretence week after week, month after month, even though you know this phenomenon, whatever it is, has touched our lives.'

'Leave Benja out of this, Huxley.'

'Dead and buried, out of sight, out of mind, is that the way of it, Hadrian? Even though you know something happened on that day that no one can adequately explain.'

'Benja was our friend. Not your witness. Not your alibi.'

'You have seen the frescoes,' Huxley flared, finally tiring of the third degree. 'And you know their significance as well as I. Somehow or other, these people abandoned their fear of death.'

'Death was friend, not foe, is that what you're saying, Huxley?'

'He's saying that,' said Sam, his eyes like blue worlds in the stillness of the candles. 'He's saying that they learnt to defy instinct, to defy the nature within that drives us to survive at any cost.'

The way he shaped the words, they sounded almost erotic.

I saw the shock pass over Anna's face, and she just managed to say: 'The gods have a way of teaching humility, Marcus. Perhaps you should remember that before you demand the truth prostrate itself before you.'

★

The glittering autumn morning was doing little for the pounding cobwebs in my head. Out on the largest of the Burnt Islands, the crater continued to blow drowsy smoke rings into the sky.

At the precipice wall, the fishermen were drawing lots to ferry across Father Nannos with his prayer book and holy water, there to bellow his fire and brimstone exorcism over the smouldering pit, now stained an ominous Lucifer yellow. Through the great portal of the church you could hear the tin votive offerings jangling in the wind, the nave ablaze with candles, the air redolent with incense.

Huxley squinted against the morning light. He hadn't slept a wink, that much obvious enough from the bloodshot eyes, the grey stubble, the charts and papers littering his desk.

'You can't give up now,' I said, alarmed at the depths of his depression.

He glanced up almost resentfully. 'We have hit a dead end. There is nothing more to go on.'

'Why not follow the light?'

'The light! It is impossibly elusive, and even if it weren't just a gaseous product of the volcano, a volcanic will-o'-the-wisp, as Hadrian insists, it is not the Oracle of the Dead. You saw what it did to Claude.'

With only a moment's hesitation, I retrieved them from my dispatch bag, placing them on the desk in front of him. Benja's shopping list with the impossible numbers, written hours before he died. His notebook, betraying a moment of epiphany before breaking off in the middle of a sentence.

336

He offered a broken grunt, part grudging thanks and part resentment that I had kept them from him for so long. Screwing up his eyes, knitting his brows, sighing, he studied the list for a good ten minutes before concluding bitterly: 'It means nothing. Except, that is, to the mind we know was already suffering its own delirium.'

Such was his mood he seemed on the verge of crumpling the paper into a ball and tossing it away, before thinking better of it. 'No,' he muttered, as if to the shadow of his own daemon. 'We must think. Allow the mind room to breathe, to perceive beyond the clutter that besieges us.'

56.

Christmas came and went, not that there was much cheer about it that year, what with Huxley's black, erratic mood. We entered the bone chilling damp of the new year, and before we knew it, were tumbling into March, icy winds and raw skies vying with the spring sun.

There were sporadic tremors, running like live wires under the ash. An earthquake that cracked a church dome, and rained coloured Byzantine plaster down on the heads of the congregation. Following a brief spell in which it merely hissed and smouldered, the eruption on the Burnt Islands intensified, cracking a shower of sparks into the night. Though there was no lava flow, it was enough to bring the vulcanologists down from Thessalonica again.

Amid the trenches, holes and slag heaps, again there were intermittent sightings of Benja the *vrykolakas*.

Watching the latest victim being dosed on raki outside the mess tent, Hadrian grunted scornfully. 'Thankfully, even Huxley will make nothing out of this.' With a glower in my direction he added: 'Isles of the Blest indeed! The Promised Land!' His arm swept over the shattered landscape. 'Then behold it, in all its splendored glory.'

Interpreting our silence as a retreat he added abrasively: 'There is your Oracle for you. As scintillating as the logic it is made from. Hear it speak: superstition, ignorance always leads nowhere.'

Catching the tremor of hesitation on her lips, he added with asperity. 'Well, Anna? Doesn't it?'

I knew what she was thinking, even as her eyes flinched from the sight of house 16 up on the rise. About Benja, losing his grip on reality; losing contact with the memories that made him who he was, loved ones just a phone call, a ship, a plane ride away. Friends, just a word away.

She replied bleakly: 'Nowhere, Hadrian? Then why is everything around us falling apart?'

'What is?' he gaped.

She shook her head, the uncertainty coming on a torn sigh. 'I don't know... Friendships. The island, that once seemed a kinder, nobler place. What we once used to value or believe in... Even our dreams at night — *like lost souls tossed about in a raging sea!'*

'You talk as if he's unleashed some ancient curse upon us.' The words were twisted with scorn.

'Well, hasn't he?' She threw him a fierce, unrepentant, glance. 'If his is a madness that engulfs us all, isn't that curse enough for you? At least the ancient thinkers knew hubris will end in nemesis!'

Drifting back from the raw winter blueness outside, Sam's eyes bored into mine and wouldn't let go.

For once I knew what he meant. 'Hubris. Madness. Nemesis. It was the heart of the legend, wasn't it,' I said.

'What legend?' barked Hadrian.

'Atlantis, of course.'

'Atlantis? I give up! I wash my hands of you all!'

Halfway through my morning rounds, I stepped into one of the town houses on the fringes of the agora. Sam was up on the mobile scaffold with his handpicked students, pretty young things all too eager to be mixing pigments for him, fetching and carrying, while he retouched the repaired plaster grain by speckled grain. A bright-eyed fawn in the high forest, the vivid spice terraces and the glowing city far below.

My eyes strayed to the work bench. Among the glass tubes of hand-made pigments, the array of brushes and spatulas, something else, spilling out of Sam's leather satchel.

A handful of painted beach pebbles, volcanic black, red or silver, the imperfect canvas, the genius of the artist, who knows what, lending these vivid snatches of our lives something timeless, something eternal, something beyond words.

Huxley standing waist-deep in a lava trench, a terracotta calix in his hands. Benja, fighting fear as he treads the temple heights at midnight, drawn by another luminous apparition. Sam himself, about to make his first acquaintance with island obsession in Le Petit Phoenix in Saint-Michel. No one could mistake the style could they; stone or fresco, they might have been painted by the very same hand.

Above my head, Sam was treading the scaffolding with a hollow thump. Startled out of my thoughts, I glanced up, something about the abruptness of the movement making the walls swim, the colours blur and run. I blinked. Shook my head, and was just blaming my restless night when I caught the tuning fork ping on my eardrums…

The thought entering my head like a cloud of ink. Benja saw the selfsame thing, didn't he. Colours, almost as metaphors, flowing one to the other: *There, where they touch, a new colour comes into being, has no one noticed?*

Suddenly my heart was pounding in anticipation and I was on my feet, treading in almost fluid silence room to room, fresco to fresco.

Everyone thought it was just another symptom of your troubled mind, didn't they, colours, forms, identities, billowing, swirling, morphing one into another as the frescoes flow like some vivid river of life splashing through the void.

Swallow into sky, bee into wildflower, leopard into antelope, dolphin into prism of light, cloud into river, saffron gatherer into priestess... Even those ardent lovers on the hillside, catching our own distant reflections.

'Do you see that?' I breathed, biting my lips in fierce concentration, as Huxley barged his way in from the bright winter daylight. 'They're like visual codes, flowing room to room, house to house... they're —'

He grunted disparagingly. 'Yes, Benja saw the same kaleidoscope of colours didn't he? And look where it got him. Devoured by his own darkness, his own delusions.'

★

Hands thrust into my pockets, I dragged myself home, leaning against the frigid night air. Every echoing step seeming to mimic my own uncertainty, the shuttered houses, the wind sounding its lament through the wires.

Thinking, maybe he's right. Maybe Benja was losing his mind. Seeing things. Hearing things.

Thinking. Maybe you are too. Thoughts hurtling this way, that way, bouncing off your dead end walls whichever way they run.

Jittery, exhausted, I fell into bed, already hearing nightmares convulsing in the dark. I could feel them clawing at my feet as I tumbled headlong into the blackness... only to find myself drifting into a long tranquil sleep, like some steamship lit up from stem to stern, plying its way through the night.

It was still dark when I sprang awake, trying to remember who and where I was. But then, just as the fog dissipated into the blue, I knew it with utter certainty. What was going on. What it all meant.

I leapt out of bed and threw on my clothes, not even daring the splash of icy water over my face for fear of losing the moment and the precious insight that came with it. Trying to beat the sunrise, I raced over to Monolithos, and hammered on his door.

Huxley knitted his brows, scowled, but at least heard me out as he led me into the kitchen, still in his tattered dressing gown.

Those orphaned strands of time. Those sporadic hallucinations carrying us off like flyaway balloons. That inexplicable encounter on the rock beds that even he had witnessed with his own two eyes, Sam, Aris, out of character, out of place, the spitting image of their ancient reflections up on the hill. Sauntering towards us over the crystalline waves, the air billowing. Aris but not Aris. Sam but not Sam. Until the bubble burst, leaving nothing more substantial than the splash evaporating on our faces.

Despising my interpretation, he scowled. 'Sam is not dead, Aris is not dead. How can it possibly be the Oracle? *How?* It makes no sense.'

'No it doesn't,' I said, struggling for the right word. 'Because they're *fluctuations*, they're *distortions* in our reality. Our perceptions of it. Our physical and mental reactions to it. They happen whenever this thing, whatever it is, comes anywhere near us.'

Aperture, anomaly, fracture, Oracle of the Dead. Nobody knew what to call it. Even the monks who had driven themselves mad or blind trying to interpret the fragments. Agonising over whether it was an act of God or a freak of nature. 'Isn't that right?' I demanded. 'They didn't know how to define it, did they? Portal of the gods, passage of heroes, rift, exception, flaw...'

'Well those "fluctuations" as you call them, led nowhere,' he rasped. 'They meant nothing. In the end, what other conclusion could I draw? These weren't objective events, merely the delusions of those who perceived them.'

'You said the same about Benja, didn't you?' I said, hurling the words at him. 'That he's seeing things. That he's losing his mind. Bewildered, terrified, suddenly finding himself thrust into these apparitions, reality rippling, buckling. It was Benja who first remarked our likenesses in frescoes, wasn't it, not you!'

'*Yes!*' our voices like echoing thunder now, rattling off the kitchen window panes. 'At first I assumed he was just homesick, that's all. His symptoms were erratic, yet worsened over time. What do you expect, on an island like this —'

'What fucking island? In the end, he didn't even know which one he was on, did he? This broken ruin under his feet; the ancient idyll he was digging out of the ash; the Isles beyond sunset you were planting in his head at every opportunity; the daydreams conjured up by Stavros and Vassilis, an island of learning and invention, a civilisation in love with nature, in love with wisdom!'

'That was just a collision of circumstance, that's all.'

'You knew and did nothing to help him!'

'It would have jeopardised everything!' he rumbled, his thunder weakening. 'The apprentice must follow his own path; he cannot be led. *The mountain must speak to innocence!*' He sighed, rubbing his hands roughly over his face. 'In any event, in their randomness of appearance they were impossible to predict.' His voice grew taut with frustration. 'Reality melting, the logic of its construction, events, personalities, colours, running into one another. Sam, whose brushwork has so come to resemble that of the fresco painter on the hill it is almost impossible to tell them apart. Aris, tossing a cast net into the sea with a skill only fluke or atavistic memory could achieve... Is it any wonder I tell you it is impossible to separate the reality from the myth, the objective from the irrational.'

Once Huxley was in the mud, it was difficult to budge him. 'We should be out there now,' I argued, 'searching high and low for them. In the ancient city, on the mountain. Anywhere.'

57.

The day was so blue and raw it seemed to be letting in the darkness of space. Beyond the mountain the stars were still glittering like ice jewels. Camp was only just stirring, the sun an orange glow beyond the mountain.

'Remember: keep your wits about you,' Huxley admonished me, as we moved across the compound. 'As it is, even if one of your fluctuations does occur, there's no guarantee we will realise it, no matter how odd or anomalous the event it creates.'

We crossed the river bridge, cut past the bakery and ceramic workshop, climbed the hill.

Moderating our pace, we moved along the house fronts bordering the square, every so often peering in through one of the windows or doorways into the silent rooms beyond, like living moments trapped in amber.

Ten minutes elapsed, and the next time I looked, an hour. 'We're wasting our time,' he grumbled. 'There's nothing up here.'

Nothing. Not a shadow out of place, nor even a disturbed speck of dust caught out by the brightening sun. Just the sea breeze, sounding its musical notes now between the temple columns.

'What did I tell you,' he said, masticating the words. 'There is no way of predicting them. Why do you think we were all so baffled by Benja's state of mind, the spells of perfect lucidity, the spells of madness, the flashes of brilliance.'

Time has that treacle-like motion about it. I'm turning in a slow arc, trying to tune out the fitful gusts from the sea, the scattering dust devils, the rustling of last summer's scorched weeds. Senses suddenly alive to the bleak sand-coloured facades gaining colour as the sun floods into the square, ochre, cornflower blue. The dry taste in my mouth. The premonition in my gut.

The wind drops. Meeting silence, a tuning fork hums in my ears. I can feel the blood pounding in my head like surf.

It comes swelling towards us, spherical ripples buckling air, the only obvious trace of their presence the air pocket weightlessness inside, the momentary tremble of the town houses bordering the square.

'Listen!' he hisses, spinning round like a scarecrow. *'Listen!'*

Warbling voices rising to a sudden cacophony, crowds mingling through the agora on market day. Traders' shouts, children's cries, a distant song. Unmistakeable this time. I can hear mountain water, plashing under the river bridge. The fluttering of leaves, the snapping of a sail in the wind.

There are invisible circles rippling all around us.

I jump back as if stung, the touch of some invisible thing walking through me, our bodies stretching and billowing as we part.

Shadows flicker across the walls of the Thalassa house. Almost missed to the blink of an eye, they momentarily gain colour, light, substance, as they disappear through the doorway. Sam, Aris, a gaggle of young students.

Huxley slumped onto the parapet wall, breathing hard, trying not to gasp. 'Get Sam out here! Aris too! Now!'

Into the penumbral light splashed with pools of sun, the frescoes seeming to swell and sigh with the nocturnal sea. The leaping dolphin, catching the first of the dappled light. Still in the half-shadow, those two young fishermen standing naked on the dock, a brace of sea bream in their hands, their faces bearing that haunting resemblance, impossible to prove, impossible to refute. 'Sam!' I called. 'Ari!'

At the far end of the room the scaffold's deserted, the work bench still covered with its paint-spattered sheet.

'Nothing. Nobody. They must have —' The words were hardly out of my mouth when I caught the movement over his shoulder, down at the quay. I stared, mute, dumbfounded, for against the flutter of the caïque's burgundy sails, there they were, Sam, the students, lending Aris a hand laying his nets in the sun.

Whatever had just swamped our senses in those air-pulsing waves had left us high and dry. I joined him on the parapet, head in my hands, feeling so lightheaded I feared I would blackout if I stayed on my feet.

'How can they be in two places at the same time, how is that possible?'

He said with asperity: 'How? Because they're illusions, that's how. You said so yourself!'

I shook my head uncertainly. 'Every time we're plunged into these moments, I don't know, they're more real than anything else. That's what I don't understand. So is the island...'

Now it was his turn to demand: 'What island?'

'The one that calls us.'

Narrowing his eyes at me, he flared: 'Snap out of it! I warned you, didn't I. We could blunder into these distortions and scarcely even remark upon it. We've been doing so for months!'

We cut across the quarry, dragging our coats behind us, the day suddenly far too warm for them.

The sky was glowing like a lamp and I was mildly astonished to find the first wildflowers springing out of the charcoal soil, splashing colours at our feet.

'Maybe they're reflections from some other point in time,' I mused aloud, adding in a voice that sounded hollow even to my ears: 'Like our own likenesses in the frescoes —'

'No!' came the retort, as though the very idea were anathema to him. 'They have the appearance of Sam and Aris, that's all. It is the truth beyond the distortion that we seek. Remember that.' With a glare at the sky, he added almost resentfully: 'It is almost as if it were using our own faculties of perception against us to avoid detection, camouflaged by the blueness of the sky, hiding in the sound of the wind. And yet there it is, nonetheless, the fracture between life and death, the meaning of all this...'

He winced, ground to a halt, bit hard into his lips, and several moments elapsed before he prised out the words. 'Except...'

'Except what?'

'Back in summer on the rock beds, remember? Whatever happened in those few surreal moments with Aris, Sam, Maria, the ancient resemblance was just uncanny. Facial expressions, mannerisms, movements... Almost as if they embodied the very heart and soul of this civilisation. No weapons, no guards, no battlements. In their eyes, you perceive an openness that knows no enemy...' He grunted, mashing the words. 'Yes, so out of character, so alien to all we know they might just as well have been ghosts!'

'Then they're just illusions, they don't mean anything, that's what you're saying.'

He said in a taut voice: 'Probably not... Except I have seen that look in Sam before, or something like it... Just once. Before he even set foot on Thera. Up on the floodlit Parthenon, still euphoric with his escape from his old life, on the threshold of another, Athens a blaze of light at our feet.'

'So how do you explain that?'

He shook his head dismissively. 'Another figment in an ocean of figments — am I supposed to be surprised by that? Such is the guile of this state of trance we are stupid enough to call reality — *so be warned!*'

Saying we had no choice but to press on, he went dashing off to the huts to collect his gear.

'You must be mad or stupid, both of you!' seethed a voice at my feet. Anna's sweat-muddied face glared up from the shoulder-deep trench, one hemisphere of an exposed pithoi buried in the ash like some dinosaur egg. 'Exactly when did you forget about the masks life forces us all to wear, you, me, everyone, masks for almost every occasion? How dare you imagine that when you see me, Sam, Aris, or anyone else, you are seeing the sum total of who we are. *How dare you!*'

'But the fluctuations…'

'Those *are* the fluctuations!' she cried. 'They are the dark sides of our worlds that sometimes just begin to creep into the twilight, they're our moods, our contradictions, our inconsistencies, our paradoxes…'

She threw up her hands in exasperation. 'Don't you understand anything? People *are* contradictory. They say one thing and do another. They feel one thing and say another. They act out one reality and dream another.'

'Does that mean we should be seeing people in two places at the same time?' but I had faltered, and it was too late.

'Maybe you should finally ask yourself what it is Marcus wants from you, and why,' she went on, glaring up at me in-between her bouts with the stubborn soil. 'Maybe you should ask what it was he took from Sam. And what it was he stole from Benja and went on stealing until Benja didn't care anymore whether he fell, jumped or was pushed off the scaffolding.'

58.

By the time I escaped, Huxley was already at the gates, throwing stuff into the Land Rover; his battered old Leica, his binoculars, a compass, a map.

'Get a move on,' he scolded.

Slit-eyed, impassive, his attention never wavered from the dust track up ahead as I recounted my run-in with Anna.

'Well, bear in mind: sometimes the dreams that frighten us most are the ones we can't resist; the sweet dream, not the nightmare.'

'That doesn't sound like Anna. I always thought —'

'Well you thought wrong.' Twisting the steering wheel between his hands, he said in a clipped voice: 'Anna lost the love of her life when she was still in her twenties. Renato and Anna. Two young lovers the ancient gods would probably have turned into constellations…'

'What happened?'

'He died on the road. Some stupid, mindless accident. Within the space of time it takes to mangle metal, crush bone, snuff out a life, her world had become unrecognisable, an inferno of broken dreams. So take heed. Such is the malice or the brute senselessness that confronts us all…'

'But she always seemed so happy, so full of life,' I said lamely, remembering the champagne laugh in her eyes.

'Well, that's what makes Anna so exceptional, isn't it. She is an alchemist of the heart, turning base grief into laughter, turning gravity into air, turning fog and drizzle into a resplendent golden day.'

'Then what's wrong, what's changed?'

Staring fixedly at the strip of dust beyond the windscreen, he said: 'She begins to see his face again. Begins to feel his touch. Begins to hear his voice. In the trench while she's digging. At home, lying in bed, the touch of his lips…'

'My God… that's why you took her on, wasn't it. Back in Alexandria. She was your first apprentice. That's the thing we all had in common: we all lost someone close to us…'

We sped up the mountainside, the sun infusing our dust cloud like a comet's tail. For the next few miles I could barely speak, but then asked him, 'What's the plan? Where are we going?'

Fighting the bends and almost running us off the road as he wrestled with the map, he just managed to jab at them with his forefinger: those scattered locations where anomalous events had been recorded before.

We're on a wild goose chase, I thought, as we drove fruitlessly from point to point. The measure of his desperation, perhaps, in seeing the anomaly slipping away from us, receding over some unknown horizon where three dimensional minds cannot follow.

By the time we pulled into the town square, the ripening moon was casting its thin shadows over the island, and the sea was restless and swollen.

Tired and demoralised, we were about to head into Alexi's for a beer when he tensed, whispering through clenched teeth: 'Do you see it?'

'See what?' Just the same old people milling about the pebble-dashed streets. The same faces. The same chairs and tables painted blue. The same lamps on the walls, as bright as moons. The same waiter with his tin tray, ferrying wine and raki. The same old men playing *tavli*, hurling the dice, the counters two-stepping across the board like soldiers in hobnail boots.

'There! *There!*' he hisses, and this time I see it instantly, on the rise of the pathway. A slight tremor in the night sky, the stars rippling as if on an unseen wave.

I hold it in my field of vision, but obliquely, already sensing that the more intently I stare, the greater its capacity to meld into the background, to mimic the flickering street lamps, the reflecting windowpanes, the canvas of stars painted over the horizon.

The pretending sky ripples, like a night-reflecting pond into which a pebble has been tossed. And at that precise moment he steps onto the pathway. Comes striding down towards us, and I can feel my heart free-falling off the cliff face.

Benja, the man who refuses to stay dead and buried, bearing down on us, still wearing the same chequered jacket, the same heavy mountain boots. At my side, I can feel Huxley's presence, like flowing water that has turned to ice.

They're not the eyes of a dead man, anyone can see that. They flicker over mine, linger briefly on Huxley as if struggling to grasp the memory or the dream in which this imposing man at the precipice once figured so large. Then with hardly a breath between us, he veers away, pulls up a chair with the *tavli* players, orders wine, lights a cigarette, makes some wisecrack about the luck of the dice. The apparition is no ghost. But flesh and blood.

'Where are we?' I whisper.

'Calm yourself,' he hisses, fighting the faint tremble in his voice.

'Why has he come back? ...Or is it we who have been transported somewhere else without realising?'

He frowns. 'Remember, these are just fluctuations, meaningless in and of themselves. It would stand to reason, wouldn't it, that where the two worlds collide like this, these great upheavals take place. We are only seeing these things at all because this is an anomaly, a mistake, a flaw. The truth, the reality, lies beyond this vain conjuring trick.'

Half-expecting the illusion to pop like a soap bubble, I blink my eyes in rapid succession.

'And yet what a beautiful flaw it is!' he marvels, his eyes drinking in every last detail of the scene before him, the starry sky with its billowing imperfections, the constellations whose shapes and magnitudes are ever so slightly off-key, the Symposiasts' tumbledown windmills on the rise, back to their former glory, their white canvas sails turning in the night wind, the broken tick-tock clock chiming the hour in Alexi's.

Suddenly, Huxley's bounding up the pathway and I don't have to ask why.

'*Wait!*' my voice yelling after him, struck by the irrational terror of being stranded here on this strange rendition of the island, wherever it's supposed to be. I chase after him, leaping up the steps towards the fake sky and the little chapel with its candle-glowing glass and white dome.

He stands outside its lop-sided door, panting.

'Has it gone?'

He nods, still trying to catch his breath. He seems dazed, disoriented.

'Are you all right?' I ask, as he wipes the sweat from his brow, and fleetingly clutches his pounding heart.

Threading our way across *plateia* again, I was not particularly surprised to find that Benja had now been substituted by Nikos the sponge diver, wearing a chequered jacket of slightly muddled design. The grumpy *tavli* players, as was their custom, offered us a curt nod as we passed.

Vowing to press on tomorrow, we said goodnight. I lingered along the precipice pathway, watching the swollen red moon tumble into the sea.

Just as I fell asleep, the day's events dripping and mutating into dream, as they sometimes do, I had to wonder if the Codex might be right after all. Maybe there really were hidden codes in the language in which this Earth was written.

59.

I awoke with a start and a gasp of chill night air.

'*Dad?*' I called, not yet realising what I was seeing was impossible. My father, gliding along the hallway in a kind of luminous mist. His eyes still held that kind, startled look I remember as a child, as though everything in the world came as a surprise to him. He hadn't aged a single day.

Propped up on my elbows, I watched as the light seemed to refract, then shrink to a single bright point as he passed through the front door, into the silent lamplit street.

By seven I was stepping into the fragments hut, ready to resume the hunt. Except it wasn't Huxley I found staring resentfully at that immense jigsaw littering the trestle tables, but Anna.

'Any luck?'

She tossed a fragment back onto the table, and a look of derision at me.

'You make it sound like a crime, Anna. *Is it?* To understand what lies over the horizon.'

'Some things are not ours to know!'

'So we're supposed to remain in fear of it forever, then, like those ancient mariners who swore blind their ships would fall off the edge of the world if they ventured too far.'

'You sound exactly like him. How well he's trained you!'

'No, it's my own freewill!'

She uttered a scornful laugh. 'No, that's just Marcus' disease insinuating its presence everywhere, even into the inner sanctum of your own mind, *his hubris like a virus!*'

The rage of the words seemed to shock even the mausoleum-like silence of the great hut, row upon row of metal shelving, boxes of shattered civilisation, disappearing into the gloom.

'I know about Renato. He told me.'

She looked about to go up in flames, or throw every last fragment on the table at me, but something held her back, maybe his presence inside, or the lingering memory of his touch, alive again.

Her eyes had brimmed with tears, and she angrily brushed them away.

'I saw my father last night,' I confided. 'At least I think I did.'

'Marcus is awakening the dead in everyone — can't you see that? — he and his hateful Ferryman.'

'You can't really believe that. It's just a lump of rock.'

'Is that what you think?' The glance was bitter, almost pitying. 'After all this time at his side, how little you have learned about human psychology, about manipulation, about reality! Do you know why Marcus had the Ferryman returned to the cave?'

I faltered. After all his talk about ancient logic, of reason defeating superstition, that very act, I realised, still nagged at me. It was almost as if he wanted us to believe he was meddling in the occult.

'Because Marcus is being Marcus, that's why. He knew it would churn up powerful emotions in all of us — even in diehard sceptics like Hadrian. Even the act alone changed our reality, changed the way we reacted to one another, made us think, talk and dream of death, and what might lie beyond. Without it, we were just actors miming words on an empty stage. But with the Ferryman back in that warren of tunnels, suddenly he had his psychological prop, he had his scenery, and he had his actors convinced of their own lines.'

'So it's all theatre, is that what you're saying? Smoke and mirrors, just as it's always been.' I shook my head. 'Is it really possible to alter our perceptions like that? So radically?'

Her eyes plunged into mine. 'Have you ever been in love, Nicholas?'

My thoughts drifted to Célestine, but at that moment she seemed farther away than ever. 'Probably not.'

'Then you have yet to discover how the entire universe and everything in it can change in the blink of an eye, when love is given or when it's taken away.'

Under her shocked hands, the shards and fragments began jangling over the tabletop. A teacup rattled to the edge and toppled over, bequeathing its own smithereens to history. Instinctively, we froze. As the tremor rumbled away, Anna jumped to her feet, exasperation yelling in clenched teeth and fists.

'Where are you going?' I called as she marched towards the door.

'To see a man about a volcano!'

I just managed to vault into the jeep as she sped out of camp, pedal to metal. Spurning the dust track for the open fields we headed south along the peninsula, violent jolts threatening to toss us out whenever we kangarooed over a bump or a dune.

Against the charcoal dust, the encampment with flapping white awnings and orange tents was visible a mile away.

As we drew up, a man with a neatly clipped beard thrust his way between the flaps, revealing the seismographs and other sophisticated sensing equipment inside, already humming and whirring.

We had met before, in Huxley's company. Professor George Matsaikis and his team of vulcanologists from Thessalonica.

We nodded hallos. There was an impatient flicker of a smile before he called back into the tent: 'Remember, we need the whole array running before moonrise.'

'Excuse me, did you say the moon?' said Anna, with a puzzled look.

He nodded, the stress of the deadline still telling in his face.

'But why the moon?'

He sighed the sigh of a professor whose students should know better. 'Why? Because it's not only the oceans that are at the mercy of the moon's potent gravitational pull. A full moon can force lava from a vent, trigger eruptions, earth tremors, even make an erupting volcano blow its top...' His eyes swept over the gashed cliffs and immense caldera. 'On an island like this, riddled with holes, you might come to expect it.'

'Then it's not dormant? I mean, apart from the odd snore or convulsion in its sleep?'

'It might doze for a hundred years or a thousand, but it would be unwise to forget that there is an ocean of magma beneath us.'

'Then how on earth are we supposed to sleep?' said Anna, only half in jest, as she gunned the engine and grated into gear.

'Well, if you're like me,' he smiled, raising his voice over the engine, 'you might get to sleep, but not without a chilli pepper dream or two. In fact, when forces collide like this, you might anticipate the odd sensation in broad daylight too.'

'What?' She killed the engine. 'What did you say?'

'Volcanoes and earthquakes,' he explained, resting his arm on the windshield now. 'Primeval forces. They can provoke spikes in the magnetic field, even minor fluctuations in gravity. The psychological effects have been embedded in mythology since time immemorial — yes, just as the full moon has always been associated with magic, madness and monsters. Of course, they even had their own gods.'

'So they can play tricks on our senses, that's what you're saying.'

'Ask anyone who's ever survived an earthquake or a volcanic eruption. They'll tell you: it's your sense of reality that seems to buckle and bend. No wonder in that, perhaps, when what was once rock solid is suddenly rippling under your feet.'

'But... hallucinations, you're not telling me it can provoke hallucinations?'

He regarded her with a flinch of a smile, perhaps wondering how deep ran the fault line or the fissure beyond those eager green eyes. 'Well, as I like to tell my students, I have no scientific proof that *vrykolakes* do not exist: I only know what the folklore tells me: they stalk the island on full moon nights.'

We drove off in a cloud of dust, Anna thumping the steering wheel in triumph. 'Finally. Finally!' she yelled over the wind.

'So it wasn't Huxley at all.' I hardly knew whether to be relieved, baffled or disappointed. 'It was just the volcano.'

'You think he didn't know?' she retorted, the words torn from her lips. 'You think the volcano wasn't all part of the stage scenery? Remember: it wiped out an entire civilisation. It bequeathed us that ghost town on the hill.'

Fault lines, molten fissures, seismic juddering. An island whose mountain volcano was once the circumference of the caldera itself. Could it all be explained away so easily?

'Wait!' I yelled. 'They must be in the log. The diary entries. We were all told that, weren't we. To keep a meticulous record of events, no matter what...' She was still gaping at me in confusion as I leapt out of the jeep and headed for the site office. By mid-afternoon, I had every anomalous event that had ever entered the camp record marked on the site map according to date, volcanic or seismic activity, and lunar phase. When at last I added the entries from Benja's last days on earth I didn't know whether to break down in tears or dance a mad jig around the desks with Maria. The red clusters said it all.

'When is the full moon?' I yelled.

'Tonight,' she replied, as baffled by my intensity as by the ecstatic wet kiss I planted on her cheek.

'No, it's more than that, Maria. It's the equinox. The sun crosses the celestial equator. Everything aligns. Don't you get it?'

60.

Huxley stood in the long shadow of house 16, staring pensively up at the wooden scaffolding. Every now and then he grunted, apparently in grudging recognition of my discovery.

'Fetch me his last notebook!' he commanded, without turning.

'Whose?'

'Benja's, of course!'

I rummaged about until I found it, buried deep in his accordion style briefcase, sandwiched between other paper.

Snatching up the binoculars, he turned between compass points, taking in one landmark at a time.

The sun was already dipping into the caldera, setting flame to the distant temple columns. 'Quickly!' he yelled, unfurling the site map. 'We are running out of time. Read them out to me!'

'What?'

'The numbers, you fool. The numbers on the shopping list!'

I flipped through the pages until it came fluttering out, that jumble of nonsensical figures that had confounded us for months, 522 salted fish, 66 wines, 22 ropes...

As I called them out, his finger went darting over the map.

'I apologise,' he said at last, in a taut voice. 'I am the fool here, not you. This mad shopping list of Benja's is no such thing... The numbers are site coordinates, with the first digits removed, no doubt to throw Guirand's spies off the scent. The others are codes for the full moon, the equinox.'

'Look,' he said, sharing the map with me while uncapping a felt marker between his teeth. 'The path of the sun.' He painted an arc over the mountain volcano as it once stood in ancient days, sky-piercing and snow-capped; over the Oracle cave, temple hill, the sunset horizon. 'That was Benja's epiphany. If there was one thing he knew inside out, it was the lengths to which ancient philosophers, inventors and architects would go to serve the cause of alignment and relationship. And here it is: a design of mathematical genius, an intricate alignment of celestial and volcanic forces.'

'But how did it work?' I said, remembering the chimney-like shaft rising up though star-flecked darkness of the Ferryman's cave.

He grunted. 'When the mountain entered one of its active volcanic phases, that inner vault must have captured, channelled and magnified the light as it burst through the deeper warren of tunnels, the surfaces forming natural obsidian mirrors.'

'That was the Oracle of the Dead?' thinking to myself, then it is all smoke and mirrors... 'So what killed him? What sent Benja flying off the scaffolding?'

When no answer came, I found myself blurting out the words in spite of myself. 'Was it you? Did you kill him? I want to know. The truth this time. And don't tell me I haven't earned it.'

'You think me capable of that?' Returning my unflinching look, I had the impression I was experiencing a landscape of him I had never seen before, one of rolling hills instead of granite cliffs. 'Perhaps you are right. Who knows what we are capable of, what goodness, what depravity —'

'Then what was it? He fell, is that what you're saying? He had nothing to live for. He jumped.'

I caught something in his look. 'Why are you protecting him?'

'Who?'

'Guirand. Doesn't Benja deserve better than that?'

He uttered a torn, reluctant sigh: 'I suppose so; what does it matter now? When we placed him in the well of the Land Rover, Claude was dribbling words along with his drool, less a confession than a boast. *He* had the scaffolding sabotaged, knowing how it would throw the whole camp into turmoil and unleash the state machinery against us. In his mind, that one act proved instrumental in his triumph —'

'*Triumph?*' I sneered.

'His encounter with the Light.'

'And much good it did him. Oblivious to the soul he had lost and to the monster he had become.'

I hesitated, not for the first time stumbling over the facts. '*But wait.* In death, Benja's eyes seemed too bright, too serene, do you remember Anna saying that?'

'Of course. He had found the Oracle. He understood how it functioned, its bending and refraction of light.'

'No. That eureka moment came the night before in the *kalivi*. So too the utter relief of knowing that the hallucinations had been real all along. From that second on, they had become a thing of beauty to him, not fear.'

He threw me a vexed look. 'Then what?'

'He writes about the Wolf Moon, rising; the February full moon. He even remarks about the compasses going haywire that morning, about the tremors striking in the night.'

'Then what? What did he see?'

I gazed up at the scaffolding, remembering vividly the incredible view it commanded, the ancient city an island flooded with early morning light, a sea of shadows all around.

Crouching there, the weight of the revelation was too much for me, and I subsided back into the dust.

'He saw them. Don't you understand? Levitating over the ancient city. He saw the Isles.'

61.

Darkness was gathering swiftly. Of the setting sun, barely an ember remained.

Approaching the crest of the hill, the temple columns were like black ink hieroglyphs against the star sown sky.

'Look,' he murmured, dragging me back a few feet to take in the sight of mighty Orion, finding perfect mathematical harmony between the columns.

We were still staring in silent awe as the full moon rose between the gashes in the crater wall, so heavy, so blood-red it could barely lift itself out of the sea.

And then it began. Across the excavations, sporadic rays of light came bursting through the shafts and boreholes, bringing a faint luminous tinge to the crest of the hill.

By the time I caught up, he was beyond the temple grove, wading through a pool of white light. I could feel the sweat trickling from my armpits, my face turning numb. Twenty paces on, I began to understand what I was seeing: Huxley, standing outside house 34, head tilted down towards his feet, seemingly dazed by the luminescence leaking out from under the makeshift weatherproofing door, by the miniature shaft of light blazing out of the obsolete keyhole. Right under our feet, no one had to remind me, was that vivid warren of rooms where death was being greeted by rapturous faces, the music of the lyre, blizzards of petals.

Roughly, he put his shoulder to the door. Then hesitated. 'We can burst right in,' he whispered back at me. 'Or we can bide our time.'

Torn with indecision, he uttered a ragged sigh. At the keyhole, I was testing the light with my fingertips, marvelling how it made my skin glow as if from the inside. Gently, he drew back my hand. 'If Benja's to be our guide, we must wait for the dawn. After all, it is not the light we seek, but that which lies beyond it.'

Tense enough to snap, we kept our silent vigil, willing the treacle-drop hours to run, the stars to cross the sky, the moon to reach its perfect equinox. Huxley fidgeted, clenched his fists, rolled pebbles around in his palm, muttered at the sky. At the fluting of the wind, the rustle of the weeds, our eyes would scour the darkness, heartbeats thumping, bracing ourselves for another fluctuation... anomalous images reflected onto the retina of time, our own imperfect doubles rippling out of the frescoes. They were almost conspicuous by their absence.

At last the island was regaining its form, shapes without colours or textures emerging into the bloodless light, the craggy face of the Prophet rising brokenly into the sky. At the keyhole, the shaft of light was diminishing. We scrambled to our feet.

'Now!' he rasped, as bright flames caught the charcoal of the dawn sky.

He put his shoulder to the door, and it went scraping roughly across the flagstones.

Planting our feet with care we crossed the threshold, eyes interrogating the gloom. I heard his breath quicken. Among the far shadows, there was still a single point of light, white and ethereal.

We advanced across the marble floor as if on eggshells, and had barely achieved five paces before it flared, sending our hearts into our mouths and our shadows across the walls, hair flying in a sudden unearthly gust of wind, voices ringing in our ears.

Just as abruptly it blew itself out, leaving us standing there under the high vaulted ceiling, struggling against what our eyes were showing us.

Nothing. A bare room, just grand enough to have been a hall of some description in its ancient heyday, filling up with thin grey daylight, and an emptiness that echoed at every word or step.

Six stone arches in rapid succession and then, after a longer interval, a seventh that — with no land or other island feature in sight — appeared to lead out into the limpid blue sky. I sniffed at the curious scent lingering in the air that I knew but couldn't place, something reminiscent of honey, cinnamon and cloves.

'We should have done it!' he rasped. 'We should have been in here, watching, waiting, and to hell with the consequences.'

A rustling drew our attention to the timber roofing supports.

A startled dove, that's all, drawn by the brightening sky beyond. On fantail and beating wings it passed under the sixth arch and quickly reached the seventh, formed by two great stone columns.

An unlucky blink might have missed it entirely: that slight tremble in the sky, that rippling blueness, into which our speckled dove simply vanished without trace. There was a brief fluting of birdsong, and the breeze that swelled over us tasted of forest.

Several seconds later Huxley said in a stunned voice. 'Summon the others. They have a right to know.'

Almost every emotion you could think of was in that billowing tent, its canvas snapping in the wind. Hadrian, sliding each word under the microscope lens, convinced that here lurked either delusion or devious logic. Stoical Nestor, whose loyalty to his Kapítán could be counted on even if the ship were to go down with all hands. Maria, unconsciously trying to hug the strangeness out of herself. Sam clapping his hands together like an autistic child finding some deep, inexplicable reason to rock with laughter.

'You heard what the volcanologists said,' objected Hadrian, on an octave of indignation. 'The full moon, volcanic activity, the seismographs going haywire!'

'Like lie detectors,' observed Anna, with a pointed glare at Huxley, 'flicking over the paper, recording every suspicious twitch and murmur.'

'Your so-called ghosts and doppelgangers are merely volcanic mirages, Huxley, that's all, not apparitions from the dead. Whatever you think you've found up there on the hill, there is nothing mystical about it. Just some ancient mechanism flooding the tunnels with light, ingenious enough, I admit. Just sad pilgrims overcome by the opiates of their own gullibility and the most potent drug known to man: desire... *Apparently no different even in this day and age.*' He uttered a disparaging click of the tongue.

'What would you have us do?' said Anna, her voice stumbling between incredulity and dismay. 'Walk in there...'

'I want you to do what you are paid to do. Your jobs. Examine, decipher, interpret.'

Nestor nodded grimly. 'This thing has been tormenting us ever since our shovels first bit into the ash. We should know what it is, whatever it is.'

'We know what it is!' rasped Hadrian. 'Theatre. Psychological manipulation. No different from any of those dark necromanteia dotted over the ancient world, whose corrupt priests fleeced the living by conjuring up the dead.'

'Then I take it your scientific curiosity has similarly reached a dead end.'

Having successfully painted himself into a corner, Hadrian muttered: 'Oh, no, Huxley. Another ritual debunking, why not?'

Snapping out orders, Huxley said: 'Nestor: I want a tent pitched closer to house 34. We will need shelter, a place to rest. But not too close. We would not wish to draw attention to ourselves.'

'What about security, Kapítán? You can't have those *touristas* wandering about up there or, God forbid, those reporters and cameramen!'

Every pair of eyes settled on Huxley. The adoring feature writers were one thing, their flowery prose still evoking the glories of Atlantis whenever they put pen to paper. The dirt-diggers, however, quite another. Cynical, world-weary, these feral hacks could sniff out a suspicion as instinctively as a jackal scents carrion on the wind. They had even been caught slinking past the guards, scrambling under the wire, trying to insinuate their way into the site office.

'That's what comes of getting into bed with tyrants, Huxley,' said Hadrian, arms folded across his chest. 'Of course the foreign papers set the dogs on us. Who else would willingly fraternize with criminals, but criminals? You wanted the publicity; you wanted the fame: well now you have it by the bucketful!'

'We could post extra guards,' suggested Nestor.

'No. That would only pique their curiosity.'

'Then what?'

'A diversion,' said Anna, as if the words had a foul taste.

Huxley nodded in grim satisfaction. 'Yes. Mr Louganis, you will resume excavations in the southern sector... and make a big spectacle about it.'

'It won't be enough, not for those jackals,' argued Nestor. 'We need something for their noses, something they can sink their fangs into.'

'Give them,' said Huxley, hesitating only briefly, 'their fill of carnal desires. Show them the frescoes that can still bring a blush to the faces of our pretty young students. I regret having to do so, believe me, because I can already hear the shocked, indignant cries of all the pious hypocrites out there.'

'You can't do that!' cried Anna. 'There are people who would take a sledgehammer to them without so much as batting an eyelid. There has to be another way.'

'We have to be practical,' growled Huxley. 'We have to be pragmatic.'

'*What about principle!*'

'Principles confine us, they do not set us free.'

He ordered razor wire fences erected and put Tassos on sentry duty, that lumbering barnyard animal of a youth with thickset eyes, who could be trusted to march up and down with a hunting rifle over his shoulder and nothing even vaguely curious in his head.

It was hard just focusing on the odd jobs that had been assigned to us, the hours all shot to hell, in tattered pieces, spinning off in every direction, and pulling us with them.

I was helping Nestor put up the army tent below house 34, in a field that the spring rains had turned into a sea of poppies. When a harried Huxley happened by, I asked: 'Is it dangerous? Is it stable? How long can it last?'

As I spoke, I realised I had been worrying about it for hours. If the phenomenon really did owe its existence to some flaw or rupture in the physical fabric of the universe, who was to say death couldn't enter our world from the other side, first as a trickle, then a flood?

'Death will always be dangerous to those who cling to living,' he snapped, already tormented to distraction by our incessant, childish questions.

Over the guy ropes, he turned to Nestor, saying: 'Take Aris aside, Nestor, make him understand the gravity of the situation, tell him: be on the lookout for prowlers; people who pretend to be who they are not, people in disguise, people who may even resemble ourselves; trust no one.'

Catching my wondering look, he snapped: 'It's just a precaution, that's all.' Adding with distaste, 'These doubles or variations of us, we don't even know what they are or where they come from...'

The experience had unnerved him far more than he cared to admit, I could tell. Ghosts of the dead were one thing, ghosts of the living quite another.

'What about the Comte? Shouldn't he know?'

'Know what?' he growled. 'What is there to know when we know nothing ourselves!' Narrowing his eyes at me, he added with ruthless humour: 'If it's Célestine you're pining after, you would do well to set your heart on snatching her from the clutches of King Hades himself, because that is the only way the Comte would ever contemplate relinquishing her. One word: *knowledge!*'

As he spoke, it was as if some forgotten dream had flared into my eyes, and I was seeing them on some far-flung island, Célestine, Jean, walking through a forest of tall silver birches, shafts of sunlight striking between them.

By day's end, everything was in place, the tent pitched, canvas army cots sprung together, a wicker hamper stuffed with food and drink packed by Huxley's housekeeper, Myroula.

For an hour or more after the nightfall, the only source of light was the intermittent glow from Huxley's pipe, casting our faint silhouettes against the canvas.

And then, almost imperceptibly, it began again, a white, almost liquid luminescence seeping out of house 34.

I heard Hadrian rustling in his clothes as he struggled out of his chair, his scientific honour insulted again.

He lumbered up the hill, wheezing indignantly, until at last he stood at the plank wood door, peering at the curious light that appeared to be penetrating the leather of his shoes, revealing the outline of his feet and toes in a kind of fuzzy aura.

62.

Drifting silhouettes in the twilight, we made our silent way towards the temple heights and house 34. Dawn was almost upon us. So, too, the inescapable moment of truth.

At the plank wood door Huxley turned to us, his stubbled face curiously golden in the rising sun. Lips parting, he was all set to repeat his admonishments about rules and procedures when, with a sharp intake of breath, his eyes caught a movement over our shoulders.

'My God,' he hissed. 'Who has betrayed us?'

Against the bloodless tephra I almost missed him entirely. A wan figure in black robes and stovepipe hat, riding a charcoal mule: Huxley's blood-and-thunder nemesis, Constantine Nannos.

Hurriedly, we descended the hill, if only to throw him off the scent.

Arms folded defiantly across his chest, Huxley was already standing like a stone sentinel in the middle of the street, aiming to block the priest's path.

A war of words appeared inevitable, accusations of sorcery and devil worship and God knows what else. Any moment now, the priest's reinforcements would arrive, that cloud of dust at the gates heralding the arrival of the police, even a contingent of conscripts from the barracks.

The old man dismounted with difficulty, a wince of pain creasing his lips.

Smouldering eyes scorching each of us in turn, he swept towards us, robes billowing like a spinnaker in the wind.

Face to face, he locked Huxley's arm in his and wheeled around, the movement as ruggedly graceful as a Cretan dance. The fluid motion now had both facing, not ghost houses or temples or the hive of activity in camp, but the blue caldera as limpid as an eye.

'I have not told another living soul, Huxley, so spare me, I beg you, unnecessary pretence.'

Even in profile, you could see the shockwave breaking over him, his eyes widening, then flinching. Perhaps, in his self-obsessed way, he had underestimated this Orthodox priest, whose genius in reading and plotting conspiracy was as old as Byzantium itself.

Huxley's volcanic eyes swept over the rest of us, no doubt hunting for some convenient scapegoat for later sacrifice. With what little grace he could muster, he steered the Papás towards the field tent, a curt gesture of the hand commanding me to follow.

At Huxley's sullen bidding, Father Nannos subsided into a chair around the camp table, again with a wince of pain, sweat beading his brow. I brought him a glass of water, for which he nodded his thanks. I glanced at Huxley. Beyond the brooding eyes you could almost hear the scheming of his mind like restless insect wings.

'Then I won't conceal it from you, Papás,' he began, with a curious air of defiance. My eyes widened in shock. *What was he doing?* 'There is some force up there on the hill we cannot explain. But what? True, I have long held out the hope that it is, as ancient legend attests, a window on the world that awaits us. But what if I am deceived, what if it is nothing but an ignis fatuus, a volcanic phenomenon that merely corrupts our perceptions of reality?'

'I come to you not out of some idle curiosity, Huxley. I come to you because I am dying.'

The canvas awning snapped in the wind, startling me almost more than the revelation itself.

Propping up his head with both hands as if it had suddenly swelled in weight, Huxley replied: 'It might well be dangerous, Papás, whatever it is. For all we know, it will kill us all.'

My eyes darted at him. For a second I could barely hear them over my own galloping heartbeat. I told myself: it's just a ploy to get the priest out of our hair, that's all.

'When Stavros Sanassis sprang the truth upon me, that my life could now be measured in days or weeks, it was to see everything under the sun change in shape and meaning. Perhaps I am a weaker man than my vanity once had me believe, because I find myself in the desert, under a mute sky, no longer certain that faith alone can be enough to sustain any of us.'

Thoughts meeting in battle, Huxley regarded his old adversary through narrowed eyes. The word 'no' was already on his lips, and to hell with the consequences, when the priest said:

'What if only nothingness awaits us, for all the hymns and prayers we have cast up into the sky? What if heaven is but the figment of fragile men who merely wish it to be so? My expiring soul, I feel sure, would let out an anguished cry so deep it would echo between the stars themselves. Yet for all that, I would know truth before the lie. I would choose certainty above the doubt that is faith's constant companion. Will you help me, Huxley. Will you help an old dying man peer beyond the glorious vanity of his own mind?'

Pensive, silent, Huxley remained immoveable in his canvas chair, the fingers of his right hand digging into his temple. I watched him clench his jaw several times in rapid succession, and if I hadn't known him better, might even have concluded he was fighting back his emotions.

'Then you shall join us, Father,' he said in a measured voice, oblivious to my bewildered look.

I broke the news to the others. Hadrian grumbled: 'There has to be an ulterior motive, mark my words, whatever's been cooked up for us up there. *The Papás?* He detests the man!'

63.

Despising the conventional route, Huxley cut across the poppy fields, leaving a trail of bloodied petals in his wake.

Crossing the agora, he maintained his relentless pace, obliging the rest of us to press on after him. Anna, her face numb with trepidation. Father Nannos, skirts hitched up about his ankles, muttering prayers into the lark's blue sky. A florid-faced Hadrian, the good doctor still convinced he's on his way to a ritual debunking, where scepticism will run through the unknown like a dose of salts.

We found Aris marching up and down temple square, a blade of grass between his teeth, a hunting rifle slung lazily over his shoulder.

'What was Nestor thinking?' said Anna, in a vexed, incredulous voice. 'Aris doesn't need a gun!'

By the time we entered the last stretch my heart was pounding in my chest with an echo I could feel in my fingertips. There it was, looming up before us, that innocuous looking house with the number '34' chalked onto the faded blue and ochre facade. There was no turning back now, whatever was waiting for us.

With a shove, the crude plank door swung open, grating over the stones.

Eyes finding focus far beyond our expectant faces, Huxley said in an mechanical voice: 'I shall not be joining you. Not this time.'

The same word burst out of our mouths in a bewildered chorus: 'What?'

'The man who has moved heaven and earth just for this moment?' cried Anna.

'If I were to join you,' he rebuked us, 'there would be no scientific control, none whatsoever. The experiment would lose all validity.'

Hadrian muttered, 'Of course. The necromanteion always needed its priest, if only to pull the strings, light the incense, make the shadow puppets dance...'

Pre-empting any further argument, he reeled off our instructions. We were to approach the seventh arch side by side. We were not to communicate or distract one another in any way.

'And a word of caution,' he added. 'A red line now marks the floor at the seventh arch. Do not cross it. Do not be tempted even to put a toe over it. I say that because, if you do, I cannot vouch for the consequences.'

Nothing more was said, not even a few last words of encouragement. He merely nodded his head dismissively, his mouth set in a firm, impassive line.

'Courage, children,' said Father Nannos, turning to face the cold echoing chamber and its sequence of arches. 'Courage!' as Hadrian's nostrils twitched at the bittersweet scent in the air, reminiscent of cinnamon, cloves, some sultry resinous spice.

We moved as one, bunching together a little as we passed between the great stone columns. I could already see the danger line marking the marble flagstones in fire engine red.

Nearing it, something of the phenomenon itself or its imperfect camouflage became apparent in the glow of the sky; indistinct, like a heat haze that shimmers over a summer horizon.

Three more steps, and I'm thinking, *there's so many things left unsaid*

Mist. It rises from the marshes like a gangrenous fever. My feet squelch through putrid mud, the bony fingers of the trees scratching at my face, the dust moths fluttering into my eyes.

Panic clutches me by the throat. I'm hammering on the back of my eyelids, trying to wake up, trying to break out. Except I know I'm not asleep.

The bog marshlands of the Styx and Acheron. The abode of the dead, where five rivers meet. Greyness as far as the eye can see. The sky entombing us like a concrete slab.

A ragged column of dead stumble towards the river, men, women, children with mute bloodless faces, driven on by the cracking whips of the guards, the snarls of the dogs.

Sam, Anna, Father Nannos, they're shuffling into line, their faces, their eyes already dead.

The path strikes through the marshlands, the reeds cackling as we trudge between them single-file.

I was supposed to remember something, what was it? Something among the memories already seeping away into the numb black river.

'*Dad? Is that you?*'

It is, an apparition between the bone-splintered branches, between the matted hair leaves. Calling out with words that have no sound.

He comes stumbling towards me through the swirling dust, his face splotched with hollow shadows where the wry mouth, the startled eyes used to be. Miming words at me.

What is he saying?

'Fight, Nico! Fight them! Do not give up. Not ever! Rage against the fools who have created this place! The Realm of King Hades! Say it Nico, say it, you remember what! Tell the guards! *No, don't run!*'

But I am running. I'm running as fast as my buckling legs can carry me. Ducking under the branches entangled with lichen grey hair, crashing through the splintering reeds, flying headlong into the marsh. The stinking mud squelches around my ankles as I wade through, each step heavier, more impossible than the last, the fetid water up to my chest, up my chin, up to my nostrils.

Unceremoniously, the guards fish me out, their blank dead stares as inert as the entombing sky.

I don't know what it is. I can feel the numbness spreading through my limbs like curare, then the poisonous thought that comes with it: You can't do it. You don't have it in you. Why struggle against the eternity that claims you.

Drink! command the guards. *Drink!* the miming silence ringing in our ears.

The River of Oblivion. It glides by at our feet, swollen with fading cries.

Something I am supposed to remember word for word. No, something that *will* remember, that's it. Something of me that will forever remember.

Say: 'I am the son of Earth and Starry Heaven. Please give me something to drink from the River of Mnemosyne.'

As the words rumble out across the barren landscape, even the grey pall that is the sky seems to quiver in surprise. It sounds like thunder, the pattering of rain.

If only for an instant, the fog lifts over the marshes, bringing with it an insinuation of sun. Between the rising veils, I catch a fleeting glimpse of them: sentinel trees against the skyline, the slope of a distant mountain.

'Then kneel at the river of memory,' mouths the guard, finding some remnant knowledge of this forbidden rite buried inside. I stumble to my knees. The water. It's almost luminous as I lift my cupped hands to my lips…

If ever I was asleep, in dream or in death, I awake to a fast-flowing river, all blue and green under the ancient platanos trees.

The other side must be the far edge of the world, the boundary that separates all that is from all that is not.

A wooden punt comes gliding up to the shore on the swirling current, and there's no mistaking the identity of the tall figure standing at the stern, his face obscured by a black cowl.

'You'll carry me to the far shore?' The Ferryman offers a single abrupt nod, motioning me to take my seat, reserved for me by name.

At least his hands aren't all bone and gristle, I think, taken by surprise by the inexplicable laughter bubbling up inside. The punt wobbles and dips as I step aboard, and no sooner have I taken my place than we slide off the grassy bank, the little boat pirouetting in the current.

'But I can't pay you anything,' I say in sudden consternation, rifling through my empty pockets.

Punting pole spearing the riverbed, we hesitate, begin to turn. 'No! Wait!' my fingers retrieving a silver drachma from my shirt; only one man can have put it there. The Ferryman studies the coin intently before pocketing it with single abrupt nod; an understanding, apparently, between principals.

Several white egrets go darting up the river in a spray of light and water, the tips of their wings feathering the ripples into a different pattern. A kingfisher dips between the rushes.

'It is a beautiful river,' I say, 'not at all what I imagined, not at all what the legend had us believe.'

'And what is it that it had you believe?' His voice is almost resonant, as if it had assumed the dialect of the river itself.

'That you are all about darkness and grief, the end of everything we know.'

'Then it has never occurred to you, that perhaps the dead resent being dragged to life as much as the living to the dead. If you had listened intently enough, you might have heard it in the first unhappy shriek of the newborn babe.'

'You would know that far better than I.'

'Not I. I ferry souls to the other side, and were it not for their laments and tumbling memories, I would know nothing of the worlds beyond in either direction.'

We drift diagonally across the river. Every so often, the Ferryman will correct our course, driving the punting pole between the clacking riverbed stones, as if by some sixth sense that anticipates the shifting currents.

I'm spellbound by everything I see. The water's buoyant lilt over the shallows. The concentric ripples at play in the deep. The motion of the trees in the wind. The exuberant clouds over the distant peak. The surge of resplendent light through the forest.

'Why are the colours so intense?'

'You would expect anything less, where two worlds collide?'

Two worlds. Two banks of the river. His very existence, his language, his concept of the universe, is bound and shaped by them.

'But what if we don't cross the river at all?' I ask. Playing the innocent, just like that. 'What if we were to head downstream instead, let the current take us where it will?'

But answer comes there none; unless, that is, I am supposed to divine the gurgling water or the hollow clopping of the riverbed stones.

'Why won't you answer me?'

'Because there is no new combination of words that you can find that I have not heard before,' he replies at last. 'When they sit in my ferryboat, sooner or later everyone pleads and bargains. For their life, for their past, for their destiny, that which now cannot be changed.'

'You mean to tell me you have never had the curiosity? You have never once wondered what it must be like, beyond the borders marked by the river bank?'

For the first time I can hear his breath, nasal, laboured.

'Do you even know what lies downstream?'

He shakes his head in that abrupt, taciturn way of his.

'Then upstream?'

Again that motion of the head, almost imperceptible beyond the shadow of the cowl.

'Then what malicious god has imprisoned you here? What petty deity has condemned you to ferry the dead for all eternity? Back and forth, back and forth.'

'Each has his own fate, that which cannot be deviated by mere will or wish.'

I think to myself, what would Huxley say now? What trick would he pull, what subversive piece of logic that would defeat or befuddle his opponent?

371

'All rivers spring from the hills and flow to the sea,' I argue, 'that is *their* fate, and yet you defy their destiny every time you punt this boat from one side to the other. How do you explain that?'

He must have caught me mid-blink, because the gasp's still in my chest. And there I go, swept away on the swirling current, dazed, winded, my shoulder still smarting where the punting pole has struck its glancing blow, toppling me overboard.

'So you *can* cheat destiny,' I yell, as I tumble over the shallows.

'You imagine it so?' Words so dry they appear to float towards me like fallen leaves.

64.

When I came to, it was to find myself still sitting under the sixth arch, alone. Scrambling to my feet, I made may way out into the brilliant sunshine, the wind tugging at my shirt.

Checking my watch, I was surprised to find that barely an hour had gone by, not days, not weeks.

Maybe it was just the euphoria of making it back in one piece, escaping Hades like some golden warrior of legend, but somehow there was a resonance, a vibrancy, a poetry to the world I had never quite realised before, that flight of migratory birds crossing an indigo sky, those darkening wave patterns running through a sea of poppies.

My tongue was swollen with thirst, my stomach hollow and churning. I needed water. Fighting the wobble in my legs, I made my way towards the sailcloth awning that Nestor had strung between the southern temple columns.

Just then our guard turned the corner and stopped dead in his tracks. I kept on walking. Aris raised his gun, squinting as much from the glare off the flagstones as from his own fierce reckoning. But as we came face to face, he lowered the rifle with a grin, apparently satisfied that in my face he had found something that was undoubtedly, genuinely me. I was relieved.

Huxley glanced up from his papers as I flopped down on the temple steps. There was no disguising the look on his face, tense, expectant, interrogating. I could only imagine how excruciating it must have been for him, forcing himself to play by his own ground rules, resisting the impulse to fire questions at me point blank.

Avoiding my eyes, he handed me my notebook and pen. 'Sit over there and write,' he ordered brusquely, banishing me to the farthest corner.

After sloshing water into a glass half a dozen times just to take the edge off my thirst, I did just that, catching the odd glimpse of my fellow travellers as I put pen to paper. A wan Father Nannos, panting in little bird-like gasps, being helped into the jeep by Maria. Anna, weaving between the temple columns, a quiet song on her lips, and that magic carpet look in her eyes I hadn't seen for months.

No sooner had I put down my pen than Huxley ordered us all back to base camp.

Playing up like children, we crowded under the awning or into the tent itself, grabbing whatever places we could find among the folding chairs or the camp beds.

'In view of his frailty and exhaustion,' proclaimed Huxley, grating his teeth at the hubbub, 'I shall read from Father Nannos' account myself.'

It was enough to kill the teasing and bickering at a stroke.

I glanced at Sam. There it was again. That look I had only ever seen in trapdoor moments of unreality, Cycladic blue eyes that carry no guard, no gun. I caught Huxley's frown and knew he'd seen it too.

★

'That marvel in the sky!' Huxley began, the Papás' words lifted by the wind billowing into the tent. 'I can tell, child, that you are burning to know what it permitted these old, unworthy eyes to see, yet I must beg your indulgence a moment longer. Because I would not wish anyone to be deceived by these, the vestments and trappings of my church, my robes, my crucifix, my book of prayers. You see, I came to you less as a man dying in flesh than a man dying in faith.

I see that surprises you, yet it is in ritual most well-rehearsed that truth can best be disguised — from oneself even more than from others.

Keener eyes than mine might have seen it in my stoop, in my cantankerousness, in the mechanical way I performed every rite or duty, in the dull advice or comfort I dispensed to the needy.

Yet as a boy I was drawn, not drummed, into the priesthood. I marvelled at the lives and adventures of the saints. In the jewel sky of night I knew the existence of God without recourse to faith or scripture. Yet when next I looked, when next I asked, my whiskers were grey, my eyes had dimmed, and in place of the boy with the yearning heart I found an embittered old man losing his reason to be. In the heavenly sky now, not stars of wonder, but dead pinpoints of light.

Abroad, I had heard, there were men of science who had declared that God was dead. But I could not fathom their meaning. Did they mean that we had imagined God all along? That He had gone away to die by the wayside, unrecognised and unwanted? Or that our logic had slain him as surely as a steel sword slashing through flesh and bone on the battlefield?

When Stavros Sanassis broke the news to me, I knew there could be no hiding place anymore, even as I climbed the steps to the church, and stood under its echoing dome.

Sweep away all the clutter, as a dying man must do, and what is left? Take away the icons, the devotional candles, the tin votives, the incense, the relic bones, and what is left? An empty building in the shape of a church. A painted universe above our heads.

I know nothing of your will, nothing of your purpose! I cried, the words finally tumbling from me. *I cannot even explain the meaning of life to a child, nor of death to the bereaved!*

And so it was I came in search of epiphany to that ancient house on the hill.

Of those exquisite images that have somehow survived the brightness of day, I will tell you: I saw angels drawn in light. I saw gardens and wondrous trees. Joyous faces, and all manner of creatures, their earthly strife forgotten.

I saw men and women I took to be saints, their bodies all aglow, their heads ringed by a golden nimbus. I thought I recognized Aghios Giorgios and Aghios Spyridon but, as I passed them along the way, their great faces beaming kindness, it seemed they remembered neither their great deeds nor even their own names. They had found eternity, and the serenity that abides there.

I came to a child under the teeming stars, head thrust back between his shoulders, drinking in the sky. *Who are you, child?* I asked. *Who has abandoned you here, all alone?* As a shooting star drew a taper of light across the heavens, he spun around, his young face snatching my voice away. I knew this child. His eyes, they were brimming with wonder, yes, but something else, something more precious than all the sacred scriptures in the whole wide world: that unspoken instinct that recognises kinship, a single soul between the stars. I remembered then: the child I once was. The child I shall ever be.'

'Well, that's it,' said Huxley, snapping the book shut, his mocking grimace drawing puzzled looks from around the tent. Maybe it was just the Christian mythology that had rattled his cage; or was it the ghost of his own father?

Sam was next, the euphoria that had kept him company all the way down the hill already wearing-off, judging from the uneasy shadow now passing along the battlements of his eyes.

★

'I got to the line. Stared into that elliptical patch of sky. Not blue as it should be, but black, blacker than night,' he began, the first halting words finally submitting to the hypnotic memory they contained, like summer meadows remembered in amber cells of honey. 'There's nothing there. *Nothing.* No, wait. Just a faint speck of something. A pinhole in a black formless Void... Or is it an exploding star? I watch as it sweeps towards me, swelling in size and magnitude... Until I realise, no, it's *you*, you're the one who's streaking towards the light.

There, where it touches, I appear to be turning into light myself, and the more of the light I become, the faster I streak through the blackness.

Up close, it's like a luminous beating heart. Like a nebula, with towering clouds of celestial dust, waterfalls of light, coloured pebbles of stars.

The orbits of these worlds, they paint infinite circles across the Void, patterns, forms of relationship that would take an eternity and a universe like this to understand at all.

I'm thinking, there's lives of me in each of those worlds, isn't there, and maybe it's the shock of realising it, but suddenly I'm hurtling towards the mantle of some random globe of light, I'm tumbling out of the sky.

At least it seems that way. Because the next thing I know, I'm walking out into the sunshine again, squinting against the glare. Crossing the agora, on the lookout for Aris. Except something's not right.

Everything's not right.

Under my sandaled feet, there's newly milled stone. In the gardens, moist earth, blossoming trees. Under the river bridge, cascading water. To the north, the pyramid volcano, soaring over the city, two miles high, its summit still white with summer snow.

Donkeys with laden panniers enter the square, hooves clattering across the flagstones. Farmers' carts, piled high with watermelons, grapes, purple figs. I'm threading my way between the market stalls with their bright awnings. Children playing tag, saffron gatherers, farmers, fishermen, artisans, young women in spice-dyed robes, boys whose beauty could rob you of your senses, people I've seen a thousand times in the frescoes, come to life, flesh and blood.

What am I doing here? Who am I? But it's just a passing thought, isn't it, some kind of existential angst, like you have sometimes.

Unconsciously, my hands obey the ritual, gathering a new batch of herbs, spices, minerals. Saffron and cayenne, lapis and indigo. Second nature to me now, as I cross to the townhouse on the crest of the hill, its sky terraces facing west, the sun streaming in through the windows to meet a kaleidoscope of colour, a timber scaffold balancing against the walls.

Thalassa, insisted my boss — *I want everything about the sea.*

So I will give him what he wants, dolphins and sea horses, mermaids and Posidonia meadows, octopus and fishy shoals, but what else... *What else?*

Daydreaming, my gaze is drawn through the open windows, down into the marketplace below. That's when I catch sight of him, weaving between the market stalls, a fish basket on his bare shoulder.

Aris. Or whatever he calls himself here. Not quite as innocent as he pretends either, judging from the silver dagger concealed at his waist, or the insolent bow he offers the temple priest he passes on the hill.

The light of him passes through the window, enters my eye, causing the pupils to dilate, the iris to quiver, the idea to flood the mind. Why not? After all the frescoes I have given this city, haven't I deserved the immortality? To place myself there on the quay, disguised as a fisherman myself, a cast net slung over my shoulder, a brace of sea bream in my hand.

I whistle down to him as he passes under the windows, and Phaestos, he needs little coaxing to climb the stairs, strip off his clothes, and stand there against the blue prism sea.

Sea salt serpentines across his skin. Now and then his glance drifts to the sleeping bunk I use on long hot summer afternoons like these, and I know it won't be over when I'm finished with him here, even as our likenesses finally emerge from the wet plaster.

There is something about his beauty... far beyond the tangle of golden hair, the summer skin, the impossibly long eyelashes, the tongue-wettened lips; it's hard enough just to still the shake in my hands — *me!* behaving like some lovesick boy — fumbling now with the brushes and paints, swallowing hard, trying to concentrate, knowing I'll have to paint from memory or imagination a phallus far less swollen, far less demanding than that... After all, what would the master say?

Trying to escape that feeling... this beauty cannot be contained or controlled, can it. Not in flesh. Not in pigment. Not even in ideas flying between the worlds that we are.

No. There is danger, I sense that already, even if I don't know why... It's in his question, "Where is the master of the house?" his muscles tensing until he hears that the master is on his estates on Keftiu. It's in his silver dagger with the ebony handle, hidden in that bundle of clothes on the floor, a warrior's knife, not a fisherman's. It's in those restless glances down to the temple square, priests and pilgrims coming and going. It's in those cornflower blue eyes with their seductive parody of innocence, like so many of the youths in this glistening city.

The journey back was a sensation I can hardly describe, except to say it felt like I was being decanted into a kind of physical receptacle, a glass jar. Like one of those stupid street mimes in Paris, who silently try to feel their way out of the invisible walls that contain them.

That's what bothers me most, I suppose. Somehow, the experience has altered me inside, it has known my soul. You think any of us can go back to living as we did?'

'Next!' said Huxley, tossing his head in a vague gesture of disgust.

Anna. Scrambling off the camp bed. Pulling up a chair. Opening her notebook, closing it, the record too clumsy, too dry. Taking a deep breath, oblivious to Huxley's darkening mood. A sunflower pointing its beaming face towards the bruise-black clouds of a gathering storm.

★

'Oh, I don't even know what I should call it, an act of God, an act of nature or an act of man, but whoever, whatever, is responsible I don't care!

You all know the foreboding I felt: that whatever presence lingered in this abandoned city, it spelt something dark and ominous for our lives. Perhaps what you don't know is that in some secret place inside I did keep the vigil, I did keep the flame alight, hoping against hope that we would meet again, somewhere, somehow.

378

When I lost Renato, you see, something inside me also died. From one fractured second to the next the world became a different place. One in ruins after the Bomb has hit.

I caught the scent in the air as I passed under the arches, the summer orchards, the river, a scent so potent I

I find myself in the Via Amelia, walking under the plane trees with their deer-dappled bark. Along the river now with its bright circles and languid currents.

There it is in the distance, the *Pensione Galileo*, with its tall windows and narrow little balconies.

I can hardly walk for my own heartbeats, like dizzy waves breaking across the shore, passion and dread, passion and dread.

I slip past the *senora* at the front desk, why I can't imagine, for her smile scatters across the little foyer, warm and knowing.

One flight of stairs and there I am, *camera cinque*, the peeling grey door whose unassuming face so cleverly disguises a love too vivid to be contained beyond anything else.

I hesitate, hand mid-air, ready to knock, the thought just crossing my mind that I'm losing touch with whatever part of me is still on the island, staring into this sweet distortion.

It doesn't matter. I can hear him scrambling off the bed, his hand on the door, and the door flies open.

And it is him, it is! living, breathing, with those soul-mischievous eyes that seem to shine with the laughter of some half-forgotten world. *Renato!*

"Where have you been, Anna?" a torn smile, a frown, melting, as he gathers me up into his arms, smothers me with kisses. Oh Mnemosyne, it's as if I had never forgotten those sweet lips at all, that inquisitive tongue, the fading just the amnesia of pain.

He pulls away in reproach, bright curls tumbling into his eyes: "You have been gone forever, Anna! You should have written, you should have called!"

And before I know where I am, there I am, floating upon the crisp white sheets, wet, naked, plunging into the hot blood of our souls. Ready to catch the wave surging towards us, lifting us, thrusting us into the sky, and as that star-trembling moment comes, *heart-stopping, echo pounding*, as souls collide and the light bursts all around, how can I describe it, I am everywhere, I am everything… *in your love I can see from one end of the universe to the other!*

Renato's at the mirror now, running his hands through his hair, putting on his shirt.

"Don't go, Renato," I call out to him, still flopping on the pillows, as tense as honey.

"I have to, my love," he says, knotting his tie, tossing the words at my reflection instead of me. "A few days on the road. I will be back before you know it. I promise. May God strike me down if I tell a lie."

Strange, it seems little more than a premonition now, doesn't it, a dream you forget over breakfast.

An accident. A black crushing hole where my heart used to live. The shriek of tearing steel, the wail of ambulances. *But how, when?*

Running a red light, that's it, too much espresso in their veins, too much anger, chasing money, strangling time by the throat. A tremor runs through me; it's like touching a live wire.

It's going to happen all over again, isn't it. He's going to die all over again. I can't live through that, I can't, not again. How will you do it, Anna? the panic pounding in my head making it difficult to think at all. *How will you alter what has already been written? How will you defeat what fate has already conspired against you?'*

Under Huxley's glower, the camp sceptic took his place.

★

'I did not appreciate the experience one bit,' sniffed Hadrian, 'whatever it was. For the record, I continue to harbour the unwavering suspicion that we are being credulous or, even worse, deliberately deceived. That said, I could not miss the opportunity of experiencing this so-called phenomenon first-hand, if only to be in a better position to challenge and refute some of the more asinine and far-fetched explanations that were bound to cling to its discovery.

I was conscious of an indistinct yet curious odour, a sweetness shot with spice, that I could not place. Interrogating that patch of shimmering sky, I mentally patted myself on the back because, clearly, I was experiencing no effects whatsoever.

I glanced at my watch. Half an hour had passed. *This is ridiculous!* I muttered, and turned to leave, all the more irritated by my companions, apparently lost to some morbid state of trance.

Just as I turned on my heel, I caught the faint echo in my ear. Where was it coming from? Not that dubious patch of blue, no, but from everywhere, the arches, the columns, even the skin of my companions.

Ever so faint, ever so beguiling. And oh yes, even if I had never heard it before, I knew what I was hearing now. Of course I did, the idea had captivated me for years as a boy: the *music of the spheres!* That mathematical pulse of sound that Pythagoras himself deduced all heavenly bodies must emit as they move in relation to one another. I was hearing what was impossible to hear, that which is inaudible to the human ear. Stars, planets, nebulae, galaxies, composing their own exquisite symphony through the vastness that is space.

Thankfully, I fought the temptation to surrender to that siren song tooth and nail. And indeed, it was with a sense of utter relief that I finally emerged into the spring sunshine once more, my feet planted on *terra firma* once more.

As to the true nature of this phenomenon, this invention, this artifice, we are still all at sea. Whatever the truth, I feel compelled to end on a note of caution. That this *thing* might pose a risk to life and limb goes without saying. But what of its effect upon our minds, our lives, our concept of reality — something so inherently subversive?

Yes, subversive! How else can one possibly regard it? Can there be any greater nightmare for science — or even religion for that matter? To find oneself in a universe where, *ipso facto*, there is no objective truth worthy of the name. Where fact and falsehood, truth and illusion exist simultaneously, simply depending upon the angle from which reality is being perceived? Where indisputable truth there is none — merely interpretation?'

Huxley's eyes jerked open and he said in a clenched, sarcastic voice, 'Et tu, Mr Pedrosa?'

65.

As I closed my notebook, he snorted derisively. Even the musical beauty of the Styx had failed to move him. I threw him a puzzled look and, as our eyes met, he blew up in our faces.

'What *is* this?' he bellowed, leaping up from the table, the chair tipping over behind him. 'You all entered house 34 at precisely the same moment and left only minutes apart — yet none of you saw even remotely the same thing. *How is that possible?*'

'Let me get this straight,' said Hadrian, leaping gratefully at this I-told-you-so moment. 'Are you finally admitting that your *Oracle of the Dead* is no such thing?'

'Without a single common thread linking your experiences?' He shook his head in loathing. 'No. We are no closer than ever. All we have is mythology, metaphor, symbols, no different than it ever was!'

Sensing Anna about to object, he silenced her with a swift and brutal gesture of the hand. 'How else would you characterise it? The Papás, his afterlife replete with saints and angels, the lion laying down with the lamb! You, Anna, reunited with the man of your dreams, not on some far distant shore, no, but in the Pensione Galileo the day before he dies… I could say the same for all of you, yes, even you, Hadrian, with your music of the spheres from your emotionally stilted childhood. In reality they are merely the projections of your own personal aversions and desires, that's all. Of the objective truth that lies beyond you, your own minds and personalities, there is nothing, nothing at all!'

'You're all the same,' said Sam. 'Take one step out of your own minds and you're lost. Did it never occur to you that whatever's in there might be showing us far more than that — far more than afterlife?'

'What do you mean?' Huxley bristled. 'What are you saying?'

'That it *is* an oracle… just not the one you were expecting. Instead of the future, it's showing us something else: possibility in the making, variations of ourselves in other places, other times.'

Huxley glared at him. 'Do you know what you're saying? If I accept that, I accept that there is no truth at all — no universal concept of truth.'

'Is that a problem for you?' The words sounded abrasive, even insolent, until he added, almost as an afterthought: 'Each experience was
unique to us individually — what does that tell you?'

Hadrian squinted, like a man trying to find the end of a lost thread.
What was Weed Boy really saying? Was he actually conferring upon
this thing the rudiments of purpose, even logic?

'Whatever is out there,' added Sam, 'it knows us far better than we
know ourselves. That's what I've been saying.'

A sudden gust from the sea billowed into the tent, snapping the
canvas.

'Are we talking about God now, is that what we have been reduced
to?' demanded Hadrian, on a surge of irritation.

'Or fate,' insisted Sam, with grim vanity. 'One that might still
determine our path, who we are, who we might become. Imagine:
events being formed out of molten possibility.'

Finding the idea impossible to stomach, Huxley angrily waved him
off: 'If that were true, how many universes would there be? How many
versions of people and places and events? We would be creating them
with every thought, every permutation of the moment...' He trailed
off, the words drowning in their own dismay... 'No, no, I will have
none of it. The Codex promised truth, not meaningless figments of our
own psyches.'

Another argument broke out around the table, each voice trying to
shout down the other.

He was still pacing back and forth, fingernails digging into his
scalp, when the thunderclap shocked us into silence. 'Look at you!
Do you even hear yourselves? Still blabbing about fate, karma, divine
providence, natural phenomena. Is it any wonder I tell you, we are no
closer to the truth than ever before!'

'Then look for yourself!' cried Anna, her patience in tatters. 'Have
you even looked?'

'Of course he hasn't,' said Hadrian. 'He wanted the results from
his guinea pigs first. Just in case anything were to go wrong. He was
afraid.'

As that revelation broke over us in all its impossible absurdity, I
thought we would die laughing, tears streaming down our faces.
Huxley spun around to face us, the fear, the hope, splintering through
his anger. Then in one darting movement he was gone, like a dead man

who has left all his possessions behind him, pipe and tobacco pouch, notebooks and papers, dusty crumpled hat. Nobody moved, nor even said a word. Silence, tranquillity settled upon our eyelids. I realised something then. Whatever lives or stories we had found in 34, parts of us were still there, living them.

When hours later Huxley finally reappeared it was with the semblance of mirage, not flesh and blood, an indistinct form flickering between perpendicular gashes of shadow and sun.

Anna splashed water into his glass. He drank copiously, then demanded more.

Exhausted, he slumped into his chair, the sweat trickling in rivulets along the crease lines of his face.

'Do you know what I saw?' he rasped, his hands clenched, his knuckles white.

The ambiguity had vanished without trace, and if words can ever be translucent, then each of them in turn would have revealed the barb and the venom cloud that had poisoned them.

'Shall I tell you?'

All eyes were upon him, not even daring to blink.

'*Nothing!* That is what I saw! Nothing but an empty patch of sky. Do you know what that means?'

'It means this thing is playing tricks with our own minds,' said Hadrian indignantly. 'There is the appearance of substance, and yet when you analyse it dispassionately, it has all the objectivity of a nightmare. I warned you, didn't I? It is inherently subversive.'

A bleak glance, and Huxley returned his defeated look to the detested tephra at his feet. 'Is that what you believe? Given what you saw or think you saw, I cannot help but wonder if this is an oracle that has, after all, spoken the truth. That beyond this jumble of lust, guilt and desire, there is nothing, nothing at all. Would the Codex be proven wrong if that were the case? — no, merely our interpretation of texts so arcane we can barely understand them at the best of times.'

He tossed us the line almost contemptuously: '*And ye shall know the truth, even if the truth shall know thee first...* But that piercing fragment could mean almost anything — even that there is no truth at all.'

Exasperated by his self pity, Anna said: 'It could also mean that whatever's in there is reading our minds, reading our souls. But not yours, apparently — *or is it?*'

'We all experienced different things,' I added, clumsily. 'Maybe there's a reason for your... blindness... in there.'

'What are you saying, Nicky?' said Sam, a sardonic voice from the camp bed. 'That he deserved it?'

'He's right, you do deserve it, Marcus,' said Anna mercilessly. 'Just face it. Even in beauty all you see are the seeds of corruption and decay. You crave innocence for its purity, yet despise it for its naivety.'

Huxley was glaring at us; the acrid words like smelling salts. 'Fools!' he snarled. 'What do you know about anything?'

'Didn't I tell you it was a danger to our minds?' Hadrian shot back. 'Didn't I?'

Anna leapt in, thrusting her own indignant words between them. 'Why, because we are finding a way to nourish our souls? What's so wrong with that?'

'Because it is *not real!*' Hadrian barked back at her, and I saw Huxley blanche, as if the idea, in all its heretical simplicity, had only just dawned upon him.

'You're always saying the world is illusion, Marcus. Well, if that's true, then everything we have ever seen and everything we have ever known is illusion, so what does it matter? Renato is flesh and blood. I was there, and nothing's going to steal him away from me again do you hear, not fate, not you, not anyone!'

And suddenly we were all at each other's throats again.

'So now you see how it is, Professor Almighty,' said Hadrian, hurling the words at Huxley. 'The man who wanted us to relinquish our illusions. Who wanted us to step out of ourselves. Who wanted us to see the universe from outside our own bodies, even our own consciousness!' He grunted in disgust. 'And now look what you have reduced them to, craving their fool's paradise almost more than the air they breathe.'

That's when Huxley dropped his bombshell, his flecked-stone eyes crushing each of us in turn. 'House 34 is off-limits. I will not be responsible for aggravating other peoples' delusions. I expressly forbid it.'

66.

Dead dreams eating him like quicklime, Huxley sealed himself up at Monolithos, slamming the doors, bolting the shutters.

Mindful of the risks, Anna, Sam and I followed our morning ritual to the letter, clocking-in at the site office, collecting our gear from the lock-ups, heading off for the huts or the trenches. But then one by one we would drift off towards the hill, trying not to draw attention to ourselves as we passed under the vigilant eyes of Galatea and her students.

Luckily Nestor's diversion was working, and the journalists and cameramen were already besieging them, their curiosity stoked by coils of razor wire, then the vision of jug-eared Tassos, patrolling the perimeter with his hunting rifle and his toy-sentry march.

'The rumours are true then,' they demanded, hurling their questions through the razor wire. 'There are thieves and traffickers about.' They craned their necks, lifted their cameras high over their heads. 'What's so valuable? What's Huxley hiding in there?' Imagining treasures that would dazzle King Midas himself.

To their feral eyes, Galatea's blank stare only served to incriminate her all the more, so too the busy bee behaviour of her students, the digging, the coming and going, too diligent, too industrious by half.

'Poor Galatea,' commiserated Anna, as we walked up the last stretch together. 'Digging for 18 months and look what they've got to show for it. A few burnt out shells of houses, a few cracked amphorae. No wonder she was so baffled by Nestor's insistence about the razor wire and Tassos with his gun... *I hope it's not loaded!*' she added, casting him a dubious look. 'The idea of handing that oaf a real rifle with real bullets!'

Leaving the cacophony far behind us, we reached the crest of the hill, cutting diagonally across the temple square. Aris was slouching up against house 34, rifle at his knees, a stem of grass between his teeth.

Anna touched him lightly on the shoulder. 'Be sure to keep a good lookout, Ari. Call us if you spot anyone, do you understand? Any of those reporters sniffing their way up here. Nestor, Hadrian, even Professor Huxley.'

'*Especially* Professor Huxley,' I murmured.

Tongue between his teeth, he whistled a fluting bird call so oddly mesmerising, Anna asked: 'Where did you learn that, Ari? It's beautiful.'

'I don't know,' he shrugged, with a bashful grin. 'I don't remember.'

'Well that will be our secret call then, use that. Whenever you need to!'

As we pushed our way through the plank wood door, I murmured back at her: 'It's a golden oriole, isn't it?'

'Is it? But how? There can't have been an oriole on this island since —'

'Since there were people in these houses. Forests. Rivers.'

★

I went tumbling over the rapids, the Ferryman a receding figure midstream under the sky tall plane trees.

I bobbed through a wasp-waist gorge under towering red cliffs, then felt the surf breaking over my face with a salty sting. I could feel the riptide tugging at my feet, and before I knew it I was being swept out into the open sea. There was no land in sight in any direction. The sun arced across the sky. Then the stars. Once, twice, I must have passed out, bursting awake only as the choking water entered my lungs. I lost count of the hours, or could it have been days. But then through my blurring vision, I saw their distant silhouettes undulating against the watermelon skyline, and I knew it with utter certainty. I was being carried towards the Isles.

Stomach growling, tongue parched and swollen, I slumped down beside Anna on the temple steps. I had been away for hours, just struggling to stay afloat, struggling to stay conscious, willing those sinuous shores ever closer as they rise against a star-drenched sky.

Glancing up from the notebook propped against her knees, she handed me her flask of cool water.

The breeze was sounding its musical notes between the temple columns, the poppies and wind anemones in sweeping waves across the slopes.

No need for words.

★

Her thoughts drift along the lazy meander of the river, smiling at the deer-dappled plane trees, at the Pensione Galileo on the corner.

Her head turns on the pillow. The drab pastels of *camera cinque* bleed into her eyes.

It's Wednesday, and the horrid clock on the wall is ticking away in that hollow mocking way it has, *his life and hers, her life without his.* And she knows what she has to do.

She imagines it. The audacity of it. Renato, cheating death, cheating fate, that malignant force still conspiring to murder him at the same crossroads, the same traffic lights. Hours from now.

Head sinking back onto the feather-soft pillows, she turns to him, planting that prescience in his love-drowsy head, warning him about running the lights, turning amber, turning red, the traffic jam all psyched out on stress and caffeine and jobs that barely feed the wallet, let alone the soul. She has the mental image in her head as she struggles to make it obey her own thoughts, flying through time. She can already see it hurtling through the spitting rain, the black Alfa that will run the lights and almost tear Renato in two.

She will fight the screeching tyres, the shriek of crumpling steel, the wail of the ambulances, the smell of blood on the asphalt.

It will obey. *It will obey.*

'I will be back before you know it,' he says. 'Friday night, I promise. May God strike me down if I tell a lie.'

She wiles away the time, walking along the riverbank, running loving fingertips over the dappled bark of the plane trees. She spends hours in the Pensione, not knowing what to think or what to do. Tries to read but can't. Gazes out of the window but sees only the snarling traffic in her mind's eye.

She paces back and forth, waiting for the phone to ring. Waiting for the rap on the door, the two Carabinieri standing there, too tall for the doorway, fumbling for words.

For an hour or two, she takes refuge outside.

Where has the time gone, she wonders. Too long ago, you spent your childhood summers here. But it was different then.

The great old farmhouses, the orchards and wheat fields, they have given way to roads and factories and dirt you can't scrub off your hands, can't wash out of your soul.

As the moment takes her, she crosses the red fields, lifting the raincoat high over her head in a whirlwind April shower.

Comes to a rambling farm, ramshackle and derelict, not much different from grandfather's farm, even the rusting old tractor in the barn with its smiley radiator face and bulging headlamp eyes.

I'll bet the whole family used to sit out here under the trees or the trellised vines, she's thinking, every summer Sunday a feast of goodness, water and wine.

Their fading echo seems to well up on the wind, talk, laughter, the kids chasing each other into the tall fields of maize, the light-drawn image of herself, an impudent little tomboy with a sweet smile and mud-spattered knees.

The world is slipping away, she thinks, right under our noses. People, woods, songbirds. *But where are you going?* the thought striking her from some odd uncharted angle. *Can't we come with you?*

There's a loud rap on the door and her heart leaps into her mouth. It wants to run away, doesn't it, leap out of the window, carried away even in the filthy dirty river.

She wills herself to the door, takes a faltering breath, thinks she's going to crumple to the floor just at the sight of them standing there, their caps squashing-up against the lintel.

But no! it's him, it's Renato, in flesh and blood.

And with that look that always sends her weak at the knees.

You will not have your way with us this time, fate, she thinks. No, not this time.

They lie glistening and exhausted upon the crumpled white sheets, sunbeams straying in with shadow leaves through the tall windows.

'I feel all aglow inside,' she says, a murmur across the pillow.

'That is because I have plucked a star from the deepest heavens and placed it in your heart,' says Renato with a deadpan look.

Wherever does he find the words? she giggles. No. So corny, but that's love all over. Given half the chance it will turn water into wine and even bestow upon the cold, empty universe a soul born of itself. Yes, that's right, she murmurs to herself, her gaze drawn to the splash of sun and rain at the window, every little leaf, every sailing cloud in the sky. It's funny I've never noticed it before.

'What are you mumbling about?' he says, turning, nuzzling her ear.

'Love,' she says.

'My love?' he teases, stealing a kiss from her lips as she catches the cheeky look in his eye.

'Perhaps.'

There's a youthfulness about her, isn't there, in the fiery redness of her hair catching the afternoon sun, in the bright emerald clarity of her eyes, in the hope that sees horizon.

'Do you know how much the Alpha fool missed him by?' she gushed, thrilled to have worked her magic. 'Millimetres, Nico, split seconds, the place where fate and circumstance are supposed to meet and come to an understanding. Renato, he just got the fright of his life, that's all. Not a graze, not a scratch. Just screeching tyres, blaring horns, the usual volley of curses, and shouts of blue murder.'

Sam thrust his way though the plank wood door, squinting against the light.

Sensing something different about him Aris stiffened, advancing a few wary steps along the street just as Nestor had taught him, rifle raised, a shout of challenge on his lips.

If the transformation was unmistakable, even haunting, at least I had seen it before. Sam's angry, trigger-happy soldier, the one who's forever patrolling the battlements, denying entry, had deserted his post again.

I squinted, not quite believing my eyes as he threw his arm carelessly over Aris' shoulder, an easy gesture no one who knew him would ever have imagined him capable of; a string of words passed between them and suddenly both were grinning ear to ear.

Strange, I thought, how even the simplest of gestures had disarmed our own guard as well. It is almost as if... no, that's not possible — *is it...?* almost as if the influence Sam brings from the other side is enough to evoke the other Aris as well.

'Maybe Sam was right,' said Anna, staring hard. 'Even if Aris has no idea what's going on behind that plank door, maybe he already senses that something of his own soul exists beyond it.'

Seeing Sam saunter towards us, hands thrust lazily into his jeans, she added with a serious look: 'Do you think we might be turning into our other selves? That the longer we stay on the other side, the more we become like them?'

The implications were just sinking in when we heard Ari's whistle from 34. He was motioning down the hill. Sam turned. I scrambled to my feet, my eyes sweeping over the street, temple square, the fields.

'Hadrian,' I said with a start. He came lumbering up the hill towards us, but then made an abrupt turn into Huxley's field tent, still pitched halfway down like some mute canvas totem to his failure.

'False alarm,' I called, breathing a sigh of relief.

'You're a very good boy, Ari,' said Anna, surprising him with a kiss. He shuffles his feet, an awkward smile blushing the peach fuzz of his cheeks.

We were hungry, starving, famished, and with the water flask dry, also parched. Playing the innocent, we wandered down the hill with some grand plan about firing up the samovar, maybe even drawing straws for a run down to the mess tent.

'Look who it is,' said Sam, his uncharacteristic nonchalance catching Hadrian off guard. Huxley's second-in-command treated us to a paternal once over, then a disapproving frown, before returning to his milky tea and, taking pride of place on the camp table, a plate of Myroula's honey cakes.

He gaped as we tore into them, stuffing our mouths until all that was left were crumbs.

He said at last: 'I take it you have expended little thought on what this thing is, much less the validity of its effects upon you.'

Anna stifled a giggle.

'Look at you!' the words coming on a squeal of disgust. 'You don't even care if it's reality or chimera, worse, if it's malignant or benign!'

'No, we don't care!' retorted Anna, with a defiant toss of the head. 'Must we doubt and question everything under the sun? Why not just say: *it is!*'

Sam said: 'It's just as the Codex says. We lose what we have become. Become what we are not.'

Hadrian snorted: '*We become what we are not!* Of course. Illusion. It is the *definition* of illusion.'

'No, it is the definition of reincarnation. The transmigration of the soul. Somehow, it's making them visible to us. Our other selves. Our parallel lives.'

Hadrian caught his restless glance up the hill. 'I'm warning you, Sam. Don't you dare make this worse than it already is. Don't you dare drag Aris into this. How old is he anyway? Nineteen? Twenty?'

He wagged an admonishing finger in Sam's face, trailing off only as he found himself slipping into those blue pools of eyes. 'I'm just saying,' he added, shifting uncomfortably in his chair. 'If something were to go wrong, it won't just be Huxley falling in on you like a ton of bricks, remember that. You're hiding from everyone; the teachers and students, the labourers, the dirt-diggers snooping about the compound. Everyone!'

Regaining his composure with a slurp of tea he sniffed: 'Whatever it is, it can't last. Once this volcanic activity subsides, it'll go out like a broken light bulb, and good riddance!'

'Don't say that!' Anna flared. 'Why do people always want to spoil everything? What makes them say things like that? Spite, envy, jealousy, *what?*'

Flinching, he said: 'Have it your own way, Anna. Go on believing it's your faithful genie of the lamp, if that's what you want, here to grant your heart's desire.'

67.

The days are liquid, they flow like quicksilver.

April, flooding into May and the full-blooded days of spring, corn poppies and wind anemones giving way to undulating fields of chrysanthemum.

We were neglecting our duties more brazenly than ever, going through the motions just to cover our tracks. A dazzling smile for Maria in the site office, a taciturn nod at Nestor, who could be relied upon to report anything suspicious to his Kapítán, an awkward wave for Hadrian. Then through the plank wood door, the ivory marble underfoot so weathered and water-smooth it seems to be rippling through time.

I must have lost track of the hours. I stumbled out of 34 and into the perpendicular shadows of the sun. I was dizzy. I slumped down beside Anna on the temple steps. The May sun was reddening our faces, the marble columns still night-cold against our backs.

'I'm nearly there,' I said. 'There are islands, hundreds of them, maybe thousands, scattering into the blue. There are mountains and forests. Peaks with snow. Silver torrents. But not a single town, not a single house or meadow...'

I shook my head. Tried to outstare the ancient street, the ghost houses on the hill, the sacred grove with its petrified trees, if only to know which of my realities was indisputably real.

My latest encounter had left me strangely abstracted, strangely numb, as though whoever was supposed to be me now really did exist in two places at the same time.

'Don't you think you're losing touch with who you are,' I confided. 'Here, I mean?'

Anna nestled her head on my shoulder, flyaway hair tickling my nose. 'Don't worry, Nico.'

But I was worried. 'Don't you think you're spending too much time in there?'

She drew away sharply. 'What about you? You think that just because you're trying to get to the Isles, just because that's your dream, it makes it better than mine?'

'Did I say that? I didn't say that.'

Relenting, she motioned towards Aris, leaning up against the façade of 34, the habitual stem of grass between his teeth. 'Sam's right. Aris feels it too, even with that thick stone wall between them. You can almost see the change coming over him.'

'That's just the teenager in him, isn't it. Rebelling against the Colonels, the establishment, the medieval village smothering him.'

She narrowed her eyes at him, murmuring: 'I don't think so, Nico. Even if he can't put it into words or pictures, day by day that other part of him is becoming ever more tangible… Like an image struggling to emerge, an insight struggling for recognition… This Phaestos — who is he anyway? What does he want, what is he doing? A simple fisherman like Aris, a dagger in his belt? — I don't think so! Even Sam… I mean the fresco painter… knows that. And if he's not just a common thief, what's he got to rebel about anyway, in an idyll like this? Whatever's going on between them, it's crossing into our own time as well. Aris — he hardly knows who to be anymore, does he.'

'I don't know,' I said, scrambling to my feet, feeling nauseous.

'Hadrian was right, there is something exquisitely subversive about this.'

'He didn't say exquisite.'

At least we could still tell the difference between our selves and our other selves, I thought, our form and our reflection. At least we could still do that. Couldn't we?

'Why can't Sam just be content with what he finds on the other side?' I said, irritably. 'He must know that Aris is not Phaestos, he's just not.'

She looked up at me, shielding her eyes. 'He's in love, of course. Didn't you know?'

'Sam is incapable of love,' I said, more abruptly than I had intended. 'Everyone knows that. He as good as admitted it himself.'

'Sam is, yes… But I didn't mean Sam'

Maybe she was right. They were crouching behind an ancient wall as I crossed the terraces back to camp, the joint ember-first in Sam's mouth, the smoke streaming between Aris' eager lips. If anyone found them at it, there would be hell to pay.

Wondering what day it was, I wandered down to the field tent, thinking, you should remember this, what day was it yesterday? Blinking against the Cycladic light, I could still see, as if flash burnt onto my retinae, the forested mountain slopes, the islands scattering into the sunset.

'Wait!' Anna called, skipping after me between the ancient houses, one hand saving her straw hat from the wind. She looped her arm through mine, but then clicked her tongue at the sight of Hadrian sitting out under the awning. 'Not another third degree!'

'At least he's brought the honey cakes.'

She giggled, then said: 'You're not still worried are you. I know you, Nico, you're such a worrier!'

I shrugged. I didn't think I was, but I was worried about this.

'You have to surrender to it!' the words coming like a song. 'Body and soul! Just like me, just like Renato.'

She threw a smile into the sky, as rapturous as a lark's song. 'Term's finished now; the students have all gone home on their cycles and Vespas, we're leaving Roma. The whole summer stretching out before us! Any day now, we'll be heading south. The Aeolian Isles, Stromboli, Vulcano, Filigudi. Renato has it all planned, we have the train tickets, the boat tickets, everything!'

'You didn't mention being here,' I said, in a hollow voice. 'You didn't mention that, Anna.'

She frowned in irritation, sweeping past Hadrian to fill her mug at the samovar.

'Have you read this?' he spluttered indignantly, shaking some tattered back issue of Popular Science at us, one of those old magazines that the students were always leaving behind. '*Have you?*'

Seeing Huxley's imperious image staring back at us from the front cover, I flinched. '*Atlantis...?*'

'No!' he snapped, tapping the offending page with disdain. 'A different science altogether, assuming that that is not an oxymoron.' He cast a dubious eye over us. 'These quantum physicists — they claim that if one were to travel far enough along the curve of the universe one would eventually come face to face with oneself, one's own doppelgänger... *Preposterous!* They claim that there are fault lines running hither and thither through the fabric of space and time, squashing and distorting reality.'

'Maybe they're right,' said Sam, pushing his way past us, filching a couple of honey cakes as he went.

'So that explains your magic carpet rides does it?' He flung the magazine across the tent, its pages fluttering loudly in complaint. 'That we can't even say what it is — it's an affront to us all!' Adding, as he squirmed in frustration: 'These anomalies are supposed to be unstable. If this is one, and I'm not admitting it is mind you, the tremors and rock falls, the bubbling fissures out on the Burnt Islands, would all attest to it. The full moon set it off, that's what we thought. So why is it still here at all?'

The exasperation still lodged in his throat, Hadrian struggled to his feet, feeling suddenly bilious, and I knew why just from the loathing glance; he's just noticed the love bites on Anna's neck, the youthful beauty in her face; he's seen the blue and ochre pigment staining Sam's fingertips, knowing it can only have come from the house on the hill.

★

There it was again, an oriole darting between the trees on a lilting cry.

We made for the door, blinking into the sheer sunlight.

Several seconds elapsed before we even caught sight of Aris, astride one of the exposed walls, motioning frantically down the hill.

Just when I was thinking, I can't deal with this. Not with Huxley, not with Nestor, trouble of a different kind sprang into view.

I couldn't believe it. Equipped with pliers, they were actually cutting their way through the wire fencing into the restricted zone.

What with their angular faces and mousy hair I recognised them at once. Jackson and Platt, the most dogged and aggressive of the red top reporters. Fed on malice and mythology, they had had their suspicions about Huxley from the start, and if it wasn't Benja's manslaughter or worse they were intent on pinning on us, it was fraud or trafficking or collusion with the Colonels.

Brushing off the dust, they struggled through onto the ancient street and, with one sniff into the wind, were following their noses right up the hill. Someone must have tipped them off, it was the only explanation. Past the petrified trees. Past the water fountain. Any minute now there'd be a confrontation, questions, accusations, threats. Behind me, I heard the click as Aris cocked his rifle.

'What do we do? What do we do?' whispered Anna, in no state to do anything at all.

Just when I was thinking, that's it, they've caught Nestor off guard, we'll have to face whatever's coming, their heads jerked towards rubber-faced Tassos, loitering with intent outside house 22, as a pair of labourers in thick gloves coiled razor wire around its perimeter.

Sure enough, they took the bait, eyes darting left and right as they scurried along, notepads and cameras at the ready.

'Wait here!' I yelled, and ran down to do my own bit to feed the lie.

By mid-afternoon, the entire press corps was crowding into 22, pushing and shoving, flash bulbs and pulses alike sizzling at the erotic frescoes.

Huxley's great secret was out, and you could see the obvious dawning in their awestruck eyes as they moved from room to tantalising room, the gas lanterns held aloft in their hands. No wonder Marcus James Huxley had kept these pornographic frescoes from the public eye. No wonder. What else could he do, what alternative did he have? The censors wouldn't allow publication of a single image, not without cropping, masking, blurring.

Out at Monolithos, Huxley must have imagined the world was falling in on his head.

I wondered how he would endure it. Not the shouts of pious outrage, but those other fools already committing pen to paper, voice to tape, and myth to credulous minds... that the shocking scenes were Huxley's missing evidence, his crowning glory, proof positive of Atlantis' fall into darkness and depravity.

68.

Cutting through the Thalassa house I stopped dead in my tracks, squinting against the glare from the windows up ahead, heart thumping in my chest. Thinking, it has to be another fluctuation; another of those freak moments the anomaly likes to conjure up out of thin air. This time, the fresco painter, the young fisherman, Phaestos. Thrust against the vivid pigment sea, a wall of glittering light prisms, a shoal of startled fish.

Blinking against the bright amorphous daylight from the street, finally the scene springs into focus.

No. It *is* Aris, his head thrust back against the ancient sea.

It *is* Sam, his lips, his tongue in search of the boy beyond.

Sam's coaxing him down onto the ground, tearing at his clothes, fingertips tracing the huge cock straining the denim of the boy's jeans.

I retreated into the street, thinking, doesn't he even know the difference, can't he tell it's just Aris? Shouldn't someone say something?

I was already turning the corner when I heard advancing footsteps, crunching over the pumice-littered path. I thought to shout a warning; too late.

Through the ancient window, I saw Aris' head jerking up in alarm. His startled look finding my face in a momentary flicker of relief... before slamming right into Tassos; rifle braced behind his neck, a broken-toothed leer twisting his mouth, buried eyes still feasting messily on everything he'd seen.

You could almost hear the ramifications, like blood-spilt heartbeats, like giant's footsteps pounding over the ash. Aris, being swept away on the flash flood of his own emotions. Apprehension, panic, the reluctant realisation that the worst thing that could possibly happen is already happening.

The moment hesitates, then bursts, the shockwaves radiating out all around us.

Far too late to save himself, still he lunges at the futile hope of it, the rage exploding in his chest, bursting into his mouth.

'Queer! Filthy fucking queer!'

Alarmed, Tassos retreated several steps. Gaping stupidly as Aris' fists quickly became smeared in blood, Sam too dazed even to lift his hands to defend himself.

They tumbled out into the sunlight, into the street. Aris would end up killing him, I was sure of it, Sam's head staved-in with one of those ancient stones just an arm's length away.

Crumpling under the barrage, his mouth was already dribbling blood, a gash opening over his eyes, that were still registering only amazement.

'Ari!' I bolted over, throwing myself between them. Could feel his blind rage exploding over me, blows raining down on my back, thumping the air out of my lungs... until finally, he recognised me.

In that young face, not even a grim satisfaction could be found. Merely the implacable reflection of the mind that had made it all possible. Not Sam. Not me. Just the cretinous Tassos.

Abruptly, Aris scrambled away, bolting between the houses, a smirking Tassos breaking into a whistle as he about-faced and marched down the hill.

In the ugly stillness that remained, it seemed all too obvious.

Everything was going wrong.

Our worlds colliding in ways we could never have imagined. Wherever they touched there was turmoil and convulsion.

'Why did you do it?' I said, angrily. I was ransacking my pockets for something to mop up the blood, but had nothing. In the end, he tore a strip off his already ripped shirt and dabbed his split lip with it, wincing.

'I don't know.'

'You must know! Aris and Phaestos, they're not the same. You can't transplant one to the other. They're not the same, are they?'

He pushed me away, scrambling to his feet. 'Like the island,' I insisted, hoping to drum some sense into him. 'The one we stand on. The one we dig out of the ash. The ones we dream of. The ones we see in 34. They are not the fucking same!'

He stole a glance along the street, probably hoping that by some miracle Aris would be coming back to him, and they would tell reality to go to hell.

'Look, it's not like Aris sends my heart diving off a cliff, if that's what you think. It's not even the risk or the thrill of it anymore. Or the sight of people clinging to the wreckage of their own ideas about reality. Or wanting what I can't have. A week ago, I might have needed the risk, chased it, I don't know why — just to get out of the fog, just to feel alive, just to prove I wasn't dead.'

'Then what?' I yelled.

'Aris, Phaestos, they have to reach each other, that's all...'

'Why? What is Phaestos doing? He's just a fisherman, isn't he? Well, isn't he?'

He clammed up, and wouldn't or couldn't say.

Considering the pummelling he had just taken, the absence of the soldier in his eyes was more startling than ever.

Seeing that look was to know how wrong I had been to pretend, even for the sake of simplicity, that the worlds we had come to know were irrevocably separate, that here I was real but beyond I was not.

Words becoming ever more difficult to speak as his lips swelled, he said in a murmur: 'If you ask me, that's the trick, the secret of how this thing works. It's not transporting us anywhere; it's plunging us into their consciousness.'

'You know what you're saying?' I flared, feeling a queasy billow of dismay inside. 'You're saying we're simultaneously alive in different places, different times, different possibilities...' My voice petered out, like some path swallowed by the forest.

But then he said something so startling I had to wonder where else he can have learnt it, if not from some other perspective beyond the plank wood door. 'Those variations of us, I think they're always trying to reach out across the Void, one to the other. They have to reach each other. I mean how else could we ever discover who we really are?'

The words made some kind of improbable sense but all I could think of at that moment was Phaestos, staring into that same hole in the sky, as peripherally aware of us now as we were of him. Had he put Sam up to this, as a means of reaching himself? Too unnerving even to contemplate, I thrust the idea aside.

He threw me a glance, his eyes already puffed up and turning purple. 'Next time you make the crossing, Nicky, remember to look. Say: show me my life one hundred degrees east. Say: show me my life if Célestine had stayed with me. Say: show me my life if my father had never died.'

'Shut up Sam. Maybe you should put some ice on those bruises. It might reduce the swelling in your brain.'

When Aris failed to show up for work the next day, Nestor said with a vexed brow: 'That's not like Aris. What's come over him? He knows we have a ton of supplies due in this week.' Adding with an irritated sigh, 'I suppose I'll just have to send one of the men down to the village to fetch him.'

'No don't,' I said with a start. 'I'll go. I'll go after work.'

I could already sense it in the heaviness of the air, in medieval streets barely wide enough for two mules to pass, in windows painted infinite Cycladic blue, in the picture postcard views with their whitewashed stones, basil pots and cascading bougainvillea. The slur-thick voice of Tassos, his spittle and malice still flicking off one tongue after another, as contagious among these huddled dwellings as the winter flu.

As I neared Aris' crumbling house, hemmed in on all sides by its neighbours, I could hear the words thumping like detonations, his stump-armed father in a murderous rage, vowing to disown him, kill him, if he didn't kill the foreigners first. I heard his sister sobbing, his mother shrieking at her mutilated man to leave the dynamite alone, hadn't it destroyed enough already. I heard a roar and another barrage of cries as I stole away under the neighbours' invisible seething gaze.

Bloating under the tentacles of myth, before the week was out that one stupid kiss had been transmuted into abominations every bit as unspeakable as those in Marcus Huxley's evil frescoes. Aris must have been possessed by them, went the whispers, those debauched images that deserved the same fiery hell that had consumed their godless creators.

To their disobedient sons and daughters falling under the same spell they would shout, scream, light a devotional candle. *Do you want to end up like Aris? Those pagan devils, like an animal without a soul?'*

★

Across the rippling ivory marble, I entered 34.

The sun must have found the sky. Shafts of light stream in through the whale-singing sea.

Ribs of light play a symphony composed for reflection and water. The music floats, drifts, weaves all around me, so mesmerising to the soul that the body, forgotten, goes sinking down into the welcoming sea grass, fronds swaying back and forth in the breeze currents.

How many seafarers have been seduced by that same sweet siren song, I wonder, like me, drowning in rapture.

But not now. Not today.

My staring eyes, they're filled with sky, a bright blue dome reflected onto the retina of the sea, catching there the tumbling slopes of an island, steep crags, silver ripples along the shore, footprints in the sand, mine.

Striking deep into the wooded hills of the island is a stony path, and I take it, making a swift ascent.

Here and there comes a dashing torrent, rock pools bubbling silver between the trees.

Reaching the forest line I emerge into crystal sky, the path meandering between two rounded hills. A mountain lake appears. Rising out of its slate-blue waters are two great stone windmills, their white canvas sails catching the wind.

A piercing whistle scorches the air like a bullet. The sky trembles.

It must be Aris, I'm thinking, on the other side, but it's nothing like his fluting call.

Irritated, I try to push it away, still making for the lake and the windmills, but there it is again and again, like a shrieking kettle now, and I could feel it dragging me back, dragging me down.

'What are you *doing*, Hadrian?' cried Anna, if anything, even more incensed than I.

'What do you think?' he squealed back at us. 'Trying to save you from yourselves!'

'*How dare you!* Do you know where I was? Do you know how close I was?' She was rambling, like a sleepwalker chased into the incoherent light. 'Half a day's sailing from the islands... Stromboli, Vulcano, Filigudi... Renato is going to ask me, I know he is. He has it all planned. The moment, the place. We'll leave the rat race behind us forever. Rent a little house up there in the village with its own trellis and vine; we'll grow capers and herbs, buy an old boat and do it up and fish along the shore; in a few years, who knows, maybe there'll be a child on the way.'

The hulking shadow lodged in the doorway looked fit to burst. 'Do you hear yourself, Anna? Do you hear what you're saying? The *insanity* of it!'

Sam stirred angrily, his face still bearing the livid bruises of his encounter with flesh and blood rather than more intangible shadows of desire.

'Why don't you mess up your own life, Hadrian, instead of everyone else's?' To which Anna offered an insolent smattering of applause.

'And if Huxley should find out?' he blustered. 'Don't think he won't fire you all on the spot. Don't think I won't tell him if I have to.'

'You wouldn't dare,' she said dangerously. 'You wouldn't dare betray us.'

The mood spoilt, we traipsed back to camp, our mouths dry and stomachs growling. We pushed our way into the mess tent, jostling into line for the tin trays. I had the impression that everybody was staring at us, the chattering students, the bespectacled teachers.

I slid onto the bench next to Hadrian, still moping over the way we had treated him.

'Aren't you overdoing it?' I said in a forced whisper. 'Can't you see how happy Anna is now? Sam too, come to that — at least, when he's not here.'

Munching mechanically on his food, he said in disgust, 'Next time you're at home, look in the mirror, if you dare. You began by spending half an hour at a time staring into that thing. Then your free afternoons. Then every waking moment you could snatch without getting caught. One of these days you won't even know how to get back, you'll lose yourself for good. Nothing will bring you around. Nothing!'

★

'We need Aris!' cried Anna, as we wandered into the deserted temple square. 'Who else can we trust to keep meddling fools away? That Tassos? I won't have him anywhere near me!'

'So, talk to Aris,' I flared. 'If you think it's that easy. It isn't.'

'He has to grow up. Sam may have been reckless, yes we know that, but don't tell me Aris didn't know, don't tell me he doesn't feel it inside. Why else would he be fighting with himself, answer me that! One demanding, one denying the recognition of the other?'

'Maybe he doesn't want to, maybe he can't,' I said, ambushed by her vehemence.

'All right, I'll go down there myself,' she declared at last, but with the look of someone who knows they'll have to pull themselves together first.

I stared hard at the plank wood door.

If this was the Oracle, at least the Codex was proving its point. It didn't predict the future.

69.

Barely an hour later I was summoned to Monolithos, not the best of all possible omens.

'Ask him!' said Anna, with a rare streak of insolence, as I hurried off to the Morris. 'Ask him if he's Braille-read the causes of his own *blindness* yet...'

'Are they obeying my orders?' he demanded abrasively. 'Are they staying out of 34? I am relying on you, Mr Pedrosa, to keep me informed.'

Cutting a bizarre figure at the kitchen countertop, his hands were pummelling bread dough, a striped apron looped around his neck, his cheek dusted with flour.

'Yes, of course,' wondering if he'd catch the lie in my voice.

Glancing up, his flecked eyes interrogated mine. 'Very well then,' he said at length, motioning me to the bench seat. 'Sit. And pay attention. Because I have been thinking.'

'About what?'

'About what was said in the heat of the moment up there. That this thing can alter its appearance according to whomever is staring at it.'

'So?'

'What does that say to you?' he challenged me, his voice hardening. 'What does it remind you of? Think! A creature that suddenly assumes the colours of its surroundings, melding into the background.'

'The chameleon. The octopus. The —'

'Yes! And why? Why do they behave in such a way?'

'I don't know. To become invisible, to defend themselves against attack —'

'Yes! To defend. To protect. That's when it struck me. The Oracle is throwing out these distortions precisely for the same reason. To fool us into thinking there is nothing there of substance. The question is, how can we trick it, how can we force it to reveal its true form? How can we persuade it that we're harmless?'

'That is difficult to do,' I gulped, 'when it can read your soul.'

'Is that what it's doing?' he retorted in a flurry of anger, but quickly relented. 'You may be right. Whatever intelligence it does possess, complex or rudimentary, malignant or benign, we cannot be certain it's not overhearing everything we think and say. Even now it might be devising some means to foil us, even from within ourselves.'

'Why are you so convinced that the truth lies beyond illusion at all?' I demanded, fighting the nauseous mix of fresh bread and madness.

He took a shot of wine, so dark it was almost grape purple. 'Because I have come to realise that Sam was right, even if it was just a fluke. He stumbled upon a truth more profound than he can ever have imagined.'

With a flourish, he drizzled virgin green olive oil into a glass bowl.

'Right about what?' thinking, it can't be that resin-sticky idea about events being hammered out of molten possibility, can it, variations of every moment blurring through some invisible dimension. *Wrong.*

'Reread in that light, even some of the more obscure fragments of the Sais Codex begin to make sense. Think of it. The Oracle that is "learning the truth", the Oracle that "will yet divine the future". But I would go further even than Sam and his fuddled brainwave.'

I was almost too afraid to ask. 'How much further?'

He turned from his bread making, his fingers clogged with dough, his eyes, fixing mine, assuming a clarity just too incongruous for the manic chaos beyond.

'Listen to me now, and pay attention. If you really want to know what you all witnessed in house 34, it was the raw strands of existence itself.'

Unlatching the oven's cast iron door, the heat glow surged out at us. Face glistening, he took the baker's paddle down from the wall, and shunted the loaves between the embers.

'Or to use another analogy,' he added, with a bloodcurdling smile, 'we are seeing fate not yet kneaded or baked.'

'Then what is its value?' I objected. 'What is the difference between illusion and events that are purely hypothetical?'

'The difference, Mr Pedrosa,' he said, clinking his glass against mine as if sensing triumph close at hand, 'is that possibility has the latent potential to become real, whilst illusion does not. One can nurture possibility, but to nurture illusion is to hunger and die.'

'Then you'll open up 34 again?' almost tripping over my own eagerness.

'I told you. I am not interested in the superficial fluctuations this thing is kicking in our faces — seemingly infinite interpretations of every event. Not facts, not truth.'

'But we're all responsible for the destinies we create, aren't we? For ourselves, for each other.'

'We are merely fate's sightless guinea pigs,' he erupted. 'What more proof do you need of that than a world aching from war, hunger, disease, pointless tragedy? One might almost be tempted to believe that fate were purposely fabricating events simply to feed upon our reactions, hopeless, pitiful or defiant, I don't care.'

So stark was the transformation it was almost as if another Huxley had entered him, forcing the departure of the other.

As he rambled and raved, I realised how his madness was coming in fits and starts, a few moments of clarity, a few insights bordering on revelation, then jagged splinters of thought that seemed capable of lacerating flesh, drawing blood.

I could feel the icy sweat trickling down my back.

Elysium, the Isles of the Blest, the transcendent realm — it has to be a trap, I thought, in sudden panic. Anyone could see that from Huxley himself, shrinking, descending, as if through the chequered floor tiles, into his very own hell.

It was then that he spoke those words that made my blood run cold, and I knew he must have been scheming about it for days.

'Staring into the rift cannot be the same as crossing through it. That much must be obvious to any fool.' He grabbed me by the shoulder, the fingertips digging into muscle. 'If only we could follow someone through, see what they see with their own eyes as they pass away. That, Mr Pedrosa, is *revelation*... Think of him as a pioneer, a golden hero, being catapulted beyond the stars, beyond everything that is fake in this sham world.'

He flopped down at the kitchen table, his eyes brightening at the audacity and ingenuity of his scheme. 'Well, what do you say? Do you have anyone in mind?'

'What?'

'A brave volunteer. Someone prepared to leap through to the other side; if they're fortunate enough, even to return to tell the tale.'

'But how will you see what they see?' I objected, far less interested in the mechanics of it than finding something, anything, to humour him.

'Nestor will find some way,' he replied confidently. 'He will devise some rig that will allow us to dangle our volunteer over the rift, suspend him, as it were, between one state of being and the other, just far enough to penetrate the mantle and peer beyond the distortion, beyond the camouflage, into the pure, unadulterated truth beyond.'

70.

There he was, back on sentry duty, rifle braced across his knees, sullen eyes searing the camp below.

'What do you expect?' said Anna. 'The stench of gossip in the village, like a cracked drain. His father's curse. He's been hurt, humiliated. And he'll never live it down. It will always be there. A stain. A sin. A sickness.'

'How did you ever convince him to come back?'

'I don't know, Nico. We were sitting there for hours on the *Persephone*. At first he wouldn't even look at me; he just sat there, sewing his nets, pulling the thread between his teeth, glaring daggers... But he was in two minds, I could read that even in his silence.'

'*Two minds?*' the unintended irony giving me a start.

As Sam passed, still bearing the scars of their last encounter, Aris regarded him through narrowed eyes. He was guarding his emotions well.

We were still sitting there, our backs against the temple columns, as the stars emerged. Then I must have fallen asleep because the next thing I knew, Anna was gently nudging me awake. 'Listen, Nico!' she whispered.

'What is it?

'*Listen!*'

The words were welling out of the darkness, but I couldn't decipher even one, not for the life of me. Oddly lyrical, like rolling clouds, they were in a language I had never heard before.

'Who is it?' I asked, stirring.

Barefoot, she stood, taking several light steps over the undulating marble towards 34.

'It's Aris,' she whispered back.

His eyes were wide open, words were tumbling from his mouth, but for all that, he wasn't awake. Not here anyway.

We crouched down beside him. 'What's he saying?'

Unnerved, Anna said: 'I don't know. If it's Minoan he might as will be speaking in tongues. *I don't know!*'

'Should we wake him?'

The question was hardly out of my mouth when the torrent of words bubbled fluidly into Greek. Several seconds later, he came to. 'What is it?' he asked in alarm, fumbling for his gun.

'Nothing Ari,' said Anna. 'You were just dreaming, that's all.'

He swallowed hard, blinked. She handed him the water flask.

'I don't suppose you remember anything. Where you were, what you saw?'

'There were people,' he said at last, in fierce concentration. 'Hundreds of them. Running for their lives, the earth chewing them up like monster's teeth. They're running for the boats, crying, screaming... Some of the houses are on fire.'

He shook his head in bewilderment. 'Just a dream.' Embarrassed, fearful, he scrambled to his feet.

When we were alone again, she said: 'It might just be autosuggestion, that's all.' Catching my look, she added: 'All right then, but we have no evidence that these people ever evacuated the island, you know that.'

★

We pushed our way through the plank wood door, squinting against the ethereal afternoon light, heads swimming from the unfamiliar ground underfoot, somehow too solid to be real.

From the colonnade's perpendicular shadows, a bumblebee silhouette flickered into the sun.

'Look at you!' it squealed, morphing into Hadrian. 'How futile, how pathetic...!'

About to open my mouth in protest, he cut me off, hand slashing air. 'No! Don't for a minute think I'm excusing myself...'

Pointing an agonized face at the sun he slumped onto the marble steps, wrenched off his glasses, thumb and forefinger rubbing deep into the sockets of his eyes.

His face crumpled in self-loathing. 'No, I am worse than the lot of you put together... preaching water, drinking wine! At least you make no bones about your obsession with this thing, while I carp and complain yet still can't tear myself away.'

'*You!*' A gleeful smile appeared on Anna's face. 'Where did you go? What did you see?' Squeezing his arm in encouragement.

His lips trembled, dry, wordless, as if his confession would only contaminate the air.

'It was the music,' said Sam brutally. 'The music of the spheres. That's what brought him back. Even while he was lecturing us from his pulpit. He couldn't resist it.'

'Because I still heard it!' he cried, twisting a plimsolled toe in the dust. 'If ever so faintly. Yet whenever I stopped to listen, it would fall utterly silent and I'd hear nothing, not a single note. Then just as soon as I wasn't paying attention, wherever I was, in the hut, in the trenches, under the shower, there it was again, sweet, sublime, *yes!* irresistible!'

Sam said, 'So you crept up here when no one was looking.'

Hadrian nodded in revulsion. 'One minute I was crossing the threshold, the next, catapulted into the farthest reaches of the universe. By which I mean where it begins or where it ends, who can say. There was a cloudburst of stars, like a luminous breaking wave. And then it began. The music... So exquisite, so divine, it seemed to hum through every fibre of my being — no, that's not right — as if my very essence had become an instrument itself in that wondrous symphony of light and sound.'

He uttered an anguished sob, burying his face in his hands.

Pirouetting between the temple columns above us, Anna sang out across the excavations through cupped hands: 'What—have—you—done—to—us, Marcus?'

'Don't you understand?' Hadrian called up angrily. 'I tell you this because I am all at sea — not because I think I have landed in *Elysium!*'

She flopped down beside him again, her euphoria deflating like a child's leaky balloon.

'We already know they're not illusions,' Sam warned him. 'And we're sick of you pretending they are.'

'Maybe they are not,' conceded Hadrian. 'But does that make them real? No! In fact if there was no one to shake you out of that morbid trance, a year from now some passer-by would probably find you on the marble floor, a sack of dust and bones, no matter how much glorious food you had stuffed into your mouth in that other world of yours.'

'So what does that tell you?' said Sam. 'That this reality is preeminent, demanding our homage like some jealous god? No, if anything, it's us, marooned on this barren, tortured rock who are figments, the shadows of who we really are on the other side.'

'Snap out of it, Sam.' There was a sadness, a frustration, a disgust churning in his voice. 'We have not seen eye to eye on many things, it's true, but I will not sit idly by and see you destroy yourself, I will not!'

He drew Sam towards him, a brotherly gesture I found astonishing in someone of Hadrian's stiff English reserve. Roughly, Sam shook him off.

'If you want to make yourself useful, Hadrian, just make sure you keep Huxley and his lapdog Nestor out of my way... This is my life now. Up here. I will see it through.'

Hadrian bit hard on the corner of his lips and I thought for a moment he was going to cry.

Sam booted a pumice stone across the street until it cracked against a wall. 'You just don't get it, do you, Hadrian? Even after everything you've been allowed to see!' He snorted with contempt, 'Admit it, you probably still think our other selves are imprisoned on separate worlds in separate times!'

Hadrian shuffled his feet, evidently not wanting to admit anything.

'Don't you understand? The entirety of one is always present within the other — even if it's only sleeping potential, even if it's no more evident than a gesture or a look or a lost thread of dream inexplicable to us.' He clenched his fists, trying to find the words, trying to wring out their inner meaning. 'Part of you is always there. It's there now, don't you understand? Living its life. Surrendering to the music.'

'That's why we brought Aris back,' said Anna. 'Even after everything that's happened. That's why you should keep Marcus away for as long as possible.'

An explanation that seemed no explanation at all until the implications sank in, like some slow-acting poison.

'You can't think he will make the crossing,' said Hadrian, so aghast at the idea his face had gone numb. 'You can't think he will appear in Aris' mind. That Aris will recognise him, give him life, give him consciousness!'

Sam's defiant look said otherwise, and Hadrian sagged against the temple column, his eyes rolling in dismay.

'We have to know what Phaestos knows,' affirmed Anna. 'If only to preserve the Oracle. To know what it would wish of us.'

Struggling to his feet, Hadrian threw a look of such unrestrained hatred at 34 that in myth or legend it might have torn stone from stone. 'I told you from the outset,' he rasped. 'Whatever is in there is inherently subversive, inimical to logic, to freedom, to life itself!'

★

411

We crouched beside him in the moonlight, incomprehensible words streaming from his lips again, his eyes rolled back so far in his head his pupils had vanished. 'We have to wake him!' said Anna in alarm.

'No! We have to wait it out.'

'It is Minoan,' mumbled Sam, 'I recognise some of the inflections. I —'

A tremor ran through Aris' body, head to foot. He lurched forward in a sudden fit of coughing.

Bewildered, he glanced at each of us in turn, even Sam, not even rebelling against the gentle touch of his shoulder. 'I was dreaming again. Wasn't I?'

'Yes,' said Anna, trying to control the tremble in her voice. 'Do you remember, Ari? It's important you tell us if you remember what you dreamt.'

He blinked, screwed up his eyes. 'I was running. Running through the streets. There was a knife in my hand...'

'You remember the ebony grip,' said Sam. 'You remember the silver blade?'

'No —' Whatever terror he'd witnessed seemed to come alive his eyes. 'I remember the blood on my hands. I remember the bodies in the street. *I remember the tyrants!*'

'That's all right Ari,' said Anna quickly. 'Pay it no mind. It was just a stupid dream, that's all. It's a wonder we're not all having the same nightmare. Those vile Colonels. Tanks on the streets in Athens.' She planted a kiss on the top of his head.

Sensing my look as we walked down to the field tent to turn in on the camp beds, she snapped: '*What?* He was rambling, that's all. You heard him! It doesn't mean anything!'

'No. It means Phaestos is here. In his head, in his soul, in his spirit...' I was struggling for the right word. It seemed that one did not exist.

71.

Nestor's jeep came hurtling towards me along the vineyard track. Seeing the Morris he flashed his lights and slowed to a crawl. As we inched past each other, I was about to ask what the 'Kapítan' wanted, but caught the harried look in his eye, the rolls of technical drawings on the passenger seat.

'You are late, Mr Pedrosa,' came Huxley's brusque voice from the terrace.

Above our heads, swifts went soaring through the June sky. He seemed oblivious to them. Waves of air, first warm, then cool, came undulating up from the sea.

I slid onto the stone bench opposite him, realising with a start that he was reviewing our first logs from 34, going through each one, line by line.

'You wanted to see me,' I said, already tensing under his predatory gaze.

'Yes. I am vetting the logs for our volunteer.'

'What for? What's the use?'

Bristling, he ground the words between his teeth: 'Because whatever's in there, meddling in our lives, corrupting our senses, playing God, we will have the truth of it, *whatever the cost!*'

'Why do you have to talk like that?'

'Like what?'

'Like the most cynical, embittered man alive.'

'Why, because I am driven, that's why,' he replied, with that peculiar look of bleak, almost corrosive, defiance he wore sometimes. 'Do you think I was always like this? *Do you?* No... once I was like you, like Benja, like Sam before his own bloody-mindedness got the better of him. I too could find infinity in the vanishing of a summer's day. I too could look upon the world and know its inner purity. There among the rolling hills, the patchwork fields, the meander of the river, the splash of water over the shallows.'

'Because you can't see it,' I mocked him, 'it's not there anymore?'

His eyes narrowed. 'No. There is a greyness in the air that obscures the sun. The fields are poisoned by greed. The river is contaminated with our own stupid sins. The child carries the germ of its own spiritual death. Cynicism is the virus that hatches in our own blood...'

'That's what Anna meant, wasn't it,' I said, in sudden revulsion. 'About craving what you must destroy. About corrupting Sam, corrupting Benja. It was their innocence, their naivety, their idealism, you drank like blood.'

'Call it the disease of living,' he said with finality.

'No, it's you. People like you, people like Guirand. Feeding off us like some guilt-ridden fetish, until we've nothing left to give. Until we're just as old and bitter as you —'

'Don't be so melodramatic,' he snapped. 'It is life that poisons love, not I. It is life that makes the young old and turns beautiful dreams into ash, not I.'

That's when the realisation finally hit me: it wasn't the truth about life and death he was turning the world upside down for, and never had been. It was the cure for his own disease.

'You want to break into heaven,' I taunted him. 'Well anyone can, can't they, as long as they have a stolen key or a pair of wire-cutters!'

'Not I, Mr Pedrosa, *you*.'

'Me?'

He added with acrid humour: 'You shall be my guide; the blind-man's guide.'

'You think you can cheat it,' I said incredulously, getting to my feet. 'I won't do it. You can't make me. Not this time.'

'Do you think I don't know what you're all up to in 34 any chance you get?' he boomed, with one shot flushing my reluctance out into the open like a doomed quail. 'What kind of fool do you take me for? Admit it, whenever you're not staring into that thing, you're craving it. You're all so transparent it's pathetic.'

Our eyes clashed in fury, but even then I could not quite find the man I needed to hate.

72.

Brooding, furious or ecstatic as the mood took him, Huxley remained behind locked doors at Monolithos, trying to breathe life into his blue-faced brainchild.

He had no peace. Chattering birdsong woke him at the crack of dawn, and he would think of death. As the sun rose over the midsummer sea, the cicadas would start up, their dry ratchet song bruising the still air. Then under the relentless sun they would reach their hellish crescendo, infesting his mind. *Couldn't anyone silence them? Kill them, crush them into dust?*

Only Nestor beat a path up there these days, poring over blueprints of wood and iron contraptions on the Kapítán's desk.

His hounded eyes became a welcome sight to me during those long summer days; it meant that the machine remained marooned on the drawing board, beset by maddening technical problems.

I heard nothing more until Maria, repeating pillow talk, whispered something about Nestor being at the end of his tether, what with the Kapítán still demanding the impossible — a contraption of ropes and pulleys that could dangle a man in any direction other than that dictated by gravity.

'How was it?' said Sam, as we left 34 side by side, blinking against the blue glare of the sky.

'Flat,' I said, feeling more seasick than I usually did back on solid ground.

'You have to let go!'

'I got as far as the windmills in the lake but there was no one there,' I replied, through gritted teeth. 'I walked on to the next bluff, and saw the land and the golden fields sweeping away down to the sea, all glistening in the sun and the rain. But there were no people...'

'You see?' said Sam, lighting a cigarette, fighting a devilish grin. 'Even your otherworld is boring. You are given the chance to see anything, become anyone, and what do *you* see? Fields!'

I wasn't in the mood to see the joke.

'It's paranoia,' he added, pronouncing judgement as only Sam could, squinting up at me from the temple steps. 'Face it, Nicky, you can't let go because Huxley's always inside your head, checking every thought, every move.'

Counting to ten I just managed to stop myself blowing up in his face, but by six, already knew he was right. That, after all, was what Huxley had wanted from the very beginning, and what he was now plotting to achieve by mechanical means with Nestor's contraption.

How are you going to defend yourself against him? comes the thought, on a spasm of raw fear. *Somehow, you have to regain your clarity, your presence of mind. You have to resist it. This addiction to beauty, to everything that means anything.*

In search of moral support, I cornered Hadrian down at the field tent. 'Maybe you're right…' I said, casually tossing out the words as I poured tea. 'Maybe we should stay out of 34. You know, just in case…'

He raised an eyebrow at me: 'Alas, I cannot concur.'

'*What?*' I almost drenched myself in hot tea.

'If anything, it is our atavistic superstition that is inherently subversive, our terror of the unknown. That part of us that must forever be king of the castle, that can never say… *surrender!* No, Master Pedrosa. We must follow this to its logical conclusion, whatever the outcome. We can do no other.'

I decided to go it alone. It wasn't easy.

I fought the cravings with gritted teeth and buckling willpower. Flung my body into the sea, willing my mind to recognise the breath-snatching clarity of the splash. Ordered myself to eat even when the food tasted like sawdust. Forced myself to shepherd a new batch of students around camp, ignoring their bleating whispers and curious, sidelong glances.

I watched the others come and go, unsure if the emotion knotting me up inside was pity or envy. Each time, so it seemed to me, they emerged from house 34 with an ever more tenuous grip on the reality to which they returned.

I don't think Anna ever quite forgave Hadrian for shocking her out of her trance. Every day since, she's been trying to get back to her unfinished chapter, find her lost place on the page, rejoin the stream of events as she left them.

They're still heading south, it's not that. Still sitting side by side in the swaying railway carriage, their fingers entwined. Watching the sunflower fields blur by outside, the breeze tearing through the open window, fighting the lingering stench of stale cigarette smoke and spilt wine, the clackety-clack of the rails in their ears.

But something's different. Something's not quite right. Maybe the glow about them, now faintly diminished, the one that used to draw the wondering glances of passers-by in the street. Maybe something missing from his eyes, something that was there before.

And so back she tumbles to the present, or at least, the one that pretends to be so, emerging from 34 like a sleepwalker, gliding past without a murmur.

Every time she tells herself the same thing: there must be some way of getting back there, to the page I was on before.

But no, it's wrong, all wrong! The chapter is not the same. There are nuances she has never seen before. The sentences are different, the penmanship belongs to a different hand, the imagination stems from a different mind or a different mood.

But in the end, she knows she has to see it through.

★

As dawn breaks, there they are on the summer horizon, the first of the islands. Arm in arm, they take in the sights from the railings as the ferry steams into Vulcano, holidaymakers, pilgrims in search of a cure, right there along the shore, squelching into the hot mud, floating in bubbling springs.

That night she draws up a chair at the *Giallo Rosso*, wearing a summer dress as blue as a bluebird's egg. Across the table, Renato, his face, his body, all brown from the August sun, unruly curls tumbling into his eyes.

He reaches over, squeezes her hand, tickles the dips and hollows between her fingers. The mood is getting to him. The dusky red Aeolian wine. The stars that someone has just sprinkled into the sky. And then the sex-drenched moon that heaves itself out of the sea. A summer breeze billows in, worrying the candle on the table, and the sputtering flame is momentarily reflected in their own eyes.

The *primo piatti* arrive, and his attention begins to wander. To the two dotty old ladies who appear to be running the place singlehanded, one behind the open hatch in the kitchen fussing over steaming pots and flame-spitting pans, the other ferrying plates to the tables. And all the while he's talking, just small talk, wondering why everything in the place is done up like a Soviet flag, blood-of-the-revolution red, hammer-and-sickle yellow, chairs, tables, awning, everything. His restless gaze shifts to the neighbouring tables, to affluent faces flushed with candlelight, to clinking wine glasses and tinkling laughter. He sloshes more red into his glass and almost kills it in a single draught. He's drinking a lot these days isn't he, she thinks, and feels the curious twist inside, as if the revelation had been known to her all along.

'Maybe their husbands were die-hard *comunisti*,' she jokes. 'Maybe they fought Franco in Spain and died on the battlefield, a single bullet felling them both.'

'Don't be stupid!' he rebukes her, the underlying aggression giving her another start. At the nearest tables, heads jerk towards them and he scowls. 'I'm thinking that, for a working man's trattoria, it has become far too bourgeois, that's all.'

'You don't like it?' she asks, and she hates the anxiousness in her voice. The way she feels responsible for the emotions on which they float, like two souls on a raft in the wide open sea. But it was always like that... *wasn't it?* Basking in his happiness. Shivering in his anger or sadness.

He splashes more wine into his glass, drains the carafe, orders another. He's getting drunk and the *secondo* hasn't even arrived yet.

Strange, she thinks. All those months ago, we used to live for the dream, leaving the rat race for good, a little house up there on the fringes of the village, its windows drinking in the sea. Now it's just pretend isn't it, just make believe, a child's fantasy. What would we do here, without jobs, without money? What were we thinking?

Then just at the corner of her eye, she catches it. The look. And for a tumbling heartbeat, almost convinces herself she's never seen it before.

Not in Renato.

That look he has for the woman two tables down, the one with the pearl necklace and the sheer black dress, too daring for half the women in the world. The look that's been darting over her shoulder the whole time, lingering, exploring, eager for conquest, for intimacy, for lust. She kicks him hard on the shin and he yelps, the table grating over the tiles, the glasses chinking in complaint as he plunges down to rub away the pain.

But that's Renato all over. You could never stay angry with him for long, could you, not with those puppy dog eyes, that devilish grin.

She taps the pencil across her teeth, brings pencil to paper, letters appearing across the page like charcoal hieroglyphs:

"So we amble along the seafront in the still, humid air, leaning into each other's arms. Drift back to the hotel, climb the creaking wooden stairs to our room under the eves, fumble with the key in the lock. The door creaks open and Renato murmurs, no, don't turn on the light. I stand there in the moist shadows, and can already feel the perspiration running down my neck. Through the open window, there's hardly a breath of air, just a wash of moon that seems hot to the touch.

His shadow turns to me, takes me roughly by the arms, begins to kiss and lick my neck, the soft-hard tongue poking its way between my lips, insisting I take all of it in my mouth, thrusting in and out in a teasing little play of what he knows will come. He's pushing me back across the room, one step then another, until my knees give way against the bed. And suddenly we're falling, falling down onto the trampoline mattress, bouncing up and down, up and down, tearing at each other's clothes.

The heat and sweat and saliva makes us slither all over the sheets.

And when we can take it no more, he lowers himself down upon me, that hot, blood-throbbing part of him thrusting its way inside me, higher and higher until love... love finds its impossible climax, and there we are again, in that nameless instant, that timeless place... that *meraviglia!*

It comes sweeping towards me, wave after wave, streaking my soul across the sky. Painting it there in pure white light.

The utter stillness floods over me, where I lie on the cusp of the moment, waiting to see you, feel you, know you again. Eternity.

But what is it, something's wrong, tonight I can't even *see* the wave, much less catch it. There's something sordid about the room, sordid about his lust, sordid even about the moonlight. I try to thrust away the poisonous thought. That it's not me he's making love to at all. That under the cover of darkness he's giving his desperate kiss of life to the pretty girl in the trattoria instead. Trying to paint her face and body onto my blank form, trying to..."

She squinted up at the sky. 'Will you write the rest down, Nico, if I tell you? I don't think I have the strength left in me anymore. But up here, where it's harder to go on telling lies to oneself.'

'Why don't you end it?' I said, reluctantly taking the pencil and logbook. 'Forget about 34. Forget you ever saw it.'

Wearily, she shook her head. 'Fate is having its revenge for what

I did, don't you see that? Whatever happens in there, I have to know where it will end. I have to let it follow its course. Just in case, you understand. Just in case it has the capacity for mercy. Just in case love can triumph after all. You will write it, Nico, won't you.'

I wrote. Renato and Anna, they return to Roma. Chased by billowing autumn cloud. The filthy concrete streets, too hard for feet that have known summer sand.

She returns to her job at the university, watching the students running across the piazza ringed by smog-eaten statues. The students sputter up on Vespas. They have sunburnt faces and their skin still smells of summer.

You think you'll live forever, she murmurs, looking down on them from the casement windows, you think youth is eternal. And instead of bitterness, she's surprised to find a smile on her lips.

Renato goes about his buying and selling, racing north, racing south. Maybe he's settling down, she thinks, grabbing an espresso and a brioche on her way to work. Maybe we'll make our life together after all. At least we'd still have the islands for the holidays.

Sometimes, he's away for days and she doesn't hear anything until his keys are jangling in the lock and he lurches into the apartment, dead on his feet, sometimes, already half drunk and trying to hide it.

The confessions are shy at first. 'She didn't mean anything, Anna. It was just some girl down on her luck.' He still has that puppy dog guilt in his eyes, the one she can never quite tell is put on or not.

Then before she knows it, his confessions are turning brash, aggressive, as if she's trespassing on his rights, as if she's not even worth the effort of the lie anymore. Pulling a face at the dinner she's kept warm for him on the stove, he drains another bottle, slamming it onto the table, all the women he's ever had entering the kitchen in a boastful slur, women who don't judge, women who don't expect anything from him, women he's met on the road in some cheap motel, yes, women he's had in their own bed while she's out at work, why not.

In the shine of his face, the glint of his eye, there's a kind of slick mendacity, the travelling salesman trying to make another pitch, another sale.

One last day, she says, pushing open the plank wood door. Just to be sure. Just to say, I gave it everything I could.

Just to know with perfect intimacy the contempt that comes with familiarity.

Just to know what love looks like as it withers and dies.

He comes barging in through the front door, already drunk, reeking of cheap perfume.

She shrinks back against the wall as he snarls, raising his hand to strike her across the face. And she realises it then in the hissing vacuum the moment has bequeathed. *I don't know you anymore, Renato. Whoever you are. I don't know you. The man I love is not even in this room anymore.*

The door heaves open, and she blinks against the dazzling light.

She looks gaunt, washed out, her hair flecked with grey, her skin assuming the pale, translucent quality of ghosts that come gliding through solid walls.

'I would give anything to go back, Nico. *Anything.*'

She catches my look of surprise and says, 'No, I mean back to the beginning. Back to when he was dead and buried and the dearest boy in the world.'

73.

Sam shoved his way through the plank wood door. Squinting against the glare, he slumped down beside me, rifling through his pockets for his sunglasses, snatching the water flask.

Rivulets streaming down his neck, he gulped it dry. 'This is getting harder and harder,' he sniffed, wiping his mouth with the back of his hand.

'What is?'

'Going. Coming back,' and in his face I noted another shared trait among the travellers in 34. The impassive way he spoke, as if the facial muscles that lend us the expressions of our emotions had been frozen, plunged into ice.

Going. Coming back. The words echoed, their implications all the more unnerving to me now that my head was clearing.

'So stay out of 34,' I said, more harshly than I had intended. Thinking, but he's right, isn't he, he's thinning, diluting, like a pigment in water, a dream lost to the morning. More real to the ancient island now than he is to this one.

He froze, eyes darting past me to the crest of the hill. *Voices.* There they were again. Welling up on the wind. No mistaking them now, nor the sound of boots ringing out over the flagstones.

Huxley. Marching up the hill with Nestor at his side, blueprints pleated under his arm, the habitual tool belt slung around his hips.

'Sam, wait!' I yelled.

But Sam was already making a run for it, vaulting over the nearest wall.

Huxley and his foreman were still arguing over blueprints and schematics as they emerged from 34, fingers jabbing or sliding over the plans. I had rarely heard Nestor so vociferous, nor his voice so ragged with stress.

Reimposing his command in camp, Huxley took his angry inspection to the huts and lock-ups. At the sight of the woman with the gaunt face and tangle of grey hair humming absently to herself outside the site office, Huxley's pace slackened uncertainly, until the shock of recognition bled into his eyes.

Barking for Maria, he retreated several steps, as if fearing contagion. Seconds later she appeared at the door, eyes flaring at the mere sight of him standing there, remorseless, tyrannical.

'Take Anna home,' he commanded. 'She does not belong in my camp in that state, nor in any place of work for that matter.'

'Professor Almighty!' Mutters of insolence just teetering on the brink of something far more spectacular. 'Just know this,' she cried, loudly this time. 'You have brought this curse upon us!'

Deftly, Nestor jumped between them, deflecting Maria from the object of her fury.

Words hissed between them, and Maria was still smouldering as she broke away to coax Anna to her feet.

'Get to work, Nestor,' he said sharply. 'You have your orders.'

'No. First I will have my say, Kapítan.'

Hearing that defiance from the man he had once considered no more likely to mutiny than scuttle the ship, Huxley's eyes narrowed in suspicion.

'Can you not see what is happening all around you? The lives in ruin, the friendships destroyed?'

'That's enough,' snapped Huxley, his voice low and dangerous.

'Look at what you are doing to your friends, Kapítan. Anna, more dead than alive, the memory of the one man she ever loved, shattered, destroyed. Sam, making a fool out of himself with Aris, people sniggering behind their backs, children throwing stones after them, calling them names. My own Maria who, thanks to this madness, cannot even walk past a mirror without jumping out of her skin. And now Hadrian, whose common sense we once all relied upon to keep the ship afloat, lying in his tent, writing and writing, trying to find the notes to some impossible symphony written in the stars!'

'What was I to do? I forbade them all from entering 34, you know that.'

'Do not take me for a fool, Kapítan. You knew they would disobey you! It is what you wanted! You watched your friends destroying themselves — and for what? To know something only God can know.'

'God will not deny me knowledge,' rasped Huxley, the thunder in his eyes. 'Not as long as I have one last breath left in my body.'

'You are using them, exploiting them!'

'I am using them as Life, God or Fate uses us all. How else are we to make the truth reveal itself?'

'Listen to what you are saying, Kapítán. Do you hear yourself?'

'They are explorers, Nestor — I thought you at least would have understood that. One day society will laud them for their courage and their vision.'

'Bury it!' came Nestor's reply, the words hissing between his teeth. 'Bury the damned house! Return it to the ash grave where it belongs!'

'Now, when we are this close?' the dismay and suspicion making his eyes dart.

'Oh, we are always close, Kapítán. Every time I hear you say the same thing — one more step, one final great push and we will be there… But even when we have arrived, Kapítán, there is always another place to be.'

'You've never wondered, Nestor, is that what you're saying? What it must be like when we cross the frontier, what it must be like to know eternity?'

'No, Kapítán. I have no wish to live forever. Sometimes, things are all the more beautiful because they are fragile, because they will die.'

Huxley shook his head dismissively. 'I cannot turn back now.'

'Then maybe you should ask yourself what happened to the ancients in this ruined place,' said Nestor, anger and disgust scalding his voice. 'Maybe you should ask yourself that, Kapítán, as you and your friends become as feeble as ghosts.'

'I have not set foot in 34 for weeks,' said Huxley, seething at the implication. 'Even when I did, I saw nothing, you know that as well as I. I am not under its influence. I am not under its spell. I remain as clear-headed as ever.'

Nestor uttered a bitter laugh. 'Ah, Kapítán, is that really so? I think not. I think you saw *this*.' His arm swept over the tortured landscape of shafts, slag heaps, and exhumed houses. 'I think you imagined yourself in *this* place and *this* time, more desperate than ever to know what lies beyond your own death, more willing than ever to sacrifice friends and loved ones. Anyone or anything, just to know your precious truth.'

The words hit him hard. 'What do you mean?'

'Do you even care about the dig anymore? The new streets running west, your work in the fragments hut, the restoration of the frescoes. You have abandoned everything you worked for.'

'It's over. There is nothing more to find.'

'Then how is it you still cannot answer the most basic question of all: what brought these people to ruin? Did they die in the volcanic blast, or perish upon the sea?' He tossed a glance of contempt at the hill. 'Did that Oracle of theirs save or consume them?'

'Let Hadrian dig,' taunted Huxley, 'if he can tear himself away from his sheet music. I have no time. Not when we are almost ready to make the crossing.'

'Then have it your own way, Kapítán,' said Nestor, wearily. 'I wash my hands of it. I will make you your contraption, I will even show you how to use it, but never dare tell me that I never warned you.'

If Huxley had won his argument he didn't show it. His face remained impassive, and he offered only a stiff, silent nod as he watched his muttering foreman walk away to load the timber, ropes and pulleys onto the truck.

'You think he might be right, don't you?' I said sharply.

He shifted uneasily on his feet as if, prying into his subconscious, I had exposed some humiliating inner flaw or weakness.

'Of course he's right!' he bellowed. 'If time were on my side, perhaps I would return to the fragments hut, and perhaps I would spend the rest of my life trying to piece them together — thus dutifully learning my lessons in futility in 50 years instead of ten...'

Taken aback by his bitterness, I said: 'Is that what you think?'

'I cannot face them anymore. The fragments. The shards and splinters. That shattered, broken universe that I am expected to piece back together. Sifting, sorting, cataloguing, trying to find that one missing piece that will make all the others fall into place; that one piece that, for all I know, may no longer even exist except as dust.'

'Then why not resume the excavations around 34?'

'Students and teachers up there, are you out of your mind?'

'Then order the others to dig. Anna, Hadrian, Sam.'

'What use would they be?' he retorted, but then hesitated, quizzing my eyes. 'You want to help them. You think that if I give them each a trowel and a brush and order them back to the trenches, things will go back to the way they were. An admirable motive, Nicholas, yes, but when you can turn back time, when you can undo fate, when you can walk on water, let me know.'

'Of course I can't!'

'No, you cannot,' he said, spitting the words between his teeth. 'Why else would we be plunging ourselves into that rift in the sky?

Why else are we prepared to take the risk, stake everything we have? Because that is the knowledge we demand. To know the mechanism of fate as a watchmaker knows the workings of a clock.'

He watched grimly as the Berna grated into gear and took the back route towards the hill.

'Well?' he demanded. 'Are you ready? Have you prepared yourself mentally, as we discussed?'

Now it was my turn to exact a price. 'No. Not unless you get the others back to work.'

'Why, occupational therapy?' he mocked. 'To save them from themselves?'

'No!' I yelled. 'Because you know Nestor's right. You know there are still secrets buried on the hill.'

74.

'How much longer, Mr Louganis?' Huxley bellowed, head thrust back between his shoulder blades.

The gruff answer was crushed between echoing mallet blows and whistling pulleys: 'Maybe hours. Maybe days. Maybe never.'

At first, I couldn't even tell where the voice was coming from. But then, following the contraption's elaborate array of beams I finally spotted him, draped over one of the highest struts, a bunch of nails in his mouth. The more I stood and stared, the more I began to understand the logic of the design, the intricate array of ropes and pulleys, the belts and stirrups that would propel Huxley's guinea pig towards that rift in the sky and then duck him over the edge. Me.

Once the nausea of that realisation had passed, I knew I was ready for the crossing; at least, as ready as anyone ever could be.

Biting his tongue lest a rash word send his right-hand man walking off the job altogether, Huxley turned on his heel, his eyes bleak and dry.

Predictably, his order to resume digging up on hill met with no reaction at all, not even rejection or indifference.

'You see,' he shrugged, drawing some perverse satisfaction from being proven right.

'And to think they once believed in you,' I said, skewering the words to his back, 'even admired you.'

I found Hadrian sitting under the temple columns, humming to himself, still lost to that symphonic echo from the luminous edges of time.

The music of the spheres.

Sometimes, it's almost there on the tip of his tongue, and he'll start scribbling in a frenzy before screwing the paper up into a ball and tossing it away with a howl of frustration.

'How will I do it, Pedrosa? How? I sense it, I hear it. How will I ever find the notes and intervals to express it? The universe distilled into the clarity of a chant, the chime of a glass bell, the west wind through the aeolian harp, the flute of the woodwind forest at dawn...'

Evicted from 34, Sam was hardly faring much better. Prowling the ruins, in full view one minute, vanishing into thin air the next, the hunted look on his face said it all. Huxley had no right to banish him from 34; Nestor had no right to build his ridiculous cowardly contraption over something so sacred.

I was strapped in, my waist and chest buckled into the harness, my feet twisted back into the leather stirrups. Offering some rudimentary means of control by way of the train of pulleys above, my hands remained free to work the ropes.

Balancing on one of the crossbeams, Nestor avoided my eyes as he fussed over me. He muttered, 'You don't have to do this, you know,' stealing a furtive glance at the Kapítan, scrutinising our every move from the undulating marble way down below. 'There would be no shame in saying no, in turning your back on the whole damn thing.'

I shook my head, unable to choke up a single word, so loudly was the fear pounding in my chest.

'Have it your own way,' he grunted, clamping a pair of earphones over my head so as to maintain contact via radio. A microphone was looped around my neck.

Then, with the last of the buckles checked and fastened, he threw a glance at the seemingly tiny figure far below. 'We are done, Kapítan,' he called. 'Pedrosa is ready for the crossing.'

Huxley offered an iron-stiff nod of satisfaction, his face impassive.

I watched as Nestor clambered down the scaffolding, as agile as a monkey, then caught the sudden hum of the wireless as the vacuum tubes lit up. Huxley snatched up the microphone.

'Imagine it, Nicholas!' and through the hiss and crackle of the earphones I could hear the thirsting eagerness in his voice. 'Moments from now, we shall know the truth! We shall land upon the Isles!'

The sun, all squashed and distorted, was plunging into a vermilion dusk, but still we waited, hardly daring to breathe.

Then out of the streamers of cloud they rose up, as if from a molten sea.

A constellation of islands. Mountain silhouettes snaking across the skyline. Lakes, rivers, glistening.

Huxley nodding his assent, Nestor released the pulley brake. Gathering pace, I went gliding towards the sunset, trying hard not to resist or pull back against the harness. Seconds later, I realised: I had no control. I was going too fast, shrieking towards the mouth of the vortex.

With a presence of mind that may have saved me, Nestor wrenched back the pulley brake. I jerked violently to a halt, winded and bobbing on my strings.

'You are on course!' insisted Huxley's tinny voice in the earphones, evidently annoyed that I had not trusted his foreman's trigonometry.

A few more feet went by, a smoother ride now that Nestor was getting the hang of the ropes.

With another application of the brake I was dangling over the edge of the rift, and for the first time, could plainly see its rippling distortion.

I gave my OK, but had to chase the words out of my mouth.

Gingerly, Nestor released the pulley brake, and I went sailing towards it like a dandelion seed. I could see the minute particles begin to fizz and sparkle even before my intruding feet made contact.

It's a curious feeling, that effervescence tingling through the skin, the blood, the bones, that creeping sense of disembodiment, a flowing from one state to another.

But I've been here before among the swaying fronds of sea grass. Gaping up as a fish might at that strange other world painted onto the viscous surface of the water. The convex shores of an island, pebble beaches, an iris sky.

Then before I know it, I'm bobbing to the surface, spluttering for air; I can hear Huxley's faint mechanical voice, ever more insistent. 'Can you hear me? Where are you? Respond at once if you can hear me!'

Finding my own voice at last, I call out across the divide, the seawater still giving bubbles to my voice. I can hear their relief and elation as I come through on the other side, Huxley almost on the verge of tears.

Watching the islands scatter into the blue. Hearing the birdsong from the trees. The music in the wind. I try to explain. This isn't like sitting cross-legged on the rippling marble floor, staring into that hypnotic patch of moonstone sky. Not because the colours are more vibrant, or the sensations more intense. It's because the world that holds me on a thread has receded to a pinpoint. Even Huxley himself is but a distant voice in my head, and the memories I brought with me are growing fainter by the minute.

'You must remember!' rasps the voice. 'You cannot allow yourself to forget. I want you to describe everything you see, every last detail, every last sensation.'

The windmills in the lake. They have always intrigued him, if only for the wrong reasons. He sees them almost as an astronaut might, finding a footprint beyond the Earth. Evidence that we are not alone. Proof that there is intelligence beyond the vanity of our own minds.

The air is markedly cooler up here. The path snakes its way between soft, undulating hillsides and then, almost when you least expect it, the lakes appear, a string of them, beaded onto a silver river.

Choosing my words with care, I describe the windmills to him, their white canvas sails turning in the wind, the small waves splashing against their stone walls.

'There are no people,' Huxley hisses. 'Why not? Move down through the fields! Look for houses, look for livestock, look for gardens. There can't be windmills without people.'

Apprehension wells up from the pit of my stomach. Suddenly, I can't help thinking I shouldn't be here at all. Can't quite shake the feeling that, somehow, I'm the one with the pair of wire cutters in his hands, I'm the one trespassing over sacred ground.

Along the broken path crossing the mountain slope, crystal water takes its euphoric leap from the rock face. Above, prism clouds go tumbling over the peak, suffused by sunlight.

I may not know how to put it into words, but I feel a presence up here that does not belong to us or to anyone.

There is a language up here, a different tongue, I begin to tell him, thinking that he might remember all those important things he once had to say about allegory, metaphor, about being on the borders of dream when familiar objects, familiar faces, begin to morph into other things, other selves, but what? The true face beyond, or yet another symbolic representation, another metaphor, another variation on a theme?

He won't listen. 'You are there to find the City of Light,' he berates me, 'not to walk the desolate mountains.'

'How do you expect to hear it,' I reply, 'when every sound is drowned out by your own voice?'

'We have to know where we are,' he insists. 'Without human contact, we have nothing. Everything else is just guesswork.'

There's just no reasoning with him.

As I turn my back on the mountain and begin my descent, I make a promise to myself. When all this is over, I'll come back alone. Next time, I'll devote myself, and nothing will intrude to distract me.

Nothing will come between us.

A shiver runs though me as the wind chases me down the path and blusters in my ear, because I know what it's saying. I always promise the same thing.

'Where are we now?' he demands, vexed by my prolonged silences.

'We're moving down through the patchwork fields,' I reply. Along pathways transformed into glistening torrents by the rain.

I can feel him in my head more than ever now, watching, analysing, waiting. The worst thing is the distortion in my ears, the fluctuation in the signal that, when it's at its most faint, makes his voice resemble mine.

I know, I should have been paying more attention to the gurgling paths and where they were carrying me than to every childish distraction along the way. I might have noticed how the path had chosen that moment to dip and twist, while the torrent itself just goes diving headlong between the trees.

Before I can think I'm somersaulting down the mountainside, branches thwacking me left and right, finding my feet, falling, almost at the edge of the bluff before my knees finally give way.

The last stretch I crawl on all fours, knowing, even without Huxley's crushing presence, that I have to see, have to know. What lies beyond this sky-piercing rock?

Fingers digging into moist earth and tufts of seeding grass, I raise myself up.

The whole world seems to fall away.

My gasp sets the startled warblers scattering from the trees behind me.

It isn't the beauty of the wooded plain or the conical hills that rise up here and there from the alluvial soil. It isn't even the serpentine coast vanishing into the rose-blue mists of summer, or the constellation of islets offshore, or the torrents that go tumbling down the mountainside.

It's that I'm struck by a peculiar sense of déjà vu. Of having been here before. But when, how? This doesn't make any sense at all.

Clustered around the bay, scattering across the green foothills beyond, blue and ochre houses, hilltop temples in their own leafy groves. Avenues paved with stone. Terraced gardens and vivid spice fields.

Beautiful, astonishing, but that's not why I'm still lying here, gaping like a fish.

It's because of the waterways curving in from the sea, entering the city on their own perfect arc, like ripples radiating across a pond. It's because of the ships with fluttering sails entering the canals from the bay, drifting under the arching bridges.

I know this place.

If I squint hard enough, I can even make out the hilltop temple and house 34, from whose ruins I am still dangling, 3,500 years from now.

'Well?' Huxley's distant voice demands, more irascible than ever. 'Speak, damn you!'

My fists clutch at the grass where I lie, but at that moment all I can feel is the lava dust between my fingers, the furnace heat of the bleached bone mountain at my back.

'It's Atlantis!' I yell, the words stumbling over each other in their shock and disbelief. 'Plato's Atlantis! Just as you described it.'

The last thing I heard was the panic in his voice, yelling at Nestor to winch me back, knowing it's all gone wrong.

When I came to, Nestor was fussing over me, unstrapping the belts and harnesses. Huxley standing at his side, with the pallor of someone who has just seen a ghost.

We made our way down to the field tent, Nestor lending me his arm. I was somehow surprised to find that it was morning, and felt oddly disoriented by the missing hours.

Once we were in the shade of the awning, Huxley brewed up strong Russian tea with milk and sugar. Something for the shock, apparently.

He glared at me, as if somehow my loyalty had been tested and found wanting. 'When did you first suspect it? When did you realise you weren't on the Isles at all?'

'Only when I got to the bluff.'

I imagine I was meant to see his disappointment in me as his eyes shifted away from mine.

'Don't you see, Kapítán?' Nestor broke in. 'That's just what I've been saying — the secret must be up here on the hill, right under our noses!'

Huxley poured tea, and I could tell by the clenched jaw and abrupt movements that he was trying to smother his own anger.

He began interrogating me about what I had seen from the bluff, sector by sector, the orchards and spice fields, the tree-lined streets and city landmarks.

'But there was something different about the hill.'

'What was different about it? Think! Visualise it!'

432

Fingers at my temples, I was squinting so hard my eyes hurt, the image from the bluff already so elusive it was like an evaporating dream.

'A sacred grove? A shrine. A workshop —'

'No! That wasn't it!' I threw up my hands in frustration. 'I can't remember. It's hopeless!' Then just as the memory blinked into the harsh midsummer daylight, I caught a final semblance of form and substance.

'No, wait! It was a building. Bigger than all the rest. An edifice. Four storeys high at least. And walls, I remember seeing walls circling the temple heights...'

'Is it important, Kapitán?'

'That we shall see,' he replied grimly. 'Illusion cannot be made of stone.'

We clambered into Huxley's battered Land Rover, barely able to see because it was so stuffed with supplies. Raising an immense cloud of dust, we cut across the pumice fields, a hundred yards on meeting the track that ringed the eastern sector. Beyond the barbed wire, the students and teachers were as indefatigable as ever, digging, brushing, mapping, cataloguing.

'Look at all the ash they've shifted,' I observed, my voice rising over the headwind. 'Especially Galatea and her students.'

'Much good will it do them,' he said, with a vague sneer. 'They will never find anything remotely of value there.'

The implications snatched my breath away. 'My God, that's why you assigned them the east in the first place, wasn't it. You already knew from your own test drills they would find nothing! It was just a smokescreen to get them out of your hair, to fool the authorities into supporting you... Their very own archaeological ghetto...'

Taking the back route, we climbed towards the temple heights and lurched to a halt, brakes squealing.

Huxley surveyed the scene through narrowed eyes.

'There,' he said at last. 'It can only be there: that patch of wasteland between 34 and the temple grove.' He stood behind the wheel, leaning on the windshield. 'And beyond, on the sunrise edge of the agora. We need to follow the lay of the land as it falls towards the eastern perimeter.'

'You won't be shifting that ash with your bare hands, Kapitán,' said Nestor. 'It could still be thirty feet deep at the bottom of the slope.'

'Then get the machines in, Mr Louganis, get the moles in.'

I should have known. Huxley never did anything by halves. If there was one exception this time, it was that he was leading from the front, returning to the trenches in person rather than commanding events from the imperial tent. By the end of the first day he was wearing bandages around his blistered fingers.

There was something frantic about the digging that I had never seen before, and I didn't realise until the second night what it reminded me of: the distraught victim of an earthquake, who can still hear the faint breath of a loved one beneath the rubble.

At Huxley's tent the hissing lamplight was making the canvas glow and was painting his bent, elongated silhouette onto the slanting roof.

Like the sullen silence about camp, the distortion only served to reinforce the impression that I hardly knew him anymore.

I slumped into a chair opposite him. He was munching distractedly on sandwiches, his eyes finding focus in some other place and time. Such was the nature of his obsession. He was already thinking about tomorrow, wishing it were daylight, his thoughts those of a general, plotting the next ambush or advance.

'We have to do something to help them,' I said, words breaking the silence like a limb torn from a tree. 'Anna, Hadrian, Sam.'

Briefly, his eyes found some kind of tenuous focus between mine. 'So work with us, Mr Pedrosa. Take a shovel in your hands for once instead of a pen. Dig until we find the truth. Who knows, you might even save your friends. You might even break the spell that has captivated them.'

I had grown used to his callousness, even his bouts of clarity and madness, but even I wasn't prepared for the morbid chuckle he emptied over the rim of his teacup as some dark, twisted joke occurred to him, at whose expense I could not tell.

75.

'Come quickly, Kapitán!' His voice burst over the ruins like a strangled cry.

'What is it?' Huxley already on his feet, the shock of premonition cracking through him as Nestor came bolting towards us.

Dread painting all kinds of feverish pictures in my head, I chased after them. I was seeing men crushed in the machines. Armed soldiers at the gates. The rift swelling uncontrollably across the sky.

Still at a run, we reached the temple heights, our feet clattering across the square.

Barging through the plank wood door, Huxley stiffened then froze in his tracks, so abruptly I almost went colliding into his back. I peered over his shoulder.

Sam was still there where Nestor had left him, dangling upside down in the ropes, as limp and lifeless as a puppet whose strings have become hopelessly entangled. His eyes were wide open, blue and empty. I broke into a cold sweat. Knees buckling, I subsided against the nearest arch, gulping deep draughts of air.

'Nestor, help me cut him down.' Huxley's command was a whisper, almost as if the sight of the body might offend the living, or that its very existence belittled his faith in the afterlife.

Hadrian came blundering in behind us, taking in the incomprehensible scene through finger smudged glasses.

We watched as they cut the climbing ropes, unbuckled the belts. The remaining cords whined through the pulleys and Sam flopped into Huxley's arms just as a sleepy child might embrace his father.

Biting her lips, Anna jerked her head away, the sight too bitter to bear.

Gingerly, Huxley laid Sam on the rippling marble floor.

Stirring from his stupor, Hadrian said, 'Do you think it was deliberate, Huxley, I mean, that he took his own life? I could understand that, if what he saw on the other side were even half as glorious —'

'*Pull yourself together man!* Sam would never have committed suicide. *Never!*'

The sheer ferocity of it made Hadrian jump, and in the bruised dignity that now crept into his raisin-in-dough eyes, it was possible to see a shadow of his old pompous self.

'I only meant that I know what he was going through,' protested Hadrian. 'So do you, Huxley, if only you'd care to admit it to yourself.'

'You have to bury the body quickly, Kapítan,' interrupted Nestor. 'This August heat! These flies!'

I could hear the crazy ratchet song of the cicadas outside, thrumming the air like a ten-gallon hangover. Beyond the thick stone walls that shielded us, it must have been 95° in the shade.

Sam's covered body lying at my feet in the well of the Land Rover, we sped towards Phíra in frenzied silence.

We were blurring past the cemetery when Huxley slammed on the brakes, just on the off chance of finding Mad Yanni there, digging graves or plucking bodies out of the soil.

As luck would have it, we found him propped up against a headstone, sucking on a huge red watermelon, spitting out black pips everywhere. Knowing his reputation I expected protracted negotiations, but only a moment or two passed before he lifted his grey stubbled face, squinted up at the silhouette that was Marcus Huxley, and gave a single brusque nod. Maybe it was too hot even for Mad Yanni to be bloody-minded.

'There is a grave already dug,' explained Huxley, as he climbed back into the Land Rover, his head half inclined towards Anna. 'But nothing will happen until evening — not with this heat.'

'Will someone write to his family?' I asked.

'He had no family,' cried Anna. 'None that wanted him or wasn't ashamed of him. We were his family!'

No sooner had Huxley rapped on the door of the doctor's house than Stavros Sanassis appeared in person, just about to set off on his rounds. Reading our faces, the affable smile vanished in an instant. With the brisk precision I had come to expect of him, he leaned over the tailgate, pulling back the coarse blanket to reveal Sam's pale, almost translucent face.

'My God, how did it happen Marcus?' he gasped, as we crabbed awkwardly along the corridor, Huxley and I at Sam's shoulders, Stavros at his feet. We were about to turn into the surgery, when he added breathlessly: 'No, not in there. There's little enough space as it is and my other patients will not appreciate it. In the *apothiki* out back — at least it's cool in there.'

We laid the body out on a narrow bench against the whitewashed wall, beside barrels of wine, jars of olive oil.

'You will need a death certificate,' said Sanassis, fighting his emotions. He hesitated, peeling back Sam's eyelids, gingerly touching the livid black bruise around his neck.

'He shouldn't be lying in here,' said Anna, quietly. 'Not in the gloom like this. We have no flowers for him!' She began to weep and I could feel the sting rising in my throat.

'It can't be helped, Anna,' said Huxley, not unkindly.

'How can you say that?' she sobbed, and even Sanassis must have realised that the words weighed far more than petals.

'You know they won't allow him to be buried on consecrated ground, Marcus, not if he took his own life.'

Huxley stiffened. 'He did not kill himself, Stavros. You have my solemn word on it.'

Sanassis glanced up at him and then back to the body and the telltale welt.

'We frequently use climbing ropes at the dig,' explained Huxley disingenuously. 'You know how reckless Sam could be. He was climbing alone, without supervision. He must have slipped, fallen, become entangled in the ropes.'

'You shouldn't have moved the body, Marcus. If the police get wind of it, well, you know what they'll make of it, there'll be hell to pay.'

'Manolis, Chondro, those simpletons?' growled Huxley.

Sanassis frowned and said almost in rebuke: 'Not anymore, Marcus, where have you been? We have police of quite a different order now. Torturers. Criminals. Manolis and Chondro, they're at their beck and call, fetching coffee, souvlaki, cleaning the toilets, or else sitting at their empty desks, staring into space, their minds no doubt finding some kind of vacuous kinship there.'

'I didn't know,' said Huxley, with a dazed look.

Sanassis let Huxley stew for a good few minutes before saying: 'Very well, then. I shall issue the death certificate.' Just as I looked away I caught his penetrating glance, and could feel the scepticism it carried.

Ten minutes later Huxley was rapping on Father Nannos' door.

We waited, our nerves wound tighter than a clock spring. Just as we were about to give up and head for the church, we heard tip-tapping steps. The door rattled open, but it was not Father Nannos.

'The Papás is not well,' said the toothless crone who now stood there, stooping towards us on bandy legs, leaning heavily on her cane. Huxley scowled. 'I have a boy to bury,' he explained in broken Greek. 'Kindly inform Father Nannos that it is I and I am in need of him.'

A moment's hesitation and she hobbled back a few steps, the door opening with her. 'Wait here,' he muttered over his shoulder, and stepped inside.

Too hot, too dazzling under the midday sun, we took refuge in the milky sweet shadows of the fig in the priest's tiny courtyard garden.

For a good ten minutes we sat in drifting silence, until Anna said absently: 'Sam sensed it from the very beginning, didn't he? I mean that everything we experienced in 34 was somehow uniquely attuned to who we are and who we might become. No wonder Marcus got so furious hearing it.'

I said clumsily: 'What about Renato? I suppose you still wish you had never set eyes on him again.'

She squeezed my hand. 'I can rage at Renato day and night, Nico, I can curse fate or God or the entire universe for everything that happened, but the hardest thing to admit is that it was made for me. I kept asking myself, again and again, *why is this happening to us? Fate, are you trying to make me pay, is that it, is it just revenge?'*

She leaned forward intently, eyes fixing mine. 'Then I realised. I was wrong. *So wrong!* Fate wasn't teaching me a lesson — it was the other way around. Fate was *learning from me!'*

I blinked, trying to take it in, trying to make it make sense.

It was late afternoon by the time we gathered outside the church gates.

From his house on the slope, the Papás appeared. He had been ill, everyone knew, but the sight of the frail, gaunt figure that met us at the gate still shocked me to the core.

'I shall be all right,' he said, raising himself up with a sharp breath. He gazed up at the deepening sky for a moment, if only to avoid our doubtful stares, as if they, like magic spells, had the power to undo conviction.

Our ragged cortège was a work in progress, taking shape as people drifted in to pay their last respects. Students and teachers from camp, Sam's own restoration crew, several gruff labourers, and every single surviving member of the Symposiasts.

'Oh sad day, sad day indeed!' lamented Vassilis Nafpliotis, as dapper as ever in a dark blue tailor-made suit; silver hair, silver moustache, groomed to perfection.

With a self-conscious twitch, Alexander Vouris nodded his assent.

Alexis Pangalos pushed his way through the milling crowd.

'We haven't seen you about lately, Nico,' he growled good-naturedly, clapping me over the shoulder, sizing me up through narrowed eyes. 'Have we, Stavros?'

The doctor replied distractedly 'No indeed,' his eyes darting anxiously up and down the street.

'The kids and I, well we were even beginning to wonder if you had sailed off into the sunset without saying goodbye…'

'Me…? No… just busy, that's all. I haven't been in Phíra for weeks. I've been bedding down at camp.'

An awkward moment passed as my defensiveness passed under the collective magnifying glass.

'We are here to honour Sam as much as to say goodbye,' said Nondas the barber, his words almost lost to the surrounding hubbub. 'Yes I know Marcus thought he had a cheeky mouth, but still. He was a good boy. I will not hear a word said against him…' His voice rose in volume as he cast his eye about the mourners, just in case there were gossips about.

'Hear hear!' boomed Pangalos, his look searing the crowd for fools.

And suddenly they were all reminiscing about our last wine-drenched symposium at Monolithos, about Sam springing that strange interpretation of Atlantis upon us, almost lost to the streams of history. Plato's Conundrum.

'How did it go?' pondered Vassilis Nafpliotis, tilting his head up into the evening sky. 'That's right, I remember now. In this curious exegesis, the island is neither mythical, nor legendary, nor even real in the accepted sense of the word. No, it is an ingenious metaphysical device that propels Atlantis through time, one age, one land to another. And wherever it settles, there is it possible to witness the same purity of mind and purpose that built Atlantis, the same corruption that bought it to ruin. The two sides of man, if you will, the human nature to which we are enslaved, the divine nature to which the soul aspires…'

Sanassis glanced sharply at him, biting his lips. He looked older, wearier, his face bearing an anxious shine, his eyes ringed with dark sleepless smudges. 'I only hope the police won't interfere,' he muttered. 'There's a death certificate, yes, but you know how even in a child they see a criminal.'

'You cannot so much as step outside your own front door without tripping over them,' growled Pangalos. 'They or their back-stabbing informers. Now they're on the ropes, what do you expect? Students rising up. Musicians, writers, poets, philosophers; men of vision, marching, singing, speaking out! Any day now we shall bring them down, the Colonels and their quislings. And they shall lie broken in the dust, like the fascist statues they are —'

'Alexis!' they hushed him in one voice, Stavros muttering: 'It is still not too late to be dragged away in chains.'

A couple of Galatea's brawnier students stepped forward, and we hoisted the crude pitch pine coffin up onto our shoulders. Then at last we were on our way, Father Nannos leading our procession through the narrow cobbled streets, staff in hand, censer billowing smoke.

Even under the weight of the coffin, I could hardly believe my own eyes. It was high summer, no one had to remind me, but the transformation, it was like falling asleep in one dream and waking up in another.

Tourists like locust swarms, seething through the clogged streets in their straw hats, flip-flops and shorts, the stench of sun lotion trailing them like a vapour cloud. Every few yards our cortège would lurch to a standstill, unable to pass until, amid chaos and shouts, they would skip out of the way, gawping pink faces flinching in shock at the sight of the Papás and the coffin bearing down on them. Sometimes, they would lunge for their cameras instead, the clicks and flashes exploding in our faces.

Ferries, cruise ships, motorboats, yachts, catamarans. There were hundreds of them, steaming, streaking, blowing into the caldera.

Rent this, sell that signs, now plastering one building after another, cars, mopeds, boats, rooms.

In the streets hawking souvenirs, plaster busts of Plato, plastic miniature temples, gaudy paintings of the Lost Isle, even genuine Atlantis pumice stones for the bathtub.

We were passing them left and right. Silver and gold boutiques for the better heeled. Chic sunset bars, the thump thump beat colliding with classical violin. Discos and nightclubs still reeking from last night's booze, their big city spivs lounging in the doorways eyeing street talent, while the hired help slops out for the evening shift.

Short-tempered waiters dashing between the tables, ferrying food, drink, money, the cash registers jangling. Atlantis cocktail hour, Atlantis Paradise, Atlantis this, that, the other, and the stench of cheap smoking meat from the souvlaki stands.

When two loyal fans recognised Huxley from his face in the popular press, they thrust their way forward, and even with the coffin on his shoulder, badgered him for autographs.

Much to their chagrin the great archaeologist stared stonily straight ahead, crushing his emotions as he always did between the granite millstones of his life, expediency and survival.

Abruptly, he came wading between the tables, the last person I expected to see, not here, in full view of everyone. Aris. He nudged me aside, taking my place under the coffin, all to the catcalls and hisses of a gang of half-juiced youths, probably his neighbours and childhood playmates.

Pangalos glared at them, raised his fist, corking the words in their mouths.

'Well done, Ari,' called Stavros. 'We shall make a philosopher of you yet.'

We were almost out of the souk, and into the elegant beauty of the town heights when the two red-top reporters, Jackson and Platt, darted out at us from one of the sunset bars, almost upsetting their beer boots in the process.

'How did he die, Huxley?' they slurred, hurling the question against his impassive face, then his profile, then his back. 'Will there be an inquest, Huxley? This is the second death, isn't it? Or were there others?'

Behind their plastic sunglasses, a pair of uniformed police officers threw us murderous looks. It may have been paranoia, yet in those grotesque faces I couldn't help reading a comfortable intimacy with torture.

If the Church was still hand in glove with the Colonels, no one would have guessed it from Father Nannos as he swept by with a thunderous look, hiding his infirmity, shepherd's staff in hand.

We were on the final stretch now, closer to the evening sky, our procession snaking along the crater wall. A breeze blew across the caldera, cooling the sweat on our brows.

Over the Burnt Islands the sun receded, turning lava bays and inlets into silver lakes and rivers.

Sam would have liked that, I thought. Wouldn't you, Sam?

'He's here with us now,' whispered Anna, giving me a start. 'Can you feel it?'

The sun went tumbling into the sea just as we gathered around the open grave. The heat was already ebbing, and the cicadas grew quieter, slower, like a clock winding down.

The Papás recited his lilting dirge over the coffin. The sprig of basil quivered in his hand and holy water welled from Sam's eye like a teardrop.

The coffin lid was brought and a final shadow passed over his face as it was fastened shut. Mad Yanni stepped forward with the ropes and deftly looped them around the coffin. Then it was lowered into the earth, lurching back and forth.

The first handful of earth went scattering over the wood like a hollow pelting rain. Anna tossed a flower into the grave. Aris roughly brushed away a tear from his cheek. At his side, Maria was burying sobs into Nestor's shoulder.

Watching the Papás hobble down the cemetery steps, the evening light glowing in his face, Huxley muttered: 'It seems everyone is leaving us. All the friends we knew. Where are they now? Still I cannot say, I cannot know.'

76.

The finds seemed insignificant at first. Yellowing shards prised out of the earth like teeth from an old jawbone. A few gourd-shaped amphorae and kitchen bowls, virtually intact, their exquisite designs evoking a summer morning, a flight of doves, a honey bee, an apple blossom, a still moment that knows eternity.

I was beginning to feel like I had been caught lying.

But then beyond the petrified trees, at the eastern limits of the temple grove, the picks began sparking off stone.

Inspecting the find, Huxley ran his fingers over the exposed limestone, chipping away at the clinging earth.

'What is it?' said Nestor crouching at the lip of the trench. Wary of Huxley's mercurial temper, his moles had retreated several steps. 'Is this Nico's wall?'

'It is the summit of a wall,' grunted Huxley, adding defiantly, 'but what kind of wall? Look at the massive build of it, the sheer size of these geometric blocks!' He scrambled out of the trench, barking at the moles: 'Well, what are you waiting for? Bring in the machines!'

We were digging day and night. Under the harsh August sun, under the dazzling carbide lights.

Mechanical diggers biting into moon dust. Conveyor belts rumbling down the slope, spewing ash and rubble over the cliff face. Picks and shovels deepening trenches inch by inch until the jealous ash relinquished its dead.

Wooden crates balancing on their bare shoulders, the moles ferried potsherds back to the sorting hut. Huxley watched them with bleak, defiant eyes, probably already knowing he was cursed. There seemed no end to them, these shards and fragments of things, these bits and pieces that wouldn't fit together however hard he tried.

'Where is Anna?' he demanded irritably, snatching another potsherd off the tabletop, the magnifying glass flooding its fractured light back into his face, a line of taunting hieroglyphs, the broken eye of a child, or was it a dolphin or a deer. 'I cannot understand her. Abandoning us now, when we need her most. Can that be right? *Can it?*'

'No!' he barked, as if sensing collusion. 'It cannot. Only pushing on will make sense out of all this, Benja's death, Sam's death, the lies and distortions this thing is throwing in our faces.'

The door swung open, the hut flooding with August light.

The moment chimed like a glass bell, for there stood Huxley's absent soldier, not in her habitual boots and fatigues, but in a blue summer dress. It could only mean one thing. She had no intention of returning to the trenches. She was deserting him.

'I expressly forbade you to go anywhere near 34,' he glowered, catching the magic carpet look in her eye.

Flopping down into one of the canvas chairs her bright laugh echoed irreverently around the hut. 'I have not been in 34, Marcus,' she said quietly. 'I have been out on the sea in our sailing skiff. I have been out to the rock beds under the tamarisk. I have been roaming the island. I have been watching the swifts soaring through the summer sky...'

'What is that to me? *Nothing!*'

Their friendship went darting between them like an orphaned shadow.

'Because I would never have believed it possible, just how different the world can look if only we alter course by a single degree.'

'Then live the illusion if that is your heart's desire, Anna. Believe in the soul of the sea, the innocence of a child, the beauty of a flower, and say yes, therein lies the glorious truth...'

'I won't plead with you, Marcus. I just wanted to ask you to remember what it was like when you could still surrender to a summer's day.'

'Surrender,' he mocked. 'While we are at war? Not while there's a single breath left in my body!'

Her lips held a wry smile. 'Then I have had my say.'

'Anna truly believes that the whole wide world can be saved by love,' he taunted, as she headed for the door.

'Oh no, Marcus,' she said, turning back to him, the words as bright as a child's poem. 'I believe that it is saved by love.'

★

We hurtled past Nestor's giant propellers, Huxley blind at the wheel as we hit the storm, pumice rattling against the windscreen like hail.

Seconds later, we emerged into the abrupt clarity of the temple heights. On the eastern slopes, Galatea's excavations were inching towards us, the upper storeys of some unidentified building now rising from the holocaust ash. Any day now the two sectors would meet, even if Huxley continued to wall them off with his own disdain.

Squinting against the sun, Galatea's favourites, Christos and Helia, waved up at us with the same bright enthusiasm they brought to everything. I waved back, luckily without getting caught. Under the tense gaze of the trench moles, Huxley was in confab with his foreman, checking progress at the limestone wall. A good thirty feet of geometric stonework had been unearthed, if barely to waist height.

'We are moving at a snail's pace,' he reproached Nestor. 'Until we know the length and breadth of it we are lost to guesswork; we are nowhere!'

Proving there was still method to his madness, he made a point of amending the site map, unfurling it over the hood of the Land Rover, then barked at the moles to get back to work.

When a solitary figure in the distance crossed his line of sight, he scowled. 'What's he doing up here?'

Aris. Looking ever more like his ancient image peeled from the dust, hair tumbling to his shoulders, filaments of gold striking the sun. Still keeping his solitary vigil outside house 34, rifle propped up against the wall.

'He's up here day and night, Kapitán,' shrugged Nestor. 'I've explained there's no need anymore, not with the rest of us up here, but he won't budge. He says he is waiting.'

'*Waiting?*' Huxley looked set to pounce, but then said dismissively: 'Then leave him. He has no purpose, and we have no time.'

We shifted ash by the ton, the exposed limestone walls rising ever higher from the fire-scorched earth.

Huxley stood below them, the bafflement and frustration of it telling in his clenched fists, his sweat-muddied face.

'I do not understand!' he seethed.

'But why, Kapitán?' said Nestor, sailing blithely into Huxley's gathering storm.

'Because these aren't temple or sanctuary walls, that's why!'

He had finally spoken the obvious out loud. 'Anyone with eyes in their head can see that. They're citadel walls, look at them!' He scrambled down the embankment and into the moat-like ditch, that only served to reinforce their martial appearance.

'They're six feet thick in places. Six feet! What does that tell you?' He went scurrying along the ditch like a man possessed, glaring up at the walls as if he would have them under siege. 'And here,' he yelled back at us, from what looked like a breach in the wall, where first one and then a second angular block had been unearthed. 'A fortified gateway, you can tell from the massive buttress stones.'

'But didn't Plato's legend say that?' called Nestor, before I could stop him. 'Isn't that the evidence you've been ransacking the island for all along?'

Huxley glowered back at us, uncertain whether he was the brunt of sarcasm, ignorance or the malevolence of fate itself.

'Where is Hadrian?' he yelled. 'Is it too much to ask that I should be able to rely on his intellectual capacity, his academic experience? And Anna? Where is Anna now that I need her. Where is Sam?'

He glared at the ancient houses, at the fake innocent blue sky and in typical Huxlian fashion ordered in more men and machines.

If this was war, he now waged it with a vengeance, trench by trench. Against the ever-looming citadel walls, the timber scaling contraptions looked like siege machines.

77.

I cut across the *plateia*, hoping to run into Stavros Sanassis or one of the other Symposiasts. Maybe they would know what to do. Maybe they would understand. As the swarm of tourists thinned, their clothes rustling like locust wings, I spotted an agitated Nondas Maharis at his shopfront. Something was wrong. 'Nondas!' I called, the sun glancing off his bald crown as he scurried between his possessions littering the street, his barber's chair, his mirror and basin, his striped barber's pole, everything.

'Well they did it, Nico,' he said, stooping to rescue a hairbrush, a comb, a bottle of cologne, before they were trampled under passing feet. Straightening up, he tossed a look of contempt at the café across the square where the crafty old landlord and his slick new tenant were still gloating over their success. 'They must have broken in during the night, changed the locks.'

'Where's Stavros? Where's Alexis?'

He sank into his barber's chair as if the world had just caved in on him, a pallor creeping over his face, as passers-by cast us quizzical looks. 'They came for Alexis before dawn, Nico,' adding bitterly, 'Of course! While all the *touristas* are still fast asleep in their beds and the town's deserted. Frogmarched down to the quay at gunpoint, Alexis' voice booming out *freedom! freedom!* despite the beating it earned him, you know how he is.'

'Can't we do something? There must be something we can do.'

'They are torturers, Nico! Murderers. Even the lawyers are afraid to speak.'

Fighting the current, I made my way through the jam of bodies, the stench of smoking souvlaki competing with wafts of noxious perfume and rancid sweat.

Escaping into a side street I ran into Anna, on her way to the cemetery to bring flowers to Sam's grave. Stavros Sanassis must have happened by too, bag in tow, his days now a mess of sunstroke and hangover cases, and young men prone to accidents while in police custody.

There was a shocked angry look to their faces and they didn't answer when I said hello. But then I saw her too. Angeliki, the little handicapped girl who used to run up to strangers, a bunch of wild-flowers in her hand. There, at the far end of the weed-choked garden, little fists clutching the bars of the storeroom window, swaying back and forth, whining, trying to get out.

'That's no way to treat a child, Kyria, any child, much less your own! Have you lost all sense of decency?'

A weary voice called back from the clothes line: Angeliki's mother, pegging up the bed sheets, the exhaustion and the summer heat telling in her face. 'I'm run off my feet as it is, Doctor. Washing, cooking, cleaning day and night, just trying to make ends meet. *What can we do?*'

She tossed her head scornfully at the rent rooms, souvenir boutiques, ice cream and souvlaki stands left and right. 'The neighbours, they complained that Angeliki was driving away the *touristas. Just look!* they screamed, *she's throwing stones at them now, pelting them with stones! Only yesterday we had to bandage some Englishman's head!* Then the police came hammering on the door, threatening to drag Angeliki away, saying they'll put her in that lunatic asylum halfway across the sea, haven't you heard of it, you must have, that place where children are chained to the beds and live in their own filth. Is that what you want? Is it?'

We threaded our way through the streets. 'Is this the island we have dreamed into being,' remarked Stavros, through numb lips. 'Ask Plato: what shall we create when innocence is a liability, a source of shame. Once lost, it can never be regained, not in this lifetime.'

Seeing my chance, I leapt at it: 'It is almost as if we were inside the Conundrum, Stavros, isn't it. Almost as if everything that's happened since our symposium has been about Plato, about Atlantis, about that metaphysical device they say he invented.'

He threw me a quizzical glance, probably wondering if I needed tablets like Benja.

'You don't believe me? Maybe you should visit camp. Maybe you should speak to your friend, Marcus. Maybe you should see what we are digging out of the ash!'

His eyes narrowed. 'Sam didn't die in the climbing ropes did he, Nico? Did he?'

78.

Nestor's lank figure appeared between the dunes on giant strides. 'Kapítán!' he called breathlessly. 'Come quickly!'

Irritation creasing his face, Huxley glanced up from his trowelling.

'You won't believe your eyes! A triumph Kapítán! Your crowning glory!'

Dumbfounded, Huxley hurried to catch up as his foreman led the way; moments later, we were scrambling down the scarp towards the eastern perimeter.

Gingerly, we negotiated the barbed wire. Then crossed the plank bridges traversing the maze of trenches that Galatea's students had carved, Huxley more than a little taken aback by the energy and devotion they had brought to the archaeological wilderness he had sentenced them to all those months ago.

Shinnying down a makeshift ladder, we came to an exposed wall in tricolour volcanic stone, an imposing arched doorway, and Galatea's anxious, startled face, her devoted students Christos and Helia at her side.

Snatching a gas lamp, Huxley plunged inside, light hissing at the ancient darkness, his eyes darting over the images peeled raw from the ash, willing his mind to understand.

He emerged blinking into the bright daylight. Then with an indecipherable nod — of recognition, of congratulation, *what?* — he thrust his way past Galatea, past Christos and Helia and clambered up the ladder.

Stony-faced, he swept past the milling students jabbering their praises at him, their eyes glittering with admiration, their hands ringing with applause.

'What was it?' I asked, panting as we climbed back up to the temple heights.

'A fresco.' I noticed he was avoiding my eyes, almost as if he were somehow ashamed of the truth, or even responsible for it.

Reluctantly, in fits and starts, he began to explain, almost wincing as he did so. 'It decorates the entire length of one wall. *Go and look for yourself!* Thirty feet or more… Ships with sails and fifty oarsmen each. Warriors armed to the teeth, raiding foreign coasts, plundering villages. An auction of dark-skinned slaves, their arms and feet bound tight by rope and chain. Grown men, women, children; the spoils of war. A public sacrifice, offering a hecatomb to the gods.'

He caught my uncomprehending look and rasped: 'Don't you understand? The fresco is not simply recording a historical event, *it is celebrating it!*'

I understood the moment I set eyes upon it, this fresco painted by a different hand, for a different master. A fleet of triumphant men-o'-war returning home, the warriors with their boar's tusk helmets, tall spears and bronze shields, the rowers at the oars keeping time to the drum. The citizens of the great city in festive mood, drifting towards the harbour to greet their returning heroes, people watching from the windows and rooftops of the towers and multi-storey houses. There is even a canal depicted, arcing through the island under the citadel walls.

Somehow, the discovery possessed power beyond reason, contaminating even the idealistic purity of the earlier frescoes, the dolphins, the swallows, the saffron pickers, the isles levitating above sunset.

It was as if their artists had become guilty by association, their motives, their honesty, now fatally impugned. Somehow, even the blue and ochre houses, the temples and fountains, had become suspect, as though their naivety had always concealed a lurking corruption.

'But what kind of building is it?' I asked, as I recorded the discovery in the log. 'It's not a residence, is it? Or a workshop? What was its purpose?'

He sat at the trestle table, gingerly touching his forehead with tapping fingertips, as if trying to still the tumbling thoughts beyond. 'We don't yet know. We are digging. We are digging.'

79.

'Stavros, look!' cried Huxley with a demented laugh, on all fours in the ash. 'Animal bones! After all these years of fruitless digging! *Animals!*' With a look of numb dismay, Sanassis advanced towards us, as baffled by the looming citadel walls, as by the sight of his old friend scrambling about the rubble, raving to himself, hands plunging into the ash dunes, fingers probing for bones.

Up to his elbows, he retrieved them one at a time, curious bleached shapes virtually unrecognisable to the untrained eye. 'Can we have been so mistaken? Or did the market stalls extend all the way along here as well, those selling meat and livestock, perhaps?'

After some fumbling with both hands, the ash crumbling and falling away as he tugged, there it was, a large skull still bearing a pair of horns. An ox.

When several minutes later he drew out a slender bleached bone, Sanassis flinched. Swallowing hard, he sank to his knees, gently retrieving it from Huxley's hands. 'That's not an animal bone, Marcus,' he said quietly. 'It is a human fibula.'

I saw the recognition seeping reluctantly into his eyes: that this had to be the sacrificial square depicted in Galatea's loathsome fresco.

While Huxley drafted in the moles to clear the tephra, Sanassis wandered back towards the temple, hands thrust deep into his pockets, face creased in thought. Under the sailcloth canopy strung between the temple columns, he found Hadrian humming to himself, musical notes and intervals dashing over the page. 'Stavros, what do you think?' his smudged glasses aiming a look of anguish at the sky. 'If I eliminate every source of polluting sound, will I hear the music then? I have already blocked out the sea and the birds and the senseless chatter of human beings. Thank God there are no whispering trees or babbling brooks in this godforsaken place, but what am I to do about the flapping of the moths at night, or worse, the moaning of the wind through the wires?'

Sanassis glanced back at me in dismay, then walked on, following his suspicions all the way to 34. Aris stirred as he approached; they exchanged a few words, and the next thing I heard was the plank wood door scraping over the stones.

Lest Huxley realise the risk I stood before him, blocking his line of sight, peppering him with technical questions about removing the tephra without endangering whatever was lurking below.

I was still scraping and brushing when a shout welled up on the wind.

Seconds later, the weatherproofing door burst open and Sanassis staggered out on buckling legs, coughing and retching.

'Marcus! Nestor!' came the ragged, delirious cry. Aris scrambled to his feet and was already shouldering Sanassis' weight as I dashed over, snatching a water flask as I went. Sanassis subsided onto the temple steps, still gasping for breath.

I handed him the flask, which he almost drained in a single draught. 'What did you see?' I pressed him, as Huxley and Nestor came running. *'What did you see?'*

'Marcus!' he gasped. 'You must fence it off at once! The fumes, they must be seeping in from below.' He blinked hard, fighting for words, his speech still slurring, the ground still reeling. 'Not that I remarked anything at first, just that curious smell reminiscent of — *what?* — cloves, cinnamon, opium, something like that. It was only the stench of sulphur that brought me round at all. *How can you not have known?'* He struggled to his feet, examining the face of his friend, as if not quite recognising him anymore. 'You have people at risk. Their lives! Their sanity, like Benja, like Hadrian! And for what, Marcus? Is this how you would exploit them? I never took you for a cynic, no, not even when you insisted on playing the Devil's Advocate to provoke us all…'

Huxley scowled, turned on his heel. 'Get him out of my camp!'

What is he saying? I thought, as Sanassis descended the hill, still remonstrating with Nestor as he went.

'What is he saying?' I yelled. 'That it's all drugs, that it's all illusion! One big fucking conjuring trick. This whole thing. This whole place!'

Huxley spun around in fury, but had no words even to speak.

80.

Agonisingly, hour by hour, the form began to emerge under our trowels and brushes.

'What is it?' I asked, as Huxley, grimacing, rubbed away at the stubborn ash deposits with his calloused hands.

A perfectly round stone, ten feet in diameter, dipping at its centre, and with carved sloping gutters at its circumference. Using his fingernail, he scraped until the last film of ash was loose, blowing it away to reveal something darker beneath, the colour of nicotine.

'It is as I thought,' he said, in a staccato voice. 'This is an altar stone. This is blood. The priests assembled here. Offered their blood sacrifices to god or gods. Animal. Human.'

'But I thought it was the agora, the marketplace.'

'In a way, that's exactly what it was.'

'What?'

'What I mean is,' he replied, his voice twisting with scorn, 'kings, princes, satraps, merchants — in the Oracle's heyday they came from far and wide, their ships bearing tribute in gold, silver and precious stones, eager to divine the will of the gods in the questions that preoccupied them most: trade, war, alliance, marriage, heirs to thrones, the spoils divided or torn between them. Ask now how many enemies the great Oracle will create.'

'But I thought it was knowledge of the dead they were after... The Ferryman. The passage. The worlds beyond.'

'Knowledge of fate,' he glared. 'The child of Life and Death and their eternal titanic clash. They would interrogate the darkness, seeking the lost knowledge of their ancestors. They would wring prescience from their fallen kinsmen, all to know what omens, favourable or ill, already shadow their every thought, their every step, endangering their kingdoms, their colonies, their estates. Somewhere up here will be the treasury, you can bank on it.'

When a man's heavy gold bracelet was discovered by a jubilant Christos and Helia one house beyond the war frescoes, he said with a mirthless smile: 'The temple treasury. What did I tell you? This is

453

where the tributes were stored. If history is anything to go by, it would have been jammed with treasure, floor to ceiling, if only to shame the pilgrims into outdoing the generosity of their rivals. After all, there were futures to buy.'

'Then where's the rest of it?' I said, throwing a glance into the bare dark rooms.

Nestor's moles shovelled, drilled and blew their way through the ash until finally there it was, an ominous shadow against the corn-flower sky: the citadel's massive western gateway.

We stood beneath it, dwarfed by its towering presence, intimidated by its purpose, by the sheer weight and size of its reinforced buttresses and limestone blocks.

Huxley was inspecting the ground on all fours, running his fingers over the exposed earth.

He shouted for Nestor, beckoned me over with a curt toss of the head.

'Look,' he said, adding with sarcasm or pathos, it was difficult to tell: 'Here is your crime scene... In a way, you were always expecting to find one, weren't you?'

Eyes probing every inch of ground, I was trying to make sense out of what we were seeing. A chaotic series of intersecting footprints, a few shards of pottery, several scattered arrow heads, a dozen pitted round stones like shot-puts, a single bronze dagger.

To the tall approaching shadow of his foreman, he said: 'We need a plaster replica of these footprints without delay. And bring the monorail camera. We cannot go further until we have catalogued everything here.'

'Well?' he demanded, already scribbling notes, and making a rough sketch of the scene.

'I don't see it,' I said. 'Something happened, but what? There must have been soldiers or sentries here, because of the arrow heads.'

'Ask yourself why the footprints have been preserved like that. Ask why there are black stains on the stone buttresses.'

For several minutes he watched me sweat and struggle, but then finally relented, directing my attention back to the crime scene, using his pencil as a pointer. 'The black stains are scorch marks. Fire.'

He hooked one of the potsherds by the loop of a broken handle.

'The pottery fragments are the remains of hydria — three-handled water jugs. They must have been shattered in the mêlée, dropped as the defenders slithered over the wet ground, or else thrown down when the gates were being battered open.'

He traced the outline of a footprint with his finger.

'The chaos of footprints, stamped as if in clay — they tell their own story of panic, the defenders running back and forth in a frenzy, trying to douse the flames at the gate. So much water was thrown that the ground became sodden. But then, as if in a kiln, it baked hard from the sheer ferocity of the fire, capturing their doomed footprints forever.'

He added in a taut voice: 'And if you ask yourself why the footprints are flecked with ash, there can be only one explanation: *the volcano is erupting...*'

'But the enemy,' I argued. 'They must see the mountain's on fire. Why would they even take the risk —'

'Fed on blood and plunder, Mycenaean warriors like these would pluck triumph from the jaws of death itself. Even under the darkening skies, the snowing ash, they'll already sense that those once mighty and intimidating walls are in reality as weak as a man's bones crumbling from disease.'

An arms-akimbo shadow at our backs, Nestor said: 'If I remember my Plato, Atlantis was under attack before it sank beneath the waves, isn't that right Kapítán? Suffocating in tyranny, riddled with corruption...'

81.

Edging ever closer, the two sectors were now only yards apart. More gingerly than ever they scratched away at the tephra, Galatea and her students on one side, Nestor's moles on the other. 'Can you hear us?' they called through the ash, but the voices from beyond seemed as muffled as ever.

Wielding picks the students had advanced another three feet, when the ash wall collapsed in a sudden whoosh and an immense cloud of dust.

Seeing bottomless pits and grinding fissures, they leapt back in panic, imaginations running wild. But as the dust settled, they were left staring, not at Nestor's helmeted moles tunnelling in from the other side, but at a gaping hole to the east, still snowing ash. After several moments of deliberation, Galatea invoking every archaeological god she could think of this side of the Nile, they squeezed through into the bloodless light beyond, scarcely daring to breathe.

Wide-eyed and trembling, one of the student runners came bursting into the agora to fetch us.

Climbing through, our helmet lights and torches swept through the devouring darkness, highlighting dust. Such as it was, the air was thin, stale, difficult to breathe. Christos was guiding us along footprints in the ash, the shock still telling in his face. At our backs, the bright hole in the hillside receded like the light marking the mouth of a tunnel.

'We shouldn't be in here at all, Kapitán,' murmured Nestor, casting an anxious glance at the roof of compacted ash above us. 'One shout, one tremor, could bring the whole lot down on our heads.'

'A courtyard of some description,' muttered Huxley, his eyes roaming left and right. 'Ringed by buildings — look, you can still make out the scorched façade, the windows.'

Grey stumps and pillars littered the ground here and there. 'Petrified trees,' he remarked, adding with asperity, 'is that what I was dragged down here for?'

You could even make out the dappled bark, the tree rings.

Flickering carelessly over Christos' bare back, his torch brought

Galatea's face looming out of the darkness, wan with shock, Helia at her side.

Eyes straying to the discovery at their feet, Huxley's march across the buried courtyard abruptly lost all momentum, as if the will to know had deserted him.

There were nine altogether. Nine corpses lying in a tangled heap, dark holes where their eyes and mouths should have been.

'The hot ash must have turned them to stone,' said Galatea, wincing at the monstrous faces.

His dry lips bleeding where he had bitten into them, Huxley said, 'Not before they died. Look, there.' He pointed to one of the charred figures, a scream set in stone on its face. Something was protruding from its throat. Disguised by the embalming ash, it looked as if it might once have been a crossbow bolt or a broken arrow, but Huxley was adamant, examining the object at close quarters. 'A dagger,' he concluded. 'If you look carefully, you can even make out the hilt.'

'Silver blade and ebony handle,' I murmured absently.

With a sharp intake of breath, Huxley stiffened. 'Galatea: be so kind as to take the cast. If there is a single face to be found on the inside of those grotesque masks, I want to see it.'

Bleak eyes probing the tangle of bodies, he added: 'Nestor: fetch Aris.'

'But why Kapítán? What's the use? Aris is just Aris.'

'No one is who they say they are! *No one!*' The volume was enough to send grains of ash singing down on our heads. Our eyes darted to the entombing roof in alarm.

Lest Galatea and her brood overhear him, Huxley thrust me aside, whispering through gritted teeth, 'it's possible the boy still retains some atavistic memory of this moment, you know that.' He added with asperity: 'Sitting up there, hour after hour, the knowledge entombed within his head just as these bodies are entombed within the ash itself.'

Not a moment too soon we climbed out into the late summer sun.

'But I don't understand, Kapítán. The enemy was at the gates. So who were these people? Why are they at each other's throats? Why are they killing each other? *Who is fighting who?*'

'Dig! *Dig!*' he barked, as if digging might finally lay bare the clockwork mechanisms of fate itself. 'Clear the ash. All of it! Blow it to kingdom come!'

Coaxing him away from his silent vigil, I led Aris through the broken crust, into the hillside and the shadowless twilight.

Under Huxley's relentless gaze, he approached the ash-embalmed bodies with a look as inert as stone. Just as I sensed Huxley reaching his flashpoint, demanding reaction, Ari's hand strayed towards the tortured face of the scream, fingertips exploring the contours of the stone, lingering over the forehead and the brow. Was that a wince, a flicker of anger or grief? Whatever it was, I can't have been the only one to think it's out of character, it's out of place.

Was that the unconscious recognition he had been waiting for? Memories made of something other than synapses releasing their fountains of light.

Huxley dismissed him with a gruff nod. 'Don't tell me he's not hiding something,' adding with a clap of thunder, '*Even from himself!*'

★

The days ran like watercolours, bleeding into the fibres of time.

Back on the surface, the moles had shifted enough tephra to trace the long path of the great walls, striking out from the gateway on a north-south axis.

As the implications percolated through him, Huxley stood under their gashing shadows, surveying this new reality that had emerged like a disease, too numb to move.

'We have been deceived,' he called at last, his voice tolling across the excavations like a funeral bell. 'By the ash, by our own wishful thinking, *worse*, by that which we always guarded against — *appearances!*'

'What do you mean?'

'Don't you see? *Don't you understand?*' He threw up his arms with a fractured laugh. 'All this time we have been digging in the inner sanctum of the island. Yes, almost as if we had been digging in a monastery, oblivious to the raging world beyond its ancient walls and tranquil gardens. A place virtually immune to the flow of time, while all around, the years have come and gone, and things have changed beyond recognition.'

Hand over fist, he scaled the great walls until he stood atop them.

Wind tearing at his words, he yelled: 'These fortress walls didn't even exist when the temple was built. They were thrown up much later,

458

and you can see, they will end up ringing the entire site, the agora, the houses, the Sacred Way.'

'But why?' I shouted up at him. 'To keep people out? To protect those within?'

He scrambled down, grazing his arms and ripping his khaki shirt in the process. He didn't seem to care, nor even notice the occasional drop of blood that now splattered into the dust.

'Whatever it was before,' he said at last, the words spitting from his mouth like bloodied, broken teeth, 'this place became a prison, its walls encompassing everything. These people... they became prisoners within their own city, their own island, their own minds, the earliest frescoes evoking an idyll already dead.'

82.

The risk too great for Galatea's inexperienced crew, Nestor's moles took over, burrowing deep into the hillside.

It looked like a silver mine now, a black hole carved out of the lava crust, shored up by wooden beams and struts.

'A hundred yards more,' gasped Nestor, his lamplit face oddly flushed against the tephra. 'Once past the temple we'll join the warren of tunnels running towards the mountain, I'm sure of it.'

Kicking out the dust behind them, the moles scratched and burrowed until they hit native rock. Then they struck out in opposite directions, until at last there was an exultant yell. The drifts of remaining ash fell away almost effortlessly, revealing the cavernous mouth of a tunnel, hewn by magma and steam aeons ago.

We waited for the OK to follow them in, gritting our teeth, screwing our feet impatiently into the ash.

'To hell with it,' muttered Huxley, about to barge his way in when we heard a strangled shout, a voice swallowed by a beast: 'Stay back, Kapítán!'

Seconds later, they burst out of the shaft, coughing and retching, one even crawling out on all fours, as another dragged him by the arm.

'Gas!' gasped Nestor, an unfamiliar delirium swimming in his eyes. 'The air's toxic down there. Sanassis was right.'

A dangerous edge to his voice, Huxley demanded to know what he meant.

'We were directly under 34,' explained Nestor, still breathing hard. 'There were small shafts rising up between the columns. Manmade. Carved out of the volcanic rock. I saw them with my own eyes, a baker's dozen of them in three rows, like the pipes of a church organ.'

Hadrian stood at his shoulder, blinking incredulously. It was his first day back on the job and he could hardly have chosen a worse one. 'It was all psychological manipulation, volcanic fumes, is that what you're saying, do my ears deceive me...?'

'We need to clear it,' insisted Huxley. 'Sink a ventilation shaft, maybe position one of the fans here at the entrance.'

Once the air was deemed safe to breathe, we entered the shaft, moistened bandannas pulled down over our noses just in case.

'By rights we should have gas masks,' muttered Nestor, calling back to us: 'The moment anyone feels light-headed, dizzy, strange, don't think twice, *shout!* The dose is unlikely to be constant; if anything it will come on a belch from the magma chamber, half a mile under our feet.'

We pressed on. Then out of the gloom our darting torch beams caught splashes of colour from the manmade walls up ahead. With a deft sweeping motion of the hand, Huxley brushed away the dust, uttering an exclamation of disgust as the lurid image emerged; frescoes of the journey to the other side, isles rising from the sunset, yet these different than the rest, as though some rancid imagination had been ordered to produce vision by threat or patronage. A heaven made of conquest and possession.

'Behold — the elixir of religious delirium,' declared Huxley, with implacable derision. 'What can we deduce from the evidence? This: having paid their tribute, initiates and devotees would make their way into this maze of volcanic tunnels, into the inner chambers...'

'But how can that be?' rambled Hadrian, stumbling after us as we resumed our exploration. 'Must the facts fit the picture, Huxley, or the picture the facts?'

We entered a larger chamber, its ceiling only visible at all because of the torches in our hands and the sudden bright reflective quality of the rock. Our giant silhouettes twitched across the walls with the motion of shadow puppets.

'Here are your facts, Hadrian,' said Huxley in a voice as caustic as sulphur itself. 'Devoting their lives to illusion, engineers achieved an almost perfect manipulation of natural and volcanic light. Glancing off the obsidian mirrors, reflecting off the white stone with its glittering flecks of crystal. Already high on their own adrenalin, our gullible pilgrims enter this ingenious mise en scène. Marionettes, flickering over the white walls plunging ever deeper into the heart of the volcano, evoking their own escaping souls, or the ghosts of their ancestors. On the same bogus plays of light appear the banks of the Styx, the far shore, the asphodel meadows of Elysium, the Isles of the Blest... The sulphurous breath of the volcano wafting in now, sweetened, perhaps, with jasmine or poppy seed incense, the potency heightened with opium resin or some other hallucinogen, sending our devotees into mystical frenzy before they hear the Oracle speak, words echoing through the coiling tunnels, persuasive enough, hope the shepherd priests, to fleece them of their gold, their land, even their power.'

'But even if that were so,' objected Hadrian, drawing a sidelong glance from Nestor, 'that doesn't necessarily invalidate our own experiences does it? Does it, Huxley. No priest told us what to see, what to believe...'

Huxley scowled. 'The universe is predicated on deception, Hadrian, every last atom of it, or had you forgotten? We seek the truth even though the truth is impossible to know or attain. Cynicism is not a malady of the spirit but the only logical response to a reality that is all fabrication and duplicity. Every last truth or belief we ever thought we knew will end up here, in a tomb of ash, mountains ground into grains of sand...'

'You are wrong,' stumbled Hadrian. 'I know what you're saying once made immaculate sense to me, but you are wrong.'

The coiling tunnels seemed to snatch his voice and echo it back at us, gathering something of its own dark malevolence along the way.

'But aren't we constantly creating and recreating the universes in which we live?' I said. 'Isn't that what Plato meant?'

Huxley shook his head at us, his mouth twisted in contempt.

The tunnels closed in around us, forcing us into single file. For ten minutes or more, we were corkscrewing through rock, losing all sense of orientation.

Abruptly, we spilled into another sequence of cavernous chambers, these formed by solidified lava, blacker than night.

The numb silence seemed to ring in our ears as we interrogated the feeble beams offered up by our hand and helmet torches. The tapering side tunnel that went plunging ever deeper into the darkness, barely wide enough for a child to crawl through. The peculiar stains to the vaulted ceilings. Scorch marks, perhaps, along with flashes of brimstone yellow sulphur.

Wary of the cloying air, we followed Nestor's swift lead and pulled the bandanas down over our mouths and noses.

'We can't stay long, Kapitán, not in here,' came the muffled warning.

As the restless beams glanced over some dark, formless shape at the mouth of the tunnel, I edged forward to investigate.

A stupid thing to do. The shock propelled me backwards, smashing me into the wall. The blood was already trickling through my hair, into my eyes. I began gasping for air.

'What is it?' yelled Nestor, darting over.

Torches converging, they leapt out at us.

Five little children sitting in a huddle, their clawing limbs and insect-like faces still miming the same death agony that had claimed them as the magma vents ruptured.

Caught in the blast, they too had been turned to stone, cruel volcanic effigies buried under the ash.

'Why, Kapítán? Who are they? What are they doing here?'

'They are the seers,' rasped Huxley with a twisted grimace, ripping away his bandana. 'Children, fed on poison to divine the will of the gods. Can't you see them? Held underground merely as a pretence, their skin turning as translucent as grubs in the soil. Can't you hear them? Pitiful bleating voices echoing through this coiling inner ear of tunnels — almost like the lost children within us, dreaming some nightmare that we are living. Voices amplifying as they reach the temple priests in the Necromanteion above, interpreting the prophecy according to their overlords' will.'

He took a lungful of dead poisonous air. 'Don't you understand? In the hands of the priests, death has become a dark and fearful place. A land of shadows and corruption.'

He thrust his way out of the maze, so carelessly that chutes of ash rained down on our heads as he barged into the supporting beams at the shaft entrance.

I found him on the southern slopes. He used to survey the entire site from this high vantage point, the king of the castle atop his mound of grey rubble, flecked with crushed particles of civilisation and the lives that had known it.

No longer.

The shock was still leaching its way through his bloodstream like some ancient disease. His face, as bloodless as the dead dust itself. His hands, trembling. His beleaguered eyes, staring straight through me, through ash and solid rock, through limpid blue sky.

At that moment, I knew he was seeing the same thing as me.

Plato's shimmering ghost.

No, not some nebulous apparition that comes gliding through solid walls, but something else, something made of light, mind and infinity. A presence capable of bending time and space to its will. Whatever it was, however it functioned, it had never been so close or so tangible.

Across the peninsula, there were archaeological ruins as far as the eye could see. Yet somehow, it was the idyll this ancient city had once found in our hearts and minds that now lay in ruins more complete than time alone could ever have achieved.

'Why don't you just fucking admit it?' I yelled, hurling the words at him.

He barged past, scrambling down the scarp.

'They were losing the fairest of their precious gifts,' I taunted him. 'What was that? What did Plato mean by it?'

83.

I watched him climb the hill, a charcoal figure against the firestorm sky. His shadow flickered between the temple columns, as if the dusk sensed his desperation, and then he was gone, the plank wood door grating closed behind him.

Seeing him strangled in the ropes, asphyxiated by volcanic gas, throwing himself off the high beams, I wondered if I should raise the alarm, indecision making me pace back and forth under the emerging stars. I threw a questioning look at Aris, who silently shook his head, eyes glittering in the marble reflected starlight.

It wasn't until midnight that he returned, the crunching of pumice under his boots jolting me awake.

'What happened?' I leapt to my feet.

'Have you forgotten the rules?' he rasped, fighting for breath, his darting eyes momentarily finding their curious focus on Aris. 'I need pen and paper. *Now.*'

Walking him down to the field tent he leaned heavily on us, his head lolling first to the sky then to his own stumbling feet.

Keeping our silent vigil we watched him write in a fierce trance, the lamplight casting his pointy silhouette over the canvas. Watched, as his hand fought cramp, his scrawl chasing along the lines.

The last of his energy spent, his head almost touching the table, I brought up the Land Rover and drove him home through the muffled darkness, white dust billowing in the mirrors. He could or would not speak. There was a feverish look in his eye and every so often an involuntary shudder would run through him.

I had hardly switched on the lights before he dragged himself into the front room, crumpling onto the sofa. I brought him mountain tea sweetened with honey, but he seemed more delirious than ever, eyelids twitching, limbs jerking to the nightmare still raging within him.

I snatched up his notebook. The words were like shells over a battle-field, the detonations ringing in my ears, the earth and stones bursting into my face.

★

I hauled myself up, one beam, one rung at a time, this ladder into the sky I had Nestor build for me.

Finally, I had reached my point of no return, I knew that. To turn back empty-handed — no. Not again. Trudging back to the fragments hut, where the puzzle at my fingertips threatens to shatter my mind into a million shards and smithereens.

My palms were slippery with sweat, my teeth gritty with dust. The last rung behind me, I heaved myself up onto the swaying platform, dangling in the sky on timber and rope.

I fumbled with the straps, buckles and stirrups, but swiftly lost patience. What use was this glorified safety harness to me? I had to know the truth. Once and for all. However bleak. However glorious.

I leapt, plunging into the blueness. My eyes were wide open, and all around my head the silver bubbles fizz like the falls in a mountain torrent.

Who is there?

Is anybody there? Damn you, is anybody there!

What is that, do you hear it...? If ever so faintly, my eardrums hum to the sound... a whisper welling up towards me...

Until, there it is, tuned to perfection, yes! — your own hollow shout. Echoing back at you through the vast dark emptiness.

So this is the answer you have always craved. This. The true meaning of what lies beyond us.

Nothingness. Oblivion.

Is that the true meaning of it? I yelled at the top of my lungs. *I will not back down now; no, not before man, God or eternity. Is this your meaning of Life? That it has no meaning at all, no higher purpose than this, a futile struggle to survive, to eat or be eaten? Then take it! I shall be glad to be rid of it. I shall be glad to be dead!*

I began my descent, rung by rung. Passed between the arches. Wrenched open the door. Lifted my distracted gaze to the temple heights, and one, two, three heartbeats later, the shock wave hits me and almost blows me off my feet.

Conscious of my own quickening breath, my homespun robe, my sandaled feet, I find myself hurrying towards the agora, trying to think, trying to remember, *who am I, what am I doing here?*

Gardens pass in a blaze of summer glory, then the sacred grove with its ancient trees. *Where is everybody?* The streets and squares deserted, the only movement the plash of the fountains.

On to the nearest vantage point, the high crest of the hill, the breathtaking image already there in my mind's eye. Houses and temples clustered around a crescent bay so pronounced it might have been drawn by a compass. Canals and waterways, arcing in from the sea like concentric ripples across a pond. Cutting between rounded hills. Bringing a stroke of blue to the farming villages they pass through, the sail-wing ships seeming to glide between the houses.

Ripples forming islands within islands, just as Plato will describe two thousand years from now.

And before you ask, yes, the coincidence has struck me, but that is all it is, coincidence; the way this ripple effect that crosses the island might be seen as a visible representation of the Conundrum itself. Variations radiating out across time, across possibility, human souls, island souls, what's the difference, that's what he would have us understand.

My eyes roam over the blue and ochre houses with their polished stone and sky terraces. Linger over the seashell windows of the Thalassa house, with its exquisite frescoes of the sea. I almost expect to find him standing there as I pass, Sam, I mean, or whatever name he goes by here, gazing down from the scaffold, fulfilling his commission for the master of the house.

A shiver runs through me, in spite of the sultry air. I know why. I'm rebelling against the implications; the daunting idea that Sam, through some lucky instinct or collision of thought, may have been right after all and that here and there, somewhere or other, we are always alive. It is only consciousness that flits from one life to the other, awakening, brightening, fading.

But no, no, I cannot bring myself to believe it. I cannot.

If that is how we exist, as permutations in numerous places at the same time, then where is the truth? Where is the one real us? Where is the island we have sought, its true face, its true countenance?

At last the citadel walls loom up before me, geometric limestone blocks whose workmanship alone beggars belief.

Still there is not a single soul. The villas and apartments deserted. The beds made, the stoves cold, pots and pans neatly stowed away.

Scaling the high ramparts I'm almost at the highest steps when the muffling effect of the great walls abruptly gives way to a deep, distant roar. Beyond the northern towers that eclipse it from the streets below, the mountain now looms over us like some vengeful god of legend, huffing and puffing, poison thundering from its cone, seething into the sky.

Atlantis, its annihilation almost upon us. Don't tell me fate doesn't have a sense of humour just as black and twisted as our own!

Along the curve of the shore, under beams of sunlight breaking through the deepening gloom, I can make out the beached Mycenaean ships, their reinforcements still flowing towards the citadel like some dark disease. The forward contingent already has the western gates under siege, the battering ram raining sparks, catapult stones blasting the ramparts, the fiery volleys of the bowmen arcing high over the walls.

There is something desperate and futile about it now, the fire-blackened gates buckling under the ram, jars of sloshing water being passed back and forth along a ragged line to douse the flames, the citadel guard, slaves, slithering over the slick mud.

With a final splintering, the gates burst open and in they surge on a triumphant roar, broadswords clashing against shields, skin, bone.

Javelins at the ready, broadswords drawn, reinforcements come charging across the square on a blood-curdling war cry. Drill, discipline, war; they have erased all emotion, all humanity from their faces. How will I ever explain my presence here? Eyes blazing, footfall juddering through the soles of my sandals, they raise their swords, about to cleave my head in two, then... plunge straight through me.

I gaze down in astonishment, the mute cry still in my throat. Watch, as my body quivers, becomes translucent, then virtually invisible. Watch, as it trembles back into being, as insubstantial as a shadow to the wind.

No wonder the guardsmen didn't strike you down! the realisation coming on a stab of dismay. *No wonder they marched right through you.* You are ghost, not flesh and blood. Neither here nor there. Neither dead nor alive.

And what futile truth am I supposed to glean from this — another morsel of a reward, perhaps, that will open some other trapdoor in time?

Yet the ghost, it seems, he has some will to live after all; I even catch myself wondering how I will ever find my way home again. At least, back to the time I once knew or believed to be my own.

Past the great houses on the hill, cocooned in that inexplicable serenity. Then on towards the eastern gates, wide open, abandoned. I pass under the great stone portal, and there they are, making their way along the broad avenue sweeping down towards the waterways and harbour wharves hollowed out of tricolour volcanic rock. A caravan of carriages and carts. Horses snorting, neighing in panic. Elite troops marching in parallel columns, with denser defensive lines front and rear, some still chanting their wretched paean to the people's glory.

It can't be long now. The sky's darkening by the minute, a baleful purple, like an angry bruise. Intermittently, lightning crackles dementedly through the clouds.

The thrum of the volcano conducts its way through everything, quivering even my own reflection, mimicking the sensation of skin. Tremors strike without warning, the earth cramping and twitching through its epileptic fits, walls shaking, statues teetering, cobblestones wrenched like teeth. Now and again even I throw out an invisible hand just to stay on my feet, such is the guile with which existence convinces us we are.

The snowing ash is falling thick and fast now. It comes floating down from the sky, just as snow should, mesmerising, oddly beautiful. Strange to think that, in it, I can read my own future, see my own purgatory.

Under the shadow of the great walls, I find myself in a warren of unfamiliar streets and alleyways. Hovels. Cave-like workshops. Three-storey slum tenements. By the look and stench of them, each slave family assigned a windowless room the size of a cubicle. Deserted.

This sector was never on our excavation plan. Even if it survives the blast of the volcano, it will take us another thousand years to get here.

As I weave my way through the maze, trying not to get lost, another piece of the jigsaw tumbles reluctantly into place, the unadorned facts staring back at me from the open windows and doorways. Meals abandoned on the tables. Pots still bubbling away over stoves and hearths.

Oh, how blatantly we were deceived three and a half millennia from now! Unearthing those fine abandoned villas up on the hill, as likely as not the estates of merchants and noblemen, long since in exile. The limits of our archaeological horizon the summit of a hill, where beauty and ingenuity were on display for anyone who could afford the price of admission. Without other finds to contradict us, why else would we suppose that not everyone lived like this, among gardens and fountains, spacious rooms with breathtaking frescoes, running water, windows opening onto sea and sky.

The alley turns a blind corner, then another, as it dips towards the sea. A blast of wind hits me, funnelling between the houses, then a murmur welling into a roar.

And then all hell breaks loose, lament, terror, desperation amplified a thousand times, and a thousand times again, rolled up into one awful wave.

Sweat, fear, filth and sulphur, that's the unmistakable stench as they come churning along the street like so much flotsam to the storm, the remorseless flood crushing my ghost against the wall, the shouts and shrieks of the children too much to bear.

Fishermen, farmers and saffron pickers. Artisans, bakers and blacksmiths. Deserting soldiers, slaves and beggars. Musicians still with their drum and kithara in tow, the skin and the strings sounding their own lament in the crush. Young women with babies hugged tight to their breasts. Students from the academy, schoolchildren, teachers. Running. Running as fast as their legs can carry them, jostled, crushed, down to the harbour front, in search of a boat, a ship, anything that can float.

The sky dims. The thrumming underfoot becomes a pounding heartbeat you could confuse with your own.

A young woman happens by, striking even at first glance. No, not for the cornflower blue dress ripped to the thigh, or the intense Minoan eyes that might leave this world forever before the day is out, but for the water vessel held protectively to her bare breast like an infant. Compared to the pottery we have exhumed from the ash, exceptional, as round as a gourd. Possibly an antique in its own right, a family heirloom, the vivid depictions running across its circumference evoking the island's past. Halcyon days lost to time. Memories, residing now in the mausoleum of myth.

I edge closer, if only to catch a glimpse of its lost innocence, its curious mingling representations of heaven and earth. Stargazers, spice gatherers, a priestess meditating upon the soaring swifts, a regatta of sailing boats upon a bright sea, a hilltop village without a rampart in sight, islands scattering into the blue —

In the tightening crush, she stumbles, almost falls, the precious vessel slipping from her grasp.

I watch as it goes tumbling through the lurid twilight as if on some reluctant patch of time. Watch, as it finally surrenders to the inevitable, striking the rough stones underfoot with a hollow thud, cracking into two jagged hemispheres, earth, sky, the domain of the mortals, the domain of gods.

Her anguished cry is all but smothered by the stampede, frantic feet kicking, trampling, crushing.

Under bloodied soles the hemispheres shatter, a thousand fragments bursting out like shrapnel.

In the vacuum the moment bequeaths, as everything else achieves a perfect hissing stillness, jostling feet, snowing ash frozen in time, I watch the fragments twirling through the air like some improbable symphony born in the heavens.

Some I have even seen before, I just know it; that one there with the petal of a blue flower, that one, bearing the fingers of a human hand; that one, the fractured face of a god, a forest, a village among blossoming spice fields... Fragments of heaven and earth, life and death. Fragments of great city squares and wild mountains. Fragments of God. Of humans. Of animals. Fragments of body and soul...

'Those whom the gods wish to destroy...' I catch the murmur on my lips, even as the moment resumes its ear-splitting chaos. 'They first make mad.'

Don't you see? Don't you understand? I've been toiling over these shards and fragments for longer than I can even remember, bits and pieces that wouldn't fit together however hard I tried, and still the mystery defeated me.

Awake or asleep, sealing fractures, cementing cracks, assembling, demolishing, my mind closer to madness than an answer. I didn't even recognize it in the mirror, when I caught a stranger staring back at me. Demanding the fragments form the picture they were hiding from us, never suspecting for a moment that that was the picture all along. Brokenness. Madness. Thoughts, strangers to emotion. Words, strangers to the mind that conceived them. Actions, strangers to the heart that would believe them...

471

84.

Ash flies in a sudden squall. Frantic crowds are pressing towards the gated wharves. There aren't enough ships. Sentries are pushing them back, people falling in the crush or bludgeoned to the ground. Others, skirting past, go scrambling down a steep escarpment to the shoreline, wading or flailing about in a sea already choked with pumice.

Ships brimming with people are cleaving their way out of the harbour under oar and sail, a desperate flotilla of anything that can float, war galleys, merchantmen, slave ships, fishing boats, reed and papyrus rafts. The sails flap feebly in the wind, then suddenly billow and tear in the demented gusts sweeping down the mountain, several vessels turning turtle as sea and pumice slosh over the side.

Sparking as they go, fireballs streak across the sky. Out in the bay, beyond the farthest arcing canals, the molten hail has turned at least two fleeing ships into flaming torches. Survivors, some on fire themselves, are hurling themselves into the sea.

Intermittently a few stragglers stumble by, burdened by the elderly or the infirm, negotiating fallen walls and masonry, a tooth-jagged fissure now taking its ravenous bite out of the paved street up ahead.

On the far edge of the mountain now, an incandescent lava flow comes churning through the forest, torching trees as if they were paper. The sky darkens by the minute, ash clouds and fire bestowing upon the island the eerie light of an eclipse.

They come looming out of the blizzard, six young acolytes grappling with a six foot god carved out of flood basalt, its vivid prism eyes undaunted even by the eternal night, almost upon us.

A stumbling stride behind comes their pointy-faced priest, in fine flowing robes notwithstanding the odd cinder or scorch mark.

Then billowing out of the smoke, other silhouettes: four loping slaves, a stout reed cage perched upon their shoulders. Crouched inside, tiny fists at the bars, a little albino child with pink docile eyes.

The temple guard, or what's left of it, brings up the rear, a pair of dishevelled youths in bronze helmets, their wretched faces smeared in blood and pasted with ash.

Thrusting out his hand at the fleeing ships below, the priest utters a torn cry, and bellows them on.

They're barely into their stride when he motions them to a stand-still, pointy beard quivering, frantic eyes devouring the sickle blade of light magnifying now on the far horizon.

The full moon. Massively, it heaves itself out of the sea, drenching the charcoal sky and snowing ash in blood. He utters a hoarse cry of triumph; then, weeping, sinks to his knees in supplication, a raucous chant erupting from his lips.

Fumbling at the barred door the acolytes draw the child from the cage, with little pretence at ceremony laying him down upon a broad volcanic stone at the roadside.

Unremarked at their feet, the Ferryman is already succumbing to the snowing ash, waiting for us; it's drifting into his ears, into the crook of his elbow, into the hollow of his chest, his lapis eyes.

As pale as a grub dug out of the soil, the pink-eyed child lies in the hollow of the black stone, mute, passive, even as the priest raises his silver bladed sacrificial knife to the sky, a murmur of a thirsting prayer on his lips. Even as the blade plunges down, making its deft incision. Even as the hot blood spurts over the stones, a child raised in darkness, somewhere along that coiling inner ear of tunnels, tuning the voice of their devil god to the understanding of man.

But now it's the priest who lowers his head, putting his ear to the child's lips, exhorting him to speak in the delirious tongues of omen, the emerging landscape that bleeds into his eyes as he passes to the other side.

If it's prophecy you want, Priest, I can already tell you. A life too late, I divine it from the fissures cracking open the streets. The citadel walls that eclipse the sky. The quarries brutalising the mountain. The forests razed for war. Those heavenly palaces up on the hill. Those slave tenements on the fringes of the swamp. It's been there all along, hasn't it, a reality becoming manifest day by day, hour by hour. Not at your probing fingertips, you sick fool, not in the entrails of a bird or a lamb or a child, but in the fractured light of your own eyes.

Whoever would have imagined that my anagnorisis would come from a figure such as you, robes flying, the draught sweeping the ash into a flurry, eyes exultant even as your god erupts in demented fire.

But that's what you've been waiting for all along, isn't it, for a thousand years and thousand years again, the moment when the world cracks apart and this abandoned child, Humanity, shall know the truth of all truth. That which hides in Apocalypse, the end of days.

But that's the strange thing about truth isn't it, Priest.

Once proclaimed, everything at variance becomes a lie.

Once enshrined, even as a deity of an idea reclining upon its throne in the palatial vanity of your own mind, every doubt, denial or deviation becomes a heresy.

Oh Priest, we have more in common than either of us would dare admit. Demanding the truth reveal itself, while cursing the contradictions that would deny us. Ripping away its disguise, only to find another dissembling face beneath.

Faces that blaspheme the truth, even by the mere act of existing.

The infallible truth our species killed, tortured and crushed spirits to attain. The One Truth we razed mountains for, poisoned drinking wells, burrowed through a hundred feet of volcanic ash for.

Those variations that taunt and humiliate us with their brute protean genius, that baffle, perplex and frustrate us as we employ every means at our disposal to reduce them to a word, a formula, an equation or a prison cell.

Assailing us at every turn — distortions, anomalies, mutations, lies.

Except… they were never any of those things, were they Priest?

If you want to know what they were… they were us.

They bestow upon us the greatest gift anyone can ever know: possibility.

The means to change reality.

★

Dividing and dividing again, the dirt track loses itself in the sprawling marshlands, the air more putrid than ever. *What is that stench? Worse even than the gagging stench of sulphur.*

It materialises out of the gloom like some long-forgotten nightmare peeled raw from childhood. A shanty town of rotting, splintered shacks and lean-tos, some almost subsiding into the swamp.

Raw sewage festering in open ditches, fighting the reek of marsh gas.

If not for the juddering of the volcano it would be peculiarly silent here, the Oracle, even the citadel itself, spared the sight of this abomination by its own towering walls.

You have to get off the island before it's too late! cries an inner voice. *You have to escape. Now!*

Scouring the marsh paths for the most likely route, their shadows are upon me before I even know it.

So curiously mute, so curiously inert, at first you might mistake them for cruel wax effigies, the lost souls who inhabit this place. Crippled slaves, soldiers broken in mind and body, women and children staring blankly into the snowing ash.

I take to my heels, any path will do. Between the crushing reeds and billowing mosquito clouds, I almost tear right through him.

Sitting there in the dirt and the muck. A grubby-faced child.

A crudely carved wooden boat sailing the stinking puddle at his feet, a young reed stem as a mast, a reed leaf as a sail, his absent eyes lost to some far horizon beyond the sun.

Fate. Every time I hear the word, I can taste the rancid old tea in my mouth, the acrid stench of the lime kilns in my nostrils.

One by one, they tremble into being from the viscous air: the yellowing walls, the palm leaf crucifix above the iron bed, the sagging mattress with the rumpled bed sheet a size too small. Father, the crook of one arm shielding his eyes, the half-pint of village arak almost slipping from his sleep-weak grasp, dog collar all skew-whiff at the neck.

And down on the wooden floorboards, under the languid ceiling fan, me. There's something in my hands, a painted tin ship, that's it, pitching through the waves on some infinite imaginary sea, oblivious to the dust rolling about the floor.

My eyes stray to him, yet flinch at the sight.

There's no mistaking it. There's something of me in the child I once was.

I can read that young face better than I can read my own, the sullen tug of the mouth, the resentment in the eyes that refuses to be acknowledged, the defiance that will one day challenge even the gods themselves, screaming that primal scream into the claustrophobic sky: *nothing is impossible, nothing!*

What is it that makes me despise him so?

Not that stupid dog collar that would look better on a dog. Not that leather-skinned Bible on the nightstand whose metaphor codes and lost analogies defy all but futility, and that without doctrine or dogma would look different according to the capriciousness of the weather, or the mood of an eye. Not the pretend faith that through force of tick-tock discipline will go through the motions expected of it. Scribbling the Sunday sermon with a shot of arak to loosen the tongue, or should we say the bonds of emotion, tied to a chair like a kidnapped child?

But no, no, that's not it.

Then perhaps it's the sight of him, stooping into this palm leaf hut or the other to console the bereaved. The missionary pamphlets in his hand less a means of instruction than a plea of innocence for his God, the Accused. His reluctant forefinger smudging over the gaudy pictures of the life hereafter, where for the meek and the virtuous, there shall be no want.

The kingdom lies beyond, my boy. Beyond. *Where beyond?* In the heavens. *Where in the heavens?* In the sky. *Where in the sky?* A patronising look lurks in the thickset eyes as he fields my sticky questions. Answers sliding glibly off the tongue, not because the questions are childish or naive, but because the deeper implications don't bear thinking about. Not in a world that will always be like this, bequeathing its split personality to the blood of its own future.

He scowls at the indignity of it, having to explain again and again the dubious sanity of Our Heavenly Father, loving kindness one minute, brutal, vengeful, arbitrary the next.

I see it lurking in his yellow jaundice eyes. The priest who no longer believes in God, about as much use as a doctor invoking Charon to cure the sick. Not that he would ever admit to such a thing. Not Father in his tyrannical weakness, who long ago swore eternal allegiance to whatever divine or temporal authority demanded it of him, state, church, fate, what did it matter?

The Real World, that's what you called it. More than God Almighty apparently, it had power over everything under the sun, decreeing what is, what is not, what can be, what cannot.

It wasn't like that in the beginning, though, was it Father? In the beginning, you were indefatigable. You rose with the dawn, you toiled into the night. You dug wells, gathered firewood, met government functionaries, even the ambassador. You pleaded for medicines, food parcels, tools to till the soil.

You went door-to-door, collection tin in hand, a humble smile on your face, begging for charity. Up to the rich houses on the hill with their leafy gardens and turquoise pools. Sometimes they'd put in a farthing, hoping you'd think it half-a-crown, sometimes they'd even write you out a cheque for the Mission, no doubt enduring their sacrifice as stoically as Christ himself on the blood-sticky slopes of Golgotha.

Do you know, Father? When they told me you were never coming back, that old heap of a plane tailspinning into the cloud forest, your body succumbing to the scavenging ants, the plane to rust, I didn't know whether to cry out in grief or euphoria.

What is that sound beyond the window draped with a hessian sack, in-between the drone of the flies? *Go and look!* I whisper to the boy. *Go now!*

Obeying his inner voice, he scrambles to his feet, tip-toes to the flimsy screen door, opens it just a crack lest the afternoon glare break through his father's eyelids.

That's when I see it. Smell it. Taste it. The memory buried inside, leaking its filthy poison. There, beyond the compound ringed by palms and papaya, beyond the makeshift chapel with its crooked wooden spire, beyond the cherub-faced Buddha at the temple shrine dreaming of non-existence.

People in tin shacks and wooden crates, scattered over whatever hard ground they can find between the malaria swamps and the open sewers.

The war-mutilated, dragging themselves through the dirt on stumps. Men drunk on arak. Mothers at the fouled river, raising water that will kill their own children.

Skeletal pye-dogs lying in the dirt. Beasts of burden, their running sores and open wounds infested with flies; sinners reborn, say the wise men, accorded their divine justice.

I understand the gagging stench now. After all these years of never quite recognising it for what it was pretending to be.

I saw it living there. In the eyes of a broken-toothed woman old before her time. Not poverty, not famine, not even death… But futility. Hopelessness. That which dares call itself Fate.

I was bursting to tell him. I have been bursting to shout it out for 40 years. *Get up!* Get us out of this flea-ridden pit with the blood-splattered mosquitoes on the walls and the sticky fly paper coiling down from the ceiling. Burn the children's Bibles to light the cooking stove. Get up off the bed! *Get up and do something, Father!*

85.

I brought him another mug of hot sweet tea, but still couldn't rouse him. He seemed more feverish than ever, his forehead scalding to the touch, his skin and clothes drenched in sweat, his lips moving to inaudible words. Sporadically, his heart would pound in his chest, then fall so silent I could barely find his pulse.

Alarmed, I ran down to the village to call the doctor.

On about the tenth ring, Despina answered, saying Stavros had already been called out on another emergency. She didn't know when he would be back.

I hurried up to the house, through the darkness and spitting rain.

Sometimes, there would be a gust from the sea, and it would cry plaintively at the windows. I lit a fire to drive off the damp chill, brought him another woollen blanket to feed the fever, pillows to prop up his head. Pacing up and down, I didn't know if I was saving him or killing him. Every so often my eyes would stray towards his notebook and to his other self, still beyond the ink and the paper, the island's death roar about to echo across half the world.

★

Another tremor strikes; this one sharper, longer than ever, making you wonder if it will ever stop. Trees utter an unholy groan as their roots are torn from the soil. An avalanche of smouldering rocks comes pelting down the hill. On the fringes of the city, a raging torrent of water bursts from a ruptured canal, flooding streets and farmland, sweeping away houses like toys. Several tall buildings sway and totter, then crumple to the ground.

Up ahead, house 34. At last.

I pass under the arches, willing Nestor's towering contraption to appear, the crescent island, the caldera, an inverted image suspended in the sky.

By the sixth arch, my hands are fumbling over the bare stone blocks, inch by inch. I'm trying to suppress my own sense of panic.

There is nothing here. *Nothing. It has vanished without trace.*

Out into the snowing ash again, bumping the walls like a confused bee, peering in through every door and window.

What's that? A movement at the corner of my eye, once, twice, then again and again. A shadow, no more, then a hollow thud. It's only in shuffling through the ankle-deep ash that I realise what it must be: songbirds, falling out of the clouds.

The doom-black sky over the mountain crackles in a sudden frenzy of lightning, not white, but blue and green and red.

A rag-tag contingent of the temple guard comes charging out of the sulphurous twilight; a dozen dead-eyed young men armed to the teeth. Bronze helmets shadowing their eyes, 7-foot javelins in their hands, bows and quivers slung over their shoulders.

As they cut into a narrow side street, I give chase, first one corner, then another, just quick enough to catch the sole of a disappearing sandal or the billow of a cloak.

Over the citadel walls, the immense moon rises, a breathtaking blue.

We blast into the hilltop square, under the temple columns' stuttering shadows. Past the great sacrificial stone with its congealing blood. Past the treasury, its cedar wood portal still ajar, its great hall virtually bare, spilt jewels like cat's eyes glittering from the floor.

Of course... That caravan of laden carriages and carts, making for the ships with its own elite guard, beating off anyone who would stand in their way, even their own wretched people. Too late for the enemy, for all their mad drunken lust to conquer the hill; the island's own tyrants have already robbed it blind.

Yes, and they'll still be savouring their triumph as that immense wall of water sweeps towards them, the island crumbling in fire at their backs.

The troop clatters along a high gypsum wall, then barges into a courtyard ringed by two- and three-storey houses.

Wait. I have seen this place before, and in the same bone-chilling twilight, the entombing ash above our heads.

Still warm, the bodies lie in a mangled heap on the blood-gummed stones, and there is that sweet sickliness in the air that reeks of death.

The spindly lad with the crossbow bolt in his back. In black robes, the hollow-cheeked priest, Aris' silver-bladed dagger in his throat. In bronze and leather armour, a wide-eyed youth who in better days might have been immortalised in marble instead of lava. Spreadeagled beside them, the young man who once committed his own likeness to pigment in the Thalassa house. Sam, or whatever alias his soul goes by here, the blood drenching his arms, trickling towards those dead graceful hands, the blue and ochre still staining his fingertips.

One courtyard to another, and off the dead-eyed faces of the boundary walls the shouts and the clashing bronze echo back and forth like the demonic shrieks of poltergeists.

At the rasping paean of their commander, the temple guard advances under shield. Arrows, javelins and broadswords rend the air as they clash, mortal enemies, brothers.

Can't you see everything's already lost? I cry. Can't you see the mountain is on fire? Don't you know the barbarians have already stormed the gates? Who has God on their side? Tell me now, if you dare. *Who is fighting whom?*

So far from anywhere now even this brute madness finds an implacable logic far beyond your broken capacity to understand it, lost among the fragments that spell the name of your disease.

Blessed by the gods. Of course you are.

86.

I heard the front door open, creaking on its hinges as it always did. 'Nico. Where's the patient?' Bringing in the damp chill with him, Sanassis shook off his overcoat in the hall, blinking into the bright kitchen lights, his head wet with drizzle.

'Thank God you're here. He just collapsed onto the sofa. I couldn't lift him. I didn't know what to do.'

'I'm late, I know, but Father Nannos is in a bad way, and refuses to be taken off island to hospital.'

To my eyes, the patient was just as delirious as ever, matted hair plastered to his forehead, the sweat beading his skin.

'You were right to call me,' said Sanassis with a grimace, dropping to his knees, prising open his bag.

He was a good ten minutes into his examination when, with a nod towards the blankets and the olive wood fire in the grate, he murmured: 'You did well, Nico. We need to feed the fever, not suppress it. You'd better bring some fresh sheets and pillows. These are wet through.'

Hurrying back from the upstairs cupboards I hesitated at the doorway, the fierce words catching me off guard. 'What is hubris, Marcus? Defiance of the gods, is that it? Who is the engineer of fate? Who creates reality? *Answer me!*'

Huxley struggled feebly against the weight of the blankets, the words tormenting him like mobbing shadows in a nightmare.

About to protest, I caught the doctor's glance and understood.

He shook his head in frustration. 'If we can't bring him round we might lose him altogether. He needs catharsis almost more than rest, but how much is too much?'

Feverish, disjointed words were erupting from his cracked lips. Fate. Nemesis. Streets running with fire.

★

Oracle priest bellowing them on, the temple guard advances under shield, the archers at their rear sending a volley of incendiary arrows darting high over the courtyard.

481

Ghost or not, terror still has me by the throat as I dash between the lines, the arrows whistling down through the ash, spilling their liquid fire.

A searing pain strikes me in the chest and, glancing down, I'm amazed to find grief leaking out of my chest in lieu of blood and flame. It's the first time I've seen their faces up close like this, this band of rebels in dented armour and cracked leather, hardly more than children most of them, boys, girls, taking cover now among the sacred trees. *Aris, is that you...?* It is. Or should I call you Phaestos. Hair the colour of straw, wide searing eyes lined with kohl. He's ducking down between the trees, arming his crossbow, again and again, firing desperate volleys at the advancing enemy, trying to beat them back.

It's futile. They're on the brink of defeat, anyone can see that, half their number fallen, their ammunition all but spent.

Phaestos reloads his crossbow, pausing now to find true aim through the ash fall, steadying his hand, holding his breath. With a muffled whoosh the bolt leaves the bow, darting far across the courtyard, missing heads by a whisker left and right, its trajectory finally swallowed by the blizzard. It's over. You've failed. In the sheer chaos of the moment, the collision of pointless tragedy, I almost miss it: the howling priest crumpling to the ground, the bolt through his forehead. Suddenly leaderless, the guardsmen scatter for cover. The youngsters regroup, tend their wounded, advance across the courtyard, still covering their backs... *So that's what you're fighting over...*

★

Looping the stethoscope into his bag, Sanassis slumped down at the kitchen table with a heavy sigh, blinking hard and rubbing his eyes. 'I can do nothing more for him. It is up to Marcus now.'

'You saw something, didn't you, Stavros? In house 34...'

He took a shot of wine, draining the glass, and poured another. After first avoiding my eyes, there was now something piercing about his look.

'I was never satisfied with his explanation for Sam's death, you know that. *Strangling himself in the climbing ropes...* Not that anything made much sense to me anymore, what with the mad tyrants reigning in Athens, the island I grew up in that I barely recognise anymore, the monstrous things you have plucked out of the ash...'

He hesitated, chewing his lips, then to my surprise yanked open the kitchen door, pitching his words so that they might just reach the ears of his delirious patient in the next room.

'Thinking to understand Sam's death, I exchanged a few words with Aris but couldn't get a straight word out of him, his mind elsewhere as it always is these days. So I ventured inside the ancient house with the 34 chalk marked on the wall, my eyes widening in amazement at that wooden contraption rising into the vaulted ceiling, puzzling over its purpose, the pulleys and ropes and cantilevers. Cautiously, I began to scale the lower rungs, then, gaining confidence, hauled myself up to the crossbeams.

'When I came to I found myself lying face down on the flagstones, hardly knowing who I was, much less where I was. I came staggering out, coughing and retching. I saw blurry figures running towards me.

'Once I had recovered my senses I hurried back to the surgery, still trying to convince myself it must have been some kind of delirium induced by the volcanic vapours leaking in from below; a faint brought on by lack of sleep; the incessant worry. I had barely slept a wink in a fortnight; tossing and turning, worried sick over Alexis, and who'll be next... The kids in Alexander's class, perhaps, plotting something stupid; or Aris, the rebellious streak in him growing more reckless by the day. Last week they were puncturing the tyres of the patrol cars; yesterday it was firecrackers, tossed into the police station. Some of these thugs have killed for less... And what on Earth did you mean, confronting me with that crazy idea that Plato's Conundrum is here amongst us, shaping our lives, creating reality? What is Atlantis anyway? Does anybody know...? Such was the wild torrent of thoughts churning through my head as I made my way home.

'I stopped dead in my tracks, gaping at the sight of my neighbour's donkey in a parched field; the word *poleitai*, For Sale, painted onto her side in big white letters. Who needs a doctor now, I raged, spitting feathers. A psychiatrist would be of more use!

'Past the Atlantis sunset bars, discos and nightclubs. Past the hotels with turquoise swimming pools, sightseers still thronging the streets. Past the tavernas with their nouveau riche clientele, ordering up a prize mullet to adorn the table, eating a quarter, and stubbing out their cigarettes in the rest!

'Well, why not, I thought, as some shiny monstrosity of a new car on the upper road blared me out of the way, sending me sprawling into the dirt. Such is the reality we dream into being, isn't it. *Our human bloody nature!*

'The words, Nico, they snatched me away as if with the potency of some long-forgotten scent, and in that instant there I was again, that lost memory from the house on the hill rendered in such brisk clarity you might imagine memories never perish at all, but go on living their own lives within us.

'It was a fine autumn day, and the fact that I was now gazing down from the high ramparts of the Acropolis was no more peculiar to me than finding the caldera or the Burnt Islands in my bedroom window...

'The wooded hills of Attica, rising like islands from the rose mists of dawn. Red-roofed houses scattered among the olive and lemon groves, irrigation channels glistening between them. An Athens that knows Plato by sight, not merely by name. Oh, come what may, I would have my answer now, *and from the horse's mouth!*'

87.

'I cut across the agora, less a manifestation of flesh and blood, truth be told, than some elemental particle of light, in a thousand places at the same time; anything that reflects — the canopies of the market stalls, the dew of the grapes, the eyes of the hawkers and punters, the eyes of the russet tomcat darting between their feet.

Finding myself in the maze of paths and garden walls beyond, I allowed the brilliant reflections of the Iridanos stream to propel me through the Potter's Quarter, as far as the Dipylon Gate and the road to the Academy.

On the rise beyond the quadrangle, above the river Cephissus where the kids cool off in summer, there it is, a modest house sheltered by tall plane trees.

The old man has flashes of silver in his beard; he sits at the window in a charcoal chiton, chestnut eyes surely fainter than in his youth, yet no less intense for all that. The boughs and turning leaves find reflection there, so too the young scribe who commits words to wax at the long table between them.

"Beyond the Pillars of Hercules," Plato begins, his voice melodic, the songbirds his chorus, "there lay an island among islands, whose people had the means to cross one to the other..."

A flicker of amusement crosses the young man's earnest face, and he bites his lips as if to contain it.

The stylus is cutting through wax word by word, line by line, as if this last great dialogue were an epic poem recited from the ends of time.

"Are you happy and content?" I taunted him, sheer rage refracting me through the blue glass pitcher on the table, glancing me off the mirror by the door. "Do you know what they are saying? Philosophers, historians, scholars, who have devoted their lives if not their sanity to you. They're saying you were fooled by those itinerant windbags in the agora, Magian sorcerers, Egyptian priests, garrulous sea captains with their fishy tales about seamonsters and mermaids, lost islands levitating between the clouds...

"They say you only ended your last dialogue midsentence because you had lost your thread! The only Conundrum you had entered was the baffling cotton wool senility of your own mind...

"No! Don't tell me that is the sum of it, not after everything we have been through. Friends compelled to seek the truth and killed for the dream of it. Our ancient city, where once we could meditate upon the echo of a lost idyll, now the picture of brutality and superstition. The tyrants in Athens killing youngsters in the street, boys ordered to shoot their own brothers, children tortured! Friends imprisoned on dead, waterless islands, who may themselves be dead before the week is out! Jealous, twisted people informing on their neighbours, peering out from behind the curtains as they're dragged away in chains, stealing their land, killing their animals, settling old scores. Answer me. *What is Atlantis!*"

The birds fell silent. Amid a flurry of autumn leaves a sudden gust caught the window, evicting my reflection and tossing it across the room. Then before I knew it, there I was, in the bright irony of his eyes, cartwheeling through the black pupils, past the neuron flares and synaptic fountains of light... into a summer garden not far from the sacred Acropolis itself, water splashing between the orange trees.

A misshapen face appears at the garden gate, bulbous nose and straggly remnants of hair.

Socrates. He comes bustling in, threading his way to the fountain where the friends have gathered again, taking advantage of the coolness of the water.

Their reflections captured in the sky-limpid surface, I'm conscious of young Plato examining every face and gesture.

That legendary ugly mug of Socrates, belied in an instant by those mischievous twinkling eyes.

The tall, dignified figure of Hermocrates, the would-be peacemaker among the warring city states of Sicily.

Pythagorean cosmologist Timaeus of Locri, whose mane of silver hair is only accentuated by those jet black eyebrows and tranquil pools of eyes.

Seated between them, a youthful Critias, whose charisma alone can seduce the eye. Still in his twenties and poised for greatness, judging from the curious indulgence Socrates affords him; so much so, you might even imagine he was the apple of his eye.

With each falling globule from the water spout their reflections tremble, faces distorting and running into one another as the ripples effect their perfect circular motion across the surface. Unremarked by the others, Plato leans forward, a look of utter captivation entering his eyes.

There's a mixing of wine, a breaking of bread, words that have the bright resonance of musical notes. Socrates, wondering aloud how the most idyllic civilisation might look. Youthful Critias, recounting his tale, heard generations earlier from the lips of the revered Solon himself: the eternal legend of Atlantis.

Everything is as it should be, isn't it.

Except… for that same nagging doubt, that unsettling feeling that something's out of place, and always has been. Flaws. Anomalies. Contradictions that have driven grown men to drink or distraction for two thousand years. Characters who appear to be different versions of the same soul. Like Socrates in the image of Plato. Like Critias in the image of Solon. Words born in one mind yet spoken implausibly by the lips of another. The intricate interlacing of time, or the absence of it. Time itself, a picture of the ripples in the fountain, the image of eternity. Impossible. *Impossible!*

The weight of bitter defeat upon me I turned away, and if not for the breeze through the sweet fig above, might have missed it altogether, meeting the water. That fierce, calculating gaze of Plato's.

Of course! the shock almost causing me to refract into thin air. *The flaws are not flaws at all. The contradictions are no such thing. The anomalies are meant to be there! That is where the Conundrum hides. In the personalities of each.*

Peacemaker Hermocrates. Timaeus, cosmologist of the transcendent realm. Socrates, the philosopher who famously claims to 'know nothing', yet here acts as the very catalyst for the legend to be retold at all, pondering aloud the qualities of an ideal society.

Great souls one and all, and yet who is it that relates the legend of Lost Atlantis? Who speaks the words of Solon? Not Socrates. Not Hermocrates. Not Timaeus. But *Critias*. The future despot. The future murderer.

Listen, Stavros! Listen to the words, I yelled inside. Listen to him speak of a once luminous people, plunging into the darkness… A people growing visibly debased, yet ever convinced of their own glory. Listen to him speak of the human and divine nature, the goodness at the heart of the universe.

Save for Plato's own delicious irony, nothing could make Critias speak such words... Nothing except time itself, that is.

Time, that will turn this bright young man into one of the most rabid of the Thirty Tyrants, inflicting their reign of terror upon Athens. Citizens murdered, friends robbed, homes seized, children thrown into the street, families sold into slavery. The rule of law established by Solon lying in shattered ruins upon the ground.

Young idealistic Critias, and his future shadow, the ruthless opportunist who preys upon goodness, in the firm belief that the 'divine nature' is a fallacy, and thus a weakness that the victor must exploit... Yet the victor will become the vanquished, the tyrants meeting their wretched end at the hands of the rebels. Pandering to the mob and the clamour for vengeance, they'll put Socrates on trial for corrupting the minds of the young, and it will be Critias' loathsome name, submitted as evidence against him, that will help sentence him to death.

So now at last I had my explanation for the curious affection with which Socrates indulged the young man. For in Critias, you see, he perceives far more than a tyrant in the making, or the monster that can awake within; he perceives a metaphysical principle, a vision of the universe at work. Who Critias is; whom he might become. The presence of infinity within every soul.

He sees the legend of Atlantis being enacted upon the shores of Critias' own mind, and knows that it is not fate but possibility, self knowledge, that brings us closer to heaven or hell.'

★

'Yes, Stavros, it makes perfect sense, everything fits into place... I —'

'No wait, Nico,' he said, his hand staying mine. 'There's more. The most important part of all...'

★

'I felt myself slipping away or coming to, when something yanked me back with a jolt.

Over their faces the ribs of light were passing in rhythmic waves, the tyrant in Critias fighting to emerge from the child, the youth, the young man, when within that wavering distortion I caught something else: Marcus' unmistakeable likeness.

The same stubborn jaw. The same splintered eyes. The same beguiling voice.

An optical illusion. A trick of the light. Yet disquieting enough when in the last six months we have all asked ourselves the same question. Who is Marcus Huxley? Do we even know him anymore?

Yet as the ripples again found Plato's own reflection, I read something altogether more shocking in those intense eyes. Design. Premeditation. The vision of a metaphysics so pure, it can warp or create reality.

Within the instant it takes for a particle of light to travel a life, there I was, back at the Academy, autumn leaves falling through the ripe balsam sky.

Plato is reaching the end of the dialogue, and with such melodic fluency you might imagine he has roamed Atlantis with his own two feet.

He has the young tyrant-to-be speak those immortal lines about a once noble people falling into iniquity. Losing the fairest of their precious gifts. The divine nature within fading, adulterated once too often by the mortal admixture, until it's the beast inside that has gained the upper hand.

Shedding his disguise Zeus, God of gods, returns to Olympus amid a volley of thunder and lightning bolts. Incandescent with rage, he summons the Deathless Ones to hear his judgement.

The philosopher pauses. The young scribe lifts his head expectantly.

"It is better we leave it there, Timón," says Plato, offering only an indulgent smile to the young man's bewilderment. "It is better this way. It is better that we end in a broken sentence. You understand."

But if Zeus was incandescent, so was I.

"What the hell do you mean by it, Plato?" a fortuitous gust at the window lending voice to my cry. "You and Socrates? This myth, this legend, this hoax, this mind-boggling riddle, or whatever else it's pretending to be."

Can you even guess how many minds it will enter?

How many moments it will shape, how many lives it will transform?

How many ages and civilisations it will travel, as if with the immortality of light itself. Can you?

Abruptly the gust subsides, acquainting me with my own stunned silence.

But yes... of course you can... That has been the intention all along, hasn't it? I see it in the irony of your lips, the tranquillity of your eyelids, the steeple your hands form as you dictate.

You are imagining it even as you speak, aren't you, everything here upon this world, blowing out from the Forms in one almighty blizzard of light, a rainbow cascading through the Void.

Master of human psychology, every element falls into its accorded place, like some metaphysical model of the universe itself. Elements that are like jasmine to the soul on a summer night. Elements that will evoke our wonder or childlike curiosity. Elements that appeal to our lust for knowledge, or the vanity that demands every mountain be conquered and every riddle laid bare. Elements that appeal to our sense of adventure or discovery, those tantalising islands over the next horizon. Elements meticulously designed to obsess, muddle or confound, yes, even those who will doubt and despise every enciphered word of it, their fingers jerking over the lines, breath whistling indignantly through their nostrils, teeth grinding at the blatant gullibility of the world as one incongruity after another leaps off the page at them.

You devoted pages and pages to the island's landscape and architecture, its people and gods, even going so far as to provide weights and measures to lend that extra bit of verisimilitude to confound the nit-pickers. Such is the labyrinth of detail in which we all lost our way, torches sputtering and dimming the further we ventured in.

Once released into the febrile air of the agora, you know just how contagious it will become, like the ripe spores of some delicious sickness.

What is Atlantis? your Conundrum disguised in a riddle far more banal and enticing to the human psyche: *where is Atlantis?* You'll hear the trilling echo like summer crickets even in your own lifetime, as Atomists, Cynics, Sceptics, Pythagoreans and whatever have you, debate and declaim around the city.

The garrulous sea captains who'll swear blind that they have passed between the towering Pillars of Hercules, defying those great rock inscriptions that exhort them to venture no further, and yea, have espied submerged streets and temples in the shallow waters beyond. The Egyptian priests who'll declare they have beheld the ancient papyrus in Sais with their own eyes. The travellers who'll carry the legend to Athenian colonies far and wide. The adventurers who'll sail west in search of the Lost Isle's remains — if not for its vanished idyll, then at least for its buried treasure.

Such are the waves these ripples will make though time, your Atlantis dialogues entering more minds than even a god could guess at. Forget about the Pillars of Hercules: explorers will plant their hopeful or defiant flags of discovery on six continents, and in every one of the seven seas.

And then it will begin all over again, won't it, whatever idyllic island, pristine shore, sunken rock or desolate peak has been speared through the heart, the flag of discovery snapping in the wind.

Some South Seas isle or Antarctic ice ridge. Some Bahamian sandbank or Pacific atoll. Some Aegean island among islands. The cast of characters will take to the stage.

Fresh faces, different voices, changing scenery, yet oddly familiar for all that. You'll recognise something in their mannerisms, or perhaps their compulsions, their ambitions and desires. A word or a phrase will jog your memory as they deliver their impromptu lines, oblivious to how many interpretations have been spoken before. Enacting the same eternal allegory on tyranny and freedom, honour and iniquity, the human and divine nature as rages on the metaphysical shores of Atlantis itself.

"They were losing the fairest of their precious gifts," the boy recites from the wax.

His eyes meet Plato's returning gaze from the window, momentarily amber with the falling leaves. "You cannot tell me what it is, Timón?"

"Something that belongs to the light… is born in the light…" The boy's eyes narrow in fierce concentration until, catching his breath, he says at last: "*It was their love of life…*'"

88.

Huxley was still delirious, and losing fluids so profusely Sanassis began muttering about needles and drip feeds. As it was, he did what he could to relieve his patient's thirst with sips of water from a cup. He cocked his head to catch the words still streaming from Huxley's cracked lips.

'Half his soul is still marooned in that place, Nico. Streets running with blood and madness.' He frowned anxiously, adding in a murmur: 'I was wrong. I thought to hear us would help him back, speed the catharsis. Now I wonder if it won't prove too traumatic for him. I'd administer a sedative in a trice, but who knows if it would save him or push him over the edge?'

★

The roar of the volcano reaches its thundering crescendo, fissures streaking across the courtyard, walls tumbling, the sky in a mad frenzy of lightning.

At the far colonnade a coiling stairway plunges below ground, into a labyrinth of passages probably not even mapped, so deep do they burrow into the mountain, scalded by steam, scorched by fire.

I find myself passing through deepening degrees of shadow until the blackness is as thick and as sticky as pitch, and only gravity, the weight of my feet upon stone, tells me which side is up and which is down.

A glimmer of light catches my eye and at first, such is my disorientation, it is hard to tell if its source is the breeze-torn flame of a lamp a stone's throw away, or the speck that marks a nebula on the tail end of time.

Then just when I least expect it, it springs into focus. And there it is, the Oracle of the Living, hanging in the darkness like a patch of cornflower sky. Beyond, the shimmering ruins at Akrotiri. I can even see my own tent and the camp table under the saffron awning. I can see the trenches and the fragments hut and, for the first time that I can remember, the sight no longer fills me with dread, as though something in there were pulling me apart, one thought, one emotion, one conflict at a time.

If I listen carefully, I can even hear the pickaxes biting into ash and the *tink tink* of the trowels as they strike pumice.

Drawing closer, I watch as the image ripples, then clears again, every other moment, like a skipped heartbeat.

Something is being thrown into it, but what?

One more kink in the tunnel, and my answer emerges from the shadow and the flame. A procession of people, snaking back into the coil of the labyrinth.

Faces curiously blank, eyes curiously expectant as if, beyond all appearances to the contrary, they still sense something beautiful out there, a life worth living, an eternity worth fighting for.

Faint but insistent, finger drums and water bells sound from the shadows, spelling out some ancient system of harmonics and consonance, the likes of which Hadrian almost gave up his life for — the music of the spheres.

The beat rumbles through me like a poignancy remembered, I know why. I have seen these spirit-souls before, if only in the blink of an eye as our picks bit into the ash crust. That curious refraction of light I might have blamed on a sleepless night, or the echo of some forgotten dream. Elemental particles of consciousness scattering into the blue, finding home now on a blustery street, in the humming silence of the temple heights, in the glance of a friend or a passing stranger, in a memory roaming the unconscious.

The fisher boy Phaestos comes jostling up the line, the silver dagger missing from his belt.

As if in premonition, I see myself walking through camp, past the dock and the moored *Persephone*. And Aris will be there, shifting crates or mending nets, casting me that shy baffling smile that is his yet is not, betraying a knowledge that, whilst present, does not quite reside in his own consciousness.

I threw myself headlong into the vortex, knowing, even as I did so, that the people gathering there to jump themselves could feel the frigid draught on their goose-bumped skin.

As I flew, I saw the volcano explode, a white-hot sheet of flame devouring everything in its path, forests, houses, temples, animals and people, the guilty and innocent alike. If divine wrath there is or can ever be, I have seen it.

89.

We were dozing in the kitchen when a voice roused us. 'What is hubris, Stavros? Is that what you demanded of me? What is nemesis?'

'You should be in bed, Marcus,' said Sanassis sharply, springing up from his chair to examine his dishevelled patient. As grey as the snowing ash, he was still unsteady enough on his feet to need the doorway to prop himself up.

Firmly, Stavros took him by the arm, nudging him back to the front room. 'You need rest, and plenty of it. Mug after mug of mountain tea. A nourishing soup... *Doctor's Orders.*'

'Do my ears deceive me, Stavros,' he rasped. 'No? Then it seems we are the fools who tread the boards of this metaphysical theatre, enacting its divine comedy through the ages... Seeking the far distant Isles with our dying breath, even if we never left their shores for a single heartbeat. Palace or slum. City street or mountain peak. Raging battlefield or oasis of serenity. We could travel a thousand miles, a thousand worlds, a thousand lives away, and still we'd be here. The island idyll, brightening, fading. That's what Plato meant, wasn't it? Worlds within worlds. Islands within islands. Souls within souls. Each holding some facet, some reflection, some residual memory of the other. Each embodying everything it might yet become. Demonstrating the concept of relativity *before relativity even had a name!*'

'What did I tell you?' demanded Sanassis, in a sarcastic appeal to the ceiling. 'It is easier to ask a fish not to swim, a bird not to fly! Well, at least his fever has broken. At least his eyes aren't rolling back in his head anymore!'

Satisfied his patient was on the mend Sanassis took his leave, ducking as he swept out of the front door into the spitting rain. Still in the glow of the porch lamp, he turned almost as an afterthought and said: 'He's had a traumatic experience, Nico. Don't expect miracles. Revelation can sometimes be hard to live with.'

Clutching the blanket to his chest Huxley slumped back onto the pillows again, staring up at his own crooked silhouette cast by the firelight, as if not quite believing it belonged to him.

He gripped my arm, interrogating my eyes. 'You know it always tormented me, what the White Lighters really found in the light.' Thinking of Célestine and Jean, I resisted the impulse to pull away. 'I could never quite decide whether to admire or despise them. Something out there had touched them in ways I could never bring myself to accept. They had returned stripped of their fear of death, yes, but also with an optimism about life *impossible, impossible to understand!* Kids with dewdrop eyes, men and women in their prime, ancients already half-crippled by the years. Wherever we found them, in the ghettoes of New York, in the temples of Tibet, in the Black Country factories, crossing mountains or raging torrents or city streets, it just didn't matter. They always carried something of that unspoken knowledge within. Luminous, indefinable. Often years after the event — that kiss of life at the roadside, that electric shock to the heart on the operating table. Wherever they had been during those few moments while they were dead, they came back with it blazing in their souls. And not just the light, something else: that irrepressible idea that anything is possible. *We can feed the starving. We can make the deserts bloom. We can bring peace to the battlefield...* It didn't matter if they were eight or eighty; they'd pester us with it incessantly, almost as if they were deliberately trying to obscure the real secret that lay beyond. *Why isn't it possible?* they'd insist, again and again, with an obstinacy you'd expect from children. *Why? Give me one good reason! Just one!'*

Momentarily, his eyes found some kind of tenuous focus in mine. 'And you know what, I never could, not really... What was I supposed to say? That it's human nature to deprive a child of food? To engineer our survival through the death or misery of others? To hasten the world's end so that we may live another day? As though any fool now is expected to believe that goodness has never existed in the human heart. That it's all just atoms and molecules... Or maybe I should have said, no, it's the mortal admixture getting the better of us. It's the light fading away.'

★

I called Huxley into the kitchen to eat, and was already ladling out the prescribed soup when he appeared, slumping down at the kitchen table, more out of obligation than appetite, I could tell.

He had showered, shaved the grey stubble from his face, tamed his wild hair and might even have looked halfway presentable if not for the haunting shadows in his eyes that even thirty-six hours of sleep had not diminished.

His movements were abrupt. His manner restless. Words between us suddenly awkward.

When his voice broke the silence midway through our meal there was something almost bitter or resentful about it. 'It's just as the Scholiast prophesied,' he said, avoiding my eyes. 'Once it has awoken with us, we shall never escape it, backwards, forwards, sideways in time. Plato's Conundrum. Having learnt what I have learnt, I stand before it in utter awe — *and wish to God I had never heard of it!*'

My spoon clattered angrily into my plate. 'You can't mean that. What about the others, what about the rest of us? Everyone sacrificed something to get here, not only you. *Everyone!*'

Startled, his eyes momentarily found focus in mine. 'You have grown up,' he said, and there was something in his voice I could not quite place, something like sadness or regret.

'That is the truth that we have found. *Together.*'

'The truth is that there is no truth at all,' he countered, almost scornfully, 'merely perspectives that shift according to angle, mood, interpretation, even the weather!'

'That's not what you said yesterday,' I taunted him. 'Who are you supposed to be today?'

'I need no reminding of my own disease, but am I the one who created this schizophrenic universe? Am I?'

'That is not the truth we found.'

'Where light opposes dark, death opposes life! Is that your great truth?'

I shook my head at him in disgust, frustration robbing me of words.

'What you now call truth, I call unthinkable. Do you know when at last it wrenched open my eyes, this fool who always prided himself on the keenness of his own intellect, his own insight?'

He leaned forward, his mouth forming a thin, grim line. 'This I could not bear to write, even if my cramped fingers might have obeyed. Yes, we are all metaphor for something. That I knew. But what? Just as I took that strange leap, the ancient island exploding in searing white heat, one world's reality turning into the dream images of another, I saw their faces forming lucidly within me. I knew I had recognised them before, recognised them from my innermost being, and now I knew why...'

His eyes bored into mine.

'It was I... me... myself... I was that presence in my father's soul as he went begging door to door, euthanizing his own pity on bitterness and arak; I was the woman in whose eyes even hope had died; I was that fly-infested child sitting in the dirt, a palm leaf boat to sail the open sewers; I was the pye-dog pelted with stones. I realised then that I would never know the truth, for there is none to know that does not change its face.'

90.

We were lingering over breakfast when Myroula came bustling through the front door, chased by rude sea gusts and spitting rain. I could hear her cackling and clucking even as she made the floorboards groan in the hall.

Heaving her shopping bags onto the countertop, she signed the cross over her ample bosom, and announced in shrill indignation: 'Our dear Father Nannos at death's door, and where do we find you, the pair of you? Here, without a care in the world, stuffing your faces with bread and *marmalata!*' The talking hands eloquently expressed her opinion of such behaviour.

'We didn't know,' pleaded Huxley. 'No one told us.'

'*Ha!*'

Inside the priest's little courtyard, the street widows were hunched under the spindly fig tree like a flock of black crows. They eyed us suspiciously as we tapped at the door.

We didn't wait, but stepped inside, inching our way through the spartan living room with its wavy stucco walls and polished cement floor, on towards the bedroom, Huxley calling out the Father's name.

The door opened with a wince to reveal Father Nannos lying in his narrow iron bed, the little shuttered room all aglow with candles, heady with incense.

Fussing over the autumn flowers at his bedside, the hunched old woman who cooked and cleaned for him muttered a greeting as we entered, then shuffled out between us on bandy legs.

Above the priest's tired, cotton-white head, hangs an icon of some island saint, so old and gnarled it might have been carved from a piece of driftwood. Barely distinguishable now, the face seems to be struggling to remain, as if it too were slowly expiring, leaving this world to enter another.

Globules of candlelight swim across the walls, pass over the old man's dimming eyes, linger over his parched lips. Huxley pours water from a jug at the bedside, lifts the glass to the Father's lips. The presence of water rouses him, and when he sees Huxley, a smile appears in his eyes made of light.

I press myself against the door jamb for support. Whatever it is, the presence in the room seems to lift me like a boat on a wave. I wonder if Huxley has sensed it too. It even crosses my mind to tell him, but the moment passes like a premonition.

'Sit with me a while, child. Even if we have not always seen eye to eye, is it not true that we have been through more together than many friends or enemies ever have?'

Outside, the wind was wailing through the wires and the gusts would sometimes seep through the shutters and the ill-fitting windows, worrying the candles.

'I have sent word to Theo,' he said, 'on that sea rock where he lives with the gulls.' As he spoke, the monastery on the clifftop swam into my mind, and the monk's humorous, berry-round face.

He reached for Huxley's arm. 'To do what should be done, you understand, to observe the rituals. I have little stomach for them of late, it's true, and yet still, it seems, I am a creature of habit.'

At the priest's bidding, Huxley pulled up a chair. He had embarked on this obligation red-eyed and reluctant, but I could see it in his body language now. There was a curiosity, a guarded eagerness in the way he leaned forward over the bedside.

'Why, Papás? What would you say, is it life or the contemplation of death that has changed you?'

'It is revelation that changes people, child, not words chewed over and over in the mouth like grit. I daresay you knew that, and accepted it, long before I. The yearning to know. Not to deny faith, no, but to lead faith out of the dark stable where we lock and bolt it and feed it hay even as the meadows are blossoming outside.'

'I suppose the experience has altered us all — for all the good it's done us.'

'You are thinking of the boy who lost his life on the ropes. And perhaps of Anna, whose shadow has lengthened, or so it seems to me. But you are too hard on yourself, child, too hard on the frailties of others, too hard on the hidden motives of fate. Here as I stand on God's threshold, do you know what it is I wonder? I wonder how much time we have spent picking over our differences, picking and fussing until we no longer recognise one another, nor even remember that once we were all born of the light.'

'What do you mean?' Huxley flinched.

'Life can weigh upon us, it can burden us all,' the Papás went on, apparently oblivious to Huxley's torment. 'And yet when I stepped through that miracle on the hill made of blueness and light, I lost all sense of time, I lost all sense of the force that plants us here. It is almost as if the pressure of the world, its weight, its gravity, its demands, distorts our true selves, blurs our own true reflection, forcing us to think and speak and move in a way that is not really our own, like a palsy-stricken child. Often, we cannot find the right words to say, nor find the clarity of thought that should have us wing through the air, not stumble and crawl.'

'Then we *are* in hell.'

'No, child. You are too hard on the Earth that turns dust and water into the miracle of life. Do you know what it has taught me, my encounter beyond the doorway? It has taught me this: that if there is a difference between the eternal soul that inhabits us and the brittle persona with which we face the world, then that distance between the two is the same as the distance between each and every one of us, the same as the distance between here and that place where the soul still emanates from the light.'

Huxley grunted. 'What would you have a man do, Father? Command the points of light to converge?'

The Papás squinted up at him, troubled now by the black bitterness bleeding from his words.

Seeing it, Huxley added, 'Unlike you, I was foolish enough to expect the Oracle to reveal the truth — not infinite variations on a theme, not a theatre stage upon which we are obliged to act out our futile parables of existence until the sun rises and sets no more.'

'But is that not the truth you were seeking all along?'

'That there *is* no truth?'

'That the truth lies in infinity.'

'Infinity, Papás — or merely perpetual doubt?'

'You can say that, after everything you, your friends, even your enemies, have been through? Tell me, will you be the last one amongst us who stubbornly refuses to change, who fails to recognise the truth of himself?'

The words seemed to spring out at him from nowhere, and Huxley bit his lips, taken aback, if less by the priest's sudden vehemence than by the implications.

He was already examining the rebuke from every angle he could

500

think of, I could tell, wondering if it might be true, the faces of Guirand, Hadrian, Sam, Anna, me, reeling through his mind's eye.

At last he said in a clipped, defeated voice: 'I do not know who made us this way, Papás — life, or forces beyond our understanding that we sometimes call God — but it was not I.'

To the questioning look he found staring up at him, he added with sudden asperity: 'Am I responsible for the design of a universe where light opposes dark, where death opposes life, where every word we speak is measured against its opposite? No, not I. That is what plagues me, Papás. For if they are merely a fabrication of man and not of nature, what lies in their stead? How shall we ever escape their tyranny?'

Nannos' eyebrows twitched in wry amusement. 'You ask that of me, Huxley, whose Church divides the universe between good and evil, saint and sinner, heaven and hell?'

Nannos reached for Huxley's hand and I was struck by this strange reversal of fortunes, the dying man reaching out to aid and comfort the living.

'I envy you your faith, Papás. I do.'

The Papás chuckled weakly. 'Do not say that, child, for if our Church Fathers could peer into my heart they would cast me out as surely as Satan himself was hurled out of heaven.'

'Don't tell me you have found a new God,' said Huxley, in mock astonishment, the candles amplifying the mischievous twinkle in his eye.

'No, dear friend... I believe I have found the God my heart has yearned for since the day I first set foot on this spinning earth.'

'Then you must have found truth, Papás, for what is God without truth?' He pressed against the bed, a slow blink trying to restrain his own sense of urgency.

A faint smile creased the old man's lips. 'If there is one thing the light has revealed to me, child, it is this: Like it or not, there are as many truths in our world as there are stars in the heavens or grains of sand upon the shore.'

'For what conceivable purpose? What can be gained from condemning us to live like this?'

'But where then should it lie, child, that one shining immutable truth? Not in some old man's mind, shoring up his beliefs like a crumbling church that God has abandoned.'

'Is that where your faith resides? Once I might have believed it. But now...?'

'Now I ask myself, what can be the purpose of them, these truths greater in number than we can ever hope to count? Shall I explain them all away as you have done, as perspectives that deceive and torment us, or worse, as illusions? Must I regard them, perhaps, as the inexorable workings of Fate, with its random smiles and curses? No? Then surely as the Will of God, who alone possesses the clarity of forethought, and in whose boundless wisdom, all is known?'

Huxley pulled back, the protest already on his lips, and only a squeeze of the hand restrained him.

'After I returned home, the vision on the hill still bright in my mind, I could not help it. I had to ask. The crucifix on the wall. The holy icon. The tree in the courtyard. The church dome of Christ Pantocrator, ruler of the Universe, gazing down upon me from the heavens. *Wait!* I cried. *Omniscience? Knowing all? But how can that possibly be? How, when everything under the sun tells us otherwise?* Eyes in every shade from amber to blue. Leaves and tendrils reaching out towards the light. Skin, fur, feathers and scales sensitive to the wind's or the wave's or the soil's caress. Ears attuned to sounds that the mind may never knowingly hear at all. Currents of fate in all manner of agreement and contradiction... Perceptions that vary soul to soul, moment to moment, that if written down in some great book would fill the universe itself! What other conclusion could I draw, Huxley, answer me that! Can these be the attributes of a God all-seeing, all-knowing...? *Can they?*'

He was fighting a shortness of breath. Huxley squeezed his hand, all the more eager to wring the words out of him.

'...Using every eye, every eardrum, every tendril, every collision of experience to reach out, to explore, to understand...? Tell me, what else could bring God to life, child?'

A fond smile illuminated Huxley's eyes. 'They will burn you, Papás.'

'Too late for that, my friend — *too late.*'

The old man closed his eyes, and for a moment sleep overtook him.

When they flickered open again, he seemed momentarily confused, as if wondering where he might be. His throat was parched and Huxley lifted the water glass to his lips.

He shot me a anxious glance. 'Brother Theo,' Huxley murmured. 'What can be keeping him?'

'It's blowing a gale outside,' I whispered back. 'They'll never make the crossing, not in this weather.'

Almost imperceptibly, Father Nannos said in a faint voice, 'I would hold on till first light, Huxley, if only I can. I always detested the dark, you see, even as a child. I always despised the gloom.'

An hour before dawn the wind dropped and it was so eerily quiet you could hear the old clock tick-tocking on the kitchen sideboard.

'Will you do the honours, Huxley, and place the silver drachma on my tongue? I should feel embarrassed to turn up at the ferryboat empty-handed.'

Huxley clicked his tongue affectionately. 'Whatever will the bishop say?'

'Is that the dawn chorus I hear, or do my ears deceive me? I fear I cannot hold out much longer.'

'Yes, Father. The birds are greeting the new day.'

'Then open the shutters, child, swing open the shutters to let in the light!'

At Huxley's firm command they creaked open until they struck plaster. The blush of dawn entered the room, confusing the impetuous candles.

A smile alighted on Father Nannos' lips, crinkling the skin around his eyes.

Huxley pressed forward, his lips almost touching the dying man's ear. 'Speak if you can, Father. Where are you? What is it that you see?'

I wanted to pull him back, drag him away, but couldn't even tear my own eyes away from the faint tremble on the old man's lips, wondering if, against all odds, he might have the strength to whisper something from the other side.

91.

No sooner had the sun dawned than it was devoured by sombre grey cloud. Minutes later, the drizzle swept in. Huxley grimaced and turned up the collar of his jacket.

The black crows in the courtyard hopped and flapped as we cut a path between them, fretting over the lean pickings in Nannos' grieving house. Once our backs were turned, they would probably strip it to the bone.

We made our way back to the Land Rover, the streets oddly mute, the season like a withering autumn leaf, bars, hotels, shops, all boarded up, not a tourist in sight. There was something in the air, not just melancholy or dead, but ominous. A few late passengers were still scurrying down the cliff face serpentines to the port, dragging suitcases behind them, others crying out in alarm as their mules skated over the slick stones, the *Pegasus* a toy boat a thousand feet below.

Huxley tossed me the keys and told me to drive. I fired him a questioning look, my fingers still fumbling after a clumsy catch.

For a mile or more he remained silent, just watching the scree slopes and the twisted fig trees blurring by outside.

Then out of nowhere came a hoarse laugh. 'Who would have guessed it? That on the brink of death it is he, Father Nannos, who relinquishes his illusions. Even those he has clung to all his life, even those that formed the bedrock of his faith. Why? Because he can no longer bring himself to deny the obvious: that truth cannot possibly exist because it has not yet been formed.'

'Is that what he said?'

Huxley grunted. 'It was implied.'

'And you believe him?'

'How should I know?' he retorted, with that corrosive sarcasm over which he had such masterful command. 'Since belief itself implies that there *is* truth or at least an expectation of it.'

Turning a corner, I piled on the brakes, just managing to judder to a halt before we careened into a checkpoint.

Two police and two military vehicles parked nose-to-nose. A wooden barrier slung across one half of the road.

'What do they want?' For once the answer was quick in coming. Several military police were rooting through the adjacent field where the largest Phoenix Rising hoarding on the island had not only been felled but blown to bits, judging from the charred shrapnel that remained.

'Aris has obviously found a better use for his father's dynamite,' muttered Huxley, adding through numb lips, 'Do not look them in the eye,' as the soldiers manning the roadblock glowered at us through the windscreen.

In spite of myself my eyes strayed to theirs as they waved us down, and the next thing we knew they were shouting, demanding papers, brandishing rifles at us. At that moment I had no other impulse than to drop the clutch and floor the accelerator, a stupidity luckily averted as their superior stepped between the cars, issuing a brusque order for them to stand down.

He must have recognised Huxley from the newspapers; with a flicker of a smile, he motioned us through, offering a brisk salute for good measure.

'It is coming closer,' I said, driving off.

Misunderstanding, Huxley growled: 'Let them come if they dare! Let them arrest me, let them put me on trial!'

Climbing the stairs, he threw himself into bed, still craving the sleep that would release him.

★

Along the dark lane leading into Oia, headlights flared over the dry stone walls. After the morning's encounter I was imagining another army patrol, another stop and search, and it wasn't until we squeezed by on the narrow track, brake lights illuminating our faces in red that I saw Stavros' stress ridden face.

He wound down the window. 'Nico. You shouldn't be out alone at this time of night. Marcus has enemies, you know that, people who will not understand why the Junta has indulged him for so long. Every day it gets worse. There is talk of war, even among ourselves left and right; of American conspiracies to keep the Colonels in power. There are armoured cars and tanks in the streets. There have been more shootings. Running battles. Aren't you checking the wireless reports?'

'I think it's broken. At least, Huxley never turns it on.'

He shook his head, the ambivalence striking him with a frown, then a staccato laugh. 'Oh, if only we could all pretend that reality does not exist simply by ignoring the fools who propagate it!'

★

There was a glow at the rock face window. Not the paper lantern I was expecting, but a bare bulb dangling from the vaulted ceiling, lending the room a thin, unforgiving light. I wondered what was going on until I saw the mess littering the table, the bed, the floor.

Anna said: 'It's not the danger, Nico, the police, the army, so don't for a second think that it is.'

'He'll be lost without you. You know that.'

Lips forming a hard, stubborn line, she went on cramming books and clothes into a battered suitcase. 'Well unlike Marcus, I can't pretend there is no such thing as a lie, no such thing as the right thing to do.'

I found a place to sit on the bed, knees up to my chin. Wine was poured, and before I knew it we were halfway through the bottle and I was relating everything I could remember about Stavros and Huxley, and their travels in 34.

'They were losing the fairest of their precious gifts,' she recited in a murmur. 'Of course. The joie de vivre, la dolce vita.'

She sat back in the mess, blowing the stray wisps of red hair out of her face. A smile came to her eyes, then the rest of her face, dawning there, just like the old days, that magic carpet look.

She glanced up at me with sudden intensity. 'Tell him, Nico, when you see him next. Even if he knows it already. Remind him. And then remind him again. It wasn't the brute instinct to survive or the fear of death that once kept people here. It was their love of life.'

Placing one of Sam's beach pebbles between a folded scarf, she added, 'Somewhere along the way, Marcus lost sight of the fact that we are not fate's clumsy, senseless instruments. We can be perceptive even when half the world is wallowing in the fog, kind even when cruelty and callousness are everywhere.'

We wandered out into the night, reluctant to say goodbye. I must have been biting my lips or something, because she kissed me on the cheek and said, 'Don't be sad. I couldn't bear that.' She took my hand and squeezed it hard.

Taking in the incredible cascade of stars above our heads she said at last: 'You know, I never really doubted it… I mean that something of us should live forever.'

'Why?'

'Because somehow it's the light that makes us who we are… Just imagine there's a civilisation up there somewhere, its astronomers peering down on us through some immense telescope. You think they're seeing the two of us standing here? No, they're seeing the light that has taken all those years to reach them — the ancient city in its heyday, the volcano blowing apart. Every moment ever made, travelling by light. These days, whenever I look up at the night sky, I have to wonder where I am as the light passes this star or that. Maybe that little tomboy in the muddy dress on my grandfather's farm. Maybe I'm with Renato, climbing aboard the train, heading south. Or bringing flowers to his grave. Or with Marcus in Alexandria. The thing is, there must always be something of the light reaching somewhere.'

Her gaze returned from the flood of stars and she said: 'But there was something I forgot, something that house 34 taught me about all those people I know or ever knew.'

'What?'

'How the light of us also enters each other… and what becomes of us there.'

92.

Fearful of waking Huxley from his big sleep I held my breath and tiptoed into the house. It was a wasted effort, as the splash of light under the study door forewarned as I crept up the stairs.

My heart sank the moment I set eyes on him. Sitting at his desk under the snake-neck lamp, lips miming fragments, fingers running over the Sais Codex and his own log from 34.

Sensing my presence, he announced grimly: 'The Conundrum is still revealing itself. Layer by layer. One deception, one metaphor, at a time. As if Plato were still posing the same eternal question: how are we to understand the nature of reality? How are we to penetrate the final deception?'

As he glanced up through his half-moon reading glasses, I heaved a sigh of relief. He was still exhausted beyond measure, but this was not the same crumbling man who had descended the hill three days earlier, craving a release that even death would not bring him.

Then he thought to ask. 'Where have you been?'

I hesitated, but knew it would be wrong to spare him. He had to know.

In the end I couldn't tell which hit him harder, Anna leaving us or her insights about the light. He gripped the table as if, without its solidity, he might have flickered away as easily as a careless refraction.

He said in an awed whisper, 'We all played some indispensable part in this, you were right to trust your instincts. Each and every one of us. The Codex would still mean nothing to us without the others, and I mean everyone...' He counted us all off on his fingers, not even forgetting Aris or Maria, Dr Sanassis or Vassilis the postmaster. 'Even poor Claude before the light claimed him — it was probably that humbling revelation that ruptured his mind.'

He snatched up the Codex, running his finger over the squid-dark ink. But it wasn't the abruptness of the movement that sent my stomach into free fall. I knew, from the rapid blink of his eyes, that he was experiencing it too, that tumbling sense of premonition.

'*The pure white light that enters [...] the soul*,' he recited, punctuating even that empty space where the verse had been fractured.

He lunged for his logbook, flicking feverishly through its spider-scrawl pages. His eyes alighting on something mid-paragraph, he stabbed at it with his finger, triumph thinning with awe.

'One word,' he murmured. 'One simple word. I didn't even register it at the time, as I hurried past the hieroglyphs…'

His eyes met mine. '*Prism. The pure white light that enters the* prism *of the soul…* That is the inscription on the temple stones.'

He blinked. There was a hollowness in the room, and I think he sensed it too, as though whatever inspiration had been sweeping us along on its cresting wave had suddenly left us high and dry. Heavily, he lifted himself out of his chair and made for the door, waving goodnight without turning.

And again he slept. Slept for another two days while I paced the room or roamed the fields through the drizzle with the stray dogs from the village for company.

By the time he got to his feet and threw open the shutters, an Indian summer had settled over the island, and for a moment he just stood there, trying to convince his reluctant mind to absorb every lumen of it, the silver-green olive trees, the still rose sea, the single hot air balloon of a cloud in a sky tempted by purple.

'Do you feel better?' I asked, when at last he reappeared, bathed, shaved and in a fresh change of clothes.

'I don't know where I have been, or even if all of me has returned,' he said, patting himself down with an irony that I only dimly remembered from the past. He looked across at me. 'Yet somehow, I do feel different, it's true. I even caught myself exchanging glances with the man in the mirror and for once, do you know, I even recognised him.'

He sat down at the stone table on the terrace, and I poured him coffee.

Just then the *Pegasus* appeared, rounding the headland, steaming north, a sooty cloud panting from its funnel.

'Anna,' I said, and even if he was used to hiding such things, I saw him wince with regret. I felt partly to blame. They hadn't even said goodbye.

He shook his head. 'I cannot undo the past, Nicholas. What use is there saying goodbye as things stand today?'

Again he winced, but this time at the irony of it. 'Who would have thought it? That I, Marcus Huxley, would be demanding uncertainty in the hope that things might be better tomorrow.'

Suddenly he was on his feet, asking about the sailing skiff, still moored in the cove below the house.

'Where are we going?'

'Out there,' he said, drinking in the rose-splashed sea.

93.

Rounding the cape, we fell under the perpendicular shadow of the crater wall, red lava cliffs plunging into the caldera.

The sails fretted and snapped and as Huxley drew them in I could feel its deep water force creaking through the timber. Free of the wall, we caught the unhindered wind; moments later, we were skimming across the water.

Phíra came into view, then Oia, perched on its honeycomb cliff top.

The spray was flying into my eyes. Through the blur I could make out the jagged black boulders of the Burnt Islands. We were pitching over the waves at them, and still he made no effort to alter course.

I glanced back in apprehension but saw only a face set in stone, one hand gripping the tiller, the other drawing taut the mainsail.

Just when I'd decided he was going to sink us, he jerked the tiller hard to starboard. The sail flapped frantically, the boat shuddered from stem to stern, but there we were, gliding into a narrow inlet once formed by black tumbling lava.

Presently, the channel broadened into a luminous little bay. We moored the boat at some shattered rocks and followed a trail through the lava flow. The boulders rose up all around us, monstrous and deformed. Petrified faces, distorted in agony or leering malice. Faces of gods and men and mythical beasts.

Soon they were towering over us, concealing the horizon, distorting any sense of perspective.

'It could be a vision of hell itself,' he muttered, grim-faced as we threaded our way between the obsidian rock formations with their needle-sharp spires. 'Or the Earth itself after the atom bombs have had their day.'

Crossing a ridge between the lava dunes we found ourselves staring into one of the minor craters that pitted the island's scarred face. The rocks and scree were stained brimstone-yellow and every so often the acrid sulphur fumes would smoke into the air, scorching our nostrils, squeezing the tears from our eyes. Could he feel it too, I wondered, the tremble underfoot, so ambiguous it might even be mistaken for one's own pulse?

His eyes flinched over the shattered landscape and its twisted sculptures, his memory evoking a different image altogether; the spice terraces, the forested mountain, the sweeping arc of the shoreline.

'A place of utter beauty,' he said at last, 'reduced to this broken ruin of an island. And before you say anything, I know what you're thinking: that this could be the landscape of our own lives, the human condition.'

I meant to object, but he cut me off. 'No. I once despised the idea that these dichotomies could form the basis of reality, you know that. But I was wrong, blind, stupid. Even if they *should* be illusion, even if logic demands it, who am I to pretend that we do not evoke them like some malevolent poltergeist with every broken word we have been taught to speak, every contradictory thought and deed? They tore the ancient city apart. They tear me apart. Out there, they tear apart half the world.'

He hurled a rock at one of the lava gods in sudden fury. 'In life, we cannot understand death. In loathing, love deserts us. When we speak from the heart, the intellect fails us. When the soul whispers, the brain shouts and clamours and drowns it out.'

I took in the smoking craters beyond, turned skywards like the nostrils of a dragon in fitful sleep. This island, fire in its molten heart, engulfed by the sea.

'The ancient island was destroyed by fire,' I said absently, 'fire and water. Just as the Egyptian priests told Solon... Plato must have known that these were the destructive forces we all carry within us —'

The words must have ignited something within him because suddenly he was dashing towards the skiff, dragging me along behind him. Seconds later we were skimming across the water again, sails straining at the seams, sea hissing against the bow. I caught the crazy look in his eye, and knew he was about to do something desperate. He wrenched the tiller hard to port, putting us on a collision course for the soaring rock towers beyond the islets.

To hear the locals tell it, those lava spires mark the mouth of the volcano itself, a great Charybdis of a whirlpool, that over the centuries has swallowed more than its fair share of fools and innocents. Caïques, yachts, even freighters, they have all come to grief there, the beguiling current drawing them in like a paper boat until they hit a riptide the likes of which no sail, oar or engine can withstand. Before they know it, the monster has them in its swirling maw, the bow's going under, the stern's up in the air, and the crew are tumbling and sliding about all over the decks, knuckles white on the railings, on the ropes, on anything they can grab hold of, while they shriek for their lives.

I don't know what it was, fear or euphoria, that had me lying in the well of the boat, my muscles unwilling to lift me.

Mast rocking drunkenly against the sky, we blew into a tempest of water, spray and sunlight.

I clung to the bow, ever more doubtful that we should escape with our lives.

Seconds later we reached, then crossed, our point of no return, the boat pitching through the waves like a child's toy, the foam swelling over the sides, the spray bursting into our faces.

I was about to shout a warning. Too late. We were already there, rising onto the whirlpool's outer lip. I could see the unmistakable depression in the water. Feel the boat's deepening tilt as it began to corkscrew around. Watched helplessly, as the sea was sucked out from under us like water swirling down a giant plughole.

Whatever it was, luck, providence or just Huxley's inexpert hand on the tiller, the mouth suddenly spat us out with such violent distaste I was expecting to see the boat reduced to matchsticks all around us. For several impossible seconds we even seemed to be hurtling through the air, and when finally we hit water again, it was in a torrent of spray.

Against all odds, we were still in one piece, despite the tattered sail, the sea swishing about our ankles, our waterlogged clothes.

And there we were, drifting across a stretch of improbably calm, improbably blue water, while all around us was churning sea, mist and foam.

I peered over the side, into water so luminous it seemed certain to sting the hand that touched it.

There were strange tumbling shapes in the water, oddly mesmerising, oddly beautiful.

They come surging up from the deep and — *what's that?* — as each touches a penetrating stream of sunlight, a vivid iridescent pulse strikes through the blueness.

'What is it?' I was still peering over the side, struggling to understand, my face almost touching the water.

'Evidently,' said Huxley, 'the place where rainbows are born.'

I glanced back at him, uncertain whether I was hearing awe or sarcasm. I began mumbling something about the intensity of the colours, but by mid-sentence the words had already snatched me back in time.

'Why are the colours so intense?' I ask, mesmerised by the riverbank trees and the musical swirls of the water. To which the Ferryman replies in his riverbed voice, 'You would expect anything less, where two worlds collide?'

When I tell Huxley, he squints at me in that calculating way of his, chews his lips, interrogates the fact from every angle.

To think that only this morning he had almost admitted defeat, saying, 'the pure white light, the prism of the soul — perhaps we shall never know what it means.'

Plunging his hand over the side, the boat pitched so violently that water began sloshing in again. He was grabbing this way and that, like a fool trying to catch fish with his bare hands.

Finally pulling back, he opened his clenched fist and there it was on his wet palm — a small pumice stone, its pitted surface still bearing a fading iridescence.

'Do you remember the vulcanologist who was here, taking readings all over the island, Professor Matsaikis?'

I nodded, though I could hardly recollect the face, just the tall frame of the man, the neatly clipped beard, the jeep crammed with plotters, wires and vacuum tubes.

'I entertained him to a bottle of wine at my tent, and I remember, he marvelled at its depth and richness, all from this arid volcanic soil. To think that life springs from such devastation, he said, raising his glass to toast those primeval forces that ruled the Earth before history had even been thought of. To Life, born of Destruction. *What do you mean?* I asked, realising he was no longer talking about the vineyards flowing down to the shoreline. Lava, he said, meeting sea. You are an archaeologist. You see only the ruin wreaked, and I don't blame you one bit, not when you have to shovel through a hundred feet of ash just to find a roof tile. But don't you know? If it weren't for fire and water, we wouldn't be here at all. They were the Titans of the world before time, primordial elements, implacable foes who clashed in battle and wreaked unimaginable devastation. Towering volcanoes exploding into the sky, spitting fire and molten debris. Rivers of incandescent lava flowing down into the primeval soup. And it's there, where they meet in a maelstrom of fire and steam, that the incredible occurs: life emerges, the first cellular links of it, growing, reaching, eventually populating the earth and the oceans with a diversity impossible to comprehend.'

He leaned forward intently, the luminous water ripples reflecting into his face. 'So that's what the writers of the Sais Codex meant by the inexpressible moment! It is the moment fire meets water, light meets dark, life meets death, opposites collide, and paradox is born.'

Absently, he began stuffing his pipe with sodden tobacco, just to give his trembling fingers something to do.

'Think!' he said, an exhortation as much to his own struggling thoughts as to mine. 'Those who have been to death and back, drawn irresistibly towards the white light, *becoming* white light, glimpsing the goodness at the heart of the universe. Yes, like Célestine, like Jean! They awake with a longing for that blissful lost state and yet find within a kind of inexpressible wonder for everything they set eyes upon —'

'They returned through the prism, that's what you're saying... Through the paradox.'

'Well, what are we, if not light, refracted through this or that experience to give us our hue and temperament, life in its mind-boggling diversity?'

'But it's metaphor...'

'It is the code reality is written in,' he countered, 'streams of metaphor symbols... That is what the Codex meant all along. It's just that we were all too immersed within our own metaphors to realise it.'

He silenced me, almost ruthlessly, lest he lose his thread.

'The allusions to metaphor in the Codex always baffled me, you know that, in part because I could never fathom their purpose. If not outright fabrications, I considered them an artifice by which truth is not expressed, but disguised. To whom should the metaphor make sense, I demanded? The poet describes the world in lyrical imagery, and all too often we struggle to interpret and understand. The astronomer gazes up at the heavens and the heavens become streams of numbers, baffling formulae chalked up on a blackboard. The musician sets his eyes upon us and, lo and behold, we are transformed into sounds and intervals.'

'You are saying they are a form of language.'

'They are representations. Numbers cannot adequately express reality any more than artist's pigment.'

He caught my questioning look.

'Yes. We are all metaphor for something. There is nothing out there that is not a metaphor for something else. The further we venture from what is familiar to us, the more we rely on metaphor to describe, to convey, to interpret.'

Wherever it was coming from, the inspiration was still carrying him along in its turbulent flood, the words making sense to him only as he spoke them.

He chewed on his lips, his eyes questioning mine.

'Damn it, the clue is even buried in the word itself — why didn't we see it before? From the Latin, *metaphora*, from the Greek, *metapherein*; it implies change, yes, and transformation, but its literal definition is something else: to transfer, to carry forth... That's what the Codex meant. Not that the metaphor codes are a human invention like Linear A, or merely a human means of expression, conveniently allowing us to draw likenesses between things. No, it is the alphabet reality itself is written in, the means by which one variation explains itself to another.'

I thought I saw a chink of light. 'Is that why the Codex says those things about losing what we have become?'

He nodded.

'Then it is all about transformation, the ability to find affinity in what we are not, to become what we are not. A prescription for living, not dying.'

I added with a laugh: '*The Oracle that does not know the future*,' that Codex fragment that had so irritated me when first I heard it, so bogus did it seem.

And before I knew it, there I was, back under the molten skies of August. Sam's death has hit us hard. We're sitting under the fig in the Papás' tiny courtyard garden, and Anna's saying something, something I half-dismissed at the time, thinking it just emotion or the summer heat getting the better of her.

'And then I realised,' she's saying, with rising intensity. 'I was wrong. Fate wasn't teaching me a lesson, it was the other way around. *Fate was learning from me!*'

It was almost as if the front door had opened on the wind to reveal the old priest lying there on his narrow iron bed, the room ablaze with candles.

'Father Nannos!' I said, almost tripping over the words. 'Do you remember? He was asking you why... how could it possibly be... if truth is already known...'

Our eyes met. He knew exactly what I meant. '...Then why endow the Earth with senses and faculties at all, why produce perspectives unimaginable in variation and number? Are these the characteristics of omniscience — using every eye, every eardrum, every finger touch, every leaf and tendril, to seek, to understand?'

To the gentle ripples of water lapping up against us, he added in a murmur: 'If that is true, then beyond the prism where the light breaks there is mind... or something like it, just as Plato imagined. A convergence. A focal point where the scattered light is gathered up, focused... dare we say, "interpreted"?'

It was dusk by the time we moored the boat, and climbed the rock face steps.

I heard the old green Land Rover grating gears on the turn. A minute or two later Hadrian came ambling through the courtyard garden.

As he pulled up a chair, I could see the change in his face, the clear complexion, the pin-sharp eyes.

The night was warm and we ate outside on the terrace, the glow of the lamps illuminating our faces against the moonless sky.

When Huxley related the day's adventures to him as one might a scientific expedition, I half expected Hadrian to scoff at us. Instead, he appeared to weigh every word, a reaction I took not as a measure of mood but of the distance he himself had travelled since encountering the unknown in 34.

'Imagine,' said Huxley. 'At the point where the light converges. What awareness, what knowledge, what truth must be found there.'

He was trying to get Hadrian to admit that this was what he had seen with his own eyes beyond the plank wood door, the awesome beauty of it, the intervals like musical light waves, pounding onto some far distant shore beyond time.

Rolling the clay wine cup pensively between his fingers, Hadrian replied: 'You are implying that this is some kind of immense instrument, of which our own faculties form an infinitesimal part. You are suggesting that the universe is aware, that it is searching...'

'Look at the evidence, Hadrian, that is all I ask. Lay it out across the table, one piece, one fragment at a time, and tell me — what other conclusion can I draw?'

94.

A peal of thunder, or something like it, rumbled through the night sky.

'What's that?' started Hadrian, peering into the darkness. 'There's not a single cloud, not one!'

The words were barely out of his mouth when back came the answer, tremors streaking under our feet like magnetic current, stones grating in the terrace walls, leaves rustling frantically in the garden. As if by witchcraft, the front door swung open, then slammed against the wall.

'Move! *Move!*' cried Huxley, already on his feet and bolting away from the house, up onto higher, safer ground.

For an hour or more we just stood there among the vines, tense, anxious, wondering what we were in for next.

'It's too quiet,' said Huxley, still interrogating the night.

'I doubt even an earthquake will give the Colonels pause,' said Hadrian, a pinched voice in the darkness. A moment later he added, almost with regret: 'We have to think of practicalities, Huxley. Athens is a tinderbox. If the Colonels are toppled, you can just imagine the questions the new regime will fire at us. You, with all those papers plastered with Junta approval, courtesy of the Comte.'

I expected Huxley to roar about fools and time wasters, but for once he remained oddly silent.

By first light we were already in the Land Rover, driving between the vineyards, a dwarf sun peering through the mist.

I stole glances at him at the wheel. Something was different about him, but what? Not the lumbago a night under the olives had gifted him. Not the back-to-business khaki fatigues and trench boots. Not even the iron-brittle tension that used to wire his bones every morning when heading out to camp.

He was perhaps more incisive than usual, more determined, that's all. *You're imagining it*, I told myself. The volcano is to blame, the eerie trembling of the earth underfoot.

Looking back on it now, maybe he didn't know his own intentions any more than I did; at least, not then. Events were in the making. We were being spoken in a language we didn't understand.

Following some wordless hunch, he took a shortcut to the crater wall, along a dust track all overgrown with morning glory.

We were in for a shock, the full force of it only hitting us as we neared the edge of the precipice and saw the plumes of sulphurous smoke and ash spewing out of the largest of the Burnt Islands. There was the red glow of lava and every so often a geyser of steam would spout into the air.

In the far distance, I could make out the crowds gathering at the cliff wall. Anxious or enthralled, the whole town seemed to be there.

'To think we were standing at that very spot just a few hours ago,' murmured Huxley, 'right on the rim of the crater.'

Glaring down at the fumarole as if it were some fizzling Roman Candle, daring it to blow up in his face, he turned abruptly on his heel and marched back to the Land Rover.

Parking just beyond the gates we walked the rest of the way into camp. I wonder if he was as taken aback as I, seeing the disinterred streets and houses scattering over the cape, our memories struggling to fill in with life and colour the bleak ruined shells.

'It's sad,' I said.

'Only our lack of insight is sad,' he snapped. 'To think that I had to dig up half the cape to understand what I understand now.'

The trenches were abuzz with news of the eruption, students, teachers, craning their necks for a better glimpse of the smouldering island in the caldera.

Huxley did his best to avoid them, dodging questions, threading his way between the tents and the huts, jacket collar turned up over his ears. A flicker of amusement crossed his face as he caught sight of Galatea, Christos and Helia, trowelling, brushing, sketching, seemingly with no more time to squander on the volcano than on the Colonels themselves.

Almost at the site office, two figures darted out at us between the huts through their own fug of ash and smoke. The red top reporters, Jackson and Platt. At least no one could fault them for their tenacity.

You could read it in the edgy triumph of their faces, the smug certainty that their first instincts had been right all along. Things here just didn't add up. The figures didn't add up. The deaths didn't add up. Even the inventory of priceless artefacts didn't add up. 'All these years, Huxley,' they taunted, 'digging under the patronage of tyrants… What do you have to say to your accusers, Huxley? People like this Sarrides character, finally released from his prison island after it was proven the looted antiquities had been planted on him by his own superiors. His only crime, to expose corruption. To bring you down. These murderers and torturers have kept you safe and sound while others —'

We entered the musty gloom of the fragments hut, the door slamming shut behind us.

Potsherds still littering the trestle tables, he uttered a staccato laugh, bitter, ironic, contemptuous, sacrilegious, who knows what. 'These can be boxed up and sent on their merry way to the Service,' he said. 'Let Sarrides catalogue them — each one, piece by piece, his grasping mind never suspecting for a moment that these shards and fragments will never fit together. *Never!*'

Our looks collided.

'I told you already. I cannot reassemble a broken world, Nicholas. I cannot do it.'

'*We* can do it. All of us together. That is what we learnt.'

'No. No one can do it.'

'Why not?'

'Because it's impossible!'

'Give me one good reason. *Just one!*'

'What do you want from me? I was made for this. Every moment, awake or asleep, delivered me here. To understand the Codex. To find a way through to the other side.'

'You have found a way through?'

'The final deception is behind us. We have come to glimpse the pure reality that lies beyond. And yes, it truly is the eye of the needle...'

'I don't understand. I don't get it.'

'But you were there the whole time!' he flared.

Out of the hut and into the sunlight again, I darted after him. Did he even realise then? Did I? How clumsily I was trying to reach him.

'Just for one moment,' he added, through gritted teeth. 'Imagine what we discovered yesterday to be true. Only one logical conclusion remains. What is it?'

When I refused to reply, he squinted hard at me. 'What is wrong with you today?'

'I don't understand, that's all.'

'Of course you understand!' he boomed, his patience in tatters.

Up at the field tent we ran into Hadrian, making tea on the Primus, and dithering over which honey-gummed pastry to stuff into his mouth.

Behind the finger-smudged glasses his eyes strayed over us, and before they had even returned to the whistling kettle, I could see reflected in them the recognition that we had quarrelled — at least, in that peculiar way Huxley ever allowed.

'Now he insists there's only one way to interpret the evidence,' I said, appealing to Hadrian's stolid common sense. 'It's not some philosophical game, so forget that. No, now he's certain, adamant — beyond the point where the light breaks, there is mind, or something like it, a universe dreamed into being. A transcendent realm. A dimension of perfect Forms, which everything here so imperfectly reflects. He insists I should know what that means. But I don't know what that means.'

'Of course you do,' growled Huxley. 'You know it as well as I.'

As I jerked my head away from him, I caught Hadrian's glance and a look that said, *So here you are at last, I knew it would come to this. The impressionable boy who suddenly realises he's swum far out of his depth, the storm rising, the land out of sight. And so all the ambivalence he has ever known, certainty, doubt, bliss, terror, now collides within him.*

'It means the Isles *do* exist,' said Hadrian simply. 'They would have to. That's all.'

The childish protest was still on my tongue when the tremors went juddering through our feet again. Hadrian froze, his eyes wide with shock. The tent shook on its poles, guy ropes snapping free of the pegs. The camp table lurched sideways, upsetting a cup. A veil of dust rose from the ground like a thwacked carpet.

Huxley leapt to his feet, bolting away from the tent. It was only then, seeing him with that scalding look in his eye, that I realised this wasn't some stupid, knee-jerk reaction at self-preservation.

'It can't last!' he muttered furiously. 'Not with seismic activity like this. One shock, one tremor too close and we shall lose it forever.'

But our fire-breathing island had already fallen back into its fitful sleep, the teachers and students who had come stampeding out of the huts only moments before, already wandering back inside.

'What makes you think it will be any different this time?' I was angry at his obstinate jaw pointing up the hill, and angry with myself for having indulged him for so long. 'What makes you think it won't be snowing ash again, the island dying from your own disease?'

He spun around, the fury blazing from his eyes. 'Don't tell me you don't dream of it! Don't tell me you don't crave it! To know what lies beyond the windmills in the lake.'

He began threading his way through camp, but with giant strides that had me scrambling to keep up.

'Where are you going?' As if I needed to ask. We were already on the snaking path between the dunes, marching for the hill.

He spun around, panting, and I thought he would explode. 'What is it you want from me? What do you expect me to do? Heal the schizophrenia of the human race?'

'*Why don't you get up? Why don't you get up and do something, Father?*'

He lurched backwards in shock, never imagining for a second that anyone would dare hurl those necromantic words into his face, what with their raw power to bend time, summon ghosts.

Struggling free, he shook his head in fury and resumed his march.

Everything was just as we had left it. The sailcloth awning strung between the temple columns. The contraption that Huxley was already fussing over, wondering if it had sustained damage in the tremors. Grimly, he tossed a pebble between the columns, watching with bated breath until the blueness rippled.

Then, just as he was making his final preparations to climb the scaffold, the tremors returned with a vengeance. We barely managed to scramble outside as they hit us, wave after wave, ripping the ground from under our feet, shaking us like rag dolls.

I could hear the stones of the ancient houses, grinding back and forth like angry teeth. Then the shouts and screams from camp. From the dust where I lay, I watched the distant stick-figures staggering from the huts and tents. Above us, even the temple columns seemed to sway and totter.

From inside 34, came a loud splintering, then the deep, hollow chime of timber beams striking the flagstones.

'Go!' Huxley bellowed, scrambling to his feet as the tremors finally subsided. 'Fetch Nestor.' Seeing the doubt in my eyes, he gripped me tightly by the wrist and wrenched me off the ground. 'Go! I'll still be here when you get back. I swear it.'

95.

I tore into camp, down through the pumice-littered fields. It was only after reaching the first of the tents that it burst through my fogged senses, panting and blood-boiling, almost as if it had been three steps behind me the whole way. *Why was I running? Why was I helping him?*

I found Maria in a scrum of frantic students. Pushing, yelling, demanding to be evacuated before this crumbling island killed them all.

'*There is no ship!*' she cried back at them. '*Your tents are the safest place to be!*'

Guessing I would be on some errand for Huxley, she threw me a fierce, smouldering look. 'Nestor has gone,' she snapped. 'Gone for supplies.'

'When?'

'Not ten minutes ago.' A frightened shadow crossed her eyes and I knew it was Nestor she was seeing, driving the clifftop road just as the earthquake struck.

I ran to the Morris and managed to get it started on the roll. Moments later it was spluttering up the hill in a cloud of bluish smoke.

No sign of him along the way, just more rock falls and chutes of dust.

A wary silence had fallen over the town, people trickling back to their houses from the fields, inspecting the odd crack in the plaster-work, but concluding the worst was over. The men stood huddled in little groups, smoking cigarettes and casting sullen looks at the Burnt Islands, still blowing smoke rings back at them from the caldera.

Dusk fell in a blaze of volcanic glory the likes of which even I had never seen before. When the islands began taking shape there, I had to swear under my breath, but still couldn't tear my eyes away from their luminous forms.

Why was I helping him? *That was why.* What point was there in denying it? I did want to see beyond the windmills in the lake. I did want to thread my way along those lake and forest paths. I did want to know the City of Light.

I made another round of the town, searching Nestor's favourite haunts. There was no trace of him anywhere.

When in the gathering darkness the street cast me up at my own front door, dead on my feet, I decided to call it a night. Even if Nestor had made it back to camp, nothing would happen till first light however much his Kapítán chose to rant and rave. I lit a fire in the stove, kicked off my boots, found some stale bread to toast, a tin of fish.

I must have dozed off because the next thing I knew the chair had been kicked out from under me and I was lying on the floor, blood trickling into my eyes, the whole world shaking. After the first wave, there came another and another, each more violent than the last. Pots and pans crashing to the kitchen floor. Smoke belching into the room, the chimney pipe wrenched out of the wall.

I got as far as my hands and knees before the next wave tore the ground from under me.

There was a roar and a deep-earth rumbling as the glass cracked and then exploded from the window frames. The tall sideboard in the corner tottered, spilling its plates and cups, then fell like an axed tree.

A tooth-jagged crack split the wall from floor to ceiling. Then the whole house lurched towards the cliff drop in a storm of dust, falling masonry and shattered glass. In the abrupt lull that followed, the front door swung open of its own accord, and I half-crawled, half-stumbled into the street.

I had never known darkness like it. There was no moon. Every house light and street lamp had been extinguished. I began fingering my way along the wall, trying to make sense of the frantic lanterns somewhere up ahead, the spilt embers of some upturned stove. Screams and wails pierced the darkness. Several yards on I ran into my neighbours, a woman and a child digging frantically through the rubble with their bare hands, a father missing, a brother missing. I don't know when it hit us: that the island had probably tossed their sleeping bodies into the sea, tumbling through the star-crushed darkness, bed, blankets and all.

Dawn brought a pallid, unearthly hue to the island. In the thin light, the devastation became all too brutally apparent.

Ruined shells of houses. Walls torn from their foundations. A bedroom exposed like a doll's house, the iron marriage bed seesawing over the brink. Fissures running crazily across the street. A church dome cleaved in half. A stairway ending abruptly in the fall to the sea.

On the Burnt Islands, the plume of smoke from the crater had billowed into a cloud. Every so often, one of the minor vents across its pitted surface would release a furious geyser of steam. Where the incandescent lava flow met the sea, the sea hissed and boiled.

Out in the caldera, hardly safe herself, the *Persephone* was tacking back and forth, searching for bodies. Aris' stump-armed father at the tiller, steering with his knees, the boy up front, a grappling hook in his hands.

Dwarfed by the red lava cliffs, a flotilla of caïques and rowing boats were searching for something else closer to shore. Miracles. Loved ones who, against all odds, might just have survived the thousand foot fall.

Shell-shocked survivors stumbled about the ruins, clothes in tatters, the women's keening hurled up at the stone deaf sky. Scratching their cheeks with bloodied nails, shrieking, crumpling under the weight of their own grief. Dead, pallid faces exposed between the rubble. Bodies, lying mute and waxy on tarpaulins laid out in the street.

Moving from one ruin to the next I was pitching in wherever I could. Digging, shovelling, just as we had always done, but this time in hope of hearing a breath or a faint buried voice.

I saw Stavros Sanassis kneeling in the rubble, eyes on fire, trying to bring the dead to life, families crushed under the fallen masonry. I saw Alexander Vouris, the schoolmaster, hurling away stones like a man possessed, his timidity thrown to the four winds. I saw the postmaster, Vassilis Nafpliotis, in search of lost children among the fallen walls, his dream of an island of culture and invention still in the making.

In the thick of it, I had almost forgotten that Huxley existed.

But then, while I was helping Stavros with another stretcher victim, he glanced across at me, and in that instant read something in my eyes. Well, he had known Huxley far longer than I. They had dreamed, debated, taken philosophy to the edge of the world and back.

'You shouldn't blame Marcus, Nico.' He swabbed the grime from his forehead with his sleeve. 'If we were to judge everyone by the same yardstick, where on earth would we be?' A glimmer of a smile came breaking through his grief. 'And what use would he be here, anyway, answer me that, getting under our feet, all fingers and thumbs. Marcus was made for other things, not this.'

Just when I least expected it, there he was — Nestor, a bloodied bandage tied around his head, in a group of blanket-hugging survivors, huddled around a fire.

'Where were you, where have you been?'

Maybe it was just the blood and grime, his wounds or mine, but at first he hardly seemed to recognise me at all, looking up in confusion as he bandaged a little girl's arm.

I broke the news. 'The Kapítán needs you.'

He threw me a thunderous look. 'He dares ask me that? In the middle of all this?'

By mid-afternoon, army medics and Red Cross rescue teams were landing. Field hospitals were being erected in the vineyards, and Nestor had even offered our own tents to house the homeless.

'These people want to live!' he seethed, taking his temper out on the gearshift as we made our way down to Akrotiri. 'What time do I have for people who despise life?'

I could hardly argue with him about that, not after all the accusations I'd hurled at Huxley myself just the day before. It was only in relinquishing the memory that I realised it wasn't true, not really. In fact, there was probably not a man on Earth who loved life more than Marcus Huxley. It was just that he loved it not for what it was, but for what it had the capacity to become.

By the time I climbed the hill the sun was already glowing between the temple columns, but in a crayon and charcoal-smudged sky that seemed on the verge of fire.

I called Huxley's name, once, twice, three times. Checked his tent, empty, billowing in the wind. Circled the temple, wove between the columns. Then finally moved on to 34, conscious of the stray grains of pumice cracking under my feet. The door was ajar and I pushed it open, the shadows scattering.

I crossed the pebble-smooth flagstones, feeling the ripples that time had made upon them.

The dislodged beams and struts were still where they lay, in a twisted heap.

Snatching up a stone I lobbed it between the columns, holding my breath for the dusk luminous sky to come rippling towards me.

As it went rattling across the ancient walls outside, I fought the crushing sound of it, and what my eyes were telling me. There was nothing. Nothing but meaningless empty sky.

A dark void seemed to clutch at my soul.

There, wedged between the tangled beams, lay Huxley's upturned shoe.

96.

When I broke the news to Hadrian he nodded impassively, as though it were only to be expected from a man as irredeemably egotistical as Marcus James Huxley.

Tossing another book into the trunk he was packing, he added grimly: 'There'll be trouble now, mark my words. Grief ferments into anger, then revenge, it always does sooner or later.'

Sensing a reluctance to believe the worst he abruptly flew off the handle, his voice gaining an octave. 'Can you even imagine what those dirt-digging hacks will make out of Huxley's vanishing act. Can you? They'll listen to the village tales about holes in the sky or the Devil reclaiming his own and they'll think: Huxley is not dead. A man even his friends call arrogant, imperious, self-possessed? Never! He no more flung himself into some ancient portal than he threw himself off the cliff or into the bubbling crater. Then they'll jump to the only conclusion their cynical minds will allow: that Huxley knew he was on the verge of being exposed for his crimes, and made his getaway with as much haste as he could. Like the callous opportunist that he was, he had no qualms about using the tragedy of the earthquake as a cover, his boat stuffed with priceless antiquities.'

'It almost sounds like you believe it yourself.'

'Then just think how compelling the case will be to everyone else. In their eyes we are all accomplices after the fact — whatever that is or can be twisted to mean. Once the Colonels have been toppled, born-again democrats like Sarrides will be falling over each other to string us up.'

And he was right, I knew it, even as I fought the lucid image of Huxley clambering aboard his skiff and stealing away under the cover of night.

He wrenched the glasses of his nose, dabbing the nervous sweat from his brow. 'We have to get off this damned island. Now! Before it's too late! They won't admit it, of course they won't, but vulcanology is about as precise a science as divination. Nobody really knows what's going to happen until it does.'

'But how? There's no boat…'

The rusting military tubs that had ferried in food and blankets, tents and medical supplies, had already steamed away empty, armed guards beating back anyone mad or desperate enough to try to steal aboard. With the Junta on its last tottering legs, the Colonels were throwing their paranoid glances everywhere. No one could be trusted, neither a Colonel nor a bishop, much less the homeless or the dispossessed.

'The *Pegasus* will be here tomorrow,' said Hadrian, the thought alone restoring some of his battered confidence. 'Nestor managed to get through on the ship-to-shore, and they're making the crossing now. The captain's given his word. They will evacuate us.'

I ended up bunking in the fragments hut but found it difficult to fall asleep, a spasm of fear, a shout from the tents, a dog's bark, wrenching me awake.

Between ragged strands of dream, nightmare, reality, I found myself thinking about the final deception, what it might mean, what it might be.

For all his talk about glimpsing the pure reality that lay beyond, there had been something almost desperate about his march up the hill, his enemies closing in on him, the earthquake threatening to cut off his last means of escape.

Clawing his way over the collapsed beams, edging ever closer to that patch of moonstone sky, taking the leap, what certainty can he have had about anything? *Where* he would be, *who* he would be, even *if* he would be.

Is that the final deception, I wondered, tossing and turning amid the fragments littering the floor.

The pure white light a chimera, a clever projection of the human mind unable to conceive of a world in which it no longer exists.

Tossing, turning. Plato's eyes follow the undulating meadow down to the river; he's talking about drawing down the light from the Forms; about the perfect image of the island already there within us, struggling to emerge.

Tossing, turning, I heard Hadrian's voice welling out of a luminous blue window hanging in the darkness: 'It means the Isles *do* exist. They would have to. That's all. Such is the nature of the Forms.'

There in perfect contemplation, beyond space, beyond time.

Tossing, turning, Célestine and I are sitting under the garden walls, scarlet bougainvillea cascading over our heads. *So you've seen it, you've been there*, I'm saying, the sarcasm leaking through my voice. *The City of Light*. No wonder she's so tongue-tied, so lost for words. But no, I'm catching something else now as the scene replays, something beyond the words that so stubbornly refuse to form.

It's not because the memory did not survive the crossing as she awoke to that kiss of life on the mountain bluff; it's because the City of Light can only exist at all free of the definitions that would imprison it.

I awoke with a gasp, the heartbeat thumping in my chest, cold sweat trickling down my chest, potsherds from an upended box digging through the sleeping bag into my skin.

I knew it then without question. Huxley was wrong. The final deception is not the deception that comes last, but the metaphor that makes sense of all the others.

But what? What is it?

Wherever you are, Huxley, I hope you are at peace now. I hope the cicadas or the dawn chorus won't be driving you mad, or the mountain taunting you with its secrets, but somehow, I don't know why, that's the hardest thing of all to believe.

The next thing I knew someone was hammering on the door, shouting. *'Did you hear what I said?'*

When my eyelids finally jarred open it was to find Hadrian's plump silhouette in the doorway, the briny autumn wind off the sea impatient to get by him and bluster through the hut.

He studied my face as I lay there, propped up on my elbow, sweeping the fragments away with a dazed movement. 'Why are you so angry?' he demanded briskly. 'If it's because you think he's abandoned you, think again. He's abandoned us all.'

It was only then that I realised. I *was* angry, probably more angry than I had ever been in my life. The moment it dawned on me I had to clench my teeth just to swallow the roiling emotions about to swamp me, rage, frustration, love. With a rising sting in my throat, I blinked back tears, hiding my eyes as I rolled up the sleeping bag.

With the wireless forecasting gales and high seas, no one was willing to take bets on when the *Pegasus* would make landfall.

'We have to be ready at the boats,' fretted Hadrian. 'Ready to row out. The captain won't be willing to dawdle, not with the crater still spewing lava. The crush will be unimaginable, so take heed, be warned.'

Ninety minutes later, the camp's battered old bus was grinding its way up the crumbling track, hairpin by hairpin.

Inside, we were packed like sardines in a can, three to a row, the aisle crammed with sweating bodies.

I tried not to look at the numb, pallid faces pressing in on me, or the hands and fingers that were rigid with apprehension. Every time we lurched into a rut or a pothole, gasps would run the length of the bus like a live wire. In the crush, I caught Galatea's numb smile, hardly recognising her without the ghostly look of the dust, a glum Christos and Helia standing as sentinels at her side. So even they had deserted the trenches, finally blown back into this, the real world.

The Morris was still parked outside the post office, looking faintly smug and ridiculous. People were already jamming the serpentines to the port, some on foot, some clinging to the saddles of their mules.

'Nico, where are you going?' called Helia, a disembodied voice in the scrum.

'To get my passport,' I shouted back.

'You can't, Nico. There isn't time. It's too dangerous up there. *Nico!*'

Deeper into the warren of streets there was not a soul to be seen, the houses left standing a picture of tranquillity, windows closed, doors locked, everything neatly stowed away. The church with the blue dome was ablaze with candles, tin votive offerings chiming in the spirited wind.

I scrambled over the rubble, down to the house, hardly recognising it with its cracked face, the fig half-buried in the courtyard, the hallway littered with debris. Holding my breath, I stepped across the threshold. Tiptoed past the bedroom, grabbing odds and ends as I went, the clothes spilling out of the cupboard, the holdall squashed under the bed, the passport in the nightstand.

Keeping my back to the wall, I moved on towards the kitchen. What was left of the house ended there in thin air, and a jagged gash of bricks and masonry. Edging closer I could see the Burnt Islands far below, still belching fire and ash.

An abrupt movement drew my attention to the crumbling edge of the floor, where the wind was flicking through its pages, its bent-back spine protruding from the rubble.

Travels in Elysium. That hymn to reckless idealism penned by a youthful Claude Guirand, obsessed by islands, obsessed by the light, even as he watched them fading inexorably within.

A wave of dizziness swept over me and I let myself slide to the floor. I could feel my own hot breath turning cold on my face. I closed my eyes, wrestled with my own buckling courage, but knew I had to go through with it. Slowly, deliberately, I advanced on all fours through the shattered cups and plates, wincing as the shards cut into my hands and knees. On towards the broken edge, where the kitchen table still held its precarious seesaw balance, half in this world, half in the next.

The floor lurched, the house juddered. Dust and masonry began falling in on me. I screwed shut my eyes, feeling my own wild heartbeat echo back at me from the concrete.

When it was still again, I wriggled on, inch by inch until I could feel the breath of the book's fluttering pages.

As I coaxed it towards me, a single page between my fingertips, I couldn't help it, my eyes were drawn into the abyss as they have always been drawn by forbidden things.

The west wind blusters all about me, and the last thing I remember thinking is, I have come to know you, beautiful soul. I have come to know the wind.

97.

Along the mountain pathway my feet barely touch the ground. Pathway and I, we cross the high meadows, undulating like time-still waves that have burst into grass and flower. Higher and higher we climb, until the clouds look like blossoming crystals suffused by the sun. Above the forest line, the path meanders lazily between stone-littered hillocks. One more turn and there they are, the windmills in the lake, their white canvas sails turning in the wind.

I remember Huxley asking indignantly, 'Where are the people? Here I should die of loneliness.'

He did not understand. How could he — when everything beyond his own horizon abruptly ceased to be him? Like the soaring cliffs where the island plunges into the sea. Like the threshold of our fears, where the known falls away at our feet. I could not describe this feeling to him, not unless he could find my euphoria in the wind, the prism clouds over the mountain, the silver torrent, the soaring swift. I could not make him understand because it was the only thing I could not, dared not, put into words: that beyond the curve of our own horizons these things have always been us.

'What are you doing up there in that godforsaken place,' he would demand irritably, '— when you should be finding the City of Light? Where are the people? Whose feet tread this path? Whose hands created those ancient stone circles? Whose imagination built the windmills in the lake, and for what conceivable purpose?'

Something deeper than instinct as it was to me then, I didn't even have the words to tell him that it's only by the grace of this wild place that the City of Light can exist at all.

Mist billows up from the valley.

When at last an aperture appears, revealing the sinuous shore far below, it's not the walled city or temple hill that floods into my eyes, but stepping-stone islands scattering into the blue.

Forest envelops me in chlorophyll light. Water chimes and cascades between the trees. I cross a humpback bridge arching high over a river torrent and then, in the serendipity that appears to bring this place into being, there follows one after another along the trail.

Another turn, another dip and the first of the lower lakes appears, glowing emerald between the leaves. In no hurry to get where it's going, the path serpentines its way between them, a water necklace strung between the hills.

'Show me the City of Light! Show me the minds who have built this place; those who found their way here against all odds!'

His agitated voice rings in my ears, just as the forest track flows into a pebble-stone road undulating over the hills.

City of Light.

It rises over the next bluff like a starburst sunrise.

I wonder what it was that sent me sprawling back in amazement into the tufted grass. Not the bough-spreading trees in the streets, or the torrents that came splashing down between the houses and their wavy, undulating walls. Then maybe the soaring spires and minarets, the paper-twist onion domes, the stupas and taper-roofed pagodas. Maybe the hill gardens, with their cascading leaves and blossoms, their vivid spices. But no, that's not it, because it wasn't any of these things alone that snatched my breath away. Rather, it was the subtlety with which each flowed one into the other, creating in that streaming moment something else, something paradoxical, something beyond themselves.

If you say to yourself, that's it, that is what the legend meant all along, you are almost there.

I will not tell you about the minds who create this place, beyond the storms of time, beyond life, beyond death. I will not tell you about the light blown ships I saw approaching the islands or the mirrors that flashed from the windows of the houses to greet them.

I will not even tell you about the people I saw in the meandering streets, or how I recognised in them people I have known everywhere; or how one can find the mountain in them, or the sky, the forest deer, or the neighbour that passes them by. You know all about that now, becoming what you are not.

★

When finally I came to, the sun was fading and I was having a hard time remembering who or where I was. Wind-sped clouds were tearing across the sky and the rain was pelting my face.

As I lifted my head, something caught my attention.

At first it looked like a toy boat in a tempest, thunder claps, lightning forks, slanting sheets of rain chasing her over the sea.

It was the Pegasus. Whirlwinds and waterspouts darting all about her, black steam panting furiously from her funnel.

She was trying to outrun the storm before it engulfed her, racing for shelter and the southern breach in the crater wall.

I wondered if she would even make it, so badly was she listing in the heaving swell. Unless the captain could somehow straighten her course, she would come perilously close to the rocks.

98.

I gripped the railings with both clenched fists, bracing myself against the crazy pitch and roll. I had to wonder if I had ever seen a sky so piercing, a sea so blue and silver.

Hadrian came reeling across the deck. If not for his sense of relief in leaving the island for good, he'd probably be pea-green in the face.

Every so often my eyes would be drawn back to the rust-red island seesawing in our wake, growing smaller and smaller until finally it falls over the horizon altogether.

'Do you remember what he said — Huxley I mean? He said, before this thing is over, I will prove that death does not exist.' I could see the words being snatched by the wind and carried off in the spray. I could feel the grin breaking across my face.

'Yes, and he failed miserably,' retorted Hadrian, cocking an eyebrow at the bluish bruise on my forehead. 'For all his boasting, he proved nothing. Even after everything he put us through, what do we have to show for it? For those who are already that way disposed, hope, faith, and a few inexplicable coincidences on which to pin them, nothing more.'

Sensing I was about to object, he threw me a withering look. 'Huxley has gone, but I don't know *where* he is or even *if* he is anymore. Only he knows that — *or does he?*'

He cast an ambivalent glance back at the island. 'Admit it,' he said, forcing the hoarse words between his teeth. 'You feel it as well as I. The hypnotic spell it put us under; I don't know, the strange ways it obsessed and captivated us. It's already lifting. With every passing wave, each nautical mile we gain, its hold over us diminishes... *Well?* When you look at it dispassionately, wouldn't that be the perfect match for Marcus Huxley's final deception?'

If the final deception is not simply the last one, but the one that makes sense of all the others, then yes, I thought, why not.

'I wonder what new spell will captivate us now.'

Hadrian shuffled his feet, grunted, lips curling with distaste at the very notion, far preferring to believe that the island alone was to blame, capable of squeezing our irrationality into broad daylight like molten lava from a fissure, like delirious vapours from a vent.

Huxley's face shimmers into my head unbidden, his voice booms like distant thunder. *Didn't I warn you? Didn't I say from day one, Take nothing at face value. Trust not what your eyes can see, nor the sounds your ears can hear. Nothing is what it appears, and never has been. Nothing!*

By a few degrees, the ship shifts course to follow the cliff bound coast of some bleak Cycladic island, heaving past jagged rocks barely a stone's throw away. The sun veers east as she goes, and our shadows pass over the silver window of the saloon bar, eclipsing the roiling surf reflected there. Within our own silhouettes the interior becomes visible, things gaining substance, gaining reflection. I can see the light striking through the blue and amber bottles chiming behind the bar, the mirror catching the coffee cups and saucers sliding back and forth over the tables, some crashing to the floor.

The moment swells like a wave as it passes beneath us, hesitates, and in that briefest of lulls I see them, as clear as day, just on the edge of the eclipse. The Papás with his stovepipe hat, Anna, Benja. Sam, his arm draped lazily over Aris' shoulder. Stavros Sanassis, Vassilis the postmaster. Alexis Pangalos, his wife and kids. Nondas the barber. Nestor and Maria, arms looped together. Célestine, Johnny. Everyone I ever came to know on the island. Even the whiskered old farmer who first pestered Huxley about the ghosts flocking out of his fields at dawn. Huxley's lighting his pipe, that familiar intensity written all over his face, his lips miming something, *what is it?*

'Don't you see?' he's saying. 'Everyone helped us to get here, know it or not, like it or not.'

The deception moves, unravels, one metaphor at a time.

I blink, once, twice, as Hadrian shifts his bulk at the railing and the sun bursts through again, the window resuming its dazzling reflection of sea and sky. Over the next headland a village appears, white cubic houses, domes and bell towers following the contours of a rust red cliff top.

I can hear myself yelling, *Wake up! Wake up!* yet in a distant voice that hardly seems to be mine at all.

The ship heaves over an immense wave, the sheer force of it battering us sideways.

I jerk my head around to shout something, a question, a warning, I don't know what, and it's only then that my eyes falter over the newspaper folded under Hadrian's arm. I take a deep sharp breath, and the wet salt air stings my lungs.

The front page. It carries the same story I saw on the journey down, all those months ago. The same breathless headline: *Archaeologists Unearth Mystery Hieroglyphs.* Hadrian must have found it among the yellowing newspapers in the saloon bar, that must be it.

Strange, uncanny, I almost expect to feel the Frenchman's twisted glare on my back. I glance over my shoulder, just to make sure, almost missing him in the dense shadow of the ship's funnel. Claude Guirand, gazing venomously at the wild sea, the skull-headed cane clasped tightly between his bony knees. Who is this boy, he's thinking, falling into Huxley's clutches? How much does he know? Can his loyalty be bought?

Wake up! Wake up!

The light, incredible, is refracting this way and that. It crosses my mind to ask why the colours are so intense.

The engines are rasping, sooty black smoke panting from the funnel. Don't they realise how perilously close we are to the rocks? Hadrian utters a torn cry, our eyes darting to the bridge, through the open door, to the silhouettes wrestling madly with the helm.

There's the shriek of ripping steel against rock.

I can already see the gaping faces in the water, the wide numb eyes, the seaweed hair.

It was always about that wasn't it, books, dreams, lives, civilisations, breaking off in the middle of

Phíra, Santorini, 3 March

Dear Mrs Pedrosa,

I hasten to write this letter so that it might be with you later today, thanks to our Consular officials in Athens. I know how anxious you must be for news.

The loss of the *Pegasus* has shocked us all. With so many passengers and crew lost to the gale, on a small island like this it is hard to find a single household that is not mourning a family member, a neighbour or a friend.

Your son Nicholas was fortunate to survive at all. It was hours after the ship went down that the young fisherman Aris spotted his body, washed up on the rocks. With difficulty in the heavy swell, he and his father lifted him aboard and, thinking him already beyond help, laid him out on deck. Once back at the dock, they had him carried by mule up the cliff face path, up to the makeshift mortuary in the school house. He was pronounced clinically dead.

Seconds later, my good friend Dr Stavros Sanassis happened by and, just as he was preparing to rush to the next casualty, noticed the faint pulse in your son's throat. If miracles there are, one must surely have occurred at that moment. Stavros tells me he lost Nicholas twice in the hours that followed. He died and was revived. He died again and was revived again.

He was rushed to the clinic, then, when he had stabilised and recovered some of his strength, to one of the houses we keep in town. That was Stavros' idea because, although Nicholas was now out of immediate danger, although his vital signs had stabilised, he would not wake, nor even respond to normal stimuli. When I asked Stavros if he meant a coma, he said no, that was not it; it was shock, trauma. Almost an unwillingness to return.

So we all took turns at his bedside, talking to him, reading to him. Though the prognosis appeared bleak, it was Stavros who insisted we should, having learnt of a similar treatment in Paris.

I admit, we were dubious.

What shall we say, what shall we read? At a loss, they all asked the same question. I don't care, I replied, ancient legends, discoveries we make in the trenches, poetry that sets your soul on fire, stories from your own lives and loves and dreams, stories that bring the ancient city alive... Use whatever imagination the good gods gave you.

And so we began. I myself, Vassilis Nafpliotis the postmaster, Alexander Vouris the schoolmaster, Nicholas' own future workmates, our young students from France, Célestine and her brother Jean, even our village priest, Father Nannos.

My housekeeper Myroula even brought along her tastiest dishes in the hope of tempting Nicholas from his big sleep, opening the casserole under his nose, the baskets of assorted pies and honey cakes, the freshly-baked bread.

Adrian Hunt, my second-in-command, who barely escaped the shipwreck with his own life, took his turn in the afternoons; he even had a piano brought into the house in the expectation that music might reach deeper than the spoken word. Perhaps it did.

So far Nicholas has said very little, though he is clearly on the mend. It is almost as if he were lost for words, unable to express what he has seen. No, I don't mean the sinking of the *Pegasus*, the drowning. The feverish resuscitation in the schoolhouse, the kiss of life. I mean this, and I believe it your right to know before you set out from England: what he says he saw when everyone else thought him dead. A white light, like some bright looming star. And then beyond, he says, people, events, worlds beyond his own horizon...

— *Yours, Marcus James Huxley.*

★ ★ ★

CPSIA information can be obtained at www.ICGtesting.com
Printed in the USA
BVOW03s1341051113

335524BV00001B/9/P